DARKMOTHERLAND

DARKMOTHERLAND
SAMRAT UPADHYAY

SOHO

Published by
Soho Press, Inc.
227 W 17th Street
New York, NY 10011

Library of Congress Cataloging-in-Publication Data

Names: Upadhyay, Samrat, author.
Title: Darkmotherland / Samrat Upadhyay.
Description: New York : Soho, 2025.
Identifiers: LCCN 2024016325

ISBN 978-1-64129-472-0
eISBN 978-1-64129-473-7

Subjects: LCGFT: Novels. | Classification: LCC PS3621.P33 D37 2025
LC record available at https://lccn.loc.gov/2024016325

Interior illustration: © BormanT/iStock
Interior design by Janine Agro, Soho Press, Inc.

Printed in the United States of America

10 9 8 7 6 5 4 3 2 1

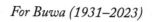

For Buwa (1931–2023)

PART I

THE BIG TWO

1.

When the Big Two struck, people got into cars and taxis, motorbikes and bicycles, and formed enormous lines to get out of the Valley. They were stopped by the Loyal Army Dais carrying machine guns. The highways out of the city had been ruptured or blocked with debris or landslides, the Loyal Army Dais said, so no one could leave. It was hard to see anything in the billowing, swooning dust. People only saw hardened, commandeering faces of the Loyal Army Dais and snouts of machine guns, and voices, shouting, scolding, haranguing. "Turn back! Back!" Small pandemonium broke out in the line, with people pushing, shoving, weeping, praying to their ancestors.

A pillion rider on a motorbike was carrying a massive boombox on her shoulder. She turned up the volume of a Beatles song that penetrated the air, telling the good folks of Darkmotherland to *get back to where they once belonged.*

———

Two days after the Big Two, a small band of protestors wearing masks took to the streets, fighting the sandy grit in the air that got into their eyes, ears and mouths, shouting slogans about accountability and transparency. It was a small group, timid and furtive, as it made its way through the rubble that cluttered the lanes of the inner city. Their masks looked like they were borrowed from the set of a 1950s movie depicting space aliens. The residents of the surrounding houses, some of which were tottering and heaving, threw things at them: small stones, bunched-up paper, old dolls, water. When the group reached the Lion Palace, these masked men and women were apprehended and taken to an unknown location, where they were beaten and tortured. Other protest groups in the days following faced similar fates. When the media tried to find out what had happened, the Rajjya officials feigned ignorance.

The media was also not its former self. A couple of high-profile newspapers simply stopped operating because the buildings in which they were housed had collapsed. A big TV station's owner died when he was buried in the rubble of his own home. The remaining media outlets, which began their operations in fits and starts, were now under the control of the Ministry of Communication. Blogs and podcasts were also monitored, or simply shut down. A popular, fast-talking host of an FM talk program was replaced by a regime media official who spoke in a slow drawl.

The Rajjya changed its face: new people were announced as ministers, cabinet secretaries, and ambassadors. The new PM declared a State of Emergency. All political activities were immediately banned, and the Loyal Army Dais went to the offices of political parties and shut them down, putting big government padlocks on their doors. This happened within days of the Big Two, before the people had a chance to assess the damage that the earthquake had inflicted. Darkmotherland had a history of sweeping changes in the government every other year, so this was not unprecedented. It's natural, Motherland TV assured its citizens, for a new Rajjya, filled with responsible adult Darkmotherlandites, to emerge at a time of such unfathomable tragedy. After all, the Big Two had happened under the old Rajjya's watch, hadn't it?

Billboards with photos of the new PM, clad in daura suruwal and wearing a dhakatopi cap, multicolored and tapered at the top, sprung up at key intersections. His right fist was thrust in front of him, and, underneath it, the words, "Pure Darkmotherland." The Loyal Army Dais began patrolling the streets in greater numbers. The Big Two was so named because this bhukampa was as big as, or even perhaps bigger, than the big one that had struck the country in 1934.

2.

Planning for a counteroffensive began in Beggar Street. A massive rally was envisioned, similar to a protest years ago against the monarchical rule that made tens of thousands of people take to the streets.

The entire Darkmotherland is in ruins, Kranti thought, and these fuckers are scheming to bring down the new Rajjya. Kranti knew that Bhaskar, if given the opportunity, would join the Beggars. As it was, Bhaskar liked to listen to the Beggars, who sat at the feet of their leader, Professor Shrestha, Kranti's mother, in the living room, while Kranti fumed by herself in her bedroom next door. The house was small: an average-sized living room where the Beggars gathered, a tight kitchen, a tiny room for Kranti with a narrow bed and a desk on which sat an eight-inch TV, and a larger bedroom for Professor Shrestha. Behind the house was a lawn, one that Dada, when he was alive, talked about being a perfect space to construct an in-law suite, where he wanted Kranti and her husband to live. "A son-in-law suite," Dada liked to joke.

Voices in the house carried, so when she lounged in her bed or worked at her desk, Kranti heard everything they said in the living room. Sometimes she peeked her head out and called to him, "Bhaskar, can you come back in?" The Beggars looked at her, then at him, then at Professor Shrestha. They knew Professor Shrestha, whom they respectfully addressed as Madam, ran a liberal household, but this was too liberal, wasn't it? Allowing your daughter and her boyfren to cuddle in her room while people discussed important matters, such as the fate of the nation, only a few feet away? But of course, the Beggars weren't going to say anything to their beloved Madam, or to Kranti, who they knew had always been a difficult daughter. Amongst themselves, the Beggars whispered that Kranti's hostility toward her mother had increased after her father's suicide.

She'll take Bhaskar away from me, Kranti often thought, just like she took away Dada. Madam Mao. This was the nickname that

Professor Shrestha had received, from her critics and the Rajjya. In her mind, this is how Kranti referred to her mother. She needed to leave Beggar Street once and for all and whisk Bhaskar away from Madam Mao's pernicious influence.

Kranti also fretted over whether Bhaskar's family would accept her.

Bhaskar laughed when she expressed her worries to him, in her room and in cafés across the dusty valley. "Darkmotherland is devastated, we've just had a koo, and you're worried about what the Ghimireys will think of you?"

Kranti knew she was being irrational, given what had happened to Darkmotherland, but her mind had abandoned the rational course long ago, after Dada's death. Now she latched on to one worry and stubbornly clung to it until it consumed her. It seemed as though the destructions in Darkmotherland were only a backdrop to her personal drama. When she looked at it objectively, she saw it. Half of the country *was* in utter ruins, as Bhaskar said. A major highway out of the Valley was ruptured. Rice and dal, the two staples of the Darkmotherlandese diet, were scarce. Bread had disappeared from the market. The price of eggs had quadrupled. The poorer residents scrounged for nettles and other grass for their greens. Prostitution was rampant, and, for some inexplicable reason, so was gambling. Dead bodies were strewn by the sides of the roads, often unclaimed by relatives. Hospitals overflowed with patients struck by diseases that had no names—that attacked their vocal cords, made them bleed profusely, or forced them to speak in languages that sounded like radio static.

Bhureys, a derisive nickname for earthquake refugees, kept pouring in from the mountains, cramming the city center, especially the core of Diamond Park and the Parade Ground, now called Bhurey Paradise. "A paradise for halwais and honeys," Bhaskar's elder brother, Aditya, said, using the street slang for pimps and prostitutes. Bhaskar had relayed this to Kranti. Aditya could barely contain his disdain for Bhurey Paradise, Bhaskar said. "A cesspit for crooks and looters, rats, and homeless and disease-infested humanity." He applauded the Fundys for prowling the Bhurey Paradise for signs of "hotbeds of immorality," for roaming the area with lathis, and picking out honeys and halwais to beat.

—

When the earthquake hit, Bhaskar and Kranti had been eating in the Head in the Clouds restaurant in the Tourist District, the very place where their romance had started.

Bhaskar had picked her up from her work at Bauko Bank, where she was a clerk in the section that handed out loans to farmers and small businesses. She'd started working not too long after Dada died, partly to drown out the voices in her mind. Although the job could be boring, she liked the routine and her coworkers. At times Professor Shrestha seemed to suggest that Kranti wasn't ambitious in terms of her career, but Kranti largely ignored her, thinking, *Look at where your ambition got you—you led your husband to suicide.*

At Head in the Clouds, Kranti was in the middle of a sentence when there was severe rattling, then the floor of the rooftop restaurant had convulsed. "What the—" Kranti said, clasping the table with her hands. But the table had bucked and flown away from them and disappeared over the edge of the roof. The rooftop swayed like a swing. Loud *booms* sounded around them. Birds swarmed the sky above, raising hell. The house across the street burst into dust. She clung to Bhaskar, and the two of them crawled across the rooftop, where large cracks were appearing. At the top of the stairs, the dishwashing boy lay slumped, his head against the wall at an impossible angle.

They struggled to get to the bottom through the churning dust and rubble in the staircase. On the street, bodies were scattered, some writhing and moaning. Debris—almirahs, chunks of concrete, iron bars—blocked their way as they moved toward the Tourist District chowk. A wooden beam hurtled toward them from a nearby house, forcing them to let go of each other. Bhaskar became lost in the eddying dust. "Bhaskar!" she cried, and she thought she heard him respond, but how could she be sure in the cacophony of screams and shouts and wails surrounding her? She heard a rumble, and when she looked back, she saw a stampede of sheep charging toward her. Sheep? In the Tourist District? Why? (Kranti never found out. Later, there were reports of several species of animals, both domestic and wild, frantically running through the streets in packs when the Big Two struck—jackals, goats, chickens, bulls, wildcats, and, according to some, even rhinos.) The sheep charged past her, as if they were late for an appointment, and somehow, behind the last sheep was Bhaskar, the side of his face cut and bleeding.

"This way," Bhaskar said, taking her through an alley. They reached another chowk, which appeared to Kranti like a photo from a bombed-out courtyard in World War Two. Then she realized that she and Bhaskar had passed through that chowk dozens of times in their strolls through the Tourist District. Finally, they found shelter in the nearby Iconic Guest House, where the daughter-in-law of the owner, her face normally charming but now marked with worry, ushered them to the garden (she knew Bhaskar, as half of the Valley did). Guests and the hotel staff were sitting and standing, conversing in panicked voices.

Kranti and Bhaskar sat by themselves in a corner, and she told him, clasping his arm tightly, "Earlier, when we separated, I thought I had lost you."

Perhaps the fear of losing Bhaskar had made it important for her now that the Ghimireys liked her. She didn't like feeling clingy, hoping to gain the Ghimireys' approval. But what choice did she have? She couldn't imagine a life without Bhaskar.

—

"Who'd have thought the Hippo would end up grabbing power like this?" Professor Shrestha said to the Beggars. She refused to call him by the name that the entire Darkmotherland had begun to call him: PM Papa. Instead she called him the Hippo because he was ugly like a hippo—short and fat, with an insanely wide jaw, squinty eyes set high on his face, and each ear the size of a thumb, and small tufts of hair on his head. She had been calling him the Hippo for many years, ever since he'd come after her when she was a young political activist at Tri-Universe University. She was already known then for her stubbornness, for fighting authorities. The two had collided over the years, as she'd established herself as an admired and reviled force of dissent in Darkmotherland, and he had risen in power, starting as an influential party operative to become the home minister. And now the prime minister in what was clearly a koo.

The Beggars were a small group of dissidents. There had never been more than twelve Beggars since their formation, but now they were reduced to only five. Some Darkmotherlandites laughed at them, called them impotent because most often they congregated in Beggar Street and complained, discussed, and planned—but rarely took action. They did publish pamphlets and brochures at Mothercry Press, an "underground publication," as the Beggars liked to call it. But people said that it was so called not because it was clandestine but because the press was located in a basement apartment of one of the Beggars. Mothercry Press produced pamphlets, brochures, manifestos, caricatures, essays, and occasionally, small books that called for revolution. Its operation was erratic. Sometimes it went for months without any activity, then suddenly it would publish a flurry of papers and pamphlets. Even before PM Papa, every year or two the Poolis Uncles had come knocking, bothered by the depiction of the Rajjya in a cartoon or a guest editorial.

Professor Shrestha was a former academic given to theorizing, pontificating, but largely holding a pacifist view. A big fan of the Mahatma, she was a fighter of injustice, but "with no teeth," as many said derisively. She was more of an *intellectual* dissenter, rather than someone who'd take up arms for the cause. Her battles lay in the arena of the mind, often her own mind.

Yet many admired her, for her defiance of authorities, her determination, her refusal to join political parties for her own benefit. "I'm happy with my lot," she said about her small group of devoted Beggars: Murti, Prakash, Vikram, and Chanchal. "Beggar Street is where I'll stay and fight."

But that was precisely the problem: the Beggars were often holed up in Beggar Street, sitting around and fuming and complaining, or admiring Mothercry Press publications they considered subversive but that were mostly ineffectual. The more radical groups in Darkmotherland scoffed at the Beggars, often asking, "They can talk the talk but can they walk the walk?" It wasn't as if Professor Shrestha, and a handful of other Beggars, hadn't gone to jail for their activism over the years. But they'd go in only for a night or two, at most a week, then be released. Often it was over participation in a protest march that had gotten out of hand, or an article in the Mothercry Press that the Rajjya admitted, reluctantly, crossed a line. The Beggars were certainly not like some of the more chomping-at-the-bit, or even violent, larger groups that had operated in Darkmotherland since the monarchy years, groups that occupied state buildings, held Rajjya officials hostage, or even set off bombs in markets or blew up electrical grids. The Beggars were, as some said, genuine beggars, begging for scraps in the political dissent in Darkmotherland.

Part of the problem was that Professor Shrestha was the sarbe-sarba of the Beggars—the be-all and end-all. She was the only one who had the name, the clout. When Darkmotherlandites thought of the Beggars, Professor Shrestha's face loomed large. The others—Prakash, Murti, Vikram, Chanchal—were mere minions.

But since Papakoo there had been a sense about the Beggars, about Professor Shrestha, that things were about to come loose, on the verge of breaking and inflicting damage, or perhaps being damaged themselves.

There was a brooding air to Professor Shrestha's dissidence now, a fuming, smoldering quality. It was as though she was waiting.

For something. For someone. Kranti was beginning to feel that that someone was Bhaskar.

—

The Valley still swirled with large funnels of dust. Occasionally thick and furious enough to carry off flowerpots, windows, puppies, even little babies, these dust bowls didn't erupt from buildings that the Big Two had demolished—they appeared to have come from somewhere else. People swore that these swirls actually carried off babies. "I saw it with my own two eyes," a woman from the Exercise Lane said.

Once, there was a sighting of a giant swirl of dust as high as a house ("like a surf wave from Maui!" a well-traveled witness exclaimed), that was not fast but slow, lumbering through the street, nearly groaning, pausing every now and then to rest. There was an eye in the center of that dust swirl, like the third eye of the Pothead God.

They were still discovering bodies buried under the rubble. The hospitals were so overcrowded that tents had been erected in the streets outside, and patients walked the neighborhoods carrying saline bags, leaky tubes up their noses. There were long lines everywhere—at community taps, grocery stores, and Rajjya buildings. At internet cafés—those that were still standing—web surfers discovered that they received "Page Blocked" notices whenever they tried to access Facebook, WhatsApp, or TikTok. The streets now swarmed with stern-faced Loyal Army Dais and Poolis Uncles. Dusty vans with megaphones roamed about, telling people what they couldn't do. Orange-robed Fundys were seen everywhere, carrying tridents and yelling slogans with foam-spitting mouths. "Bom Bholey!' they shouted in praise of the Pothead God. "Pure Darkmotherland!" they bellowed, thrusting their right fists in front of them. They attacked couples in parks and public places, unmarried couples, but also married couples they found holding hands, or necking, or sharing an ice cream cone behind a swirl of dust. Usually, they thrashed the men and called the women sluts.

"Why doesn't someone simply up and shoot the Hippo?" Professor Shrestha said in Beggar Street as they discussed the rally. "Put a bullet right through that black heart? Or axe him in the brain?"

It was as though she didn't care that now, a few weeks after the Big Two, there were immediate crackdowns on those who spoke out against the new regime. Motherland TV identified dissidents by name, listed their family members, and called them unpatriotic. Then the Loyal Army Dais and Poolis Uncles knocked on their doors. These arrests were often televised, and often Home Minister Dharma Adhikari, with his long neck, was at the front, leading the way. Detention camps cropped up overnight. The locker rooms in the Ten Chariots Stadium became prison cells for hundreds of detainees.

Professor Shrestha stopped pacing and fidgeting and stood still, her face darkening. She always turned slightly darker during such instances of impotence and quiet rage. Her chin tightened and her lips narrowed. The Beggars knew this moment well. They had seen it over the years, and they simultaneously dreaded it and welcomed it. The time for the fight had arrived.

Sangharsh, Professor Shrestha called it, her catch-all phrase for the struggle.

3.

The Beggars chanted and raised their fists. Some of Professor Shrestha's neighbors had never cared for her activism and her loud-mouthed protests and wouldn't hesitate to call the Poolis Uncles. The neighbor who lived in the next house, Mr. Sapkota, always kept an eagle eye on the Beggars from his rooftop. He's seen their numbers dwindle over the years, from close to fifteen to now merely a handful. Even with the post-earthquake dust swirling about him, he watched the comings and goings at Beggar Street, sneering, complaining loudly about the riffraff that inundated the neighborhood.

The Beggars discussed whom to contact, how to contact. The phones, especially landlines, were probably tapped by the Rajjya. As it was, the Beggars were already using codes to talk about their scheduled meetings. "The weather forecast calls for no rain" meant that a meeting was happening. Or, "The highway is blocked because of landslides" was to confirm that a meeting had been postponed. But one could never be sure whether one was talking to a true dissident or an undercover agent.

The leader of another group within the Sangharsh said, "No, I'm not happy with everything PM Papa is doing, but this is a moment to Rebuild and Restore, so I'm not going to go out and dance on the streets saying my liberties have been violated. Rebuild and Restore now. Liberty later." Had he become a Papafan? At minimum, he was no longer a Papee, those considered not sufficiently supportive of PM Papa's vision for the country. Being labeled a Papee was stigmatizing and meant that your neighbors could shun you and you could be demoted at work. People were terrified of being labeled a Papee, which meant sinful and corrupt in the native tongue. They said that being a Papee was like starting an apprenticeship to become a Treasonist.

Every day there were stories of bureaucrats in government offices, those deemed insufficiently supportive of the new regime, who suddenly found themselves losing their fancy titles and their plush offices. Some were simply let go. In offices throughout Darkmotherland, PM Papa's ministers installed loyalists to powerful positions. Banners loudly proclaiming "Pure Darkmotherland!" appeared overnight hanging in front of Rajjya buildings.

So this much was certain: the Beggars and other groups in the Sangharsh, which were now fewer than before after the Big Two because many were scattered and disorganized, couldn't hope for a tremendous show of strength.

"The Hippo has become even more emboldened to crush dissent," Prakash said, "now that he has received a pat on the back from President Corn Hair."

They talked about the Amrikan president's tweet of congratulations to the Hippo, for "rising up from the ashes" of Darkmotherland. Motherland TV had shown that tweet for days, claiming that President Corn Hair's endorsement demonstrated his high regard for Darkmotherland under its new ruler. Papafans had made the tweet viral. PM Papa had immediately tweeted back, saying that he hoped Darkmotherland would one day be as prosperous and powerful as Amrika had become under President Corn Hair. "Congratulations to the Best President in Amrikan History for Making Amrika Great Again!" PM Papa had tweeted. Overnight, red caps with MAKE DARKMOTHERLAND GREAT AGAIN on them had appeared in the market.

But launching Operation Papa Don't Preach, as the big rally came to be called, wasn't as easy. Communication among the various groups in the Sangharsh was erratic and unreliable. The damage from Big Two made phone communications hard. Mobile phones often suffered from little to no signal, especially in areas where the dust devils were strong. Strong connections could abruptly die. Someone talking to his mother could suddenly find himself negotiating the price of spinach with a local farmer. There were instances when people's mobiles caught words in other languages, so two lovers exchanging endearments over their phones found themselves listening to a woman cursing in German, "Scheisse! Scheisse!" Some people complained that their phones, especially in the mornings, transmitted a fast, gravelly voice, saying "baby baby" every other word, followed by a wolf's howl and an old Angrezi rock song.

More problematic was the danger that the Rajjya was listening in to their phone conversations. The Ministry of Communication had given itself carte blanche authority to tap into people's mobiles and landlines, and so Poolis Uncles actively monitored those they suspected of being Treasonists.

A date was announced for Operation Papa Don't Preach, but the planning was thrown into chaos because two active groups within the Sangharsh backed out, giving vague excuses such as "lack of wherewithal" or "death in the family." It was quite likely that they'd received a visit from the Poolis Uncles. Or their families had been threatened. The Rajjya now encouraged people to act as moles within their community, even within their families, and report suspicious activities. They would be doing these suspects a favor, the Rajjya said, catching them before they went too far, before they reached a point of no return. It was a patriotic act. The snitches would help PM Papa purge the country of impurities, build a Pure Darkmotherland.

Another date for the rally was fixed, but it coincided with a major religious holiday when many people would be going to temples. It didn't look like the rally was going to get off the ground.

Then the Poolis Uncles intercepted a message between Prakash and a man from another Sangharsh group. The Poolis Uncles had come to the house of this person, whose name was Ramchandra, and taken him away. The Poolis Uncles had listened in on a phone conversation between Prakash and Ramchandra, and heard about Operation Papa Don't Preach. But they hadn't been able to identify Prakash because he had used a burner phone. Ramchandra had been interrogated, then tortured for hours about Operation Papa Don't Preach, but he'd insisted on his innocence: He was talking on the phone about the singer, since his daughter was a fan. Yes, Madonna was too old for his daughter, but she'd watched the pop icon sing "Papa Don't Preach" on YouTube and was smitten. One Poolis Uncle who seemed to be aware

of who Madonna was had scolded Ramchandra about what kind of a
father he was, anyway, for allowing his daughter to listen to that filth.
Then the Poolis Uncle had applied electric shocks to Ramchandra's
body, to his eyes, to his penis. "They've rendered him a eunuch, those
bastards," Prakash said, "permanently damaged his eyes." When the
others asked him how come Ramchandra hadn't given away Prakash's
name, Prakash said that his father, now dead, had saved Ramchandra's family from financial ruin years ago, so Ramchandra felt a strong
loyalty to Prakash and his younger brother.

The next day, at the gathering in Beggar Street, Prakash told Professor Shrestha what they were thinking: they suspected that Bhaskar
was a spy for the Rajjya.

Of course, it was Prakash who'd speak for the Beggars. He was
the bluntest in the group, unafraid to offer his opinions with anyone,
even Professor Shrestha. He had a bit of a temper, and increasingly
expressed dissatisfaction with how passive the Beggars were when it
came to physically confronting the authorities. "He's a hot-blooded
one," Professor Shrestha often said of him, "my dear Prakash." She'd
heard that Prakash was even grooming his younger brother, Gokul, to
become a dissident. He had, in fact, wanted to bring Gokul to Beggar
Street, but Professor Shrestha had nixed the idea since Gokul was
merely a teenager.

Now Professor Shrestha stared at Prakash in disbelief, then said,
"You must be out of your mind."

"Madam, please hear us out," Murti said softly. Murti had been
with Professor Shrestha the longest, at times acting like she was her
madam's attendant, fiercely protecting her from criticism. The other
Beggars mildly complained that she had a special access to Professor
Shrestha that they didn't have.

Professor Shrestha turned to Vikram and Chanchal. "You two
also?" They nodded. Big and bulky Vikram considered himself a bodyguard for Professor Shrestha. "My gentle giant," Professor Shrestha

called him, but everyone suspected that Vikram was smarter than he let on.

Chanchal, so named because of his restless, mischievous eyes, was always smiling and fluttering about—he moved quickly, like a truly chanchal fellow. Over the years he'd turned into the gofer for the group—making tea in the kitchen, fetching samosas from the restaurant, and running other errands.

"This is a genuine concern for all," Murti said, putting her hand on her Madam's hand. "Bhaskar does belong to a family that is benefitting from the Hippo's rise."

Bhaskar himself had talked about the muted sounds of glee in the Asylum when PM Papa had arisen from the dust and destruction of the Big Two. "Mind you, how long after the Big Two did we learn that he was in control?" Bhaskar said to Professor Shrestha. "In just a couple of days, hoina? And here was my family, as though my father himself had won the election. First there was the relief over the fact that the Asylum had remained unscathed, even as most of the country was destroyed. Then, the news of PM Papa's ascension. My family could barely contain their joy, never mind that some of the Ghimirey & Sons businesses had suffered damage—the roof of the shoe factory had caved, several cars in the Mercedes Benz dealership had been destroyed, the big machine at the Gyani Biskut had stopped working and would probably have to be replaced at the cost of crores. But that was no reason to be unhappy because Ghimirey & Sons could do so much more with PM Papa in power. Aditya talked about the various projects that he could now push through. Chaitanya wondered if this was a time to lobby PM Papa that their father be given an important position in the Trade Ministry, perhaps even as the minister. Can you imagine? The entire country's infrastructure had come crashing down, and here were Ghimirey and his two Sons and two-daughters-in-law clinking champagne glasses and toasting to a brighter future. Sure, there was a brief scare when a mob of looters rattled the gates of the Asylum, but a quick call by my father to PM Papa and the Loyal Army Dais came within seconds and fired tear gas to chase the mob away."

Ghimirey & Sons made or sold shoes, wine, bicycles, children's books, computer software, cigarettes, and vodka. "Impossible to keep track of what your family business does," Kranti sometimes told Bhaskar, who said he couldn't either.

"One day I'll look up in the sky," Bhaskar said, "and see a cloud floating by with a Ghimirey & Sons stamp on it."

"The company name should have been Ghimirey & Two Sons," she said. "What have you done for the empire?"

"Nothing," Bhaskar said. "I am the black sheep."

Professor Shrestha came to Bhaskar's defense with the Beggars, "Bhaskar and Kranti were together before the Big Two, before the Hippo, so your theory that Bhaskar is a spy is nonsense. This is precisely the kind of thing the Hippo wants, to create division among his enemies."

Tiredness had come over her, and along with it some uncertainty, even though it was insane that she was doubting Bhaskar. Still, she couldn't help but dwell upon the time Bhaskar entered their lives a year ago—the blossoming romance between him and Kranti, and how quickly Professor Shrestha came to view him as someone not only good for her daughter, but also a like-minded son she'd never had. She'd been impressed by his disdain for a life of privilege, by his sensitivity toward the poor and the downtrodden, his quick mind, his witticism, and his Aquarius-like all-encompassing view of the world. She wondered now if that had all been a scheme.

If there had been a scheme, then that meant Bhaskar had seen the Big Two coming and the rise of that Hippo. Absurd. But could it have been that the Hippo, after he came to power, had managed to persuade Bhaskar to spy on Professor Shrestha? Even more absurd. What could PM Papa give Bhaskar that he didn't already have?

Could Bhaskar have been forced by his family members into spying? If Bhaskar was indeed a spy, then this explanation was the most logical. Professor Shrestha found herself sinking into further absurdity: the alliance between the Ghimireys and the Hippo had started years back, when Bhaskar was a teenager. Bhaskar's brain-washing could have started then, at a time when Professor Shrestha had emerged as an enemy of the rich, and later he could have volunteered to make Kranti fall in love with him to gain access to Professor Shrestha.

Her line of thinking was so outlandish that she couldn't believe she had gone there. Oh, the depravity of the mind, how low it could fall!

She wanted to put her foot down to the Beggars, tell Murti et al. to knock it off. But that wouldn't do anything to diminish their suspicion.

She finally came up with the idea of officially inducting Bhaskar as a Beggar. Thus far Bhaskar had been at the periphery of the group. Sometimes he sat in on the Beggars' meetings, but mostly he spent time with Kranti, often in her room. The Beggars' induction ceremony would be a brief one, but it would require him taking a pledge after being questioned by the other members. Professor Shrestha would even allow Murti to question him privately.

⏤

PM Papa loved them, of this the Ghimireys were certain. Bhaskar thought differently. "That man has no true allegiances, Kranti," he said. "He will turn against you at a moment's notice." The Ghimireys, too, sensed that it would be a bad idea to anger PM Papa; he needed to be pleased at all costs. Otherwise, he'd stop bestowing his favors on them and open doors for the other business magnates in Dark-motherland, like the Srinivas, or the MOM Group, or Shakya Inc. Even as they clinked their champagne glasses, the Ghimireys knew this, and their minds were already looking forward to more deals and contracts and partnerships that would enrich Ghimirey & Sons, and also benefit PM Papa.

Much of the enrichment was already happening. Under PM Papa's tenure, business deals and bids were quickly made easier for Ghimirey & Sons. Documents that needed the Rajjya's authorization were stamped and pushed through with alarming ease, especially under the chaos of the Big Two. Ghimirey & Sons received, within days, many major rebuilding assignments for the Rajjya. In an unprecedented move, PM Papa fully privatized waste management for the Valley, and within days after the Big Two, Ghimirey & Sons won the bid, even though the company had no previous experience in waste management. A facility in the outskirts of the Valley, near the City of Devotees, was rapidly built, so speedily that people said they'd never seen any building or factory constructed so fast in Darkmotherland, ever, let alone after being devastated by a colossal earthquake. One week Raddi Tokari wasn't there, the next week it was—with towers, large drums, cranes, and compressors all at the edge of a forest spanning about twenty hectares. Aditya, as the eldest son, was in charge of it. Ghimirey & Sons was also building a new luxury hotel half a kilometer away from Raddi Tokari, one with a mountain theme. They said that Raddi Tokari was one of the most profitable of all Ghimirey & Sons businesses, even more profitable than the hotel. The waste management facility was guarded by a special battalion of Loyal Army Dais, and Aditya was working directly with General Tso to ensure its smooth running. Some people wondered why a waste management operation needed to be protected by the military, why the Rajjya would be involved when it was contracted by a private company. Then the news came out that the Son of Yeti, a near-mythical rebel in the mountains who had risen to oppose PM Papa, was scheming to target waste management facilities throughout Darkmotherland.

Why waste management? people asked.

Why not? others answered.

This was how many conversations went in Darkmotherland:

Why?

Why not?

—

The Big Two fucked with people's minds. It gave them false memories, it made them hallucinate. Their parents who'd perished in the earthquake appeared in their kitchens to lecture them. They answered phone calls from their dead children's schools telling them their children had fallen out of trees or broken their necks. Women were stalked by men from their distant pasts. Furry creatures climbed inside children's blankets and requested bedtime stories. College girls, raped by ghosts at night, awoke to sore cunts and bloody sheets.

The Big Two made people go insane. A well-respected spice merchant was seen around town drumming dhintang, dhintang, dhintang on his madal all day long, making everyone wish he'd died during the Big Two. A housewife stood in the middle of the street, directing traffic with ladles and pots.

The Big Two fucked us like no one has fucked us before, people said.

If it weren't for PM Papa we would have been fucked even more.

They admired the statues of PM Papa that had appeared, almost overnight, on major intersections of the Valley. PM Papa on a horse, extended arm holding a sword, wearing a crown sort of like the autocratic ruler of yonder years. Every now and then, people were seen praying in front of a statue, leaving fruits at its base. A woman, her mind stolen by the Big Two, made it a point to circle all of PM Papa's statues in the Valley, all twenty-four of them, like a pilgrimage. She was interviewed by Motherland TV, where she punctuated her answers with "Pure Darkmotherland!" while jabbing her fist in the air in front of her.

—

She'll get Bhaskar killed, Kranti thought.

"She's a witch, Madam Mao," she told Bhaskar in her room.

"Don't speak that way about your mother," Bhaskar said. His long body, clad in immaculately white kurta suruwal, struggled to fit on the small bed Kranti had had since her teenage years, one that Dada had bought for her. Bhaskar's feet jutted out of the bed's end—he was more than half a foot taller than she was. He leaned over and adjusted the fan by the bedside so that it would rotate more smoothly, drive out the dust that continuously drifted in from outside.

Bhaskar sounded just like Dada. And just like Dada used to say about Professor Shrestha, he said, "She is like Gandhi, or Martin Luther King."

Bhaskar had begun admiring Professor Shrestha soon after he graduated high school, when he happened to read her book *Cry the Cursed Country*. The book lambasted the long history of the nation's oligarchs, monarchs, autocrats, and dictatorial politicians and advocated a transformative revolution. It was a classic, a favorite among the communist rebels during the Maoist Civil War, taught in Western universities by left-leaning professors, and now banned by PM Papa. Well, not banned explicitly, but the book was no longer available in those bookstores that were still standing after the earthquake.

Motherland TV was on in Kranti's room, on low volume as usual, barely audible, but the anchor Hom Bokaw's slurred monologue was soothing. Hom Bokaw's last name was something else but he was called Bokaw because with his prominent white beard he resembled a billy goat. Despite his speech impediment, he was the most popular anchor in Darkmotherland, and his job was to offer extravagant praise of PM Papa.

"Is he always anchoring on Motherland TV?" Bhaskar asked. "Doesn't he ever go home to sleep?"

Professor Shrestha and the Beggars were in the living room, poring over a leaflet that they'd just produced in Mothercry Press that depicted PM Papa as a fat cat sleeping on bags of money, as skeletal-like Darkmotherlandites stood around him, begging.

Kranti and Bhaskar could hear them discussing whether they could reactivate Mothercry Press's Facebook page under a different name. The account had been shut down, as many others had been, by the Rajjya soon after the Big Two.

"Crymother Press?" Vikram suggested.

"We just have to be very careful about what we post on FB and Twitter now," Chanchal said, his eyes dancing across the faces of his colleagues, Kranti imagined.

She told Bhaskar that last night she'd dreamt that the Son of Yeti was waiting in the mountains, his hand cupped over his ear, waiting for a signal, his extra-large penis ramrod straight, perky, alert, twitching. She'd cried out and awoke with a jolt.

"There is no Son of Yeti," Bhaskar said, pinching her nose. "He's PM Papa's creation."

Kranti also harbored similar doubts, then she doubted her doubts, which was how her mind worked. "The Wanted poster looks real," she said. The Son of Yeti had mountain features: wide cheekbones, small eyes, and a Genghis Khan mustache.

"Photoshop."

"His eyes," Kranti said. "The anger in them. He's real. He wants to harm this country."

"Kranti, Kranti," Bhaskar said. "You shouldn't go by your feelings so much. Your feelings have deceived you in the past, remember?"

She'd become irritated with him. "Not every feeling I have is mistrusting and paranoid!"

He stroked her hair. "Sorry."

She softened. "Besides, since you've come into my life, I've been better."

⌒

Bhaskar's induction ceremony took place when Kranti was at work. Murti took Bhaskar to the other room for questions. There were snickers and guffaws, as usual, about what she might be doing with him. "Untoward? Untoward?" Prakash said. "Something untoward happening in there?"

Bhaskar's vetting process was quick, and Murti emerged smiling. The oath-taking was also brief. Bhaskar committed himself to the work of the Beggars. Murti watched him, but not with the kind of scrutiny they had anticipated. Whatever Bhaskar had ended up saying to her in there, he had charmed her. My charming Bhaskar, thought Professor Shrestha. Hell, he had even managed to charm Kranti, who had been a grump as far back as Professor Shrestha could remember.

4.

Professor Shrestha referred to Bhaskar as "the son I never had." She made it sound a bit like a joke, but she repeated it often enough that listeners, mostly the Beggars, deduced that Bhaskar was a replacement for her daughter. Kranti *could have been* a daughter who was adoring and admiring, a daughter who *could have* taken up her mantle, those words suggested. After all, hadn't Professor Shrestha named her girl "Revolution"?

Kranti had been born during the days of the monarchy. Professor Shrestha was in the last stages of pregnancy when she'd been arrested for leading a demonstration that had turned violent. Her water had broken soon after they threw her behind bars, so Kranti had been born in a jail cell, a fact Professor Shrestha often repeated to relatives and friends, and especially to the Beggars. As a toddler, Kranti's tongue couldn't put the *k* and *r* together, and she often said "Kanti" when people asked her name. "It's Kranti, silly, not Kanti," Professor Shrestha said to her daughter in front of the Beggars. "Kanti means beauty, and yes, you are beautiful, but what this country needs is not beauty—it has beauty oozing out, ad nauseam, everywhere— but a revolution. Get it? For centuries we've been brainwashed with this baloney that we're a land of beauty, of beautiful people, and look where it has gotten us. Tell me, child," she addressed her daughter, but the intended audience was the Beggars or whoever happened to be in the room, "is there beauty in starvation? Is there beauty in backbreaking labor on a farm, owned by someone else, for which you only get a fistful of rice? Beauty in marrying off your twelve-year-old daughter to a forty-year-old man? So, no, you're not Kanti but Kranti, a symbol of the coming uprising."

Kranti was too young to fully understand what her mother was saying, but even then she hadn't enjoyed her mother's hectoring. As

she grew older, and her mother's diatribe on Kranti vs. Kanti continued—someone new would always mishear her name—Kranti felt
that her mother used her name as a political fusillade. When Kranti
was fourteen she told Dada privately that she wanted to change her
name. "Kranti is a beautiful name," Dada said. "It's an unusual name,
especially for a girl. Makes you special. Why you worry so much?"
That was one of Dada's favorite expressions for Kranti: Why you
worry so much?

"I hate it. It sounds horrible."

"Shh." Dada was always worried that Professor Shrestha would
hear Kranti's increasingly outspoken pronouncements.

"Why are you shushing me?" Kranti said. "She should hear this."

"The name means a lot to your mother."

"Then she should have used it for herself. Professor Kranti. Perfect!"

Despite himself, Dada let out a chuckle, which emboldened Kranti
to chant, "Professor Kranti! Professor Kranti! No peace, no shanti,
I'm a rebel, don't wear no panties."

His face mirthful, Dada scolded her, then placed his palm over her
mouth to prevent her from continuing, so Kranti chanted against his
palm, "Fofeffo Famphi! Fofeffo Famphi!"

Professor Shrestha walked in and said, "What's so funny between
father and daughter that I'm being left out of?"

While the Beggars gathered in the living room, Dada cooked
snacks for them in the kitchen. Kranti watched him and said, "You
and I will never be Beggars."

"Then what will we be, Kranti?" he asked.

"We will be anti-Beggars," she said. "We will be against Beggars.
Yes, Dada, you and I should start an Against Beggars movement. The
Against Beggars Brigade." Kranti had always loved wordplay, and she
rejoiced in this opportunity. "Or the Beggars Go to Hell movement.
Or maybe you and I will be chairmen of the Beyond Beggars Asso-
ciation."

"Shhh!" Dada said. "They will hear. Better Than Beggars?"

"Bureau of Bully The Beggars."

It had seemed unfair to the teenager Kranti, and she'd expressed this much to Dada, and also to her mother, that the Beggars pilfered Dada's creation to name their sorry group. The name, a distortion of Baker Street, had originated with Dada, a big fan of Sherlock Holmes, and he'd given the house its name, Baker Street, saying he could imagine Sherlock walking into his home in the Valley's autumn fogs. He'd even had a plaque made and hung it on the doorway: 221B Baker Street. Then, in small letters beneath the address: Holme of Sherlock Holmes (Dada was proud of his wordplay). But some people had a tough time pronouncing "baker" and soon it turned to "begar" and finally they settled on Beggar. The street itself, which had an unpronounceable local name, found an easier sound in Beggar Street.

—

Sometimes Kranti smiled just at the thought of Bhaskar. He'd come into her life in Tri-Moon College, about a year before the Big Two. He pursued her. He used to tease her when she passed him by on the campus grounds. He would be sitting on the lawn in front of the main building, along with two or three of his friends, and he'd begin singing, "Talking about a revolution."

She didn't know the song, or even that he was singing to her.

"He's addressing you, you idiot," one of her classmates said.

"What?"

"It's a Tracy Chapman song, ke."

When she still didn't get it, another friend said, "Hello! Revolution. Kranti. Isn't that your name?"

She looked back. He was grinning. So were her friends. What an idiot, she thought. If only he knew that she hated this name of hers that was given to her by her mother.

A few days later he found her alone in the hallway. She was late for class.

"Won't you speak to me?" he asked.

She didn't recognize him at first, then she did. Oh, the handsome fellow. She didn't say anything, but she didn't make a move to go past him.

"Are you afraid of me?" he asked.

"You think too highly of yourself."

He touched her arm, and, although for some reason it didn't feel like an encroachment, she had no time for him. She left him and went to her class.

She thought of him on her way home. There had been a boy or two at her high school whom she thought she could be interested in. But the initial interest always fizzled out once she discovered how immature and silly they were. And after Dada's death, which happened during her first year at Tri-Moon, she didn't even want to spend time with her friends, let alone become interested in boys. In fact, she'd quit her studies then, managed to find a job as a teller in Bauko Bank, struggled with delusions and the paranoia that her mind pushed her toward, but found a strange hiding place and solace at work. Professor Shrestha had tried to talk her out of quitting college, but she herself was depressed over Dada's death and couldn't move beyond a weak protest. For Kranti, the bank job had eventually turned out to be a blessing because of the perfunctory and mind-numbingly boring nature of her duties as a teller, enabling her to mask her symptoms. After three years, the pain over Dada's death had subsided a bit and she'd returned to college.

Bhaskar wrote letters to her, called her at home, called her on her mobile, passed messages through her friends, all of whom were jealous.

"Ghimirey & Sons!"

"Ghimirey & Sons is after you!" they said.

"Stop making a big deal of this, please," she told them.

"You are such an idiot, Kranti," they said. "One of the most eligible bachelors in town has taken a liking to you, and you are such a scaredy-cat."

"You can have him," Kranti said. "And all the other sons. You can have old man Ghimirey too for yourselves."

Then, she didn't see him for a few days, and his absence gnawed at her. Her eyes darted across the campus, across the classrooms; she searched for him when she came across a cluster of boys. The thought crossed her mind that she should have at least said hello to him. A small hello hurts nobody.

One afternoon when she reached home, he was there, talking with her mother. He sat at her feet, like many of Professor Shrestha's pupils did. Kranti hesitated at the doorway, wanting to turn around and leave, and return after he was gone. But they had seen her.

"Kranti!" Professor Shrestha said, smoke twirling from the cigarette on her finger, "you didn't tell me you had such a handsome boy as your friend."

Kranti went and stood in front of them, her heart beating rapidly. "Why are you here?" she said, something raw and burning in her throat.

"Kranti," Professor Shrestha said soothingly, "why talk like that to a friend who's come for a visit?"

Bhaskar continued to grin, looking up at her, his arms wrapped around his knees. She couldn't meet his eyes and looked away.

Professor Shrestha observed them. "Why don't you two go out for a walk? Obviously you have things to talk about."

"But, Madam, I need you to protect me," Bhaskar said, leaning against Professor Shrestha's legs and cowering.

"A joker, aren't you?" Professor Shrestha said, tousling his hair. "A joker and an intellectual. Kranti, where did you find this rascal?" Before Kranti could answer she said, "Go, go, you two need to sort things out." She took a long drag of her cigarette.

Outside, in her frozen anger Kranti refused to speak to him and walked rapidly, clutching her books against her chest and realizing, with added fury, that she'd forgotten to leave them at home.

"Kranti," he said, as he attempted to catch up with her. She was a fast walker, always had been to her mother's annoyance, so he was always a couple of steps behind, even though he was the one with the longer legs. Beggar Street was at the edge of the Tourist District, and so it was toward the Tourist District they moved, she propelled by her aggravation, he calling out her name, "Kranti, Kranti." They passed tourists with their stringy hair and their cameras.

Near the main chowk of the Tourist District, where lanes converged, she stopped and turned to face him, words surging up her chest and to her throat, but not coming out.

He clasped her hand. "A few minutes with me, please?"

She shook her head no, but she really wanted to say yes. She was tearing up, she realized, because no one wanted her company like this, except Dada. A couple of shopkeepers were watching them from their doorways.

He gently tugged at her arm. "It's a nice afternoon, please." He noticed her wet eyes, and wiped her tears with his palm, right there in the middle of the Tourist District, close to the shop where she'd bought Dada a Grateful Dead leather jacket.

He led her into a nearby doorway and up some narrow stairs. She could have simply turned around and escaped. But she didn't. They climbed four stories until they were on the roof, decorated with some tables and chairs, and a few uniformed waiters standing idly, looking at the chowk below. They sprang to attention when they saw Bhaskar and Kranti, who were then seated and fawned upon. The waiters, clearly familiar with Bhaskar, completed his order before it left his mouth; they nodded their heads and smiled and said, yes, sir, just like the last time. Bhaskar referred to them by names: Batman, Mukhiya, Shiva, and Goru. He joked with them about Batman's mustache and Mukhiya's obsession with the lottery. He asked how Shiva's father was faring with his cancer treatment. She wondered if he'd orchestrated this, reserved the entire rooftop—why weren't there other customers?—asked the waiters to be prepared for his arrival with a girl, anticipated that Professor Shrestha would ask them to go out, knew that she'd storm into the Tourist District, knew she'd stop right at the chowk below the restaurant.

After the waiters disappeared there was silence, except for the noise from the Tourist District below and the chirping of the birds from the telephone wires. She could see the tops of the surrounding houses. The sky was brilliantly blue. Not a whiff of cloud—was that also his orchestration? She found herself smiling.

"A suka for your thoughts," he said in Angrezi.

"Isn't this too much?" she said, but the smile didn't leave her face. She ought to have been angry.

Music sounded on the roof—there must have been speakers hidden behind the giant potted plants scattered all over and controlled by the waiters below. Some New Age music with a soothing melody. She closed her eyes.

"Will you dance with me, Kranti?"

After a moment he called her name again, and it felt like he'd been calling her name for years now. She opened her eyes. He was holding out his hand.

"Here?" she asked.

"Here."

She gave him her hand and they stood and began dancing. He held her like a ballroom dancer, moving around the rooftop in between the tables.

She had never danced before. Never, as she was the shy type and thought she'd make a fool of herself and cause others to laugh at her. Yet, here she was, in the middle of the Tourist District, with this impossible, dashing guy, at a rooftop restaurant named, even more impossibly, Head in the Clouds. The waiters, who'd come up with drinks, were now watching. Heads poked out of the windows of the surrounding houses. Spectators. She was gliding, effortlessly, and soon it was as if they were floating in the air below a clear blue sky.

During the Big Two, seconds after Bhaskar and Kranti escaped Head in the Clouds and found shelter in the Iconic Guest House, the entire four-story building that housed the restaurant, the travel agency, and the pashmina and gemstone shops below had been dragged across the street, as though by a giant invisible hand from above. It had then toppled onto the Happy Ending massage parlor where scantily clad honeys, often escaping hard lives in their villages, used their soft hands and mouths on pilgrims, who were also escaping hard lives in their villages. Batman, Mukhiya, Shiva, Goru—had all perished, along with the honeys and the pilgrims.

"Now it should be named Dead in the Clouds," Kranti couldn't help quipping to Bhaskar.

⁓

After she and Bhaskar became intimate, Kranti thought that, once and for all, she would be able to stop drugging herself with Paagalium, which she'd been taking since Dada died. With Bhaskar by her side, she was going to get better, on her own, without relying on these pills and suffering their horrible side effects—they made her drowsy or hyper, or infuriatingly, both.

She loved him. His gregariousness intimidated her. He had an easy way of dealing with others, embracing them into his world. People flocked to him, and he appeared to know everyone in town. In cafés, there was often a constant stream of visitors to their table.

"Oho-Bhaskar! Haven't seen you since the Big Two."

"Bhaskar, I want you to meet my aunt."

"You never phone me back, Bhaskar! Would it have hurt to at least send an SMS?"

"How's your father, Bhaskar? Please give him my greetings."

Often it was impossible to be in a crowded café without people constantly interrupting their conversation. Kranti experienced a variety of conflicting emotions then. Thrill at watching Bhaskar, his way of dealing with people, making them feel important, his memory of the details of people's lives—houses bought, children birthed, jobs changed, exams passed. But she also experienced intense social anxiety, felt that as soon as they were out of her earshot they were going to make disparaging comments about her, about her looks, about her sorry family situation, about her mother. On occasion Kranti asked that they go to a more secluded restaurant. He willingly obliged.

"Do you feel uncomfortable with all these people around?" he asked her.

"I feel nervous," she replied. In return he squeezed her hand and said nothing more.

She hadn't told him about Poe, hadn't told him about the paranoid feelings about Murti and the other Beggars she'd had after Dada died. She had only said that for a long while her "head hadn't been right." She worried that talking about her demons would bring them back. Only Professor Shrestha knew of the extent of her depression and paranoia, and even then her mother tried to hide it from the rest of the world. She used the euphemism of "rog" to refer to her daughter's mental illness with the Beggars and others, and even when it was just the two of them. Kranti feared that once Bhaskar learned of her mind's proclivities, he'd wonder what kind of life he was getting into with her. He'd love her, yes, but he'd love her sadly.

—

One afternoon, on the way to watch a movie, they'd walked past the scene of a mass wedding. It was presided over by none other than Swami Go!swami. The Rajjya was encouraging, facilitating, and even funding these weddings, to create new families to replace the old ones lost in the Big Two. Hundreds of couples sat on thin carpets that were laid out on the street, which had been blocked to traffic, near the Queen's Pond. The men wore the traditional daura suruwal and dhakatopi and the women wore red wedding saris. At the end of the street on a raised dais sat Swami Go!swami and about half a dozen priests chanting wedding mantras into microphones.

Swami Go!swami sported a thick moustache and dark beard that came way down to his chest. It was so dark that it looked like it was colored. He had a lustrous shiny face and shinier eyes. He was made even more radiant by the bright red robe he wore, distinguishing him from the other saffron-robed sadhus, as if the bright red meant that he had reached an even higher plane than his subordinates. He had amazingly white teeth, so white, Bhaskar said, that whenever he broke into a grin, one expected to hear a jingle from a toothpaste commercial. Spiritual leader, yoga master, Ayurvedic healer, Vaastu expert, astrologer extraordinaire, with an encyclopedic knowledge of the scriptures. He was the swami of all swamis. The exclamation in the middle was for even further encouragement, like saying "Go! Swami, rise to an even higher plane." A superman of swamis.

Now, as he supervised these quickie weddings, he was surrounded by beautiful white women wearing snow-white robes, robes so white that sometimes the women seemed to dissolve in the extreme whiteness.

Uncharacteristically, Bhaskar appeared to be moved by the scene of the mass wedding. "It's nice," he said, "that people can come together like this." She made fun of him then, asked him whether he too wanted to be seated cross-legged on the street, putting tika on the forehead of his new dulahi. "Sure," he said, "I'm open to anything."

The Worldlight Cinema Hall was still operating, even though its balcony section had collapsed during the Big Two. Now it only offered first class and second class, with moviegoers watching the film surrounded by debris. Wooden beams, loosened by the earthquake, creaked throughout the showing. Plaster fell off the ceiling. Loose wires hung from walls.

The movie was about a leftist guerrilla hiding from Rajjya forces in a village during the Civil War. It was a film with plenty of melodrama and poor acting, with some bawdy romance thrown in.

Perhaps he was still thinking of that wedding scene when, in the dark theater, he kissed her and told her that it was time he took her to visit his family.

No, no, no! she cried inwardly, and at once she had trouble breathing. The dilapidated movie theater, Bhaskar's sweet words, the timing of his invitation—it all felt like a trap. She said to him, "I need to go to the bathroom, okay?" And she exited, went to the big windows in the foyer, and looked out at the street, not seeing anything.

The anxiety attack came swiftly. *I can't do it,* she said to herself. She was acutely aware that Bhaskar was waiting for her return, and with each passing moment he'd be worried, but she needed space to collect herself. All she was doing, however, was panicking, freezing. Next to her was a man—perhaps he too was bored with the movie—and he was watching her intently, his eyes beady like Poe's. It was as though this stranger understood that she was evading something and would go to Bhaskar to tell on her. She was about to shout at the man when he looked past her and greeted a friend.

This was not the first time they had talked about her visiting the Ghimireys. But in every previous instance it had been an event in the future, something that was far away. Bhaskar had been upfront about what the Ghimireys were like—their priorities, the high regard in which they held themselves. "It will take considerable adjustment on your part," he'd said in a matter-of-fact tone, as though he was worried that she had a too-rosy picture of his family. Yet in the past few weeks, Bhaskar had brought up the idea a couple of times. "Listen," he'd said, "if we are getting married, the sooner you find out what makes the Ghimireys tick, the better, don't you think?"

"Oh, I'm sure it'll be fine," she said, but as the topic started cropping up frequently—it seemed that Bhaskar himself wanted to get this over with—she became fearful.

She returned to her seat in the theater.

"What took you so long?" Bhaskar asked.

"I needed fresh air. What did I miss?"

"The heroine's father is up in arms about their union."

They both laughed. And Kranti thought: *Had Dada been alive, he'd have been very happy with my union with you.*

Bhaskar appeared to sense that his mention of his family had triggered something in her. On their way back to Beggar Street, he said, "We don't have to live with them, but at some point you should meet them."

She squeezed his hand in solidarity, as if assuring him that she'd come around.

She went to bed sad that night at having disappointed Bhaskar. In the middle of the night, the sadness turned into something else. He was not telling her something. What it was, she didn't know, and then she did: *they have already rejected me.* They had learned about her by spying on her. For how long, she didn't know. They'd commissioned people to observe her. These spies reported back to the Ghimirey family: yes, this girl and Bhaskar meet almost every day. The Ghimireys knew that Bhaskar spent a lot of time at the house of the famous Madam Mao, but did they know that Bhaskar literally sits at her feet to take in her communist wisdom? The spies report that the mother and daughter live in a small house on the other side of the Tourist District. Only one-storied, which immediately signals a lack of wealth. The father was a simple cook, a chef in a hotel, who committed suicide. Then, there's the caste issue: the mother and daughter are descendants of the historical settlers of the Valley, clearly a lower caste. Yes, true, Professor Shrestha is nonconforming, and she hardly speaks the language of her caste. Still, lower caste. The Ghimireys are Brahmins. High Brahmins.

The next morning Kranti had dark circles under her eyes. She was supposed to meet Bhaskar but she didn't go. He called her mobile and texted her; she didn't answer. The home phone rang; Professor Shrestha picked it up. "O-ho, Bhaskar," she said. She was always pleased to hear from him. I wish you had been this pleased with Dada all the time, Kranti thought. But she knew her mother was simply happy that she had found such a nice, smart boy. Her daughter who'd started talking to herself in her room, who'd turned hateful and bitter, who'd seemed to lose her grip on the world. Bhaskar had injected joy in Kranti's life, in Professor Shrestha's life. He was so full of verve, so filled with goodness, so honest about himself—Kranti could see these thoughts her mother had about Bhaskar. Her mother also wondered what Bhaskar really saw in her insecure and disturbed daughter. As Kranti sat in her room listening to her mother speak to Bhaskar on the phone, she could see everyone—not just Bhaskar's family but taxi drivers, waiters in restaurants, girls at checkout counters in well-lit department stores, men who hung around shops drinking tea—wondering about her and Bhaskar, just like her friends in college had

wondered, often silently but sometimes aloud, about what Bhaskar
saw in her:

What is so special about her?

Well, she is kind of pretty.

Average pretty— not like Julia Roberts pretty.

Certainly not Aishwarya Rai pretty.

Not all right in her head, is she?

Maybe the handsome middle son from Ghimirey & Sons likes
these demented ones.

It's a passing interest. He's a do-gooder type, you know.

He wants to cure her?

Of course, and once she's cured, he'll move on to someone else.

The voices continued inside her and she didn't even hear Professor
Shrestha calling her.

"Bhaskar is on the phone," Professor Shrestha said through the door.

Kranti made an attempt at getting up but couldn't.

"Kranti? Did you hear? It's Bhaskar."

"Tell him I have a headache."

"Shall I bring the landline into your room?"

"No, I'll call him later."

A minute later, Professor Shrestha cautiously opened the door and
peeked into Kranti's room. "Had a fight with him, did you?"

"Always nosey, you."

"Just talk with him."

"You two never leave me alone."

Professor Shrestha stared at her. "Is it coming again?"

"Is what coming?"

"Rog, rog." Of course, Professor Shrestha would use the euphemism for "sickness."

"My rog has gone all rogue. Now leave!"

Later, Kranti heard her tell Murti on the phone that the Beggars
couldn't gather at the home that afternoon.

Apparently Murti disagreed, for Professor Shrestha said, "Yes, yes,
I'm aware that we need to get those posters ready, but we'll do it

another day." Professor Shrestha listened, then said, "Murti, why are you being such a dunce? It's simply not possible today." She hung up. It was rare for Professor Shrestha to hang up on Murti, so she must have felt especially guilty this time. Even after all these years, Professor Shrestha went into bouts of guilt over Dada's suicide, and over the state of her daughter. She should feel this way, thought Kranti, because she is culpable. Professor Shrestha sometimes said out loud, especially after a couple of pegs of whiskey in her, "I should have let him know more often—how much I loved him."

"But you never did," Kranti would say if she was nearby. *You never did.*

"You don't know what your Dada and I went through together." Professor Shrestha would launch into a nostalgic soliloquy, punctuated by long spells of silence, about her and her Mani during their heyday. Kranti would listen, half-dismissive of Professor Shrestha's fabricated emotions, half-curious because she could never get enough of Dada. "He was so handsome in those days, your Dada. On the chubby side, for sure, but with a good-looking, charming face. I fell in love with him instantly. Two seconds—I was gone. You know where we met? On a bus while traveling on By-Road. I was going to a dissident gathering in the City of the Brave; he was on his way to help a friend start a restaurant. We sat together. At first he was nervous, even as I could tell that he wanted to talk. When I realized that he'd never gather the courage, it was I who asked him what time it was. The time! Everyone could see that I had a watch on my wrist. That gave him an opening, and he asked my name and everything, and he began telling me jokes. I was howling inside that bus, with everyone staring. But I had never been the type who cared about what other people thought, so at the end of the bus ride I asked him for his number."

———

Dada had never complained to Kranti about Professor Shrestha, never uttered a word against her. On the contrary, he'd always spoken highly of his wife, to Kranti and others. "You must be very proud of your mother," he often said to Kranti. "Why you worry so much?" But Kranti knew that he was hurt by the enormous amount of time Professor Shrestha spent with other people, with her students, with activists, with human rights workers, with the Sangharsh, and after Kranti was born, with the core group of her disciples who formed the Beggars. At times Professor Shrestha treated Dada like a noker-chaker. She ordered him around, asked him to fetch things around the house for her, and became irritated with him for petty reasons. Since they had no nokerchakers—they never had, because Professor Shrestha claimed that keeping nokerchakers was akin to keeping slaves—it was Kranti's father who ended up doing most of the house-work. Her mother was too busy with her students and her politics. Professor Shrestha didn't think it was out of the ordinary for her husband to be in charge of the daily management of the house, didn't think that she ought to share the burden. So, even though he worked long hours at Hotel Thunderbolt & Diamond, the boutique hotel where he was a chef, it was Dada who fed Kranti her breakfast while her mother wrote her books behind the closed door of their bedroom. It was Dada who ironed Kranti's school uniform, then prepared lunch for her to take to school in her tiffin box. It was Dada who accompanied her to the bus stop, a few neighborhoods away near the Durbar, even after Kranti was old enough to walk alone.

Often the father and daughter walked leisurely, Kranti clasping Dada's arm. Daddy's girl, her classmates at the bus stop teased her. One classmate said to her, "The only man whose arm I'll hold will be my man's, not my father's." You can have all of your men, Kranti thought. I'm happy with my father.

Dada listened to her when she worried about an exam, when she couldn't decide on a dress to wear to the school fair, when she was con-flicted about acting in a school play directed by a demanding teacher. Professor Shrestha had mostly been unavailable, or if she had been, she had listened to Kranti with a distracted look, her mind engaged with an essay she was composing, or the speech she was planning to deliver at a gathering, or the agenda for a forthcoming meeting. Conversations with her mother led to explosions of anger, with a tearful Kranti running to Dada, who then soothed her.

"You have to make do with the mother you have," he told Kranti. Not only make do, but be proud that her mother was making a difference in so many people's lives. "We are all born for different purposes in life," he told her during their walks to the bus stop or to her karate class in the next neighborhood. "Your mother has come into this world with a miraculous mind." A miraculous mind, he often said about his wife. Yes, a miraculous mind, Kranti agreed, but an empty heart. When Kranti sarcastically referred to her mother as Madam Mao—during those early years she barely knew who Mao was, only knew that he was someone whose name often appeared on the lips of those who gathered in her house—Dada gently reprimanded her, told her that she should treat her mother with respect.

Dada also existed in the periphery of the circle of supporters and acolytes who surrounded Professor Shrestha. When Kranti was a teenager, their house was always crowded with the Beggars. Her father made tea, prepared snacks, provided shawls and blankets on cold days, arranged for fans during the summer. He ran errands, acted as Professor Shrestha's assistant. Yet she barely acknowledged him when others were present. His role in her public life was so marginal that some Beggars treated him as though he were indeed a butler or an attendant. They grew annoyed with him if the fans stopped working, or if somehow there were not enough snacks for everyone. They mocked his profession: "It must be very easy for you," they said, "to slip into the cooking role at home, hoina, Chef-ji?"

During those times he retreated to his record collection in his bedroom. He had an eclectic taste in music: jazz, classical sitar and vocal, Mohammed Rafi, and lately, classic rock, mainly the Beatles and the Rolling Stones. He lay in bed and listened to his CD player, his eyes closed. This was his escape, and even Kranti didn't bother him when he was in his music-listening mood. He had a couple of same-age friends, including a pilot who sometimes came to the house, with whom he discussed music and his newfound love for rock. At one point, the Eagles were his new favorite. He often crooned to Kranti about how her eyes gave away her lies. In the kitchen as he rinsed the dishes, he pointed a soapsuds-covered finger toward the window, which was so foggy that you could hardly see anything, and sang about seeing an iridescent light on the horizon.

Kranti helped Dada in the kitchen when the living room was crowded with the Beggars, but she did so with resentment, banging the pots and pans, cursing the Beggars when they laughed loudly or when they treated her father disrespectfully. "Why doesn't she hold these meetings elsewhere?" she fumed as she and Dada worked together in the kitchen. "Why does she need to bring her minions to the house? Go to a hotel, rent a room, and you can laugh all you want with your Madam Mao."

"Shhh," Dada cautioned.

Arguments often erupted between Professor Shrestha and Kranti.

"I have so much homework to do," Kranti shouted, "and I can't concentrate with all of these idiots around me."

"Talk like that about my people and I'll slap you," Professor Shrestha said.

"Hmmph! And I'll slap you back so hard I'll make you crap."

Once, upon hearing her daughter's retort, Professor Shrestha did slap her, and Kranti was so enraged, especially given her mother's talk of non-violence, that she leapt upon her mother. Dada had to intervene and clasp her from behind and lead her out to the lawn as he gave dagger-looks to his wife, who appeared shocked that she had indeed hit her daughter.

"She's an uncaring, unfeeling witch," Kranti cried out on the lawn, her cheek stinging from the slap. "Boksi!"

"That's not true. You shouldn't say such things about your own mother."

"It's true! It's true!" she cried, shaking. "She doesn't care about us. She doesn't care about you." She turned toward him as if he were the one who was uncaring.

He led her away from the house toward the main street, stroking her back as they walked.

"She cares about me," he said. "Trust me, she cares about me."

"She treats you like a dog," she said flatly, now a bit calmer.

He stopped her, wiped her tears and said, "What do I need her respect for? I know who I am. I know that deep inside her heart she loves me."

"People who love *show* their love."

"She needs me, Kranti. And I don't mind. At this point in her life when she is doing great things and teaching great things to others, it's okay."

"What great things? You are so gullible."

"Why you worry so much?" Dada said.

She didn't want to argue anymore with Dada, so she slipped her arm into his and they went to a nearby eatery for chhoila and kachila. He told her jokes, and at first she remained serious, but he continued telling his jokes, and finally she cracked a smile.

— ⌣ —

Kranti heard Bhaskar talking to Professor Shrestha in the hallway, then he was at her door. He came and sat on the bed next to her. She didn't look up. He put a hand on her shoulder, gently massaged it, inquired if it was something he did.

That's when she turned to him. He was startled by her appearance, and she could see herself too in the slim mirror behind him. She hadn't changed out of the kurta suruwal from the day before, and her makeup—she'd started wearing makeup after she met Bhaskar—was smeared all over her face, the mascara running down her cheeks.

He stood and shut the door.

For a moment she observed him, his handsome face, his broad forehead, and her heart broke. Tears streamed down her cheeks. "Why are you with me?"

He wiped away her tears.

She averted her face and said, "Your family despises me."

He watched her momentarily, as if waiting for her to laugh and tell him she was joking. Then, he said, "Why? Did you hear anything? Did someone tell you something?"

"I just know."

"Did someone from the Asylum come to talk with you? Chaitanya? Priyanka?"

"No! No!"

"Then what is it?" Understanding dawned on him. "Oh, I know. It must have been Shambhogya bhauju."

"No, Bhaskar, no! No one from your family has come to see me."

"Then what is the reason for this?"

He pressured, but she couldn't bring herself to say the word "spy," that she was convinced his family was spying on her. But that was the problem: her conviction wasn't convincing, even to herself. A voice inside said: *Knock it off! No one's spying on you.* At other times, it was a certainty. A pedestrian looking away, the cat next door staring at her, a neighbor bent over her waterspout—all signaling that something was afoot.

She told Bhaskar that his family thought she was not worthy of him. He expressed his bafflement, asking her why she was underselling herself. They were both lying in bed, she half-turned away from him, her kurta suruwal soaked in sweat because she had been writhing in it for so long.

He placed his palm on her shoulder and asked, "Don't get angry with me, but is this like what you were experiencing when Dada died?"

She stopped breathing and closed her eyes, wishing this moment had never arrived. "What do you mean?"

"You had said something about your mind being deeply disturbed then. I was just wondering if, you know, whether you are feeling the same things now."

She told him it was nothing.

"Kranti, you know I'm not going to think less of you because of this."

"I don't want to talk about it," she said. He knew that she'd struggled with depression in the past, but if he knew the full extent of her mental illness, he'd no longer want to be with her, and she couldn't imagine being without him.

He hovered over her in bed, sometimes putting his chin on her shoulder, sometimes pressing his cheek softly against hers, imploring, cajoling. "No," she said.

"Please," he said, and then suddenly Kranti was watching herself, watching herself and Bhaskar together, from somewhere up above, and she saw how ridiculous the whole thing was—she denying, he imploring, both of them but one soul, one soul—and she ended up bursting into laughter, then crying, covering her face with her palm, then laughing again.

"What did I say?" Bhaskar said, smiling.

What must he be thinking of me? she thought. What a dolt I am. She could have slapped herself right there, for all the drama. "It's nothing," she said, smiling.

"If it's nothing, then why are you lying in bed like this, huh?" Bhaskar said, tickling her, and she tried to protect herself and couldn't and she tried to tickle him back and couldn't and soon he was kissing her.

—

On her way home from spending time with Bhaskar in a café, she spotted a man in the Tourist District who had been watching her from under the awning of a shop and who quickly looked away. On another occasion in Lord of the Heavens chowk, she sensed something and looked up to note a woman on a second story window of an old, teetering house. When their eyes met she turned her face sideways to address another person inside the room, then returned her gaze to Kranti. Another time in a microbus, a man sitting in front of her repeatedly turned around, his neck craned at an impossible angle in the overcrowded van, and he finally asked her who her parents were, where she lived. She refused to look at him and got off at the next stop. The man got off with her and followed her for a while before he turned down another street.

—

Palatial, it had a total of fifteen rooms, Bhaskar had said of the Asylum. Some rooms were never used. A few years ago Aditya had all the windows replaced with traditional carved windows he'd commissioned from a famous artisan in the City of Beauty, and the house had been featured in *Valley* magazine. An atrium courtyard was in the middle, with a small fountain and a lush garden, where parties were held in good weather. The centerpiece of the courtyard was a human-sized statue of Darkmother, multiple arms, tongue down to her chin, eyes kohl-rimmed, large and bright, glowering at her devotees as though watching their every move. Prithvi Raj prayed here for half an hour every morning, and the other Ghimireys and the nokerchakers bowed their heads for blessings when passing by. Balconies ran around the second floor where all the bedrooms were, affording a view of what and who was below in the courtyard.

The subfamilies lived in distinct sections on the second floor: Aditya and his wife Shambhogya, and their son Shaditya, who was away at a boarding school in Bharat; youngest son Chaitanya and his barren wife Priyanka; Bhaskar; and Prithvi Raj and Muwa. "Once you get married," Prithvi Raj told Bhaskar, "I want you to take two rooms, in anticipation of the little one that'll come." Bhaskar had declined, saying he and his future wife wouldn't need more than one room.

"Why did you say that?" Kranti teased Bhaskar. "I need five rooms."

The Asylum had not suffered a scratch during the Big Two. It had swayed and rocked gently, as if it were enjoying a gentle breeze, as houses across the Valley, and across Darkmotherland, had toppled and crumbled. The Ghimireys liked to say that it was Darkmother who had saved the Asylum and its inhabitants, "as if Darkmother has a special affection for the wealthy," Bhaskar told Kranti. His family often attributed their financial success to Darkmother. And why would Darkmother favor them? Because Prithvi Raj was a Darkmother devotee, had been since his teenage days back in the village.

His family genuinely believed they were good people, pious people, worthy of such blessings.

Bhaskar mocked the name of his house. "You know why it's called the Asylum, don't you?"

She'd heard it from Bhaskar before: the Ghimireys, in their high-mindedness, had arrived at the name of the Asylum for their mansion as a symbol of refuge, even though they had never given anyone shelter, not even after the Big Two, when so many people had been rendered homeless.

"But the real meaning is that it's an asylum for the wealth they hoard," Bhaskar said.

On the ground floor was also a gym that no one used, a table tennis room, and a small theater with its own popcorn machine and soft drinks dispenser. Shaditya, when he returned home from his boarding school, sat in the theater once in a while to watch movies. But there were big TV screens in every room, so even the downstairs theater mostly remained empty.

On the lawn by the side of the main house was a small temple, God's Room, that Muwa had built for herself. She spent a lot of time there.

The Servants Villa was a building next to the garage, and that itself had five or six rooms.

"Instead of us having two rooms," Bhaskar said to Kranti, "why don't we adopt those khateykids and give them a room or two here in the Asylum?" Khateykids, ranging from ages eight to sixteen or seventeen, roamed the Valley, begging or scrounging around for food in garbage dumps, sometimes collecting glass and plastic to take to recycling centers for a few paisas. With many kids orphaned or rendered homeless by the Big Two, khateykids had multiplied recently. A small group lived on the pavement outside the Asylum: beggars and vagrants, high on glue, begging or gambling or quarreling. They flocked to Bhaskar when he stepped out of the Asylum, and followed him to the Tourist District, where he rendezvoused with Kranti for an evening stroll.

The Ghimireys donated to orphanages all over the Valley, Bhaskar said ruefully. At every major festival, Ghimirey & Sons fed the hungry and donated blankets. Prithvi Raj, wearing a shiny, expensive shawl, gave alms to the homeless and down-and-outs who lined up on the way to the Lord of the Animals Temple. Ghimirey & Sons donated money to ashrams and orphanages. "You know what the motto of the company is? Every Challenge an Opportunity. They are opportunistic all right."

The Ghimireys tried hard to get rid of the khateykids who had made their home on the pavement outside the Asylum. The Poolis Uncles came by several times a month and a few times even the Loyal Army Dais had come. They beat the khateykids, sometimes to bloody pulps. The khateykids would disappear for a few days, then show up again. Shambhogya complained frequently. Aditya said that one day he'd fetch his gun and shoot them, one by one. But sometimes a gun wasn't even necessary. Once, a khateykid died in the hospital after he got thrashed by a Poolis Uncle, and the hospital merely pronounced he'd died of "preexisting conditions."

The khateykids loved Bhaskar. Rascals, Bhaskar called them, gave them high-fives, and asked how their business was going. The business of thieving, he whispered to Kranti when he and his posse met up with her. He picked up the smallest one, a young girl, Rani, and carried her in his arms, holding her brother Subhash's hand as they roamed the Tourist District, even though the Ghimireys disapproved of that neighborhood, which was a haven for shady touts, unkempt khaireys, and sometimes high-class honeys who pretended to be tourists themselves as they solicited among the foreigners.

The khateykids tugged at Kranti and asked for money. Bhaskar scolded them, saying that if given a chance they'd sell both Bhaskar and Kranti at the fish market. "Isn't that what you did to your parents?" he asked them. "Didn't you sell them at the fish market?"

There was a magical quality about Bhaskar that made these khateykids surround him, tell him their stories, want a smile from him, a reassuring nod of his head, pat on their back, or a gaze that let them know that finally, finally, here was someone who understood them.

5.

Once, near the now-collapsed White Tower, a man and a woman were eating in a restaurant on the top floor of a mall. The roof of the mall had been blown away by the Big Two, but a massive blue tarp had replaced it and business was going on as well as it could. The man, observing the Bhurey tents on the Parade Ground, casually remarked that the Parade Ground resembled a war zone.

Bhu-kampa (earthquake) rey-fugees, a.k.a. Bhureys. A majority of these Big Two survivors arrived after making arduous journeys across the ice-covered mountain passes, and their family and friends died in the process. By the time they reached the Valley—and they were still coming, even weeks after the Big Two—they often looked like bands of bedraggled patients. They spoke of entire mountain villages demolished, burying all the inhabitants. Some villages, they said, had simply disappeared, swallowed by the big maws the Big Two had opened. They spoke of a wind that blew at ferocious speed across the mountains, one that made all rescue missions impossible.

The man's young wife—the couple had just married—said that she had seen images online of such camps in Aafrika, maybe Somalia or Sudan.

"Our country is a failed state now," the husband said.

"You think so?" the wife said.

"Yes, look at this," the husband said. His voice became emotional. "How long can this go on? North of our country is unreachable. The Son of Yeti now controls not only half of Darkmotherland, he's getting ready to invade the Valley. Everything is in shambles. Inflation is up through the roof. And yet here we are, paying two thousand rupees for a plate of momos. What else would you call it? A failed state." The man had gotten so carried away with his soliloquy that he hadn't noticed how loud he had become. His wife, focused on her momos and the eloquence of her husband, whom she adored and admired, neglected to tell him to lower his voice.

A group of young men sitting at a nearby table approached. "Pure Darkmotherland!" they said.

"Pure Darkmotherland!" the couple responded.

"What were you saying just now, bhaiya?" they asked.

The husband and wife looked at them.

"You were just criticizing PM Papa, weren't you?"

"No, no," the husband said. "I was just—"

"Failed state?" one of the youths said. He had a yellow bandana tied around his head. Papa's Patriot. Papa's Patriots often demanded—and received—free drinks and food in restaurants, and that's what they'd been doing at the next table.

"I didn't mean it that way." Sweat had formed on the husband's forehead.

"Then how do you mean?" another youth said, pressing both palms on the couple's table and leaning towards them. The waiters and the manager watched but didn't interfere. Other customers were watching from the corner of their eyes, glad that it wasn't them. They had discovered that they experienced pleasure when people were publicly interrogated and humiliated like this. Not knowing how it would end also provided a distinct element of thrill. Ah, this is what life is like, they thought. One needs to be put in one's place every now and then. There was simply too much freedom before, too much la-la-di-da-oh-aren't-we-a-happily-liberated-bunch exuberance in this country. Too many people saying whatever they wanted to, on Facebook, Twitter, Snapchat, WhatsApp, Whassup, Instagram, Whambam, Whatnot, TikTok, Crapshoot, Whatevah. Everyone clamoring for attention, everyone having an opinion and having the need to express it as if expressing one's opinion as emphatically and as eloquently and as pithily as possible was what made one important, as if silence was no longer a virtue. And everyone was always shouting for rights: third-gender rights, women's rights, marginalized people's rights, pregnant women's rights, single dads' rights, Christians' rights, Muslims' rights, Buddhists' rights, atheists' rights, vegetarians' rights, pacifists' rights, momo eaters' rights, kothay eaters' rights, dancers' rights, prancers' rights, taxi drivers' rights, prostitutes' rights, youths' rights, sleuths' rights, animals' rights, homeowners' rights, street hustlers' rights, street vendors' rights, street artists' rights, scam artists' rights, smokers' rights, children's rights, retards' rights, blowhards' rights, yoga practitioners' rights, priests' rights, teachers' rights, students' rights, adult learners' rights, adulterers' rights, writers' rights, non-writers' rights, beggars' rights, caterers' rights, dress makers' rights, carpet weavers' rights, porn stars' rights, widows' rights, anarchists' rights, laugh therapists' rights, weep therapists' rights, cab drivers' rights, cab passengers' rights, rights-advocates' rights—when was it going to end?

Now, with PM Papa there was a semblance of order in this country. Sure, there are restrictions now, a clamping down, a tightening, but it's good to be constricted like this. Good to know what you could do and what you couldn't do. Good to shut down all these rights seekers. Life is simpler this way, clearer, better managed.

"You have a pretty wife," the youth with the yellow bandana said. He ran his index finger on the wife's cheek.

The wife didn't say anything but looked at the husband, who said, "You misheard, brother."

"We heard what we heard," another youth said.

The yellow bandana slipped into the seat next to the wife. "My legs are tired. I should sit down," he said. It was a small booth, so he was squeezed against the young wife. The husband reached across the table as if to claim her but quickly withdrew his hand.

"And you were saying?" the yellow bandana said.

"I said I wasn't criticizing PM Papa." The husband's voice became hoarse.

The yellow bandana shifted so his body was now touching the young wife's. "So, what exactly were you saying?" One of his hands disappeared under the table. "I want you to describe in detail what you thought the conversation was about so I can be convinced. And take your time, I'm in no rush."

The husband was stocky enough that he'd have easily beaten the yellow bandana. But he wouldn't have been able to fight all five

Papa's Patriots, so in the end he'd have been defeated. Still, people would've said he tried to protect his wife's honor. Hadn't an ancient god launched a full-scale war to reclaim his pure and devoted wife from the multi-headed demon? Didn't the husband of the young wife in the restaurant, like all Darkmotherlandites, have such super-hero models to follow?

The yellow bandana's hand roamed under the table.

In the end, people said that nothing much happened. Well, nothing, except that the young wife was molested in public by the yellow bandana, his hand roaming freely over her kurta suruwal, caressing her thigh, pressing her boobs, hovering over her crotch, while the rest of Papa's Patriots formed a protective circle around the booth, barring the other patrons and waiters from viewing. But the body curtain was also a pretense: these Papa's Patriots didn't care if others saw. No one said or did anything, anyway.

They raped me, the wife thought afterward, in the months and years that followed, even later on in life after she was a mother and a grandmother. They raped me and you did nothing about it, she told her husband silently, in her mind, and she held this accusation within her, like one holds a talisman close to one's chest, until the day she died. They never referred to the incident again. In fact, that evening, after locking herself in the bathroom and having a good cry, she emerged as someone who had accepted what had happened and was ready to move on. They stopped going out to eat in restaurants, but beyond that, she behaved normally toward him. They made love and had babies who went on to have their own. Yet, every once in a while, he'd find her staring at him as though she were lost in secret thoughts about him.

———

Kranti and Bhaskar had recently had their own encounter with Papa's Patriots. Returning from meeting a friend who had been con-valescing in the Brave Hospital after a massive head injury suffered during the Big Two, they had marveled at the tent city of Bhurey Paradise spread out before them. Bhaskar had wanted to go see his friend Kabiraj, who taught with him at Streetwise School and lived in Bhurey Paradise, but Kranti said that she wasn't in the mood to traverse through the tent city. She had met Kabiraj before, knew that he was a poet of some note among the Valley's upcoming bards. A round, not-too-attractive fellow, but charming in his shyness. He was sought after as a tutor in the Valley, and also taught at Streetwise, but only an occasional class. The day Bhaskar had taken her to Streetwise to show her his workplace, Kabiraj had been there, but so shy, oh so shy that she'd asked Bhaskar afterwards, "Is he always like this?" Mostly around pretty women, Bhaskar had said.

When Kranti said she didn't want to go to Bhurey Paradise, or to see Kabiraj, the couple walked toward the Queen's Pond. A government vehicle went by, using a megaphone to enumerate the details of the Treasonist Act, which had just been signed by PM Papa. Kranti felt Bhaskar's hand tightening in hers as the announcer kept repeating the word "treason" as though it were a contagious disease. Some people were staring at the government vehicle in confusion. "How large?" they asked one another, regarding the number of people who could gather under the Treasonist Act.

Inside Mitho Chiya, the tea shop near the Queen's Pond, Bhaskar and Kranti heard conversations around them.

"You mean we can't drink tea together like this?" customers whispered.

"Large means very large. Dozens and dozens."

"You mean as in we-plotting-a-kranti large?"

"Yes, more like we-gonna-topple-PM-Papa's-Rajjya large."

"Shhh!"

"But I was just—"

"PM Papa jindabad!"

"PM Papa 24/7!"

There was subdued laughter, which vanished when two Papa's Patriots entered Mitho Chiya, announcing, "Pure Darkmotherland!"

From Motherland TV on the wall Hom Bokaw was enumerating the countless ways in which PM Papa had saved the country from the brink of disaster. Once Papa's Patriots entered, the tea drinkers watched Motherland TV in silence, seemingly unable to peel their eyes off it. The man next to Bhaskar and Kranti clapped and said, "Bravo! Bravo!" at the television. But most men slurped their teas, their eyes glued to Hom Bokaw.

"How many of you here are together?" Papa's Patriots asked. Kranti felt heat rise up her chest, to her face. She clutched Bhaskar's hand under the table, hard.

No one answered.

"How many?" one of them shouted.

Two men raised their hands timidly, then Bhaskar and Kranti.

To the two men, Papa's Patriot's asked, "What's your relation?"

It looked like the two men were friends but they went into a convoluted explanation about how they were distant cousins who also grew up together and went to the same college and now just hung out together occasionally. But they were so busy with work that this was the first time they'd hung out like this. "In a long time," they finished, breathless.

Papa's Patriots glared at them, then turned to Bhaskar and Kranti. "And you?"

"Boyfren and garlfren," Bhaskar said.

All the heads inside Mitho Chiya turned toward Bhaskar and Kranti.

One Papa's Patriot, wearing a yellow bandana that said PP, put on a thoughtful expression. "Incredible. No shame anymore."

"Well, what can we say about shame," Bhaskar said.

Kranti held her breath. Why couldn't Bhaskar shut his mouth?

"Openly declaring themselves boyfrens and garlfrens," the young man said. He couldn't have been more than eighteen, younger than Bhaskar or Kranti. "This is against PM Papa's vision of Pure Dark-motherland."

"True," some of the men in the tea shop muttered, men who until a moment ago hadn't cared whether Bhaskar and Kranti were lovers or siblings or playmates.

"Something wrong with us being a couple?" Bhaskar asked, before Kranti could stop him.

"Are you having sex?" Papa's Patriot Two asked. He said sex in Angrezi, making it sound like sax.

The audacity of the question generated a subtle gasp in the room. Kranti dug her nail into Bhaskar's thigh.

"And you," Papa's Patriot One pointed at Kranti. "What is your deal? Are you a—"

"Slut?" the whisper came from a customer in the tea shop.

Bhaskar was about to get up, when Papa's Patriot Two said to Papa's Patriot One, "Let it be, yaar. He's probably already getting a hard-on listening to you. Just imagine what he does to her tonight, and you can also get your rocks off."

Papa's Patriot One stared at Bhaskar and Kranti some more. Kranti looked away but Bhaskar met his gaze. Then Papa's Patriot One raised his fist in the air and shouted, "PM Papa jindabad!"

For two seconds there was silence in Mitho Chiya, then all the customers, except Bhaskar and Kranti, raised their fists and said, "PM Papa jindabad!"

Papa's Patriot One raised his fist again, pointedly, looking at Bhaskar and Kranti. "PM Papa jindabad!"

Kranti elbowed Bhaskar, and now the two of them also raised their fists and said, "PM Papa jindabad," Bhaskar reluctantly, of course.

Later, as she and Bhaskar left Mitho Chiya, Kranti said to him, "Please don't do such things again."

He mimicked the Papa Patriot. "Well, are you having *sax?*"

"Perhaps you can take it lightly because you're a Ghimirey & Sons. It's not the same for the rest of us." She didn't tell him, then, that she had been on the brink of a panic attack in Mitho Chiya.

When Bhaskar related the incident to Professor Shrestha that evening at Beggar Street, she shook her head but said nothing, as if things had become so unbearable that she couldn't speak anymore.

A few more people came into Beggar Street one day, people Kranti hadn't seen before, people with funny faces, with furtive looks. There was something more radical about this new breed—it was in the way they carried themselves. They wore very simple shirts and pants and wore slippers, never shoes, which Kranti was sure was a statement of some sort. They were three men and a woman, infamous as the Gang of Four, Kranti learned. The woman was distinctive in how small she was, with a dark, somber face. The others, including the Beggars, called her Amma. The three men seemed to defer to her, mostly with body language, their faces half-turned toward her, as if they were looking for clues from her that would then tell them what to say, how to act. The Gang of Four didn't fawn over Professor Shrestha like the Beggars did. They appeared cautious about her, perhaps even disdainful. They mostly listened, rarely offering opinions, watching, judging, evaluating, always alert to the sounds outside. But it was clear that they had brought in a new, more pernicious energy among the Beggars. After the Gang of Four left, the Beggars whispered among themselves, at times arguing vehemently. Words such as "dangerous" and "risky" were thrown around. Although Kranti didn't catch everything, she understood that the Gang of Four had come at the invitation of Prakash, whereas Murti, along with Professor Shrestha, was opposed to being associated with them.

They came again after a few days. When Kranti left her room and crossed the living room to go to the bathroom, Amma watched her. She did not smile but there was a brightness in her eyes; they seemed to suggest she knew exactly who Kranti was. Kranti also learned, after they left, that the Gang of Four were among the most wanted by the Rajjya for subversive activities, so they were actually underground, which meant that they were certain to be labeled Treasonists and executed if caught.

The coming of the Gang of Four to Beggar Street signaled that the Beggars had also moved to a different stage. They were no longer satisfied with sitting at the feet of their Madam and complaining about the injustices of this world. They intended to do something.

Kranti especially saw it in Prakash, whose jaws had become tighter in the past couple of weeks.

Kranti wondered if Mr. Sapkota would recognize who the Gang of Four were, or suspect that they were on the Wanted list of the Rajjya. Did Motherland TV have a Darkmotherland's Most Wanted show? She didn't recall seeing one. Only the Son of Yeti was featured regularly on Motherland TV as the country's most wanted criminal.

"I'm afraid that something bad is going to happen to you," Kranti said to Bhaskar in her room that evening. She had dreamt last night that Prakash had something strapped to his chest and he was shouting something that sounded like "Long live Palestine," then he blew himself up.

"It's not that easy to die," Bhaskar said, as though he had caught a glimpse of her dream.

They argued. She told him that it *was* easy to die, as the Big Two had amply proven. And the people who'd disappeared, either in the earthquake or by PM Papa, they're most likely dead.

"Well, *Bhaskar Ghimrey* is not going to die," Bhaskar said. "Bhaskar Ghimirey has work to do to save this country."

"If Bhaskar Ghimirey continues to listen to the Beggars," she said, "he will soon be out of work." She put air quotes around "out of work," suggesting he'd no longer be able to work, then, realizing that she'd just wished death upon her lover, apologized profusely.

He stroked her hair and said that he'd been thinking that there was no reason for them to live in the Asylum after they got married. She expressed her fear that the Ghimireys would then blame her for taking him away from his family. She was worried about living with the Ghimireys but also terrified of living without them? He told her he didn't understand it.

"The Ghimireys." He used a deep movie-actor voice, moving his hand slowly through the air as though reading a marquee. "Can't live with them. Can't live without them."

Kranti couldn't help but raise both her arms in the air, fists clenched, and shout, "The Ghimireys! Yay!"

—

Their favorite café was Tato Chiso, with its comfy sofas, giant TV, and a portico with a nice view of the Tourist District, which was bustling with khaireys, rickshaw pullers, and hawkers. Tourism had made a rapid comeback after the Big Two. The Rajjya had launched an aggressive Visit Darkmotherland campaign, and incredibly, tourists had started trickling in, with the numbers increasing every week. President Corn Hair had doubled the Amrikan foreign aid to Darkmotherland, which sped up the process. The damaged airport had been repaired, and steps were underway to turn the airport terminal into something other than the large, chaotic third-world bus station that it was. And even PM Papa's critics, now increasingly silenced, were forced to credit PM Papa with such an astounding revival of tourism, at least in the Valley. Before the dust of the Big Two had even cleared, he'd propagated the idea of disaster tourism, and the Western tourists, already pre-inclined to romanticize adventures in the dust and squalor of Darkmotherland, had warmed up to the idea. Many of them were spiritually disenchanted, and saw an opportunity for finding one's true self in a faraway land that had been ravaged by a natural disaster. Where else would the chance of discovering nirvana be heightened but in a dirt-poor country that was suffering? President Corn Hair's tweet, touting Darkmotherland as a "beautiful mountain nation" that was worth a visit, had also helped double the number of Amrikan tourists. It was becoming clear that President Corn Hair and PM Papa were developing a bromance via Twitter.

Tourists were under strict warning to steer clear of politics, not to make observations or statements critical of PM Papa or the Rajjya. The Loyal Army Dais patrolled the Tourist District in small groups, always on the lookout for anti-government activities. Still, once in a while a tourist, deliberately or otherwise, violated the instructions.

And for them, too, the punishment was swift: a heavy fine, or jail, or in some instances, immediate deportation. Just recently, from the Tato Chiso portico, Kranti and Bhaskar had observed a tourist being beaten up by Papa's Patriots; the khairey had been distributing leaflets with photos of Che Guevara and words about rising up against Rajjya's oppression.

One Saturday Kranti met Bhaskar at Tato Chiso, where he'd arrived with an entourage of khateykids who made their home outside the Asylum. Usually there were two or three, but today there were half a dozen scraggly, unkempt kids, wearing rags—some shoeless and dirty, bounding up the stairs, shoving and cursing and finding themselves amidst well-dressed customers with their laptops and foreign tongues.

The head waiter refused to serve them. "We don't allow khateykids in here."

"I don't see any sign that says no kids allowed," Bhaskar said. He made a show of searching for the sign. He pointed through the glass to the inner room, where a family of khairey tourists with small children were sipping handcrafted drinks on a sofa. "Only khairey kids allowed? The fairer they are, the better?" This elicited muted giggles from the khateykids and a smile or two from khairey tourists at the adjacent tables.

"If we let khateykids in here," the head waiter said, "our business will decline."

"I don't see any of your customers leaving," Bhaskar said. "Do you?" he asked Kranti. She put her hand on his arm, pleaded no with her eyes. He stood and asked the customers at the adjacent tables, most of them tourists, "Are any of you planning on walking out because of these ragamuffins here?"

Some stared, some smiled uncomfortably. One bearded khairey, his face red from having just scaled the mountains, said, slightly uncertainly, raising his fist, "Khateykids jindabad?"

This led the khateykids to raise their fists and chant, "Khateykids jindabad!"

"Go bring some cakes," Bhaskar said to the waiter. "And sand-wiches."

"Sandwiches for these badazzes," the bearded khairey said.

The waiter left with a scowl.

When the snacks and drinks were brought, the manager also appeared. It turned out he had recognized Bhaskar as a Ghimirey. "For today, I'll let you do this, Bhaskarji," the manager said, pointing at the khateykids, who were attacking the sandwiches and the cakes. The little girl, Rani, was slurping on her mocha without taking her eyes off Bhaskar. "But surely you understand the deeper problem? Bad habits they'll acquire, don't you see? Then they'd want to have these expensive drinks and snacks all the time. Do you think it's good for them?"

A few fashionable-looking young girls climbed up the stairs, saw the khateykids on the patio, scrunched their noses and averted their eyes, conferred in low whispers, then went back down.

The manager opened his mouth as if to call them back, then turned to Bhaskar. "Do you think it's good for them, you swooping in like this and feeding them rich food, and they return to their thieving and begging and glue-sniffing—what good will come out of it? You'll spoil them and they'll bother the tourists. Will the tourists want to come here then?"

Bhaskar exaggeratedly smacked his forehead with his palm, as though he was a dunce for not having thought of the damage he was inflicting upon Darkmotherland's tourism.

"You know how hard it's been to attract the tourists here again, after the Big Two?" the manager continued. "Do you think the Rajjya will approve of what you're doing? As it is, they're trying so hard to develop our country. Have you heard of PM Papa's new initiative?"

"Which one?" Bhaskar asked. "Every day there's a new one."

The manager brought his voice down to a whisper. "Maybe as a Ghimirey, you can afford to mock them, for you will be protected, but we commonfolk will be hauled to jail, understand?"

"I don't think anyone is safe in this regime," Bhaskar said, not bothering to lower his voice.

Kranti pinched Bhaskar's arm and asked the manager, "Which initiative is this?"

"It's a long-term, major beautification project for Darkmotherland. It's called Darkmotherland: Better Than Sweejerland."

"Huh?" Bhaskar asked.

"PM Papa wants to make Darkmotherland better than Sweejerland. Within ten years."

Bhaskar laughed a big fake laughter that had other customers looking their way.

"So, we are to do everything to attract more tourists. The entire tourism industry has received directives. Athithi Devo Bhava. You've heard PM Papa say it before. Guest is God."

"Sweejerland has roads that go all the way into the Alps."

"Not to worry, PM Papa has great plans for a Highway into the Himalaya."

Bhaskar made a clown face and looked at Rani, who giggled.

"We will build expressways that will take us all the way to the base of our mountains, within a few hours," the manager continued. "There will be a system of cable cars and funiculars and high-speed trains that'll traverse across Darkmotherland. We can have cappuccinos in Tato Chiso in the morning, lunch in a heated restaurant at the base of 25,000-foot-tall Elephant God Mountain, dinner in a jungle safari in the far west around a campfire as we watch indigenous people dance with drums and masks, then take a late-night train back to the Valley for ginger-honey hot lemon at home." The manager looked wistful; he was already on that fantasy trip.

"And all this will happen within ten years?" Bhaskar said.

"Are you doubting PM Papa?" the manager said. "Maybe I should visit the local Poolis Uncles Station for a chat." He brought his voice down to a whisper. "I'm kidding, of course, but what you're doing with these kids doesn't fit with this Better than Sweejerland project. All these Bhureys with their filthy tents? You'll see—they'll be gone soon."

"Where?" Kranti asked. She thought of Kabiraj.

"Who cares? They'll probably be put in trucks and dumped off somewhere. Good riddance, I say. Pests and thieves, all of them."

"You and my brother will make best friends," Bhaskar said.

"Adityaji?" The manager's face lit up. "I've met him. I hope to be like him one day. But Bhaskarji, please, now that they've eaten, can you take them away?"

But Bhaskar said, "Ready for another round, khateykids?" The khateykids nodded happily, and Bhaskar summoned the waiter and asked for more mochas. The manager threw up his hands and left.

The next time Bhaskar and Kranti took the khateykids to Tato Chiso, they had a confrontation with the owners, a husband-and-wife team, who were waiting for them at the top of the stairs. "Pure Darkmotherland!" they said.

Bhaskar grunted.

"Bhaskar Ghimirey, are you not?" they asked. The husband wore a tight-fitting tailored suit and his wife a glittering sari. The duo had opened up a string of Western cafés across the Valley in the past decade, some of which had attracted record customers after the Big Two.

The restaurateur said he knew Bhaskar's father. "Is Ghimireyji aware that his middle son—you are his middle son, hoina?—goes around town doing stuff like this?" He pointed to the khateykids, who, faced with this suited-booted man, had become somewhat subdued.

"They can't come here," said his wife. She had a large hairdo, and a heavily made-up face. Her face and body hadn't moved, only her lips.

"You come from such a good family," her husband said. "And you pull such stunts."

"These khateykids are patronizing your business," Bhaskar said and pushed his way past the restaurateur, signaling the khateykids to follow him. They took the same table they had last time. "Look at the menu and tell the waiter what you want," Bhaskar instructed his brood after he handed them menus he grabbed from a shelf nearby.

This was meant partly as a joke, as some of them couldn't read. The most literate of them was Subhash, who had completed ninth grade in his village before his stepfather's brutal ways forced him to come to the Valley.

Subhash squinted and said in his subdued way, "Listen, brothers and sisters of the khateykidsdom, you can have a mock-a-java or kapu-chino or allah-cartey." Bhaskar waved his hand at the group of waiters standing next to the restaurateur's wife—her small army. They didn't budge. Bhaskar climbed up on his chair and, as if he were making an announcement, loudly read from the menu. He had the attention of everyone in Tato Chiso. A handful of customers from inside had also drifted to the patio. Pictures were taken; a photographer from a newspaper happened to be at the next table. Bhaskar and the khateykids posed for him, fingers held up in peace signs, flexing their muscles, standing on the table in dance moves, and making faces. A reporter who was with the photographer asked questions about who Bhaskar was, and who the children were. The bouffanted wife yelled at the khateykids; her husband signaled her to be quiet and instructed the waiters to serve the kids. He stood with his hands in his trouser pockets, a pained expression on his face, but somehow smiling at the photographer.

Bhaskar and Kranti took the khateykids to Tato Chiso several times after that, but he encountered no resistance. To the contrary, the restaurateur greeted Bhaskar, addressed the khateykids fondly, ordered some bakery items for them on the house, then produced his in-house photographer to snap pictures. The publicity had been good. Tato Chiso was hailed on Motherland TV as not only a great coffee shop but also a charitable organization that didn't discriminate.

—

Bhaskar and Kranti took a handful of khateykids to a barbershop near the Queen's Pond that serviced both the Bhurey Paradise clientele as well as those in the surrounding areas.

With this mop on your head, Bhaskar said, ruffling Subhash's hair, you will be a special target for Poolis Uncles. Bhaskar had told Kranti that the boy was not all right in his head. Imagine, Bhaskar had said, having to leave your mother and your siblings behind because of your stepfather's viciousness. And on top of that the poor boy had encountered greater problems once he arrived in the Valley. Kranti imagined that Subhash had suffered from typical Bhurey problems of poverty and homelessness, but Bhaskar said that a honey named Jharana had taken him under her wing, and the two of them lived in Hotel Kyalifornya, a hotbed for prostitution, next to the Old Buspark. But after a few months Jharana had disappeared, and Subhash was convinced that she had been murdered by her halwai. The boy had already been traumatized by his stepfather, Bhaskar said, and he lost a woman whom he loved, and who loved him. Jharana, Kranti had said. Waterfall. What a beautiful name. Yes, she had been like a cool, soothing balm to our Subhash, Bhaskar said.

The barber greeted Bhaskar heartily, which meant that he was a regular customer. Kranti would have thought that he'd visit a more upscale hair salon. Then she was surprised that she was surprised—this was Bhaskar.

The barber was cutting a man's hair, and there were two other customers in queue. The topic of conversation was the Son of Yeti. They were speaking about the kind of society the Son of Yeti wanted, what he'd create if he were allowed to take over.

"He'd redistribute the wealth of Darkmotherland," the customer in the barber chair said.

"Really?" the barber said as he carefully snipped away a tuft of hair near the ear. The barber said that he hadn't been able to sleep because he was so afraid of the Son of Yeti. "Everyone is saying what a monster he is."

By everyone, the barber meant largely the Rajjya, whose roaming vans blared through their loudspeakers about how dangerous the Son of Yeti was, how he was amassing support in the east, in the west. Make no mistake, the loudspeakers declared, the Son of Yeti is real, and he is coming, and the only person who can save us from him is our beloved PM Papa. A pre-recorded paean to PM Papa then burst through the loudspeakers, which often sounded like a jingle for an ice-cream truck. Rajjya officials and Fundys often took out processions, shouting slogans against the Son of Yeti, extolling the virtues of PM Papa. They stopped to assure worried citizens, "As long as PM Papa is alive, the Son of Yeti will not be able to touch a hair on your body. If it weren't for PM Papa, the Son of Yeti would already be ruling us."

"The Son of Yeti means business," the customer in the barbershop said. "He's out to destroy Darkmotherland."

The barber stopped scissoring, the blades very close to the customer's right ear, as though he were getting ready to chop off the lobe. Subhash was reminded of his stepfather back in the village, who had taken it upon himself to cut all the children's hair. He'd let his hatred come through in the careless way he used the scissors on Subhash's head, making him yelp and cry out in distress. One time, Subhash had run away from his stepfather because the scissors had slashed the top of his right ear, making blood stream down the ear canals.

"Does the redistribution of wealth mean that I will have to give up my shop?" the barber asked.

"What else do you think it means, barber-ji?" a customer waiting for his haircut teased. "Do you think someone like the Son of Yeti will spare you because you're what, pretty? Because you have a Salman Khan haircut?"

The barber quickly glanced in the mirror to check if he indeed looked like the popular actor. Kranti and Bhaskar looked at each other and smiled. "But wait," the barber said. "If Son of Yeti gives this barbershop to someone poorer than me, then suddenly that poor person will become richer than me. Wouldn't the Son of Yeti then have to return the barbershop to me?"

"That's not how it works," Kranti said. "You keep taking from the rich and giving to the poor until everyone is very poor." Remembering a Charles Dickens novel, she added, "So poor you can all hold a bowl and say, 'Please, sir, can I have some more?'"

Concern marks appeared on everyone's forehead. The barber began to talk, fast, half to himself, half to those in his shop, his scissors moving around his customer's head haphazardly. "If the barbershop is taken away from me, I'll start cutting hair on the streets. Cheaper clientele—laborers and Bhureys—but perhaps there'd be more of them?" He paused to do some silent mental calculations, the scissors snipping away at the air, its sound helping him think. "With these poorer customers, I'll have to charge one-fourth of the price I'm charging you all, but with twice the volume I'll make half of my current income. I'll survive." The scissors, as though heaving a sigh of relief, again attacked the customer's hair. "My family will have to trim on the luxury items. Maybe more than trim—maybe a buzzcut. No more movies, except perhaps once every few months. No more fancy Angrezi-medium boarding schools for my little ones; they'd have to attend Rajjya schools and eat the pitiful after-noon snack served in the cafeteria. New clothes only during the Ten-Day Festival."

The barber was getting more agitated as he spoke, and Kranti became worried. She didn't want to subject the khateykids' heads to those unpredictable scissors (the current customer was already making "ouch" and "ayaa" sounds). Although Bhaskar tried to reas-sure her, she suggested they take the khateykids elsewhere. The line is also long here, she whispered to him.

"Let's go to another barber," Bhaskar told the khateykids, who were disappointed. They'd never sat on a chair in a barbershop before and were looking forward to it.

They went to a footpath barber next to the Brave Hospital, and although initially the khateykids were resentful, after a while they enjoyed the way the old barber treated their hair with great care. After cutting their hair, the barber even massaged their heads, making pop-ping sounds as he pummeled their scalp with his pruny palms.

Feeling light and floaty, the khateykids walked toward the Tourist

District with Bhaskar and Kranti. On the walls near the Brave Hospital and the Queen's Pond area were large Wanted posters of the Son of Yeti.

"They weren't here yesterday," Subhash said.

Kranti rubbed his freshly shorn head and said, "This feels good, Subhash. Does it feel good?"

Subhash nodded, his eyes on the Son of Yeti. A broad face, small, slanted eyes, a drooping mustache, and a formidable chin with a stubble of growth.

"Do you really think this is what the Son of Yeti looks like?" Kranti asked Bhaskar, who responded that the Son of Yeti looked exactly like how each individual wanted him to look.

A few other people had gathered to observe, including some children. The posters were large, each the size of a small car, and which, at close range, had the effect of crowding your consciousness, as though Son of Yeti had sneaked into your brain.

Bhaskar said that the posters were placed strategically at major intersections, the slanted eyes looking at you as you waited in your car for the traffic light to change, or as you watched the traffic Poolis Uncles blow the whistle and wave you on to cross on foot on the cracked asphalt.

The khateykids began teasing the Son of Yeti. They moved to the poster's left and to its right, shouting that Son of Yeti's eyes followed them no matter where they went. They flattened themselves against the wall next to the poster to avoid his stare, but even then Son of Yeti's eyeballs zoomed in their direction.

A young man smoking a cigarette said, "In reality, he's actually handsomer than how he is depicted in the poster. He's no chink."

Another person, a dark man from the south, said in a soft voice, "He's actually from the terai, fed up with decades of discrimination and abuse our southern brothers have faced at the hands of the hill folks. He's disguised as the Son of Yeti because that's the only way he can garner support in the mountains."

Others shushed him. One man threatened to report the dark man to the authorities for making it sound as though the Son of Yeti was a good guy fighting for justice.

Some more people congregated around the poster and joined the conversation. The Son of Yeti was a mountain giant, a progeny of the Yeti, a creature erupted from a fissure in the mountains after the Big Two. No, he was simply a large human being, a mongrel, a fusion of the dark-skinned Madhesis from the plains and the lighter-skinned Pahades from the hills. No, he was a creation of the Pothead God. Son of Yeti was a strong-limbed destroyer, like the Pothead God, and he too walked around half-naked. Except Son of Yeti had clearly oriental features, with high cheekbones and slanted eyes. "Like Bruce Lee," a person opined. A woman said that the mongrel mixture was a product of the great hostility between the Madhesis and Pahades in recent years, a quarrel between folks in the plains down south and the hill folks up north that had, before PM Papa took over, threatened to split Darkmotherland in two. The Son of Yeti was a union between these two ethnicities, except it was not a good union, but a bad one. The woman continued to say, with authority, that his followers, the Yetifolk, were growing by the day. They too walked around naked on the snow, marauding villages, claiming women and girls as wives, and recruiting young men. They were nomadic, moving from one earth-quake-devastated village to another, seizing territories, killing those who opposed them, and comforting those who turned to them for guidance and sustenance. The Lord of the Winds protected them. The Son of Yeti had by now collected hundreds of followers, perhaps thousands, and he was gathering strength and waiting for the right moment to come down the mountains and take over the Valley.

The woman was unstoppable. The Son of Yeti is nearly seven feet tall, with muscular limbs, and strong teeth. He has a large head. His jaws are so broad so he can chew large chunks of human flesh.

"You worried about the Son of Yeti, Bhaskar Uncle?" Subhash asked as they moved on.

Bhaskar made a nervous, frightened gesture. "Of course! What if he wants to send me to Heaven?"

"Don't worry, uncle," Subhash said. "As long as I'm alive, the Son of Yeti will not be able to touch a hair on your body."

"What will you do?"

"I will beat him up like this." Subhash punched the air in front of him, making *dhissum, dhissum* sounds. He performed a few martial arts kicks, drawing chortles from other khateykids.

"I am so happy you're here to protect me, Subhash Uncle," Bhaskar said.

6.

PM Papa sucked Rozy's cock. He loved Rozy's cock. He loved to fondle Rozy's cock with his thick cucumbery hands. It was a beautiful cock, slightly angled, thin, on the longish side, with a soft glisten on its mouth. Unlike Rozy, who was dark-complexioned, his cock was relatively fair, wheatish in color. Rozy kept his pubic hair shaved, so the cock looked unencumbered, ready to be loved. There was a wart on the shaft's underbelly that PM Papa could feel with his tongue. "This is mine," PM Papa said during lovemaking as he caressed Rozy's member. Mine only, he cooed.

PM Papa's first experience was with a peon who worked in his district office when he was running for elected office, years before the Big Two, a couple of years before he got married. A young, handsome man with a slim nose and an earring, the peon was assigned to take care of PM Papa's needs, and it didn't seem unnatural for PM Papa to reach out one day and stroke the young man's cheeks. Soon PM Papa was licking the peon's nipples and fumbling with the buttons of his trousers. The peon didn't resist, for he knew that it was infinitely better to be on PM Papa's good side than the bad one. The peon shyly asked for money and favors, and that seemed natural too. As PM Papa's career took off, so did his appetite for men, a secret that remained hidden from the public, but not from his wife. For the most part his desires for men were purely sexual. PM Papa asked the especially effeminate ones to sit on his lap and he love-talked to them, whispered into and nibbled their ears and said things that made him feel good.

But Rozy was different. PM Papa felt an attachment to him that he hadn't felt with any other young man. Maiya, he called Rozy, like a man addressing a garlfren or a mistress. Within days of meeting him, which was soon after the Big Two, he'd secretly bought Rozy a large piece of land, sitting pretty on a hill, in a prime location in the City of Glory at the southwestern edge of the Valley. More than two centuries ago, the Founding Father, when he was on his rampage to conquer, had cut off the noses of the inhabitants of the City of Glory for resisting him. It was a pretty town, with ancient temples and bahals, that sat upon a hill overlooking the Valley. The piece of land hadn't cracked during the Big Two. Within a couple of years I'll build you a house there, PM Papa said.

But I don't want to live apart from you, Rozy said. I want to live with you, in Humble Abode. Rozy was referring to the prime minister's residence, which had received that nickname after PM Papa moved in, although with its phalanx of security guards and sniper-carrying Loyal Army Dais on its roof, it was far from humble. PM Papa projected an image of being a humble man. "I am a humble man," he said in his speeches. "I am like you, a regular Darkmother-landite. I work hard, I provide for my family, I am a full-blooded patriot. I will die for my country, my beloved Darkmother."

PM Papa smiled and caressed Rozy's arm. I too want you to live with me, he said, but right now that's not possible.

PM Papa knew that there were rumors that he was gay—there had been for years—but things were fine as long as they remained rumors and the Fundys weren't too bothered. The Fundys were a crucial component of PM Papa's rise to power. They had financial support from Bharat, where they also had a stronghold, and they wanted to make sure that their version of fundamentalism crushed all alien religions.

When PM Papa fantasized about a future with Rozy, he knew that he'd never abandon his wife, no matter that she was dowdy and religious-minded and melodramatic. He also felt an allegiance to her, a duty, an obligation. She had been with him for years, long before he even became a minister. She had believed in him, had understood his political ambitions, even though she hadn't understood his desires for men. Yet, when he imagined his old age, once he became feeble and walked with a cane, it was Rozy he'd be leaning on for support. It was in the house in the City of Glory, which PM Papa would convert into a mansion, that he saw the two of them together, not in Humble Abode, which PM Papa would bequeath to his wife. PM

Papa already had a name for the mansion, Palace of Glory. It would be bigger than the Asylum—it had to be; PM Papa's mansion could not, under any circumstance, be seen as secondary to the Ghimirey's residence. And it would be more beautiful than the Asylum. But the design for the Palace of Glory had come to PM Papa from his admiration of the Asylum, especially after he'd seen it featured in a magazine some years ago. He'd been jealous of the praise of the atrium, the statues, the fountain, the picture windows, and the skylights. When he was a home minister, he couldn't build something like that, but now as PM Papa he could. It would be his signature mansion, one that would be famous throughout the world. It would have Palace of Glory carved on its front façade.

In a future scenario at the Palace of Glory, Rozy would give him a small kiss before going to the mall for shopping, possibly with an entourage of aides and bodyguards, for PM Papa didn't see himself relinquishing power. *Prime Minister for Life!* he thought to himself. He liked the title. Had anyone in history received that title? Probably some Aafrikan dictators. He ought to consult with an Aafrikan dictator to get some ideas. Several members of his Cabinet, now referred to as Papa's Cabinet, had indeed suggested, repeatedly, that PM Papa be made Prime Minister for Life. They said part of the reason Darkmotherland never developed was that too many people came to power and raked in profits at the country's expense. We need a steady helm, they said. PM Papa has proven himself. You're a patriot, they said. All of Papa's Cabinet members were carefully chosen by PM Papa. His Minister of Finance, Artha Shashtri, was an old codger who'd bankrupted a couple of banks, but who was an ardent supporter of PM Papa. The Department of Education was headed by a Sanskrit scholar, Shiksya Pradan, with no administrative experience, but whose devotion to PM Papa knew no bounds.

"We need to rule this country with an iron fist," PM Papa said to his cabinet during a meeting in the Lion Palace. "It's best if we start injecting this title into the public's mindset right now so that they get used to it. And it's for the good of the country. We can't let these pests and vermin return to power."

His cabinet members heartily agreed. They applauded the idea. They sang praises of his rule. They saw, in his pronouncement, the longevity of their own power. As long as they pleased him and did his bidding, they could continue to rake in millions. They had already begun transferring money to foreign banks. Some of them also had contingency plans of quick escape should PM Papa turn on them. Every night they prayed that the day would never arrive. Sometimes the brave ones also plotted against PM Papa, but often only in their own minds, thinking about what they could do, who they could collude with to uncrown the Hippo. But they could trust no one other than themselves. Some of them didn't even trust their own families. Even in their homes they offered praise to PM Papa. "PM Papa jindabad!" they said after dinner, never knowing if their homes were bugged. They looked at their wives suspiciously; they never criticized PM Papa in front of their family and relatives. And of course, they couldn't trust their colleagues. Once, the Minister of Agriculture, Kisan Karmi, had gently complained to the Minister of Finance, Artha Shashtri, in privacy, that he failed to understand why, despite repeated requests, PM Papa hadn't authorized an adequate budget for the agriculture sector. It's the agriculture sector that's been the most devastated by the Big Two, Kisan Karmi said, for it is greatly affecting our food security. We need more fertilizers, more equipment—fast. The next day at the Cabinet meeting the Minister of Finance casually mentioned that Kisan Karmi didn't seem to be supportive of PM Papa's vision of the country. The entire table turned to look at him, and Kisan Karmi went on a sobbing, whimpering defense of what he said—denying, deflecting, pointing his finger at Artha Shastri, pointing his finger at other ministers in random. That afternoon he lost his position, then the next morning his entire family had been sent off to a labor camp in the Far West.

General Tso wasn't averse to the idea of Prime Minister for Life, but he thought that it was a bit too early. Darkmotherlandites needed to believe that they still enjoyed most of the freedoms the country had before Papakoo. We need to give the impression that not much has changed, he told PM Papa, who looked disappointed. PM Papa didn't buy into the "benevolent dictatorship" that General Tso seemed to be espousing. It was a mode of governance that had transformed Singapore, General Tso said, made it one of the most affluent and successful nations in Asia. But PM Papa didn't think that Darkmotherlandites could be controlled by benevolence. No. Darkmotherland needed strict discipline, draconian decrees, swift and cruel penalties, PM Papa said.

"Let's start slow," General Tso said. In contrast to PM Papa, General Tso was of a normal build, maybe even on the thin side. He had a slight paunch.

"Meaning?"

"Let's start with His Excellency. We'll add that to your title."

"You mean His Excellency PM Papa?"

General Tso nodded.

"His Excellency PM Papa." PM Papa stood and said out loud, testing his new title. He repeated it, putting out his palm as though introducing himself to the public. "Ladies and gentlemen, please welcome His Excellency PM Papa." He shook his head, tsked. "I like it, but it's missing something." He made a fist. "It doesn't have any oomph!" He went to the window and looked out at the massive lawn in the back, where Loyal Army Dais patrolled with machine guns. Snipers lurked on the roofs of the buildings of the Lion Palace. "His Most Excellent Excellency PM Papa?" He turned to General Tso. "How does that sound?"

"It's redundant, hajur," General Tso said. "Excellency means excellent."

PM Papa was doubtful that they meant the same, but he didn't want to consult the dictionary right now, so he let it slide.

"How about His Sovereign Excellency PM Papa?" the general suggested.

PM Papa tried it a couple of times, tasting it, his tongue moving in and out as he formed the words. "Nice," he said, "but doesn't sovereign apply to nations? Meaning independent?"

"Yes, but also supreme leader. We can use it as a place holder until we're ready to introduce Prime Minister for Life."

"His Sovereign Excellency PM Papa," PM Papa announced again to his imaginary audience, then smiled ear to ear (looking indeed like the Hippo, thought General Tso) and clapped his hands and said, "Brilliant!" He came to General Tso and slapped his back, hard. "That's why you're my favorite general."

General Tso nodded. At times he thought that PM Papa, whose craftiness and decisiveness he admired, was also a narcissistic fool. But General Tso had pledged his loyalty to this man, and, if there was one thing he shared with PM Papa, it was the high value he placed on loyalty.

The chief of the Army's first name was Dinesh, with a long and unpronounceable last name, but he was known as General Tso because he had a penchant for the Chiniya dish, and images of him eating the sweet and spicy chicken with chopsticks had appeared in the media frequently, even before the Big Two when he served under the previous prime minister, who was now imprisoned in Khor, the vast underground prison inside the Durbar. General Tso had a gruff, rapid-fire, scolding voice, which helped his image as a tough fellow (he had been at the forefront of the battle with the Maoist rebels during the Civil War). On TV he stood at ramrod attention, looking kind of sad and muted, as he read from a paper in his hand. Usually, they were long reports of rescue efforts and stern warnings about law and order. "I have given the Loyal Army orders to shoot on sight those who create chaos on our streets," General Tso barked.

In Gufa, PM Papa's private den in the Lion Palace, where decisions regarding all the monumental changes in the nation were made, Rozy was on PM Papa's lap. Gufa was perceived in the public imagination as a vital organ of the state machinery, yet very private, like an inner sanctum. During all the previous administrations' times, the prime minister's office was an important but ordinary place. Now it was a sacred space that was going to generate the goodness that would begin healing the wounds of the past.

"Do you like what I'm doing for Darkmotherland?" he asked Rozy now.

Rozy didn't know what to say, and, rubbing PM Papa's chin, he ended up saying, "It's barely been a few months since the koo. You have so much more to do." PM Papa's eyes clouded a bit, and Rozy hastened to say, "The entire country's fate rests on you now, Papa." That seemed to mollify him a bit, for PM Papa nodded. "It's hard to imagine what Darkmotherland would be like if you'd not taken over," Rozy said, further satisfying PM Papa. Rozy knew to offer praises, carefully measured, to PM Papa. His cabinet, of course, fawned on him. The only one who didn't offer him praise was General Tso, but PM Papa appeared to have reconciled himself to his army chief's gruff and taciturn nature. Perhaps it had something to do with General Tso's ethnicity—Bhoteys tended to be the strong, silent type, PM Papa had said a couple of times to Rozy, which is why they did so well in the army. But even if General Tso didn't offer him effusive praise like members of Papa's Cabinet and the Lion Palace staff, he admired PM Papa. Of this, PM Papa was sure, as he'd indicated to Rozy. And PM Papa admired General Tso, his ruthlessness, his cleverness, his marshalling of his men so that the koo could happen fast, with little fuss.

The opportunity for the koo had also materialized quickly. One moment Giridharilal Bhagirath Kumar was in his minister's residence, watering his roses, and the next moment he was the most powerful man in Darkmotherland. It was as though the earth had split open, which it had: the ground where he had planted his roses had literally cracked and a garden snake had crawled out. PM Papa knew the snake was a sign for him to make his move. Just to be sure, he'd called this woman he knew, even as houses were collapsing around him and people were screaming and running for cover. Yes, the time had come, Awnty had confirmed over the static of their mobile connection. "Shall I do it?" he'd shouted into his phone, and Awnty had said, "Now or never."

But the idea for a koo hadn't come about in the instant that the Big Two happened. It was years in planning. It was something that he and General Tso had discussed intermittently, ever since the two had met fifteen years ago, right before the crown prince had gone on a killing spree and wiped out most of the royal family. The chaos and confusion in the immediate aftermath of the Royal Massacre had seemed like an opportune time to step in, but the new king, who had a droopy mouth, had been speedily throned, and he had turned out to be quite draconian himself, dismissing the parliament and jailing journalists and firing at protestors. Then the Maoists went on a killing spree, and General Tso was stationed in the hills to fight the rebels; besides, any attempt at insurrection at that time meant taking on the Maoists as his enemies. General Tso was against it. He was only a Brigadier General then, and he didn't think he could pull it off. Then the Maoists gave up their arms and turned into corrupt politicians themselves, and the Droopy Mouthed King was kicked out of the palace. Things went back to being peaceful and inept and corrupt and helpless. But still, nice. General Tso rose up the ranks to become the Army Chief of Staff. Then the Big Two happened.

PM Papa often said in his public addresses that he had arisen to heal the harms of the past. For too long his country had suffered under rulers who had taken advantage of his country's innocence. The "mother" in Darkmotherland was always emphasized by PM Papa— the mother as nurturing, innocent, and ever-giving. Those who went against the mother, who betrayed her, were enemies. There was an urgent need to return Darkmotherland to its original purity.

"Do you think I'm a good leader?" PM Papa asked Rozy.

"Of course you are," Rozy said, batting his eyelids. "You are the best."

PM Papa nuzzled his chin into Rozy's neck and said something in a muffled voice.

"What?"

Again, he said something, but with this time with his mouth moving down to Rozy's chest, where it looked like he was attempting to lick Rozy's nipples through his shirt.

The Hippo, Rozy thought derisively. How Rozy hated that body, that fatty fat body, the way the fat jiggled on PM Papa's stomach. The chest hair. Oh, my God. How could a short, round person be slathered with so much hair? But the most repulsive features were his jaws—broad and rocky, as if they were designed to chew raw flesh.

Rozy lifted PM Papa's head by clasping his temples with his palms and asked, "Saying what?"

"I want to have a baby with you," PM Papa said, looking at him like a doe-eyed child. A very ugly doe-eyed child.

Rozy let out a hoarse laugh. "You crazy," he said. "You outright crazy. I can't have a child."

PM Papa put his hand on Rozy's belly. "I want to put a baby in there."

Rozy reached into the air and seemingly plucked a baby out of the air above him and said, "Oh, here's one," then placed the baby on his belly. "There! There's a baby in there now."

PM Papa rubbed his hand slowly across Rozy's belly. "I'm serious. Nothing would please me more than impregnating you."

"But how?" Rozy cried, repulsed by the image. "How? It's a physical impossibility."

"I'm sure there are ways."

"Keep dreaming," Rozy said, not too harshly. He didn't want to anger the big man.

"Are you making fun of me?" PM Papa snarled. "I am PM Papa now, bujhyau? I can make things happen."

"Immaculate conception?" Rozy asked.

"I'll consult Awnty."

"Who's Awnty?"

"Just some woman I've known for a while. She knows how to do stuff."

"What stuff?"

PM Papa waved his hand dismissively in the air.

"What about your wife?" Rozy asked. "What would she feel about it, you producing a child with someone like me."

"Well," PM Papa looked at Rozy, a bit helplessly, Rozy thought. "She hasn't been able to give me a child, has she?"

Rozy stroked PM Papa's chin. "And why is that, PM Papa? Why hasn't your beautiful wife given you a baby yet?" Rozy knew why, the woman was barren. And not beautiful—Rozy hoped that PM Papa had caught the tinge of sarcasm when he called his big-nosed wife beautiful. Rozy also knew that the lack of a progeny cut PM Papa deeply. It might not have mattered much when he was only a home minister, but once he'd become PM Papa, with the kind of absolute power he had, he felt a keen need to have an heir. Why? To carry on his legacy? Rozy had wondered about that. Was dictatorship passed down, from son to son? But what if it was a daughter? Could a daughter be a tyrant? Rozy's knowledge of history wasn't great enough for him to know this, but he'd heard people call Indira Gandhi a dictator.

PM Papa had lamented, mildly, to Rozy about his lack of a child. He'd said it only to Rozy. If he said it to anyone else in his administration, they would know, immediately, that's where his weakness lay, and they might find a way to exploit it so they could oust him. In a culture where a man's virility was closely tied to his ability to sire a son, this could be used to question his manliness.

"You know why," PM Papa said. "We tried so many times, but it looks like she's barren."

Or you are, thought Rozy, but he knew better than to say it.

"Will you give me a baby, Rozy?"

Rozy only hmmmed.

"Come on, maiya, you don't think I'll make a good father?"

Rozy tried to wrench himself away from him, but PM Papa's grip was strong, and Rozy wiggled on the round man's lap. "Let me go," he said. "You never stop."

PM Papa let him go. Straightening his shirt, Rozy walked to the window.

"Maiya, what's the matter?" PM Papa asked.

"You're always interrogating me, and my head feels like it's going to explode."

"Why are you acting like a prima donna?" PM Papa said.

Rozy swiveled. "Why do you treat me so? Like I'm any other slut you can find on the street? You have a wife at home. You should be pestering her for a baby."

PM Papa had indeed found Rozy on the street, in the immediate aftermath of the Big Two. And yes, Rozy was a bit of a slut. What else would you call someone who sold his body for money and creature comforts, like he was doing now with this round man?

Initially it wasn't like this. When they first met, Rozy had willingly and gladly succumbed to PM Papa. But Rozy was in a different state of mind then: vulnerable, weepy, shaken. PM Papa's extended hand had felt reassuring, protective. But the revulsion had grown within a few weeks.

"You know you're not like anyone else, maiya," PM Papa said and stood, and coming close, kissed Rozy's neck. Rozy felt like flinching but of course he wouldn't. He had done this type of thing—been with men he found physically unattractive, even repulsive—and he wasn't going to let his true emotions surface now, when the most powerful man in Darkmotherland was besotted with him. Rozy needed to be patient, to relax, to picture himself, when he was having sex with PM Papa, as floating in the big blue sky. Rozy would know when the time was right. Careful. You should never take for granted PM Papa's affection for you. These days when he had sex with PM Papa, Rozy closed his eyes, as though he was in the throes of ecstasy, and gently drifted to his big blue sky, found wisps of clouds where he lay down for a blissful nap, the soft heat of the sun warming his face.

Rozy had seen what PM Papa could do. There was that case of the blogger, for example, who had not stopped writing articles critical of PM Papa's regime despite repeated warnings. On the third week of Papakoo, Rozy had overheard PM Papa on the phone. "Swarga pathaideu telllai," PM Papa had grunted into the phone. Dispatch him to heaven. The next day the blogger's teenage son was found dead in a hotel in the Tourist District. The Poolis Uncles determined that an unnamed khairey who'd returned to his home in Germnee had murdered the boy. A warrant was issued for the khairey. Questions were raised by the government media about why the blogger's son, who was good-looking and slim, was alone in a hotel room with an elderly khairey male, and the young man was declared a homo.

Rozy had asked PM Papa, not long after the incident, about who he thought was behind the teenager's killing, and PM Papa, biting on the biscuit that Rozy had served him, murmured something about how the blogger had angered many upstanding citizens with his blogs. "It's unfortunate," PM Papa said, "that they targeted his innocent son." PM Papa sipped his tea and said, "Well, maybe not so innocent. What was he doing with an old khairey in that seedy hotel?"

PM Papa had gone out of his way to please the Fundys. His speeches were filled with anti-gay rhetoric. He said his administration would "hunt them down." He spoke of "rehabilitation" and "conversion." The most active LGBTQ organization in the country, the Neel Diamond Society, was now all but shuttered, its leaders either beaten or in jail. It had adopted "You Don't Bring Me Flowers Anymore" by Neil Diamond as its motto song, signifying the heartaches suffered by sexual minorities in the country. But that was before the Big Two. Now, under constant attack from Fundys and Papa's Patriots, it had more or less disappeared.

As powerful a man as PM Papa was, he was also filled with paranoia. He didn't trust anyone. He was constantly suspicious of his ministers. He wondered if one or more of them was planning a koo. Just last week, the aviation minister had been fired and his property confiscated because he had flown to Bharat for high-level talks without PM Papa's express authorization. The aviation minister was handpicked by PM Papa after the koo, so there was no reason to doubt his loyalty. There was nothing untoward about the trip, yet PM Papa was certain the minister was, as he put it, "plotting." He had hidden cameras and recorders installed throughout the Lion Palace to monitor suspicious conversations. He had bureaucrats in Darkmotherland sign oaths of allegiance to him instead of the constitution.

—

Rozy lived in a flat a few blocks east of the Parade Ground, right at the edge of the Bhurey Paradise, that had been bought for him by PM Papa within days of the Big Two. It was a temporary residence for a year or two, until the mansion was built in the City of Glory. Rozy liked his flat. It had a tiny kitchen—barely any room to move—a bedroom, and a small balcony, where he could step out for fresh air. But what fresh air? Most of the Valley was smoggy and dusty. Still, when he stepped out to the balcony early in the morning, just as the sun came up, the air seemed a tad cleaner, and with the sun's rays casting a yellow hue on everything, one could even pretend that the Big Two hadn't happened. At this time, the Valley would be in the process of waking up. The Big Two had exhausted everyone, and their bodies ached at night after having inhaled all the smoke and dust during the day. From his balcony, Rozy would see an occasional car trundling by, or a man furiously pedaling his bicycle carrying containers of milk, or a small group of children in school uniforms shouting. It was incredible that despite half of Darkmotherland ruptured and rendered askew, these small kids who could barely wipe their noses wore ties around their necks, and, having just been fed breakfast by their parents, chatted excitedly and aggressively about their new toys as they made their way to school. Every day, Rozy got up in the morning and wondered about this: How did people not only survive but go on about their lives? But then what about the impossibility of the fact that he, Rozy, was having sex with the prime minister of Darkmotherland? Not only the prime minister but the most powerful prime minister in Darkmotherland's history! When he allowed

PM Papa to go down on him, Rozy watched a movie of himself—his arrival in the Valley from the Town of Lakes, his becoming a boyfren of rich and powerful men, and finally PM Papa. There was an inevitability to Rozy's journey, he knew, and thus being under the grip of PM Papa didn't surprise him.

You are going to be the death of me, Rozy told PM Papa silently when PM Papa sucked him off. Or I'm going to be the death of you. *Death of you, death of you*, he thought as he thrust his cock into PM Papa's mouth. He thought of the kitchen knife: how easy it would be to plunge it into the man's thick neck.

As Rozy cooked his morning meal—rice, dal, and a vegetable or two—he recalled his parents, wondered whether they survived. He had tried to get to his parents after the Big Two. The day of the earthquake he'd found a microbus to take him to the Town of Lakes. Everywhere people were getting into cars and taxis, or other vehicles that were not already damaged, or hopped on their motorbikes and bicycles, to get out, to escape, or rush to their hometowns to discover the fate of their loved ones.

The microbus was jam-packed, with some people on the roof and others hanging out of the door. The driver was giggling, maniacal. He was also charging twenty thousand rupees per passenger, whether they could find a seat or not, on a seven-hour ride through the foothills of the mountains amidst the still shuddering ground and the hurricaning dust. "The Big Two Express!" the driver kept shouting. "Prepare for the ride of your life!" When the passengers had complained about the price-gouging, he had turned to them angrily and said, "Do you realize the risk I'm taking? Who knows what the highway is like? You don't want to ride, get the fuck off my Big Two Express." Other passengers, like Rozy, who had been unable to connect via phone with their families in the Town of Lakes, had scolded the complaining passengers, and urged the driver to get moving; they wanted to get to their loved ones by nightfall.

The lines of vehicles waiting to exit the Valley were long, but, Rozy saw that everyone was being turned back by the Loyal Army Dais, and the Big Two Express was also refused exit.

The fate of his parents worried Rozy, even though they had disowned him and refused to recognize that he was their son. He imagined them buried under the rubble of the old house, his childhood home, and his heart ached. He walked all the way to the international airport a few kilometers away. He had the absurd thought that perhaps the planes were flying. Maybe the Rajjya had added more planes since the vehicles weren't running. He had enough money to afford airfare (although, he worried that airfares would have also skyrocketed); he'd carried whatever cash he had, and, along with a bag stuffed with clothes, had left his apartment, afraid that the building, which still seemed to be shuddering, would topple.

At the airport Rozy was laughed at by the Loyal Army Dais strapped with machine guns, as ancient-looking soldiers carrying old rifles with bayonets looked on. The oldy soldiers seemed to be from an earlier era, perhaps from World War I, with grim faces and large hats and khukuris swinging from their hips. "What fantastic plane do you think could take off among these dust devils?" the Loyal Army Dais asked Rozy and other desperate residents who'd gone to the airport.

One soldier said, "No one's leaving. Go home. Be patriotic. Dark-motherland needs you."

With an anxious heart, Rozy had returned to his flat. He was relieved to discover that his building had somehow survived with only a few cracks on the walls. Every few hours there was a rumble from the earth, and the ground swayed and his neighbors clasped each other in fright. Some of his more affluent neighbors in the surrounding houses were sleeping in their cars. Rozy stayed in his room. One neighbor knocked with an offer of food (some stale bread), but Rozy said he wasn't hungry. Later that day he came out of his flat and stood at the balcony outside his room. With his hands on the railings, he could sense a tremor that had to be running the entirety of the earth. It was as if the ground was revving up to erupt. He wondered if he'd get electrocuted for clasping the iron railing, if somehow when there was an earthquake, the current was activated. There were reports of powerlines falling on people, of a stray cord lashing out at passersby, frying them. A child was said to have died in his yard because the marbles he'd been playing with had somehow become electrically charged.

He could hear his neighbors murmur below. They spoke of collapsed buildings and ruptured streets, of echoing subterranean cries impossible to trace in the panic and the dust.

This was the Age of Darkness invoked in the scriptures, his neighbors were certain, a period of extreme hardship for good people. But the counterargument was also offered that the Age of Darkness had existed before the Big Two—the Maoist Civil War, long lines for petrol, shitty public transportation, shittier roads, loadshedding, dance bars, brain drain, leaking sewage drains, and the politicians' sewer brains.

Nothing like this, came the retort. Looting and rioting was all around. Shops were ransacked, homes burglarized, and even homeless people were mugged. The entire Valley was in total chaos. The dust devils had made everything dark, and anyone could come after you in this swirl with a knife or a gun.

It's like 9-11, Rozy's landlord said. Like bombs are being dropped all around us.

At the mention of bombs, a handful of planes, their propellers rattling like aircraft from the previous World Wars, flew in the dark and smoky skies above.

"Watch it, watch it," someone said, as though the planes were going to drop bombs on them right there and then.

"Where are they going?" a neighbor asked.

"More important, where are they coming from? Do we have planes like these in Darkmotherland?"

The planes, their propellers rattling, flew low in the sky, as though they were running a reconnaissance mission.

"Ghost planes," Rozy's landlord said.

"Ghost planes?"

"They are mirages, created by our own delusions, warning us that Armageddon is on its way."

He was mocked by others for calling them mirages. "They aren't delusions or illusions or whatever. I see them with my own two eyes."

"They're most likely sent by Bharat," another neighbor said.

"True, Bharat," others concurred. "Bharat always had designs on us."

At the mention of Bharat, there was an avalanche of curses.

"Hold on," another neighbor said. "Are you suggesting that Bharat caused the Big Two?"

"They are the most cunning people in the world."

PM Papa was talking on Motherland TV in Kranti's room. He looked younger than his real age, although the chyron said it was a recent speech. In many of his speeches, which he purportedly gave on the premises of the Lion Palace in front of massive, adulating audiences (which no one remembered taking place), he appeared younger and younger. In one instance he even looked like he was barely past his teens.

"Forces of darkness," PM Papa was saying on Motherland TV to the roaring applause of his live audience. Kranti nodded. *Yes, forces of darkness are upon us,* she mumbled. "But as long as I am here, and I expect to be here for a long time," PM Papa said, "I will not let them harm Darkmotherland." Kranti felt grateful for his words. PM Papa, she murmured. She rolled the name in her mouth: Peee Emmm Papaaa. Then quickly, Pampapa. She imagined playing tabla on his head: *pampapa pa pam papapampam.* She imagined Dada bending over in laughter at her air-tabla and the breathy noises from her lips.

Had Dada been alive, he'd most likely not have referred to PM Papa as the Hippo. "Some might also call me the hippo, no?" he'd have said, patting his stomach. What would Dada have thought of

PM Papa and the way he had exerted extreme control over Dark-motherland? He wouldn't have been as perturbed; he most likely would have retreated into his music. If Kranti had expressed concern, he would have said, "Why you worry so much?" Of course, he never said that to Professor Shrestha when she fumed about the direction of the country; he always took her concerns seriously. He'd have gravely nodded his head in those moments when Professor Shrestha ranted about the damage PM Papa was doing; he'd have consoled her. With Kranti, he might have said, "Perhaps this is what we need right now. Perhaps, eventually, this is all for the good of Darkmotherland. We have to look at this positively. We have to always look for the positive, even when it seems like everything is negative." He'd have not said this in front of his wife, for he never wanted to displease his wife, but he'd have said it to Kranti because he was always open with her.

And now, with PM Papa on Motherland TV speaking about the country rising from the ashes of the Big Two to move toward unprecedented heights, Kranti was thrown back to the time when Dada was alive and he escorted her to school, except she imagined that the Big Two had already happened and Bhaskar was already in the picture. Dada was going on about what a great guy Bhaskar was and how Kranti was lucky to have found him.

"But what about Madam Mao?" Kranti said. "What to do about her?"

"Shhh," Dada said, smiling. "Don't call your mother that."

"She is taking Bhaskar away from me."

"Your mother would never do that."

"But she is!" Kranti cried. "She is! Why are you defending her?"

"I'm not defending her. Bhaskar just has a lot in common with her, that's all."

It hurt her that Dada said so, for she wanted to hear that Bhaskar had more in common with her than her mother.

"So, if we used our positive minds, could we try to imagine that PM Papa saved us from disaster? Huh? Huh?" Dada gently shoved her shoulder with his, then became more animated as he talked. He waved his arms about. He made swooshing sounds as he described the calamities that would have fallen on Darkmotherland without PM Papa. He made gargling, hacking sounds to demonstrate the kind of lawlessness that would have taken over the country had PM Papa not ruled with his iron fist. With his words, Dada painted a picture of marauding savages turning neighborhoods into drug dens and graveyards, giant trucks flattening homes and huts, looters and pillagers emptying stores of basic commodities, such as rice and wheat. He told her about lack of food and other basic necessities, of children going hungry, citizens dying of heat and thirst in their homes. "You see, my dearest daughter, if you put your positive hat on, you might say PM Papa is a necessary evil in our times. So, why you worry so much?"

Kranti awoke from this brief reverie to the sound of the roar on Motherland TV. The roar was from the crowd that had gathered to listen to a young PM Papa in front of the Lion Palace. "Roar!" the crowd roared.

PM Papa raised his hand in benediction and said, "I am your warrior. I am your vengeance."

Kranti began to weep. On Motherland TV a young and smooth skinned PM Papa was looking at her, smiling. "My dear Kranti," he said. "Everything will be all right. Why you worry so much?"

"Dada," Kranti whispered. "Dada."

———

The biryani was so fragrant and delicious that Rozy thought he had died and gone to heaven. The eatery was in the Old Buspark next to Hotel Kyalifornya and run by a man with a long beard and a skull cap. Rozy had been coming here about once a week, even before the Big Two. He loved the biryani, and he loved to listen to people talk. He hadn't told the owner, Ali Miya, that he now worked as valet to PM Papa. He'd merely said that after the Big Two he'd found an errand-boy type of job in the Lion Palace and didn't want it advertised, and

Ali Miya had promised his lips were sealed. When he went to work at the Lion Palace, Rozy wore daura suruwal, with a dhakatopi to hide his growing neck-long hair. And that's how the public saw PM Papa's valet on Motherland TV—in the shadowy background during Papa's cabinet meetings, or in the periphery when he accompanied PM Papa for inaugurations and official visits. When he was not in the Lion Palace, however, Rozy wore a red Make Darkmotherland Great Again cap, a minor disguise that seemed to work, as no one asked him whether he was the same person seen alongside the most powerful man in Darkmotherland.

Ali Miya's place was cramped and jam-packed, even as his customers complained about how the price of a plate of biryani had tripled since the Big Two. Ali Miya explained that on top of the already skyrocketed price of meat and rice, the Fundys extorted money from him. "Filthy Haji, they call me," Ali Miya said, "but they don't hesitate to take my money, so what choice do I have but to increase my prices?"

"And when the Fundys discover that you put beef in your biryani, Ali Miya," a woman joked, "they'll chop you up and throw you in the biryani."

A customer with a horse face paused mid-chew. "There's no beef in this biryani, is there?"

Ali Miya assured him that that his food contained no beef.

"But once you go home," a second customer said, "you eat beef, hoina?"

"If a Haji doesn't eat beef," the woman said, "what do you expect him to eat? Donkey meat?"

"Hajis will eat anything," the second customer said. "Isn't that right, Ali Miya?"

"Even a dog?" someone asked.

"Even a dog's carcass," the woman said.

"Killing a cow is sin," the horse-faced customer said. "A cow is a goddess. No one should be allowed to kill cows in Darkmotherland."

"In this matter, the Fundys are right," the second customer said.

"No one's killing cows here, bhai," Ali Miya said. "Personally, I don't even eat beef."

"You couldn't eat it even if you wanted to," the second customers said. "PM Papa has banned it, rightly so."

"Of course, that's what's best for our country. PM Papa knows best."

"PM Papa jindabad!" some customers shouted, then returned to their eating.

"He should ban all the other religions, too, while he's at it," the horse-faced customer said.

Ali Miya asked the horse-faced customer if he'd like some more raita. It would be foolhardy for Ali Miya to argue with a customer, Rozy knew. Just last week, a Muslim owner of an upscale diner in the Palace Boulevard had his restaurant destroyed because he'd exchanged words with a customer, who'd then summoned Papa's Patriots.

Rozy normally remained on the quiet side during these conversations, but now he felt that he needed to speak before something untoward happened. "Arre, live and let live, Horsy-ji," he challenged the horse-faced customer. "Our Ali Miya here is the most kind-hearted being. Do you know how many people he's helped and given shelter to after the Big Two? I'd rather have ten more Ali Miyas than one more horseface—" He caught himself and stopped speaking. The horse-faced customer stared at Rozy, surely noting his feminine face and tight clothes, and seemed about to say something but then resumed chewing.

At Ali Miya's, customers murmured about the damage caused by the Big Two. A woman said that tears come to her eyes every time she walks by the White Tower, which is now a stump.

"Forget about the White Tower, a meaningless monument to our shitty history," someone offered. "We will soon have the giant statue of PM Papa." It was hard to tell in what tone this person had said it, whether it was in admiration or a sense of irony. He himself seemed to have realized that he could be taken the wrong way, so he quickly added, "I can't wait. It'll be a thing to behold." He was talking about the giant statue of PM Papa that had begun construction across the street from the Brave Hospital, on the Open Stage area, in between Diamond Park and Parade Ground. The Bhureys there had already been chased away by the Poolis Uncles, their tents destroyed. Currently, only the statue's base had been completed, but once erected, it was going to be the largest statue in the world.

Bigger than that independent activist's statue in Bharat, PM Papa had boasted to Rozy. Certainly bigger than the several well-known statues of the Awakened One throughout Southeast Asia. "After it's completed"—PM Papa had wagged a finger at Rozy—"no one will be able to forget me. Understand, maiya? Ever."

For a few moments, even obligatorily, Ali Miya's customers emphasized the importance of the statue for the morale of Darkmotherlandites in the aftermath of the Big Two. The topic again turned to the devastation caused by the earthquake.

"Half the country is in ruins."

"Entire villages have been decimated."

"Everyone is flocking to the Valley now."

"What's going to happen to our Valley?" the horse-faced man said. "All these vagrants and riffraff tenting in our parks and streets."

"Our Valley?" Rozy challenged the speaker. "Remember you also came here from somewhere else."

"PM Papa will take care of all of them soon," another customer said. "A big-time beautification plan is about to launch, I heard."

"Yes, the Better Than Sweejerland Project, I also heard," the horse-faced man said. "It'll be a wonderful thing to behold. Imagine not having these smelly drifters and grifters around. Ahahaha! I can't wait for that day."

Rozy was drinking a Tuborg beer with his biryani. A couple of other customers were also drinking. The Fundys disapproved of alcohol, too, but their efforts to ban liquor hadn't met with the success of their campaigns against homosexuality and alien religions. Darkmotherlandites had to draw a line somewhere, and so they kept their booze.

Slightly tipsy from the beer, Rozy recalled how a day or two after the Big Two, shots had rung out in the streets, sometimes on and off for hours. People stayed indoors, or in tents or shacks, thinking bandits had gone on a full rampage, that soon it'd be a free-for-all. Perhaps the bandits would burn everyone alive. Those who were camped outside, the most vulnerable, clasped their loved ones closer.

Soon, however, there were announcements from megaphones in roving vehicles, assuring the citizens that everything was okay, that it was safe to come out, or open your eyes if you were already out. Just watch out for the dust. "Hear ye, hear ye, hear ye," a van stationed near the Queen's Pond said. "The unsavory elements of our society have been taken care of. Anyone who tries to rob or loot will be shot. Hear ye, hear ye. This is a message from our Venerable Prime Minister Giridharilal Bhagirath Kumar."

So, in all likelihood the shooters were the Loyal Army Dais. So, who were the bandits? Maybe there were none?

Rozy had wondered what had happened to Prime Minister Subba. Did the Big Two kill him?

On cue, the megaphone announced, "The former prime minister has been deposed."

"What does that mean?" people around Rozy asked.

"He's sick," one know-it-all type said.

"No, that's indisposed. This one is deposed."

People recognized the new prime minister. Giridharilal Bhagirath Kumar, a.k.a. the Hippo, as he was frequently called. He was the Home Minister, a thick-jawed man who looked like he could bulldoze through obstacles. Or, using his maw, chomp his way through the tough problems. He'd been notorious for making some hardline moves, had been in and out of power in the government.

The megaphone announced: The new prime minister has come to the rescue of Darkmotherland in this calamitous time. He is a reincarnation of our Founding Father. He has appeared to us like a father would, ready to protect and provide for his family.

That day most people around Rozy had scoffed. Of course! As if!

They remembered that this Giridharilal Bhagirath Kumar was a guy who, even when he was not a minister, kept appearing in the news for making controversial comments. His dumpy figure, grotesque but energetic, added to the outlandishness of his claims. One time he'd said that the then-prime minister loved his own dog, a large Tibbati Mastiff—*really* loved him. No one remembered which prime minister it was, for Darkmotherland had a history of changing prime ministers like they were badly tailored daura suruwal, prime ministers who, when they were replaced, rode into the sunset with engorged bank balances. The bestiality claim had remained in the news cycle for weeks. Even as columnists and reporters pointed out the absurdity of the accusation, they couldn't help but provide the details of it. Images of the dog playing with a ball in the prime minister's yard were shown on Motherland TV, as were photos of the prime minister embracing the pet. After some time, it was clear that the prime minister's political reputation had suffered an irreversible damage.

PM Papa had emerged from the rubble and ashes and dust of the Big Two. For many, he was a savior, the right person at the right time for Darkmotherland.

"He's talking care of things, like a father would."

"Yes, he's like our papa."

"Our prime minister, our Papa."

Of course, they realized that they could no longer call him the Hippo, either because it was too derogatory for a savior, or because they feared consequences.

Thus a new name for the new prime minister seemed to arise organically across neighborhoods. "PM Papa."

As Rozy had roamed the Valley in a daze that calamitous day, chants had arisen in the streets, even as the dust blew into people's eyes and noses. "PM Papa! PM Papa!"

The megaphones quickly picked up on the name: "That's right, folks! PM Papa will save us from disaster."

As if in obeisance, the dust devils relented somewhat, and things became more visible. The electricity came back on. "PM Papa has been working day and night to restore electricity," the roving vans announced. "Now the Loyal Army is running and guarding the hydroelectric power plants. No more power outages in our country anymore. Anymore. Not for a second."

Rozy was in the Monkeygod Gate Square when the bit about power outages was announced. It was greeted with loud, raucous cheers; some people openly wept. They'd never known a time in their lives when they hadn't experienced long stretches of blackouts in a single day, so to have no power outages during this calamitous disaster was a miracle. PM Papa must be an emissary of Darkmother, who'd sent her guy to pave the way for her ultimate appearance in fulfillment of the ancient prophecy.

That afternoon, the big outdoor screen standing tall and imposing among the rubble in the Monkeygod Gate Square came alive. Swami Go!swami, who had a one-hour show on Motherland TV every afternoon, appeared on the screen, sitting on a raised platform, flanked by several holy men and one holy woman. They all had supremely peaceful faces, as if they had already reached a higher spiritual plane where nothing could touch them. Swami Go!swami told stories from scriptures, in a long-winded fashion, that ended with a moral that escaped Rozy. It started to drizzle, and Rozy left Monkeygod Gate Square. On the way to his flat, it started to rain heavily, but instead of seeking shelter Rozy continued, getting soaked.

Soon after the rain stopped, a car slowly inched past him amidst the rubble in the Tourist District, close to the science college. The back window rolled down and a man's thick head popped out. "Hoina, where are you going, swinging your hips like that?"

Rozy's clothes were still damp. His shirt, which he hadn't changed for three days, clung to his skin. Rozy didn't remember whether he smiled at the man, but he remembered saying, "What is this that has fallen from the sky?" Even as he said it he knew what this man in the sleek black car wanted. Too many cars had slowed down alongside him since he left the Town of Lakes. But this was the first one after the Big Two. Perhaps there was symbolism here. In that instant, Rozy also recognized that this was PM Papa, from posters on the wall, from images on TV.

"Is it the sky?" PM Papa said. "Or is it the earth? I thought it was the latter."

"My head isn't straight, so I don't know."

Just then it began to rain again, and Rozy stood there, allowing the rain to splatter his face and run down his cheeks in rivulets, as though he were crying.

"Well, maybe I can help you set your head straight again," PM Papa said.

Rozy observed PM Papa, who had a slightly crazed, unattractive, yet welcoming face. He didn't know what it meant that the most powerful man in Darkmotherland wanted him right now. He was shivering in the rain. During those early days of the Big Two, the air turned warm to cold, and vice versa, in an instant.

"Come," PM Papa said and opened his car door.

—

Kranti, home early from Bauko Bank due to a headache, found Bhaskar sitting with the Beggars watching TV. The conversation died when Kranti entered the room, and there was uncomfortable shuffling. "You look pale," Bhaskar said. "Can I make you something?" It was odd for him to offer because he never cooked anything in Beggar Street, nor was he expected to—the Lord that he is, thought Kranti uncharitably, then was surprised at her own criticism. She didn't want Bhaskar to do *any* cooking at her house. She remembered vividly how Dada, despite slaving himself in the kitchen for the Beggars, had been the subject of their derision and ridicule.

The Beggars were nearing the end of PM Papa's biopic, released just days before with much fanfare. It had been showing continuously on Motherland TV since its release. The biopic was so bad that the Beggars were simultaneously seething and hooting at the screen. Murti was making sarcastic comments under her breath. Prakash, as usual, was hurling invectives. Vikram was standing by the door, arms crossed at his chest, frowning at the screen. Chanchal was restlessly moving back and forth between the kitchen and the living room.

Made in the immediate aftermath of Papakoo by a poor, desperate filmmaker, initially the biopic had been passed around privately. It was so ridiculous that it could be taken as mocking, although everyone knew it wasn't, and it was so ridiculous that it had become a viral sensation. Unsynchronized dubbing, overacting, dance sequences that were not relevant to the story—but once the Rajjya approved of it, it acquired an official status. Now, it was showing on Motherland TV.

There was PM Papa as a teenager, depicted by a young actor who, with his portliness, resembled the adult PM Papa to a remarkable degree. Tears streaming down his face, PM Papa massaged the feet of his blind mother. "Giri," the blind mother said. "I am not going to survive much longer. You have to go out and—" The camera zoomed in on the blind mother's face. The filmmaker had found a real blind woman, eighty years old, a pauper who needed the money to pay off debtors who'd otherwise confiscate her property in the chaotic aftermath of the Big Two. The camera must have become jammed at that precise moment because for about twenty seconds there was a static picture of the blind woman's eyes that were half-closed and vacant, creases zigzagging across her face, a globule of snot falling down from her nostrils. The blind actress had cried so realistically—toothless mouth open without sound, tears in her white-marble eyes—that the viewers often wept. The screen then switched into a song-and-shimmy scene on a beach that was clipped from a B-grade movie where a beach vendor splits open a coconut and dancingly hands it to the heroine, who raises it up in the air and lets its creamy white milk cascade into her mouth.

Watching on Motherland TV, families in tents and tottering houses, as well as homeless folks gathered on the sidewalks, clapped their hands in delight at this abrupt shift from the suffering blind old woman to the bosomy heroine with a body that yearned to be touched. Even though the dancing scene was an error, an inadvertent insertion from clumsy editing, repeated viewing gave the impression that it was a conscious choice, a moment of high art where the beach scene pointed to what could be, instead of what was, or perhaps how joyful and attractive the old blind woman was in her younger days. That's what the critics said, especially after it became clear that the bio had become wildly popular. Cinema at its finest, the critics from the Rajjya Academy said, combining the heart-touching story of PM Papa's difficult childhood with the techniques of high art. By drawing attention to its own ineptitude and crude and jarring presentation, the Rajjya Academy critics said, the movie informs us of who we are as people and who we are going to be as a nation.

In the few days since the biopic had been released, *Darkmotherlandtimes* was already speculating intensely that PM Papa's blind mother in the movie was an incarnation of Darkmother herself. So was the bosomy heroine, for wasn't Darkmother a shape-shifting goddess, one that could inhabit any body, be everywhere at once, give form to the formless, see everything simultaneously? Capitalizing on the unanticipated popularity of what he had created, the filmmaker had already changed the title of the biopic. Previously it was *The Great PM Papa*, now it was *Darkmother's Favorite Son*.

In Beggar Street, Chanchal, who fancied himself a movie buff, threw a sandal at the TV at the conclusion of the film, eliciting more laughter.

By this time Kranti had already gone into her room and shut the door. She could hear muted voices from the living room. She went to the door and pressed her ear against it. They were talking about the Gang of Four, still discussing whether it'd be a mistake to get involved with them. Prakash said that there was no other way. "I'm tired of churning out pages at Mothercry Press," he said. "Just words. They're useless. They do nothing. We need to start assembling a Dojjier, as Amma has suggested. There needs to be accountability when the big day arrives."

They discussed the Dojjier. Kranti understood that it would be a record of atrocities committed under PM Papa's regime, so when the regime was finally toppled, those responsible could face justice. Documents, photographs, testimonies. The Gang of Four had suggested that if the Beggars weren't up to armed rebellion, then they could at least do the necessary paperwork.

Murti said that Amma scared her. "Amma will go in a burst of flames," Murti said. Chanchal said something that sounded like a slight reprimand.

"It's not a bad idea," Professor Shrestha said. "But we must be careful."

"We're always careful," Prakash said. "Too careful."

"Prakash, my brother," Professor Shrestha said, "being cautious makes us see the long-term, helps us make decisions not guided by our animal impulses."

Prakash said something, or made a guttural sound, resulting in some cross talk. Kranti supposed Murti was mildly reprimanding Prakash, which she often did.

"Okay, okay!" Professor Shrestha said, raising her voice. "The Rajjya must not get a whiff of this Dojjier. It's one thing to produce pamphlets espousing freedom and justice, quite another to create a record of their crimes."

"The Hippo probably has files on all of us by now," Prakash said. "If they can do it, so can we."

"There's certainly a file on Madam," Murti said. "Probably this thick." Kranti imagined Murti indicating ample thickness with her hands.

Then Bhaskar spoke. Kranti held her breath. She didn't hear anything. He was whispering. The bastard! It was as though he knew that she was listening. She pressed her head hard against the door, bumping it against the wood, making a slight thumping sound. The living room chatter stopped. She could imagine them shushing each other. There was shuffling of feet, then Professor Shrestha's voice sounded close to her door, "Kranti, how are you feeling?"

Kranti didn't speak. She just wanted to hear what Bhaskar had been saying to the Beggars. Had they already brainwashed him? Had she, Madam Mao, filled his head with all that Sangharsh nonsense? "Sangharsh! Sangharsh!" she used to say exasperatedly to Dada. "I'm so tired of hearing that word. Such a harsh word. Ghaaarshhhh." Dada pointed out that it had the word "harsh" in it. Do something with it, he was suggesting, and of course that was all Kranti needed. She led Dada in using "harsh" in a litany of imaginary conversations:

—We must continue our resolve for our . . . *harsh*.

—Don't be too *harsh* on our . . . harsh.

—Let's see, how many people are currently in our . . . harsh.

—Murti, you are not seriously . . . *harshing*.

—That horse is giving birth—what a . . . harsh.

There were more whispers in the living room, then there was a knock. She opened the door for Bhaskar and went to her bed to lie down.

Closing the door behind him, Bhaskar followed her and sat on the bed. "Shall I rub your head for you?"

She shook her head. "Stop worrying about me. Worry about yourself."

He stroked her cheek. "What's the point in worrying about yourself?"

"You are more gullible than I thought," she said. "What were you khush-pushing out there?"

"I'm just fed up."

"With what?"

"In general." He sighed. "He's taken a new title now. His Sovereign Excellency PM Papa. Who knows what's coming next?"

"You can't stop talking about him. You have the Papa Derangement Syndrome." She'd heard a colleague at work say that's what dissidents had.

He laughed, but she didn't laugh with him. "I despise them," she said instead.

"Who?" He knew who but he didn't want to hear it.

"Them," she said, jutting her chin toward the door. "That Prakash. Just watch. One day he's going to get hanged in the public square."

"Shh," Bhaskar said. "Public square? What do you think this is? A fantasy novel?"

"We don't have public squares?" she said. "What do you think our durbar squares are? And you're supposed to be the smart one? That's what our Madam Mao is constantly telling me." She mimicked her mother's slightly gravelly voice. "That Bhaskar—smart as a whip. Oooh. Oooh." She made it sound as though her mother was in the throes of orgasm.

"Don't," Bhaskar said, smiling.

She stopped.

"And don't wish hanging upon anyone, even your worst enemy."

"His eyes. They are the eyes of a madman. How can you even have a conversation with Prakash, I don't understand."

"I like his dry humor."

"And that Murti—I can't even. Oh, Chanchal. Do you know how many times I've wanted to smack him into sitting still?"

Bhaskar moved his head and arms about quickly, in a shaking, fluttering fashion, imitating Chanchal and hoping to make Kranti smile. He imagined that's what her father would have done.

But Kranti wasn't smiling. "He's a snake, though. All of them are snakes."

"Even Vikram?"

Kranti said nothing. Vikram, with his quiet, polite ways, was the most palatable of the Beggars, but she wouldn't be sorry if she never saw him again, along with the others.

"Okay, forget it," Bhaskar said. "Let's talk about something else. Do you want to go to Tato Chiso? They've added hakka noodles to their menu."

Hakka noodles did sound enticing, but Kranti didn't want to give in. She wanted a concession from Bhaskar—what kind, she didn't know.

Bhaskar held her in his arms. "Noodles? Slurp, slurp?" He made sucking sounds close to her cheek, as though he were eating spicy food that was making his tongue burn.

Kranti freed herself from his grasp and stood.

"Is that what you want, for me not to go to the other room?" he asked.

She said nothing.

He stood in front of her. He looked handsome and heartbreaking in that white kurta suruwal. "All you have to do is give me the word," he said, "and I won't go." She shifted away from him. "Okay, I won't go." He lay on the bed.

In the living room an argument had broken out between Murti and Prakash. She was advocating for more caution when it came to the Gang of Four, and he was saying the time for caution had passed. "Enough!" Prakash was yelling. "We must act now! Now!" He sounded like a howling jackal.

"Pretty soon you'll sound like him," Kranti said to Bhaskar, quietly.

"Now! Now!" Bhaskar said in a high-pitched voice, mimicking Prakash, but softly so the Beggars wouldn't hear.

She was amused, a bit, because it was such a Dada thing to do. Oh, how she missed him right now. To Bhaskar, she said, not cracking a smile, "You don't seriously think what's happening in Darkmotherland is a permanent state of affairs, do you? There's simply no way he'll be able to hold on to power for long." She said it, but she wasn't convinced of it. PM Papa seemed here to stay, at least for a while.

"We all know he's smoothing the way to declare himself prime minister for life. That's very permanent."

"I don't believe that's going to happen."

"You're a strange bird," Bhaskar said, smiling. "On the one hand, you have so much confidence that things in this country won't get worse. On the other hand, you are quite sure that things will get bad for me."

"This is not about logic," she said. "This is how I feel, and I trust my feelings." She knew that she wasn't making much sense right now, at least logically—so Bhaskar was right in that regard—but she felt betrayed. She felt *strongly* betrayed. He had chosen the Beggars over her, he had chosen her mother over her. How could he? She, Kranti, had given so much to him—this thought came out of nowhere, inexplicably, even though it was he who had brought smiles and laughter into her life. Still, she had loved him with her whole self, and this was what she was getting in return? "Go," she said softly to him. He reached out to touch her, but she said, "Please, Bhaskar, please don't touch me right now. Please."

He withdrew, then said something, but the words didn't register with her. "Please, Bhaskar!" she said, raising her voice.

In the living room, the Beggars went quiet.

"Go!" she said to Bhaskar, turning away from him, then immediately pouncing upon him, as if she were going to pummel him. "Why don't you go to them?" she whispered. "Go to her. That's what you want, isn't it? You admire her so much that you might as well"—and before she could stop herself—"sleep with her."

DEATH AND REBIRTH

7.

Dada had admired a jacket during one of their strolls through the Tourist District. It was a leather jacket, hung on the doorway of a shop, with a grinning skull imprinted on the back. Beneath it were the words GRATEFUL DEAD. Dada had laughed at the words, fingered the jacket and commented on how soft it was, how smooth to the touch. "But what does grateful dead mean?" he'd asked her. "How can one be gratefully dead?"

"It's some sort of a hippie name, Dada," Kranti said. She was already nearing her second year at the Tri-Moon College. "Be grateful that it's not Hateful Dead."

The shopkeeper had poked his head out and said, "It's lambskin leather, that's why it's so soft. The best leather there is."

"It's the best because it's dead," Dada said to Kranti. "Get it?"

"This Grateful Dead here is a rock band," the shopkeeper said. "Very popular in Amrika. Here, I'll play their music."

On the stereo inside sounded the twang of a guitar and a soft, raspy voice. It hardly sounded like real music, more like a bunch of teenagers tuning their guitars. But Dada swayed to it, and Kranti watched him briefly, then asked the shopkeeper how much it was.

When the shopkeeper quoted the price, her father stopped smiling and swaying. "No wonder they're grateful to be dead. With that price!"

On the way home Dada shook his head and chuckled. "Grateful Dead. Wah! Wah! How come I'd never heard of them before?"

"Well, maybe they're not as popular in Amrika as the shopkeeper dai claimed. He might be saying that just to make you buy the jacket."

But the next day, Kranti found Dada listening, eyes closed, to the Grateful Dead in his room. He'd borrowed their CD from a music shop in the Tourist District. "They're good," he said to Kranti. "Half the time I don't understand what they're saying. Sugar magnolia— what is that? Ke bhancha, ke bhancha! But I like them!" He asked her to listen to a song called "Box of Rain," and even she, who normally didn't listen to much music, liked how soothing the song was.

"Now box of rain I understand," Dada said. "Paani ko baksa. It's like that bucket of rain we catch underneath the roof during the monsoon."

Kranti smiled. "You should buy that jacket, Dada."

"And who's going to pay for your wedding?"

She eyed the jacket on the way back and forth from college. A week before his birthday, she stopped at the shop and struck a bargain. She had always been frugal and had saved money over the years from the dakshina she'd received during the Ten-Day Festival. She'd also saved much of her pocket allowance instead of spending it on clothes, like her friends did. She took the jacket home and hid it in her room.

Rozan's parents had stopped loving him when it became obvious to them that their boy was *unnatural*—he acted effeminate and he liked boys. They discovered this about him two years after he himself had discovered his attraction to boys.

By the time he was thirteen, Rozan wanted to hang out with girls and wear frocks like they did. Every time he looked in the mirror, he knew he was in the wrong body. He didn't like the fact that he had a penis. It felt wrong. There were days when, peeing in the outhouse, he felt disgusted with the thing he held in his hand.

He felt ashamed, and confused, and tried to convince himself that other boys also felt as differently as he did.

One time he walked into the girls' lavatory and sat on the commode and peed while sitting down. It felt like the most natural thing to do. None of the toilet stalls had doors, so when a girl came in and saw him, she giggled and ran out. As Rozan hastily pulled up his trousers, half a dozen girls burst in. Within minutes, the news of him peeing in the girls' toilet spread throughout the school. A teacher marched up to him and twisted his ear as punishment.

When his friends teased him and asked him about it, he told them that he'd done it as a dare.

Another time, he and a good friend where sitting on a wall, looking out at a field where some girls were playing hopscotch. "Do you ever feel like you could be a girl?" he suddenly asked his friend.

The friend looked at him curiously and shook his head. "Girls are weak. Why?"

"Nothing."

"You wish you were a girl or what?"

Rozan said no, but without meeting his friend's eyes.

"Really?" the friend shoved him. "Why don't you go play with them then, kaley?"

The understanding that his friend didn't feel like a girl further confused Rozan, but he couldn't stop from looking into the mirror and thinking that he was a girl. The spelling of his name was Rojan during his childhood, but he started writing *z* instead of *j* when he was around eight. Somehow, the Angrezi alphabet *z* looked right to him. I am not like the other Rojans, he'd thought then. By his early teens, however, even Rozan dissatisfied him. Then, one day, he found a tube of lipstick that his sister Reshami had left behind when she married and moved away. Rozan applied the lipstick. In the mirror he saw his rosy lips and it felt like a natural look for his face. He tried out various feminine names for himself. Roshi. It sounded too much like rishi, an ascetic. Rozani: too long—it stumbled around his tongue for too long before emerging. Roz. Not bad. Rozy. Yes! My chosen one, my Rozy. "Timi Rozy," he whispered to his image. "Rozy," he said to himself and kissed his lips on the mirror.

His sister had also left behind some clothes for when she visited. He found a pair of panties in them, and he gingerly picked them up, smelled them, and put them on. He walked around in his room, in those panties, sashaying, cupping his breasts.

Then the crushes on other boys started, and along with it, a recognition by his classmates that Rozan was different. They began to tease and harass him. Chakka, they called him. Homo. No wonder he calls himself Rozy these days. Sounds like a woman's name, doesn't it?

Many times Rozy returned home from school in tears, his clothes torn because a group of boys had assaulted him on the playground. He tried acting the opposite, tried acting macho. He went to a gym, which was in the basement of a man's house, but quit after a couple of weeks because he found it difficult to lift the weights. And he was more interested in admiring other boys and men with their bulging biceps and sweaty glistening chests. He asked his school's sports teacher whether he could join the boxing club, but the teacher laughed at him. "You want your face squashed like a bug? That's what the other boys will do to you."

By the time he was in ninth grade, he had given up on trying to be manly. During school picnics and events he hung out with girls, who on the whole were more accepting of him than the boys were. He felt ashamed of himself, ashamed of his desires. They felt natural but he knew they were unnatural. He had some girls' clothes he'd secretly bought in the market. He wore them behind closed doors in his room. He put on his skirt, and he felt so happy. Then he was wracked by such deep anxiety—he knew that these feelings would never go away, no matter how hard he tried to squelch them.

8.

Kranti didn't tell her mother about the Grateful Dead jacket, not because she thought Professor Shrestha would object to it, but simply because she didn't want her mother to have the pleasure of this secret. She had persuaded Professor Shrestha that on Dada's birthday the three of them should go out to a fancy restaurant to celebrate—one that featured live ghazals since Dada loved ghazals. Initially, Professor Shrestha had mentioned a meeting she had to attend, but upon seeing Kranti's tight face she had acquiesced. Dada's work shift ended at five, when the dinner chef at Hotel Thunderbolt & Diamond took over, and they waited for him to return home. Kranti clasped the bag with the jacket to her chest. She wanted to surprise Dada as soon as he walked through the door. She ignored Professor Shrestha's query about what she was holding.

A man from Hotel Thunderbolt & Diamond called at five-thirty P.M. You must come quickly, the voice at the other end told Professor Shrestha. The mother and the daughter rushed out, Kranti throwing the bag into the closet. A taxi hurtled them toward the hotel, which was on the way to the Self-Arisen Chaitya. By the time they reached Hotel Thunderbolt & Diamond, Dada's charred body was being pulled out from a kitchen closet. It looked like someone had given him a mud bath. His mouth was agape, revealing pink gums against his blackened face.

One of the gas containers inside the closet had exploded. An employee had broken down the door, wrenched the fire extinguisher from the wall, and managed to douse the flames in the burning closet. But it was too late for the chef. No one knew why Dada had gone into the closet in the first place. Usually, it was the kitchen custodians who handled the containers. And why was the door to the closet locked from the inside?

Suicide. The word was whispered in the aftermath. Professor Shrestha had to be hospitalized for two days. Kranti felt no pity for her. She visited the Brave Hospital to take care of her mother, all the time wishing that it was her mother who had died and not Dada. He loved Kranti too much to abandon her like that. She wanted to believe it was an accident, not suicide. But late at night when she couldn't sleep, her mind went over what happened in Hotel Thunderbolt & Diamond's kitchen that day. Her father, because he was mild-mannered and always telling jokes, was popular among the hotel staff. She saw him smiling, joking, then entering the closet, locking the door behind him, opening the valve of a gas container, and holding the flame of his lighter to the tube where the gas was hissing out.

After Dada's death, Professor Shrestha took to alcohol and cigarettes. There was hardly any communication between the mother and daughter. Kranti kept to her room, her door locked. She still expected Dada to walk in through the front door, smiling, eager to retell a joke he'd learned that day. The Grateful Dead jacket was in her closet; she hadn't taken it out of the bag since his death. She wanted to burn it, but she wondered if it would cause her father harm, wherever he was, up in heaven or somewhere. One day, as she stared at Dada's garlanded photo in the living room, the irony of the band's name on the jacket hit her. Grateful Dead. She shook her head at her mind's attempt to link the band's name to her father's death. The band had picked out its name randomly from a dictionary! At least that's what Dada had said. There was no connection. But your death was also random, she told her father in her mind. You left me randomly, Dada, she thought, then chuckled. Professor Shrestha was seated on her favorite green sofa where she did her smoking and drinking. Sweetly, with a sad smile, she asked, "Did you just now remember one of your father's jokes, Kranti?"

—

One day Bir invited Rozy to his house for a game of cards. Bir harassed and bullied him when others were around, but fondled and kissed him when they were alone. Because he was smitten by Bir, who was brilliantly handsome with his chiseled face and his soft mustache, Rozy had welcomed the private caresses and kisses. This was the first time that Rozy had been invited to Bir's house, and he wondered if Bir was punking him. Perhaps Bir had also called his aggressive friends, and the evening would be spent in mocking and name-calling Rozy—homo, hijra, queen, chakka. Sometimes a double slur—darky homo. Rozy decided not to go, then he thought of Bir's lips against his—Bir was a gentle kisser, and he always murmured that Rozy had such pink, succulent lips—and changed his mind.

So, Rozy went, his throat dry, his hands shaking a bit. At one point in his walk he was even besieged by the impossible idea that Bir had invited him to let his parents know that he and Rozy were boyfren-garlfren now. The term "garlfren" applied to himself made him happy. He envisioned taking Bir to meet his parents, and he laughed inwardly at its absurdity.

Bir had lit a candle in the living room, but that was because loadshedding had plunged the entire neighborhood into darkness moments before. Bir was sitting on the sofa, his face in half-shadows. "No one in the house?" Rozy asked.

"Why do you want anyone, faggot?" Bir asked.

Rozy paused in the doorway. Bir's words hurt, like needles into his chest. "Did you call me here to speak to me like that?"

"How would you like me to address you? Sweetie? Dahling?"

"I came only because you invited me."

"Come here." Bir's voice was now soft.

"Any of your friends here?"

"Just you and me, sweetie."

Rozy hesitated. Bir was gazing at him with a smile, and gradually Rozy became hopeful. "Why are you looking at me like that?" he asked Bir.

"Today is a special day."

Rozy told himself to relax. The dance of the candle flame took on a romantic flavor. He went to Bir, who asked him to sit on his lap. Shyly Rozy did, feeling Bir's arousal against his thigh. It pleased him, and he himself became aroused, then became shy about it. "Why are you sitting here in the dark?" Rozy asked.

"I've been thinking of you."

They kissed. Rozy wiggled himself against Bir's lap, and Bir stiffened more. Not too long ago, in a deserted alleyway next to the school's football field, he'd thought about sucking Bir's penis, but that really it was too early to take such a bold step. Today I might just do it for him, Rozy thought. Rozy had never sucked anyone off before, although he'd fantasized about it, especially when he'd gazed at photos of actors in magazines, or sometimes even underwear models. "Where are your parents?" Rozy asked.

"They've gone to a wedding. They won't be back until midnight." Bir pulled out something from behind him. "Here." He handed it to Rozy.

"What is it?" Rozy asked, taking it close to the candle. It was a piece of clothing, soft and flimsy.

"It's a nightie."

"A nightie?"

"Yes, a nightie, and you're going to wear it."

Rozy was pleased, but he wondered if Bir knew that he liked to dress up in girls' clothes. "Chyaa!" he flung the nightie to the floor, in mock disgust. "I'm not going to wear it."

"Pick it up."

Rozy shook his head.

"Pick it up, whore. I bought it with such love for you and—"

Again, the harsh words, and the happiness building up inside Rozy vanished. "Please don't call me that."

"What? Whore? Randi? Slut? That's what you are."

"Then I will leave."

Rozy stood from his lap but Bir restrained him. "I want you to wear it for me. I want you to look pretty for me tonight." His voice was pleading.

Rozy dithered between hurt and hope. Perhaps Bir would finally confess to him how much he loved him, how much he desired him. He just had a rough way of talking—Rozy would have to train him, gradually. A pronouncement of love by Bir, even in the privacy of this living room, would make Rozy forget about all of Bir's nastiness. He knew there was a soft side to Bir. He just needs some time, Rozy thought, I can change him. "Why should I do it? You don't even love me."

Instead of answering, Bir pulled Rozy toward him, kissing him on the mouth, this time slowly and with passion. He said, "I'll show you how much I love you after you wear it and become pretty for me."

"Promise?"

"Promise."

⌒

Instinct told Kranti to burn the Grateful Dead jacket. If she kept it in her possession, Dada's soul would unhappily roam the earth, forever. She didn't know why she thought this. Dada hadn't even worn the jacket, so it was not as though his soul could be trapped in it. Then she wondered if the purchase of the jacket had contributed to Dada's death. After all, he had thought it too expensive, but Kranti had gone ahead and bought it anyway. Perhaps that had displeased Dada's atma and he'd decided to end it, once and for all.

All of this thinking was so absurd! Kranti wasn't sure she believed in the whole concept of a soul to begin with. Yet, a week after Dada's body was cremated, she had returned to the Lord of the Animals ghat, thinking she'd burn the jacket at the same place. But once she reached the riverbank, she became disoriented. She didn't know east from west, north from south. The ground spun, and suddenly the monkeys who roamed the vast temple complex, those vile filthy creatures, came up to her and sat in the lotus position. One monkey, a leader type, a big motherfucker with an ass that seemed to have been branded by red hot embers, said, "Today, young woman, we are going to teach you how to meditate." And he upturned his palms on his knees, hands forming a circle by touching the tip of the thumb and the index finger together, and said, "Now chant OM." The next moment he rolled over in a burst of giggles, and the rest of the monkeys also chanted OM, followed by spasms of belly-aching laughter.

A skinny female monkey with glassy eyes noticed the jacket

Kranti was clutching and said, "Well, looky what we have here" and attempted to wrestle it away from her. Kranti held on to the jacket, clutching it to her chest and kicking the skinny bandaria vigorously. One of the kicks landed on the monkey's chest and she was catapulted into the arms of her leader, the one with the badass embers.

The leader wrapped his arms around the skinny bandaria and said, "Mon amor, mi mono." He closed his eyes and puckered his lips in anticipation of a kiss. Another monkey, robust and handsome with thick eyelashes, came up to the red-bummed monkey and smacked him on the side of the head.

A full-scale war ensued among the monkeys. Monkeys screaming and scratching, pummeling and kungfuing, and swinging and biting. More monkeys descended on the cremation ghat to fight. Monkeys from the immediate neighborhoods and monkeys from far neighborhoods. Monkeys as tall as bamboo poles, walking on two legs. Monkeys who resembled lions and tilted their heads and roared. Monkeys with white fur and blue eyes who gave the impression that they wanted to return to the old colonial days when the white folks ruled the world. Monkeys with chips on their shoulders. Monkeys with donkeys on their backs. Monkeys with their tails on fire. Monkeys with no desire. Monkeys who called one another, "Sire, Sire."

Kranti took the jacket home and draped it on a hanger from her closet handle, the skull-side facing her. What had she been thinking by wanting to burn this jacket? She'd heard Dada singing in the shower about trucking, rattling off the names of Amrikan cities.

Now, as she walked into the kitchen, she found herself saying, "Trucking, trucking," repeatedly, as Dada had done.

Professor Shrestha watched her fetch a glass of water from the kitchen and spoke. "I thought you had a test coming up."

"Been trucking, mamaw," Kranti told her mother. Then she couldn't resist, "But no fucking."

She hastened to her room and slammed the door, delighting in her mother's horror, which she couldn't see, but knew must have been carved into her face.

9.

Kranti hadn't been to college since Dada's death and Professor Shrestha didn't question her about it. Kranti's schooling had always been Dada's domain, in any case, and Kranti would have been furious if her mother had started showing any interest now. But Professor Shrestha only sat on her green sofa, ensconced in cigarette smoke. Before Dada's death she used to smoke a cigarette or two a day; now the pack remained clutched in her hand or on the couch's armrest as she sat all day long sipping whiskey, smoke curling and twirling in the changing light.

Once in a while Professor Shrestha put an old song in the CD player and a plaintive voice rang through the house, reaching Kranti in her room, the lyrics quite proper for the occasion: "my drunkenness today has become a screen for me." It was one of Dada's and Professor Shrestha's favorite songs, from their romantic days before Kranti was born, sung by a legendary Darkmotherlandite vocalist. As she listened to the song, Kranti stood in the middle of the floor in her room and pointed her finger at her mother, through the wall into the living room. The world is corrupt, Kranti silently told her mother. And you are the corruptest of them all. Kapti corrupty, Kranti sang softly. Mirror, mirror on the wall, who is the kapti corrupty of them all?

—

One day a raven outside her window spoke to Kranti. The raven said, "Your father killed himself. Do you understand, Kranti? Your father walked into that closet and lit the match."

Great, Kranti thought. Now birds are talking to me. She remembered the poem by Edgar Allan Poe she'd read in the Angrezi literature class last year. She didn't remember all the details, but hadn't the dark bird in that kabita taunted a guy who was crestfallen over the loss of a lover, and drove him to madness?

"He offed himself," the raven said. "Do you hear? Your father. Offed!"

"Where do you come off, you offing Poe, talking to me like this?" Kranti said. "Fuck off! You know nothing about my father." She scolded him further in a trembly mocking voice, "Nevermore. Nevermore."

"Who are you speaking to, Kranti?" her mother asked from the next room.

"The fuse was lit," Poe said. "In his brain, I mean." The bird appeared thoughtful. "And also in the gas of course. Sad. Sad. Did he think of you in that last moment, my dear Kranti?"

Kranti shut the window and latched it, but she could still hear him jabbering, at times a murmur close to her ears.

—

Poe followed her wherever she went—out in the street, in the market—flying very close to her ear, mumbling, cajoling, consoling, heckling, mocking, telling her that her father couldn't take it anymore. She waved him away with her hand, and he fluttered and squawked, flew away and returned again. Passers-by looked at her, this young woman swatting away at invisible things in the air.

Poe appeared in her dreams, a giant bird with juicy eyes.

Professor Shrestha expressed worries about Kranti talking to herself. It was not a good habit, she said, standing at Kranti's door, whiskey on her breath. People had begun to return to the house again, students, admirers, the Beggars, and once again the house was becoming noisy. The Beggars had begun to hold their meetings.

"See?" Poe said. "It proves my point." Poe made fun of the Beggars— Murti's clingy obsequiousness towards Professor Shrestha; Prakash's sullenness, his temper; Vikram's dull muscularity; Chanchal's furtiveness; Baral's constant sarcasm.

Kranti stayed in her room when her mother's minions congregated in the house. Every now and then Professor Shrestha came to the door, asked her to come out to mingle. Or Murti came and talked to Kranti in a saccharine voice. These were the same people who hadn't seen Dada when he was right in front of them, who treated him like he was a nokerchaker.

"Chef-ji, can you make us some tea?"

"Chef-ji, how about the delicious alu sandeko you make?"

"Chef-ji, can you arrange some more cushions?"

It was this constant harangue, this demoralization that had driven Dada into that closet at Hotel Thunderbolt & Diamond.

A tear streak glistened perpetually beneath Poe's liquid left eye.

—

Rozy shed his clothes in the darkness, then put on the nightie, which was of a soft material, yet slightly scratchy. He'd kept his underwear on, but Bir said it had to come off too. Rozy felt vulnerable. A strange excitement was also building up in him at the thought of where the evening was headed, at the promise of hearing words of love from Bir. His arousal was showing through the nightie, and he felt disgusted, wished it wasn't so blatant and obvious. After tonight's confession he was going to demand that Bir no longer hide their relationship.

Rozy had gone to the corner of the room to put on the nightie. He returned, hiding his erection with his palm, a coffee table separating him from Bir. He made a move toward the couch again but Bir raised his hand and said, "Now it's my turn to come to you, sweetie." He came around and stood in front of Rozy, groins touching, so that Rozy could sense Bir's bulge straining against his trousers. Rozy expected to be kissed by him. Instead, Bir's hands started kneading Rozy's breasts as though they were a woman's. It hurt, and it tickled. "Where are your boobs?" Bir asked. "How can you be a woman without boobs?"

"That hurts, Bir."

"Without boobs you're merely a hijra, aren't you? A transvestite. A man who thinks he's a woman." He continued squeezing Rozy's breasts, harder and harder. He then lowered his head and pressed his lips against them, over the nightie, sucking on the nipples one by one, sucking deeply as if he were trying to extract something from Rozy's body. His words were upsetting, but Rozy had never seen Bir as hungry as this. He stroked the back of Bir's head, hoping that from now on it would be Bir who'd be hungry and needy, and therefore, more loving. Could Rozy dare to feel happy about what was occurring? Rozy's nightie had two spots now soaked with Bir's spittle. Bir stopped sucking and raised his head, like a drinking animal in the woods alerted to an unusual sound. "What was that?"

"What?" A brief moment of panic. Had Bir's parents returned home early?

"Something moved down there," Bir said. "I need to investigate." He lowered himself to his knees. His hot breath was now steaming against Rozy's erect cock. Rozy tried to hide his erection with his palms but Bir pushed them away and said, "What is this?" His right hand grasped Rozy's penis over the nightie. "I expected a cunt down here, but I'm discovering a cock." Bir stroked Rozy's penis, and Rozy became afraid that he'd ejaculate immediately. "Shouldn't you have a cunt down here? What are you doing carrying around a cock? But what a beautiful cock it is. A beaut! Half my size but lovely. And so fair, unlike the rest of you. I think I need to kiss it."

"Bir, please," Rozy moaned.

But Bir was already kissing and slurping Rozy through the nightie. Dogs were barking in the distance. Rozy hadn't expected things to move so quickly, but what was happening was also thrilling. Bir lifted the nightie and took Rozy into his mouth, swallowing him whole. Pleasure shot through Rozy and he quickly discharged and went limp. Spitting and coughing, Bir cursed Rozy, then pulled him down, so that both were now sitting on the floor. "Who told you to come in my mouth, motherfucker?"

"But, Bir, I—"

Bir slapped him, then, as Rozy was reeling from the sting, shoved him to the floor, face down. He yanked Rozy's nightie up to his waist, widened his buttocks with his right hand, unbuckled his pants with his left, and placed his cock against Rozy's anus.

Rozy protested and squirmed. But Bir had placed his elbow against Rozy's shoulder blades, and there was no way of escaping.

"Making me suck your cock, you filthy whore." Rozy felt something enter his anus, but it was not Bir's penis but his finger, first one, then two. With his free hand Bir appeared to have reached for something under the couch. Just then the lights came on, and out of the corner of his eyes Rozy saw that he had a small bottle in his hand. Rozy became terrified. Was Bir going to shove the bottle into his anus? He's read about men doing it to women when they were raping them—inserting bottles and iron rods into vaginas. Then a small relief—the bottle had oil, which Bir used to lubricate his penis. He placed his cock on Rozy's already aching anus.

"This is how you should have been fucked not only by me, but by everyone." He thrust into Rozy, and the pain was unbearable. "Isn't that true?" Bir said, grunting and breathless.

The pain was searing through Rozy's stomach and thighs. It was as if his flesh was tearing up inside him. "Not like this, please," Rozy gasped. With each thrust, the pain escalated; blood trickled down his thighs. "Please don't do this to me, Bir!" Rozy cried.

Panting, Bir said, "Isn't this how you homos like to be fucked?"

The assault continued. Rozy lost consciousness for a few seconds—it could have been minutes, he couldn't tell. His cheeks felt cold against the bare floor, and he inhaled dust and sneezed. A cockroach quickly ran across his forehead, scampering over his eyes.

Finally, Bir shuddered, and collapsed on top of Rozy, breathing heavily. Rozy felt Bir's fluids inside him. Rozy continued to weep, and Bir brought his mouth close to his ear and said he was sorry, he couldn't help himself. If only Rozy wasn't so sexy, if only Rozy hadn't seduced him. But, he said, if Rozy told anyone that Bir had sucked him off—Bir's tongue darted in and out of Rozy's ear—"I'll take a knife to your face. But if you want to tell a friend or two that you tasted my monster, I have no problem with that." Bir pushed himself off Rozy and sat cross-legged on the floor. He lit a cigarette, and after taking a drag, launched into a soliloquy. "God, you are a beautiful creature—everyone knows this. If they could, half the men in this town would love to take you behind the bushes. They don't because they're afraid of being called a homo. But I don't care. Let me put it this way. I don't care anymore if people know that you are my lover. If someone asks me, I'll even say it out loud, yes, that beauty with the Rozy lips is my lover. You know, I never thought it'd get to this point." He took a deep drag on his cigarette, blowing the smoke at the ceiling. He was relishing his epiphany. "I will readily admit that you are my lover, that I love fucking you. You'll let me fuck you every night from now on, won't you, sweetie? Oh, that beautiful cock. I have never seen anything as beautiful in my whole goddamn life. You have a pretty face, my Rozy lips, but who wouldn't salivate once they got a good look at that gorgeous thing! Come to think of it, why should I be ashamed that I sucked on that beauty tonight? I shouldn't, and I won't." Bir laughed loudly, then continued laughing. He had discovered something wonderful about himself. He lifted his finger in the air. "I will, in fact, declare to the whole world that I sucked you off. Yes, tomorrow I will announce it to my friends. Sunil, Mahesh, Bhairav, all of those idiots. The first thing in the morning. But"—he asked Rozy, who was lying face down on the floor, bleeding— "how should I say it? Should I lead up to it, tease them a bit first? Or should I be bold and declare it? Why do I have the feeling that I'll do the latter. Hello idiots, guess what I did last night? Guess. Guess. What will those fuckers do then? Disown me? Avoid me? Not believe me? They might think that I'm playing a sick joke. But would a real man like me, a marda, even joke about taking another man's cock in his mouth? Wouldn't he be afraid of being called a homo?" Bir paused. "Or maybe I am a homo." He whispered the word a few times, as though now discovering new tones and flavors. "Homo. Ho-mo. Hey idiots, I am a homo. I sucked our pretty Rozy last night and I loved it."

10.

One day, when Murti was gently knocking on her door to coax her out, Kranti thought it was entirely possible that the Beggars had plotted to drive her father to suicide. They could have decided that he was a nuisance, an obstacle to their closeness with their Madam, and schemed to mentally torture him so he'd end up taking his life. It was conceivable that they'd discussed triggers that could propel him toward self-harm. "Is there a gun in the house?" a Beggar, perhaps Chanchal, could have asked.

"It doesn't look like a gun-owning house."

"Madam is a pacifist," Murti would have said.

"But she's advocated armed revolutions!" Prakash would have interjected.

"Only as a last resort."

"Then she's not a pacifist."

"If there's a gun in the house, it'd make our task easier." This would most likely come from Vikram.

"Do you mean—?"

"Yes, he will be so desperate for relief that he'd find the gun, load the bullets, then put it to his head."

"Bam!" This would be Prakash.

"But he doesn't look like the violent type."

"What has that got to do with anything?"

"Is he a pacifist too?" Chanchal would have said, mockingly.

"If he's not the violent type, would he use a violent method to kill himself?"

"Only as a last resort."

"Ha! Ha!" Chanchal.

"He might not see it as violent. Only quick and painless."

"Do you want a painless death for him?"

"I want an excruciating death for him, so slow that it'll take decades for him to die." This would have to be Murti, given how she wanted Professor Shrestha all for herself.

"I want him to feel as if he's getting an injection with a large needle every minute, and each injection is more painful than the last," Prakash would have said, half joking, but also meaning it.

"Why? He's not a bad fella," Chanchal would say, smiling. "He makes us tea, and he fries us pagodas."

"He's sucking Madam dry," Murti would respond.

"Why the sexual imagery?"

"Folks! Folks! Please. A gun is not ideal but if that's what gets the job done, then that's what needs to happen." By this point all the voices would begin to merge in Kranti's head.

"But what if there's no gun in the house? What then?"

"Then that's a problem."

"What if we plant a gun in here?"

"Yes, we could buy one on the black market and put it in a place where he'll find it."

"Where would that be?"

"Under his pillow?"

"But what if Madam's hand reaches under his pillow? They sleep in the same bed."

"Why does she continue to sleep with this pathetic mop?"

"What if, once he discovers the gun, instead of shooting himself he shoots her?"

"Oh my!"

"He wouldn't have the nerve!"

"You don't know what desperate people end up doing."

"So no gun under the pillow?"

"A gun anywhere in the house is a risk, as that could give him ideas other than what we want."

Of course, the Beggars wouldn't know that Dada already owned a gun, one he'd bought in Old Dilli back in the day. Kranti imagined them discussing other options. Where would they conduct these discussions? Obviously not in Beggar Street? She took in a sharp breath—of course, very much in Beggar Street. Why not? Her mother had, on occasion, allowed them access to her home even when she was out lecturing at the university, or when Kranti was at school and Dada was at Hotel Thunderbolt & Diamond. On occasion, when Professor Shrestha had been out of the Valley, perhaps even out of Darkmotherland, somewhere in Germnee or Amrika for a presentation or a conference, there'd be a knock on the door on a Saturday, and there they'd be, the Beggars.

Kranti remembered one such incident when her mother had gone to Bangladesh for a seminar. Only she and Dada were home, and the Beggars had appeared, led by Murti.

"But mother is in Dhaka," Kranti had informed them at the door.

"We know that, Kranti," Murti had said with annoying intimacy. "But Madam told us we could use the house for a meeting."

"I have homework to do, and I need to prepare for exams." The exam part was not true, but the thought of these people in her house on a day of leisure ruined her mood.

"We will be quiet," Prakash said, defiantly.

"Can't you go somewhere else? Maybe a tea shop?"

"Why are you failing to understand?" Prakash said. "Madam has already given us permission, and this is our house too, hoina?"

Kranti was thinking of an applicable retort when Dada came to the door and, in his typical congenial manner, invited them in and served them tea and snacks. Kranti fumed in her room. Murti and the others began to converse loudly. Her father came into Kranti's room and tried to placate her. "What harm would it do to let them have a small bit of space in the house? Your mother has given them permission, so you can't really blame them, can you? Besides, they've become like members of our own family now."

"Why can't I have peace and quiet in my own house on a Saturday?" Kranti asked him angrily, not caring that her voice traveled.

These people never leave me alone, she'd thought. Just a few days before, Murti had come into her room, perched herself on the bed, and gone on and on about Professor Shrestha, how she needed to watch her blood pressure, which Murti claimed was linked to many other diseases. Murti had acted as though Kranti was her confidant, or that she was Kranti's confidant—this presumption had incensed Kranti. She'd interrupted Murti at one point and said, "Blood pressure or flood pressure, we all are going to die one day." Murti had become quiet then and left the room. Kranti chuckled to herself for a while, muttering under her breath, "Blood pressure or flood pressure, blood pressure or flood pressure."

And that Prakash. She'd run into him outside the house once and he'd said, out of nowhere, "You can try hard, but you'll never even be qualified to lick your mother's shoes." The comment had taken her breath away. She was about to say something when he said, "Have a bit of humility. It'll do you good." He'd left her standing there, stunned, and walked into the house, as though he were its rightful occupant and not her. She'd recovered and charged into the house, thinking she'd call him out in front of everyone, especially her mother, but he was in the bathroom, and she waited, then after a while realized the futility of saying anything to him—her mother would probably come to his defense—and, kicking the bathroom door, stormed to her room and slammed it shut. She hadn't come out until after the Beggars left, and she hadn't spoken to her mother for a couple of days.

For some time after that Prakash walked around with a smirk, as though he'd had a victory of some sort, which, she realized in dismay and anger, he had.

"Ask them to go away," Kranti told Dada that afternoon when her mother was in Bangladesh.

"Shhh," Dada whispered. "They will go away soon, and then it will just be you and me."

But the afternoon turned into evening, and they continued to occupy the living room, laughing and talking animatedly, treating the house as if it were their favorite tea shop. Every half an hour or so they summoned Dada for something.

"Another round of tea, Chef-ji?"

"More bhujiyas, please."

"Can you fetch some lalmohan from down the street?"

Sometimes they called him to settle a verbal dispute. But even when they included him in their conversation, they accompanied it with condescension and mockery. There was always an allusion to the superior intellect of his wife. "You are so lucky," Murti told him, "to live in such close proximity to such a great mind, day in and day out. Don't you consider yourself lucky, Chef-ji?"

"I consider myself very lucky."

"You married up, for sure," Chanchal said, smiling, his fingers fluttering up to indicate Dada's climb.

"I married into the clouds," Dada said.

"Consider this," Murti said. "Madam could have married anyone in this world. Anyone. I'm sure that many handsome, powerful men would have considered it their honor to be the object of her affections. But for some reason, she chose you."

"What do you think, Chef-ji?" Chanchal asked, splaying his palms in front of him a couple of times. "Why do you think Madam's eyes settled upon you, and not one of the scores of other eligible bachelors?"

"What is your hidden charm, Chef-ji," Prakash said, "that only Madam can see but we can't?"

There was some laughter, and Dada—the fool, thought Kranti—went along with it, cracked jokes at his own expense. "It's still a mystery to me," Dada told Prakash, "what she sees in me. I've always thought of her as a manifestation of a goddess, perhaps Darkmother herself, who has come to live in my house."

"So true, so true," Vikram said.

Dusk was falling, and someone said it was dinner time. They decided that they were going to eat there, and Dada was going to cook for them.

"We are Darkmother's assistants," they said, "so surely we deserve thirty-two byanjan multi-cuisine prepared by our Chef-ji?"

"It'll be my pleasure," said Dada the fool. And like a fool he went to the market to buy meat and spinach and tomatoes, paying for all of it out of his own pocket, and like a fool he came home and prepared their food, frequently wiping his hands on the towel with the logo of Hotel Thunderbolt & Diamond, his "good cook" towel, as he liked to say. Oh yes, they praised the dishes, especially his khasiko masu, and said that perhaps that was the reason that Madam had married him, for his culinary prowess.

"Had I met a man with such magical skills in the kitchen," said Murti, "I too would have married him—even if he performed no magic in bed."

Kranti didn't go to eat with them, despite her father's pleas. Even after he brought a plate to her room she didn't touch it. Only after they left—belching and burping—did she eat, and only after Dada came to her bed and coaxed her sweetly.

One time when Kranti came home from college (Professor Shrestha was receiving an award in the Town of Lakes, and Dada was held up at work that day to feed a large group of Bharati pilgrims who were staying at Hotel Thunderbolt & Diamond), the Beggars and a few others had congregated in the living room, comfortable and noisy. Kranti had had headaches all day at the college and now they amplified at the sight of them. She was attempting to go past them to her room when Murti called out, "Kranti, back from college? Can you make us some tea?"

"You can make it yourself—everything you need is in the kitchen."

"I checked earlier," Chanchal said. "There's no milk. Can you go to the shop and get us some milk?"

"I have to study. You can go yourself."

"We're in the midst of an important meeting," Prakash said.

Kranti shut the door to her room. She could hear them talking about her, saying a mouthy girl was turning into a mouthy young woman. "She has no manners," Murti said—"who will marry her? Who taught her to treat her guests like they are pests? How did our Madam end up with such a family? A rude daughter and a pathetic chef."

"He's called a chef but that's just a fancy Angrezi word for a cook, a bhanchhe, essentially a nokerchaker," Chanchal said. Kranti was sure that he was smiling as he said it.

"She should have married an intellectual like her, someone who shares her interests, then perhaps the child of that union would also have been like-minded and would have appreciated what we're doing." It was Prakash.

"Ha! Ha!"

"Shh. She will hear," Murti said.

—

True to his word, Bir told everyone in the Town of Lakes that he and Rozy were lovers. Rozy's anus hurt for days and he walked with difficulty, which, Bir's friends observed with a shocked bewilderment, supported Bir's claim. Initially they'd taken Bir's braggadocio as a continuation of his harassment of Rozy. But once they realized that he wasn't joking, they begrudgingly accepted his claims as proof of his manliness. A couple of them recalled their own small fantasies about Rozy, how their hands lingered on Rozy's buttocks a moment or two longer than necessary when they'd collectively bullied him. Therefore, in the final analysis, it wasn't so out of the ordinary that Bir had taken Rozy as his garlfren. The phrase "beautiful cock" was heard, but since Bir was the man in the relationship, he was deemed to have been the one wielding the cock, fucking Rozy with it, having Rozy suck it, taking it out to piss in the bushes. They said that Rozy must have been the one who referred to Bir's manhood as "beautiful cock." These homos were shameless anyway, they said, in how openly they talked about what they did behind closed doors. An immoral bunch, all of them.

Rozy was asked questions:

"How long did you keep that beautiful cock in your mouth?"

"Did it taste as sweet as sugarcane?"

"What delicious dishes are you going to feed your boyfren today?"

The rumors about Bir also reached Rozy's parents. Rozy's father beat him, asking why he was bent on ruining his life like that. "You will go to hell, do you know that?" his father said. He spit on the floor of his own house. "I am ashamed to call you my son today."

His mother cried, then she too got up and beat him. Afterwards, she stroked his face and said that he was a man, and men didn't have relationships with other men. "Chee! Chee! What were you thinking?"

Rozy didn't tell them that he was raped. How could he? How would they understand? Even if his sister, their daughter, had told them that a boy had raped her, they'd have blamed her for putting herself in a situation where she could be raped. They'd probably have berated her for defiling herself, and for bringing shame to the family. So how could they understand their son being raped by another boy?

Two days later, Rozy was in his room, putting makeup on his face, which he found consoling, when his father burst in, noticed what was happening, and started beating him mercilessly. Not satisfied by hitting Rozy with his hand, he ran into the kitchen, grabbed a large rolling pin and returned. He hit Rozy on the legs, on his shoulders, on the back, muttering with his jaws clenched. Rozy's mother refused to emerge from her room, where she was crying. Rozy's father dragged him by the neck and took him to his mother and said, "Take a look at his painted face. Now you and I can go hang ourselves." Rozy's mother stared at her son, then she didn't speak to him for the rest of the day, only occasionally looking at him as though she was wondering if he'd indeed come out of her womb.

Later that day Rozy packed a few clothes in his bag and left the house.

He had a friend named Sangeeta who was attending the medical college in town, studying to be a daktar. He shacked up with her for a few days in her dormitory. Bir came by late one afternoon, swaggering, his manhood proven. Rozy refused to see him. Sangeeta went down to the front lawn to meet Bir.

There was a maniacal look in his eyes.

"How is Rozy?" he asked.

"He doesn't want to see you."

"Did I hurt him badly?"

"I don't know what you mean." She knew his type, the machismo, the strut. These types were especially afraid of smart girls like her.

"I mean, did he complain about me?"

"Do you not have brains? If he doesn't want to see you, does that mean he's happy with you?"

Not used to being talked to like that, especially by women, Bir retorted, "And you think you're Einstein because you study daktary?"

"Rozy is not well."

"But I must see him."

To her surprise, Bir was holding back tears. She was not supposed to have guests in her room, especially not a man. The dorm rules were pretty strict, but she had a good relationship with the dorm supervisor and had managed to keep Rozy's stay a secret from the other dorm residents. But this encounter with Bir could turn into a scene. Already some students were looking out of their windows. A couple of them might even have recognized Bir as the local rat who hung around street corners teasing girls.

When Sangeeta went to fetch Rozy, there was no sign of him. He had already left through a back door that opened to a wooded area.

11.

Kranti didn't think it impossible that they discussed in Beggar Street—right there in Dada's home, a home whose name he'd come up with, a name so catchy that it'd become the name of the street on which the home was located, a name that they then adopted for their stupid group—how they could maneuver him toward his death. But they couldn't possibly have known about the gas canisters at his work, could they? Had they sent a spy to check out Hotel Thunderbolt & Diamond? Or perhaps one of them got a job at the hotel to research the possibilities?

Stop it!

Yet she couldn't stop because it seemed entirely in the realm of what could have happened. For some reason, she thought of Vikram with his staring eyes and muscular body, and she knew that he was involved. Vikram absolutely adored Professor Shrestha, but, despite his size, was bullied by Murti—do this, Vikram, do that; do you have brains, Vikram?—and he could have been instructed by her to get a job at the hotel. The more Kranti dwelled on it, the more it became obvious to her that the Beggars thought that if Professor Shrestha's ineffectual husband died at his workplace, then no suspicion would fall upon them.

Then she concluded that Vikram didn't need to act as a spy. She remembered that they had actually visited Hotel Thunderbolt & Diamond one afternoon.

It had started with some teasing beforehand in Beggar Street about Dada's job as a chef, the usual jibes and jokes, and Prakash had asked, "So, when will we actually get to see this Hotel Thunderbolt & Diamond, to see if it exists, to know that you really have a job? Or, how do we know that you are indeed a chef in a fancy-schmancy place and not a dishwasher in a greasy green-curtain joint?"

Unperturbed, Dada had said, "You are welcome to visit me in the hotel if you wish."

Professor Shrestha was lecturing at the university that afternoon. In her presence, Murti and the others were a bit more subdued, more controlled, and they were careful about openly mocking Dada. But her absence freed them.

"Are you sure you really want us to visit?" they asked Dada. "There's nothing embarrassing we'd end up seeing?"

"It's a good hotel," Dada said. "Small but classy. Boutique, ke, boutique. I'll show you."

Dada was proud of where he worked. Located at the bottom of the Self-Arisen Chaitya, the hotel had only twenty rooms, but it was built in the traditional style of the Valley, with decorative window carvings. It was popular among tourists and dignitaries.

"When? When?"

Just then Professor Shrestha entered, and they went to her like children, relating to her their latest plan, making it seem like they couldn't wait for this excursion.

"Good, good," Professor Shrestha said. "It's a good hotel."

And she too, along with a reluctant Kranti, had accompanied the Beggars to the hotel a few days later.

After Dada's death, Kranti understood that the day they visited the hotel together was when the Beggars finalized their plans about Dada. She remembered things that confirmed her conclusion. The Beggars had oohed and aahed as they'd walked into the hotel's courtyard. With its lush trees and flower garden, the courtyard was like a small oasis in the dusty bustle of the Valley. Dada had fed them chicken chili and momos in the restaurant, surrounded by beautiful wall frescoes. He'd shown them the guest rooms, which had cushiony beds and breezy balconies. Then, this memory: Murti asking what was behind the closet door near the kitchen. Dada didn't reply. Murti exchanging glances with Vikram, insisting that Dada show them what was in the closet. Dada saying that nothing is there, and Murti arguing that surely something is there. And Dada smilingly opening the closet, and Murti asking what are those, and Dada the fool, saying gas canisters, and Murti nodding aha, and exchanging glances with Vikram—a final understanding passing between the two.

"Oh my God," Kranti whispered in her room. They had known exactly what they were doing. Then doubts surfaced. How would they have known exactly what he'd end up doing? It is one thing to contemplate planting a gun in the house to tempt a suicidal man; it's another to predict that this very man would walk into a closet full of gas canisters at work and ignite them with a lighter.

The answer came to her in the middle of the night, triggered by a dream in which Murti was making strange hand signs. Kranti's eyes opened and her heart beat maniacally in her throat. They had planted the suicidal thought in her father. That's what her dream was saying. Murti's hand signals were part of her witchcraft—she did them to insert the notion in his head that he should go to work, walk into the closet and start a fire.

Poe appeared on her shoulder and said, "What took you so long?"

Kranti rocked back and forth on the bed. Her body felt cold, then hot, then cold again. She had heard Murti talk about what she called "the power of persuasion." An incident from three years ago came to Kranti, more vividly now even though it wasn't something she'd thought about recently. There were more Beggars then, she remembered, possibly seven or eight, including a man named Baral, with whom Murti often butted heads.

That afternoon Beggars were all gathered around Professor Shrestha. She was seated on her green sofa, gently rocking, mulling over something, her mind only half on the conversation her acolytes were having. Murti was standing next to her, her palm on the sofa's arm, her gesture of propriety over her Madam. Vikram, like the bodyguard he was, stood by the door, his beefy arms crossed at his chest; he often stationed himself at the door so that he'd be the first one to open it in case unwanted entities, especially Poolis Uncles, came knocking. Prakash was smoking by the window, pretending to be aloof but listening to everything and participating occasionally, often to make dismissive or caustic remarks. A couple of other Beggars were scattered around the room. Chanchal was in the kitchen, washing the dishes loudly, dropping things, cursing softly. Baral, Kranti recalled with absolute certainty, was seated on the floor, by Professor Shrestha's feet.

Kranti, having just returned to her room from the kitchen after fetching a glass of water, had her door open, so she could hear everything.

Chanchal shouted from the kitchen that the power of persuasion Murti was bragging about was essentially hypnosis.

Murti said, "No, no, it's not hypnosis. In hypnosis you can't make people do bad things. This is something else. You can actually make people do things against their will."

"Against their will?" Baral asked. "What things?"

"You can make people rob a bank, for example," Murti said.

"Nonsense!" Prakash said, blowing smoke out of the window, not even bothering to look at Murti.

"What hogwash! If such things were possible, all the banks in the Valley would have been robbed by now."

"And you call yourself my disciple, Murti," Professor Shrestha said. Her tone was critical, yet affectionate. She often said that Murti was like the younger sister she never had, which encouraged Murti to act with more leeway around the house than the other Beggars.

"Not everyone can use this power skillfully, Madam," said Murti.

"But you can?"

"I'm not saying anything."

"Then what are you saying?"

"What I'm saying is that certain people have this power, and it's practiced all over Darkmotherland, by sages and witches, and, with training, even by ordinary people." She spoke of a famous woman named Awnty, a legend in Darkmotherland, who provided consultation to the powerful.

"So you are a boksi?" This was said in jest by Baral. But because he and Murti had collided before, it came out as a goading insult.

"Who are you calling a boksi?" Murti said, her voice rising.

Kranti migrated from her bed to the door and watched, her glass of water in hand.

"Well," Baral said, seemingly pleased that he'd managed to anger Murti. "Didn't you yourself say that boksis practiced it?"

"So?" Chanchal asked. "Is this similar to the spell that boksis cast on people? Like tunamuna?"

"Calling me a witch for no reason," Murti said.

Baral smiled at her. "What do they say, a witch in time saves nine?"

"So, you're making fun of me now, Baral?" Murti said calmly. "Okay, then, if that's the way you want it." She kneeled directly in front of him, as though crowding his vision. "Now I'll plant an idea in your head: within the next week you will pick an argument with your wife over a very small thing. But it will grow into something big, then your wife will leave you and go to her maiti. She won't return for a month, leaving you to take care of your two children by yourself—feeding them, bathing them, dressing them, taking them to school. When your wife finally returns, and she will do this only after much begging and pleading on your part—the kind of humiliating groveling you never imagined was in you—when she comes back to you and your children, your wife will not be the same. She will be aloof and standoffish, and you will know that she no longer loves you. She'll even have less love than before for her children. That's what's going to happen to you."

The room turned silent. Kranti let out a small chuckle that was barely audible to even herself.

Professor Shrestha was about to scold Murti when Baral said, "Wow. Now you have me really scared. Look how badly I'm trembling." He put his right hand out, fingers splayed for everyone to see, shaking them dramatically.

Prakash and Vikram laughed.

"This Murti," Professor Shrestha said. "When she gets angry she really gets angry."

"That's because, Madam," Baral said, "you've put her on a pedestal and given her the idea that she's more important and powerful than the rest of us."

"So you don't believe in my powers, Baral?" Murti said, calmly. She hadn't moved from her kneeling position in front of Baral, and now she scooted closer to him, then put her palm out as though blessing him. "Here, I will even tell you what you and your wife will fight about. It will be over such a small thing that you will wonder, even when you're old and without love, how a petty argument changed your life forever. You and your wife will argue over a movie. She will make plans for a movie, you'll forget about it, and at the last minute when she reminds you, you will snap at her and say that you don't have the patience to sit through a three-hour Bollywood ballyhoo—yes, you'll use the word 'ballyhoo.' Instead, let's go to a restaurant, you'll suggest. At first she will appear to be fine with it, but once she changes into her sari and emerges from her bedroom, her face will be dark and she'll tell you that you never listen to her, that her wishes are never respected in this house. That she's been planning for this movie for weeks. But now you're calling it 'ballyhoo.' She doesn't even know what that means, she tells you, but it doesn't sound good. 'Ballyhoo,' she'll keep muttering. 'That's what you think of me—ballyhoo.' You will go on the defensive, Baral, as she becomes more accusatory. Then she'll leave for her mother's house."

"Oh, mighty boksi Murti," Baral said. "Will it happen exactly like you say?"

More laughter, some nervous, some guffawing. "Ballyhoo!" Chanchal said, performing a small dance. "Ballyhooooooo!"

But they weren't laughing and guffawing when Baral didn't come to the next meeting. They rationalized that he was most likely sick. And they were laughing even less about this when he didn't come the following week, or the week after. Then they heard the news that his wife had left him and gone to her mother's house.

—

Kranti's recollection of Murti's power of persuasion over Baral became highly relevant now in this new theory she was putting together about her father's death.

Another memory came to Kranti, one from a few days before Dada's death: "Why don't you come and sit by me, Chef-ji?" Murti says to Dada as he is serving them tea. Then, after he sits next to her, Murti begins whispering into his ear. A long whisper, as if she were reciting a mantra, planting a seed.

After coming to this realization about the Beggars' complicity in Dada's death, Kranti made sure that she didn't leave her room. If the Beggars were in the living room when she returned from college, she avoided eye contact with Murti. Poe encouraged her in this. "Don't look at her," Poe said. "With eye contact, she can enter your mind and control you. The power of persuasion. How to make enemies and influence people. A reverse Dale Carnegie." Whenever Professor Shrestha asked Kranti to come to the living room, she said she had a headache and needed to lie down. The gradual return of the Beggars—Prakash, Vikram, and Chanchal—had somewhat rejuvenated Professor Shrestha's spirits. Sometimes her old students dropped by. Once again Professor Shrestha began speaking about matters of the state, continued injustice faced by people in the south, the way women were still oppressed in the mountain communities in the north, and which politicians to pressure so that underrepresented groups got a candidate in the upcoming local elections. Her voice was more tired than before, but she was regaining her spark. Soon, Professor Shrestha was going to forget that only recently her husband had been cremated at the Lord of the Animals ghat.

—

Rozy had a backpack and some money, and on the bus that evening he sat next to a mild-mannered businessman, who was on his way to the Valley for business. The bus broke down halfway on their journey, and although the driver and the conductor tried all sorts of maneuvers to get the bus going, none worked. It was already dark. Some of the locals had come by and were importuning the passengers to go to their "hotels." "Nothing is going to happen until tomorrow," the bus driver said. "Y'all find a place to sleep tonight." Utter darkness surrounded them, save for the flickering lamps in the huts in the distance. "The bus will be ready at about ten tomorrow morning. For now, good night, sleep tight."

"I'm not sleeping in this hellish darkness," the businessman, who had a soft face and a sweet voice, said. He began to walk, and Rozy followed him. After about half an hour a truck trundled by, and the businessman stopped it. He spoke with the driver and they came to an agreement. Rozy got in with him. The driver was a Sikh who wore a turban and a lungi that revealed his hairy thighs. He smiled and eyed Rozy throughout the trip, asked the businessman what their relationship was. The businessman replied that Rozy was a friend. So, he's not your kudi? The driver asked the businessman. Rozy clutched his bag to his chest and stared ahead. The businessman asked the driver, politely, to mind his own business and keep his eyes on the road.

The truck stopped after the first descent into the Valley, and the driver refused to go further, perhaps in retaliation for what the businessman had said to him. It was close to midnight. The two got out. A few yards away was a sign for a hotel. When the businessman walked toward it, Rozy followed. This is my fate, he thought. From now on it's going to be like this. I'm going to be a kept man. As they stepped into the hotel, neither had doubts that they were going to sleep together. For the businessman it was going to be his first experience with a man. He had a wife and children on whom he'd never cheated before, not even with a woman. And Rozy, he was at the threshold of the Valley with an unknown man. Tomorrow he'd be heading into the heart of the Valley, into uncharted territory. No one there knew who he was. He was not accountable to anyone anymore. In the bathroom of the hotel room, before he headed to the bed where the businessman was waiting, Rozy put some lipstick on. He observed his face for a while, fingered his lips, and whispered, "My love, my red, red Rozy."

Kranti was especially vigilant about Murti's access to her brain. She found some prayer books in Dada's old cupboard (he was the most religious in the family) and memorized the Monkeygod Forty Verses and recited them whenever she felt that Murti was close by, either in person or in spirit.

One time she ran into Murti outside the home. That evening, Kranti, in a rare moment of intimacy with her mother, had agreed to cook dinner—she had learned, ineffectually, to make a few dishes from Dada, who used to be amused by how much mess she made in the kitchen—and was on her way to buy vegetables. She bumped into Murti right as she reached the Stone Fish Market with its strong smell of spices, oil, and fresh vegetables from the local farmers. The market was like a hub with spokes—roads and alleys—that branched out to other neighborhoods. It was swarming with shoppers as usual. "Standing room only," Dada used to joke whenever he and Kranti visited the market. The father and daughter always invariably circled the Temple of the Goddess of Grains ("Maybe the goddess can make Madam Mao's existence more grainy?" Kranti quipped). She observed the fish on the ground—now enshrined as a stone fish—that had fallen from the sky, "during a time when dinosaurs roamed the earth," Dada intoned, every time, even after Kranti countered that there were no dinosaurs in Darkmotherland's ancient history because the gods and demons slayed them with their battle-axes and their thunderbolts.

Kranti looked away but Murti called her name and approached. "Where are you off to, Kranti?"

Kranti avoided looking at Murti, who might be able to plant ideas through the eyes. "Just going to the market," she said in a low voice.

"What? I didn't hear you." Murti cupped her ears and leaned closer.

"To buy vegetables."

"Here, I'll go with you."

"No need."

"I'm in no hurry. Besides, I rarely get to talk to you these days."

Murti linked her arm into Kranti's, who was forced to move. *O Monkeygod, the ocean of virtues and knowledge,* she chanted silently.

"I have been thinking about you since Chef-ji passed away," Murti said. "How hard it must be for a young girl like you to be deprived of your father. My father, he's still alive and I get his blessing every year on Observe Your Father's Face Day. I can't imagine what I'd do if he passed away. He's already eighty. So, I feel for you, Kranti."

Cognizant of my lack of intelligence, Kranti muttered feverishly under her breath, *I focus on you, O Son of Wind, to remove the blemishes of my corrupt mind.*

"I also wonder what actually happened in that closet in Hotel Thunderbolt & Diamond," Murti said. "We never got a clear answer, neither from the Poolis Uncles, nor from the hotel management. Everyone says it was an accident, but was it, really? I often wonder what Chef-ji's state of mind was that day, what made him walk into that closet, what made him—"

Murti didn't complete her sentence, and Kranti found her breath stuck in her throat. The arm that linked hers now felt like a claw. Murti's breath, when it hit Kranti's nostrils, was stale, acidic. Perhaps poisonous. If she breathes hard on me, Kranti thought, she'll turn my face ugly. Murti tightened her arm that was linked with Kranti's as they came upon the vegetable sellers. This was the moment that this boksi was waiting for. Perhaps Dada was not even her real target, perhaps she needed to get him out of the way so she could have unobstructed access to Kranti.

Kranti need to flee. Instead, she was compelled to ask the price of the dew-soaked spinach. The farmer, who was squatting next to his vegetables and smoking, quoted a price that seemed reasonable, and she was about to pay for it when Murti reached out and picked up the two bunches of spinach Kranti had identified. Murti's knobby fingers clasped the spinach and caressed them before she lifted them for inspection. Something transferred from her fingers to the wide leaves, Kranti was sure. Murti tried to hand the spinach to Kranti, who refused to touch them and said, "Now from up close it doesn't look good. Won't buy it."

"What are you talking about?" the farmer said. "You won't find crisp spinach like this in the entire Darkmotherland."

"Nope."

"Kranti, it's good saag," Murti said. She brought the spinach close to Kranti's face, as though forcing her to inhale its invisible fumes, or whatever she'd put in it moments ago.

"It's wilted," Kranti said, stepping back and averting her face.

"Where?" the farmer said, standing. "Show me."

"Your saag is a real drag," Kranti said.

"What?" the farmer said. "After molesting it with your fingers for so long, you have to buy it now."

"Molest?" Kranti said, laughing. "I didn't even touch it."

"Your mother did."

"Then make the molester buy it! And she's not my mother!"

Kranti walked away. Murti threw the spinach back on the basket and hurried after Kranti, who went to another seller and bought some spinach and a small kauli, making sure that her elbows were angled out so Murti couldn't come near them. Now aware that she'd done something to annoy Kranti, Murti watched without saying anything.

On the way back Kranti hurried and Murti kept pace, talking breathlessly about how Kranti shouldn't be angry all the time, her father would have wanted her to be happy. She should also think about her mother, whose loss is equal to hers. Kranti should take care of her mother, Kranti should be strong.

Every time Murti's body touched hers, Kranti flinched and quickened her pace so that by the time she neared home she was power walking, with Murti close at her heels, lecturing her with gasping breath. Inside the house Kranti threw the vegetables on the kitchen counter and went to her room and slammed the door. She had been vaguely aware of her mother's figure in the living room as she passed through it—a dim shadowy figure shrouded in her cigarette smoke.

"Kranti, you're back?" Professor Shrestha said.

Then there were whispers between her and Murti.

That evening Kranti didn't participate in any of the cooking, even though she was the one who was supposed to make dinner. Professor Shrestha came to her door twice during the course of the evening, but Kranti didn't go. Professor Shrestha and Murti ate at the small table that was in the dining room, the very table where her father used to lay out a variety of dishes for their small family.

Professor Shrestha and Murti whispered as they ate. They were talking about her, Kranti was sure:

Oh, what to do about her?

She has become such a difficult child.

She will become the death of me.

Yes, she will become the death of you. She will suck your bones dry is what she'll do.

I am at my wit's end, Murti. What should I do?

Kranti's imagination carried the conversation further, at an increased pitch. Later that night she awoke to a silent house. Her pillow was soaked, her nose clotted with dried snot. She used a hand-kerchief to wipe off her nose and sat up. She stood and opened her bedroom door. She needed to eat something but she wasn't going to touch what they, what Murti, had cooked. No way in hell, she whispered to herself as she made her way in the dark—there was a sliver of moonlight coming from the window—to the kitchen.

Professor Shrestha had indeed left some food for her in a covered plate but, giving the plate a wide berth, Kranti scrounged around in the cupboard. She found a two-day old loaf of bread, slightly hardened, that she chewed hungrily, her face white in the moonlight streaming through the window. As she mumbled she became aware of a shadow in the living room. Murti? Was she lying in wait for her in the dark? But it was her mother. She was seated on her green couch.

"Madam?" Kranti whispered.

Of course she never called her mother Madam, but she often thought of her as Madam, even Madam Mao, and this seemed like the perfect moment to address her that way, even though she knew her mother couldn't hear her whisper across the room. The figure didn't move. Chewing her bread slowly, aided by the moonlight,

Kranti went to her. Hungry? She expected her mother to ask, but Professor Shrestha's eyes were closed. A half-empty glass of whiskey sat on the arm of her chair. The ashtray was filled with cigarettes. Kranti crouched next to her, watching. The Professor had aged since Dada died. Dark circles under her eyes. A stress line now permanant on her forehead.

"They killed him, Madam, you know that? They plotted and schemed and that Murti, your favorite disciple, she planted thoughts in Dada's head."

When Professor Shrestha didn't wake, Kranti whispered, "Madam? Madam Mao? Hello? Anybody home? Nod if you can hear me?"

—

At college there were rumors that Kranti had, as one girl put it, "gone off the deep end." Some of the rumors, Kranti was convinced, had been started by Murti. Kranti often dreamt of Murti. Sometimes during her afternoon nap she dreamt of her mother and Murti whispering and woke up to them actually murmuring in the living room. When she opened her door and stepped out, they stopped whispering and pretended they were busy with something else.

I am not a fool, Kranti told her mother one evening after the Beggars left. I know what you and Murti are up to.

What are you talking about?

Do you think I'm a fool, Professor?

Professor Shrestha sighed. Kranti, let's go see a daktar, please. I beg you.

Professor Shrestha had brought up the idea of a psychiatrist before, but Kranti had been scornfully dismissive. Why don't you get yourself checked out first, Professor? she'd said to her mother. She'd stomped away to her room, then returned immediately with another hot thought. She did this frequently with her mother now—storm away in the midst of an argument, then storm back to further escalate it. Yes, it's you who should get yourself checked first. You never loved your husband, never loved your child, but that Murti, you love her more than anyone else.

That's not true, Kranti, Professor Shrestha said. She glanced toward the window, as though worried that Sapkota, who was their closest neighbor, would hear how crazy her daughter sounded.

A few weeks later a woman came by the house, a friend of a friend of her mother's. Kranti later discovered that she was a psychiatrist. Professor Shrestha and the psychiatrist pretended they were old friends who happened to meet on the street after a long time, but over tea and biscuits the psychiatrist casually began plying Kranti with questions. Did she enjoy college? Did she have friends? What were her ambitions? Any hobbies?

A few days later Professor Shrestha gave her a few pills. Take these, they will help cool your mind.

What are they?

Paagalium capsules.

Kranti took them for a couple of weeks. The pills did calm her down, then in another wave of resentment toward her mother, she stopped taking them. Her suspicions about Murti returned with full force.

It was not another psychiatrist that Professor Shrestha took her to see next—it was a witch daktar. So, here was an atheist, one of the leading Marxist thinkers of the country, one who had railed against things religious and the superstitious, and here she was taking her daughter to be cured by a shaman. The helplessness was marked on Professor Shrestha's face. Kranti wouldn't have gotten better, even if she could, just to enjoy her mother's desperation.

—

Over the next few years Kranti sometimes took Paagalium, sometimes didn't, depending upon her moods. "My moods!" She laughed to herself. "Of course my moods!" When she felt good, she stopped taking them, determined to prove herself normal. The side effects were also a trap. She felt better when she took the medicine, but also felt groggy and disoriented. Sometimes the Paagalium made her feel nauseous. But when she stopped, the voices would return, and she'd begin to feel that her world was collapsing and she'd reluctantly reach for the bottle with the capsules. The man at the pharmacy had no problem giving her a supply of Paagalium whenever she needed it.

MADEMOISELLE REVOLUTION

12.

The ground shuddered less than before, like a child who is gradually beginning to calm down after a sobbing frenzy. Most of the dust devils either disappeared or they turned into pathetic versions of themselves, often swirling in a corner, sighing and whining, mocked by children, kicked. Once in a while a dust devil that seemed to be on its deathbed leapt out and attacked its tormentors. A child was badly mauled by one such dust devil and had to be rushed to the hospital.

Darkmotherlandites said that the Big Two was finally on its way out. Not so fast, others said, it's paving the way for the Big Three.

But overall Darkmotherlandites were feeling relief. Cracks in the roads began to be repaired by the Rajjya more earnestly now. More roads out of the Valley were reported to be open, at least partially. Still, the Rajjya cautioned, through state media, through Motherland TV, that the Son of Yeti hadn't relaxed and that people needed to continue to remain alert, to support PM Papa in all his endeavors, to notify the Rajjya of any unpatriotic activities, such as scheming, plotting, and conniving. Collusion, Hom Bokaw said. Watch out for unsavory elements in collusion with the enemy. Report them.

Motherland TV was showing a ceremony in the Lion Palace. PM Papa was being honored with an additional title, so now he was officially His Sovereign Excellency Darkmotherland's Favorite Son PM Papa.

⁓

The Beggars cried out Bhaskar's name when he came—Kranti heard their voices from her room, especially Murti's, and that's how she knew he had arrived. He greeted them by name as though they were old friends, saying something specific about each of them. Murti, looking young and ravishing as usual. Prakash, what brilliant essay have you composed today for Mothercry Press? Chanchal, any good movies you've watched lately? Vikram, is it my imagination or are you getting more buff?

If that's the way he wants it, she thought. The past couple of weeks, after their falling out, after she told him in anger that he ought to sleep with her mother, every time he had visited he had stayed in the living room, not even bothered to knock on her door. Not that she'd have opened it for him, but even hearing the knock would have been a consolation, for it would have been a reminder of Dada, who also used to knock on her door, gently calling her name, after she locked herself up in her room following an argument with her mother. And she probably would have opened the door for Bhaskar, had he been persistent enough. But he stayed in the living room, in a semi-circle with the Beggars gazing at Professor Shrestha as if she were a deity. Kranti had been in many dark places in her mind in the last couple of weeks. She had been weeping over Dada, haunted by memories of how she'd thought the Beggars had schemed his death; Poe had come visiting.

In the living room Bhaskar and the Beggars discussed Operation Papa Don't Preach, that stupid rally that never got off the ground. She heard Gang of Four being mentioned. Prakash said something that sounded like, "No, they won't accept it" and "the day has arrived," with sounds of alarm from Professor Shrestha and Murti. Bhaskar advocated patience, then wondered if he ought to talk to Amma.

They discussed the minimal progress they'd made on the Dojjier. People don't want to talk, don't want to give statements, Prakash complained. He had some photographs of the Loyal Army Dais loading protestors into trucks, which was not really a proof of state crime, as many democratic countries also arrested protestors if they got out of hand. Prakash did have a recorded interview with an ex-journalist, who had been very forthcoming about how he was muzzled by the Rajjya for some mildly critical articles on corruption among the country's bureaucrats. The recording went into details about the harassment and abuse the journalist had suffered at the hands of the Poolis Uncles. They'd raided his home and scared his family, ransacked his office, showed up at his young son's school and alarmed his teachers, and sent doctored photos of the journalist in compromising positions to his relatives and friends. Now this ex-journalist wanted Prakash to delete the recording, saying he was having panic attacks at the thought of being discovered by the Rajjya. Patience, Professor Shrestha advocated—let's get some more people on record but not without their consent. Chanchal said he was trying to get an audio interview with a prominent human rights lawyer in exile in the Hague—he'd somehow managed to flee Darkmotherland soon after Papakoo—to get his take on what was happening in the country, how the Hippo was violating international human rights every day with his actions. Some of these stories should get out now, Professor Shrestha said, to the *New York Times* and the *Wall Street Journal*, to tell the world about the Hippo's atrocities.

Kranti couldn't take it anymore, so she'd changed into pants and a shirt and left her room. As she crossed the living room, she could sense Bhaskar's eyes, and the Beggars' on her, but she didn't look at any of them.

"Kranti," Professor Shrestha called softly.

A few blocks from her home, in the Tourist District, Kranti found Kabiraj standing in the middle of the road, gazing at the sky, feet straddling a gash on the asphalt created by the Big Two. Short and pudgy, a notebook in his hand. A dark, scraggly growth of beard. He resembled a thoughtful gnome. Taxis and motorbikes and rickshaws wove past him, honking. His lips were moving.

Recently, Kabiraj had come to Beggar Street and sat with Bhaskar and the Beggars, listening to Professor Shrestha as he scratched his beard. Kranti was in the kitchen, making tea for herself (and determinedly not making tea for the group in the living room), and whenever she happened to glance toward the other room she found Kabiraj looking at her. Every time, he quickly looked away, a red blush on his face. At one point when their eyes met, she raised her eyebrows, as though asking what he was up to. He looked away and wiped his face, his fingers getting entangled in his beard (God, all that facial hair!). She kept her eyes on him as she stood in the kitchen and slurped her tea, loudly, her aggression partly coming from her anger at Bhaskar, who would not disengage from the Beggars so he and Kranti could go out.

"Oye!" she said now to the thoughtful gnome as he stood in the middle of the road.

He didn't seem to hear.

"Oye, Kabiraj!"

Kabiraj continued to look like an idiot, standing in the middle of the road gazing at nothing.

"Oye, King of Poets!"

He titled his head to look at her. It took him a moment or two to recognize her, then he reddened. "Eh, Krantiji, how are you?"

"What Krantiji? Am I your boss? Call me Kranti."

"Heh, heh," Kabiraj said.

"What is going on?"

"I was ... I think ... I am ..." He stammered, scratched his beard, then his scalp.

"You should get off the middle of the road."

He glanced at his feet, seemed to realize where he was, then shuffled to the side of the road opposite where she was standing. He looked at her sheepishly. She wanted to cross over to him but suddenly there was a stream of cars and tempos and motorcycles that blocked her way. She could see his hand scratching the top of his head. The wall behind him was completely filled with window-sized posters of PM Papa with the slogan Darkmother's Favorite Son.

She finally found an opening and rapidly crossed over. He flattened himself against the wall, appearing to ready himself for an attack. And she was upon him, asking him how he was, what he'd been writing. He repeated, "Nothing, nothing," as he clutched his notebook close to his heart.

"Are you writing love poems?" she asked. "Is that what you're doing?" She tried to snatch the journal away from him, a vague image arising in the back of her mind of a similar scene from a movie she and Bhaskar had watched, a movie filled with British accents. And as if reenacting a famous scene from that movie, she tried to seize his journal again. "Gimme," she said.

"Krantiji, it's private," he whimpered.

Something had come over her. Why are you so weak? she wanted to ask him. Why are you cowering in front of a woman? She felt pity for him but also a surge of aggression. "You shouldn't be like this," she said, tugging at his journal.

"Like what?"

"So secretive. Be bold."

His face crumpled. He was hurt. "I'm not Bhaskar."

"That you're not." Her body was very near his; he had closed his eyes. Their breaths were mingled now against the wall. She was aware that they were now attracting the attention of passersby. Papa's Patriots could be in the vicinity—they also prowled the Tourist District to ensure that no khaireys were acting "licentiously."

"Either you let go of your journal," she said, "or it's going to tear because I'm not giving up." Even her voice sounded different to her, like that bully from school who used to torment her friend Megha.

"It's got all of my writing in it."

"So," she said in a raised voice, "do you want it intact?"

He let go. Flipping through his journal, she could tell quickly that they were love poems. She leaned against his body, right there against the wall on the street, in view of everyone walking and of the traffic that was zooming by. Beggar Street wasn't too far away, and Bhaskar could easily come by on his way home to the Asylum. The possibility of discovery emboldened her, and she pressed herself tighter against Kabiraj, her breast now touching his chest. She wanted Bhaskar to see this. Did I give you the impression, Bhaskar, that I was weak and withering?

Her body still glued to Kabiraj's—he couldn't leave because she had his poems—she read a poem out loud, pausing and laughing because they were so filled with lofty sentiments toward the woman with whom the poet was in love. "Who's this woman?" she said, jabbing her finger at the journal.

"No one."

"As I suspected. Why?"

"Why not?"

"Don't pull that Darkmotherlandite shit on me! Answer. Why no one?"

A dilapidated truck trundled by, hurling smoke in their faces. She backed off, cursing, but then immediately sidled up to him again.

"It's just a poetic device," he said, coughing a bit.

She laughed a long and hearty laugh, which made a couple of street sweepers look in their direction. "Oh, so women are only devices for you?"

He sputtered.

"If she's a device, why have you made her in flesh and blood? Luscious lips. Hair like a dark river. Mesmerizing eyes."

"It's a literary tradition." He was annoyed, but he also seemed to know that right now she was powerful, so he said softly, "All poets do that. The love spoken thereof can stand for something else."

"Spoken thereof? What insane guff!"

"I am—"

"Stand for what?"

He looked at her in confusion.

"You said it can stand for something else. For what can it stand? Am I not speaking clearly enough for you? Should I say, 'What lovest doth ith standeth fo, heth?'"

"For—for—"

"Love stands only for love, do you understand?"

A couple of pedestrians had now stopped in their tracks and were watching curiously. Would someone recognize her and tell her mother? Your daughter was in a near-compromising position with a short, ugly bairagi type of man in broad daylight. What would happen if the Fundys caught her, an unmarried woman slithering against a man in broad daylight?

The thought of being caught by the Fundys, however, emboldened Kranti further. What better way to teach Bhaskar a lesson? When she and Bhaskar went out in public, it was often Kranti who was afraid that a Fundy would come and ask whether they were married. Bhaskar wasn't afraid of them, as he wasn't of Papa's Patriots. He said that they didn't have the right to ask questions about other people's relationships. How do we know that at night they themselves aren't ramming one another up their asses? he asked, then grabbed hold of an imaginary buttock in front of him and thrust his hips. Kranti cried that that was disgusting, but she couldn't help but snicker at the picture of the Fundys, excited by the hand-holding of couples in parks, having a go at one another at night.

"Why are you always so nervous with me?" she asked Kabiraj as she leaned against him. He was fully backed up against the wall now, his arms in a hands-up position as though she had a gun twisted into his tummy.

A car came dangerously close as it tried to squeeze through them, forcing her even closer against his body. She liked it. He was trembling like a deer, as a romantic poet might say. His lips quivered, a slight tremor from his body passing on to hers. So delicate, she thought, something which made him even more desirable. Then, suddenly, unpoetically, she had a vision of momos squirting juice in her mouth. When was the last time she'd been to a momo place? She and Bhaskar used to eat momos regularly, especially at Mofo Momos, before the Big Two, especially when they were attending Tri-Moon College.

"You like momos?" she asked, gesturing at him that they ought to get going.

He looked at her as though she'd asked him a trick question, but he started walking.

"Is the answer really that difficult?"

"What are you asking?"

"Read my lips," Kranti said, then slowly enunciated, "Doooo youuuuu liiiiiike momooooooos?"

He stared at her in utter disbelief, then said, "What kind of a question is that? Is there a Darkmotherlandite who doesn't like momos?"

Now they were walking next to Tato Chiso. She looked up and saw the bouffant-haired owner at the balustrade, watching the street with her arms crossed. Her eyes settled on Kranti, but did she recognize her?

Emboldened, Kranti clasped Kabiraj's arm. "I wish there was a shorter version of the word Darkmotherlandite. By the time you finish saying it, I'll have taken one long nap and woken up."

Kabiraj shied away from her closeness, but he didn't try to wrench his arm away. "But that's what we're called," he said. "We live in Darkmotherland. We're Darkmotherlandites."

"Doesn't the 'ite' part come from Angrezi?" Kranti said. "Couldn't we have come up with our own native version?"

Kabiraj seemed to warm up to this conversation. "You mean like Darkmotherlandbasi?"

Now they were across the street from the Asylum. Kranti wondered if there was anyone at the Asylum, watching her movements. Well, Bhaskar was at Beggar Street, but could a Ghimirey be at the window and able to detect who she was? Or a spy enlisted by the Ghimireys could have been following her all along, starting from the moment she ran into Kabiraj. For a brief moment, she was seized by anxiety, thinking that if the Ghimireys spotted her arm in arm with another man, that would be a surefire way to rule herself out as a bride.

"Or Darkmotherlandi," Kranti said. She put her finger to her chin in an exaggerated thoughtful pose. "But, landi sounds too much like—"

Kabiraj blushed.

"Cock," she said matter-of-factly. She was thrilled that she had uttered the word "cock" in the middle of the street, and right in front of the Asylum.

Kabiraj blushed more.

"But even if we were to use Darkmotherlandi, we'd soon Angrezify it to Darkmotherlandese."

"But that sounds like we are a land full of geese, and we're not particularly known for our geese," Kabiraj offered.

"Peace, brother," she said. "What else do you have?"

"There's no getting around it," he said. "We Darkmotherlandites are doomed to a long name."

Now they were walking next to the Durbar, the palace turned museum, where she used to come with Dada to get on her school bus. Sometimes Dada paused to chat with the sentries, which wasn't allowed, but Dada, the charmer that he was, brought smiles to the guards' faces. Every time Kranti passed by the Durbar, she remembered Dada, as she did now. Oh, how she missed the jokes that he used to regale her with on the way to the bus stop.

"Say something funny," she instructed Kabiraj.

"What?"

"Entertain me. Say something funny."

He appeared perplexed, but also intrigued, and he finally said, "Okay, want to hear a ditty?"

She nodded.

"We call ourselves Darkmotherlandites, check us out, we are dynamites."

The rhyme was funny in how convoluted it was, so she laughed.

They sauntered past the Home of the Bell, white with a domed top like a fireman's hat, the Valley's official clocktower inspired by Big Ben in London. With its four clock faces, the Home of the Bell served as the nation's timekeeper. It was said that its ringing was heard in the farthest corners of Darkmotherland. At the Open Stage, the giant statue of PM Papa was about one-third finished. The statue was still in scaffolding, with the area cordoned off. A small crowd had gathered beyond the cordon, making appreciative noises. Observers marveled at the statue's shoes, each of which was the size of a Boeing jet. Two legs arose vertically from the shoes, clad in what appeared to be the tapered daura of the national dress. The admirers were talking about the speed of the construction, how in no time the torso and the head would also appear. The entire statue was made of iron. An elderly woman said she wished *everything* in Darkmotherland was built as quickly, then realizing her mistake she slunk away before anyone could accuse her of leveling criticism at the regime.

"More jokes please," Kranti said, as they entered the lane next to the Brave Hospital, where the dusty compound was filled with patients who couldn't find beds inside. Many were moaning and groaning, some with bandaged heads, others with arms and legs in casts, still others walking about with contraptions for intake of fluids and oxygen.

"We, Darkmotherlandites, during the Ten-Day Festival we fly kites," Kabiraj said.

"Mmmmm."

"We, Darkmotherlandites, we drink, we get into fights."

"That last one was lame," she said. "Maybe you should stick to your poetry."

He appeared slightly hurt. "But you didn't even like my poems." He was sulking.

She stroked his arm and said, "Ofo, baba, I don't have to like your poetry, as long as you like it. But since you like momos, I'll take you to a good momo place."

"Mofo Momos?"

"You've been there?"

"Is there a Darkmotherlandite who hasn't been to Mofo Momos? What's their slogan again?"

"The Fundys might have erased it again. Let's go find out."

—

"Mofo Momos: Motherfucking Good!" was still there, but upon closer scrutiny, Kranti and Kabiraj saw that somehow the *d* in Good was missing, so now it read "Motherfucking Goo!" When the shop first opened, the Fundys had tried to close it down, but momo-lovers came to its defense. The place has the best momos in the Valley, they said, even though it's run by a khairey. The Fundys had even written over the sign, painting over Mofo with Motherland. But Na-Ryan had repainted it back to Mofo, with an added challenge: "Mother-fucking Good!" Mofo Momos was so popular that there was usually a line of people wanting to get in. The last time Kranti had been here, with Bhaskar, the Fundys had blacked out "fucking" and painted "is" over it, so that the sign read, "Mother   is   Good."

Na-Ryan was a garrulous fellow who entertained his customers with nonstop talk and banter. He was a transplant from Amrika, although he had disavowed being an Amrikan, especially after the ascendancy of President Corn Hair. It was said that his real name was Ryan but that he'd added the prefix Na to reject the topsy-turvy world he'd left behind. Bhaskar had asked him a couple of times whether that rumor was true, but Na-Ryan only said, "I am named after the Preserver God." Closing his eyes in mock devotion, he played an imaginary khartal in his right hand, impersonating an ancient sage known to play his castanet as he chanted the name of the Preserver God, "Naa-Ryanaa. Naa-Ryanaa." Those who knew Na-Ryan whispered that PM Papa's Twitter exchanges with President Corn Hair had Na-Ryan in conniptions in private, but he masked it in public.

Mofo Momos was packed, despite the momo prices that had nearly tripled per plate since the Big Two. It was a small restaurant, smack in the main chowk of the Tourist District. Momos were being cooked in three giant-sized pots, the steam rising up and clouding the ceiling. The back wall of Mofo Momos had collapsed during the Big Two, and a gaping hole now opened to an alley where mangy dogs patiently waited for the meat-filled dumplings to be thrown their way. Even our dogs are momo-crazy, Kranti said to Kabiraj. Na-Ryan had named these regular dogs after the people who had forced him to leave Amrika: Corn Hair, Don Jr., Eric, Ivanka, Jared, Pence, Pompeo, Barr, etc.

Na-Ryan spotted Kranti and waved, then pointed at Kabiraj and mouthed, "Who?" Kranti put her arm around Kabiraj to indicate a friend, drawing stares from other customers, mostly men. Na-Ryan cooked his momos wearing a black topi on his head, a lungi tied around his waist, and a white ganji that started out snow-white when the restaurant's door opened in mid-morning, and ended up a yellow-purple after becoming drenched with momo-juice by the time he closed shop. He also stood on a step stool from where he held forth, on any given topic of the day, or several topics mixed into one.

Today, he was talking about Darkmotherland's past. "I've been living in Darkmotherland since the light showed up in the Valley," he said, rubbing his belly, which was often filled with his own momos.

"What is this khairey talking about?" a young man asked.

"What?" Na-Ryan said. "You morons choose to live in utter darkness? It's your own history."

"What light is he referring to? Bud Lite?" This came from a tourist who was struggling with the tongue-burning spicy chutney that was served with the momos. Na-Ryan was proud of that chutney, prouder still that it was homemade by his delightfully expressive Darkmotherlandese wife.

"Ah, of course," Na-Ryan said. "What can I expect from you heathens? You don't even read your Lonely Planet guides anymore. You damn khaireys with your Bud Lite. Bud Lite! You don't think it's your responsibility to know how it all began before you go traipsing around this gorgeous country?"

Of course, some of the locals knew this history; it had been hammered into their brains since they were in kindergarten, but they smiled and kept quiet because they liked to hear Na-Ryan go on and on as his massive pots hissed and whistled and sputtered in the background.

"Well, listen, you morons," Na-Ryan said. "The Valley was a lake in the ancient times, and suddenly"—he stopped his wild arm movements and slowly lifted up his right arm, palm cupped as though he were holding something in it; everyone became quiet; even the momo pots stopped wheezing and fizzing—"there arose in the midst of the lake a luminous light, self-arisen, inside a lotus." He held up the light in the air for a minute or so, and all of his customers, the native and the tourists, watched. It seemed that in his hand was a lotus, and inside it, indeed, a soft-glow light—some customers swore he was cupping a small bulb.

"Gentle Glory, the bodhisattva residing in Tibbat, heard about the flame in the lake and came swooping down."

Na-Ryan flapped his arms in a gesture of flying and momentarily it seemed that he was indeed floating on the steam rising above his momo pots. "He couldn't see the flame clearly, so he took his wisdom-realizing sword and"—Na-Ryan picked up a long and large ladle and sliced the air, making his customers take steps back to avoid being smacked (they were, however, sprinkled with hot chutney)—"cut a hill to drain the lake so that the holy site would be accessible to all."

"And the lotus became a hill, and the flame became the stupa," someone said. "Yes, yes, we know."

"Tatashthu!" Na-Ryan said and held up his palm in blessing.

Kranti and Kabiraj found a bench, and soon a boy brought them piping hot plates of momos. The two ate in silence, enjoying the hot, spicy momo juice that spurted and surged inside their mouths.

"How does Na-Ryan manage to get all this meat when good meat is not even available in the Valley?" Kabiraj asked.

The customer sitting next to him nudged him and pointed to the dogs. "Do you notice how every week or so there's a dog missing? Where's Ivanka? Hmm? Have you seen her lately?"

His cheeks bulging with momos, Kabiraj gave him a stare, and the customer said, "Na-Ryan is supposed to be a resourceful fellow, and I hear he still has ties in the Amrikan community, and you know these Amrikans, they enjoy a high life no matter where they live. They can't live without their meat."

After they finished and drank water, Kranti said, "Well, if that was Ivanka, she was certainly tasty," and burped.

Kabiraj laughed.

"What? You've never heard a woman burp before?"

"I thought young, educated woman didn't burp," Kabiraj said, clearly with a sense of irony, then let out a long, satisfying burp himself. As if on cue, several of the customers burped one by one so that Mofo Momos rang with a symphony of burps.

"Okay, now that it's settled," Kranti said, "where do you live?"

"In Bhurey Paradise," he said.

"In a tent?"

"Yes."

"You're a Bhurey?"

"I've always been a Bhurey." His face, chubby and adorable, indicated he thought she was crazy to think anyone but a Bhurey would live in the Bhurey Paradise.

"Why are you a Bhurey?"

"What kind of a question is that?"

"It's an intelligent question. Some are born Bhureys, some achieve Bhureyness, and others have Bhureyness thrust upon them. Which one are you?"

Was that a smile on his chapped lips? "Ah, a Sexpear quote, applied to our native situation," he said.

"I wasn't asking for your commentary upon my pronouncements," she said. "Which one are you?"

He pondered that for a moment. "All three."

"How so?"

"I was born a Bhurey."

"How so?"

"I lost my parents when I was very young, and I have been wandering from dwelling to dwelling—"

"All right, all right, enough with that sob story, I get the point. What about the second one? How did you achieve Bhureyness?" She realized that she was enjoying this all a bit too much, querying him like this for what sounded like an entrance exam for a Rajjya post; she had forgotten about Bhaskar, her mother, and the Beggars.

Kabiraj answered, seriously and earnestly, as though he too had slipped into the role of an interviewee, "I achieved Bhureyness by actually living the life of the Bhurey to its max."

"What does that mean?"

"Well, I live in a tent, I cook for myself on a stove, I can go for days without bathing, all my neighbors are Bhureys, who also sometimes can go days without bathing, I am treated like filth by non-Bhurey folks, even though I tutor their children in basic subjects like math and science, even writing. But being treated like this is fine too, as that means that I can only go up from here, not down. There are days when I go hungry, and there's a hollow inside my stomach. Each day I wallow in my Bhureyness, so yes, I have achieved Bhureyness."

Wow, she thought. For a shy fellow, this guy certainly had a way with words. His name wasn't "king of poets" for nothing. "Okay, the last one," she said softly. "How has Bhureyness been thrust upon you?"

"I didn't ask for Bhureyness, did I?" he said.

"Hmmm," she said. "Go on."

"Well, did you ask to be the daughter of Professor Shrestha?"

Even this pudgy poet has to bring up her mother.

"Could we say that being the daughter of someone people refer to as Madam Mao was thrust upon you?"

"Okay, okay, I get your point. You pass. Now we must celebrate your passing of this important exam."

He watched her in befuddlement.

"Come," she said, taking his arm. "I know exactly what your reward will be."

Kabiraj tried to gently wrest his arm away from her. She sidled closer to him, and his face turned beet red.

"You look as though someone told you the Big Three has arrived," she said, laughing.

He didn't even smile. "Where are we going?"

"We are going to your tent in Bhurey Paradise."

"What about Bhaskar? What will he think?"

"He can go to hell."

As they walked out, Na-Ryan was performing his signature act: juggling about a half a dozen piping hot momos. At some point he'd start catching them with his mouth, and swallowing them. Or he'd catch them and overarm them to the dogs like a cricket bowler. As Kranti and Kabiraj stepped into the bustle of the main chowk of the Tourist District, she heard a customer of Mofo Momos say, "I wonder what Na-Ryan's mother thinks of his restaurant name."

13.

Kranti and Bhaskar made up. It was inevitable, Kranti thought; Kabiraj was a distraction.

She had missed Bhaskar in her bones. It had been especially hard because he had continued to come to Beggar Street and sit with the other Beggars in the living room. When she needed to go out, she'd open the door to her room, their eyes would meet, then she'd quickly cross the living room and exit. She felt his eyes on her even in those few seconds it took her to make her way through the Beggars. She knew he wanted to speak to her, although at times she felt that he was looking at her amusedly, as though her behavior was childish, petulant. His mocking gaze infuriated her.

It took some coaxing and cajoling, and submission, on Bhaskar's part before she relinquished most of her anger and they got back together. She was reminded of when he pursued her in college and showed up at Beggar Street, then charmed her mother, then her. The sequence this time started with him leaving the Beggar Street gathering and following her when she left for a walk to get away from all that noise about the Papa Don't Preach rally. It seemed that every day there was a government crackdown of some sort, which meant the big protest—"the Darkmother of all protests," Chanchal said—was perpetually deferred. It's never going to happen—this big rally. Dada, she addressed her father in her mind, all talk and no action, these Beggars. May this silly Papa Don't Preach never become realized. She blessed them as she left Beggar Street that day. She suspected that it was Bhaskar who'd come up with the name for the rally after hearing her play Madonna in her room to drown out the loud voices coming from the living room. She never asked Bhaskar because she was too afraid it'd turn out to be true. These fuckers have ruined Madonna for me eternally, she told her dead father.

When Bhaskar caught up to her that day, he was breathless. "Kranti, where are you going?"

I'm going to meet Kabiraj, she nearly said. It would have been priceless to see his face. But as it was, he was perspiring, the usually unflappable Bhaskar, her Bhaskar. Oh, God, he looked so handsome, even with rivulets of sweat running down the side of his face. "Isn't that village back there missing an idiot?" she asked.

"It's already filled with idiots," he said. "One more idiot—what difference does it make?"

She walked even more swiftly, as though she were flying. He gave up after a while and simply stood, calling her name.

He followed her out of Beggar Street a couple more times, and the third time she relented. He held her on the street, not far from Mofo Momos. "Did you miss me?" he asked.

She did a shake of her head that could have been a yes or a no or even a maybe.

They kissed, right there on the street. Bold, Kranti knew. Some pedestrians had stopped to watch this native couple acting as though they were khaireys with their public display of affection. She wondered what Dada would have thought of this moment, had he been walking with her to the bus stop. "Look, Kranti," he'd have said to his young daughter. "Look at those two, kissing on the street so openly. Wah, wah! What boldness! What badmashi!"

Later in the room she told Bhaskar that she didn't think he was an idiot, but if he continued cavorting—"and yes, I mean cavorting"— with the Beggars and their deity, then they were finished. Forever.

That afternoon she made sure that the noises coming out of her throat during sex, meant for the Beggars, were louder by a notch or two. It was silly, this sense of victory she felt over her mother and the Beggars, but in the back of her mind it was as if she'd avenged Dada.

—

That day, after she and Kabiraj overstuffed their tummies at Mofo Momos, she had insisted that Kabiraj show her where he lived.

Reluctantly, Kabiraj took her toward Bhurey Paradise, clearly worried that Bhaskar would find out.

She'd made love to Kabiraj that afternoon in his tent, which was small but comforting to her. The tent had some bare essentials—a sleeping bag, a suitcase stuffed with Kabiraj's clothes, a guitar with broken strings, and an extra-large radio that was bandaged and duct-taped, but functioning—playing a raga that was identified by the announcer as Bhimpalasi, "a raga that creates a sweet and tender mood."

And sweetly and tenderly, accompanied by the soft twang of the sitar, was indeed how Kabiraj explored her body. Shyly. It seemed as though after Dada's death, this type of affection had been lacking in her life. She knew it wasn't true. She had received much love from Bhaksar, but—she struggled with this thought—he loved Madam Mao more. He loved his Sangharsh more. *Harsh*, yes, Dada, *harsh*, but true.

After reconciling with Bhaskar, Kranti considered confessing to him that she'd slept with Kabiraj. But what would she say?

"Bhaskar, you remember the time we broke up? Well, what can I say?"

"Bhaskar, I have something to tell you, something you won't like at all."

"Bhaskar, I have been bad. How bad, you ask?"

"Bhaskar, do you believe in forgiveness?" He did, she knew. If she'd told him, he'd have forgiven her. He'd have been hurt, but he'd have told her he understood. To hide his pain, he might have joked with her. "That fast, huh? How long were we apart? A month? Six weeks?"

"I felt alone."

"So did I."

She wouldn't have been able to answer him, and he'd have teased her about choosing pudgy and ugly Kabiraj of all men, and she'd have objected to his ridiculing a person's physical appearance. She'd have said that what mattered was what was on the inside, not the outside.

"Did you have a relationship just to get back at me?"

"You needed to be taught a lesson," she'd have said, but she'd felt something for Kabiraj, too, hadn't she?

———

In the late afternoons into the evening, Kranti would lay in her bed, back to the wall, head propped on the pillow, with the TV on. This was partly to drown out the voices of the Beggars but also because she found the steady stream of propaganda that emanated from the small Sony TV strangely soothing. Dada had bought it for her when she passed her School Leaving Certificate Exam. She was fond of the TV, old and cranky as it was, and had declined Professor Shrestha's offer to replace it with the latest brand from the market. Most of the time she didn't even pay attention to what was on the screen; she was either talking with Bhaskar on her mobile, reading a book, or looking through old photo albums of herself and Dada (in some of the photos she had blotted out Professor Shrestha's face). Once in a while, she'd glance up at the Motherland TV, and there was Hom Bokaw, praising PM Papa solemnly. "Bleffed with the generosity of FeeM Fafa, our counfry is heading towarf the rife paf." The songs and dances were mostly nationalistic now, in words and in tone. There were frequent pictures of Loyal Army Dais marching, their arms and legs in unison. They looked smarter and more fight-ready than the army was before the Big Two, and even during the monarchy years of the Royal Army.

When Bhaskar was in the room with her, he would ask to turn it off, and Kranti would ask him to leave it on. Just background noise, she'd say.

But it was more than background noise; it was a retort to the constant blabber from the living room that didn't leave her alone. "Never forget, okay?" Kranti often heard Professor Shrestha say to the Beggars. "Always remember what it was like. The purpose of this Rajjya is to play tricks on your memory, so that you will forget what life was like before and you'll think this is how it always was. You'll forget the marches and the demonstrations that toppled the one-party rule, that got rid of the monarchy, the rallies that fought for women's rights and minorities' rights. They want you to think that none of that happened, that the Hippo had always been there, that he had been with us since time immemorial, even though it's only been a few months."

"That's why the Dojjier is important," Prakash said. "We need to record this, witness it. They want to normalize. Don't let them normalize."

"De-normalize!" the Beggars chanted.

The Beggars complained that if one were to listen to Motherland TV, it was as if PM Papa had been leading the country since Vedic times. Motherland TV and Motherland Radio, and *Motherland Daily*, which was free and distributed abundantly, said that all the previous rulers—the feudal monarchs from centuries ago when the Valley used to be three distinct kingdoms; the Founding Father who swooped upon the Valley and united the country; the succession of self-serving, demented, dictatorial, or cowardly monarchs; the oligarchs who usurped power from the monarch and drove the country to grinding poverty for more than a century; the democratically elected prime ministers of the more recent past—were corrupt, leeches, vermin, suckers of the patriot's blood, destroyer of customs and traditions, flagrantly disrespectful of gods and goddesses and spiritual protectors, and looters and hoarders of Rajjya property. In a frequently played reenactment documentary on Motherland TV, they were shown with hooked noses, rubbing their hands together in greed, a caricature of the people of another ancient religion. The followers of these past rulers rioted and demolished prized monuments and statues of benevolent deities. The country suffered plague and pestilence during their rule. Black-and-white photos of dry lands with no vegetation and starving children were shown on the screen, even though those photos were not of Darkmotherland, but of a famine-ridden land in Aafrika or of the notorious repressive regime of North Korea.

The veracity of the images that they saw on TV began creeping into the conversations of Darkmotherlandites—in cafés, in butcher shops, in shopping malls, in sari arcades. "Oh, yes, we were a deeply impoverished country ruled by madmen," people said. Or, "If it weren't for PM Papa, we would have been murdered in our sleep by these dark men, and our women would have been raped."

Even Kranti, who should have known better, became grateful for PM Papa. When the anchor on Motherland TV said, "We need to make up for lost time," she felt indeed that time was a precious commodity, that for too long she, as an individual, not just Darkmotherland, had also wasted her precious time. She had lost her precious time, her youth, with her mother.

So, one day she proposed to Bhaskar.

They were in her room, entangled in bed together. She was smelling him, the faint smell of coconut shampoo in his hair (probably manufactured by Ghimirey & Sons, she thought). She was running her fingers across his bushy chest ("you are hairy like a gorilla," she'd teased him a couple of times). Then she buried her nose in his shoulder and said, in a muffled voice, "Let's do it."

He thought she meant make love and he said, "But we just did."

"No, silly," she said, her mouth pressed against his collar. It came out as "no, frilly."

He caressed her hair. She could feel him rise down there. Then, he lifted her head up with his palms and said, "Oh, you mean—?"

For some reason she felt shy, and she burrowed her face into the crook of his arm again and said, "Yes."

He was silent for too long, so she jerked her head up and looked at him.

He watched her for a while, then said, "How did this come about?"

"You don't want to do it?"

He sighed, as though he was annoyed that she brought it up.

She sat up in bed, suddenly unsure. She nearly wanted to slap herself on the side of the head for being foolish.

"What's the matter?" he asked.

She shook her head and looked at the wall. She had a garlanded photo of Dada, smiling, right above her bed. Silly mistake, Kranti, Dada seemed to be telling her.

"Something wrong?" Bhaskar asked.

"Forget it."

"Forget what?" he said. "What were we talking about again?"

"I said forget it!" she said, then attempted to get up from the bed, to get out, to go somewhere, she didn't know where, maybe walk out, continue walking until she disappeared.

He pushed her down with his hands, then he tickled her, then he was on top her, grinding himself against her, rubbing his chin against her face, asking, "What did you think, huh? What did you think?" He was laughing. "That I don't want it? Idiot! When all this time I was the one who'd been saying we should do it?"

She slapped his arm with her palm, pummeled his chest with her fists. "How could you? How could you put on that face knowing full well I was serious? Torturer!"

And that led to a gentle, languorous, dreamy session of love-making, for both of them felt that they had reached another place, and there was only a future of togetherness, even as both of them knew—didn't they?—that it was illusory.

—

She didn't know what he told his family about her. She kept imagining various scenarios, every one of which had her being ridiculed, maligned, criticized or made fun of. Every few days she asked him whether he'd approached his family, and every time he said that he was waiting for the right moment, which was odd because Bhaskar never waited for the right moment. There was nothing calculative about him. He was supposed to go straight to his family and tell them that he was to marry Kranti and that was that, so what happened?

The matter was further exacerbated by Professor Shrestha. She was elated when Kranti and Bhaskar informed her that they wanted to get married, but she balked at the idea of having to perform the duties that traditionally fell upon the mother of the bride. An argument ensued between the mother and the daughter in Beggar Street the evening they told her. Bhaskar had stayed behind so he and Kranti would be together when they delivered the news, which they had during dinner. Professor Shrestha had made fried chicken, especially for Bhaskar, she said. The Beggars had already left, grumbling because Papa Don't Preach couldn't be held on the scheduled date—an Aafrikan dictator was coming to Darkmotherland on a state visit. Security would be at a heightened state then, and it would be suicidal to attempt a large, anti-Rajjya gathering that could potentially turn violent.

Professor Shrestha said she couldn't be expected to fraternize with the Ghimireys, who, she reminded Kranti, were the antithesis of everything she stood for. "I won't go to the Asylum for the wedding," she concluded.

Kranti accused Professor Shrestha of considering herself too good for the Ghimireys.

"As it is, the bride's mother doesn't go to the groom's house," Bhaskar said as he gnawed on the chicken bone he was holding. "She welcomes the groom's family to her home, minus the groom, according to the customs of your caste. But I will come to fetch you, since, according to the customs of my caste, the groom from a family wedding has to go fetch the bride."

"Since when did you become an expert on wedding customs?" Kranti asked.

"Yes, Bhaskar, I can truly see you becoming a staunch upholder of our caste rituals," Professor Shrestha said, looking at him fondly.

Bhaskar sucked in, loudly, the marrow of his chicken bone, making an insanely slurpy sound.

Kranti glared at him, partly for his lack of manners and partly for his nonchalance at her mother's diffidence.

"So, you're saying I'm expected to welcome the Ghimireys to this house?" Professor Shrestha asked, as if already wearied by the thought.

"You know, Kranti," Bhaskar said, "I really don't expect Madam to sacrifice her principles to please my family." He burped, then stretched his arms, as though he were ready to go lie down after a satisfying meal.

"You can't rely on her to accommodate her principles for her *own* family, let alone yours," Kranti said angrily. She pointed her index finger at him, as though warning him not to encourage her further. "Case in point: Dada."

—

The discussion continued for the next several days. Bhaskar pleaded with her in the privacy of her room to be kinder to her mother. Kranti responded that it was the height of irresponsibility for her mother to not want anything to do with the Ghimireys. Professor Shrestha repeatedly expressed her reluctance to be an active mother at the wedding, at times presenting it as her inadequacy and her lack of know-how of the rituals. At other times she presented it as defiance ("there's no way I could welcome the Ghimireys into this house with a straight face"). Finally, after days of back and forth, she said that she'd be willing to attend the ceremony and perform kanyadan. She had one caveat, however: she'd do it not at Beggar Street but at the Asylum, if the Ghimireys would be open to this unorthodox arrangement of the bride donation ceremony.

When they were alone in her room, Kranti said to Bhaskar, "How convenient for her. She doesn't have to do any work. Your family will do everything. All she has to do is show up."

"But, Kranti, this is even harder for her—the Asylum is enemy territory."

"But what about your family? They'll accept this arrangement?" She looked at Dada's photo, as though pleading to him for support.

"Do they have a choice? Either that, or a court marriage."

"No, no. No court marriage, Bhaskar, please." They'd discussed this option before, and although on one hand it was simple—go to the court and sign the marriage certificate—Kranti felt her anxiety intensify when she thought about how a certificate from the court, instead of a drawn-out three-day ceremony that was meant to cement the relationship in the eyes of the gods, would make her less legitimate among the Ghimireys. She imagined the large family, the elegant daughters-in-law, the opulence, the expectations—and a part of her shrank. *Madam Mao's daughter*, she heard them thinking.

14.

From the day that he'd told his family about Kranti, it had been one difficulty after another for Bhaskar. He had delivered the news about the wedding during dinner, and for a while it was received in silence. Only the clanking of cutlery could be heard.

Aditya, his fork near his mouth with a piece of mutton on it, was observing everyone with near sadistic pleasure. "A fine way to deliver the news, Bhaskar," he finally said. "Badhai chha, badhai! And let me guess—this is more an announcement, than a seeking of permission?"

"Correct," Bhaskar said.

Bhaskar's association with Beggar Street had been a point of contention in the Asylum before. Privately, the Ghimireys had fumed, but in front of Bhaskar they'd restrained themselves, only expressing their disapproval, every now and then, that they didn't understand why Bhaskar spent time at the house of someone who clearly hated Ghimirey & Sons.

"Are you going to give us a chance, Bhaskar babu?" Shambhogya said. "We have so many girls from great families you could potentially choose."

"Kranti is from a great family," Bhaskar said.

"Who is Kranti?" Prithvi Raj asked, then nodded quickly. "Oh, yes, Madam Mao's daughter." He asked for some more food from Shambhogya, even though the nokerchakers were moving around the table, refilling their plates and replenishing their drinks. The old man always turned to Shambhogya, as though the food wouldn't taste the same if she wasn't in charge of serving him.

Chaitanya laughed his snorting laugh. "Madam Mao. What a card."

Aditya and Chaitanya made fun of the name, talked about how perhaps the professor should commit suicide like her namesake, Mao Tse-Tung's wife.

"What ugly talk," Muwa said. "Wishing that someone kill herself, and someone who has a reputation for being brilliant." She was a slow eater, and it seemed that she'd become even slower recently; she'd have barely finished eating a few spoonfuls when the others were ready to get up from the table. Increasingly, she asked that the nokerchakers bring her food to God's Room because she didn't feel like coming to the main building.

"Sure, Madam Mao is a brilliant mind," Aditya said, "and we're all people with low IQs. That's why we are Ghimirey & Sons. And she's what?"

"A rabble-rouser," Chaitanya said.

"She has no idea what PM Papa can do to her, if he wants," Aditya said. "He'll crush her like an insect." He rubbed his thumb and forefinger.

"PM Papa jindabad!" Chaitanya said, looking challengingly at Bhaskar.

"Madam Mao murdabad!" Priyanka said and sniffed the air. She had a slightly upturned nose, so it often seemed that she was smelling the air for clues.

"Enough!" Prithvi Raj said. "Bhaskar is trying to tell us something, and you two are braying like donkeys."

"Bhaskar is sleeping with the enemy," Aditya said.

"No one in this house controls their tongues," Muwa said, throwing her napkin down on the table. Most of her dal-bhat was still on the plate. "I'm leaving. You all can fill me in later about issues of real significance that were discussed here today." She left the room. It was too late for her to go to God's Room, so she'd probably head up to the bedroom she shared with her husband, and she'd be asleep by the time he retired for the night.

Shambhogya got up from her chair to go after her, then changed her mind and sat back down. She sighed. "I'm worried about her."

For a brief moment, everyone was silent, then Aditya said, "Muwa will do what she wants to do, what she's always done."

Shambhogya asked the nokerchakers to leave the room. After they left, Shambhogya said, "Everyone, please, watch what you say. No need to air our dirty laundry in front of the nokerchaker class."

"Bhauju," Bhaskar said. "They *wash* our dirty laundry, so they know our dirt."

"Now, you're also joking, Bhaskar babu!" Shambhogya said. "Please don't. So, you have already made the decision about Kranti?" In the absence of the nokerchakers, it fell upon Shambhogya to serve the dessert—homemade syrupy gulab-jamun. Priyanka tried to help but Shambhogya said, sharply, "Let me!" With Bhaskar her voice was gentle. "You're not even going to give us a chance to meet her first?"

"What Shambhogya really means, my bewkoof bhai," Aditya said, "is that we would really prefer you to give this more thought. Now, I've heard about her but I haven't seen this girl, this Kanti, what she's like."

"Kranti," Bhaskar said. "It's not Kanti but Kranti."

"Kra, kra," Chaitanya instructed Aditya. "Kra, kra black crow, have you any—?"

"Beak?" Priyanka said, leaning forward across the table toward her husband.

Shambhogya gave both a scathing look.

Aditya met Bhaskar's eyes, his lips slightly curled, as though he were suppressing laughter. "Of course, Kranti. How could Madam Mao's daughter be named anything else but revolution? Now, I'm assuming you being the handsomest of the three brothers and all—"

"According to *Himdesh Magazine*," Priyanka said.

Himdesh Magazine had done a multiple page foldout feature on the industrial magnate and his three sons, in various poses, as though they were fashion models. They had declared Bhaskar "mega-handsome" and "one of the most eligible bachelors in town." This was soon after the Big Two, when everyone knew that the relationship between the Ghimireys and PM Papa had become stronger. Bhaskar hadn't been happy about the photos, but he'd gone along with it.

"Since you're so pretty," Aditya said to Bhaskar, "there's no question that Mademoiselle Revolution is also pretty?"

"She's pretty," Priyanka said, nodding vigorously.

"You've met her?" they all asked at once.

"I saw the two of you in the Tourist District once," Priyanka said to Bhaskar.

"What were you doing in the Tourist District?" Chaitanya asked his wife.

Shambhogya frowned. In the Ghimirey household, the Tourist District was an unappealing place, filled with touts and chatters and dirty and wild-haired khaireys—not a place for women from respectable families.

"I had to pick up a pashmina shawl. There's a good shop there."

Prithvi Raj, who hadn't spoken for a while, said, "Next time just send a nokerchaker to the market if you need something. We don't want people talking. Besides, who knows what can happen to a woman there."

"Yes, Sir," Priyanka said. She gazed adoringly at her father-in-law across the dining table. It was a semi-fake adoration, performed more out of need for his approval than love for him. Priyanka frequently complained to her husband in the privacy of their bedroom about how Prithvi Raj doted on Shambhogya. What does she have that I don't have? she grumbled. She called Shambhogya fake and expressed frustration that the old man didn't see that.

"Okay, so Mademoiselle Revolution is pretty, we've established that," Aditya said.

"She's prettier than me," Priyanka said, "but she's not prettier than Shambhogya di." She locked eyes with her husband.

"How is that relevant to the matter at hand?" Shambhogya appeared peeved, but with Shambhogya, one got the sense that every time someone mentioned her stunning beauty, she checked something, perhaps a scoreboard, inside her.

Meal finished, they moved to the living room, where the nokerchakers brought them after-dinner digestives and desserts: liquor for Aditya and Chaitanya, hot honeyed lemon-ginger tea for Prithvi Raj and Bhaskar, black tea for Shambhogya and Priyanka, and cute little barfis for everyone. Harkey also brought a tray of supari, lwang, dalchini, and alaichi, along with a small box of mukhwas that the

Ghimireys chewed on contentedly, savoring their aromatic flavors in their mouths.

For a while they talked about other topics: the opening or closing of a highway to the east or the west, the small repairs that needed to be done in the Asylum, the hiring and firing of management in Ghimirey & Sons. They talked about the visit of the Aafrikan dictator, which was concluding. Thank God, Aditya said, that the streets had been cleared of the khateykids for the two days that the Aafrikan dictator was in Darkmotherland. They talked about the multiple medals on the chest of the Aafrikan dictator, who was a general who'd led a military koo in his country. He was dark-skinned and tall, so when he and PM Papa stood together for official photographs, the tall Aafrikan dictator in his army regalia and the short PM Papa in his daura suruwal, they made quite a pair. Motherland TV showed the two of them in the Lion Palace chatting, offering praises to one another. PM Papa said that he admired the way the Aafrikan dictator had run democratic elections despite challenges from hostile elements within his own country. "Your people love you," PM Papa said. "This is proven by the fact that you received ninety-eight percent of the popular votes."

The Aafrikan dictator had laughed and said, "True, true, at first my people didn't love me, but now they love me." He then returned the praise. "I love your vision of Pure Darkmotherland. It is important that we remain true to our cultures." Then both had made noises about their nascent countries emerging from centuries of colonial rules (even though technically Darkmotherland had never been ruled by the Angrezis). The Aafrikan dictator had then asked whether PM Papa would allow him to sing Darkmotherland's national anthem, and lo and behold he had sung it in a surprisingly melodious voice: *More beloved than our heart, our one and only Venerable PM Papa.*

The Ghimireys spoke highly of PM Papa's rapport with the Aafrikan dictator, how world leaders all over admired him.

Finally, Aditya found a gap in the conversation and turned to

Bhaskar. "Okay, now we've established that Mademoiselle Revolution is pretty," Aditya said, "but not as pretty as my wife but hopefully prettier than our pretty boy here. Still, she has to be more than pretty."

There was silence, and a rare gratitude toward Aditya to returning the conversation to this urgent matter.

Prithvi Raj spoke up, after a pause, but it was clear he'd been dying to say it. "I'm sure that this girl is nice but what about everything else, Bhaskar? This is not a decision to be taken lightly. Aditya is right."

"You know who we were planning for you?" Aditya said.

"Who?" Bhaskar asked.

"Srinivas's daughter."

Bhaskar expressed confusion.

"Srinivas. Owner of Turruck."

Bhaskar pretended to fall down from his sofa, his hand to his chest, nearly knocking over his glass of green tea on the coffee table. "Why didn't you tell me this before? This changes *everything*. When can I start?"

"No wonder Muwa left the table," Shambhogya said. "Everything is ha-ha-he-he to you guys."

"Okay, sorry, bhauju," Bhaskar said, getting up and sitting on his sofa.

"Srinivas is very interested in this relationship," Aditya said, in a serious and somber voice that he brought out when he wanted to convince his listeners. It was as though he were channeling his father. "You know what that means for Ghimirey & Sons, don't you?" Turruck was the largest trucking company in Darkmotherland, and although the business had suffered because of the Big Two, Srinivas had just made public their ambitious plans to expand in the south. Rebuild, Restore, Drive the Economy—his company had revealed this as its new motto, in alignment with PM Papa's Rebuild and Restore program.

"Together Ghimirey & Sons and Turruck will become a powerhouse in Darkmotherland," Chaitanya said.

"Let me see," Bhaskar said, using his hand in the air to build an imaginary vista. "Every Challenge an Opportunity to Rebuild, Restore and Drive the Economy."

"A partnership with Turruck will bring us great rewards," Aditya said, still managing that solemn voice.

"Am I marrying Turruck or Srinivas's daughter? Or Srinivas?" Bhaskar asked.

"But Bhaskar babu, you know that in our culture you also marry the family," Shambhogya said. "And the Big Two has made it even clearer how important such liaisons will be. How important family bonds are."

"And our heritage," Chaitanya said.

"And our religion," Priyanka said.

"The only thing the Big Two taught us," Bhaskar said, "is how easy it is to dupe everyone. Look at how PM Papa has controlled everything."

Shambhogya shushed him, then stood and went to the door. She opened it. Harkey was standing outside, apparently waiting for further orders but also listening to their conversation. Shambhogya turned to the room and asked if anyone wanted refills. They all shook their heads, so she told Harkey he could return to the kitchen to wrap things up for the night. This time she locked the door from inside before returning to her seat. In a whisper she said, "You never know these days. One of the nokerchakers could be a . . ." She raised her eyebrows.

"What?" Bhaskar said. "A double agent? A spy for the Rajjya?"

"The caste question is big for me," Aditya said, standing up, as though he was suddenly getting tired of the meandering conversation. Aditya could shift from a joking, jovial mood or a calm, wise one to an angry, hectoring one within seconds, and his son Shaditya, when he was home from boarding school in Bharat, and the nokerchakers were often the victims of it. "I am simply not in favor of going outside our circle for an alliance."

"Caste is certainly an issue," Prithvi Raj said. "This will be the first intercaste marriage in our family, in our clan perhaps."

Aditya said that the Ghimirey name would be sullied. Chaitanya added that the Fundys could raise a ruckus outside the Asylum during the wedding that would then be broadcast on television sets. As it was, Swami Go!swami was pressuring PM Papa to make it difficult to issue certificates for intercaste marriages, which he said ran contrary to the principles of Pure Darkmotherland.

The conversation was left unfinished that day, everyone dissatisfied, but it was picked up again the next night as they were finishing up dinner. Muwa had her meal delivered to God's Room, so she wasn't there.

Aditya raised the issue of the Fundys again, how much trouble they could create with an intercaste marriage at the Asylum.

"Who gives a rat's ass about the Fundys?" Bhaskar said in exasperation. "You all do realize, don't you, that the Fundys feel they can do whatever they want because they have the Hippo's blessings?" Bhaskar said.

"Yes, keep calling him the Hippo," Aditya said, "and one of these days I don't know what'll happen to you."

"Shhh," Shambhogya said, as Harkey entered the room. He looked at Bhaskar, as though he'd heard and understood what Bhaskar had just said. Harkey asked Shambhogya whether they were ready to move to the living room for after-dinner drinks.

"Say digestifs, Harkey," Shambhogya said. "How many times have I told you?"

Harkey mumbled, obviously unable to pronounce the Franceli word.

"You need to practice so that you know how to say it proper when we have guests."

"Huncha, hajur," Harkey said obediently, bowing his head slightly, and left.

"He'll never learn," Priyanka said. She addressed Prithvi Raj, "I've tried teaching him so many times how to say digestif."

"How will you teach?" Shambhogya said. "Even you don't know how to say it properly. It's not die-gest-tif. You don't pronounce it like you're digesting something. It's dee-ges-teef." Shambhogya used her two years of Franceli language classes at her boarding school to deliver a perfect pronunciation. "Say it. Dee-ges-teef."

Priyanka blushed in embarrassment and mumbled something. She and Chaitanya exchanged glances. Aditya sneered at Priyanka.

They all migrated toward the living room, with Chaityana chanting in a barely audible whisper next to his wife's ears, "Dee-ges-teef, dee-ges-teef."

Shambhogya sat next to Bhaskar and cautioned him against using "the Hippo," especially around the nokerchakers. Prithvi Raj added that although PM Papa was a friend, he wouldn't tolerate disloyalty. Besides, the Fundys had a point: Where would our culture be if everyone went for intercaste marriage?

There was a lot of cross talk then, with Bhaskar mostly on one side arguing that intercaste marriage was the least of Darkmother's problems, and the others saying, some gently, some aggressively, that there was no country without culture, without tradition.

Shambhogya said that, frankly, apart from the cultural issue, her main concern was what it meant to marry the daughter of someone who was so openly hostile toward the Ghimireys, what they stood for, their very existence. Bhaskar tried to reassure her that Professor Shrestha wasn't against their existence per se, but that she had to admit that Ghimirey & Sons had profited greatly from riding on the backs of the poor in Darkmotherland.

"Look at the way he talks." Aditya was now a fully angry, aggressive Aditya, his voice dripping with rage. He stood and went to the bar area, then returned to where everyone was sitting. He often paced the room when he was agitated. "Pretty boy. He's already drank everything Madam Mao has poured down his throat. How much is Madam Mao involved in this rally that we keep hearing about? Some rally with a stupid name."

Bhaskar merely shook his head at his brother, smiling. He knew Aditya, his moods, what his essence was, and had learned to deal with it accordingly. During their childhood squabbles, Bhaskar had never gotten mad at Aditya (nor at Chaitanya, but then Chaitanya had always been much more agreeable), no matter what Aditya said, no matter what accusations and cruelty he hurled Bhaskar's way. One suspected that Aditya was baffled and vexed by Bhaskar's endurance.

"No, seriously, when is the sun going to shine on your scalp?" Aditya said. "The rest of the world looks up to Ghimirey & Sons, and you treat us like criminals."

"Do we need to get into that discussion again?" Shambhogya said. She appeared tense, but they all knew she would never lose control—it was simply not in her nature. She was too well-bred for it. But in high-stress situations like this one, her body became tighter and her voice turned softer, with an unmistakable edge. She needed to be fully in charge of the small world she occupied, and any threat to that control made her intensely alert, like a threatened animal. To Bhaskar, she said, "If you and Kranti get married, is Professor Shrestha going to stop talking about us as if we're criminals sucking on the bones of poor folks?"

Bhaskar shrugged. "I can't guarantee anything. She's her own person." At the beginning of this, he'd thought that he'd announce the plans for the wedding, then quickly mention that the kanyadan would be performed by Professor Shrestha. He would say that in the absence of an adult father figure on the girl's side, it had to be Professor Shrestha who'd give away the bride to the groom. And that this would happen not at the bride's home but at the groom's, another violation of the custom. But now, in light of his family's resistance to the wedding itself, raising the kanyadan issue was out of the question.

"I've heard Madam Mao really likes Bhaskar babu," Priyanka said. She had managed to squeeze herself between Chaitanya and Prithvi Raj and had taken Prithvi Raj's hand in her own, fingers entangled.

"Where do you hear these things?" Shambhogya asked Priyanka testily. "How come you are the superspy all of a sudden?"

There was a knock on the door and Harkey and Shyam Bahadur entered, each carrying a tray with the digestifs. They placed the drinks on the coffee table. Tonight, it was brandy for Aditya, coffee for

Bhaskar, wine for Chaitanya and Priyanka, and green tea for Shambhogya and Prithvi Raj. On small plates were petite bites of gourmet dark and white chocolate gifted from a business partner who'd just returned from Germnee.

Plopping a piece of dark chocolate into his mouth, and suddenly reminded of the deliciousness of the mistress he had on the side, Aditya said, "She's not a spy, is she, for her mother?"

Shambhogya shushed him, then flicked her fingers imperiously to the nokerchakers to exit. After they left, she chastised her husband, briefly, for uttering what he did in front of the nokerchakers.

Prithvi Raj took a sip of his green tea, and Priyanka quickly asked him in a whisper whether it was to his liking. If not, she said, she'd go get him another one. Shambhogya heard it and asked her why it wouldn't be okay when Shambhogya herself had instructed Harkey on how to prepare it. It's perfect, Prithvi Raj said to Shambhogya. He told her that after having three sons, he'd regretted not having a daughter, but little did he know that Shambhogya was destined to come into his life as his daughter— that's what God had in mind for him. He looked up at the ceiling. "Hail Darkmother," he said.

"Hail Darkmother," Shambhogya said.

"So, Bhaskar, you'll give us some time to think this over, I hope?" Prithvi Raj said.

Bhaskar paused only a moment. "There's nothing to think over, Sir. Kranti and I are going through with this."

Now the silence was heavy. Prithvi Raj stood and left the room. Priyanka stood to follow him, presumably to bring him back, but Shambhogya tersely instructed her to let him be, that he was tired.

"You shouldn't make Sir feel so helpless about it," she said to Bhaskar. "He's getting old and he feels these things deeply. There's the caste issue, and there's Professor Shrestha's opposition to everything we are, even though she hasn't mentioned us specifically."

Priyanka said there was an interview in *Himdesh* before the Big Two, when the editor was more left-wing, when Professor Shrestha had specifically mentioned Ghimirey & Sons as a major contributor to the country's corruption.

The discussion continued the next day, this time before dinner in the atrium, with just Shambhogya and Aditya present. Shambhogya didn't want the others around, so it was just her and Aditya with Bhaskar. Soon Bhaskar learned why: Shambhogya asked him to meet some potential brides, just to appease Sir and Muwa. Bhaskar argued that that would be deceptive, both to the girls and to his parents, but Shambhogya pleaded, saying it was a compromise for peace.

Bhaskar shook his head, not convinced; Aditya made a caustic remark.

"Can you come here for a second?" Shambhogya stood and headed to a corner of the atrium. Aditya's expression said "I'm being summoned!" and he went with her. There, next to a statue of Dark Ferocious who glared at them, fangs bared, they whispered, and it was clear that Shambhogya was scolding him. Snatches of their whispered disagreements reached them: "never listen," "strategic," "patience" and "charts." Finally, judging from Aditya's bowed head, it was clear that he had caved.

They returned to their seats, and Shambhogya said that all she was asking for were a few weeks to get "everything sorted out."

"And what'll I tell Kranti?" Bhaskar asked. "Oh, I'm just taking a gander at some high caste beauties, I'll be right back?"

"Tell her that we're happy with the proposal," Shambhogya said, "but our astrologer is working on an auspicious date."

"But that's not true," Bhaskar said.

"That is somewhat true, Bhaskar babu. We will have to consult with Jyotish Jeevan, you know that, like we did with all of our weddings."

Bhaskar ruled out involving Jyotish Jeevan, saying that the astrology stuff worked only if you believed in it. Witches, jhankris, soothsayers—who runs their lives by these beliefs?

Shambhogya asked, softly, what would happen if Kranti turned out to be a manglik? Mangliks, with their pernicious Mars, harmed not only their husbands but the entire family. Jyotish Jeevan would be able to prescribe remedies before the wedding to ward off any inauspiciousness.

Bhaskar wasn't persuaded, so he walked away.

The next evening, Shambhogya came to see him in his room by herself. She apologized for pursuing this matter, but asked that he please, please agree to see some girls?

Bhaskar, who was proofreading an essay for the Mothercry Press, said, "With the understanding that I'm going to say no to all of them?"

Shambhogya nodded.

"What about the caste issue? Aditya-da is strongly against it."

"I'll bring him around."

"What about Sir?"

"I think he's more worried about Professor Shrestha than about the caste issue. But will you talk to Professor Shrestha, Bhaskar babu? After all, if we're going to be one family, it's not unreasonable to expect that she not attack Ghimirey & Sons."

Bhaskar remained silent. He had no intention of speaking with Professor Shrestha.

"Will you agree to what I've said, Bhaskar babu?"

Bhaskar nodded. "But no jyotish, please, bhauju. I don't want to hear that nonsense."

"Just a quick look?"

Bhaskar said, "If you insist on Jyotish Jeevan, then I won't look at any girls."

"All right, all right," Shambhogya said. "No astrologer." She put her hand on his arm. "It's very important that this family stay together."

—

It was advertised as a friendly wrestling match.

In the Ten Chariots Stadium, PM Papa was seated next to the ambassador of Sweejerland in the VIP section, flanked on the other side by General Tso. The Sweej ambassador's pretty blond wife sat next to him. Rozy was seated behind PM Papa. Papa's cabinet was out in full force, fat cats wearing daura surual and chewing paan, some with their wives, some without, in seats around Rozy, the fat cats eyeing him with fascination, some with disdain, some with lust (Rozy was experienced in this), whereas the wives mostly eyed him with disdain, some fear (who was this creature?), and some with pure hatred. Swami Go!swami was seated a few seats behind with about a dozen other top swamis from Kailashram, all of them stroking their beards, excited by the sight of two nearly naked men grappling with each other. The Fundys were jabbering away in their Fundy-talk, their eyes glistening, likening what was about to unfold to the wrestling matches of the ancient Vedic times, when the fierce mallayudhas in their loincloths and their oil-and-mud coated bodies attacked and pinned their opponents to the dusty ground as kings, queens, and dignitaries applauded. The Fundys assured themselves that the primeval sages approved of these physical battles between two muscular men, so it was okay for them to participate in this spectator sport along with PM Papa and the Sweej ambassador.

They had all come to see Bangara Singh. He had emerged after the Big Two—suddenly seeming to appear out of nowhere—as the fiercest of Darkmotherland's wrestlers. His popularity had soared overnight after he defeated two of his most well-known competitors. Bangara Singh had two fangs that protruded prominently from his mouth, lending him a vampire-like look. He leapt upon his opponents, no matter how big and bulky, and quickly sunk his fangs into their necks, making them flail and howl. Bangara Singh wouldn't let go, of course, and the opponents would then stagger around the stage, their sole wish now to dislodge Bangara Singh from their necks and flee. Speculations already abounded that Bangara Singh was a progeny of the great Bharati champion Dara Singh, who was known as the Iron Man of wrestling.

The Sweej government had taken PM Papa's Better Than Sweejerland initiative lightly, laughing it off; they were confident that Darkmotherland wouldn't come close to becoming Sweejerland, let alone be better. In fact, one right-wing politician in Sweejerland, after hearing about PM Papa's initiative, had appeared on Sweej TV and said, "That hell-hole of a country, that Darkmotherland, won't even be one hundredth of Sweejerland, even in multiple lifetimes—they believe in reincarnation, don't they, those primitives?—no matter how hard they try." But the Sweej government and its people, most of them anyway, had taken the initiative in a good-humored way, saying it was good for a third-world country to aspire to become better than Sweejerland. It also spoke highly of Sweejerland, the Sweej ambassador had said to Hom Bokaw on Motherland TV.

So, when PM Papa had proposed a wrestling match between Darkmotherland's most popular wrestler Bangara Singh and Sweejerland's most popular wrestler, Sweej Cheej, the ambassador had acquiesced in the spirit of good Sweej bonhomie. Sweej Cheej was a world-renowned wrestler, famous for deceiving his opponents with a charming smile and an affable attitude. He was thin, blonde, and smelled faintly of sweet cow's milk. His face was pockmarked with large holes—a result of the release of carbon monoxide during his birth. He was so fair-minded that even when he pinned his opponent to the ground in a tight lock, he asked them whether they were okay and whether he should loosen his hold a bit. But opponents would take him lightly at their own risk—Sweej Cheej had never lost a match. They said that even Hulk Hogan was skittish about going to mat with him. So, you couldn't blame the ambassador for thinking that Sweej Cheej would quickly subdue Bangara Singh and everyone would go home happy.

But the match went wrong right from the start. Bangara Singh, who'd entered the ring to a deafening cheer from his fellow countrymen, refused to shake hands with Sweej Cheej, who initially appeared unnerved by the rudeness. The ambassador quickly looked at PM Papa, as if to say, I thought it was a friendly match, but PM Papa waved a hand in the air, smiling, as if to convey, What can you say? He's a true Darkmotherlandite. The ambassador nodded and laughed, unwilling to relinquish his ingrained Sweej geniality.

But his good-naturedness didn't last long. Bangara Singh, who was half the size of Sweej Cheej, kept prancing around the ring, as though teasing Sweej Cheej. The physical contrast between the two was remarkable: Bangara Singh was short, wiry, and dark. His skin color was burned by the intense heat of the south where he'd learned wrestling in the dust and mud in his poverty-stricken village. Sweej Cheej was tall and gangly—twice the height of his opponent—with skin that had turned translucent from growing up in the cold of the mountainous Alps.

Bangara Singh ducked and squirreled away, always out of the reach of his opponent. Sweej Cheej stood still, smiled and beckoned him with his hands, reminding his third-world opponent that it was all good and that he should engage. But Bangara Singh ran circles around Sweej Cheej, who, as he attempted to keep his eyes on his opponent, became dizzy.

"Why is he jooing jat?" the Sweej ambassador asked.

PM Papa, splayed his palms, and responded in a true Darkmother-landite way, "Why not?"

The ambassador was about to reply, "But that's not wrestling," but he held his tongue.

Of course, it was not true wrestling, for Bangara Singh was playing the clown. He would charge into Sweej Cheej, but instead of grabbing him, he'd pinch him on the thigh and dart away, drawing howling laughter from the crowd. One time, Bangara Singh managed to squeeze himself under Sweej Cheej's legs and come out from the other side and kick him from behind so that Sweej Cheej was thrown to the ropes. Sweej Cheej was no longer smiling, nor was the ambassador. Then, suddenly, Bangara Singh had a gada in his hand, not the modern kind but the kind that was wielded by the gods in ancient battles. It had a spiked, spherical head the size of an extra-large soccer ball on the top, and looked to be the type favored by the Monkeygod—not surprising as Bangara Singh was known to be a fierce Monkeygod devotee. The crowd went wild upon seeing the gada, and since Bangara Singh had produced it out of thin air, it wasn't unreasonable to assume that Monkeygod himself had blessed him with it to aid his victory.

The Sweej ambassador protested, saying, "It's not fair! It's not wrestling!"

PM Papa responded that it was free-form wrestling and that it was the Darkmotherlandite way of wrestling passed down by the ancient gods. "You shouldn't insult our heritage," PM Papa said.

"Then let my wrestler also have a weapon," the ambassador said.

PM Papa waved his consent, and soon enough, someone from the embassy handed Sweej Cheej a weapon that was passed down to the Sweej by *their* ancient gods—the Sweej Army Knife. It was a larger than normal Sweej Army Knife, and Sweej Cheej wielded it valiantly as Bangara Singh attacked him. Alas, the force and weight of the gada was too much for the Sweej wrestler, and soon he was running away with Bangara Singh chasing him around the ring. Bangara Singh was fast and agile. He cornered Sweej Cheej at one point and thrashed him with the gada repeatedly, climbing on his pale shoulders and battering him with his weapon. Clasping his bloodied head, Sweej Cheej staggered around the ring, his knife having fallen from his hand—Bangara Singh victoriously sitting on the top of his head.

"Not fair, not fair," the Sweej ambassador said. "Please stop the fight."

PM Papa stood, and waving his short hand in the air, shouted at Bangara Singh, "Finish him off!"

Rozy leaned forward and whispered, "What are you saying?"

PM Papa shouted even louder, "Finish him off!"

If anyone had been uncertain about what had been said, they were all certain now. The ministers in Papa's cabinet stood from their seats and shouted, "Finish him off!" Upon hearing this, the swamis seated behind them also stood and shouted, "Finish him off!" The entire stadium erupted into shouts of "Finish him off."

Grinning, showing his fangs, Bangara Singh acknowledged his mission and swung his gada in the air, slamming it down on Sweej Cheej's head. He then stood on Sweej Cheej's shoulders, like a circus performer, and brought the gada down, hard, on Sweej Cheej's skull, repeatedly. The head didn't split, but brain matter begin to ooze out of it, slowly, like melted cheese.

Above the stadium, small planes circled, towing massive banners behind them that read "Better Than Sweejerland."

15.

Whenever Kranti asked him whether he'd talked to the Ghimireys about their wedding, Bhaskar said he'd "initiated the conversation." The need to be accepted by the Ghimireys was growing in her every day. She felt it as a dryness in her mouth, palpitations in her heart, a nervous way of turning her head as though someone from the Asylum was watching her.

The notion grew inside her that the Ghimireys had dispatched someone to spy on her, find out what her motivations were in having this relationship with Bhaskar. Because the Asylum was right next to the Tourist District, which was a couple of neighborhoods away from Beggar Street, the palatial home was often on her route. Every time she was near it, she imagined voices inside it talking about her:

"When a girl like that is after our Bhaskar, it means she wants something."

"Well, it's clear what she wants, isn't it?"

"Hmm. I wonder how Bhaskar met her, under what circumstances."

"Do you want to bet that she's the one who lured him into the relationship? Who wants to bet?"

"Entrap."

"Seduce."

"If she thinks she can so easily access our wealth and our reputation, she has another thing coming."

"Go snoop on her. Find out what she's thinking."

Kranti kept an eye out for men and women enlisted by the Ghimireys to spy on her. Since she knew the Asylum employed many nokerchakers, she was wary of the nokerchaker types near her. Whenever she thought she was being watched by a figure in the street, she'd feign nonchalance, at times even throwing a smile at the observer. She wanted to make a good impression so that they'd report back that Kranti was a warm, cheerful person. She became quick to smile and nod at strangers, even people that couldn't possibly have been spies.

One time she was certain that she was being followed by a man wearing a red shirt, who kept fluttering around the edges of her eyes. But whenever she turned to look, she couldn't spot him. She ducked into a jewelry shop, then waited by the door for the moment when he'd pass, but only a man in a yellow shirt went by. She hurriedly exited as the shop owner called after her, asking what she wanted. Another time there was a young woman wearing a turban who was photographing her from across the street. Incensed, Kranti strode toward her, ignoring the honks of the traffic. She was about to snatch away her phone when she saw that the woman was actually taking the photo of a young man a few feet away, also wearing a turban.

In more hopeful moments, Kranti thought that she and Bhaskar could easily live in a flat by themselves. They could build their married lives away from the Asylum, without the large family and the nokerchakers, escaping the Ghimireys' stifling expectations of a new buhari. Yet Kranti knew she wouldn't be happy if she took Bhaskar away from his family. The Ghimireys would certainly blame her for it. She'd blame herself for it, and it would be further proof of her own inadequacy, her inability to rise to one of life's many challenges.

She didn't tell Bhaskar about the spies. He would worry, about her, about her mental health, what living in the Asylum might do to her. He would take it as a sign that they should indeed live separately. "And forget about a proper wedding," he'd say. "We'll get the court documents, and if anyone wants to visit us, they can come to our flat."

One day Bhaskar came to Beggar Street and told Kranti that yes, everything was fine, that his family had okayed the wedding.

"They have?" Kranti asked in disbelief. She was sitting on her bed; he was standing in the doorway.

"Would I lie to you?"

No, Bhaskar wouldn't lie, she knew that much. But there was a small shadow over his face—he wasn't his usual self. "Is everything okay?" she asked.

"Where is everybody?"

She told him that Professor Shrestha was attending a talk program, and the Beggars were at the Mothercry Press, working on the Dojjier. She watched his face, to see what his reaction would be to her mentioning the Dojjier. At first, he seemed to avoid her eyes, but then she continued to stare at him, and he said, "Oh, you know about the Dojjier?"

She said that she lived in Beggar Street. Did he really think that she was stupid enough not to know what went on? He said that he'd never thought she was stupid; it was just that he didn't know how interested she was, how curious. They argued quietly in her bedroom, with Dada's portrait watching over them. She said she was curious only because she was afraid. He said the work of the Dojjier was important.

"We need to witness, we need to record," he said. "For posterity, for who knows what's going to happen to us tomorrow?"

"Oof, Bhaskar! There you go again," she replied.

He watched her for a few seconds, then asked her whether she knew that PM Papa was moving to take control of the judiciary system in Darkmotherland. Papa's cabinet was now going to appoint all Supreme Adalat judges. The Darkmotherland Bar Association would be under the jurisdiction of the Ministry of the Interior.

Kranti knew this. Motherland TV had broadcast a speech by PM Papa. He was seated on an ornate chair by the fireside in the Lion Palace, where he had emphasized the need for a reformed judiciary to root out the rot that existed among the judges and lawyers in the country. "I need you, my dear Darkmotherlandites," PM Papa had said, almost sadly. He thrust his fist into the air for emphasis. "Pure Darkmotherland!"

But Kranti didn't want to get into a discussion about PM Papa, so she said, "Shall we have some tea? I'm dying for some tea."

Bhaskar, probably realizing that he wasn't going to get far in this conversation with Kranti, forced a smile and said, "With cinnamon?"

They moved to the kitchen, where she put some water to boil. "Are they happy about it, Bhaskar? Your family?"

He watched her, smiling, a forced smile, she thought. "Why wouldn't they be happy?"

"Bhaskar, please." She ground some cinnamon to put into the tea.

"Yes, they're happy."

She watched his face, and she knew that they weren't happy.

"Trust me, they're happy. They will be happy."

She experienced a mild panic attack right there, in front of Bhaskar, and desperately she tried to hide it. She felt her heartbeat accelerate as she poured tea into the cups. She handed a cup to Bhaskar but her hand was shaking.

"What's the matter?" Bhaskar asked, but she shook her head and said that she had to go to the bathroom. There, she sat on the commode, taking deep breaths. It was as though Bhaskar was about to discover something really bad about her, but she didn't know what. It felt like if she married him, then her whole life—and his—would simply fall apart. She put one hand on the wall to brace herself while she sat. She could hear Bhaskar calling after her, asking whether she was all right. After a while she came out.

"Not feeling well?" Bhaskar asked.

"Felt nauseous all of a sudden."

They went to her room, where she lay down and he massaged her forehead. "Why do you take such a burden on your shoulders?" he asked.

"There's no burden," she said.

"Did you have a panic attack?" he asked.

She shook her head and closed her eyes.

"You might need to push through this."

"Push through what?" she mumbled, not opening her eyes.

"Whatever happens, my family will accept you."

She pondered his words for a moment. Did it mean that they didn't accept her now? That they'd refused to accept her? But she didn't want to ask. She realized that she was afraid to ask.

"We must march forward," he said.

She laughed and opened her eyes. "What are you? An army general?" She mimicked him. "We must march forward."

He lightly tapped her cheek and said, "Cheeky, cheeky."

She sat up and raised her fist. "March onward to the Asylum, Madam Mao's daughter."

Bhaskar too raised his fist and said, "Breach that barrier!"

Then they both laughed, but Kranti's laughter was tinged with anxiety. She wondered if Bhaskar's was too. Did she detect real anxiety, or was she imagining it?

"No, seriously," Bhaskar said. "All that needs to be done is the working out of some details. Then we'll finalize it. No more delays."

"What details?"

Bhaskar was vague, something about Shambhogya wanting to make sure that the wedding date was auspicious according to their family astrologer.

After he left, she felt that the walls were about to cave in on her. She needed to get out of the house, so she ended up going to see Kabiraj.

—

Shambhogya informed Priyanka and Chaitanya about her pact with Bhaskar—she'd concluded that it was best if they were kept in the loop, just for strength in numbers—with strict instructions not to reveal it to Sir and Muwa. Let them believe that Bhaskar is serious about meeting these prospective brides, she told them.

"That's my boy," Prithvi Raj said when Shambhogya told him Bhaskar would look at girls. "I knew he'd come around. The Ghimirey blood runs strong in all of us." He gave credit to Shambhogya, and said to Aditya, "If only you were half as savvy as your wife is, Ghimirey & Sons would have been *numero uno* years ago. We'd be doing better than Srinivas, or the MOM Group, or even the Kapadias. Maybe we should give Shambhogya a room in our office, next to yours." Aditya was about to respond when Shambhogya cautioned him with her eyes. The old man was half-joking, of course, women in the Ghimirey household would never work. Their place was firmly within the boundaries of the Asylum walls.

But Muwa became suspicious when Shambhogya informed her later that day, as they sat in the atrium before dinner, that Bhaskar hadn't yet arrived home. Prithvi Raj was upstairs, making some calls. "Bhaskar agreed? What changed his mind?"

"Shambhogya's magic," Aditya said. "You don't know what a gem you have in your daughter-in-law."

"I know what a gem she is," Muwa said in a deadpan voice.

"What about me?" Priyanka said, sounding hurt. "Am I not a gem too?"

"You all are gems," Muwa said. "Precious gems. And I—I'm a misshapen rock in this family."

"And of course, your favorite son, Bhaskar, is a diamond in the rough," Aditya said.

It was a cool evening, and the Darkmother's statue watched over them. Shambhogya loved gazing at Darkmother's face, the fierceness in her eyes. She had the nokerchakers bathe the statue in milk every morning, then give it a vigorous wipe so that it gleamed throughout the day.

Muwa said to Shambhogya, "I'm just trying to picture my Bhaskar listening to you and saying, 'oh, yes, of course, I'll do exactly as you say.' Bhaskar is not a fool."

"And we're not either," Shambhogya said. "You underestimate us. Do you want some green tea before dinner, Muwa?"

Muwa waved her hand dismissively. "What will Kranti think when she finds out he's looking at other women?"

Shambhogya said there was no need for Kranti to know, but Muwa was unhappy. Kranti expected Bhaskar to talk to his family, not have his family parade a bunch of girls in front of him.

Shambhogya stood and went to the Darkmother's statue. She ran her finger over the statue's right arm—dust. "Ofo!" she said. "Did they not wipe Darkmother properly this morning?"

"It's from outside, Shambhogya-di," Priyanka said. "There's no way to avoid the dust from the Big Two."

"Maybe you can supervise the nokerchakers better," Shambhogya hissed at Priyanka. "It'll be so embarrassing, if at our next party our VIP guests see the dust. And on Darkmother, of all things!"

Priyanka muttered something under her breath.

"All I'm trying to do is prevent chaos in the Asylum, Muwa," Shambhogya said. "Why is everyone being so difficult?" She looked at Muwa, then Priyanka, and, finally Aditya.

Muwa said they were playing with an innocent girl's feelings. Kranti, too, had a right to her dignity.

Chaitanya and Aditya accused Muwa of caring more for outsiders than her own family. Shambhogya put up a hand as though preventing them from attacking their mother, but she didn't say anything. It was good if the old woman was put in her place. She was mostly holed up in God's Room anyway—what did she care about the well-being of the family?

As though reading her thoughts, Aditya said, "Muwa had always wanted to be a sanyasin, detached from the trappings of this world." He pointed to the atrium, as though demonstrating how ridiculous it was to think that this beautiful space was a trap.

"Maybe we should pack up things for her," Chaitanya said, "and send her off on a pilgrimage to Bharat until this issue is resolved."

—

The Bhureys eyed Kranti as she crossed the Diamond Park to the Parade Ground. There were whistles and catcalls. Smoke rose from the coal stoves burning next to the tents; evening meals were being prepared. Vendors walked about hawking their wares: tiny bottles with syrups to cure impotency and cancer, breast enhancement contraptions that looked like iron bras, rabbit innards fried with peanuts, fritters, and stale bread. A man held up what looked like a small python wrapped around his arms, but it turned out to have the head of a cat, which mewed and purred. A diseased monkey hopped around on stilts.

Tents crowded the park. Kabiraj had told Kranti that before the Big Two, the honeys, along with male prostitutes, known as homeys, and thirdgender prostitutes, who were called frens, had free reign of the Diamond Park, especially once the sun went down. Now, small scuffles broke out, for some Bhureys were angered by the honeys, homeys, and frens. They were collectively known as bhalus and they solicited clients amidst them. Wives were afraid that their husbands would be lured. Husbands became worried that their wives would start eyeing the homeys.

"Where are the Poolis Uncles when we need them?"

"The Poolis Uncles are not going to do anything."

"Call the Fundys!"

And, now and then, the Fundys did appear in their saffron robes and bandanas, shouting, "Bom Bholey!" And just like that the bhalus were nowhere to be found. Kabiraj said that not too long ago a honey was raped by Fundys near the toilet in the corner of the Diamond Park. It was a mystery how they'd accomplished it, with all the tents all around them. The honey later said that one Fundy had clamped her mouth, while another held a trishul to her throat while they had done her behind the bathroom. Four of them, one by one, had raped her, calling her derogatory names throughout, while occasionally chanting "Bom Bholey!" In general, however, the Fundys were more lenient with honeys than they were with homeys and frens, whom they beat mercilessly, calling them freaks and disgraces. On Motherland TV, Swami Go!swami said that God didn't want his children to tolerate these abominations. He stroked his beard; his eyes filled with a strange brightness. "It is like cancer. And cancer is the most dangerous of diseases. Does anyone say that cancer is okay, and that it is natural, that we should accept it? No, everyone says cancer needs to be cured. So why not homosexuals and thirdgenders?"

It was now several weeks since she'd come here with Kabiraj. She was overwhelmed by the number of tents. She couldn't remember which was his, or what path to take. More catcalls came her way, and a man in garish clothes donned by the pimps in Amrikan movies—a grimy rainbow-colored robe, a white hat, dark glasses, and a stick—stepped in front of her. He moved his body spastically, then looked at her in wonder. "These pretzels are making me thirsty," he said.

"What?"

"Pretzels," he said. "See?" He opened his hands. There was a piece of sel in them.

Just a few yards back, Kranti had seen a vendor cooking the donut-shaped sel in dirty oil. "That's a sel, not a pretzel."

"Pretzels, pretzels," the man said. He thrust the sel in front of her face. "Eat, eat, you're all skin and bones."

She shoved his hand away and said, "Buzz off!"

The man did another twitchy move with his entire body, as though he were being electrocuted, then he smiled, anticipating her comment.

When she didn't comment, his face turned sour. "Didn't recognize?"

She waved her finger near her head. "A total cuckoo?"

"Kraymah." He waited expectantly.

A vague image came to her mind, of an eccentric character from a movie or a show, but she didn't know where it was from. She couldn't even be sure whether it was an Angrezi character or a Darkmotherlandese one. But who had time to engage with this whackadoodle in Bhurey Paradise? Kranti tried to get past him in the narrow area between two tents.

He blocked her way with his stick. "Where do you think you're going? No one gets past Kraymah so easily." Then he put his free hand out and cried beseechingly, like an actor in a melodramatic movie, "Kraymah! Kraymah!"

"Will you let me through?"

"Name's Mukesh Dalal. Work is booty dalal. Get it?"

"If you don't let me through, I'm going to scream." She was beginning to feel anxious. This was Bhurey Paradise, after all. Every day bad things happened here—beatings, rapes, disappearances. Comical as this character was, there was something ugly about him. He'd said his work was booty dalal—that meant pimp, didn't it?

"What's the hurry, chickadee?" He raised his stick and gently caressed Kranti's cheek with it. "Everyone calls me Mukeshbro, affectionately."

Kranti pushed the stick away, but he was still blocking her way, so she said, "I'm looking for a man named Kabiraj."

"Describe him." Mukeshbro stopped swaying.

"Short, pudgy, with a poet-like beard."

"I ain't no poet, my beauty," Mukeshbro said, "but I know a poet when I sees one. He's a good poet, that man."

"Well, where can I find him?"

"Go down that street," he said, bending at his waist and pointing with his stick to the pathway between tents, "then take a left at the first three-way boulevard, then a right at the communal tap, which then curves into a boutique avenue that will lead you right to Laj Mahal."

"Laj Mahal?"

"The Palace of Shame. The Poet-King's words, not mine."

Kranti memorized the instructions. "And the color of Laj Mahal is blue, isn't it?"

"Yes, bootylicious. Blue, the color of poets."

"Thanks," Kranti said, and glared at him so he'd lower the stick. He didn't, so she put his hand on it, thinking that any moment he was going to raise it and strike her. It was a standoff. She pushed the stick down and he let her as he slowly nodded his head. Gone was the herky-jerky character from earlier. Finally, she was able to push past him, feeling his eyes drilling the back of her neck as she left him behind.

She found the Laj Mahal. Flying on top of the tent was a small, frayed, rectangular flag with an image of the first ever poet of Darkmotherland, Adikabi. A cowbell hung outside the door of the tent, which she assumed was to be used as a doorbell, so she rang it.

Kabiraj's lazy voice asked her to enter.

He wasn't surprised to see her. Or at least he didn't act surprised. He was his usual shy self. He was lying on his bed on the tent's floor. The tent itself was about the size of a very small room, with narrow bedding in the corner, and a couple of old beanbags on the floor, which was carpeted with a plastic sheet. Kabiraj, because of his tutoring income, could afford a single tent. Some Bhureys in Bhurey Paradise were forced to share theirs with several other people, often family members but sometimes strangers. There was one large tent, Kabiraj had told her, which happily held more than a dozen members of the same clan, refugees from the mountains.

She snuggled next to him on the bed. "Bhaskar and I are getting married," she said. She put her head underneath the blanket on his stomach. His shirt had slid up and she felt his slightly bloated, hairy stomach. She drew circles on it, making him give out these small giggles. "Con—ha! ha!—gra—he! he!—tulations—ho! ho! ho!"

"Who do you think you are? Santa Claus?"

"Have you been naughty or nice, this season?" he asked shyly.

"I'm acting nice but I'm really naughty."

"Ho, ho, ho," Kabiraj said.

"Once I enter the Asylum, I'll not be able to come and see you," she said, although instantly she knew that she'd come to Kabiraj even after marrying Bhaskar. She knew that the pressures of being a Ghimirey buhari would be too much for her. She felt a panic attack coming even thinking about it, so she focused on Kabiraj's face, and found herself beginning to relax. What a doofus this man was, so amusing, just being with him made her worries recede.

"Ah, the Asylum," Kabiraj said. "I've always wondered what it was like in there."

"You're Bhaskar's friend, and you never went in?"

"There never was an opportunity," Kabiraj said, "but I bet you it's not as opulent as my tent."

"The pimp called it Laj Mahal."

"Oh, you met Mukeshbro?"

"He's from a different planet, isn't he, this Mukeshbro?"

"If you think *Seinfeld* is a planet," Kabiraj said.

She looked at him questioningly.

"You've never watched *Seinfeld*?"

She shook her head. "What's it about?"

"It's a show about nothing," Kabiraj said. "Mukeshbro's ambition is to become the most powerful pimp in Darkmotherland. People have advised him that he should start out small, by first being the most powerful pimp in Bhurey Paradise. And now he is. He controls many things in the Parade Ground and the Diamond Park area."

"Will you miss me once I get married and am unable to see you, dallu?" Her fingers were wrapped around his penis now, and it began to harden.

"You won't come to Laj Mahal?" He began to moan.

"I'll be too ashamed to come to the Palace of Shame, won't I?"

"So, you're not a shameless hussy?" he asked.

He was fully hard now, and she watched his face as she stroked him. His eyes were closed; it was as if he'd drifted off into a dreamland. "I am," she said, "but I will be caged. In the Asylum."

Kabiraj moaned, and he came, into her palm.

"Disgusting," she said. She spotted a small jug of water in a corner of the tent, next to a large metal box that looked like it was carried over from the previous century. Holding her hand away from her body, she stood and went to the jug and poured the water over her hand, then wiped it with a nearby rag.

"I'm sorry," he said.

She returned to him and lay next to him. "Now your turn," she said.

—

Later, they strolled through the Parade Ground. Some of the tents were so close to one another there was hardly any room to walk between them. A handful were raised about a foot off the ground and had barbed wire running around them. There were sounds of radios and televisions. Kranti thought she heard the opening of *The Simpsons*, then Homer's voice complaining in Japanese. At the communal tap, women and children were bathing, soaping and rinsing themselves. A couple of teenagers were splashing water at each other and getting scolded for being wasteful.

A thirdgender walked by in a kurta suruwal and said, in a sweet voice, "O-ho, Poet King dai, who is the gorgeous maiden?" She had a long, beautiful face, with hair that cascaded down to her waist.

"Just a poetess friend, Pyari," Kabiraj said.

Kranti elbowed him.

"Be good and control yourself around her, okay, Poet King dai?" Pyari said as she continued.

Kabiraj said that there was a group of thirdgenders who were concentrated in the middle of the Bhurey Paradise. "I have conducted occasional poetry workshops for them," he said. "Pyari is a community leader of sorts." Kabiraj appeared very much at home in Bhurey Paradise, as though it was his ancestral home. For a shy fellow, he knew many people.

Outside a tent one young girl with tattoos had a cigarette between her lips and was playing the guitar and singing. Kranti caught some words. Then she remembered—another one of Dada's songs.

"Pink Floyd," she told Kabiraj, in a showy manner. "'Wish You Were Here.' If the Fundys catch her, a young girl, smoking, with tattoos, and singing an Amrikan song—"

"Belaiti," Kabiraj said.

"I know that, idiot," Kranti said, but she didn't know, because she had never distinguished the rock that Dada listened to as Amrikan or Belaiti—they were all Amrikan to her. "But will the Fundys care whether it's Amrikan or Belaiti? For them, it's corrupt."

"We have an advanced warning system," said Kabiraj. And he gave out a long, ear-piercing yodel that went on and on, as though he were trilling and warbling in the white mountains of the Alps. With cries and whispers of "Fundys," people scurried about. The girl with the guitar stopped playing and vanished in a puff of smoke. Televisions and radios were either shut off or switched to wholesome family dramas, in which women were always chaste, or to religious programs featuring preachers who extolled the virtues of cows, cow dung, and cow urine. All of this happened within a few seconds. "Do you see how efficient we are?" Kabiraj said.

"The Bhureys will lynch you for disturbing them with this false alarm."

"Not really," Kabiraj said. He cupped his palms around his mouth and shouted, "Practice drill!" Faces peeked out from the tents and people came out.

A couple of youths approached and said, "Poet King dai, we just had a drill yesterday."

"It don't hurt," he said to them, "to be alert." He explained to Kranti that it was an apt slogan for the poor folks at Bhurey Paradise, who always had to watch out for the Fundys, Papa's Patriots, the Poolis Uncles, and even the Loyal Army Dais. "And now with the Better Than Sweejerland initiative, we have to be on constant alert that one day we're not razed to the ground to beautify Darkmotherland."

She asked him whether he watched the wrestling match, and he responded that he had to teach that day.

"The Sweej government is quite unhappy with PM Papa, for not stopping the fight," Kabiraj said. "They haven't taken kindly to the fact that their most popular wrestler is now dead. They're threatening to withdraw their embassy."

"It doesn't seem like PM Papa cares."

"He loves violence."

"Do you think we're turning into a more violent country under PM Papa?" For some reason, she immediately thought of Bhaskar.

"We're becoming like Amrika, where violence is celebrated."

President Corn Hair had tweeted about the wrestling match: "Great match. Amazing work by little dark Bangara Singh. Congratulations to my friend PM Papa, with whom I get along very well. Darkmotherland will soon be a thousand times Better Than

Sweejerland, which is as soft as Sweej Cheej. PM Papa is a fantastic leader."

Kranti took Kabiraj's hand in hers, which surprised him, and also her. Bhaskar could show up at Bhurey Paradise, you know, she told herself. What would happen then?

President Corn Hair's tweet had further emboldened PM Papa, it seemed, for the phrase Better Than Sweejerland had begun to appear more and more on Motherland TV. Hom Bokaw said that the wrestling match had proved that Darkmotherland was already better than Sweejerland. And it had all happened under the strong leadership of PM Papa.

Kabiraj walked with her to the exit of Bhurey Paradise, near Diamond Park, where Mukeshbro was sitting on a wall. He and Kabiraj exchanged pleasantries. Mukeshbro looked Kranti up and down, smiled a goofy smile, then made a joke about how popular she'd be among his pilgrims. "There's a nice income to be had in this profession," he said, "especially in this time of such outrageous inflation. Within a few years you'll be able to buy yourself a half anna piece of land and start fantasizing about your dream house, fulfill your Darkmotherlandite dream."

"She lives in a mansion already," Kabiraj said.

Kranti elbowed him. She didn't want her identity known.

Mukeshbro mistook her elbowing for something else and said, waving his arms about frenetically, "Sure, sure, if you live in a mansion, I own a piece of cheese on the moon, maybe Sweej Cheej." Mukeshbro laughed at his own joke. "But let me tell you, I'll be living in a mansion long before you, as soon as in a couple of years."

He jumped off the wall and launched into a soliloquy about his ambitions. He paced the ground, moved his arms about, and caressed his chin in a thoughtful manner. He spoke rapidly, at times as though he had verbal diarrhea. He was ditching the lower-class pilgrims for businessmen and foreigners. That's what he wanted—all of his honeys servicing these rich pilgrims. "Oh, yeah!" he exclaimed, pointing his index finger at Kabiraj and Kranti. But there was competition in that sector. He complained of another man, someone named Badal, who dominated the high-end market. That's why Mukeshbro was on the lookout for hot-looking potential honeys, like Kranti, who'd appeal to these discerning clients. Mukeshbro was trying hard to become the sole supplier for the Valley's top manpower companies and cater exclusively to agents from the oil-rich Khadi countries who came to Darkmotherland on business. He had a burning ambition to become the kingpin of honeys, serving only luxury pilgrims in four- or five-star hotels.

When Kranti pointed out that the Fundys were on a mission to eradicate prostitution altogether—where would Mukeshbro be then?—he waved his hand at her dismissively, saying, "Bahhh! Our prostitution business is a driving force of our economy. PM Papa wouldn't mess with it. He's a man of the people."

Mukeshbro boasted that he was cultivating friendships with powerful Poolis Uncles and gifting a live goat to the Inspector General of Poolis Anand Chhetri in the next Ten-Day Festival. He was going to carry the goat in his arms to deliver it to the IGP's home. He paused his pacing and asked, "Can you keep a secret?"

"Sure, Mukeshbro," Kabiraj said. "We will take your secret to our funeral pyres."

"Wah! What an expression," Kranti said to Kabiraj sarcastically. "A versifier of pyres. They don't call you a king of poets for nothing."

Mukeshbro leaned closer and whispered that he and IGP Chhetri were in a partnership to service big-time businessmen from the Khadi who were interested in coming to Darkmotherland for a pilgrimage. "They have special tastes, you know," he said. "We're going to supply young honeys to this big hotel next to the Raddi Tokari Factory."

Kranti knew that the Raddi Tokari Factory was owned and operated by the Ghimireys. The big hotel that Mukeshbro was talking about—didn't that also belong to the Ghimireys?

Accompanied by their families, prospective brides were brought into the Asylum for viewings. They were beautiful girls, some even stunning, with lithe bodies clad in saris, oval-shaped faces featuring slim noses and long eyelashes, and cheeks that dimpled when they smiled. They spoke Angrezi, were experts in the culinary arts, had charming demeanors, and were not overly ambitious about their own careers, but displayed enough curiosity about Ghimirey & Sons to demonstrate that they'd make good business wives. One young woman, who was attractive enough to have sought a career in modeling, had an MBA from Harvard, but she dropped heavy hints that she was more interested in "homemaking" than in entrepreneurship.

Muwa had now quieted down; perhaps I'm no longer fit to make judgments on any of these matters, she thought. Her heart went out to the girl, Kanti. No, it was Kranti. What a name! Only a revolution-minded woman would name her daughter "revolution." Recalling the dinner conversation the other day, Muwa experienced mild anxiety about Madam Mao. Was she as difficult as it was rumored? Was she really trying to get her daughter into the Asylum in order to turn their world upside down? Perhaps this world did indeed need to be turned upside down—this little bubble? This last thought of hers made her blanch. Of course, Muwa wouldn't want any harm to fall on her family. If this Kranti was really bad, Muwa wouldn't support this alliance. But, Muwa concluded shortly, her Bhaskar would never select a girl with a duplicitous or scheming heart. She had already formed an image of the girl—slim build, a kindly face, and guileless, just like Bhaskar.

Her Bhaskar. Why did Muwa feel so much more for him than she did for her other two sons? After all, all three were born from the same womb. Perhaps she saw in Bhaskar an image of herself, another alien in the Asylum. Illegal alien, as Chaitanya had mockingly called his mother once.

The mocking, silly Chaitanya. Stupid Chaitanya. And the scheming, conniving, power-hungry Aditya. People always asked her how her middle son turned out to be so different than the other two.

Not interested in family business, pounding the pavements wearing his sandals, always in a kurta and faded jeans, hanging out with riff-raff and the khateykids. "Is he even your son?" sometimes people joked, and she smiled along with them, but later thought angrily—he's more my son than the other two combined. She felt protective toward him, something she didn't for the other two, as if she knew something bad was going to happen to him later on. Even when Bhaskar was born, she had nursed the feeling that something awful was going to befall her middle son. During his birth she had been in labor for hours, the contractions ripping apart her body. Any moment now the baby will come, the midwives surrounding her had said, but the baby stubbornly stayed inside. After close to twenty-four hours, the contractions became so intense that she pleaded to the midwives to kill her. Even then the baby seemed to be clinging to the walls of her uterus, refusing to emerge. The midwives tugged and pulled. Prithvi Raj was on a business trip somewhere, and Aditya, then five, was at his boarding school in Darjeeling. She was alone. Finally, when Bhaskar came out, all slathered up, he sported such an angry face that she felt she had done something wrong by bringing him out.

When all those prospective girls started coming to the house, gorgeous girls with both smarts and culinary skills, Muwa wanted to confront Bhaskar. Is this you? she wanted to ask him. I can't believe you agreed to this. But she didn't because she was afraid everyone would criticize her of not caring about the family. She thought she would leave the Asylum to seek out this Kranti girl herself. She knew where Beggar Street was—not too far from the Tourist District—even as she rarely left home. Recently, after the Ghimireys became aware that the relationship between Bhaskar and Kranti had progressed to a seriousness they hadn't anticipated, Muwa had recalled seeing Professor Shrestha's photo on the cover of an issue of *Himdesh Magazine* that was still lying around somewhere.

She'd retrieved the issue and read it, painfully slowly because she wasn't accustomed to reading and her eyesight had become poor. Professor Shrestha's life appeared remarkable to her, so different from her own. Here was a woman whose intellectual ferocity was marked on her face: a wide, broad forehead with a singular vertical crease in the middle like a tika carved by the gods themselves, a large, formidable nose, a strong, resolute chin. No wonder she was respected and feared—and reviled—by so many in Darkmotherland. PM Papa wanted to take her down. Rereading the article and gazing at the photo, Muwa had wanted to meet Professor Shrestha. She imagined asking her questions about her life, asking where she got her tenacity, how she managed to keep going strong, year after year, how she survived all those times in jail. Muwa couldn't imagine herself in jail, along with common prisoners, sitting on a dirty floor amidst the stench of urine and feces, being harassed by guards. She would curl up and die. But if someone like Professor Shrestha was in the same cell, Muwa might draw strength from her, and survive. Yes, Muwa could see herself holding hands with Professor Shrestha in a jail cell, looking at her for guidance. Muwa had wondered what her family would think about her desire to feel camaraderie with a woman who was quoted in the magazine as saying that Ghimirey & Sons are "sucking dry the blood of the poor" for profits.

Muwa watched the parade of girls come to the house. Smart women, beautiful women, some possibly more beautiful and smarter than Kranti, yet they conducted themselves as though they'd come for a job interview at Ghimirey & Sons. They were sycophantic, adoring of everything they saw in the Asylum. They were witty and demure at the same time. As the potential groom's mother, Muwa was supposed to be interested, involved, and evaluating, but the most she could do was say, "Please have some more biscuits," or "How crowded the Valley has become," or "I wonder when Darkmotherland will fully be restored to how it was before the Big Two." She made excuses to leave the drawing room and go to the kitchen, as if to supervise the nokerchakers.

Bhaskar joked with the girls, teased and charmed them—he'd always been good with women—yet it was clear that he had no intention of moving forward with any of them. Muwa was glad to observe this. The other Ghimireys might have also sensed this, but the girls and their families surely didn't, for Bhaskar was cordial and smiling all the time. It would be hard to tell he was faking it. Muwa was sure that they'd heard about Bhaskar's liaison with Kranti, but they might have assumed that for his wife he'd want to choose someone from a more high-class family.

16.

The idea of Professor Shrestha doing kanyadan at the Asylum instead of Beggar Street encountered strong resistance from the Ghimireys when Bhaskar brought it up over dinner. Yes, they understood that the girl didn't have a male figure, an uncle or a cousin, who could donate the bride, but why couldn't Professor Shrestha give her daughter away at her house, as the custom demanded?

Bhaskar made excuses.

Aditya, who'd been watching his brother's face closely, concluded that he knew why: Professor Shrestha didn't want the Ghimireys at her house. They all stopped eating, the clanking of the cutlery paused, and looked at Bhaskar. Shambhogya asked whether that was true. Aditya said something about "no good two-penny communist filth." Priyanka opined that to allow the wedding to happen in such a circumstance would be a disgrace, which drew a rebuke from Muwa, who asked her youngest daughter-in-law not to speak "out of her station." Chaitanya defended his wife.

For a while there was much cross talk, then Prithvi Raj, in a hurt voice, asked Bhaskar why he had put his family in such a difficult situation.

Bhaskar responded that the simplest thing to do would be for he and Kranti to get married in court, then move into a flat. Problem solved, he said, and left the dining room.

—

Shambhogya called for an emergency meeting the next morning, minus Bhaskar and Muwa, in a corner of the atrium. They all sat on benches next to a life-size statue of a battery-powered dancing Pothead God whose legs moved and whose hips gyrated.

It had been drizzling all morning, and they could hear the pitter-patter of the rain above on the skylight. Shambhogya said that letting Bhaskar have a court wedding would be bad for the family. Aditya and Priyanka were of the opinion that they shouldn't give in; otherwise, it'd be a victory for Madam Mao. Shambhogya countered that if Bhaskar married Kranti in court and lived elsewhere, then not only would Madam Mao be victorious, they would also lose Bhaskar.

It was hard arguing against this logic. Prithvi Raj bemoaned that he had such grand hopes of inviting PM Papa to Bhaskar's wedding, but there was no way that could happen now with Madam Mao's daughter as the bride. If only they could have Jyotish Jeevan take a look at her chart, like he'd done with both Shambhogya's and Priyanka's charts before their weddings. Shambhogya took the opportunity to mention how accurate Jyotish Jeevan had been in forecasting Priyanka's childlessness (Shambhogya knew that it was a sore spot for Priyanka. Child-bearing was one area in which Priyanka had clearly proven herself inferior to Shambhogya. Priyanka and Chaitanya had tried many remedies over the years—special pilgrimages, Ayurvedic medicines, Tibbati shamans, organic dieting—but none of them had worked.). Priyanka defended herself, saying that there was a dasha on her chart that needed to be removed.

They all began to complain about what an impossible place Bhaskar had put them in.

"Everyone stop!" Shambhogya said, standing to make herself heard. "Instead of moaning and groaning, can we talk about what we can do? We have to make the best of the situation."

"It's hopeless," Aditya said.

"For someone running a major company in Darkmotherland, you sure are a beacon of optimism and hope," Shambhogya said.

Aditya looked at his wife. She was getting bolder and bolder with these pronouncements now, even in front of her father-in-law. And Prithvi Raj didn't reprimand her. Aditya couldn't let her get away with it. If she continued to disrespect him, he'd have all the more reason to spend time with his mistress; he'd put her up in a flat in the northern side of the Valley, near the Temple of the Old Blue-Throated Floating

God. And if Shambhogya didn't change her ways, maybe one day he'd tell her about this mistress and watch the reaction on her face.

"Bhaskar babu is going to marry Kranti," Shambhogya said, "but perhaps there's a way we can spin this to our advantage."

"Go ahead, spinmistress," Aditya said.

"Or is it spinstress?" Chaitanya asked.

"Okay, I don't want jokes," Shambhogya said. She was now pacing, clearly a leader who expected silence from her troupe as she arrived at a decision. "How about . . ." Everyone could see her mind churning. She stopped. "How about we tell everyone that this wedding is a union of two opposite forces, that it is our way of letting the world know that we value peace above everything else. We are the good guys."

"That's a lousy spin, spinmaestro," Aditya said.

Shambhogya sighed and sat down. She raised her palm, as though to silence unruly subordinates. This was an opportunity for PM Papa to be magnanimous toward his enemy, she said, to show his citizens that he's truly a compassionate leader. When Chaitanya said that the Fundys aren't going to like him sharing the stage with Madam Mao, Shambhogya responded that it actually allows PM Papa to come out on the top, to show that he's willing to extend an olive branch to even his sworn enemy.

Slowly, the others began to warm up to this idea, and they began to see that sharing the stage with Madam Mao could be good publicity for PM Papa. An added bonus could be, Shambhogya said, that it'd help undermine the Papa Don't Preach rally. Once the rally folks saw PM Papa and Madam Mao in the Asylum, it would demoralize them. But the planning for getting him to the Asylum would have to be carried out in utmost secrecy. Madam Mao shouldn't get a whiff that he was coming. Aditya would ask the chiefs of Motherland TV and Motherland Radio to keep it under wraps until the last minute. Then it'd be broadcast live. The Rajjya media frequently carried live coverage of PM Papa's surprise visits to factories and ministries. The need for secrecy was always explained this way: PM Papa has too many enemies who'd want to know his routine and want to harm him.

Prithvi Raj gazed adoringly at Shambhogya and told her that she should have been a politician. Aditya remarked caustically that his father shouldn't give her ideas.

———

Even on very difficult days, she didn't touch Paagalium, merely looked at the bottle as it sat on her bedside table. She was determined to grit her teeth through this, no matter the pervasive anxiety in her, now like a faint odor of gas in her nostrils, over the impending wedding. What would Bhaskar think if she backed out? More important, what would the Ghimireys think if she withdrew? Whenever she thought of the Ghimireys, her body went hot and then cold, then hot again. They wouldn't approve of her. They didn't approve of her now. They would never approve of her.

She became physically sick. Feverish. She stayed in her room, Poe whispering in her ear, telling her the nightmare she was entering into. Bhaskar came to see her. She pretended to be so sick that she couldn't even use her throat for words. Bhaskar sat by her bed for hours, even neglecting the Beggars in the adjoining room. In half-pretend, half-real delirium she asked him hoarsely, "So, what do they say, Bhaskar, what do they say?"

"Were you expecting a message from them?" Bhaskar asked, stroking her burning forehead.

"Bhaskar, please. Are they still okay with this?"

"You need to stop asking whether they're okay. They are very okay. You are okay. I am okay. So, they will be okay even if they're not okay."

"They're talking about me, aren't they?" she asked in near panic.

"What?"

"I can hear them."

"Where?"

"I can—" She managed to catch herself before she said anything foolish that would give her state of mind away. It was hard. Even as she watched him, she was thinking that he had something up his sleeve, that he too might be plotting. Plotting to leave her?

A wedding date was fixed. Kranti got word that the Ghimireys wanted to meet her. She was terrified, and Bhaskar said, "You don't have to meet them before the wedding if you don't want to. It's just a formality."

"But I must!" she cried. "What bride wouldn't want to meet her new family?"

"Damned if you do. Damned if you don't."

She knew she hadn't made things easy for him. As it was, he was the only conduit between the two families, relaying information back and forth, an unusual and unorthodox position for a groom. Professor Shrestha didn't want anything to do with the preparation. "I will do the kanyadan at their place," she said, not even willing to say the Asylum. "But leave me out of everything else." Kranti was certain that the Ghimireys had complained to Bhaskar about the whole thing—how the wedding was being prepared, the fact that they hadn't yet gotten to meet the bride, that the bride didn't want to meet them beforehand, that the bride was the daughter of their long-time enemy. It's a miracle, thought Kranti, that they'd even agreed to the wedding.

She paused.

But had they?

She asked Bhaskar again whether he was pulling her leg.

"About what?"

"That they're okay with this?"

"Of course, they are," Bhaskar said. "Why would I lie to you about such a thing?"

"But you're not telling me something."

"What?"

"Whatever is happening at the Asylum."

"Nothing is happening at the Asylum," Bhaskar assured her. "Nothing ever happens at the Asylum except the business of making money."

When Kranti accused her mother of not doing enough regarding the wedding, and not making overtures to the Ghimireys, Professor Shrestha said that she didn't care what Kranti thought. The plans for Papa Don't Preach were having a lot of difficulty coming together, and she was distracted. The Gang of Four was getting impatient, saying that they were ready to take more forceful action. Among the Beggars, too, there was dissension. Prakash, too, thought that they ought to stop dithering. "We need to go for the jugular," he kept saying. "Jugular. Strike at the jugular—that's what we must do." The others were afraid to ask him what he really meant by the jugular. Storm the Lion's Palace? That had been brought up by the Gang of Four, but Professor Shrestha had immediately discounted it. Murti, too, advocated for a more balanced approach. "We need balance," she said, and no one asked her what she meant by that. The Rajjya hadn't relented on its crackdowns. Two more presses with left-leaning sensibilities had been shut down, their editors imprisoned. Mothercry Press had been silent for weeks now, more because of Professor Shrestha's instruction rather than Prakash's wishes.

Professor Shrestha was warming some milk for herself—she found it helped with her sleep. Prakash worried her more and more. She suspected he was meeting the Gang of Four without her knowledge, outside Beggar Street. When she'd questioned him a couple of days ago, he'd first said that he'd only been talking to them on the phone, trying to coordinate their planning, but then in the end he admitted that he'd gone to visit them. Where? Professor Shrestha had asked, her mind racing. Prakash had declined to divulge where, saying he had sworn to them that he wouldn't tell anyone. "The less you know, the better," Prakash had answered. Then, seeing the disappointment on her face, had added, "For your own safety, Madam."

As Professor Shrestha waited for her milk to boil, Kranti came into the kitchen and said, out of the blue, "You think that I'm marrying above my station by marrying Bhaskar, don't you?"

"What?" Professor Shrestha said, barely paying attention to her. Her mind was still on Prakash. She'd cautioned him, saying that the Rajjya could be spying on them, spying on him, and he could easily get labeled as a Treasonist. More important, she didn't want such a direct link between the Beggars and the Gang of Four. He'd laughed at her, saying that she'd invited them to Beggar Street in the first place. She said that she regretted it now, that she feared she'd put everyone in danger. He said it was too late. They were tied to the Gang of Four, whether they liked it or not. Besides, Prakash said, they're the only ones who can do something about PM Papa.

"Aha!" Kranti wagged her finger at her. "Aha!"

"Aha what?" She turned around to face her daughter, and in that moment the milk boiled over. Cursing, Professor Shrestha turned off the gas and used a towel to stem the flow of milk on the counter. "Look what you did," she said to her daughter.

"What?" Kranti said belligerently. "I caught you . . . in your evil thinking."

The very phrase "evil thinking" did something to Kranti's mind. It led her to believe that her mother was harboring evil thoughts about her, that she was using her own daughter as a pawn to attack the Ghimireys. A pawn. So, Kranti accused her mother, wagging her finger close to her face as Professor Shrestha wrung the towel dripping with milk at the sink, of using her own daughter as a pawn. Professor Shrestha asked her whether she'd stopped taking Paagalium, and Kranti said she wanted her to take Paagalium so she'd be like a zombie who'd be easier to control. She tilted her head, closed her eyes, and stuck her tongue out. "You want me to be a zombie. Maybe a bambi?" She fluttered her eyelashes and hopped around the kitchen like a deer.

Professor Shrestha made it as though to strike her with the milkwet towel, then, abruptly tossing it in the sink, retreated to her room.

"I am not a dumbie!" Kranti shouted after her.

The idea was suggested to her by Poe, in a whisper in the middle of that night when she couldn't sleep. He called her "Lassie" and crooned to her that his bonnie lay over the ocean. She turned on the light and paced the room. Her hand reached for the bottle of Paagalium. No, no, no, she told herself. Could it be true, what Poe said?

That night when she turned the TV on, there was PM Papa, smiling at her, calling her. Your mother will love it if you and I are friends, won't she? he said.

What about Bhaskar? Kranti asked. Will you protect him if I come?

PM Papa smiled back at her from the TV. Of course. Handsome Bhaskar. I will protect him.

The next day, she asked Bhaskar whether he'd met PM Papa when he visited the Asylum as a minister. Bhaskar said that he was only a teenager then and his memory about the day was fuzzy. Aren't you curious now about meeting him, she asked, and he said that he was afraid his blood would start to boil if PM Papa was in the same room.

Kranti hadn't told him about her little daydream, her talk with Dada about PM Papa and his exhortation about a positive mind, let alone about the message from Poe. You shouldn't be too angry at PM Papa, she said to him now. I want to meet him.

He appeared startled, then asked her if she really wanted to see the Hippo.

She asked him not to call him by that name, and in response, he shouted "Hippo" multiple times.

They were in her room, and since Beggar Street was in an alley, the noise wouldn't carry to the main street, but someone nearby could hear, and Mr. Sapkota was always listening. Watching the fear in her eyes, Bhaskar said, "See? That's precisely my point. Why do you want to meet a man you're afraid of?"

"I was fearful for you, but I'm not afraid of him," Kranti said. "I've done nothing wrong."

This was only partly true. She *was* afraid of him, but not for the reason that she ought to be. Poe had told her that PM Papa wanted to see her, and after she got over her initial disbelief and panic, she had come to believe it.

———

Bhaskar stayed for dinner that night. At one point, he let it out to Professor Shrestha that Kranti wanted to meet PM Papa.

Professor Shrestha, with roti inside her mouth, asked, "Are you out of your mind?"

An argument ensued. Kranti said it was none of her mother's business who she met and didn't meet. She threw the question back at her mother: Had she, Kranti, ever stopped her from meeting who she wanted to meet? Her minions, for example?

Professor Shrestha asked Bhaskar why he was marrying her daughter. What did he see in her?

Bhaskar shook his head and smiled, as if it was all mildly amusing. If he was having doubts about what Kranti was turning into, he wasn't going to show it.

They returned to their eating in silence, then Professor Shrestha wondered why in God's earth would PM Papa want to meet her daughter.

Kranti, waving her curry-dipped fingers in the air, said, "Maybe he'd want to meet me precisely because I'm your daughter." She couldn't help but add, "So-called daughter."

Of course Kranti had no clue how to go about arranging a meeting with PM Papa, why he'd even want to meet someone like Kranti, especially once he learned that she was the daughter of his nemesis. For a moment, her original impulse, which had seemed like a possibility, however remote, now appeared ridiculous, outlandish. But to her mother she said, "I will show you by making it happen."

Professor Shrestha was dismissive of her claims and said that she could keep dreaming that the Hippo would give her an audience.

They finished eating and moved to the living room, where Professor Shrestha sat on her green sofa, and Bhaskar and Kranti on the other sofa, holding hands. Kranti was still sulking.

"If meeting him is what Kranti really wants," Bhaskar said, "I can try to make it happen."

Mother and daughter looked at him. Kranti scoffed. Professor Shrestha asked him why he'd want to facilitate it. Bhaskar said that perhaps once Kranti met him, she'd get over him.

"Get over him?" Kranti laughed and jerked her hand away from his. "He's not some beau I need to get over after a breakup!"

"It is like you're obsessed with him," Bhaskar said. Was there a hint of resentment in his voice?

Kranti denied she was obsessed, accused *them* of being obsessed with PM Papa. "You really have Papa Derangement Syndrome," she said. "Maybe if you leave him alone, everything will turn out to be fine." She said they should stop trying to be the managers of Darkmotherland. Poe had used that phrase: your mother wants to be the manager of Darkmotherland.

Professor Shrestha and Bhaskar exchanged glances, then, drawing a long breath, Professor Shrestha said she needed a drink. Bhaskar, the dutiful future son-in-law that he was, went to the kitchen to pour her a glass of whiskey (the bottle of Jack Daniels used to be in the living room, on a table, but on occasion the Beggars, especially Prakash and Chanchal, helped themselves a bit too easily to it, so now Professor Shrestha kept it on a shelf in the kitchen).

"Thank you, my son," Professor Shrestha said when Bhaskar handed her the glass. She used her other hand to clasp his fingers, and thus they were, the two of them, against Kranti, it seemed. And, as though confirming this alliance, Bhaskar asked Kranti whether she wanted to bet that he'd be able to arrange a meeting with PM Papa. Kranti, her eyes on their intertwined fingers, said yes. Bhaskar said ten thousand rupees would be a nice sum; she said that the paltry sum would mean nothing to the "Middle Son of Ghimirey & Sons."

"What do you propose then?"

"Yes, if you lose," Kranti said, "you'll get me out of this hellhole as quickly as possible."

"There you go," Professor Shrestha said. "It's about me."

"And if I win?" Bhaskar said.

"What do you want?"

"We will live in a flat instead of the Asylum."

"When?" Kranti asked. "On the wedding day?"

"If not, then soon thereafter."

She didn't think Bhaskar could pull it off. PM Papa was known for his sense of self-protection, and to think that he'd give an audience to the daughter of Madam Mao was outlandish. But what if Bhaskar somehow managed to arrange it? She had no intention of honoring that part of the bet. They'd first live in the Asylum anyway; later, she'd simply put off moving. What she was doing, or thinking of doing, wasn't right, but she couldn't imagine leaving the Asylum so soon after the wedding and being a target of criticism by the Ghimireys.

Professor Shrestha protested the bet. "Bhaskar, what nonsense have you gotten her into? If you arrange this meeting, the Hippo will use this as a photo op to tell the world that even Madam Mao's daughter is a Papafan!"

It was strange to hear Professor Shrestha call herself Madam Mao. Bhaskar said that the meeting would be kept a secret. He'd make sure that this condition was agreed to beforehand.

Kranti made convoluted rationalizations for herself. If she was going to enter the Asylum as a Ghimirey buhari, then she needed to know about PM Papa and what kind of a man he was. After all, he was a friend of her future father-in-law. And after all, PM Papa himself had spoken to her, hadn't he? Hadn't he said, "My dear Kranti?" Or was it Dada? Or was it Poe? That was the thing with this rog; she heard voices, and sometimes they were real voices, and sometimes she was not sure. But she was sure of this—the Ghimireys needed to be happy with her. And for that, PM Papa's blessing would be wonderful. And she could try to persuade him not to harm Bhaskar.

17.

In bed, Shambhogya had glasses on her small, fine face and was reading a Jane Austen novel. She was in her nightgown, which made her very fuckable, Aditya thought.

But with Shambhogya, instead of feeling virile like he did with his mistress, he felt emasculated. Shambhogya was prettier, more educated, and a perfect buhari for the Asylum, but she had a mind of her own that now increasingly conflicted with his. She's smart, yes, but she's only a woman, he wanted to tell his father. She can't do the things I do. She can't conduct tough negotiations like I do, yet you value her opinions and dismiss mine. I am your son who has made Ghimirey & Sons even more successful than it was, and my plans for an international hotel chain will make the Ghimireys a worldwide name. Perhaps emboldened by Sir's attention, Shambhogya had started speaking her mind even in the bedroom, which used to be a place for softness, cuddling, and lovemaking. Now, with Shambhogya leading the charge on the Bhaskar-Kranti matter, the air had turned more discordant.

He wondered how she'd react if she knew that he kept a mistress. He had his mistress in a one-bedroom flat with electricity, hot and cold water, and security guards at the gate. What would his wife think of his mistress who wore high heels, even inside the flat? There were costs to her upkeep, and secrecy from his family, but his mistress was so delicious and clearly quite accommodating, and he needed some stress relief, didn't he? He was, after all, the eldest son. Chaitanya was getting better at his business dealings, but he still made stupid mistakes. Last year he'd lost ten crore rupees over a bad negotiation that Aditya had specifically coached him on beforehand. Prithvi Raj expected more out of Aditya, him being the eldest son and all, yet Aditya felt that among the three sons, his father was the least affectionate toward him. While growing up, Aditya was always the first one to get beaten ("you're oldest, you should know better"), and in general Prithvi Raj was more critical of him than he was of the other two. Bhaskar was, and had always been, his favorite. Aditya failed to understand why, given that Bhaskar was the one who was the black sheep of the family.

Aditya couldn't help but shake off the feeling that this marriage would prove bad for Ghimirey & Sons. Under PM Papa, Ghimirey & Sons had received lucrative Rajjya contracts without bidding. Ghimirey & Sons was making a nice sum on inflated prices of some basic commodities. Most importantly, with Raddi Tokari monopolizing Darkmotherland's waste management, Aditya's dreams of becoming an international magnate were within reach. There were things about this project that he couldn't even tell his own family members, not even Sir and that stupid Chaitanya, especially that stupid Chaitanya. This had to be Aditya's secret, but now this proposed alliance with Madam Mao could put all of that in jeopardy. Would General Tso be angry at this new marriage partnership? Would the general then ask that the important work for Rajjya that Raddi Tokari was doing be handled by another company?

"I don't like this wedding proposal one bit," Aditya muttered to himself in bed, not sure that Shambhogya heard him. The whole thing, as he prepared to sleep, was stressing him so much that he was yearning for his mistress now. Oh, to be able to cup those succulent breasts in his hands. To kiss those juicy lips. She expressed no desire other than to be with him totally, with her whole being. Serve him, satisfy him sexually. He talked to her about his work, ranted about obtuse workers, conniving business partners, and ungrateful laborers. He even talked about home—mocked his stupid brothers, complained about his father who didn't realize his genius, and about a mother who was withdrawing more and more. His mistress listened to him, stroked his arm, his face, nodding sympathetically, sometimes seemingly moved to tears by his difficult life. He knew it was an act, but he liked it. Perhaps she thought his complaints were also an act, and that both were involved in pantomime. She was only partially right that his complaints were performative. Yes, Aditya knew that he had it better than most in Darkmotherland, but he deserved better, and he wanted even more, which made him even more deserving. Desire creates success, he told himself. He might have read it somewhere, but now it seemed like it was a powerful quote he'd invented himself. In the future when he became a worldwide mogul, it might turn into the title of a book with him on the cover.

Aditya had his eyes on the Amrikan hotel business. He wanted to create a chain of hotels and resorts, like the Hilton chain. In order to be competitive in the Amrikan market, he had come up with a mountain theme, with a simulacrum of the Himalayan range in the lobby of each hotel. Each hotel would also have a rock-climbing facility. Better Than Sweejerland indeed! That PM Papa was a genius. A model of such a hotel, Hotel Himalayan Happiness, was already up and running near Raddi Tokari Factory. Luckily, the hotel had only been halfway constructed when the Big Two had struck, so the damages had been minimal, and Aditya had sped up the project soon thereafter. About two dozen special cottages—super luxury suites, really—were being constructed behind the hotel, with rich Khadi customers in mind. Aditya had enlisted IGP Chhetri, who had recruited an up-and-coming pimp with the ridiculous name of Mukeshbro, who was going to supply these Khadi customers with honeys.

This Mukeshbro had appeared at the Asylum, unannounced, a few weeks ago. Harkey had come to Aditya and said that a guy named Mukeshbro was here to see him. Who is he? Aditya asked Harkey, the name not registering. Harkey said that he was IGP Chettri's man. Aditya then vaguely remembered IGP Chettri talking about Mukeshbro and didn't like the idea of having direct contact with him. He asked Harkey to let the man inside but keep him in the driveway. When he went down, Aditya saw that the man was wearing a robe, a patchwork of rainbow colors, that came all the way down to his knees. He was twirling a stick, wore a hat taller than his head, and had dark glasses. He came toward Aditya sporting a wide, crazy grin. There was something spastic about his physical movements, like a drug addict.

In a fast-speaking manner, Mukeshbro said that he wanted to pay his respects, since they hadn't met and had only communicated through IGP Chettri.

Aditya said that there was no need for him to come to the house like this.

Mukeshbro said that he just wanted to convey that he was capable of delivering even more "special items" to cater to any unique needs these Khadi customers might have. Then he muttered something under his breath that sounded to Aditya like "Giddy up!"

That's fine, Aditya had said. It's good to know. But please don't come to the house. I'm going to let IGP Chettri handle everything.

Harkey walked Mukeshbro outside, and Aditya observed them chatting for a couple of minutes near the gate. Harkey came inside laughing. "Where did you find this specimen, hajur?" he said to Aditya.

In bed with Shambhogya, Aditya craved his mistress, who understood him. She'd listened to him intently as he'd recounted to her his dream of becoming a mega-billionaire, with a brand that was nationally recognized, just like President Corn Hair. "I'm going to go at it alone, understand? This will be mine, mine only. I will show Sir what I'm capable of. Even though I'm the one who has done the most for Ghimirey & Sons, I'm the one who has been viewed as good-for-nothing. I'll show them all who's who, and what is what." Running her fingers through his hair, his mistress softly consoled him, assured him that given his energy and his cleverness, he was going to outsmart them all. She told him that every night she prayed to Darkmother for his success. She pointed to the Darkmother poster next to her bed. She fed the goddess sweets every day, so there was always laddu or peda stuck to her lips. Darkmother had helped her escape the clutches of a terrible woman from her past, his mistress said.

For his dreams to become real, Aditya had to make sure that he developed an even closer relationship with PM Papa. A chain of Hotel Himalayan Happiness could be at the forefront of the Better Than Sweejerland initiative. Right now, it seemed to Aditya that he was on the margins when it came to PM Papa, given how close the big man was to his father. Aditya had hinted to General Tso a couple of times that he wanted a direct relationship with PM Papa, but General Tso had merely grunted. Now that it was becoming clear that PM Papa was admired even by President Corn Hair, Aditya needed to get into PM Papa's inner circle. Unbelievable, Aditya thought, that the prime minister of a small landlocked country with minimal geopolitical value would get the attention of the Amrikan president, undoubtedly the most powerful man in the world, now made even stronger after he'd emerged unscathed from impeachment and had been reelected with an even greater margin than the previous election. It was said that PM Papa would be visiting Amrika in the near future, at the invitation of President Corn Hair. It was also rumored that President Corn Hair had said that, of all the dictators in the world, PM Papa was his "favorite dictator." Aditya had laughed at that one. Dictator or not, PM Papa was just the right person for Darkmotherland, especially for the Ghimireys, even more especially for Aditya. PM Papa's warm relationship with Amrika would prove to be extremely beneficial to Aditya in his dreams of a chain of worldwide hotels. One tweet of endorsement from President Corn Hair, for example, could make Hotel Himalayan Happiness into a recognized brand name—all over the world.

The vital work that Aditya was doing for General Tso was another important step toward realizing his personal ambitions. It was so top secret that very few people knew about it. It seemed that even PM Papa wasn't aware of all the details; he had handed the reins of this particular mission to General Tso and hadn't yet visited Raddi Tokari to see what was going on. Perhaps him pretending to not be directly involved was a prescient move. This way if the news got out in the international arena about what was happening at Raddi Tokari, he could feign ignorance, could point the finger at General Tso. If Sir knew what Raddi Tokari was also being used for, apart from taking care of waste, he too managed to keep it to himself. The Ghimireys had their hands in so many businesses and operations that it was quite possible that Sir had no idea. Perhaps Aditya ought to tell his father, just so he knew the important work he was doing for the Rajjya, for PM Papa, really. So that he would stop treating Aditya like he was a loser.

To tell the truth, when General Tso had first approached him, Aditya had been hesitant. The whole idea seemed beyond him. He wasn't even sure exactly what was involved, except that General Tso said that Raddi Tokari would be a good place to "take care" of Treasonists. That's all General Tso said, in his stoic manner: "Take care." Aditya had nodded without fully knowing at that time what he meant. "And these are Treasonists, understand?" General Tso said to Aditya. "And if we don't deal with them, here and now, they will take over just like that." He snapped his fingers. "What they really want to do is topple PM Papa, and they won't hesitate to hang him, in public." Aditya thought about that. "Once he's out of the picture, they'll hunt down their sup-porters and friends. That's me. And you. Ghimirey & Sons. Especially your father." The thought of these traitors, who probably never worked in their entire lives, lifting a hand to harm his father angered Aditya, and he thought, what do I care what General Tso does with these men? Aditya had placed one of his trusted men, Sunil Baniya, at Raddi Tokari as the manager, and he'd minimized his own visits to the factory. This way he'd be able to feign innocence if things got messy later, which he knew wouldn't happen as long as PM Papa remained in power. "This is all part of creating a Pure Darkmotherland," General Tso said. "You will play a big role in it. PM Papa will remember."

Everyone will soon know who I am, Aditya would often think after a session of lovemaking with his mistress, his head on her lap, her manicured hands stroking his forehead, her breasts close to his face, nipples nearly touching his lips.

Aroused by the thought of his mistress, Aditya's hand reached into Shambhogya's nightgown as he attempted to stroke her breasts. She struck his hand away, said, "Not in the mood!"

"These days you're never in the mood!"

"What am I?" she said. "Your cattle? For you to prod or poke whenever you want?"

"Cattle? As if you're not my wife."

"Do you think about that when you . . ."

"When what?"

"Never mind."

He watched her closely. Did she know? About his mistress? But how would she? No one in the Asylum knew he owned the apartment. He had bought it with money from an obscure account that neither his father nor his brother paid attention to, and the building's guards were bribed to keep mum.

Did Shambhogya smell his mistress on him? Aditya lifted his armpit to smell himself.

"Did you not shower today?" Shambhogya asked him without looking up from her novel.

Instead of answering her, he asked, "So, we're going to go through with this?"

"And what's the alternative? Why don't you think before you speak?"

Increasingly, this was her tone with him, impudent and disrespectful. He wanted to make her stop. But he knew he couldn't slap her, she simply wasn't that sort of a wife. Now Priyanka—if she was Aditya's wife and if Aditya had slapped her, she would have accepted it. But who would want mousy Priyanka as a wife? She was perfect for Chaitanya, who didn't have a brain of his own.

"We have to handle this very carefully," Shambhogya said, as though explaining things to a child. "If the rally happens before the wedding, then that can anger PM Papa, and he might question why we're tying the family knot with Professor Shrestha."

"That rally isn't happening," Aditya said. "PM Papa is too strong and clever for these idiots."

"Maybe. But even if there's no rally before the wedding, what if Professor Shrestha raises a stink once she sees PM Papa next to the wedding pyre? How embarrassing would that be? The entire wedding could be called off."

"You're weaving fantasies in the air. First, PM Papa has to agree to come, and I doubt that he will."

"He's already agreed."

"What?" Aditya jerked upright. "Who told you?"

"Sir did."

"When?

"Yesterday."

"How come he's telling you all these things but not me?"

"Because you're hot-headed and don't think clearly."

"Yes, yes, I'm the only one with flaws in this house." He was feeling like a petulant child, and he hated it. After a moment, he asked, "I'm assuming PM Papa is well aware whose daughter our pretty boy is marrying?"

"I believe that Sir was able to convince PM Papa that attending the event would be beneficial to him."

Despite feeling left out, Aditya couldn't help but be pleased at this information. PM Papa's attendance would bolster the name of Ghimirey & Sons in the global market. Foreign or multinational companies would want to do business in Darkmotherland, in partnership with Ghimirey & Sons, because there would be fewer bureaucratic hurdles. It would also mean that Aditya would have more leverage regarding the international hotel business he wanted. He could also perhaps find a time to talk to PM Papa about President Corn Hair, tell him how much he admired him. Aditya could say a word or two about his plans for a hotel chain. PM Papa would ask him to visit him at the Lion Palace or the Humble Abode to discuss the matter further.

Although these thoughts and the news of PM Papa's acceptance of the wedding invitation excited him, Aditya was disturbed that his father, instead of informing Aditya, had chosen Shambhogya. Then something occurred to him. "Are you sure PM Papa won't do anything unexpected during the wedding?"

Shambhogya expressed confusion. Aditya explained that PM Papa might take the moment to arrest Madam Mao. Shambhogya laughed derisively, told him he was thinking like a child. Unlike you, PM Papa doesn't think impulsively or short-term, she said.

He's very conscious of his image. Aditya protested that PM Papa might do it for publicity.

Shambhogya tsk-tsked his thinking, then said, "Once the wedding date is finalized, Sir and I are going to deliver the nimto to him personally."

"Sir and you?"

"Yes, Sir wants me to go with him to deliver the invitation because I'm better at explaining how he can use Madam Mao's presence to his advantage."

Aditya curled over to the other side and went to sleep.

—

Bhaskar didn't know how he'd arrange a meeting with PM Papa, and the more he thought about it, the less sure he was that he should even try. He'd been more troubled by Kranti's request than he was willing to admit. It had planted a seed of doubt about Kranti and whether she was a suitable match for him. Yet another part of him had also thought that coming face to face with PM Papa would be good for Kranti, to see what illegitimate power looked like. And it would be good for him, too. He needed to deal with this anger that was building up inside him. Perhaps meeting the Hippo would show him the way. He didn't know what he meant by this. Could it be that fate was propelling them toward something? Would a visit open up access between Bhaskar and PM Papa that could then . . .? He couldn't fully articulate what he was thinking, but the thought was there, in the air above him.

The only person who had the power to arrange such a meeting was his father, but what would he say to Sir, that the woman he wanted to marry, Madam Mao's daughter, wanted to meet PM Papa in person? There was already suspicion in the Asylum that Kranti might be a spy for Professor Shrestha, part of a conspiracy to bring down Ghimirey & Sons.

One day Bhaskar casually asked his father, "What does one have to do to arrange a meeting with PM Papa?"

They were in the living room. Bhaskar was seated next to Prithvi Raj, who was looking over some documents. He paused to observe his middle son and asked him who wanted to meet PM Papa. At first Bhaskar said he was asking in general, but Prithvi Raj didn't believe him, and Bhaskar admitted that it was he who wanted to meet him, then finally he said that it was Kranti also.

Prithvi Raj was pleased. "I wouldn't have thought it," he said.

"Thought what?" It was Aditya, who arrived in the living room followed by Chaitanya, then soon Shambhogya and Priyanka.

"Who is thinking about what?" Shambhogya asked.

"Does anyone even think in this house?" Chaitanya asked thoughtfully.

Prithvi Raj told them.

For a few seconds no one spoke, then Aditya burst into laughter. "Ha! Ha! He! He! The prodigal son returns."

"Really, Bhaskar babu, is this true?" Shambhogya asked, her voice still saccharine sweet.

"We really do," Bhaskar said.

"Why?" Chaitanya asked.

"He's the prime minister of this country, and we're its citizens. What's the problem? Besides, whatever happened to the Guest is God policy?"

Athithi Devo Bhava, PM Papa had said on Motherland TV soon after occupying the Lion Palace. Guest is God. The prime minister's door would literally be open to the public, at all hours, so they could come to him with their grievances, complaints, and commendations. Or just come in for some tea, PM Papa said, with half a smirk, his eyes boring into the audience through the TV skin, and his ruddy face appearing happy. A walk-in system, like the medical clinics in the West, where people could walk in with their ailments and get treated immediately. "I am Darkmotherland's daktar," PM Papa said, "and you are my patients. I am here to heal." Those words had been repeated by Motherland TV for weeks.

It was reported that PM Papa's door was indeed open to the public, but only once a week, for an hour, and even then, they got to see Bill Tamang, the chief secretary. And they were let into his office only after going through multiple security screenings. The ones who got to Gufa, PM Papa's inner sanctum in the Lion Palace, were the better dressed, upper middle-class types, not the laborers and the menial workers with their muddy feet and torn clothes.

Priyanka suggested that it could be Kranti's act of defiance against Madam Mao. Bhaskar said that Kranti wasn't as critical of PM Papa as her mother, which pleased the Ghimireys, so they agreed that arranging such a meeting might be worth a try. They were also thinking—something they couldn't tell Bhaskar—that it might grease the wheels for PM Papa's attendance at the wedding.

"And it'll be good for PM Papa, for the world, to see that Professor Shrestha's daughter is a Papafan," Shambhogya said.

Prithvi Raj finally agreed that the meeting could be beneficial to PM Papa and said that he would try to arrange it. Muwa also came in, and Shambhogya explained to her what was happening.

The Ghimireys had thought that all of them would go to the Lion Palace with the prospective bride and groom, but Bhaskar informed them that Kranti wanted it to be just the two of them. He said that she felt shy and wasn't ready to meet the whole Ghimirey family yet. "She wants to meet you all properly when she comes here as your buhari, not in the Lion Palace," he said.

"It makes perfect sense to me," Muwa said from the doorway. "Why are you all bent on giving that poor girl such a hard time, anyway? If she doesn't feel comfortable going with you all, why not respect her wishes? Why does everything need to turn into a battle of the Mahabharata here?"

"Look who the cat dragged in," Aditya murmured.

Prithvi Raj shot him a glance, then explained soothingly to his wife that he could also see Kranti's point. "As it is, a meeting with PM Papa is a big deal. We don't want her to be overwhelmed." He patted the empty space on his sofa, and Muwa sat next to him. The others hadn't seen the two in this gesture of intimacy for ages.

Finally, Shambhogya broke the silence. "I guess we can all be happy at least Kranti thinks highly of PM Papa, unlike her mother."

"It appears she has some respect for PM Papa, a recognition of what he's trying to do," Prithvi Raj said. "I'm beginning to think that she might fit in here at the Asylum."

—

At Beggar Street, when Bhaskar told her that a meeting with PM Papa was in the process of being arranged, Kranti asked him how, and he said impishly, "I have my sources."

Kranti felt a flush of anticipation. She thought of Dada, how he too would have been excited about such a meeting. They hadn't yet told Professor Shrestha, who was with the Beggars in the living room, drinking afternoon tea. Bhaskar suggested they wait until after the Beggars left to inform Professor Shrestha. But Kranti said she wanted the Beggars to know too. Bhaskar didn't agree, but Kranti dragged him next door, then informed Professor Shrestha and the Beggars.

"Unbelievable," Professor Shrestha said.

Murti asked why she'd want to meet the Hippo.

"Why not?" Kranti said, taking advantage of the Darkmotherlandite's rice-and-lentils answer to the *why* question.

"He's everything we're fighting against, Kranti," Prakash said. "And you're making it seem like it's an honor for you."

"Tremendous honor," Kranti said, thinking that she'd never forgive Prakash for his comment about not being qualified to lick her mother's shoes. "And if you were invited, you'd go too."

Prakash appeared offended. He looked up at Kranti from his lotus position on the floor and said, "No way in hell. I'd rather die than share a drop of water with such a despot."

"Okay, you can go die—what do I care? I'll sip masala tea with PM Papa."

⌣

Things became strained at Beggar Street. Bhaskar was viewed with suspicion by the Beggars, especially Prakash, who opined to Professor Shrestha that it was imperative, given the action that Bhaskar was taking, that they listen to the Gang of Four. Darkmotherland was in danger, Prakash said.

The next time she was alone with Bhaskar, Professor Shrestha asked him whether he felt that he had to fulfill every wish that Kranti expressed.

Ashamed, Bhaskar told her that he would cancel the meeting with PM Papa, if that's what Professor Shrestha wanted.

At first, Professor Shrestha said that he ought to cancel, but as they continued to discuss the issue, it became clear to her that doing so would infuriate Kranti, and also incense the Ghimireys. They might back out of the wedding, she told Bhaskar. I just wish that you hadn't started any of it, she said. "Oof!" Professor Shrestha held her head in her hands.

He knelt down beside her green sofa and gently rubbed his thumb against her palm. He couldn't bear to see her so upset. There is still time to change things, he said to her. But Professor Shrestha concluded that they couldn't go back, that she didn't want to live the rest of her life hated by her daughter. She had tears in her eyes, and Bhaskar wiped them away gently and soothed her with calming words. "I can't afford to lose her, Bhaskar," she said.

"You will not lose her. Why dwell on such things?"

Professor Shrestha spoke about how so many times in the past she'd thought that she'd lose her daughter. In the immediate aftermath of her husband's death, for example, she was convinced that Kranti would harm herself, perhaps even kill herself. "This rog of hers," she said, "I have thought many times that the rog itself would kill her." She didn't look at Bhaskar when she said rog. This was the first time that she had explicitly raised the topic of Kranti's mental illness with Bhaskar, and she waited for his reaction. What could

Bhaskar say? He nodded. "This rog is so unpredictable," Professor Shrestha said. "One moment she is fine, then the next moment she's off somewhere." Bhaskar said that he was aware of Kranti's issues and would be gentle with her; he would take care of her. When Professor Shrestha said that he might not fully realize what he was getting into with Kranti, he said that he knew and that he wanted to be with Kranti no matter what.

"That's good," Professor Shrestha said. "I'm so afraid that she will cut off all ties with me once she goes to your house. But I will not be able to live if she stops talking to me completely. You won't let that happen, will you, Bhaskar?"

"I won't let that happen," Bhaskar said. He had never seen Professor Shrestha so vulnerable. He had always associated her with a defiant energy, and now she was like a broken-down doll. Part of her weariness, he knew, was due to PM Papa.

Bhaskar consoled her, saying it'd be good to get to know the enemy.

They sat holding hands, Professor Shrestha on the sofa with her head bowed, Bhaskar kneeling, murmuring to her like a loving son comforting his heartbroken mother.

18.

Bhaskar had been in the Lion Palace before, he told Kranti, for a function that his father had dragged him and his two brothers to when he was a teenager. Aditya and Chaitanya had wanted to go; Bhaskar hadn't. It was a function that a previous prime minister had presided over.

"Tighter security now than the last time I was here," Bhaskar said to Kranti as they finally entered the main gate after an extensive security screening. There were Loyal Army Dais all over the gate, watching people, sometimes even stopping pedestrians who were walking by to ask for their papers.

"And of course, now we have monkeys," Bhaskar whispered. The Lion Palace employed monkeys to pat down people after they went through the security doors. A bunch of them hung around the gate in ill-fitting army uniforms, their caps shading their eyes. Hanu Mans, they were called, after the Monkeygod's native name. After the visitors passed through the security doors and the Loyal Army Dais used their screening rods, the Hanu Mans, who waited expectantly on the sidelines, descended upon "the victims," as Bhaskar whispered to Kranti. Four or five Hanu Mans at once, leaping on the visitor's shoulder, jumping up on the head (the women tried hard not to scream), scouring through the hair, their hands—four Hanu Mans with eight hands and forty fingers—prodding, poking, grabbing, fondling, caressing, scratching, pinching. The Hanu Mans also looked into people's ears, noses, and, on occasion, were also known to put their fingers into the visitor's rectum. "Hanu Manhandling," Bhaskar said.

Since Bhaskar and Kranti were PM Papa's special guests, they were subjected to minimal Hanu Manhandling. The Hanu Mans seemed especially eager to get their hands on Kranti. However, the Loyal Army Dais barked orders at them in monkey language, which sounded like *chee chee na gar bad mash ban dar.* Bhaskar muttered to Kranti that the Hanu Mans might be trying to emulate the monkeys from that novel, the one where the monkeys attack a single mother in the Lord of the Animals temple as she meets her married lover, the math teacher.

I too battled monkeys at the Lord of the Animals temple after Dada died, Kranti thought. Could these be the same monkeys, now promoted to Hanu Mans?

"It is some kind of a paranoid thing," Bhaskar whispered to Kranti once they were inside the gate and turned back to observe the Hanu Mans, who were now molesting other people who needed to be screened. "Ramping up the security means that the Hippo can finally claim he's that important."

Kranti shushed him, terrified that someone would hear him call PM Papa the Hippo. And in the Lion Palace! "But it's not paranoia," she whispered back. "There are many people who wish him harm."

"Sure," Bhaskar said, the look in his eyes confirming that he was one of those people. Kranti wondered if indeed Bhaskar had agreed to set up this meeting because he had something nefarious in mind. Ever since she'd told him that she wanted to meet PM Papa and he'd agreed, he'd had a strange look on his face. In Beggar Street, she'd find Bhaskar and Professor Shrestha engaged in murmurs and whispers, and she'd asked herself if he'd begun to let Professor Shrestha know his doubts about spending a lifetime with Kranti. She also wondered if it was something else. Her mother and Bhaskar could be plotting something about Papa Don't Preach. Or perhaps another thing that directly led to . . . PM Papa? Kranti shuddered inwardly—she didn't want to think about it.

As they were escorted to the main office by a guard, who walked a few steps before them, Bhaskar whispered to Kranti, "But the more he ratchets up the security around him, the more he can tell everyone how vulnerable he is. And that when he's vulnerable, Darkmother-landites are vulnerable."

She watched his face to see if she could decipher anything more than what his words conveyed. "You and her aren't up to something, are you?" she whispered.

The military escort turned back and said, "No talking, please, and walk faster."

Kranti moved away from Bhaskar and walked a few steps ahead. She was overthinking Bhaskar's words. What he said about PM Papa's security was true (it had also been amply shown on Motherland TV). PM Papa did travel with a phalanx of security guards and cars. His Hummer limo with its tinted windows was bulletproof. He always had his main bodyguard, Laxman, who was from General Tso's village and whom General Tso himself had trained and mentored, as well as two or three other bodyguards in dark suits, carrying machine guns, hovering around him. Sometimes there were sniffing dogs, some of whom also wore dark glasses. It was also rumored that on occasion, to fool his enemies, PM Papa employed a double—the rotund man walking around with bodyguards was not PM Papa, but a look-alike.

—

They waited in the main office, a large Victorian-styled room, with ornate furniture made of mahogany wood, rich and dark tones all around, from the floor panel to the curtains. They were surrounded by big portrait paintings of important past kings, but the centerpiece was an oversized painting of Jungey, the cruel autocrat from one hundred and fifty years ago. Jungey rose to power after he engineered a large-scale massacre that killed top military generals and government officials, including the prime minister. The portrait showed Jungey, with his scruffy beard, in full regalia, staring somewhere in the distance. "Maybe he's contemplating another massacre?" Bhaskar whispered to Kranti.

PM Papa emerged from the Gufa and came toward them. Kranti noticed that he was slightly bow-legged. He was wearing daura suruwal and dhakatopi—he always wore the national dress to demonstrate his patriotism. More and more men in Darkmotherland were wearing daura suruwal and dhakatopi these days because of PM Papa.

PM Papa was shorter than Kranti had imagined him to be. He barely reached Bhaskar's shoulders. He was, in the truest sense of the word, roly-poly. Roly-poly PM Papa, Kranti thought, with his ruddy cheeks and his smiling face. Kranti nearly said, "You're so roly-poly, PM Papa!" but she controlled herself. And yes, he was ugly. That jaw—she'd never seen a jaw that looked so much like a misshapen rock.

"Ah, my children," PM Papa said, as though indeed his offspring had arrived for the bring-your-children-to-work day. "Welcome to the Lion Palace," he said. "Or the Lion's Den, if you will." He laughed, a merry kind of laugh, thought Kranti, befitting his roly-poly figure. Her eyes flitted toward the Jungey painting, as though she were comparing the two dictators. PM Papa noticed, for he said, "Impressive, isn't it? This painting is the largest painting of Jungey in Darkmotherland. It was lying neglected in the National Museum until I resurrected it. Isn't it beautiful?" He stood in front of it, Jungey's stature towering over his short figure, and said, "Look at that face. What command. The eyes. They knew things, didn't they? You know these eyes speak to me, when I'm alone? I swear!" PM Papa splayed his palms, as though he knew that sounded crazy.

And when Kranti looked at the eyes, it did seem that they were conveying a message, although what, she couldn't tell.

"The autocrats weren't that bad, you know," PM Papa said, "certainly not worse than the politicians who've leeched this country for so long. They codified our laws, they established the modern bureaucracy, they kept Darkmotherland independent from the Angrezi rule. They were patriots."

Kranti could see that Bhaskar was about to provide counter-arguments, so she squeezed his elbow and signaled him with her eyes. Her heart was beating rapidly, making her wonder if she should have come to see PM Papa by herself.

"Well," PM Papa said, smiling, "I can tell that you didn't come here to listen to me talk about Jungey. Please, let's go inside." He led them into the Gufa.

Rumors about the Gufa ran the gamut. The Gufa had an electric chair where PM Papa executed his most archenemies. The Gufa was a hideaway for sexual extravaganza and bacchanalia. The Gufa was where PM Papa meditated, sometimes for hours on end, about the state of the country.

It was in fact a fairly simple room, Kranti observed, average in size, the walls adorned with some paintings of past monarchs and warriors, and a pink sofa where they now sat.

"Langotia yaar, you may call us, your father and I, tied with a sarong in childhood," PM Papa said to Bhaskar, "although our friendship doesn't go that far back. But I've never been one to care about a little exaggeration." He smiled. "It has helped my career."

He seemed to pick off some lint, although it was a leather couch, so there was no lint.

"You are handsome," PM Papa said to Bhaskar. He spoke slowly, deliberately, as if he was talking himself through a policy proposal for Darkmotherland. "Much more handsome than your two brothers. Your father too was handsome. In his early years." He laughed, as though he'd uttered a joke, his belly heaving.

"And you, of course," PM Papa said to Kranti. "You are Madam Mao's daughter. So pretty," he said. "Just like your mother. You probably don't know this, but your mother and I go way back too. Not necessarily in a good way, mind you, but we do go back. And I knew your Dada."

Kranti sucked in a breath. She knew that PM Papa had hounded Professor Shrestha before Kranti was born, but he also knew Dada? This was new information.

"I used to eat at the hotel where he was a chef," PM Papa said when he noticed Kranti's puzzled face. "The very hotel where he— well, I shouldn't. Let it be."

"Hotel Thunderbolt & Diamond?"

"Yes, that very one. I was a regular customer. I liked to hold meetings there with diplomats and government officials, and your father used to come to chat with me during his breaks. Your father made the best khasiko masu in the entire Valley. The best, I tell you. In the hotel for the khaireys it was advertised as mutton curry, but it was the purest Darkmotherlandite khasiko masu, with gravy that made you feel like you'd ended up in heaven." PM Papa briefly closed his eyes, as though he were tasting Dada's khasiko masu at that very moment.

Kranti thought, half panicked and half gleeful—khasiko masu! Khasiko masu! That was Dada's specialty. How does PM Papa know this?

PM Papa opened his eyes and looked at Kranti. He had small, beady eyes, kind of bloodshot, although he was not known as a drinker. "Your father liked to tell jokes, didn't he? Every time he came to check on me at the table he had a joke ready. Then we'd both roll in laughter, and I had to tell him to stop, stop. I tried to return the favor by telling him a joke, you know. I'd think of a joke while he was in the kitchen, and I'd rehearse it over and over in my mind, practicing the correct phrasing, the right pause. I'd wait for him to come out. And when he did, wiping his hands on a towel on his shoulder, the towel that had Hotel Thunderbolt & Diamond's logo on it, you know, the one with a thunderbolt encased inside a diamond, he'd ask how the food was. 'The food was great,' I'd tell him, even though I'd barely tasted it because I'd been so focused on the joke.

"'Did you hear the one about the rabbit and the lion?' he'd ask, wiping his fingers one by one on the towel. He'd proceed to tell me the joke, and it would be so funny that I'd double up in laughter. I might even have rolled on the floor, I don't remember."

Kranti found herself smiling. The wringing of the fingers on the towel was a typical Dada gesture. He often did that in the kitchen of Beggar Street when he cooked. And the towel with the logo—Dada's "good cook" towel.

"He was a special man," PM Papa said. "And he talked a lot about you, his daughter, and what a special young lady you were. In fact, he'd worn out his coworkers by always talking about his little girl, his favorite person in the world."

Kranti bit her lip and felt tears come to her eyes.

"I was there when he, you know," PM Papa said. Something stuck in his throat, he coughed and snorted. "You know that day." His shoulders sagged. "He was— I was— Boom!" He made a small, explosive gesture with his fingers. The sound was coming from the fingers themselves, along with a small cloud of smoke. Kranti widened her eyes to look, but the smoke had vanished. But why was she getting spellbound by what appeared to be a small act of illusion? If PM Papa was in Hotel Thunderbolt & Diamond when Dada died, she ought to have seen him when she and Professor Shrestha had rushed to the hotel. She tried to remember if there had been a stocky, hippo-like man in the hotel lobby. But her mind at that time had been frozen in panic; how would she have remembered?

"I was there when you and your mother got there," PM Papa said. He was watching her closely, as though her thoughts were scrolling across her forehead. "I saw you two come in, but I had an appointment for a haircut that I simply couldn't miss."

"Appointment for a haircut?" Bhaskar said incredulously.

"Stunning, isn't it? A dear joking friend of mine had just blown himself up in a closet and I went to get my hair trimmed. But I had no choice. You see these tufts of hair sprouting from behind my ears? They grow so fast, like little bunny rabbits, and if I don't get them trimmed every few days, they get into my ears and get all itchy and scratchy and maddening and I want to go and shoot someone with my gun." PM Papa breathed. "Do you want to see the gun I use to shoot people? Have you heard about the Russian writer Chekhov, who said if you have a gun in your story, it needs to go off by the time the curtain closes?"

"So, if you bring it out, you will have to shoot it by the time we leave?" Kranti asked.

"Will the curtain have closed by then?" PM Papa asked churlishly.

"Well, this curtain," Kranti said, drawing a square in the air with her index finger. "Our little scene here."

"No, I'm sure Chekhov meant by the time this story ends. This whole saga." He waved his arm near his head, as though to include the entire world, including the history of evolution, time, and space. "Do you want to see the gun?"

"Yes, PM Papa," Bhaskar said in a flat voice. "We would love to see the gun that you could then use on us."

For two seconds PM Papa stared at Bhaskar, as though trying to determine if he was being mocked—Kranti's heart skipped a beat— then he said, "We are in for a treat," before calling out, "Rozy!"

From a door in the corner of the room, which Kranti had thought was a closet until now, came a dark-skinned beauty wearing a rainbow-colored frock and T-shirt that said, "Bite me." The woman, with hair touching her shoulders, was quite heavily made up, with plenty of kajal around her eyes to make her lashes look long and seductive. Her lips were extra red, almost like blood. One look at her lips and it made sense why she was named Rozy.

"Rozy maiya," PM Papa said in a sweet voice. "Can you bring the gun please?"

"Which gun?" the beautiful woman asked, but the voice that emerged from her wasn't a woman's. It was a man's. Kranti and Bhaskar exchanged glances.

"Which gun, he asks," PM Papa said, laughing. Rozy was a few feet away from him, and he went toward him as though to embrace him. But Rozy shied away, saying something with his eyes, something to the effect that there was company. Kranti got the impression that this type of interaction might be frequent between the two, with PM Papa wanting to become amorous with Rozy, and Rozy gently but urgently pointing to the company that was present in the room. "Which gun, he asks," PM Papa said. "He knows perfectly well which gun I'm talking about. The Ancient Kalo Bandook, please."

"In the case or without the case?"

"Take it out of the case, please."

"Bullets in or bullets out?"

"Bullets in, please. I don't know whom I may need to shoot today." He became thoughtful. "Or is it who? Who or whom, I can never figure that one out."

Kranti glanced at Bhaskar, who looked slightly alarmed, as though he was thinking, as was Kranti, that, should PM Papa decide to heed Chekhov, he'd shoot Kranti rather than Bhaskar.

"Wipe it with a cloth if it's dusty?" Rozy asked.

"Yes, wipe."

"Should I—"

"Just bring it, please, maiya."

Rozy stood slowly, and sashaying his hips—it was a performance, Kranti knew—went back inside. PM Papa watched those hips longingly. "He's my most trusted advisor," PM Papa said. "He's my valet, but he's more like an advisor. He's in the process of transitioning. Or, shall we say, he has been transitioning for a while now. Mind you, if you see him outside, you won't recognize him. He'll appear to you like a regular bloke walking down the street wearing his Make Darkmotherland Great Again cap. Only here, in the Gufa, does he change. I love him, his presence in the Gufa. He's like a ray of sunshine in these dark, degenerate times."

Rozy returned, holding a gun that looked like it had been excavated from the ruins of an ancient civilization. It was half an arm's length, with a long snout. And it was black, black as a lump of coal dipped in ink.

"It's scary," Kranti said. "And beautiful."

PM Papa took the gun from Rozy and pointed it at Kranti and Bhaskar. "If I wanted to, I could shoot the two of you right now and no one would know about it. Well, except Rozy here, of course. Now, you wouldn't tell anyone now, Rozy, would you?"

"Why would I tell?" Rozy said slowly. "I don't want to be declared a Treasonist."

"Wouldn't that be something?" PM Papa said. "Madam Mao's daughter and future jwain felled down by PM Papa. Then disappeared." PM Papa launched into an imaginary conversation: "*What happened to Bhaskar and Kranti?* I don't know. *But they came to see you!* I don't know. *And then they disappeared.* I don't know. *There's blood on the Gufa carpet.* Goat blood. Nothing to see here."

PM Papa laughed. Rozy rolled his eyes. PM Papa pointed the Ancient Kalo Bandook at Kranti and asked, "What did you want to see me about?"

Her voice was small. "I only wanted to meet you, PM Papa."

"You like what I'm doing for Darkmotherland?"

She wanted to say that she felt he'd spoken to her, that Dada wanted her to look at PM Papa positively, but she ended up saying, "Darkmotherland needs a lot of help." She avoided Bhaskar's gaze, worried what his face would convey.

There was a knock on the door. PM Papa looked at Rozy, who went back inside his closet door. "Yes?" PM Papa said.

A man, his neck as long as a giraffe's, entered, then hesitated when he saw Kranti and Bhaskar. "Is Rozy not here, Papa?" he asked.

"He's around somewhere," PM Papa said. "What is it?"

"I need your signature here, Papa," the man said. Kranti recognized him from television—Home Minister Dharma Adhikari.

PM Papa scanned the document, then signed it. "Well, that seals their fate, doesn't it?"

The man smiled. "It sure does, Papa."

PM Papa pointed to the man and said, "This here is Dharma Adhikari. If you were looking for the most loyal dog in town, this man is it."

Kranti observed the Dharma Adhikari's face, but he didn't even flinch at the word "dog." In fact, he seemed pleased at what PM Papa had just said. Kranti recalled Dharma Adhikari boasting on television that he was Papa's most significant loyalist because he now held the position that PM Papa used to occupy some years before he swooped into power to save the country.

PM Papa dismissed Dharma Adhikari with a gesture of his hand. Once he left, PM Papa called Rozy, and Rozy appeared, this time in men's clothes, his long hair hidden under a Make Darkmotherland Great Again cap, much of the makeup on his face washed off. "How beautiful you are, my Rozy," PM Papa said. He turned to Bhaskar and Kranti. "Isn't Rozy amazing?"

Before Bhaskar and Kranti could respond, Rozy said, "Is that why you are hiding me in that smelly closet?"

"My maiya," PM Papa said, grazing Rozy's chin with his stubby finger, "You know I'm converting that room back there into something nice, just for you and me." He explained to Bhaskar and Kranti that he was in the process of building a chamber within the Gufa, "a Gufa within the Gufa, if you may. Or even better, InnerGufa. Rozy and I are going to make a baby in there." He watched the faces of his guests for their reaction. Both Bhaskar and Kranti tried to present a stoic face. "Wouldn't it be wonderful?" PM Papa said. Then, he appeared to nod to himself. "Yes, I can already see that baby. It will be as beautiful as my Rozy." When he didn't get any reaction from Bhaskar and Kranti, he said, "Anyway, that's in the works." Then he addressed Kranti, "You seem like a good girl. What are we going to do about your mother?"

It took a moment for Kranti to mentally change gears from the baby talk. "Sometimes my mother is just bark, no bite."

"Sometimes even barking dogs need to be shot, just to shut their yaps." He was looking at her steadily, as though testing her, as though what she said next would determine her fate.

Kranti froze. She had to be careful here. She thought hard, but nothing came to mind she could say that seemed reasonable. Finally, after what seemed like minutes, she said, "She's stubborn, Papa."

"The choice is hers," PM Papa said. "If she stops, then her life will be much easier." PM Papa shook his head slowly.

"Papa," Bhaskar said, and it was hard to tell whether there was a hint of sarcasm in his voice. "Madam is not going to stop just because you tell her to stop."

PM Papa swiveled the gun toward Bhaskar, and his finger circled the trigger. "No?" He was a few feet away, but it appeared as though if he stretched his arm, he could have touched Bhaskar's tummy. He inched closer toward Bhaskar, and then he sang, "Papa Don't Preach," in a soft murmur, so that the words weren't clear at first but became gradually more clear.

Kranti glanced at Rozy, who appeared more alert than before. His dull eyes were now awake, perhaps even amused. Fearful? Was he asking Kranti to do something? To intervene? "You think I didn't know, Bhaskar?" PM Papa asked. "Are you also part of this? I hear you're turning into her favorite acolyte. True?"

"Why are you using that gun as a toy?" Rozy swiftly moved toward PM Papa, who'd swiveled to point the gun toward him. "Give it to me," Rozy said, putting his hand on the barrel of the Ancient Kalo Bandook. Rozy pulled the gun toward himself, poking his belly and pressing it into his navel. "PM Papa," he said in a seductive voice. "Are you going to give the gun to me?"

"You will be the death of me," PM Papa said. His eyes were bright.

The gun was now pressed deep, with half the barrel disappearing into the folds of Rozy's belly button.

"PM Papa," Rozy said. "What'll it take for you to hand the gun to me?"

PM Papa gazed into Rozy's eyes, then whispered into his ear.

Rozy smiled. "That's it? Of course, I'll let you, but later." He slowly pulled the gun away from PM Papa. There was a minor tug of war between the two, their bodies close, until finally Rozy managed to wrench it completely away from PM Papa, who smiled, almost proudly, at Bhaskar and Kranti as if to say: What can you do—that's my Rozy.

And he did say something close to it, once Rozy left the room. "If there's anyone in Darkmotherland who can take PM Papa down, it's that beautiful creature right there. One of these days my beautiful Rozy will come to me in the dark of the night and blow my brains out, with that very Ancient Kalo Bandook, and I won't say a word. Well, how could I, hoina? I won't have a brain."

19.

Kranti bought a DVD of *Darkmother's Favorite Son* and watched it repeatedly.

"What is wrong with her?" Professor Shrestha asked. The Beggars asked Bhaskar whether PM Papa did something to Kranti for her to behave like this? Perhaps some magic? Tunamuna?

"He's not a magician," Bhaskar said. "Just a simple dictator." He said in a high-pitched voice: "Don't mind me. I'm just a simple, innocent dictator."

The Beggars, except Prakash, laughed—how could anyone not laugh with Bhaskar?—but the couple's visit had made the Beggars more fearful of PM Papa, as though now it had been established that his powers were truly extraordinary. Murti joked that PM Papa had thrown a magical lasso and pulled Bhaskar and Kranti into the Lion Palace, but it was not really a joke. The Beggars now went to the windows often to peek through the curtains. Small noises alarmed them, and they uttered a lot of *hunhs*, *hahns*, and *kanhs* in startled voices. Their eyes frequently flitted toward Kranti's door. Prakash asked Bhaskar what she was doing in there. Bhaskar said that she was watching *Darkmother's Favorite Son*. Prakash asked why she was watching it on DVD when one could watch it on one of the Rajjya-controlled TV channels all the time. Bhaskar said that on a DVD she could pause and rewind and watch certain scenes again, as Kranti liked to do. Chanchal asked him what her favorite scenes were, and he said that she often watched the scenes featuring PM Papa's mother.

Bhaskar said all of this in a patient voice. He himself did not understand what was happening with Kranti. She had put up a large, framed photo of PM Papa on the wall, adjacent to her father's. This particular photo of PM Papa wasn't flattering. His cheeks bulged, and his smile, with teeth showing, was forced. But the image also projected authority, a type of aggressive power. It was freely distributed by the Rajjya and now they were seen in many households, across the Valley but also in Bhurey Paradise.

Professor Shrestha asked Bhaskar what was wrong with Kranti. Was she serious about the Hippo's photo on her wall, right next to her father?

"It might just be her rog, Madam."

"Do you know how humiliating this is for me, Bhaskar? Me, someone who's given her life to the Sangharsh, but whose daughter, like an uneducated country bumpkin, is praying to the photo of this Hippo? I sent her to one of the best schools in Darkmotherland!"

Bhaskar didn't know what to say. He had been worried about it too. What did it mean in terms of their marriage? But he didn't want to admit it to Professor Shrestha, who would then try to pressure him into not marrying Kranti, saying that she wasn't worthy of him.

As it was, he was already facing enormous pressure at the Asylum, a pressure that he had been bearing all on his own. He had no one to confide in. He couldn't tell Kranti because he didn't want her to worry. But the situation at the Asylum hadn't been easy for him.

—

"Such a good girl, such a good girl," PM Papa said when he phoned.

Prithvi Raj hadn't expected the call, so when he saw the unknown number ringing on his mobile as he emerged from his shower wrapped in a towel, he nearly didn't pick it up. He thought it was a scam, or someone asking for donations—the Ghimireys got several such calls a week. But something told him he should answer this one, and there was PM Papa on the other line.

"Yes, hajur," Prithvi Raj said, water still dripping from his hair. He didn't want to let on that he had yet to meet his future daughter-in-law, although if PM Papa had asked, he'd have told him the truth.

"So intelligent, so demure. Pity that she's Madam Mao's daughter, no, Prithvi Raj?"

"Yes, indeed, Papa." After the Big Two, Prithvi Raj, too, had started addressing him as Papa, instead of Giri, which is the term he'd used when PM Papa was a minister. But now the power dynamics had shifted. "Papa" rolled off his tongue easily, and PM Papa also appeared pleased that even his long-time friend showed him deference now.

"She's a unique girl."

"Certainly."

"She's very, very, very unique."

"Yes, indeed."

"They do say you can't use 'very' with unique."

"Ha! Ha!" Prithvi Raj sat on his bed. He desperately wanted to change into his clothes, as he felt somewhat vulnerable half-naked talking to the most powerful man in Darkmotherland.

"But I can say whatever I want, can't I, Prithvi Raj? Tomorrow I could issue a mandate that 'unique' may not be used without 'very,' let the Angreziwallahs be damned."

Prithvi Raj imagined PM Papa's ruddy face, glowing. "Heh! True, why not?"

"I don't think you can go wrong with her, Prithvi Raj."

"You think so?" Prithvi Raj was caught between a type of ecstasy— PM Papa endorsing his daughter-in-law—and trepidation; a part of him still felt uneasy with this marital alliance. "Everyone in the Asylum likes her quite a bit," he said, lying. "But we are worried about her mother."

"What about her? What about Madam Mao?"

Somehow it didn't seem right calling her by that name with PM Papa, so Prithvi Raj said, "The girl's mother . . ."

"Say it, Prithvi Raj."

"Say what, PM Papa?"

"Say Madam Mao."

Prithvi Raj chuckled. "You like to joke."

"I'm not joking. If you can call your home the Asylum, you can call her Madam Mao."

Prithvi Raj gave an embarrassing laugh. "Madam Mao."

"Say we're worried about Madam Mao."

"We're worried about Madam Mao."

"See?" PM Papa said in the manner of someone who's proved a big point. "Half of the battle is in naming."

"Of course. I know that I could learn a thing or two from you." Prithvi Raj meant it.

"The wedding might be a good way to bring Madam Mao into the fold."

"True, although I'm surprised that Professor Shrestha, I mean Madam Mao, hasn't been taken care of already." Prithvi Raj wondered what Professor Shrestha, his soon-to-be samdhini, would think of this conversation he was having with PM Papa, deciding her fate.

There was a brief silence at PM Papa's end. Prithvi Raj transferred the mobile from one hand to another. He wondered if he made a faux pas. Would PM Papa feel offended by his statement? Would he think that Prithvi Raj was criticizing him?

"People underestimate me."

"Not me," Prithvi Raj said. "I knew what you could do even before Papakoo, when you were a home minister, that's why I've been your most loyal supporter." This was only partially true. Prithvi Raj had had his doubts when PM Papa was a minister—all that lying and exaggerating, thinking that it'd come to bite him on the ass one day—but as a minister PM Papa had also been a boon to Ghimirey & Sons, so he'd not complained.

There was another silence at the other end, long enough that Prithvi Raj thought that PM Papa had hung up. But PM Papa returned in a calm, measured tone, "You have no idea, Prithvi Raj, the kinds of things I have planned for this great nation of ours. I have been mulling over this for a long, long time, such a long time that it feels that I have been the prime minister since I was born. Ever since I was a child, when I saw that this country was going to hell in a handbasket. Corruption. Nepotism. Erosion of our values. Humiliation of our culture. All the people who have harmed or want to harm our nation need to be destroyed, made impotent."

"I agree, PM Papa." Prithvi Raj's chest swelled with pride.

"We need a purge in this country."

"True, true," Prithvi Raj said. "Pure Darkmotherland!"

"What about that son of yours?"

Prithvi Raj's heart stopped. He knew who PM Papa was referring to, but he hoped it was not Bhaskar. "Which son, PM Papa?" he asked.

"Your middle one. The Handsomest of Them All. Yes, he behaved when he came to see me—why wouldn't he, though, since even the most ardent of my enemies behaves well in my presence. But what's the deal with him?"

Prithvi Raj didn't want to say anything that would implicate Bhaskar. He knew where PM Papa was going with this. Bhaskar had come up in previous conversations with PM Papa, and PM Papa had expressed concern and unhappiness over Bhaskar going over to Beggar Street. Just youthful foolhardiness, Prithvi Raj had said then. He'll come around.

"I've been talking to him, Papa," Prithvi Raj said. "Trying to make the sun shine on his scalp."

"Black sheep."

"Hajur?"

"He's the black sheep of the family. Ba, ba, black sheep. Of the have-you-any-wool variety." PM Papa made sheep sounds. "Baaa! Baaa!"

"He's still a child, Papa."

PM Papa said that Bhaskar looked like an adult to him. PM Papa said that he knew about the rally, then, he hummed a tune that, incredibly, Prithvi Raj recognized. Chaitanya had been singing it. "Papa Don't Preach." Aditya had scolded him, called the singer a slut. Prithvi Raj didn't even know who this Madonna was—had never heard of her.

PM Papa stopped humming and asked, "Prithvi Raj, have you heard of the Gang of Four?"

"I have, Papa."

"Tell me who they are."

"The Chiniya group. Led by Mao's wife? Right now, her name escapes me."

"There are Treasonists here, in Darkmotherland, who call themselves the Gang of Four."

"Led by dead Mao's wife?" Prithvi Raj said, then realized how stupid he sounded. He recalled, in embarrassment, reading something about Darkmotherlandite Treasonists who'd taken up that name.

PM Papa said flatly, "They want to kill me, do you understand?"

"Tsk," Prithvi Raj said. "Such people need to be caught and immediately hung, Papa."

"Right? Right?"

"Of course! The audacity of these goons!"

"Is Bhaskar involved with them, Prithvi Raj?"

Prithvi Raj couldn't speak. He thought the big man was joking, but the silence at the other end lingered, so he blurted out, "No, no, no, Papa. That's not possible."

"Let's hope you're right. I have my doubts." PM Papa asked him whether Bhaskar was aware of the trauma that Darkmotherland had gone through.

Prithvi Raj stammered and said that Bhaskar was idealistic and misguided, but he would never do anything to harm PM Papa. In the end, he was a Ghimirey and he loved PM Papa.

PM Papa said that he hoped Kranti would set him straight. "She might be able to steer him toward the right path."

Prithvi Raj said he was confident she would. He could see his own mind slowly shifting toward a more favorable view of Kranti.

"She is the goose with the golden egg," PM Papa said.

"Hajur?"

"Do I have to explain everything to you, Prithvi Raj?"

PM Papa was chastising him like he was an uncomprehending schoolboy—Prithvi Raj, the magnate. But fear had gripped Prithvi Raj, and it was very important that he allay PM Papa's fears about Bhaskar. If Bhaskar was indeed involved with this so-called Gang of Four, who knew what PM Papa could do? But the Ghimirey family owed a lot to him. If it weren't for him, Ghimirey & Sons and the Asylum would have been destroyed after the Big Two, razed to the ground by the looters and the Bhurey mobs.

Prithvi Raj didn't tell the others about the full extent of his conversation with PM Papa. He didn't relay PM Papa's question about Bhaskar and the Gang of Four, didn't tell them about the golden goose comment. He only said that PM Papa had taken a liking to Kranti and thought she'd be right for the family.

—

Aditya was lying in bed alone—Shambhogya was out—when Priyanka knocked on the door that was slightly ajar.

"Yes? Does Sir want me?" he asked, sitting up. He wondered if Sir had changed his mind about going with Shambhogya to deliver the wedding invitation to PM Papa; he wondered if Sir would say, "I've decided that that's no task for a woman," as he'd been saying all these years on many business matters.

"No, I needed to talk to you."

"Oh?"

"About the wedding."

Aditya didn't like Priyanka sidling up to him like this. He didn't recall a moment in the past when Priyanka had come to him by herself to discuss a family matter. Sometimes she'd come to inform him that the food was ready, or that Sir wanted to see him, but that had been the extent of it. This private approach with her older brother-in-law was inappropriate, and he knew that others in the Asylum would also think that Priyanka was impudent and too forward.

He didn't ask her to come in. Shambhogya wouldn't approve of this. But perhaps just to spite his wife, Aditya should ask her in. He decided to wait a moment, just to see what his sister-in-law had to say.

Priyanka searched his face, as though gauging his thoughts. "Are you happy with what's going on?"

He watched her. She was audacious. She had ambitions of acquiring as much power as Shambhogya, perhaps even more. Aditya wanted to laugh in her face, yet he also admired her courage in coming to him like this. She knew that he could easily tell Shambhogya that her mousy sister-in-law had approached him alone on a family matter, and Shambhogya would raise a stink. So, this woman was a risk-taker. She wanted to be dominant in the Ghimirey household, just like he wanted dominance in the business world. He had to give her that. "Well," he said guardedly. "My happiness is not of question here." He paused. "That's what Shambhogya says."

"Why can't your happiness be of question?" She took a step in. Now she was technically inside his room. Muwa, or a nokerchaker, could pass by and see her—she was indeed ballsy. He pictured balls where her genitals would be. She probably sported those balls in that relationship with Chaitanya. "Your happiness should be paramount, Aditya-da," she said. "After all, you are the most hardworking person in this family."

"Am I?" He understood her strategy, yet he also couldn't help but be stirred by the praise. He needed to hear that because he never heard that from anyone in the Asylum, especially Prithvi Raj and Shambhogya.

"Of course you are." She chuckled. "I probably shouldn't say this, but you work harder than Chaitanya. Don't tell him I said that, though."

"Chaitanya means well, but he's not capable of following through."

"Exactly!"

"Come inside."

"Should I?" She looked over her shoulder.

"I won't tell anyone."

She stepped fully in, and he asked her to shut the door. She hesitated. "Go on and shut it," he said. "We don't want unwanted ears."

She did.

Now we both are ballsy, he thought. He was ballsy because Shambhogya could come in any minute. Yes, now both were ballsy, yet he was the one with the real balls, yes, real, hairy balls, and he couldn't let this mousy woman forget that.

She continued to stand, arms crossed at her chest. Yes, ballsy, but God, what a mousy-looking woman, so unattractive compared to Shambhogya, who, despite her commandeering ways, was one of the prettiest women around. Okay, Aditya, don't get distracted, he reminded himself. Focus.

"What are we going to do?" Priyanka said.

"What can we do? The wedding is going to happen."

"You're okay with Madam Mao as your samdhi?"

"Like I said, it doesn't matter."

"It could be a conspiracy."

He said nothing. The thought that it might be a conspiracy had occurred to him. Several times, in fact, since Bhaskar had mentioned marrying this girl. Perhaps even before, when he'd learned that Bhaskar's garlfren was Madam Mao's daughter, although at that time Aditya had mostly thought, as had the rest of the Ghimireys, that the daughter was a floozy who'd eventually disappear from Bhaskar's life. But now this was real.

"There are many people who'd love to get a piece of this pie." She waved her index finger in a circle, indicating the Asylum.

"But Madam Mao, really? She's devoted her whole life to fighting this." He also waved his index finger in a circle.

Priyanka didn't respond to his mimicry. "Before, there was no opportunity, now there's a real one."

He asked her whether she knew how Bhaskar and Kranti met. She said she had no doubts that Kranti knew Bhaskar was a son of Ghimirey & Sons when they met at Tri-Moon College.

Aditya asked Priyanka to sit down on the bed, and, after demurring for a bit, she did, toward the edge.

"Even if Madam Mao's after our money," he said, "there's nothing we can do. Now it appears that even PM Papa approves of her." He felt helpless. He didn't like the tone of his voice. He was downtrodden—these feelings were reserved for people without power. But he was

Aditya Ghimirey, Brahmin Extraordinaire of Ghimirey & Sons. He believed in caste superiority. When he was with his Brahmin friends, he usually held forth on the superiority of the Brahmin caste. He didn't do so during meetings and social gatherings with businessmen of other castes and races; he wasn't foolish. But when he was with his own kind, he often let loose, especially after a couple of drinks. "We are superior where it matters the most. Here." He tapped his head. "That's why we're so successful, from politics to scholarship to business. All of our great leaders have been Brahmins. Even the Maoist insurgents who tried to ruin this country, they were Brahmins. I despise them, but only they were successful in overthrowing the king. It's like we Brahmins can't lose even if we try." Whenever he said it, he was reminded of PM Papa, whose hagiography depicted him as a poor young man who had lifted himself up by his bootstraps. PM Papa was also a Brahmin. Earlier in his political career, he had denounced Brahminism (what a ridiculous term, Aditya thought, as though all the ills of the world came from Brahmins, as though being a Brahmin was a disease!) and adopted the caste-neutral Kumar. Aditya knew it was political opportunism, and he forgave PM Papa for it. Besides, PM Papa had demonstrated his Brahmin intelligence by becoming PM Papa, hadn't he?

The helplessness Aditya felt was not Brahmin-like either. A man of his intelligence, his business acumen should not have to feel that things were not under his control. Now, he recognized that much of the sense of weakness he was experiencing had to do with the looming alliance with Madam Mao. Part of his mind had brightened at the possibility of PM Papa in the Asylum for the wedding—how the event would be broadcast on Motherland TV, and likely picked up by the international media.

Priyanka was talking about how Aditya could try to persuade Shambhogya to not go forward with the wedding. After all, Shambhogya was his wife. Wasn't it her duty to listen to her husband?

Shambhogya won't listen to me, Aditya thought. And if she learned that he'd been talking about her to Priyanka, he'd not hear the end of it. Although Shambhogya spent much time with Priyanka (some people thought they were sisters, that the brothers had married sisters, which annoyed Shambhogya to no end), she also mocked Priyanka in the privacy of her bedroom. "Isn't she so musa-like?" Shambhogya said, then jutted out her upper teeth, raised her chin and sniffed the air vigorously. "That mouse and your brother are perfectly suited for each other." Shambhogya mimicked Chaitanya's nasally voice, which gave his speech a slightly whiny tenor: "But Aditya-da, the broker is saying that he can't get the other party to sign until he gets his commission. But Aditya-da, I only promised him fifteen percent. Now he's asking for twenty, Aditya-da. What should I do, Aditya-da? I don't know what to do, Aditya-da. Please, Aditya-da." Shambhogya inhaled deeply and let it all out in a long, wail of "Aditya-daaaaaaaa" that filled the room. Aditya shushed her, then burst out laughing. "What's wrong, Aditya-daaaaaa?" Shambhogya wailed.

Priyanka said that *she* listened to Chaitanya. She was a devout woman. She believed in obeying her husband.

She said it with such earnestness that Aditya wondered if she had some screw loose inside her. But it was true that she was pious. She had a small shrine in her own room, and she prayed there every morning, and invoked God whenever she could. Her favorite was the Elephant God. She had persuaded Prithvi Raj to install a human-size Elephant God statue right by the main door to the Asylum, one that raised his hand in blessing to all those who entered. At the foot of the statue was the Elephant God's animal, a small mouse, nose upturned, sniffing, and every time Priyanka passed by it, she patted its head lovingly.

Aditya told Priyanka that all Shambhogya wanted to do was maintain peace in the Asylum, keep the family intact. Even as he said it, he knew he didn't care if the family remained intact or not. If Bhaskar wanted to leave the Asylum and shack up with Madam Mao's daughter, or Madam Mao for that matter, good riddance! That would enable Aditya to make the case to his father that Bhaskar shouldn't receive a single paisa of the family wealth, although Aditya had a feeling that Sir would never agree to cutting off his brother's inheritance. Aditya was slightly disturbed that he wouldn't want his younger brother to get a share of the family wealth; he didn't know where such feelings came from. When they were younger, Bhaskar used to follow him around, saying "Aditya-da, Aditya-da" in his totey boli. Come to think of it, Bhaskar was his favorite brother until their teenage years, when Bhaskar started reading Trotsky, Marx, and whatnot—corrupting his brain. Bhaskar was no longer the brother of their childhood, so Aditya shouldn't feel bad about harboring these thoughts about the pain-in-the-ass he became. Let him marry that filth's daughter, let him live somewhere else. People will talk for a while, but the Ghimirey family will go on without him, and become even more prosperous than with him.

The next day, Priyanka again knocked on Aditya's door and said she'd learned something about Kranti that was going to blow everyone's mind.

20.

Aditya and Priyanka kept the news to themselves for a day or two because Aditya wanted to verify that the information was true before they revealed it to the other Ghimireys. Even then, Aditya wasn't sure that the news, if indeed true, ought to be divulged. "If we tell the others now, wouldn't it create unnecessary furor?" he asked Priyanka. "And would Bhaskar renege?"

"I don't know what you mean."

They were conversing behind a ficus tree in the courtyard atrium. "Would it be strategically smarter to reveal it close to the wedding date?" Aditya whispered. "That would then allow us to say that the stakes are too high for this to go forward now?" He had used this strategy before, but only in business, where time had been manipulated—to either back out of a lousy deal or push through a beneficial one.

"That's brilliant!"

Aditya was moved. Here was a woman, despite her small chin and twitchy nose, who actually appreciated his deep intelligence. Perhaps there was more to her than he previously thought. A faint odor of radish emanated from her mouth at this close range.

"We could even consider releasing it the day of the wedding," Aditya said.

Priyanka clasped her hand over her small mouth. "That would be quite something, wouldn't it? During the ceremony, Madam Mao will be ready to donate the bride, and suddenly you will say . . . what?"

In a thunderous, Amrish Puri-like voice Aditya spoke, "Halt this wedding!"

"Shh!" Priyanka said, finger over her lips but unable to contain herself. "They'll all ask: 'But why? Oh, why?'"

"At that time," Aditya said, "You will point at the bride and say what?"

"'The girl is loony tunes.'"

"Loony tunes?"

"You don't like it?"

"I don't know. Will the others get it?"

"'A cuckoo bird'? Is that better?"

"How about: 'This girl, her lights are on, but no one's home.'"

"'A balloon with no air?'"

They were laughing and slapping their thighs, and it was naive of them to think that no one would notice. True, the Asylum was a cavernous house, but it also had about a dozen nokerchakers who were constantly moving back and forth, up and down, carrying food, laundry, messages; they were cleaning and sweeping and dusting; they were fixing and repairing and constructing.

The next day, Shambhogya asked Aditya, "So, what was all that giggling with Priyanka about?"

"Giggling?"

"I heard that you two were quite chummy yesterday behind the shrubs in the atrium."

Aditya gaped at her, as though he couldn't believe this ludicrousness.

"I don't like you becoming bosomy with her."

"Bosomy?" Aditya asked, cupping his breasts. "With that flat-chested mouse?"

"Disgusting," Shambhogya said. "You better be careful—she's a rat."

"I thought she was a mouse."

"It's not funny, Aditya. What were you doing with her?"

"Oh, Shambhogya, it's nothing. You're just getting your panties in a bunch."

"Panties? Bunch? What kind of insane talk is that? How crude you are!"

"Okay, okay, sorry. But she was telling a joke about Madam Mao that was actually funny. Can you believe it? That mouse telling a funny joke?"

"What was the joke?" Shambhogya's eyes looked like rays of sun piercing through a magnifying glass.

"Oh, what was it? Let me remember."

"There was no joke."

"There was."

"Then what was it?"

"Wait," he said, putting his hand on his chin. "Ah, yes, it's a poem."

"I'm listening."

"Here it is." He said:

There once was a professor named Madam Mao.
She loved songs, so she told her pupils, "Sing! Gao! Gao!"
Her students got confused. "We know not how to gao.
Please, teach us how."
The Madam got pissed, chopped off their heads and said,
"How now brown cow—
can you sing NOW?"

"That's funny?" Shambhogya asked.

"It's not? How now brown cow? You know, rhymes with Mao."

"It sounds like it's written by a schoolboy. Our Shaditya can write better than that."

"Okay, how about this?" Aditya said:

There once was a professor named Madam Mao.
She loved food, so she told her pupils,
"Bring food. Food lau!"
Her pupils obliged, brought her
a whole roasted cow.
Madam Mao exclaimed, "I'm God-fearing so I don't eat beef,
but my, this is WOW!"

"Chee! Chee!" Shambhogya said. "Making jokes about eating a cow. You're a Hindu, it's a sin."

"It's a joke, not a sin." Aditya said. "And a double joke. Madam Mao is an avowed atheist."

"Yes, just let the Fundys hear that kind of joke from your mouth.

Don't encourage lewd jokes from Priyanka, okay? Madam Mao is going to be our samdhi soon, and we should all control our tongues."

"Oh, my fruit fly," he said. He embraced her and kissed her. "You are so pretty."

She softened. "You think so?"

"Yes, indeed so." He kissed her lips, gently. His trophy wife. He'd noticed how other men admired her at parties. She spoke Angrezi better than he did, with an accent that sounded vaguely Belaiti, although she'd never been to Belait. She had a vocabulary in Angrezi larger than his; she used words like "supercilious" and "embankment" and "rudimentary," words that made him want to consult a dictionary (but who had time?). She had a perfect appearance—just enough makeup, and if she was wearing a sari, it seemed to adjust to her body perfectly, fit her curves with no room for criticism. It was the same when she wore a kurta suruwal. Her clothes acquired a glittering, glistening quality when she wore them. In social situations she always had a faint smile on her lips—like the *Mona Lisa*—that made her face pleasant to look at. She was a good mother. She regularly used Skype with Shaditya, asking him about his studies and his life in the Bharati boarding school.

Shambhogya allowed him to make love to her that night, and he did so greedily, hungrily, thrusting at her hard, calling her "my fruit fly" (where did that nickname come from, he wondered). She also responded eagerly. Perhaps the stress of the wedding was taking a toll on her, although it was hard to tell with Shambhogya. As he neared orgasm, his mistress appeared in his mind—her creamy thighs, her red, luscious lips, her caressing fingers—and he quickly came inside his wife.

—

Muwa peeked through Bhaskar's door just as he was about to turn off the light and go to sleep. She startled him with her soft, ghostly voice when she called out his name. It was a shock to see her at his door so late at night, given how much she shied away from the family nowadays.

"Come in, Muwa," he said.

She came in and sat on his bed like she was a stranger in the house.

"Is everything all right, Muwa?"

She nodded.

He waited for her to speak.

Finally, she said, "There's so much clamor in this house, ever since you announced your marriage."

What a lovely soul, he thought of his mother. She had never been happy in this family, from the moment she'd come to the Valley after she and his father had gotten married. She had never been interested in Ghimirey & Sons. All this insatiable greed for amassing wealth made her feel empty inside. So, she was like him, in a way, except she had thrown up her hands in despair and retreated whereas he wanted to fight it. Also, there was an aura of unhappiness about her that he didn't have: she rarely smiled these days, and there were permanent worry lines on her forehead, and her eyes sagged. In contrast, he was still optimistic about the future—beginning his life with Kranti, his friendship with Professor Shrestha, and his induction as a Beggar, the role he was going to play in the Sangharsh. There had been brief moments when he'd wondered if it was a good idea to tie the matrimonial knot right after he took an oath as a Beggar. He was not naive. The Rajjya had proven how far it would go to suppress dissent. Something could happen to him, and happen quickly, rendering Kranti a widow. But Bhaskar was also an eternal optimist, and his entire being refused to bow down to this possibility. If he was meant to die, he was meant to die.

He put his hand on hers. "Everything will be okay."

"Why don't you two simply go live someplace else?"

He smiled. "You don't want me here in the Asylum?"

She stroked his hand. "You know there's nothing that would make me happier than to have you and Kranti live here. But these people, they won't let you live in peace."

"We'll be fine, Muwa. Kranti is a strong girl. You'll like her."

She stood, as though her liking Kranti wasn't important. "Have you heard the latest?"

"What is it this time?"

Standing, she told him what she'd heard, that Kranti was mentally unstable, that she'd not been right in the head since her father's death. He told her that he didn't care if she spent her entire life in a mental hospital.

Muwa went to the window and looked out. Without turning to her son, she asked whether it was true what they said about Kranti.

"Half this country is mentally unstable, Muwa, especially after the Big Two. Why target her?"

"They're saying that she has been ill a long time, before the Big Two, since her childhood." She said they had expressed surprise that Kranti was able to hold on to a job, given her mental illness.

Bhaskar shook his head at all the machinations that went behind his back. Kranti's work at Bauko Bank had also come up recently. The Ghimireys were of the opinion that it would be beneath the dignity of a Ghimirey buhari to work a low-paying job in a bank, as if she were a commoner. But Bhaskar had put his foot down, and they had backed off. Bhaskar hadn't told any of this to Kranti, of course, so she didn't know that her job had already become an issue at the Asylum.

He went to Muwa and put his hands on her shoulders, smelled her hair. He'd missed his mother, knew that she was going to retreat more and more into her cocoon in the days to come. "Muwa, are you okay?" he asked.

"This family," she said. "I don't think I can take it anymore."

⁓

The next evening over dinner Bhaskar quietly told them that if they were contemplating trying to dissuade Kranti somehow, he was going to cancel altogether. "We will have a court wedding," he said, "and you'll never see us again."

There were sounds of dismay, and protests that they weren't planning on doing anything to Kranti; they were only concerned that she might be mentally sick.

"Who did you hear it from?" Bhaskar pointed his finger at Priyanka and Shambhogya. "You've been spying on Kranti?"

Priyanka said that she had discovered a man—an uncle of a friend of a relative—who had been a regular at Beggar Street when Kranti was younger, a man named Baral who said that yes indeed, Madam Mao's only daughter had mental problems. She hears voices, Baral had said. She imagines people who are not there. She imagines people talking to her. She hallucinates, thinks people are conspiring against her. I haven't been to Beggar Street for years, Baral said to Priyanka, but I have heard, from other Beggars, that Kranti's mental illness has continued into her adult years. Baral had said that he was willing to come to the Asylum to testify, that it'd be an honor for him to tell the Ghimirey family the truth about this girl.

"Okay, that's it!" Bhaskar said. "The wedding's off!"

There was commotion. "The wedding's off?" Shambhogya said. "You're not going to marry her?"

"That's a really smart decision, bhai," Aditya said.

Both Chaitanya and Priyanka made noises of happiness. It was as if they'd all turned into children.

Bhaskar sighed. "I'm going to marry her, just not here. We'll marry in court. I'll live in Beggar Street until we find a flat."

Shambhogya sat down and looked out of the window.

Aditya shook his finger aggressively at his brother. "You mean you'd rather be a ghar-jwain than live with us?"

"Yes, I'd rather be a live-in son-in-law than bring Kranti here." With that, Bhaskar stood and headed toward the door.

But before Bhaskar could leave the room, Muwa slammed the table, causing everyone to jump. "Enough!" she cried, her face distorted in anger. "All of you who are calling that girl crazy, you're driving me crazy with your selfishness and your stupidity. If my son has to leave the house because of your shenanigans, then what makes you think that I'd want to live among you pathetic creatures?"

It was an impressive display of rage. No one had seen Muwa this angry before. Her nostrils were flared, her hair was as disheveled as if she'd just battled a tiger; her eyes were fiery.

Prithvi Raj tried to calm her, saying, "We're just discussing, just talking." Muwa replied that she'd had enough. She was ready to walk out of the house, there and then.

The nokerchakers were in the kitchen next door, eavesdropping. Thulo Maya had her shawl covering her mouth, a gesture she often used when she was listening intently. Harkey was standing next to a wall, alert, but his face noncommittal as usual. The others—Sarla, Mokshya, Shyam Bahadur—were pretending to busy themselves with various tasks.

"I am serious," Muwa said. "If the wedding is not happening in this godforsaken house, then you will not see me when you wake up tomorrow morning."

Shambhogya said, her voice nearly breaking, "Muwa, we don't mean for you to be so upset."

"You be quiet!" Muwa said. She had never previously told Shambhogya to shut up. "I put much of this at your feet, you with your what-about-this and what-about-that." She turned to Priyanka. "And you, if only you . . ."

"Okay, okay," Prithvi Raj said. "We'll do what you want." He instructed the others. "Okay, forget about everything now. This discussion is over, okay? We are moving ahead with the wedding. Bhaskar, no more talk of going to live somewhere else. I won't have it. You are family, and now, for better or worse, Kanti is also family."

"Kranti," Bhaskar said.

"Yes, yes, Kranti," Prithvi Raj said, throwing up his hands.

Shambhogya was waiting for Kranti on the second-floor open portico of Tato Chiso. She hugged Kranti a bit too tightly and said, "I've heard so much about you from Bhaskar babu, and I recognized you immediately from the photos I've seen."

Kranti wiped the sweat on her upper lip. She had nearly turned back a number of times on her way here.

Some customers at the other table were watching, perhaps admiring Shambhogya, her graceful movements, her white teeth, her charming speech peppered with effortless Angrezi.

Once they sat down, Shambhogya held Kranti's hand across the table in a gesture of intimacy. "How are you? How's your health?" Kranti thought Bhaskar had told her about her recent bout of flu, so she said she was fine. "I'm glad to hear it," Shambhogya said. As a Ghimirey buhari, Shambhogya wasn't expected to wander into the Tourist District, she informed Kranti, but she badly wanted to meet her, so she snuck out.

The owner of the restaurant came by in his boutique suit and fawned over Shambhogya, asking about Prithvi Raj and Muwa, ordering the waiters to bring this and that. He didn't seem to recognize Kranti from the confrontation over the khateykids; if he did, he didn't let on. When the drinks and the snacks came, Shambhogya didn't touch a single thing, saying she had stomach issues. When the owner kept on pressuring her to eat or drink something, she finally said that she was fasting. The owner appeared crestfallen.

After the owner left, Kranti asked her, "Do you fast regularly?"

"Every Monday, for the Pothead God."

"But today is Tuesday."

"Well, I said that just to shut him up."

"Then you should have this chocolate mocha," Kranti said.

Shambhogya said she normally didn't like consuming outside food and drinks.

"So you don't go out to coffee shops and restaurants?" Kranti asked. She couldn't help adding, "Bhaskar and I love trying out new places."

There was a pause. Kranti couldn't tell whether she detected disapproval from across the table.

"With all this scare of bombs now," Shambhogya said, "what's the point of going out?"

"True," Kranti said. Motherland TV had been blaring nonstop about being on the lookout for "suspicious-looking packages," like those that had been found at the city center recently. A twelve-year-old boy had spotted a bag in a pile of trash at the Lord of the Heavens chowk, with what looked like a cell phone peeking out. He rushed to the bag and excitedly opened it. Inside was a cell phone, but it was attached to two hand-sized bombs with wires running around them. The boy picked up the device, uncertain as to what it was, but a Poolis Uncle saw it and immediately called his superiors on the phone. Luckily, the bomb was defused in time. The Poolis Uncles said that the homemade bomb was filled with large nails that could have caused lethal damage within a hundred meters.

"Well, we go to restaurants in luxury hotels," Shambhogya finally said, "but only rarely, for special events where business wives are expected to attend." She looked around. "I'm sure you understand. There are too many Bhureys about these days. And who knows? Those bombs? Bhureys maybe?"

Since the incident with the Lord of the Heavens bomb, the name of Gang of Four had been mentioned. At Bauko Bank, too, she'd heard whispers about the Gang of Four. It was said that the Gang of Four had recruited some young people into its cell, especially young women, who, it was said, wouldn't come under Rajjya's suspicion because they were young women. In the bank's bathroom, Kranti came upon two of her coworkers who were saying that there was talk across the Valley that the Gang of Four was serious about toppling PM Papa's Rajjya. They shushed each other when they saw Kranti coming. At that moment, the thought had run through her mind that they were associating the Gang of Four with her because of her mother.

Kranti was pretty sure the Bhureys couldn't be behind planting those bombs, but she now wondered what Shambhogya would think of Kabiraj. No, no, bad thought for this moment.

"Ghimirey & Sons is a big name," Shambhogya said. "People will jump at the first opportunity to sully us. That's why I don't like to expose myself too often in public."

Kranti nodded, as though it was perfectly understandable.

"But you'll learn of the ways of the Asylum soon enough," Shambhogya said. She then told Kranti how lucky she was to be marrying into the Ghimirey family. After a pause she said, "And of course, we are also very lucky to have you." She squeezed Kranti's hands and looked into her eyes, probing, inquiring.

"I hope I don't disappoint you," Kranti said, partly pleased, partly anxious.

"Let's hope not," Shambhogya said, then laughed as though she were making a joke. "There will be some learning, but I'll teach you. You and I could be like sisters."

"You all must be concerned that I am Professor Shrestha's daughter. But I can assure you, and Bhaskar must have told you also, my mother and I, we are very different."

Shambhogya smiled a somewhat sad smile, Kranti thought. "You're Bhaskar babu's choice, and he's made his choice. We should all try to be happy with that choice."

A WEDDING AND BEHEADINGS

21.

The wedding was grand, as one would expect from the Ghimireys, although not as grand as the wedding thirteen years ago of Aditya and Shambhogya. That was the grandest of the grand, with decorated elephants transporting the guests, a free feast for the poor on the street outside the premises of the Asylum, a guest list that included the who's who of Darkmotherland, including the Droopy Mouthed King and his wife who briefly appeared, even though a majority of his kin had been gunned down by his nephew not long before.

The wedding of Bhaskar and Kranti had no elephants, but the poor were still fed. Food was distributed on the street outside, and, upon Bhaskar's insistence, a group of khateykids was allowed inside for about an hour to watch the ceremony and to eat.

There was a great deal of buzz around town about this tying of the knot. A Romeo and Juliet type of situation, it was said. Or, Layla and Majnu, although in contrast to the classic love story, it seemed here the girl was the "touched one" and not the boy. But the biggest buzz was about the showdown that was going to take place between Professor Shrestha and PM Papa. What was going to happen?

People visualized it almost like a quickdraw gunfight from the Westerns:

Professor Shrestha and PM Papa spot each other across the lawn of the Asylum and they freeze. The guests' voices drop to a murmur. The waitstaff, who have been serving fried prawns, mini crab sandwiches, and other delicacies, stop serving. The band that has been playing Bollywood music in a jazz style also softens, only the drummer is maintaining a barely heard marching beat. A man in daura suruwal appears with a flute, standing between the two duelists, playing the music from *The Good, the Bad and the Ugly*, which signals the official start of the duel. Professor Shrestha and PM Papa slowly move toward each other, she in her resplendent mother-of-the-bride sari, and he in his traditional daura suruwal, a dhakatopi resting on his head, his paunch leading the way. Both have guns strapped to their waists, their hands hovering over their holsters. They stop about ten feet from each other. The only sound is the flute, the soft howling *ooo–ooo–ooooh.*

Then what?

Who wins?

But nothing remotely like this happened. Throughout the evening, Professor Shrestha was the most reserved that she had ever been. It was as if she'd trained herself in the last few weeks to exercise maximum restraint. She greeted the Ghimireys with stiff namastes, not cracking a smile, but not showing a visible sign of displeasure either. "You have to admire her for this," Bhaskar whispered to Kranti at one point.

PM Papa was supposed to arrive in the middle of the bride donation ceremony but he appeared toward the end with his entourage, including Rozy. The entire street had been quickly cordoned off for his arrival, with people directed toward the Tourist District via side lanes and alleys. Starting early morning, plainclothes Poolis Uncles had scoured the area for suspicious-looking packages and activities. Half an hour before PM Papa came, Loyal Army Dais had arrived with machine guns and tanks. It was like a war zone.

As the Ghimireys went to receive him at the gate, Professor Shrestha continued with the bride donation ceremony, following the priest's instructions, throwing rice into the wedding pyre. It was as though she was determined not to acknowledge the presence of the Hippo. The Ghimireys brought PM Papa close to the wedding pyre but not so close that it would disrupt the ceremony (or Professor Shrestha herself would burst into flames!). PM Papa watched the ceremony for a couple of minutes, not looking at Professor Shrestha, his bloodshot eyes only on the bride and the groom. When they looked at him, he nodded as though to say, see, I even made your wedding happen.

The noise of the revving Army trucks outside made people wonder whether PM Papa would take this opportunity to arrest Madam Mao. Wouldn't that be something? Madam Mao arrested at the wedding of her own daughter and led away and publicly executed! That Western could be titled *A Wedding and an Execution.*

But of course, nothing remotely titillating happened. After about five minutes of watching, PM Papa said to Prithvi Raj, "I have a late-night meeting to go to."

Prithvi Raj knew this was a lie but still had to pretend it was true. "So soon, Papa?" he asked.

"The work of Darkmotherland is 24/7."

Prithvi Raj hurried over to the wedding pyre. "I need them for two seconds," he said to the priest, who said, yes of course. Normally, the priest wouldn't allow a ceremony like this to be disturbed, for it could easily bring bad luck, but this was Ghimirey & Sons, and that was PM Papa. Prithvi Raj asked the same permission from Professor Shrestha, who granted it with a wave of her hand.

The bride and the groom were brought over to PM Papa, who blessed them, then said, "I knew this moment was going to happen that day when you two came to see me at the Lion Palace."

Bhaskar's eyes strayed toward Professor Shrestha, who was stoically staring ahead. Her hands were clasped in front of her, possibly holding some grains of rice she was about to throw into the pyre. Was Bhaskar checking in with her to see if she wanted him to do something? It would be really easy for Bhaskar to do something right now, wouldn't it? PM Papa's bodyguard, Laxman, was a few feet away. Bhaskar wouldn't even have to use a gun. He could have a knife tucked somewhere in his waist and he could take it out and plunge it into PM Papa's throat.

A Wedding and an Assassination.

But PM Papa was already on the move. He waved a hand and said, "I think Rozy wants to stay. Rozy, why don't you stay?"

—

Rozy stayed behind—the man-Rozy—wearing a daura suruwal, hair in a bun beneath a dhakatopi, slight makeup on his face, so slight that had Kranti and Bhaskar not seen the woman-Rozy in the Lion Palace they probably wouldn't have known that he wore makeup. Still, Rozy attracted attention at the wedding. There were glances, unspoken speculations about PM Papa's sexual appetites, unexpressed wonder at the bizarre fact that a leader of a nation could crack down on gays and thirdgenders and yet . . . ? There was some awe in these glances (how does a thing like him get so close to PM Papa?), but most of the looks were of contempt. Something is wrong with you—they were conveying. Something is wrong with all of them.

"Rozy, hoina?" Kranti had asked when Rozy came to sit beside them at the wedding pyre, the smoke billowing up between them. Even in the brightness of the wedding lights and the shining saris and suits worn by the guests, Kranti's world had remained dark. She had dithered back and forth between anticipating the future with Bhaskar, in the Ghimirey household, and the sinking feeling that it was a mistake, that starting tomorrow the Ghimireys would hate her. She felt like she was controlling herself so she would not pass out. In all this she'd felt relief that Kabiraj hadn't come, despite getting an invitation. Rozy's face seemed like that of an angel who'd come to soothe her.

"So happy you came," Kranti whispered, squeezing Rozy's hand.

"Wouldn't have missed it for the world, saathi," Rozy said.

Kranti noted the eyes lined with kohl. Rozy was prettier than the prettiest woman in the vicinity—Shambhogya, Kranti's now sister-in-law. Kranti couldn't help marveling at this thought—she was saying that this man was prettier than a woman who was widely regarded as one of the prettiest women in the Valley.

"How are you, Rozy? My love is like a red, red rose," Bhaskar said, "that's newly sprung in June."

"Is that for me or for your new bride here, Bhaskar-ji? Rozy asked.

"Why are you calling me Bhaskar-ji?" Bhaskar said. "I hate this ji business in our country. As if the entire world will come crashing down if we don't address each other as ji."

"Ho-ji," Rozy said with a smile.

"Then I will call you mu-ji," Bhaskar said.

"Bhaskar!" Kranti lovingly chided him for uttering what was the equivalent of motherfucker, right in front of the priest, who, in the midst of his incantations, gave Bhaskar a sidelong glance.

"Where do you live, Rozy?" Kranti asked.

"Butterfly Street. Near the Old Buspark."

"Ah, near the Bhurey Paradise, where the real people live," Bhaskar said.

"Yes, indeed," Rozy said. "Can I invite the two of you to come to my flat for a meal? It's a small, humble abode, but—"

"But not as humble as the real Humble Abode?" Bhaskar said.

Rozy was smiling at him. "PM Papa jindabad," he said softly, mockingly.

The priest heard him, and in the middle of his Sanskrit incantations he managed to insert a "PM Papa jindabad!" before returning to his hymns.

On the day of their wedding, they chatted with this stranger as though he had always been their close friend. Rozy stayed with them for another hour or so, then he left, repeating his meal invitation.

—

"Are you surprised that we actually got married?" Bhaskar said that night after all the clamor had died down and the newlyweds had retreated to their bedroom, which was decorated with balloons, festoons, and rose petals in anticipation of a night of lovemaking by the bride and the groom. "This decoration—tacky like in the movies, isn't it?" Bhaskar said, hitting a balloon away from his face and chasing it around the room, slapping it repeatedly as it twirled.

"I am surprised," Kranti said. "I didn't think it would even happen."

Bhaskar grabbed a balloon between his hands and asked, "Why did we get married again? Remind me?"

"Too late now, buddy," she said. She was lying in bed, among the rose petals, feeling inadequate even among these flowers. The petals were probably the idea of Shambhogya, who probably got it from a Bharati movie, thought Kranti, one that featured a buxom heroine lying in bed with her hair spread out like a halo surrounded by flowers, and a young and handsome hero looking at her adoringly. But Kranti's Bhaskar was hitting a balloon and asking her why they got married.

She felt anxious even though she had succeeded in becoming a bride of the Ghimirey household. Dozens of eligible beauties in the Valley could have been in her position, might even have been better qualified to be in her position, but here she was.

Yet, there was no sense of having arrived. Deep down she knew that her trials had just begun and things were going to get difficult for her in this household. This moment in this honeymoon suite was merely an illusion. The floor was going to drop beneath her, soon, and she'd be plummeted below into a violent, bloody pulp. She could feel it, this crash, in the pit of her stomach. Yet in her head she was amidst balloons and festoons. Bhaskar was correct in wondering whether she'd be happy here, and although she told herself she would, now she was seized with doubt.

They didn't like her, the Ghimireys. She could see it in their eyes, the way they looked at her, the way they'd watched her during the wedding, the glances that were exchanged between them. Except perhaps Muwa, who mostly looked sad—sad not because of Kranti but because she'd always been sad in that house (Bhaskar had told her that his mother was unlike the other Ghimireys). Even Shambhogya, who had been nice to Kranti, eventually would turn out to be not so nice. There was something too well put together about her; there was, it was obvious, a great deal of tension behind that facade. Even Shaditya, who had come from the boarding school for the wedding, appeared to shy away from Kranti. A reserved boy, he clung to his mother throughout, and seemed disinterested in what was happening around him. The way the Ghimireys looked at Kranti, it wasn't merely because she was Professor Shrestha's daughter, there was something else. It was as though they knew something about her, something about her . . . mental illness?

She forced her mind away from this thought, but the only other thing she could think of right now was the Gang of Four. Should she confront Bhaskar with it, tell him to stay away from them? But he knew what he was doing, didn't he? Wasn't the whole idea of marriage about trust? She needed to trust him. For god's sake, Kranti, she chided herself, don't bring up the Gang of Four on your wedding day!

———

They'd forgotten about Rozy in the bustle of the post-wedding visitations to relatives. He called them on the house phone.

"Do you remember me?" he asked. Kranti knew the voice sounded familiar but couldn't place it, and he said, "A good friend you are. You forgot all about my humble abode?"

"Rozy?"

"Who else? I'm disappointed that you haven't yet included me in your round of post-wedding visits, saathi."

A couple of days later Bhaskar and Kranti found themselves in Rozy's flat, eating his fried fish and aloo and drinking his tea. Rozy was a good cook.

They heard Rozy's story, his growing up in the Town of Lakes, his move to the Valley years ago. He indicated that his parents had disowned him, but he didn't reveal to them the dark episode with Bir.

The food lulled them. Kranti asked Rozy how he met PM Papa. Oh, he found me, Rozy said, with a sad smile. Kranti sensed that Rozy didn't want to talk about PM Papa; she wondered whether theirs was an emotionally close relationship, or whether Rozy was merely a sex partner. She wondered how much power Rozy could exert in the relationship, whether PM Papa had him totally under his control. It did appear to Kranti from that visit to the Lion Palace that

Rozy had *some* sway over PM Papa, although how much it was hard to tell. PM Papa could quickly turn against even the most loyal of his supporters, Kranti knew this.

On their walk back to the Asylum, Bhaskar said, "All gays are good cooks."

Kranti said that was a stereotype.

"How do you know?" Bhaskar challenged her. "Do you have gay friends?"

"One of my good friends in school was gay," Kranti said.

Bhaskar laughed. "You went to an all-girls' school."

"She was a lesbian."

"You mean boarding school hanky-panky? Everyone does that!"

"She was the real thing."

She told him about Megha, the slightly butch girl who knew from sixth grade that there was something different about herself. The other students mocked her, sometimes even tried to bully her. But Megha was a tough girl and she fought back. Once, a bully had tried to tackle Megha in the schoolyard, and Megha had grabbed her by her hair and punched her repeatedly in the face. After some girls broke up the fight, Kranti had taken Megha by the arm into a classroom and applied some cream from her bag to Megha's slightly bruised chin. "You should learn to ignore them," she'd said to Megha. "They're not worth your time."

When Megha and Kranti began to spend time together, the other students called them lesbos. Megha tried to fight them, but Kranti wouldn't let her. Sticks and stones, Kranti told her. Sticks and stones. Megha told Kranti about the crushes she had on their classmates, especially the girly ones.

Once, when Kranti visited Megha in her house, Megha's mother told her that she wished her daughter was more like Kranti, more feminine, interested in more girly things. She said this when Megha was in the bathroom, out of earshot. "All of our relatives ask me what's wrong with Megha, why is she like that. And I don't know what to say to them." She looked at Kranti suspiciously. "You and Megha are only friends, right? I hope so. I will not tolerate her bringing any filth into this house."

Just then Megha returned to the room, figured out what might have transpired, and scowled at her mother. In her next visits to Megha's house, Kranti witnessed the hostility with which her family treated her. Her two brothers were openly contemptuous of her, and during Kranti's second visit, a scuffle broke out in the living room between Megha and her brothers over a minor matter. Kranti sat on the sofa, horrified, watching her friend get slapped around by her brothers. Then they'd left, laughing, and Megha had stormed out of the house, cursing, with Kranti following her, calling her name.

"So where is she now?" Bhaskar asked her,

"She disappeared. I heard that she committed suicide, but those could be rumors. Someone said that she moved to Amrika and is living in a gay village in Kyalifornya and working in a co-op store."

When Kranti visited Rozy again a few days later (Bhaskar was teaching at Streetwise), she told him about Megha.

"I know Megha," Rozy said.

"You know her? How? Have you met her?"

Rozy shook his head. "Many Meghas. There are many Meghas in Darkmotherland."

The traffic noise was loud outside Rozy's flat. Occasionally a truck blared so loudly it startled them. They talked about themselves. Rozy indicated that he'd like to keep their friendship private from PM Papa.

Kranti nodded. "But he'll find out. We're not doing anything wrong, are we?"

"No, we aren't doing anything wrong," Rozy said. "But you don't know him."

"You are with him, for now," Kranti said. "You have to make the best of the situation."

"He wants a baby with me."

Kranti watched Rozy to see if he was joking, but Rozy remained serious. "What? How is that possible?"

"I don't know. He's insistent that he wants it. He's even talking about consulting someone."

"That's crazy, that's crazy," Kranti said. "What? A daktar? Some implant?"

"What implant?"

"Is he going to put a seed in you?" Then, realizing how insane that sounded, she said, "But you're a man, you can't get pregnant."

Rozy laughed, then said, "He's enough like a hippo that he might ram a baby into me."

"Don't let him, Rozy," Kranti said.

"Let's not talk about the baby. I don't want a baby, even if I could have one. I don't like babies."

"Really?"

"Not his baby, anyway." Rozy groaned. "Argh, let's drop this line of conversation. He'll get mad if he hears me talking like this. To you."

"Why?"

"He'll see me going out of bounds, making my own decisions. He wants to control all of my movements."

They were both silent for a while.

Then Rozy said, "I have felt the same rage as Megha."

Kranti could only listen.

"It's still inside me, Kranti, this rage. One day I too might simply disappear."

"Rozy, don't say such things. You are not in a bad place." Then, even though she wasn't sure that what she suggested wasn't worse for Rozy, she said it. "You are working for PM Papa."

"Yes," Rozy said, "but I'm tired. Something's got to give. Soon."

—

Kranti was so wrong—so wrong!—in thinking that her marriage to Bhaskar would force him to turn away from Professor Shrestha. The opposite happened. After the initial bustle of the wedding died down, Bhaskar was back at Beggar Street, at the feet of his favorite madam, letting her stroke his chin, leaving his newlywed wife at the Asylum to fend for herself. One time when he didn't come home after teaching at Streetwise and didn't pick up his mobile, she called Beggar Street. "Yes, he's here," Professor Shrestha said, and she heard him say in the background, "Tell her I'll be home soon." But he didn't return to the Asylum until very late that night.

Even though Kranti felt abandoned, she didn't say anything. Besides, the Asylum kept her busy. There was so much to do, so much to learn. She had to get to know all the Ghimireys—Prithvi Raj, Muwa (with whom she formed an immediate bond), Shambhogya (who was nice to her, but there was something underneath those fine manners and impeccable words that gave her pause), Aditya (whom she was immediately wary of, and who seemed to be trying hard to mask his disdain for her), Priyanka (who clearly wanted to one-up Shambhogya in everything, but mostly fell short), and Chaitanya (who was under the shadow of Aditya, and occasionally bullied by him). Mostly, it was Aditya who made her uncomfortable. Once, she ran into him in the living room, alone. He was engaged with his mobile, but as soon as he saw her, he leaned his head back on the couch and sighed, leaving his mouth open a bit, eyes staring at the ceiling. It was such an odd gesture. Later she thought that it signaled his exasperation at her mere presence. Was it designed to creep her out, to send her a message?

Then there were the nokerchakers, so many of them, it was hard to keep them straight. There was Thulo Maya, whom Muwa brought with her from her village when she arrived in the Valley ages ago. Harkey was the lead servant who, according to Bhaskar, resembled a mafioso, and his nephew, Shyam Bahadur. Also, Sarla the cook and Mokshya the teenage girl were always present. Cheech and Chong, the guard brothers, looked so alike that even the Ghimireys sometimes got them confused. The brothers spoke in a mountain dialect that sounded half Spanish and half Himalayan. There were others who worked part time— the gardener, the dhobi, the handyman, and on and on.

There was the cavernous Asylum, probably ten times bigger than the four-roomed Beggar Street house with its two bedrooms (one for Professor Shrestha and one for Kranti), a narrow kitchen, and a large living room where all the Beggars met. The Asylum resembled the huge mansion from one of her favorite comics from childhood, *Richie Rich*. "It feels like I should take one of my traveling backpacks and go trekking from one end of this house to another," she'd said to Bhaskar.

He replied, "Who needs this much space? No one. And, when you think of it, the walls of this house are bleeding someone's blood."

She had rejected Bhaskar's dreary gloom and doom words so early. Days into her initiation into the Asylum, despite her own anxiety, she tried to attune herself to the new family and its new smells—Beggar Street smelled musty, while the Asylum smelled like rose petals. And there were the sounds that came from the multitude of nokerchakers cooking and cleaning in the kitchen, the guards at the gate, Cheech and Chong, calling each other "*cabron*," the jangling of the keys attached to Shambhogya's waist as she walked the corridors, the ringing of the bells every few hours by Muwa in God's Room, and finally, the hum that seemed to emanate from the atrium. It had a big skylight that allowed a view of the sky, the clouds lazily rolling above.

The atrium, filled with greenery and shrubbery, had statues and artwork scattered throughout. "Don't be fooled, there's not an artistic bone in anyone's body in this house," Bhaskar said. "Well, maybe Shambhogya bhauju a bit when she's not worried about dents to the family's prestige." It was Shambhogya who had given her a tour of the Asylum, with Priyanka tagging along and making odd comments here and there. It was clear to Kranti that Shambhogya was the boss.

Bhaskar agreed with her that Shambhogya was the boss. "Shambhogya bhauju will have you under her control before you know it. Be careful with her." During the tour, Shambhogya had paused at all the statues and artwork, showing them to Kranti proudly, while Priyanka tried to butt in with smart observations. But it was clear that all the major decisions in the Asylum were the handiwork of Shambhogya ("Priyanka has no taste," Shambhogya confided to Kranti one day).

The statues of gods and goddesses and the paintings were commissioned or bought by Shambhogya. She seemed quite knowledgeable about them. In front of a statue of the Goddess Playing the Beena, she'd said, "This is a replica of the famous Goddess Playing the Beena statue in south Bharat. The well-known artist Pramod Chitrakar—you've heard of him, I'm sure—I sent him to the temple to make a sketch so he'd have the most accurate replica." She explained the other artwork as well—a painting of the Shades-Wearing King ("you won't believe the price of this," Priyanka commented); a rare photo of the durbar square of the City of Beauty; apparently the oldest photograph of a bird's eye view of the Valley ("The Rajjya Museum has been trying to get this from us for years now," Shambhogya said), and so on. In front of the life-sized statue of Darkmother, both Shambhogya and Priyanka bowed their heads reverentially. "That's Darkmother," Priyanka informed Kranti, as though Kranti was foolish enough, or perhaps atheist enough, not to know who Darkmother was when the entire country was named after her. Behind Darkmother's statue was a fountain with a statue of The Thinker in the middle, through whose crown water spurted up and cascaded into the pool. "The Thinker," Shambhogya said. "You know? Rodin?"

"He's a very famous sculptor," Priyanka said. "Franceli, hoina Shambhogya di?"

"Franceli, Germnee, it doesn't matter," Shambhogya said dismissively. "The importance is in the sculpture itself, what it conveys."

Kranti looked at Shambhogya for explanation.

"It conveys—" Priyanka started.

Shambhogya stopped Priyanka with a finger in the air. "It represents the philosopher searching for the meaning of life."

"It's not the original, is it?" Kranti asked, knowing well it wasn't.

Shambhogya laughed, and Priyanka laughed with her, amused by the naivete of the new buhari, who, despite being the daughter of a so-called intellectual, was obviously proving herself to be uncultured. Kranti could have corrected them right there, saying that she knew it wasn't the original, but both Shambhogya and Priyanka seemed to

SAMRAT UPADHYAY

be in a bubble of their combined laughter that Kranti wasn't sure she could burst.

There were so many rooms in the Asylum, some empty, some furnished "extra living rooms," Shambhogya said, although why anyone would need five extra living rooms was unclear. There were separate home offices for Prithvi Raj, Aditya, Chaitanya, even Bhaskar, even though Bhaskar hadn't done a single thing for Ghimirey & Sons.

"I haven't even set foot in the Headquarter since we built it when I was a teenager," he'd told Kranti. He was referring to the Ghimirey & Sons' main office, the Headquarter, in the City of Beauty, the command center of all the businesses that the company owned.

The evening after the tour, Kranti had lain in bed in her room, waiting for Bhaskar to return (he'd said that he was visiting some friends), overwhelmed by the entirety of the Asylum. Her first thought was, as Bhaskar had said, it was all a bit too much. "It's too much," she whispered to herself. "What am I going to do?" Then she became afraid that she'd start talking to herself and the others would hear her. "You cannot, cannot do this, Kranti," she said to herself. "You cannot talk to yourself. If you do, Poe might come, and you know what'll happen." As soon as Poe's name escaped her lips, she cursed herself, "Stupid, stupid," for she knew what was going to happen next.

Poe was at the foot of the bed. "You called, dearie?"

"No, I didn't call you. I don't know you."

"Hmm, I swear I heard my name on a woman's lips," Poe said, then he sang in a raspy voice, pouting his lips, something about seeking permission to introduce himself, that he was a "raven of wealth and taste."

This was another classic rock tune liked by Dada, who used to bow in front of Kranti and sing that he was "a man of chow and jest."

Kranti threatened to unleash the nokerchakers on Poe. "I'll have them pluck off your feathers one by one and roast you alive, then serve you for dinner. With some chutney on the side."

Poe made exaggerated weeping sounds, covering his eyes with his wings. "Please, *por favor*, some kindness please, *s'il vous plaît*."

She pleaded with him to leave her alone while he mock-pleaded with her to let him stay, to be kind to him, for wasn't he her BFF? Come to think of it, Poe said, he and Kranti even looked alike, with the same beady eyes, the same beaky nose, etc.

She shut her eyes, wishing him away, but he hovered close to her ear and asked her whether she missed Beggar Street. She ignored him and focused on her breathing. Bhaskar had taught her mindfulness meditation when she felt panicky. Breathe in, one two three, hold, one two three, release, one two three.

Poe asked where was Bhaskar, the Handsomest of Them All. He looked at the ceiling. "Bhaskar wouldn't—by any chance—no, he wouldn't—but perhaps—just maybe—he's at Beggar Street, with your beloved mamaw? Maybe—even—let me take a stab with my beak—maybe the Gang of Four?"

Breathe in, one two three, hold. Kranti opened her eyes and shouted, "Get out! Get the fuck out!"

Priyanka had opened the door and was standing there; apparently, Kranti had neglected to lock it.

"What happened?" Priyanka asked. "Everything okay?"

"Nothing."

"You were yelling."

Kranti stared at her as though what Priyanka just said made no sense.

"It sounded as though you were quite angry at someone." Priyanka looked around the room, looking for that someone.

"Something might have just slipped out of my mouth."

"No, you were yelling, bhauju. Get out, or something like that."

"I was napping. I might have dreamt something bad."

Shambhogya appeared. "What's going on between two sisters-in-law? Won't you let me into your secret club?"

"I just heard some yelling, and came over to check, that's all." She locked eyes with Shambhogya meaningfully.

Kranti thought Poe had vanished, but there he was, fluttering his wings around Shambhogya and Priyanka, as though blessing them.

Kranti whispered angrily at him.

Her sisters-in-law stared at her, then exchanged glances.

"Everything okay, Kranti?" Shambhogya said. "You'll let us know if something is bothering you?"

Kranti said everything was fine.

"You look angry," Shambhogya said.

"I've not been feeling too well."

"Then why don't you rest?" Priyanka said.

"No, no, it's nothing," Kranti said. The other Ghimireys were waiting for her downstairs, she knew, and if she didn't go, they would talk about her. The new buhari acting prima donna, thinking she was above the Ghimireys. Why? Because she's Madam Mao's daughter?

"Okay, then, it's time for dinner," Shambhogya said. "Let's go down. I want to show you some things in the kitchen. I supervise dinner, but sometimes you might have to."

"When Shambhogya-di isn't here, then I supervise," Priyanka said.

"Yes, yes," Shambhogya said impatiently. "Now let's go down. Everyone is waiting."

Later, glancing from the dining room toward the kitchen, Kranti observed her two sisters-in-law in deep conversation. Shambhogya appeared highly attentive as Priyanka spoke. Kranti got the feeling that their conversation hadn't started at that moment, but was a continuation of a past thread between the two.

Poe was perched on top of the fruit basket at the center of the dining room table, clawing an orange, one nail digging through its skin.

"Scat!" Kranti hissed. She had to be careful. Muwa was sitting next to her, explaining lunch and dinner routines in the Asylum. Kranti obediently nodded to her mother-in-law to indicate she was listening. She had to make sure she didn't speak out loud, like she'd done earlier. In the kitchen, Shambhogya and Priyanka briefly stopped their conversation to look in her direction. They met Kranti's eyes, and Shambhogya smiled, then turned to Priyanka and spoke urgently. She then returned to the dining room, saying, "These nokerchakers, they can never do things properly without supervision, even after all these years."

⁓

Kranti wasn't sure how often and for how long Bhaskar went to Beggar Street, mostly because she herself was at work. And after work, once she reached the Asylum, she changed into a stay-at-home dhoti, and went downstairs to see what she could do to help. A dutiful buhari I am, she thought.

One evening, she called Bhaskar before looking for Shambhogya, but he didn't answer. She helped Shambhogya in the kitchen as her sister-in-law supervised the nokerchakers. But "helped" was a euphemism. All she could do was watch as Shambhogya commanded the kitchen staff: wipe that counter more thoroughly; make sure that the kauli is crunchy, not soggy; why have all these pots and pans remained unwashed? Did you remember to get the special small onions that Sir likes? Priyanka had gone to visit her parents that evening, so there was no one to compete against Shambhogya. Kranti felt like she was an intern, an apprentice who was tagging along to seek wisdom from a great master, feeling more and more inadequate with each passing minute.

Throughout the evening, she continued to try Bhaskar, but her repeated calls to his mobile went unanswered. This was not all that unusual, as he was not very good at checking his phone. She kept glancing toward the main door to see if she'd see him arrive. As she was in the kitchen, watching the door, the food was being transferred to the dining room. The process felt like a ceremony since the nokerchakers had to traverse a hallway with trays when they were eating.

"Where's Bhaskar?" Prithvi Raj asked at one point. Kranti replied that he must have been held up at the school. She thought she heard Aditya snicker, and Shambhogya elbow him. Prithvi Raj looked worried, and asked a couple more questions about Bhaskar. He told

Kranti that she ought to tell Bhaskar not to spend so much time out-side. Darkmotherland was getting more dangerous by the day.

By the time she went up to her room and shut the door, she felt beaten. She opened the window and peered out. The walls of the Asylum were high, but from the second floor she could see the street, the shops, and the people walking about, sometimes only their heads bobbing as they walked on the pavement next to the wall. At the front gate, Cheech and Chong sat in the guard house— she could hear their voices as they argued in their fast-talking Himalayan Spanish.

She returned to her bed. She must have fallen asleep because she woke up to Bhaskar sitting on the bed staring at her. He was smiling, but his eyes looked tired, as though he were exhausted by his own thoughts. "My sweet dulahi," he said, taking her hand in his.

"One you've abandoned." She felt guilty immediately after saying it. She didn't want him to feel that he had to make sure that she was all right at all hours, that he had to take care of her, watch out for her.

"Sorry," he said. "Time got away from me today." He let go of her hand and stood, then changed into his pajama bottoms. He liked to sleep naked above the waist, and she loved to feel his chest as she slept. Now she watched his lanky body.

"Did you go to Beggar Street?" she asked.

He stepped into the bathroom. He peed, shook himself, then pulled up his pjs. Without looking at her, he slipped into bed and said, "I just stopped by, briefly."

"Seems like more than briefly," she couldn't help but mutter. She needed to hold her tongue. She really wanted to ask him: Don't you think you ought to spend more time with me? Either in this house or outside of it? Perhaps we could go out to eat somewhere in the evening? Or even for coffee at Tato Chiso?

But she didn't say anything, and it wasn't clear whether he heard her muttering, though he was right next to her. He did say, "Just wanted to check on Madam, I thought she might be lonely."

I am lonely too, she wanted to say, though she wasn't sure whether that was true. She had been busy, but she'd felt Bhaskar's absence keenly ever since she'd stepped foot in the Asylum.

"I'm sure the Beggars haven't left her alone," she said, followed by a short laugh. She could imagine what the scenario was like at Beggar Street. Rumors had intensified in the Valley that the Papa Don't Preach rally was finally going to be held this coming Saturday. She'd heard it at Bauko Bank, and on the street, when she'd stopped by a jewelry shop on the way to the Asylum. Let's see if it happens, she'd thought as she'd overheard a group of men in a tea shop near the Asylum talking about what might transpire. "Rat-tat-tat-tat," an old man had made an imaginary rifle with his hand and shot down the protestors. Motherland TV had issued warnings against "wannabe agitators." The repercussions for anti-Rajjya activities would be swift and merciless, Hom Bokaw had said.

"Murti and Prakash and Vikram and Chanchal—are they crashing overnight in the living room now?" she asked, half-jokingly, hoping Bhaskar would divulge some crucial information. "What about the Gang of Four? Amma—she must have come to keep my mother company."

Bhaskar didn't say anything.

"That Amma and my momma, quite a pair," Kranti said.

Bhaskar spoke after a long stretch. "The Gang of Four don't come to Beggar Street anymore, so you're worrying about nothing. I'm sure Madam misses you. Yes, the Beggars keep her company, but you know what they say, that one can be alone even in the midst of a crowd."

Why aren't you thinking that about me, she wanted to ask. I too am in a crowd here, with Shambhogya and Priyanka and Aditya and Chaitanya and Sir and Muwa, and yes, the nokerchakers, my God the number of them—why do they need so many of them?

Bhaskar gently pushed his nose against her and said, "Did you miss me?"

She nodded, vigorously, then, worried that he might not have understood her, said, "More than you can imagine."

"I missed you too."

She waited for him to say more, but he said nothing for a while. She realized that he had fallen asleep.

She turned on her other side and remained awake for a long time. She missed Kabiraj, how comfortable she felt with him, with his body. She realized, with dismay, that she was actually pining for Kabiraj in this moment, while Bhaskar, her true love, was sleeping next to her. Kabiraj, her pudgy poet, her dallu. She closed her eyes and imagined being in Kabiraj's arms right now, how comforting that would be.

She wondered what the Ghimireys would think of her desire for Kabiraj, while Bhaskar was sleeping right next to her. Bhaskar with his movie star looks. The Handsomest of Them All. Shambhogya and Priyanka—Shambhogya especially—kept reminding Kranti how good-looking Bhaskar was. They were suggesting that he was too attractive for her.

One day, soon after the wedding, after hearing for the umpteenth time how good-looking Bhaskar was, Kranti had blurted out to Shambhogya, "You two would have made an excellent match." Good thing that they were by themselves, for it was clearly an inappropriate utterance.

Shambhogya said, looking embarrassed, "What are you saying?"

"Nothing," Kranti said. "Just an observation." But this is what Kranti had thought: he's as handsome as a god and you're as pretty as a heavenly apsara.

It was true. Shambhogya, although petite, had a face to die for—large eyes, a perfectly shaped nose, a slim chin. She had mannerisms that were controlled and elegant. Practiced. If she had married into a more liberal household, she could have competed in a beauty pageant, walked down a runway, and won. Kranti could tell that despite her embarrassment, Shambhogya was pleased by Kranti's comment. She wondered how Shambhogya had felt marrying Aditya, whose paunch was growing larger by the day, who walked with his feet splayed, and scratched his tummy while making important, serious announcements.

Lying next to Bhaskar, Kranti realized that she was missing Kabiraj now because when she was with him, she didn't have to constantly worry about what PM Papa was doing to the country, as Bhaskar wanted her to, especially now with the Papa Don't Preach rally so near. But even amidst the uncertainty and fear that PM Papa had unleashed, Kranti believed they could, and should, lead a secure and happy family life. If they did nothing wrong, she had concluded, nothing wrong would be done to them.

It might be a naïve view, Kranti suspected, and felt guilty about it. Any day now, Kranti surmised, the Loyal Army Dais would come for Professor Shrestha. For a brief moment Kranti relished the picture: her mother in custody, being hauled away by aggressive Loyal Army Dais. Kranti felt remorse, for there was no telling what they could do to her. Torture her. Starve her. Let her body rot away in jail. Then Kranti no longer felt remorse because she remembered Dada's charred body, and that her mother, deliberately and knowingly, tried to take Bhaskar away from her.

One early morning, two days before Papa Don't Preach, a suicide bomber blew herself up near the Humble Abode. It was only one neighborhood away from PM Papa's residence. There was nothing in that neighborhood except shops and residential houses, so it became obvious that the target was the Humble Abode. But the suicide bomber hadn't been able to make it past the strict security that extended to surrounding neighborhoods of PM Papa's residence. Also, it wasn't as if the suicide bomber had blown herself up while trying to barge through the phalanx of Loyal Army Dais that protected the area.

She had been drinking tea inside a sweets shop when two Loyal Army Dais had entered to buy some biscuits for their morning snacks. The woman, who was so young that she looked like a girl, was sitting in a corner. She seemed to become visibly agitated at the sight of the

Loyal Army Dais, who then grew suspicious at her nervousness. They also noticed that she was clad in a heavy wool jacket in the sweltering heat. So, the Loyal Army Dais lingered, chatting, eating their biscuits, talking about a recent football game, all while watching the young woman from the corner of their eyes. When the woman appeared as though she was getting ready to leave—she was clutching the jacket tightly around her—the Loyal Army Dais asked her whether she wasn't feeling hot and itchy in the jacket. The woman threw the remainder of her tea in their faces and bolted. The Loyal Army Dais chased her. She was as fast as a little squirrel, but in her panic she ran in the opposite direction from the road that led to the Humble Abode. Suddenly, she must have realized her mistake and did an about turn. However, by this time the Loyal Army Dais had already drawn their rifles and had her in their sights. That's when she blew herself up.

Fortunately, when she pulled the trigger of her bomb, she was on a grassy knoll next to a house that was under construction. The blast of the bomb was loud and she was quickly swallowed by a huge cloud of flames. No one else died, but shrapnel from the bomb pierced a Loyal Army Dais soldier's thigh. He was rushed to the hospital where his leg was amputated.

—

At Beggar Street that afternoon, there was a hot debate about whether the Beggars should participate in Papa Don't Preach given the Grassy Knoll Gal. Once again, it was Professor Shrestha who was hesitant, and once again, it was Prakash who kept saying, "No way! No way! We're not going to back down now."

Prakash was very agitated, and at one point Professor Shrestha took him out to the lawn and asked him in a whisper, "What's going on, Prakash?"

"What do you mean?"

"The Grassy Knoll Gal—do you know anything about it?"

Prakash shook his head. "How would I know?"

"The Gang of Four?" Professor Shrestha was aware of the eyes of the other Beggars at the window. She saw now that Bhaskar had also joined them.

"I have no idea."

"What did they tell you?"

"They don't tell me everything, Madam," Prakash said. He was avoiding her eyes.

"Prakash," Professor Shrestha said slowly. "This is all a bit too much. If we all get killed, then there'll be no one to fight the Hippo."

Prakash toyed the grass with his foot, then said, "And if we don't fight, what will we be? We'll be slaves to the Hippo."

"That's a bit melodramatic, don't you think?" She realized that she was beginning to sound like Kranti.

"I do have some new information, Madam," Prakash said, finally looking up.

"What?"

Prakash signaled to her that they should move away from the watching eyes of the other Beggars, and the two went to the corner of the lawn, behind the small shed where Kranti's father used to store old furniture and other knickknacks he couldn't bring himself to throw away.

The other Beggars watched from the window, wondering aloud what they could be talking about. "That Prakash," Chanchal said. "He's up to something, I don't know what. He's being very secretive these days."

"I hope he had nothing to do with that Grassy Knoll Gal," Murti said. "He's a bit too pally with the Gang of Four."

"Looks like he's found another Madam in Amma," Vikram said.

"No one can replace our Madam," Chanchal said, fidgeting as he looked out the window.

"What might be the conspiracy over there?" Bhaskar said, gesturing toward the shed.

"Who knows?" Murti said. "It's not good—I don't like it. Whatever is being said, we need to hear it too."

"I'm going to find out," Bhaskar said, and he opened the side door and went toward them as the others watched.

Professor Shrestha and Prakash were hidden behind the shed. As Bhaskar approached, he heard furious whispers, along with the word "Dojjier."

He called out before he even saw them, "What are you two colluding about? Everything okay?"

"One moment, Bhaskar, can you wait?" Professor Shrestha cried, a bit too quickly, thought Bhaskar, but he stopped in his tracks. The whispering continued, but at a much lower volume, and quickly, urgent, as though they needed to wrap things up within seconds. Bhaskar heard something about Papa Don't Preach, and "be careful, Prakash, be careful please" from Professor Shrestha. Bhaskar looked toward the window, at the three faces that were expectantly watching him, waiting for him to unlock the secret.

Professor Shrestha and Prakash emerged from behind the shed.

"What's going on?" Bhaskar said. "All that khush-phush—everything okay?"

"It was nothing," Professor Shrestha said. "Just catching up on last-minute details."

Prakash wouldn't meet his eyes.

"What last-minute details?" Bhaskar asked.

Professor Shrestha said they were discussing whether it was prudent to go forward with Papa Don't Preach given the suicide bomber.

"Well, too late now," Bhaskar said, not entirely convinced by Professor Shrestha's explanation. "Everything is in motion already. It can't be stopped."

~

"How could this happen?" PM Papa asked General Tso at the cabinet meeting.

General Tso was the only one not afraid at that meeting, which had been called two days after the Grassy Knoll Gal incident.

PM Papa had been at the Humble Abode when the suicide bomber had blown herself up. Earlier that afternoon, Shrimati Papa had insisted that he come home because she had invited the Amrikan ambassador's wife to the Humble Abode. Generally, Shrimati Papa was loathe to have her house polluted by non-Brahmins and foreigners. But khaireys, not the firangi types that roamed the Tourist District, but of the upper class, were of a different category. Shrimati Papa had swallowed her bigotry and decided that having the Amrikan ambassador's wife at her residence was worth the trouble, given what she wanted to do. She had, the morning of the ambassador's arrival, called her Brahmin priest to the Humble Abode so he could perform a puja, just to make sure that whatever impurities the khaireyni's presence would bring to the house would be purified. She had decided that she would host the ambassador's wife on the lawn, just to ensure that no impurities would enter the house proper. The ambassador's wife spoke a smattering of Darkmotherlandese, so Shrimati Papa, who didn't speak Angrezi, could potentially converse with her, but Shrimati Papa hadn't ever spoken to a khairey or a khaireyni and thought it better if her husband was by her side. PM Papa had groaned when his wife had insisted that he come home early from the Lion Palace that day so he could assist her in speaking with the Amrikan ambassador, but he had complied.

Shrimati Papa wanted to pick the ambassador's wife's brain about starting a project that would befit the wife of a powerful prime minister. Initially, she'd thought about running a book club, the kind that Oprah ran, but PM Papa had pointed out that she was near-illiterate. "Tell me how you're going to discuss a book when you can barely read and write," PM Papa had said. "What are you going to say to your book club members? Teach them the alphabet?" He mimicked her teaching the alphabet to her book club members. "'Repeat after me: kapuri ka, kharayo kha, gadhai ho ma ga.'"

Shrimati Papa hadn't cared for his mocking, especially when he'd managed to insert into the recitation that she was a female donkey. Then Shrimati Papa had thought of charity organizations, for that's what queens in the past had done. She thought of the Shade-Wearing King's wife, the one whom everyone called Queen Mother, who had started the Child Temple orphanage that was now famous all over Darkmotherland. The wives of Amrikan presidents were also famous for their own projects and charities, weren't they? She recalled hearing about the Kyalifornya-actor-turned-president's wife, who had cracked down on drug use by simply using the phrase Just Say Know. Or was it Just Say No? And President Corn Hair's wife, for example, the model-turned-first-lady, she came up with Be Best to encourage children. Be Best? Ahhhhh! So good, thought Shrimati Papa. She could come up with something short and beautiful like Be Best, but something specifically Darkmotherlandite. The Amrikan ambassador's wife could help her with this.

On the day the Grassy Knoll Gal blew herself up merely a half a kilometer away, PM Papa, Shrimati Papa, and the Amrikan ambassador's wife were sitting on the lawn, drinking coffee and eating cake. PM Papa was serving as a translator, and Shrimati Papa was extolling the virtues of President Corn Hair. She knew that the Amrikan ambassador's wife adored President Corn Hair (there were rumors that President Corn Hair had chosen the ambassador simply for his wife, who was young, blond, and pretty). For a while, the three of them sang the praises of President Corn Hair, Shrimati Papa merely parroting what she'd heard from her husband and what she'd seen on Motherland TV. The ambassador's wife gushed about how President Corn Hair had saved Amrika from the socialists and the communists. "Just like you're saving your country, PM Papa," she said, then jabbed her fist in the air and said, softly, "Pure Darkmotherland!"

Both PM Papa and Shrimati Papa instinctively jabbed their fist in front of them and said, "Pure Darkmotherland!"

Right now, Shrimati Papa was more interested in her idea for a campaign for herself, so she gently turned the topic in that direction. Through her husband, she asked the ambassador's wife what she could do. The ambassador's wife said that children were always a sure shot for elevating one's image. The Amrikan First Lady's Be

Best campaign had worked because it focused on children. It had shown the First Lady as compassionate and motherly. Shrimati Papa could think of something similar, but it couldn't sound like Be Best. Otherwise, Shrimati Papa would be accused of plagiarism, of being a copycat. The Amrikan ambassador lamented how the Be Best First Lady, as she had now come to be called, had been accused of plagiarizing the speech of the Kenyon Born First Lady. So, it had to be something distinct, something that was unique to Darkmotherland, the Amrikan ambassador said. "Oh, I know, what about the khateykids?" the ambassador's wife said. Shrimati Papa scrunched her nose. As soon as the Amrikan ambassador's wife had said children, Shrimati Papa had been dreading that she'd come up with the idea of using khateykids for her campaign.

"How are you going to respond?" PM Papa asked his wife from the corner of his mouth so that the ambassador's wife wouldn't hear.

"In our culture," Shrimati Papa began . . . PM Papa had just begun to translate when a loud boom sounded. Well, it was in the distance, but given how quiet the Humble Abode normally was in the afternoon, it sounded loud and nearby. PM Papa's bodyguards and Loyal Army Dais stationed at the gate and the roof were quickly on the alert.

"What happened?" PM Papa shouted at his main bodyguard, Laxman, who had been standing on the porch, and now was attempting to take him inside. The three were all ushered inside, down to the basement, where PM Papa had a bunker constructed soon after Papakoo, perhaps anticipating something like today. There, for the next two hours, PM Papa called people and tried to gain an understanding of what had happened. With each passing moment, his anger grew, and so did his paranoia. General Tso told him on the phone that he thought it was the handiwork of the Gang of Four. General Tso also advised him to stay down in the basement until he received a green signal from the general.

PM Papa, Shrimati Papa, and the Amrikan ambassador's wife all stayed hunkered down in the basement for the remainder of the day, then into the night (the bunker had cots), and through the next morning. The ambassador's wife cried all night, complained about the hellhole that her husband had brought her to, threatened to use her cell phone to call President Corn Hair, with whom she said she had "an intimate relationship." She did call her husband, the ambassador, who asked her to stay put. He remained holed up in the Amrikan Embassy until he knew it was safe to come and fetch her. He also promised to call President Corn Hair to see what help he could provide.

PM Papa spent the night sweating. He was certain that he had been kooed, possibly by General Tso. He should have never trusted the man. Then he thought of several others who could have engineered a koo, with or without General Tso's help. He first thought of Dharma Adhikari, who had a growing influence among the elites of Darkmotherland. Soon, he became certain that it was the Education Minister, Shiksya Pradan, who he'd always thought had shifty eyes and furtive manners. Then his attention became focused on his Minister of Communications, Prapu Ganda, who was rumored to be quoted in a foreign newspaper saying that he had doubts about PM Papa's regime (but since PM Papa couldn't find the said quote, nor the newspaper, anywhere, he hadn't taken any action).

Throughout the night, PM Papa stewed in his paranoia, certain that when the door to the bunker opened again, Loyal Army Dais would appear and take him, line him up against the wall in a dirty alley in the Fish Stone Market and shoot him, leaving his corpse for all of Darkmotherland to see. He imagined General Tso, or Shiksya Pradan, or Prapu Ganda, marching down the streets of the Valley with a megaphone, announcing PM Papa's ouster and "a new dawn for Darkmotherland." Even as he was assailed with these terrifying thoughts, he kept calling his people. General Tso said a young girl was involved, and that it looked like the handiwork of the Gang of Four, but that PM Papa should remain in the bunker until the general was sure that there were no more immediate threats. Was "remain in the bunker" code for "you're toast"? He called Dharma Adhikari, who knew little, which made PM Papa even more apprehensive. Shiksya Pradan didn't pick up his phone, confirming PM Papa's suspicion that he was involved in whatever was happening outside. Prapu Ganda sounded panicked over the phone, and kept asking PM Papa whether they—all of Papa's cabinet—were going to be all right.

Shrimati Papa was snoring next to him on the cot. A strand of snot, thin as thread, vibrated at the end of her nostrils with each rattle. Rozy! PM Papa hadn't thought of Rozy until now. He wondered whether he was safe, or perhaps whoever was masterminding the koo had already arrested him. PM Papa went into the bathroom and dialed Rozy's number. Rozy picked up the phone after about five rings, his voice sleepy and grumpy. "Why are you calling me at this hour?"

For some reason, hearing Rozy's voice made PM Papa want to weep with relief. At least this part of his world was intact. "Are you okay?" he asked him. Rozy answered, why wouldn't he be? PM Papa asked him whether he'd heard what had happened.

"About what?"

"What happened near the Humble Abode in the afternoon."

"Oh, yes."

"And it didn't worry you? You didn't worry about me?"

"Should I have?" Rozy asked, his voice still sleepy.

PM Papa's initial instinct was to get mad, to take it as a sign that Rozy didn't care for his well-being. But he realized that Rozy's lack of concern might be a strong indication that there was no koo. Had there been one, they'd have first come for Rozy, knowing how valuable he was to PM Papa. Rozy asked PM Papa where he was, and when PM Papa told him, he thought Rozy chuckled. "I'll see you tomorrow," Rozy said and hung up the phone.

The brief chat with Rozy somehow calmed PM Papa and he returned to bed. "Who was that?" Shrimati Papa asked.

"Go back to sleep. Everything is fine."

⌒

PM Papa knew that he needed to act quickly, decisively. The Grassy Knoll Gal incident turned out to be the handiwork of the Gang of Four. Poolis Uncles and Loyal Army Dais had fanned out across Dark-motherland looking for them, breaking down doors and arresting people, torturing them for information. PM Papa was worried that his enemies could take the suicide bomber as a signal that he had been weakened. He needed to show them, right away, who was boss. He needed to put the fear of God into them. So, by the time General Tso came to fetch him in the Humble Abode, he knew what to do. He immediately called for an emergency cabinet meeting. And they all came, panicked, because they also weren't fully clear on what had happened. By this time, they knew about the Grassy Knoll Gal, and they knew that PM Papa was holed up in the Humble Abode bunker throughout the night. They knew that the Amrikan ambassador's wife had been with him. Some of them might have kicked themselves for not seizing the moment and initiating a koo, for such an opportunity might not come again. Alas, it was too late, and here was PM Papa, fuming.

How did it happen? PM Papa asked. As usual, he was seated at the head of the long rectangular table with General Tso seated next to him, his eyes calmly observing the others. Rozy was seated on a chair by the door, apart from the others.

How did the suicide bomber get so close to the Humble Abode, PM Papa asked. How did she not get caught beforehand?

There was a murmur around the table. They made noises of anger. "Horrendous," they said. "Unforgivable." "Unconscionable."

"It should have never happened, PM Papa," Prapu Ganda said. "There was an error somewhere. We need to do better. We need to launch a PR campaign."

"You are the supreme leader of Darkmotherland," Shiksya Pradan said. "This is a terrorist attack."

"We'll take care of the terrorists," PM Papa said. "But who's going to take responsibility at this table?

All eyes slowly turned to General Tso, who remained calm, his gaze somewhere at the window.

PM Papa stood from his chair. In his right hand was a cricket bat. He gave it a slight twirl, then smacked it on the palm of his other hand. The cricket bat had been gifted to him two weeks ago by the captain of the national cricket team when they were hosted in the Lion Palace after winning the Asian championship. On the cricket bat was written "Pure Darkmotherland!" PM Papa had never been athletic, so Prapu Ganda had taken the opportunity to project him as a cricket player, and suddenly billboards with PM Papa wearing cricket whites and striking a ball with his bat had appeared across Darkmotherland. The billboard caption read, "PM Papa: The Man of the Century."

Now PM Papa wielded the "Pure Darkmotherland" cricket bat in his hand. He slowly walked around the table. His cabinet members experienced a collective uneasy feeling. It felt familiar, this moment, this scene they were in. Possibly from a movie they might have watched, but couldn't recall. It could have been a Bollywood movie plagiarized from a Hollywood movie—there were so many of them. Did this one involve a famous gangster of yonder years?

"You know I'm a big fan of cricket," PM Papa said. "After all, I'm called A Man of the Century." He gave a chuckle, and all the cabinet members, except General Tso, also chuckled. PM Papa waved his bat around in the air above his head. "But I didn't become A Man of the Century by myself. I am part of a team." Now he was standing next to General Tso, who still maintained his expressionless face. "And when one member of the team isn't doing his job, then that prevents me from being A Man of the Century." PM Papa swung his bat above General Tso's head, but lightly, so General Tso barely felt the swish of the air. PM Papa turned to the others. "See, I am actually an excellent cricket player, like that strapping Lamichhane guy." This drew a round of applause and "you don't say" from his cabinet members. PM Papa moved on. Now he was standing between Prapu Ganda and Rakshya Garam. "I really like being A Man of the Century," he said, "and I intend to keep it that way."

He took a wild swing of his bat, which thwacked Rakshya Garam on the temple of his head. For a short, dumpy guy, PM Papa was remarkably agile and swift. Prapu Ganda withdrew his head just in time to avoid receiving a glancing blow. Rakshya Garam's head smashed face-forward onto the table, hitting the plastic bottle of water and making it roll across to the other side, where it fell in the lap of Swastha Bigar, the Health Minister. PM Papa now raised the bat high above his head, like a khukuri, and smashed it on top of Rakshya Garam's head, cracking it. A squirt of blood shot up and sprayed PM Papa in the face, but he didn't seem to mind. Blood pooled around Rakshya Garam's hair on the mahogany wood table. The back of his head was pulpy and discolored, like a rotting mango.

Not a sound was heard in the room. General Tso's face was so bereft of emotion that it appeared he wasn't even aware what was happening in the room. PM Papa continued thumping an already dead Rakshya Garam. With each blow he rasped out, "A Man. Of. The. Century." Rakshya Garam's head now looked like a watermelon that had been thrown from a roof and lay split open on the ground below, its innards splattered.

Rozy left the room and hurried to the bathroom down the hall. He locked himself in a stall and took a deep breath, then realized that he'd soiled his underwear.

22.

The Operation Papa Don't Preach rally was supposed to start at eleven A.M. Kranti had to go to work at nine. As she walked to Bauko Bank, which was near the Dairy, not too far from the Asylum, she worried that Bhaskar would somehow end up in Beggar Street and participate in the rally. Bhaskar said that he was going to Street-wise School that day for an event, even though many schools had closed in fear of skirmishes during the rally. The Rajjya had issued an injunction against school closing, and several schools officially kept their doors open, while quietly asking their students and staff to remain home.

"Bhaskar, please," Kranti said. "Don't do anything stupid, okay? You're a married man now." He told her not to worry.

Bauko Bank was quiet, with everyone pretending to be busy with their documents and computers. The tellers were also unoccupied. Many customers had stayed away. The tension in the bank was so great that a coworker stood from his desk and began to sing, "Chyangba hoi chyangba. Suna suna hoi chyangba," an old folk song with a thumping, invigorating beat. Soon everyone gathered in a circle around him and clapped their hands and sang. "O Chyangba, listen chyangba, what are the drums saying today?" Kranti too joined them. So did their manager, a woman with grim features who normally frowned upon what she called "frivolities."

Darkmotherlandites were walking around, all across the Valley, as though they were expecting lightning to hurtle out of the sky and zap them. Rajjya vans with loudspeakers trundled through the streets, warning people. One loudspeaker didn't function well, so the words came out all garbled: "Gabhadhaba machepucha inn. Hakatari duda duluba saboteur gumba tarkari. Machapuchre fish delicious jumbo prawn. Om mane padme hum tum ek kamrey me banda."

Most shops had closed their shutters. Very few cars and motorcycles drove the streets. The eerie silence in the air was reminiscent of the old days of banda in Darkmotherland, when the entire country or the Valley was shut down because one group or another was unhappy with one thing or another.

Later that morning a rumor circulated that one of the ministers in Papa's cabinet had been murdered. Where, by whom, no one knew. It wasn't even clear whether there was any truth to the rumor. Or was it fake news, one of those alternate facts?

At eleven o'clock when the Home of the Bell went ding-dong, as if on cue people emerged from their houses—in the Tourist District, from the Lord of the Heavens chowk, from the Monkeygod Gate area, all moving east in unison. At the Parade Ground, the Bhureys joined them, and they passed the Martyr's Gate and the Temple of the Civil Goddess down the boulevard toward the Lion Palace.

Bhaskar was with the Beggars, in front with Professor Shrestha. Prakash hadn't yet joined them. Murti wondered where he was; it was not like him to miss this long-awaited rally. Professor Shrestha said he'd texted her to say that he was finishing up some work at Mothercry Press and would come straight to the rally. Chanchal said that Prakash was actually meeting with the publisher of *Cry the Cursed Country*, Professor Shrestha's magnum opus, about allowing Mothercry Press to publish copies of the book, clandestinely, of course. Prakash thought *Cry the Cursed Country* was in the same groundbreaking category as Edward Said's *Orientalism*, Paulo Freire's *Pedagogy of the Oppressed*, and Ngũgĩ wa Thiong'o's *Decolonizing the Mind*. Professor Shrestha's book, Prakash often said, not only chronicled the crimes of Darkmother's rulers but also dismantled the structures that enabled these rulers to continue their hold on power, year after year, decade after decade, century after century. When Professor Shrestha expressed embarrassment at being put on a pedestal with luminaries like Said and Freire, Prakash almost sneered at her (and Prakash could sneer!)

and said, "It's not about you. It's about the book. The book is bigger than you, Madam."

That Prakash, Professor Shrestha said after learning that he was meeting with her publisher, shaking her head, he never gives up. How will Prakash find us in this crowd? Chanchal asked. He was right. There were thousands of people, converging from various parts of the inner city, the Big Two-damaged inner city. They were joined by others in Diamond Park and the Parade Ground—LGBTQs, Bhureys, real beggars, mad scientists, a-poem-a-day poets, gigolos, pimps, Rastafarians, sushi chefs, scam artists, fake magicians, mean clowns, sudden fiction writers, rascals, ruffians, stud muffins, war veterans, roller skaters, and useless dreamers.

They had free passage. Strange. No sight of the Loyal Army Dais. No Papa's Patriots anywhere. No Fundys. What was going on? This was unusual.

From the Temple of the Civil Goddess, they approached the Lion Palace in a phalanx. They expected the Loyal Army Dais to appear and start shooting, or for the Fundys to run out from behind the trees with tridents, clubs, and spears. Or for Papa's Patriots, with yellow bandanas around their foreheads, to converge on them and start whacking them with bamboo sticks.

Nothing.

Everyone was now whispering about the death of the Defense Minister, Rakshya Garam. The government's Twitter handle, Pure Darkmotherland, had already made the news official. The obituary was brief, almost functional, as though Rakshya Garam had been a minor official in the Rajjya. A persona non grata.

They were now a couple of hundred feet away from the Lion Palace.

The big gates of the Lion Palace opened and a figure strode out, flanked by one man in an army uniform and another in a saffron robe. Behind them was the Loyal Army Dais, hundreds of soldiers, their guns raised at waist level, pointed at the protesters.

A gasp rippled through the protesters. The suddenness of PM Papa's appearance startled the crowd. There was a mild pandemonium, with some of the protestors retreating quickly. They immediately recalled marches during the monarchy years, when the army—then the Royal Army—had fired into the crowds.

PM Papa stopped ten feet from the ralliers. He raised his hand in the air, simultaneously blessing and warning them. "Friends, brothers, and countrymen," he said. "Lend me your ears."

"What? Who?" someone asked.

"Julius Caesar's friend," a protester explained. "Marc Anthony or Anthony Perkins, or whomever. I have come not to bury—never mind."

"You have my assurance," PM Papa said, "that I am the best prime minister this country has ever seen."

The protesters suspected this was a pre-emption of some sort. In a moment they would be hit by the bullets.

"For too long our country has been under siege from within," PM Papa said. His voice sounded slightly more hoarse than it usually did during his frequent speeches on Motherland TV. It also had a strange lilt, as though PM Papa had difficulty formulating the words. Perhaps PM Papa had a cold? "But I have vowed to take care of my citizens, and so I will. Heretofore, I have come out to tell you: when you protest like this, it tells all of Darkmotherland that you are enemies of the state."

There was a loud *crack!* right next to Bhaskar's right ear, and for a moment it felt like his ears had been punctured. A firecracker—that's what he thought it was. Sounds around him became muted. He witnessed panic on people's faces and saw their mouths move, but their voices were muffled.

The Loyal Army Dais quickly surrounded PM Papa, forming a tight circle to shield him. There was a great surge of people around him, some moving forward toward PM Papa, some moving in the opposite direction. A stampede of legs and arms, jostling and shoving. Just as Bhaskar's hearing was returning—a ringing sound still echoing between his ears—an elbow jabbed his lower back, throwing him to the ground. As his nose scraped the asphalt, his hearing came back, suddenly, fully, cacophonically, and it felt like his eardrums would burst once again.

PM Papa had been shot—this thought cruised through his mind. He was dead. Finally. Finally! Then, simultaneously, this thought: General Tso would come to power, maybe even Swami Go!swami.

More shots. But it sounded like they were coming from somewhere inside the Lion Palace. Every time Bhaskar tried to get up, he was pushed back to the ground, occasionally kicked by an errant foot. Then he remembered—Professor Shrestha. He had been next to her when the first shot rang out. He grunted and heaved himself up. Pain bolted through his right leg. Was he the one who'd been hit? He hobbled in one direction, then another, limping in the pandemonium. A shout: "PM Papa is dead!" A loud cheer.

"Madam!" he shouted into the pushing and jostling bodies around him. A glimpse of the big gate of the Lion Palace and he saw that the earlier cluster of Loyal Army Dais that had formed a protective circle around PM Papa had vanished.

"Madam!" he cried.

"Madam!" a voice close to him also shouted. At first, he thought it was a Beggar calling for Professor Shrestha. However, he quickly realized that someone had mimicked him. "What Madam?" the voice said, this time belligerently. The man who was mocking him was a few heads away, so Bhaskar couldn't see the face in the swarm. "Who the fuck is this Madam anyway?" the man said; a couple of people laughed, even in that surging, heaving crowd. Bhaskar experienced a flash of anger, and he lunged toward the voice, but he was shoved back, not maliciously but simply because there was no room for lunging. "Madam! Madam!" the voice continued mimicking him, as it sounded farther and farther away.

Putting his anger aside, Bhaskar shouted for Professor Shrestha, again and again. The crowed appeared to loosen a bit, and he was able to make his way to the edge of the boulevard. There was a side road that ran parallel to the boulevard. The crowd, in its attempt to flee, had also flooded this area, and from there came the faint call back from Professor Shrestha, "Bhaskar, Bhaskar. Here!"

Bhaskar nearly wept with relief.

—

They re-congregated in Beggar Street. Apparently, Murti, Chanchal, and Vikram hadn't left Professor Shrestha's side in the melee, and she was fine.

No one was sure what had happened.

"Is PM Papa dead?"

"Yes!"

"How do you know?"

"He got shot!"

"Did you see it?"

"No, but—"

"Then he isn't dead."

"But someone fired a gun."

"It wasn't one of us."

"I don't think any of the protesters fired guns."

"What do you mean?"

"The shots came from inside the Lion Palace."

"Yes, yes, I heard it too."

There was a great deal of agitation in Beggar Street. Professor Shrestha sat on her green sofa. Today, she'd broken open a new bottle of Black Label, and even non-drinkers like Murti had a glass in their hands. Chanchal was so restless that he darted in and out of the living room, sometimes moving to the lawn for phone conversations.

"Where's Prakash?" Bhaskar asked.

In the chaos, they'd forgotten about him. He hadn't come to the rally. They all checked their phones. No messages from him. They called the landline at Mothercry Press. Nothing.

"Did he even *go* to the rally?" Murti asked, angry. "Did he crap his pants at the last minute?"

Professor Shrestha admonished her not to speak of Prakash that way. She had a worried expression on her face. At one point Bhaskar found her staring at him, and she quickly looked away when their eyes met.

As the afternoon wore on, bits and pieces of news circulated through the Valley. Indeed, shots had been fired inside the Lion Palace, not outside. And it was actually not PM Papa that was shot. It was his double. Of course, the Beggars smacked their heads: Why were they thinking that PM Papa would be foolish enough to venture out among those who wanted him gone?

By evening, what initially appeared as rumors solidified as news: the culprits had been apprehended. The Gang of Four. Fear gripped the Beggars. If the Gang of Four had been apprehended, could the rest of them be far behind? Wouldn't the Gang of Four squeal? They were a tough bunch, especially Amma. The Beggars discussed whether they would cave under torture. They knew the methods the Rajjya used to make people talk—hanging upside down from the ceiling for hours, water boarding, pushing a needle slowly underneath fingernails, breaking fingers one at a time. Vikram said that he heard Madan Tumbahamphey, a well-known radical, had the skin on his face scraped off with a shaving blade—slowly, layer by layer, over days. He now resembled a zombie. Chanchal said he knew of someone whose penis had been gradually flayed over the course of a day. Professor Shrestha asked them to stop it. First, no one knew what had exactly happened, she said. They couldn't be sure that the Gang of Four were actually caught, so why were they yammering like old women? Second, even if they were caught, the Gang of Four were as tough as nails. They were made of different stuff than regular humans. Did the Beggars think that they'd cave so easily?

The Beggars tried to avoid mentioning the Gang of Four after that, but tension hung in the air.

Professor Shrestha kept looking at her phone. A couple of times, she asked Vikram to call Mothercry Press. He obliged, but there was

no answer. "Where is that damn Prakash?" she muttered every now
and then.

———

The next afternoon, the Beggars talked about how not to let the
failure of the Papa Don't Preach rally deter them from letting up
on the Sangharsh. "We can't, we can't," Professor Shrestha said. She
appeared very sad, angry. She'd confessed earlier to Bhaskar, quietly,
that she hadn't slept a wink, worrying about Prakash. The other Beggars were also agitated, wondering if the Rajjya hadn't picked him up
. . . maybe on his way to the rally?

Murti shushed everyone, pointing to Motherland TV, where Rakshya Garam's name was mentioned. She picked up the remote and
increased the volume. Hom Bokaw said Rakshya Garam had turned
out to be a Treasonist who had been plotting the ouster of PM Papa.

Bhaskar laughed. "That's what loyalty to the Hippo does to you."

Hom Bokaw said that Rakshya Garam, once he was discovered
red-handed in the Lion Palace with compromising documents, had
killed himself before PM Papa's bodyguards could reach him. "Due
to sefurity feasons," Hom Bokaw said, "fis phody had feen quikhly
chremated."

Professor Shrestha shook her head at the TV. "What does the
Hippo think we are? Idiots?"

Murti looked at her phone. "They say that his family home has
been confiscated and they've been transported to a remote location."

Hom Bokaw went on to say that Rakshya Garam's treachery
had made PM Papa even more determined to wipe out all of Darkmotherland's enemies from the face of this earth.

"Turn it off!" Professor Shrestha said, and Murti hurriedly clicked
the remote so that the screen went dark. "Let's look at those posters
again."

Chanchal pulled the posters out from under the sofa. There were
about ten of them, about six by four, exact replicas. Chanchal unrolled

one on the floor and placed books on the four corners to straighten it. They all admired the large caricature of PM Papa, resembling a hippo, with a large open jaw, housing a cluster of poor and oppressed-looking Darkmotherlandites. Beneath the image it said, "The Hippo Devours Democracy." Prakash had brought the posters to Beggar Street the other day from Mothercry Press. The plan had been to mount them on sticks and take them to the rally. But, because he hadn't showed up, the others had forgotten about them.

With the poster still open before them, as though reminding them of what was at stake, Bhaskar said that they should focus on their goals, get more money to finance the struggle. "We should hire mercenaries," he said. They all looked at him. Did he mean hire people to try to assassinate the Hippo? Maybe that was the answer. Even Professor Shrestha didn't object to what had just been uttered in her living room, whereas in the past she'd have cautioned against such talk of violence (notwithstanding the fact that in moments of anger she herself had expressed harm to PM Papa). Bhaskar spoke about approaching former high Rajjya officials for money, luring them with the promise of top positions in the new Rajjya, once PM Papa was toppled.

"You mean assassinated?" Chanchal whispered.

They heard sounds of running and feet scuffling outside.

Soon, heavy knocks sounded on the door. The Beggars scrambled to gather and hide some charts and notes that were scattered on the floor. Chanchal rapidly rolled the poster and stuffed it under the sofa.

Following Professor Shrestha's signal, Vikram unhooked the door latch. "It's open," Professor Shrestha shouted in a bored voice. A deck of cards had already been doled out and the Beggars looked up in mock-surprise at the sight of half a dozen Loyal Army Dais entering the house.

"What's the problem?" Professor Shrestha asked the army man in the front, who appeared officer-like. The Loyal Army Dais behind him all held machine guns in their hands.

"You need to come with me to the station."

"What station?"

"The Poolis Uncles Station at the Monkeygod Gate."

"But you're the army," Professor Shrestha said. "Monkeygod Gate is a Poolis Uncles Station, not an army station."

The lieutenant smacked her on the leg with his baton. The Beggars tried to rush to her, but the army men holding the machine guns blocked them. Bhaskar looked like he was ready to lunge at them, but Murti held him back.

Swooning in pain, Professor Shrestha held her leg with both hands. "I'm not going with you," she said.

The lieutenant thwacked her again. She fell to the floor. He hit her again, and again. Soft whimpers escaped Professor Shrestha's lips as she lay on the floor. Chanchal and Murti watched in dismay. Vikram was so agitated that he couldn't watch what was happening and fled to the kitchen. "Take her to the van," the lieutenant said. Bhaskar tried to argue with them, said that they needed a warrant to arrest her. The lieutenant laughed. "A warrant? What country did you come from? Amrika?"

Professor Shrestha wasn't compliant. She was in pain, that was quite obvious, but she had curled herself into a ball on the floor and wouldn't stand. When the Loyal Army Dais lifted her up by her arms, she kept her legs tightly crossed. Her face was contorted; her cheeks were shiny with tears. Her eyes were closed. The lieutenant slapped her face, hard, turning her cheek red.

That's when Bhaskar jumped at them and tried to wrench Professor Shrestha away from the men. But the two men with machine guns pushed against him, toppling him backward on the floor, making him bump his head against the coffee table. "We'll take you too!" one of them barked.

The lieutenant drew out his pistol from the hostler and pointed it at Bhaskar, now lying on the floor, the back of his head bleeding. "Should I shoot you right now, Bhaskar Ghimirey?"

Even though the Beggars were surprised that the lieutenant knew who Bhaskar was, they realized they shouldn't have been. All of Darkmotherland knew who the Ghimireys were, and by now, everyone also knew Bhaskar's association with the Beggars. So, why wouldn't a bunch of Loyal Army Dais sent by the Rajjya to specifically arrest Professor Shrestha not anticipate that he'd be there?

Bhaskar kept his cool and said, "You can't take her."

"Yes, we can!" said the lieutenant.

"Hippo murdabad!" Professor Shrestha said, her voice shaky.

"You want to wish death upon our beloved PM Papa, you slut?" the lieutenant said, giving his men the signal. The men dragged her outside to the alley, where she was watched with gleaming eyes by Mr. Sapkota.

The Beggars accompanied the men as they made their way down the alley. Murti made fervent appeals to the lieutenant, "Professor Shrestha is the pride of Darkmotherland. Please stop this atrocity, Sir."

As the men prepared to throw Professor Shrestha into the van waiting on the main street, Bhaskar tried to block their way, saying, "If you're going to take her, then you better take me too."

The lieutenant pushed him away, laughing. "We have express instructions not to touch you." The lieutenant got into the van, saying, "But not for long, Bhaskar Ghimirey."

The van drove away, leaving them in a black cloud of smoke.

⌒

Professor Shrestha was thrown in a solitary cell at the end of a long corridor. On the way to the cell, she passed by other cells, each cell containing a handful of men, sometimes even women, sometimes men and women mixed together. Her cell was the size of a small closet, with a narrow bed of stone. She wasn't given anything to eat or drink. The room smelled—of urine, of blood, of something else she couldn't identify. Her legs were swollen from the earlier beating, pain shooting up to the side of her ribs. How she wished she could have a glass of her whiskey right now.

She shouted a couple of times that she needed to use the bath-room, but no one came. "Okay, then," she said to herself and peed in a corner. She watched her pee form a narrow river and flow out of the cell. She'd always been able to pee anywhere, with ease—in the bushes, behind a building—in contrast to most women in Dark-motherland who were shy about such public exposures of bodily functions. During family outings Kranti felt embarrassed when her mother stepped behind a bush, sometimes even for a number two (using leaves to wipe her arse) when other mothers were able to pain-fully hold it until they reached a proper bathroom. "If it's coming, it's coming," Professor Shrestha said. "We need to worry about bigger things in life."

Every now and then Professor Shrestha would yell, with a parched mouth, into the hallway, "Hippo murdabad!" She knew she was asking for a noose to be tied around her neck, yet she couldn't help herself.

—

Professor Shrestha's first encounter with PM Papa had happened when she was a young woman. Pretty. People said Kranti got her good looks from her mother. The same almond-shaped dark eyes that lured you in, the same slim nose. There was a framed photo on the living room wall of Beggar Street showing Professor Shrestha from her younger days, when she was attending Tri-Universe University, about twenty-three or twenty-four years of age. When visitors looked at the photo, they said young Professor Shrestha looked like a mirror image of Kranti, even though age had changed her features now—her nose seemed to have become more unshapely, her chin bigger, bonier.

By the time that photo was taken, Professor Shrestha had already turned into an activist, fighting oppressive policies at the university, at the forefront of protest marches against the Rajjya. They weren't called the Beggars yet, but Prakash and Murti and Vikram were already a part of the larger group of about fifteen or so activists and students she led. She had, in fact, been the progenitor of the term

Sangharsh, which had begun to gain currency. At that time PM Papa, who introduced himself as Giri to people, also went to Tri-Universe University, sat in classes with the other students. But he wasn't really interested in his studies. By that time, he had a sense that he was destined for something greater. He knew that the monarchy would come to an end in the coming years, and it would have to be replaced. But by what? That he didn't know. By me? Giri? he asked himself, then laughed. But a seed had been planted. In the university canteen he sat by himself, slurping tea and observing those around him. At that time his attraction to men hadn't fully manifested itself in his consciousness. All he knew was that his eyes often followed men, their buttocks, their faces. At times he'd imagined what it would be like to hold a man in his arms. But he hadn't thought too much about it. Yes, he'd masturbated thinking about men, but he didn't masturbate that often. The time would come when this thing about men would sort itself out, he knew this. He wasn't too worried about it. He wasn't a man given to much self-reflection. He had needs and urges, and he needed to fulfill them. He felt that he deserved to fulfill them. Yes, he felt that he deserved to fulfill his desires at the expense of other people around him.

Why?

Why not?

The others were fools, stupid, or weak. They walked around fuzzy-minded about their lives, or the destiny of the country. Or they were too privileged to begin with, their brains filled with nonsensical ideas about justice and human rights and whatnot. This young woman was one of them.

In the canteen he observed young Professor Shrestha, who was usually surrounded by a group of like-minded friends, all activists, all a part of the Sangharsh.

Sangharsh! What did they know about Sangharsh, these idealistic elites? Did they know poverty, as most Darkmotherlandites did? Did they know oppression? He did. He thought of his parents, who had been hounded by landowners and usurers in the remote district where he had grown up. Did they have a sister who had died in their arms, as his sister had when he was a teenager, due to lack of money to purchase medicine? Did they have a mother who went blind in her old age and had to be nursed around the clock?

He had watched this pretty, elitist woman come to the university in her scooty, at a time when very few women drove motorized vehicles in Darkmotherland. He had thought: there she is, flaunting her elitism. One day when the classes were in session he had gone to where she parked her scooty and let the air out of both tires. Later he had watched her from the canteen as she puzzled over her flat tires with two or three of her friends. She had looked around, and their eyes had met, his fat face inside the grimy windows of the canteen and she out in the dusty area the university had designated as the parking lot.

He found out where she lived, in an alley off the Lord of the Heavens chowk, right in the heart of the city. It was an area commonly populated with the Valley's original inhabitants, those whose ancestors used to rule the various kingdoms that comprised the Valley in the medieval times. The houses in this part of the city, which was filled with narrow alleys and courtyards, were often old and crumbling. Telephone and electric wires ran very close to the windows, and he wondered if a child could inadvertently reach out with his hand and get electrocuted. He dwelled on that image, feeling the pain of the family of such a child, but also enjoying the easy manner in which a child, playing and babbling inside the room one moment, would have his life snuffed out the next. It was pleasurable to think that way, that even the most precious of lives—and who would argue that a child's life wasn't precious—ultimately held no value. It was an important lesson, one he'd been mulling in his head, this question of life and death, the preciousness of life, the total obliteration of that preciousness through death. It excited him, made him bold, as if he could go anywhere, do anything. Do anything to other people.

He stood outside a tea shop and watched her house. The owner asked him if he wanted tea and he answered no. The owner asked him to move along, as he was occupying space for paying customers. Giri said he was standing outside the tea shop, not inside, so it was not tea shop space. The tea shop owner said that the space outside the tea shop was tea shop space—don't you see the benches here where customers can sit outside and enjoy fresh air as they sip their tea? Giri said, I see the benches, but it is still not your space. This space belongs to the public.

There were a couple of customers inside, smirking at the exchange, which further annoyed the shopkeeper. One customer muttered about how plump the vagrant was. But Giri didn't budge. He continued to stand there, his arms crossed, staring at the shopkeeper as though he were the one violating Giri's space.

Professor Shrestha came to the window. She glanced toward the tea shop, their eyes briefly met. It wasn't clear whether she recognized him as someone from the university or whether, even if she did, she made much of this fellow from the university hanging out by the tea shop in front of her house. Or, whether he was like other fellows who'd followed her around seeking her affection, whether she recognized him as the same guy by the grimy window of the canteen when she discovered the flat tires of her scooty, whether, whether, whether.

⁓

It became clear in the weeks and months that followed that this man was after her. He pursued her. At first, she thought it was a romantic or sexual pursuit. She knew the type. In the past there had been men who had tried to woo her with aggressive tactics. But, she had been able to swat them down and that then slunk away injured and shamefaced. However, there was something different about this man, all that aggression in that plump body, the glare in his eyes.

He began to burst into the small meetings she had around campus, in the canteen, or when the weather was pleasant, out on the lawn, or even in the tea shop by the main road. She'd be chatting with her friends—they'd already started using the term "Sangharsh" for their struggle against those in power—when he would come and stand at the edge of the group. At first there was a slight discomfort in his presence. But they would ignore him and carry on with their conversations. Soon he began to interject. "One question," he'd say. Or, "How is that possible?" Or, "That's a bunch of hooey." They tried to ignore his interjections. Initially they did, but then he increased the frequency and volume of his comments, as though he had indeed already joined their group and had already become a valuable member of the Sangharsh. He also began to speak simultaneously as Professor Shrestha was speaking, making it impossible for others to hear her. He made snorting, coughing, and gargling sounds.

Finally, one day, they confronted him. They shouted at him. But he was unflappable. Vikram, who was only nineteen then, but already bursting with muscles (and was, as he said, "a big fan of Madam"), wanted to break his fingers. Professor Shrestha wouldn't allow it. Some of the others said that the only language a fellow like him would understand is the language of violence. But Professor Shrestha wouldn't budge. "We'll conduct our meetings elsewhere," she said. For a while they did meet in someone's house in the Serpent Pond area. One day they happened to look outside, and there he was, pacing back and forth on the street, stopping and staring at houses. He had tracked them down. It was so unbelievable that they couldn't help but laugh, or giggle rather, as they didn't want their laughter to filter out and alert the guy. "Look at him, doesn't he look like a hippo?" Professor Shrestha said, pointing her finger at him, even though he was the only one standing outside.

At the nickname, they grew hysterical.

The Hippo stopped and tilted his head, as though he'd heard the laughter inside. But after a moment he left.

Although they laughed off his appearance in the neighborhood of Serpent Pond, they became more troubled in the days that followed. There was something perniciously persistent about him.

"Perniciously persistent," they said.

"Maliciously malignant."

"It's as if he doesn't understand the word no."

"He's a loner."

"He might be a sociopath."

One day Professor Shrestha's group was holding an impromptu meeting regarding a sit-in in an empty classroom. The Vice-Chancellor had just declared that the students' demands—bathroom repairs, a bigger library, bonuses for teachers—couldn't be fulfilled that year because of budget constraints. The administration would revisit the matter the following year, he said. But the students knew that the same excuse would be offered the next time. And the budget constraints hadn't prevented the Vice-Chancellor from giving himself a raise and a bonus every year. Thus, the need for a sit-in.

But within minutes after Professor Shrestha and her group began discussing the sit-in, the door opened and in marched the Hippo with several others—Rajjya goons who roamed the college campuses in the Valley looking for anti-Rajjya activities.

"What's going on here?" Government Goon 1 asked.

"Who are you to ask us that?" Professor Shrestha said.

"You know that these classrooms are off-limits to students when no class is in session?" Government Goon 2 said.

"And you are?" Sangharsh Member 1 asked.

"Government Goon," Professor Shrestha said.

"One or Two?" Sangharsh Member 2 asked.

"And you are unpatriotic elements," PM Papa said. "I know what you're doing. You're creating unrest against the Rajjya. I could report you all to the authorities and you all"—he pointed his chunky fingers at each one of them individually as if to leave no misunderstanding— "will go to jail."

"We are just sitting and chatting!" Professor Shrestha said. "Since when is that illegal?"

"Whore," Government Goon 1 muttered.

Professor Shrestha's group exploded into protestations.

"If you don't leave, I will pull out your innards," Government Goon 2 said, raising his fist as though to strike Professor Shrestha.

But Professor Shrestha didn't flinch. She was no wilting flower: she never had been and she wasn't going to start now. "I am going to report you all to the Vice-Chancellor."

The government goons laughed, and along with them the Hippo. "Yes, report to him," he said. The three warned Professor Shrestha and the Sangharshis that if they congregated like this again, they should be prepared for whatever happened to them.

Professor Shrestha did report the incident to the Vice-Chancellor, who said, lying outright, that he didn't know who the goons were and that he'd look into it.

"And what about the Hippo?"

"Who?"

"Giridharilal."

The Vice-Chancellor feigned ignorance, but he did call Giri into his office once Professor Shrestha left. "Why are you hounding her so much?" he asked Giri.

"You're asking me?" Giri said.

Although they were both on the same side, they hadn't gotten along in the past. PM Papa thought the Vice-Chancellor was too soft, and the Vice-Chancellor thought PM Papa was more aggressive than necessary. "Speak softly but carry a big stick," he liked to say to PM Papa and other Rajjya-affiliated students and goons that roamed the campuses in the Valley to keep the students in check, especially the agitating kind.

"The problem is, Vice-Chancellor," Giri said bluntly, "not only do you speak softly but you carry a plastic ruler, like this one here." He picked up the plastic ruler on the Vice-Chancellor's desk and smacked himself on the knuckles. "See? This won't even kill a fly," and he swatted a fly that was perching on the edge of the Vice-Chancellor's desk and lo and behold not only did it manage to miss the fly, but the ruler broke in half.

The goons in the room snickered.

"I don't want you coming into my room and breaking my plastic rulers," the Vice-Chancellor said. "I also have a university to run, and I can't run it on intimidation alone."

"Well, you can't run it on plastic rulers, that's for sure," the government goons said.

"The problem is," Giri said, "you're not running it at all."

The Vice-Chancellor slammed his desk. "You're supposed to be working for me, but here you are, hurling insults."

"And you're supposed to be keeping these students in line," Giri said, "not letting them run amok." He was enjoying this. He liked confrontations, especially with people in power, or people who wanted power, like Professor Shrestha. He knew that the Vice-Chancellor was already in a weak position. He was a weak man, and he was afraid. Giri sat on the Vice-Chancellor's desk, dangling his short legs, his mid-section bulging out. The Hippo, thought the Vice-Chancellor. He stood, empurpled, but couldn't say anything. "Do you know what they're planning?" PM Papa asked. "Your good students you want to protect are planning a strike to barricade you inside your office for days, until you give in to their demands. Is that what you want?"

"Get out!" the Vice-Chancellor shouted. "Get out!" He came from behind his desk and poked his finger in Giri's chest.

—

The higher-ups must have asked the Hippo to ease up on the VC but not the agitating students. What followed were months of harassment. The Hippo would frequently show up at the tea shop outside Professor Shrestha's house (by this time the tea shop owner had come to respect, perhaps out of fear, the Hippo, who had that effect on people), then it was followed by stalking—around her neighborhood, around the campus, sometimes in restaurants where she was with her friends, one time at a picnic, where he showed up with new government goons. Her friends, those who were not Sangharshis (there were very few of those left) asked her, "What's up with the guy?" or

"Why is he obsessed with you?" Their consensus—and even some Sangharshis had come to believe this—was that he was in love with Professor Shrestha, the only logical explanation. The bastard doesn't know how to properly express his love.

There were jokes. Professor Shrestha should really go out on a date with him, at least once or twice, just to string him along, teach him a lesson. Others cautioned that rejection would make a crazy man crazier. Just let him be. He will go away one of these days.

But he didn't. He continued to show up, sometimes after weeks or months of absence, at places where Professor Shrestha was. He appeared at her dissertation viva, for example, his ruddy cheeks gleaming, and asked questions that suggested she had plagiarized, monopolizing the discussion. Then he was absent for years, and reappeared in a government post, a secretary or a lobbyist. By that time, she was already married and had become a lecturer at Tri-Universe University. He showed up at her lecture one day and appeared to be taking notes. She was somewhat rattled but managed to maintain her composure. She could have called the main office and asked them to send campus security, as the university had clamped down on outsiders coming in and disturbing the classes. But she decided against it. Calling for help would create a scene, disturb the lecture, and the students would need to know this material for the upcoming exams.

He was waiting for her outside the classroom. He was chatting with a couple of students as she was walking out. She was already becoming quite popular with the students, who were attracted to her outspokenness and her willingness to fight the authorities, especially when it came to student rights and demands.

"That was quite a radical talk you were giving," the Hippo said. His tone was almost friendly.

"It is a course on Marxist political philosophy," she said.

The students had paused and were watching this exchange.

He addressed the students, raising his hand in a query, "It's always been a mystery to me why they let such things be taught at the university these days."

"Giri-ji," she said, in a gently chiding manner, as one would a lovable yet brain-addled relative, "maybe some people love knowledge?"

He responded, playfully, tapping his head, "Some people also put junk into their brains."

"Madam, who is this man?" the students asked. "What right does he have to talk to you like this?"

Professor Shrestha raised her hand to calm them. "It seems like you don't have a life of your own, Hippo-ji? Is that why you've been pursuing me for what, ten years now?"

The "Hippo-ji" threw him off a bit, for his smile disappeared. At the mention of ten years, her students gasped. One said, "Thrash this bugger." But Professor Shrestha held up her hand again.

—

He disappeared for a while, and when the next academic season began, Professor Shrestha's lectures were disrupted by heckling sounds. Plants, she discovered soon enough. The hecklers would ask loud questions in the middle of the lecture, laugh like hyenas, or challenge her on obscure, inconsequential points. She complained to the Vice-Chancellor, who promised her that he would look into the matter. Then the heckling stopped. Soon after that, Kranti was born.

—

Years later, she heard on the news that Giridharilal Bhagirath Kumar had become the Home Minister. The news didn't come as a total shock to her. She had been aware of his political rise, first as a small-time local politician, then as a cabinet secretary, and now, after a sudden change in government following the pro-democracy movement, the Home Minister. Still, when she saw the announcement on Motherland TV, she stared at his portly figure on the screen, shaking hands with the new prime minister. "He's going to come after me," she told Dada.

"He might have bigger fish to fry now," Dada had said.

But she was right. He did come after her, in a major way. Kranti must have been seven or eight at that time. They were eating dinner when the knock came. A knock at that hour was never good. "I told you so," Professor Shrestha said to Dada. "It's him." Before they could stop her, Kranti rushed to the door and opened it. Her teacher had promised her that she would drop by the house one of these days to meet her parents, and Kranti thought it was Miss Lama who had come. But when she opened the door, it was some Poolis Uncles. The man in the front who wore a mustache and dark glasses kneeled in front of her and said, "Rani, kasto ramro bani, timilainai laijaney." Little girl, how well behaved, we should take you instead.

Professor Shrestha was taken to the Monkeygod Gate Jail, interrogated for hours about her subversive activities. The Hippo didn't appear, but she knew he was behind it. She just knew. But those were the days when there was a semblance of law and order in Darkmotherland, and she was eventually let go.

Then the ruling party went out of power, and thereby the Hippo lost his power. Then his party came back into power after a few years, and the Hippo occupied the same ministry position. Then the Big Two happened.

23.

Late in the morning of the second day—followed by the shouts of "Hail Darkmother!"—a short, squat man appeared in an army uniform with several medals on his chest. General Tso. He was flanked by two men, also in army uniforms. She had met him a couple of decades ago when he was a Colonel, at a function, one she'd gone to reluctantly, when Darkmotherland was transitioning from iron-fisted monarchy to a democracy that pretended that it tolerated dissent and a critical media. Although a favorite of the previous king, General Tso had made the right noises once democracy arrived, and he was seen as a progressive and not a sycophant of the crown. When the king ruled supreme, General Tso had been a fanatic Hindu, and his fanaticism had resurfaced after PM Papa's koo.

"So," General Tso said to Professor Shrestha.

So what, Tso? She remembered the General Tso jokes that the Beggars chuckled over.

> When did the chicken cross the road?
> Once General Tso brandished his sharp khukuri.

> Did the General think the chicken tasted good?
> He thought it tasted Tso Tso.

"Literally wallowing in your own filth, eh?" General Tso said. The river of urine zigzagged across the cell and out toward the General, who stood outside the cell, in the corridor. His shoes were brilliantly polished, and he made sure that they didn't touch Professor Shrestha's urine. She heard whispers of "General Tso" from the other cells, which were a few feet away.

Maybe I should do a number two right here, Professor Shrestha thought. She wondered if her daughter would be embarrassed by that act. Professor Shrestha could try hard to be a socialist with her poop, distributing it in small dosages throughout the cell so that this small, ugly man would not be able to stand in this cell without getting some goo on his shoes.

"We meet again, Madam." When he got no reaction from her, he said, "Did you forget, Madam Mao?"

"I remember," Professor Shrestha said.

What is General Tso's favorite TV program?
Tso You Think You Can Dance.

General Tso appeared genuinely happy. "People tell me that I'm hard to forget. Isn't that so, Madam?"

She hadn't even been paying attention to these silly jokes when the Beggars had shared them, but now they were coming to her crystal clear even in this painful state, as if she herself had penned them:

What do you call a penniless General Tso?
Po' Tso.

"Perhaps it's all the hardship I have faced in my life, Madam," General Tso continued. The General had found room enough to pace, his hands behind his back, sporting a thoughtful expression. "I don't know how much you know about my upbringing," he said, looking at her expectantly.

Professor Shrestha's throat was parched, and she knew that if she asked for a glass of water this idiot would provide it, but that would then give him an upper hand.

"I know the media has covered some of it," General Tso said.

Professor Shrestha hadn't seen much about General Tso's life story in the media. Most of the images she recalled were of him eating his namesake chicken with chopsticks, using a napkin to wipe the sauce from the corners of his mouth. Then she understood: this was a competition. General Tso wanted his bio on the screen like PM Papa's melodramatic sob story. Ah, dictators are all alike, she thought, but every dictator is unhappy in his own way. She would tell that one to the Beggars if she got out of this place.

Fat chance, she thought. Once General Tso finished his sob story, he would call his men, they would put a bag over her head, and she would be taken to an unknown location. Poor Kranti. One parent dead by suicide, the other executed by the Rajjya. But these thoughts came to Professor Shrestha dully, as though she were watching them from a great distance.

What does the army say when the General doesn't turn up for work?
General No Tso.

"I saw my whole village turn Christian," General Tso said. "They came, the missionaries, waving their Bibles, calling us heathens, offering us money to convert. And my greedy fellow villagers, they converted."

Maybe not greed, thought Professor Shrestha. Maybe poverty, eh, Tso?

"Professor," General Tso said. "I know you are anti-religion. I've heard that about you. But I hope you can see that our religion is what has made us who we are, given us our identity for centuries."

Monkeygod Forty Verses! Kranti's favorite! Maybe Professor Shrestha could recite it to make this man outside her cell vanish into a puff of smoke. *You are golden colored and your dress is pretty.* She couldn't help but add, *O Mighty General Tso.*

"And you know what happened? My family converted. First, it was my brother, my beloved brother, a few years older than me, whom I thought was my role model because he was going to join the Poolis Uncles. They managed to bribe him, show him the way of Jesus. Halleluiah, they said. Halleluiah, my foot! I say Gulaluiah, if you can pardon my cock-talk. I told him in our yard: 'Brother, what is this? What is this cow-eating religion giving you that our own ancestor-given religion hasn't?' And you know what he told me? He said:

'Listen, little brother. I have seen the light. I have been born again.' Born again! What the bloody hell does that even mean? 'Our true salvation is in Jesus,' he said. 'The Bible tells us that Jesus came down to live among us so that he could die for our sins.'

"Can you believe it? A sun-burnt khairey coming down to live amidst the poverty in our village? And die here? In Darkmother-land? When did that happen? I asked him. You and I grew up playing guchcha and dandibiyo together. We shepherded goats on the hillside, smoked bidis hiding behind trees, squeezed the breast-less chests of our young cousins and licked their earlobes. When in the world did this white guy with blue eyes and a lame beard come to our village? How come I missed all this action?' And you know what my brother did? He waved his Bible at me, then placed it on my head, like a shaman's cleansing broom. 'Brother,' he said. 'You are in the grips of Satan. Heal! Heal! Come to Jesus!' I pushed his Bible away and it fell on the dust of our yard, and he got very mad and slapped me. I swung at him, and we fought until our mother came to separate us.

"Our mother and father, both aging, had also converted, and so had our sister who then became engaged to be married to another recent convert. It seemed like my entire village had turned Christian. The remaining ones were getting tired of fighting it and would also soon convert. An old school had been renovated into a church, and people were offered conversion prayers on their porches. Dark-skinned Christian missionaries from Bharat were frequently seen in our villages, bribing people with sacks of rice or jars of oil. When I visited the village temple, I felt like I was the only one who prayed to my beloved Darkmother. I kept thinking of my long-departed grand-mother, a Darkmother devotee, who would have died of shame had she known what was going to happen to her family. Even the temple priest, who had radiant skin until a few years ago, now looked emaci-ated and never smiled. He avoided my eyes when he put tika on my forehead, and I knew then that it wouldn't be too long before he also converted. I felt such hatred toward everyone then, felt that they had all abandoned our gods. When I looked at the statue of Darkmother, I felt that she was weeping. That's when I left my village. You want to know why I'm telling you this sob story, don't you, Professor?"

You wear beautiful earrings and have curly hair, O Glorious General.

"I'm telling you all of this because you need to understand why this is happening," he said, waving his arm about.

You mean this cell? Professor Shrestha asked him silently. She hadn't slept well all night on the stone bed, and her legs were still throbbing from the whacking she'd received. She wanted to lie down on her soft bed at home.

"PM Papa is a blessing for this country, don't you see that?"

He signaled with his finger, and one of the men with him took out a bunch of keys and opened the cell door.

Okay, here it is, Professor Shrestha thought. Off to the gallows!

He stepped into the cell and sat down on the stone bed next to her. Next to her! She couldn't believe it. If she were a stronger woman with large hands, she could have strangled him, and for a brief moment she did visualize it: as soon as he sits on the bed she goes straight for his throat and strangles him. He makes croaking sounds and thrashes, but he has small arms and small hands and she quickly overpowers him. He's half-lying on the bed under her massive body—she grows in size just for this encounter, bulks up—and she slowly lays him to rest as the last bit of breath leaves his throat. He departs for his heavenly kingdom filled with his favorite gods and goddesses fawning all over him. Or she pulls out his gun, which is in his holster—as she visualized this, she was annoyed that he didn't think she'd steal his gun, that's how weak he thought she was—and points it straight at his forehead and shoots him there. The bullet cleanly passes through his brain and embeds itself in the opposite wall, leaving a small tunnel in his head, running from his forehead out the back of his head. Look, fucker, now I can read your mind. There, I see your cry-me-a-river moment where your brother turns into a Jesus-lover. There's your boy-body playing marbles in your yard, snot running down your nose. There's you, a big hurt baby, lining up to enlist in the army. There's your corrupt rise through the ranks. There are your goat sacrifices to Darkmother.

But of course, Professor Shrestha didn't strangle him, nor take his gun away. Instead, she let him take her hands and hold them, as though they were lovers. They *could* become lovers. Then she could suffocate him with a pillow over his face after they finished making love.

"I know I won't be able to convince you," General Tso said, gently rubbing his thumb on the back of her hand. "But I need to at least be able to say it before, before . . ."

Before what? Was this man going to take her out and shoot her? She hadn't heard of prisoners being shot in Monkeygod Gate Jail. The jail was in the core of the city, and the sound of shots fired would be heard in the surrounding neighborhoods. Perhaps there was a hanging room? Or an empty room with a box in the middle where the prisoner would rest his or her head and a large khukuri would descend from the air? Just across the street near the Monkeygod Gate shrine, buffaloes were decapitated every year during the Ten-Day Festival. As a child, she'd peeked through the legs of her parents to witness a khukuri, as large as a sword, descend with a *swoosh* and the buffalo's head tumbled to the ground. Blood spurted from the neck, and showered the viewers who stepped back in laughter.

General Tso laughed, a throaty, coughy laughter that, had she been his wife, would have driven her to divorce.

General Tso leaned toward her, and she smelled mint. Alcoholic? Why would that be a surprise? Darkmotherland's generals had been known, even during the days of the monarchy, for their hard-drinking ways. He whispered, "You don't think we're going to chop off your head here, do you?"

This man with his macho voice and his boozy breath was a mind reader.

"The Big Two was divine intervention," General Tso said. "It was Darkmother herself who had intervened. You know why? Because our country was being pillaged and robbed and raped, by Western forces, by Christians, by communists, and atheists like you."

We also had a fledgling democracy, Professor Shrestha mentally said to General Tso. It was as if she had lost her voice. What had happened to her? She had a better voice, a bigger, more authoritative voice than this squeak that was coming out of her mouth. Her voice commanded people's attention, made them listen. She had wielded it to her benefit in the classroom at Tri-Universe University when she'd expounded upon the evils of capitalism and colonialism, and yet here she was, moving toward silence.

"We need to purge this country of all the evils that have been inflicted upon it by these corrupt politicians."

Drain the swamp! thought Professor Shrestha sarcastically.

"Yes, drain the swamp," said General Tso.

He watched her carefully, seemingly trying to understand her. "Why do you do this?" he asked. "Why are you against Darkmotherland? Do you hate your country so much? The country that gave you birth?"

An old song penned by the Shade-Wearing King coursed through Professor Shrestha's mind: *May Darkmotherland grow and prosper— that's my only wish. Even after I die, let my hope remain alive.*

"We are trying to do something good here, don't you see?" His hand on hers had tightened. After a while he said, "Of course, you don't see. PM Papa sent me to you because he couldn't stand to look at you. At first, he thought that he'd have you brought over to the Lion Palace, but then he said, 'General Tso, I don't think that I could stand to look at her face. That's the reason that I didn't look at her during her daughter's wedding, even though Darkmotherlandites wanted me to have a duel with her. I want to tie a noose around her neck and string her up in that peepul tree outside.' PM Papa pointed to the giant peepul tree outside the window of office in the Lion Palace. I told him that I also felt the same when I saw your face, which isn't true. I don't feel like I want to string you up. I feel pity, disdain. 'Would you go visit her for me?' he asked. 'Put some sense into her?' 'Of course, I will, PM Papa,' I said."

Potayto, potahto. PM Papa, The Hippo.

"I can guess your name for him," General Tso said. "I can imagine the names that you all come up with. You do it at your own peril. Believe me, it's not that I haven't thought some choice names for him at times." General Tso chuckled. It was a rheumy, whooping chuckle.

Let me guess. *His Excellency, Prime Minister for Life, The Hippo, MD, FRSC, MPH, NSIS, CID, FBI, SINHAS, UNICEF, VPN, Lord of All the Beasts of the Earth and Fishes of the Seas and Conqueror of the Amrikan Empire in Asia in General and Darkmotherland in Particular.*

"Here, this is a good one." He leaned closer to her to whisper into her ear, and this time she distinctly smelled booze on his minty breath. He might even have tanked up before he came. "Homo Papa." He chuckled harder into her ear. "No? I think it's so funny."

There was no reaction from Professor Shrestha.

"How about Papa Chakpremi?" He waited for her. "Because . . . ?" When she didn't respond, he said, "Because he is a lover of butts. No?"

No, No, No, No Tso, Professor Shrestha thought.

"You are a dry, humorless woman." General Tso let go of her hand and stood. He signaled to the two Loyal Army Dais standing waiting outside. They came in and put handcuffs on Professor Shrestha.

She was led out of the cell, through the corridor, to the chants of "Madam Mao! Madam Mao!" from the other prisoners. She looked for other faces she recognized—fellow activists, fellow ex-jail hounds, fellow academics—but these prisoners were all strangers. Some smiled at her, some scowled, some puffed on their cigarettes and watched the smoke twirl away to the ceiling, as though they had no care in the world. In one cell, a group of prisoners were playing hacky sack; in another they were moshing to heavy metal; in another cell a sadhu-type was seated on the stone bed, right hand raised, with the palm in the wheel-of-teaching mudra, and silently preaching to a handful of his fellow prisoners; yet in another cell a play was being enacted, with a man lying prostrate on the floor and a woman bending over him in a silent scream. Thus, it went on and on, the cells never ending, it seemed, until finally, after what felt like hours, she was thrust into the sunlight out the main door.

The Loyal Army Dais led her toward the gate of the Monkeygod Gate Jail. Another Loyal Army Dai came out from inside the jail, carrying a big khukuri. She winced at the thought of how much it was going to hurt. She had seen goats who thrashed and bleated even after their heads were severed from their bodies. And chickens. During the Ten-Day Festival, when chickens were slaughtered, they scampered around the yard without their heads, clucking yeehaw!

"It's time to say adios, Madam," General Tso said.

Professor Shrestha finally managed to speak. "I don't even get a phone call?"

General Tso smiled. "Do you think this is like an Amrikan Poolis Uncles show? You've been watching too much Lah and Ahder. But I tell you, the show used to be so much better with what's his name, the main lawyer?"

"Sam Waterston," Professor Shrestha said. She hadn't watched *Law and Order*, but she had watched that movie about the Cambodian killing fields with Waterston. "Everyone should at least get a phone call, don't you think?" she said to Tso.

"Who you gonna call?"

"My daughter."

"The one who's married to a Ghimirey now?"

Professor Shrestha nodded.

General Tso shook his head. "Life is indeed puzzling, isn't it? Your daughter, marrying into a family you hate. Darkmother slapping you for your nonsensical ways."

General Tso signaled to his men to take off her handcuffs. After they did, Professor Shrestha rubbed her wrists. "I don't have a phone." This was not how she had envisioned her death, with this butcher of a man in charge, killed like a buffalo.

"Don't think this is freedom," General Tso said. "This is not. This is probation. Next time it might not even be you. It might be your daughter. Or, perhaps even better, it might be that cute boy of yours, Mr. Handsomest of Them All." He walked back inside.

Professor Shrestha watched him, thinking that he was going to come back, and then she'd be frog-marched to the spot where the buffaloes breathed their last.

"Oy, old hag," the Loyal Army Dai holding the large khukuri against his shoulder said. "Didn't you hear what General Tso said? Now scat!"

24.

The Beggars, overjoyed to have their Madam back, welcomed Professor Shrestha to Beggar Street with multiple garlands, tika on her forehead and abir in her hair. They marveled that she'd returned unscathed. Bhaskar kept saying that they ought to have taken him instead of her—he was angry about it—so Professor Shrestha hugged him and stroked his chin. She asked the others whether there was any news of Prakash. There was none.

In Darkmotherland, there were theories about why General Tso had let Professor Shrestha go. PM Papa is playing with her, the way one lifts a rat by the tail and dangles it and lets it writhe, but doesn't kill it. He's demonstrating his power over her, over other enemies of the Rajjya. The idea was also floated that he was doing the Ghimireys a favor. Perhaps out of kindness to the fact that Madam Mao was the mother of a Ghimirey now, since Kranti was a Ghimirey, even though there didn't seem to be much love between the mother and the daughter.

—

The Gang of Four were paraded around the Valley, wearing garlands of old shoes, their faces painted black. Amma was paraded slightly apart from the other three, in the front, to signal her as the leader. Her face was defiant, even when it was blackened. People watched them silently. Some whooped and cheered. Some whistled. A few wept, but then were afraid that their tears would mark them as sympathizers. Darkmotherlandites spat on the Gang of Four as they went past.

Guns and bombs had been discovered in a flat used by the Gang of Four, along with pamphlets that used harsh language against PM Papa and spoke of insurrection. Posters that showed PM Papa with a Hitler mustache.

Two days after their black-faced parade, there was an announcement about their public execution, to be held on the one-year anniversary of the Big Two. General Tso appeared on Motherland TV and talked of "swift justice." He stood at ramrod attention, looking kind of sad and muted, as he read from a paper in his hand. Initially everyone assumed that swift justice meant the insurrectionists would be executed by a firing squad in the premise of the Lion Palace, perhaps next to a building in the back that was now in rubbles. They would be lined up against a wall, soldiers a few feet away from them; on your mark, get set, go, and rat-at-at-at, and the bodies slumped to the ground.

Then General Tso announced that the men were to be beheaded.

"Beheadings? But that's not in our culture," some said timidly.

"What culture are you talking about?" came the retort. "Treason is also not in our culture. Pray, tell, where in our scriptures does it say that treason is okay?"

"It just seems primitive, that's all," the timid objectors said, their voices even more timid.

"Well, we're in primitive times. This is the Age of Darkness."

Rumors circulated that Taylor Swift herself had been procured as an opening act for swift justice. PM Papa had spoken to President Corn Hair, who was going to fly Taylor Swift on his private jet to Darkmotherland. Some questioned the rumors. Taylor Swift was virulently anti-President Corn Hair, wasn't she? Why would she do his bidding?

Why not? Darkmotherlandites answered.

A daura-suruwal maker changed her shop's name to "Tailor Swift: The Fastest Seamstress in Town." Her business dramatically increased overnight.

Singers released rap videos named "Chop It Off" and "Death By One Big Cut." Someone made a poster titled "Cruel Bummer" that showed the Gang of Four with their grinning heads floating away from their bodies.

The day of the execution was announced as a national holiday, when all Rajjya offices and most private businesses had to remain closed. At Beggar Street, Prakash's absence hung in the air. Professor Shrestha had made a few phone calls to people she knew, people in relative power—Poolis Uncles, Loyal Army colonels, cabinet secretaries—to see if she could find out his whereabouts, but every person she called didn't know, or they outright rebuffed her. Some told her that if she didn't watch herself, she could be the next one to disappear. Professor Shrestha couldn't tell if they were genuinely worried about her or issuing threats disguised as concern. One Rajjya official, who was not even in the upper hierarchy of the government bureaucracy, told her that she ought to be grateful that General Tso had let her off so easily—hadn't she learned her lesson?

The Beggars discussed whether they should watch the execution on Motherland TV, where it was going to be broadcast. Bhaskar said that he was going to go watch it live. Murti said that she simply wouldn't be able to watch such a horrific event; she suggested that they all go for a walk while the execution was televised. Professor Shrestha, worried to death about Prakash, said that she wasn't going to watch it, not because she couldn't but because she didn't want to give the Rajjya any satisfaction. The Rajjya was putting it all on public display precisely because it wanted its citizens to know the consequences of dissent.

In the back of all their minds was whether the Rajjya was going to bring Prakash out along with the Gang of Four to be executed. But the Beggars were afraid to talk about it. They were Darkmotherlandites after all, and they all instinctually thought that if they uttered it, they might will it into reality.

Kranti, too, came to Beggar Street, arriving there late in the morning from the Asylum. Bhaskar had left home early, soon after dawn. He hadn't slept well all night, she knew, because he had interrupted her sleep with his tossing and turning. He hadn't been his usual self after the news of the execution. He had become quieter, and somewhat distracted. She had already mentally begun to plead with him. Don't go there, Bhaskar, don't go there. Where? She didn't know. But she knew that she was already losing him. After the debacle of Papa Don't Preach, he was, if anything, becoming more agitated.

After Papa Don't Preach's failure, she managed to extract from him a promise that he would be careful, whatever that meant. And she had also promised him, although he hadn't asked anything of her, that she would not nag him about spending time at Beggar Street, as long as he, again, was careful. It was a truce, a weak truce, she knew this instinctively, and she also knew that it was the best that they could do right now.

One day she had slipped away to Bhurey Paradise after work and spent a couple of hours with Kabiraj. Those moments became for her more and more of what she recognized as happiness: in that small, cramped tent, with the smell of refugees surrounding her. She couldn't help comparing his space to the Asylum.

As the hour of the execution approached, it was as though the air had turned thick with tension, both in Beggar Street and in the Valley. Motherland TV was continuously showing images of the Gang of Four. One image in particular flashed on the screen repeatedly. It was a black-and-white photo, taken not too long ago. It showed the four of them, Amma in the front, holding rifles and looking into the distance. All wore scarves, which meant it was taken in wintertime. Hom Bokaw called them "Fang a Four." The Beggars kept waiting for Motherland TV to announce that a fifth person had been added to the execution list. At one point, when it became too much for Professor Shrestha, she yelled, "Turn it off!" but no one did. It was as though they were hypnotized by the TV, by the repeated images of the Gang of Four, who had sat on this very floor and drank tea with them not too long ago.

There was a knock on the door, and they all looked at each other, startled. Chanchal jumped up and turned off the TV, as though watching the news about the impending execution itself would make them Treasonists. They scrambled to get rid of whatever incriminating things might be lying around, but there was nothing. Vikram went to the window next to the door and peeked out. There's only one person, he said, I can't figure out who it is. "Oh, I forgot," Bhaskar said, went to the door and opened it. "Come on in, quickly," he said.

Kabiraj entered and stood shyly by the door. Vikram slapped him on the back, said that he didn't recognize him with his longer beard.

"Arre, Kabiraj," Professor Shrestha said. "What a surprise. It's been a while."

Kabiraj went to Professor Shrestha and touched her feet. Professor Shrestha stroked his beard and asked him how he was, said he looked fatter than when she'd seen him last. Kabiraj smiled and sat at her feet.

Bhaskar, who now sat on the floor a few feet away to make room for Kabiraj, said that since Kabiraj also wanted to go witness the execution, he invited him to Beggar Street so they could all go together. He said this looking at Kranti, who was sitting on the sofa. Had he suspected something? Why did the pudgy poet have to come? He's doing this to torture me, Kranti thought.

She excused herself and went to the bathroom and washed her face, taking deep breaths at the sink. She opened the bathroom cupboard. Her bottle of Paagalium was still there, the label fading because it had remained untouched for so long. No, she thought. No, grit your teeth and go through this.

She returned to the living room, avoiding Kabiraj's eyes.

"Are you going to come with us, Kranti?" Bhaskar asked. There was an edge to his voice, a listlessness, an unfamiliarity, as if the voice belonged to someone else.

"I don't know if I can stomach it," she said.

"I think Kabiraj wants both of us to go."

She quickly glanced at Kabiraj, who didn't meet her eyes, and looked as if he was ready to disappear into the floor. When she met Bhaskar's gaze, he said, "Look at the two of you, blushing like brides. What's wrong, Kranti? Cat got your tongue?"

Kranti said she'd go. She didn't want to be left in Beggar Street with her mother and the Beggars. She would just shut her eyes at

the moment of the beheading. Though even thinking of the word
"beheading" generated clips in her mind of beheading videos she'd
seen on YouTube.

Professor Shrestha wasn't happy that they were going to the execution. It's feeding into the Rajjya's oppression, she said. Bhaskar
responded that they *had to* witness the atrocities. "We can't just close
our eyes to the horrors that are being inflicted upon us," he said. He
looked almost angry, sulking. Even his face had become different.
Kranti had never seen him like this before. "Besides," Bhaskar said,
"if they do something to Prakash, I want to—"

Professor Shrestha and Murti cried out in protest: Please, Bhaskar,
don't utter such apashagun.

"We can't be ostriches with our heads in the sand," Bhaskar said. It
was as though he was channeling Prakash in his absence.

"That's a new one," Professor Shrestha said. "I've been called all
kinds of names but never been called an ostrich before, and by none
other than my dear Bhaskar." She stroked Kabiraj's head, which was
where normally Bhaskar's head would have been.

Bhaskar said nothing.

Murti laughed a fake, hollow laugh. She turned to Kranti. "And
you, Kranti? You sure you're going?"

Kranti nodded.

"Do you think it's such a good idea?" Professor Shrestha asked.
She pointed to her daughter's head. "What happens if it triggers
something?"

Kranti nearly said: you're my biggest trigger.

"I might end up vomiting," Kranti said as they walked toward the
Palace High School.

Bhaskar wrapped his arm around her and said, "I think it's important you came," but his voice was bereft of warmth. Kranti sneaked
a glance at Kabiraj, who was looking straight ahead, avoiding eye
contact with her, she was sure.

"Fundys!" Kranti whispered and withdrew from Bhaskar's grasp.

"Where?" Bhaskar asked.

"I thought I saw them."

But even if there had been Fundys, it wasn't conceivable that they'd have been able to monitor "licentious behavior," for the street had become swollen with people headed toward the Palace High School. Streams of Darkmotherlandites were coming from alleys and lanes that made up the center. There was excitement in the air, as though they were going to a circus or a fair that promised much revelry. Snippets of conversation could be heard all around:

"What do you think they'll use for the beheadment?"

"Beheadment? That's a word?"

"Beheading?"

"How about beheadam? Sounds kind of Sanskrit-like."

"Sounds more Amrikan to me, as in, 'Damn! My head is gone!'"

"How about be-head-gone? Head be gone?"

"I think a sword will be used."

"Not a khukuri? The national weapon of Darkmotherland—appropriate, no? To finish off these Treasonists?"

"I thought our national weapon was ineptitude and corruption."

"Shh. People will think you're criticizing PM Papa."

"Me? Criticize PM Papa? Are you insane? I have a garlanded photo of PM Papa in my living room."

"PM Papa is awesome."

"They say he's an incarnation of our Pot Smoking God himself."

"Are you saying PM Papa smokes pot?"

"No, no! When did I say that? PM Papa is the purest man alive." The man raised his fist in the air and shouted, "PM Papa jindabad!"

"Gang of Four murdabad!"

"Pure Darkmotherland!"

And within seconds the crowd was hailing PM Papa and death to Gang of Four.

The location, across the street from the Queen's Pond, on the premises of the earthquake-damaged Palace High School, was chosen strategically; it was the official boundary between the Bhurey Paradise and the more well-to-do neighborhoods to the north. It was also perfect given the centrality of its location: across from the Queen's Pond, right at the mouth of the alley that snaked into the innards of the old city, to the Stone Fish Market and onto the Lord of the Heavens chowk, then to the Monkeygod Gate. The Palace High School, as the oldest school in the country, built during the time of the oligarchs, was also vaguely symbolic.

An elevated platform had been temporarily constructed on its lawn, one that rose above the walls of the school to allow maximum visibility from the street, from where most of the people watched.

Alas, Taylor Swift didn't come. But Darkmotherlandites were excited about the jallad. He'd been enlisted from among the dark men of the south because traditionally in movies the executioners were always very dark. And this one was so dark that his skin could have been made of coal. The jallad wore the national costume: daura suruwal and a black topi on his head. From the sheath at his hip he took out a giant khukuri, thick and virile-looking, as long as an arm. The crowd let out "oohs" and "aahs" in unison. The jallad adjusted his topi and preened—he extended the khukuri in front of his face and pretended to admire his own visage on its surface. He turned his head this way and that, brought the "mirror" closer to check his eyebrows and his nostril hair. He raised the sword in front of him and did a small dance, some wiggling of the butt, and some twirling of the khukuri like a cheerleader spinning a baton. The crowd clapped. Buoyed, the jallad performed a martial arts routine, manipulating the khukuri in a series of thrusts and parries, blocks and hacks, and nunchaku-like attacks. The crowd roared. There was music, and suddenly the air became filled with the song about how everyone was kung fu fighting at the speed of lightning. Right after the singer crooned about chopping them down, the jallad stood still in mock surprise, as though suddenly remembering his mission. The music stopped. He gently drew the khukuri across his palm, drawing blood. His eyes bulged in surprise; he pretended he was not used to the sight of blood. He showed his palm to the crowd, which chanted, "He drew blood! He drew blood!" They knew the legend: if the khukuri is unsheathed, it has to draw blood. But the jallad pouted and closed his eyes and shook his head, like a toddler saying no.

"More blood! More blood!" the crowd bellowed.

The executioner opened his eyes and grinned widely, showing his insanely white teeth, bobbed his head exaggeratedly like a clucking chicken, pleased that the crowd was in sync with his needs. He widened his eyes, and jerked his eyeballs repeatedly to the left to draw his audience's attention to that direction. Soon enough, his eyes jumped out of their sockets and traveled a few inches to the side of his face before retreating into their sockets, like yoyos. The eyes stopped moving only after the Gang of Four, blindfolded and with hands tied behind their backs, were brought out onto the platform from behind a curtain. The crowd let out a roar that sounded like a rolling drumbeat in the sky.

The jallad did some quick movements like Charlie Chaplin, lifting his topi and putting it back in quick succession, doing double takes at the prisoners, leaning on the khukuri, its point resting on the floor, his finger on his chin in a thoughtful pose.

The prisoners shouted defiantly, "PM Papa murdabad! PM Papa murdabad!"

The jallad looked at his audience as if he hadn't anticipated this turn of events. He put his hand on his chin and shook his head. He wagged his finger at the prisoners. He looked at the audience and put his finger to his lips. The crowd quietened gradually, and after a while, only an occasional nervous giggle was heard. The jallad tiptoed toward the prisoners, then opened up his palms as if to say: What am I supposed to do?

He reached the first person, Amma, and sliced her head clean off. As the first head rolled away, he sliced the second, then the third, and the fourth in rapid succession. Amma's head rolled to the edge of the platform and lingered there, gently swaying, her face grim. The jallad ran after the other three heads and, abandoning his khukuri, picked them up, one by one, the blood from their severed necks dripping onto his arm. He began to juggle them, at first slowly, tentatively, then faster and faster, until they became a complete blur. Amma's head twisted toward him and observed his juggling act, a bit more sternly than necessary.

—

We love you, O PM Pap-a
Without you, we can't take a crap-a
You behead us,
while we take a nap-a
But we still salute you
By raising our headless cap-a.

—

Returning from the beheadings, Bhaskar was awfully quiet. If he felt relief that Prakash hadn't been executed, he didn't show it. His face had become whiter, slightly more plastic, more . . . robotic? Bhaskar? Her Bhaskar? Almost like a silent explosion had happened inside him but he couldn't articulate the feeling to anyone. She herself had to crouch down on the side of the street and retch. Despite herself she hadn't been able to take her eyes off the stage as the Gang of Four were executed, even as bile kept threatening to rise up in her throat. Bhaskar glanced at her, as if saying he was sorry, but his mind was elsewhere. Kabiraj looked like he wanted to hold her, console her, but he couldn't because of Bhaskar. Right there and then she knew her adventures with Kabiraj would continue, how-ever unfathomable her love for Bhaskar. And Kabiraj—he appeared to know that she would see him again: it was evident in the way his eyes didn't meet hers. In the way he looked ahead as he walked, aware of her gaze on him, not acknowledging her overtly yet still acknowledging their bond. He was telling her—was it mental telepathy?—that Bhaskar, whom she knew he liked, wouldn't be able to satisfy her completely because . . .

Because what, Kabiraj?

Because he has checked out, Kabiraj seemed to be suggesting.

In the week after the Palace High Beheadings there was an increase in incidents of people disappearing. "But where were they seen last?" people would ask, and there would be no real answer. There was the case of Somnath Rana, longtime editor of *Himdesh Magazine*, which was previously left-leaning but which had become, over time, ardently supportive of PM Papa. Rana was said to be in "PM Papa's pocket"—and he had access to PM Papa in the Lion's Palace. But then there was a falling-out, an estrangement, right after the Palace High School beheadings, which did something to the editor's brain. He flipped. An op-ed appeared in *Himdesh Magazine* that posed the question whether the beheadings meant that Darkmotherland was sliding toward feudalism. The op-ed still praised PM Papa, saying he was the right leader for the country at the right time. But the title of the editorial was: "Beheadings? Really?"

The newspaper's editorial office in Pig Alley was vandalized by the Fundys, and they beat Somnath Rana. Lying on the floor, an eye swollen shut, blood dribbling out of his mouth, he said, "I support PM Papa."

"Then stop writing such nonsense," they said. "The next time we'll burn this office down and you with it."

One of the Fundys' mobiles rang. He answered and spoke in a servile voice, "Han-ji, han-ji." He said, "Yes, yes," and moved his head and said, "Yes, yes." He shifted position, and said, "Yes, yes," then met the eyes of the other Fundys and said, "Yes, yes, yes," into the phone.

"For God's sake, please stop saying yes!" Somnath Rana shouted from the floor.

"Yes," the Fundy said and kicked the editor in the groin. "Han-ji, Swami Go!swami," he said, and hung up.

Somnath Rana obviously didn't learn his lesson, for in a few days he penned another op-ed in which he detailed the treatment he received at the hands of the Fundys. He mentioned Go!swami by name, claimed that he was fornicating with his white nubile followers, and wrote that the country, under PM Papa's rule, was "going downhill faster than to hell in a handbasket." PM Papa has established a fascist rule, he wrote. "What next? Are we going to be forced to say, 'Heil Papa'? And he printed a selfie of himself, dressed in a warm winter jacket and a woolen cap, arm raised in the Nazi salute.

The next day there was no trace of him.

—

After the Palace High Beheadings, several groups that were part of the Sangharsh simply went defunct or went into hiding. President Corn Hair tweeted a note of congratulations to PM Papa for "crushing the stupid insurgency in your beautiful country." He wrote that he also wished that the "enemies of the people" in Amrika, especially the media, could be dealt with in the same manner as the Gang of Four. He invited PM Papa to come visit him in Amrika. "Perhaps PM Papa can teach a thing or two to our opposition party in this great nation of ours and show them why they are such LOSERS."

The Lion Palace tweeted back, "Thank you, President Corn Hair, I look forward to visiting that great nation of yours and seeing firsthand how Amrika has progressed in leaps and bounds under the BEST PRESIDENT IN HISTORY."

In the streets, people spoke of the Palace High Beheadings in whispers, or not at all if they suspected Papa's Patriots or Fundys were around.

Professor Shrestha had, despite herself, watched the executions on Motherland TV. "Why?" she asked in Beggar Street, seated on the green sofa, a glass of whiskey by her side. A Surya cigarette smoldered on the ashtray next to her. "Why?"

The others had no answer for her. There was silence.

"Where is the trial?" she asked the others, as though they'd orchestrated the beheadings.

"They're saying the Gang of Four tried to assassinate PM Papa," Murti said, meekly.

Professor Shrestha's voice rose, and she waved her hand in the air. "Arre baba! Then, there's a process, hoina? Charge them, bring them to trial."

"The Treasonist Act allows them to bypass the court system," Chanchal said. He picked up the ashtray and emptied it in the trash bag by the door and put it back.

"As if," Professor Shrestha took a long drag of her smoke. "As if he even needs the Treasonist Act anymore." She coughed an ill person's cough. The Beggars knew not knowing what had happened to Prakash was eating away at her, slowly.

Professor Shrestha talked, and the others listened, for what else was there to do? They were demoralized. The Palace High Beheadings hadn't galvanized the resistance. They'd only created more Papafans. In the monarchy days, Professor Shrestha recalled, people would say that Darkmotherland needed a benevolent dictator. Your average democracy wouldn't work in Darkmotherland, was the line. Darkmotherlandites just weren't disciplined enough. But PM Papa was not benevolent; he was brutal to the core, but it seemed he was the dictator the people wanted.

The next day when the Beggars reached Beggar Street, it was locked. They called Professor Shrestha but her phone was turned off. Their first thought was that the Loyal Army Dais had whisked her away again, perhaps dragged her out in the middle of the night. Had Prakash, if he was still alive, snitched on her? Perhaps they'd tortured him and he'd told them that they'd hosted the Gang of Four at Beggar Street?

Murti called Bhaskar, who came to see them immediately. As they stood outside the Beggar Street door, Sapkota came to the roof and watched them, arms crossed at his chest. Bhaskar asked him whether he'd seen anything. Sapkota mimed "see-no-evil-hear-no-evil," then disappeared downstairs. "Could she have just gone to the market?" Bhaskar asked, but Chanchal said that she rarely did her own shopping; usually it was Chanchal or Murti or Vikram who brought her groceries and other necessities.

For a while they didn't know what to do. They called a few other people they knew to see if they'd seen Professor Shrestha, but none of them had. The four of them fanned out across the city to search for Professor Shrestha. Murti said that she'd go to the Monkeygod Gate Jail; she knew a low-level Poolis Uncle there—maybe he'd be able to tell her something. She didn't say what the "something" might be—none of them wanted to consider that she might have been arrested again. Bhaskar walked around the Tourist District, peeking into shops and cafés, knowing full well that the chances of her either shopping or sipping coffee here was remote. Then an idea occurred to him, and he hailed a cab.

The cab dropped him at the foot of the Self-Arisen Chaitya. By the time he took the hundreds of steps to reach the top of the stupa, he was out of breath. He circled the stupa, feeling more hopeless by the minute, and nearly letting out a cry when he found her sitting on the steps of a shop near the Smallpox Goddess Temple. Professor Shrestha patted the spot next to her, and he sat there, catching his breath. She asked him how he knew where she was, and he said that he remembered her saying that she had fond childhood memories of coming to this temple with her mother. And although an atheist—she couldn't care less for the zillions of gods and goddesses in Darkmotherland—she had a small affection for the Smallpox Goddess.

"Look at all these people," Professor Shrestha said, pointing to the dozen or so devotees who were praying in front of the shrine. "Do you think they already have smallpox? Or are they worried they'll catch smallpox?"

He smiled and took her hand.

"Bhaskar, something needs to be done," she said.

"Maybe we can ask the Smallpox Goddess for advice."

"Maybe she'll give us smallpox instead."

"What are you thinking?"

"Now that Prakash is gone, you are the only one."

"You know he wanted to go underground?"

"Prakash?"

He nodded and squeezed her hand. "He wanted to join the Gang of Four completely. He said he was tired of this bullshit. He felt you—we—were too timid."

"Why didn't you tell me?" Professor Shrestha's eyes watered and she withdrew her hand. She put her head in her hands and shook it. Then she stood and said, "Come."

They left the Self-Arisen Chaitya and climbed down the stairs. Professor Shrestha had to hold onto the railing that ran through the middle of the staircase as she slowly made her way down. Once in a while they stopped and observed the monkeys. Tiny, cute baby monkeys clung to the backs of their mothers who eyed potential devotees to loot. "Do you think these baby monkeys will give their mamas enormous headaches once they become teenagers?" she asked. "But right now—they'll die without their mothers." He knew she was thinking of Kranti.

They reached the bottom, and Bhaskar was about to hail a cab when she stopped him. Let's walk, she said.

Near the Sky Goddess Temple, she asked him, "Are you ready, Bhaskar?"

He knew what she was referring to, yet he thought he needed to ask, "Ready for what, Madam?"

It was like a verbal dance they needed to play before things could become openly articulated. Bhaskar had never been the type to beat around the bush. This is so unlike you, Bhaskar, he could hear Kranti saying. You've changed, Bhaskar. The former Bhaskar would have held her and said, No, I'm the same old Bhaskar. Your Bhaskar. But this Bhaskar, who was taking this leisurely stroll with her mother toward Beggar Street, was more likely to say, yes, I've changed. So what? Why haven't you changed? How can you remain so passive, so apathetic?

That's where they differed. All you need to do, Kranti was saying, was grit your teeth, close your eyes, and this would pass. This, too, shall pass. He was saying no.

Are you ready, Bhaskar?

Yes, Madam. I am ready.

—

He returned around eleven P.M. from Beggar Street. She was already in bed, and although he changed into his pajamas in the dark, trying not to make any sound, she knew he was aware that her eyes were open. She wanted to speak to him, but she couldn't formulate the words in her mind, let alone vocalize it. Something was weighing down on her chest, on her throat, on her eyes, in her head.

He slid next to her and she hoped that he'd say something, but he turned his back to her.

She waited for a minute or two, and when he didn't turn toward her—she loved to sleep on the crook of his arm—she said, "You promised me, Bhaskar."

Silence. Faint sounds were coming from the kitchen downstairs; perhaps Thulo Maya getting the kitchen ready for tomorrow.

"You promised."

She didn't expect him to speak but he did, without turning. "I promised nothing." There was a hard edge to his voice now. It crept in at unsuspecting moments, but it was there: a small coating of bitterness, of spite in his words. She didn't think it was possible, her Bhaskar changing like this. His voice had, until now, always reminded her so much of Dada, who had never spoken to her in anger.

"But you did promise," she said. "Have you already forgotten?"

He turned toward her now, his eyes flashing in anger even in the darkness. "What does it matter what I promised, what I forgot. You were there, you saw what happened."

Yes, it's happened, she wanted to say to him, but if you just wait it will pass and things will change. Take a deep breath. PM Papa will go away at some point. Or he will die. Everyone dies, Bhaskar.

Yes, but if he dies there will be PM Papa II, then III. What's your point? That we wait it out?

I'm tired of fighting. I just want it to stop.

It'll stop when things change.

Although this last bit of conversation didn't take place, it could have. Or perhaps it did take place and she thought it didn't because such conversations had already taken place several times, before Bhaskar, when Dada was alive. It disturbed her that she could no longer distinguish between the talks she'd had, the talks she'd thought she had, the talks she anticipated having, or the talks she wished she'd had. They all blended, spun, swirled, like the dust that churned in the aftermath of the Big Two—thoughts whirled and ricocheted and tumbled and somersaulted, leaving her a mess.

25.

The plan was for Bhaskar to wear a suicide vest (Professor Shrestha knew a man in a shop in the Lord of the Heavens chowk, an old, bitter revolutionary from the monarchy days, who could make it for her) and walk into the Lion Palace, seek an audience with PM Papa, and blow himself up when he was sure PM Papa was in the vicinity. Why not a gun? For Bhaskar to use a gun he'd have to make sure he was in the same room as PM Papa, which might not happen.

Why not someone else? Why sacrifice Bhaskar when only recently Professor Shrestha had dreamed of him leading the country out of darkness? The Palace High Beheadings had changed all of that. Initially, Professor Shrestha had still clung to the belief that Bhaskar was the solution. That the Palace High Beheadings would make the citizens come to their senses, that they'd realize that they were in the grips of a madman, that the only way forward was through the Sangharsh. For a day or two she'd thought the Palace High Beheadings were a turning point: the streets would soon fill with anti-Papa sentiments, citizens would no longer be afraid to express their outrage, shops would shut down, the Valley would come alive with the sound of protests.

Nothing. In fact, a shift in the opposite direction. Silence, even acceptance of the Hippo's cruelty. Acceptance of the daily erosions of their own freedoms. Along with it, Professor Shrestha's ideal of what Bhaskar was supposed to do had also eroded. It took a couple of nights of feverish thoughts for Professor Shrestha to come to this conclusion: No, Bhaskar was meant for a bigger sacrifice. It was so logical, this realization, that hovered over like a little angel in her mind in the pre-dawn hours.

She was not a fool. It was quite possible that someone else would rise to replace the Hippo. General Tso. Or even that con artist Swami Go!swami, with his long, oily beard and his sleazy white-toothed smile. But if the Hippo could be eliminated, for a brief while there would be chaos and confusion. It might just be the opening Dark-motherland would need.

The idea of martyring Bhaskar for Darkmotherland continued to press upon Professor Shrestha. Whenever guilt arose that she was orchestrating the death of her own daughter's husband, she squelched it. Kranti's worries were always about her small self; she didn't have the vision for Darkmotherland. Bhaskar did.

The suicide bombing plan, however, came with a complication. Despite being a Ghimirey, Bhaskar would still have to go through the security gates at the Lion Palace. Everyone did. If he was going to wear a suicide vest or carry a gun, the alarm would go off. Besides, the Hanu Mans would be all over him with their multiple arms and fingers. What about the Humble Abode? Since the Grassy Knoll Gal, that too had been turned into a veritable fortress: the wall had been raised higher, and more guards armed with machine guns roamed the periphery. But visitors didn't have to pass through metal detectors at the front gate; they did that only once they reached the front door to the house. It wasn't clear why that was the case. It could have been that so few people were allowed to visit PM Papa at his residence, and the ones who were allowed were those he knew intimately. Even Papa's cabinet members, for example, had been told not to visit him at the Humble Abode. To add to the security, the guards were warned beforehand about the arrival of any important guests, who were frisked. And Bhaskar now remembered that during warmer months PM Papa received guests on the lawn, under a canopy. Could Bhaskar somehow persuade Prithvi Raj to request a visit, then be persuaded to take Bhaskar along with him?

Bhaskar and Professor Shrestha plotted when no one else was around at Beggar Street, when Kranti was at Bauko Bank, when Murti and the others had either yet to arrive or had already left or been asked to leave early by Professor Shrestha, usually by feigning a headache. She didn't want anyone else to know in case the word got to Kranti. She also didn't want others to know because she worried they weren't up to the task. Even Murti, her longest and staunchest ally, had turned skittish after the Palace High Beheadings. Murti startled at the sound of the door slamming, her eyes frequently darted toward the windows, and every now and then she went to the curtains to pull them tight. The Hippo has browbeaten them into submission, Professor Shrestha thought. Prakash wouldn't have cowered, but he was, in all likelihood, dead.

So, Bhaskar would go to his father and tell him that he had some information on the Sangharsh that would be useful to PM Papa.

"But why would the Hippo believe you?" Professor Shrestha said. "Why would he believe that you'd betray your own mother-in-law and your wife?"

Patriotism, Bhaskar said. He could say he was uneasy with what the Sangharsh was plotting. He wasn't part of the Sangharsh but he was close to it and was hearing things that he thought would damage Darkmotherland.

"But what will you tell your father that the Sangharsh is plotting?"

Bhaskar was stumped. "I'll tell him that's only for the ears of PM Papa."

"Would your father buy into all of this? His son who has been so against the Hippo all this time?"

"I can convince him."

"But what if your father insists on knowing the information before he makes the appointment?"

"I'll make something up."

"Let's figure it out first."

"I'll tell my father that you have hired a professional assassin."

"Seriously, Bhaskar."

"What difference does it make what I say to him?" Bhaskar said. He stood, saying he was going to make some tea for her. "The main point is that he takes me to see the Hippo." He went to the kitchen, and she followed him and stood in the doorway, watching as he put the water to boil. He reminded her of Kranti's father, how attentive he was to her needs.

"But what you say needs to sound plausible."

"So, you wouldn't hire a professional assassin?" Bhaskar elbowed her, as one might elbow one's wife, not one's mother-in-law.

"I'm not sure."

"What am I then?"

Professor Shrestha laughed. "You're not professional enough."

"I'll tell my father that the Sangharsh has enlisted one of PM Papa's confidants as an assassin."

"That'll sound outlandish."

"Really, Madam," Bhaskar said, pouring hot water into cups, then dipping tea bags into them. "Did you forget about Indira Gandhi, who was shot down by her own bodyguards?"

"You think your father will buy it?"

He handed her the cup, which she took gratefully. Tea tasted better when Bhaskar made it, even though he used tea bags. "Why not? Darkmotherland has a history of espionage and assassins. Brothers killing brothers. Sons commissioning hits on their fathers."

Professor Shrestha said then that a gun would be more appropriate. A suicide vest with a bomb could also kill Prithvi Raj, who was sure to accompany Bhaskar. And, of course, Bhaskar couldn't kill his own father. Later, it occurred to Bhaskar that once he killed PM Papa, he would probably simply kill himself to avoid capture, although he didn't say so to Professor Shrestha. It might also have occurred to Professor Shrestha that Bhaskar would take his own life after successfully killing PM Papa, but she didn't say anything. That was best left unsaid.

~

Bhaskar went to Prithvi Raj and said that he needed to see PM Papa.

Why do you need to see him? Prithvi Raj asked.

This happened in the living room. He was standing by the window that overlooked the front lawn and engrossed in some documents in a folder he was holding.

That I can't tell you right now.

Prithvi Raj set the papers in his hand on the coffee table and asked his son to sit down. What is this about, Bhaskar? What has happened? I can't just pick up the phone and call him about every trivial thing. There is a process, a protocol.

This is important.

Prithvi Raj watched Bhaskar for a while. Son, you're not involved in this mess, are you?

What mess, Sir?

Prithvi Raj pointed toward the window. This whole mess. What's happening. The Gang of Four.

Bhaskar shook his head.

I know you were at that stupid rally. That Papa Don't Preach. Why?

I went with the Beggars.

That's it? That's all you have to say?

Bhaskar said nothing.

Let me ask you, Prithvi Raj said. After a pause, he asked, What is your relationship with the Gang of Four?

Gang of Four? Nothing.

Then why do people think that you are associated with them?

What people?

Now it was Prithvi Raj who said nothing.

PM Papa? Does PM Papa think that? Bhaskar nearly said, Does the Hippo think that? But he caught himself in time. Did PM Papa tell you that?

Prithvi Raj nodded.

Bhaskar held his head in his hands. I made a mistake, he said.

What mistake? Were you involved with them? The Gang of Four?

No, no! Bhaskar cried. But I should have never gone to Beggar Street.

Prithvi Raj Ghimirey leaned back on the sofa and said, Looks like finally the sun is shining on your scalp.

I don't know what came over me, Sir.

Prithvi Raj stood, also overwhelmed by his son's confession. He paced the room, then stopped and asked, So, what do you want to see PM Papa about?

Bhaskar said that he wanted to apologize to PM Papa, tell him how sorry he was for doubting him, for being part of the resistance. I also have some information for him. Careful, Bhaskar told himself. He had to maintain the pretense—the old man couldn't suspect anything.

What information?

Bhaskar shook his head. It's best if I tell him, leave you out of it.

You have to tell me, Prithvi Raj said. How can I call him without knowing what it is?

Bhaskar pretended to be thinking. I know something he'd want to hear.

What something?

It's valuable information. Just call him.

The look on Prithvi Raj's face told Bhaskar that he wasn't fully convinced.

It's a matter PM Papa would want to hear. It's a matter regarding his security.

Prithvi Raj's eyes widened. Really? he said, in a whisper.

Bhaskar nodded.

Prithvi Raj became thoughtful. Okay, I will call him today, but you will tell me what this information is before we see him?

Now it was Bhaskar's time to pause. Would his father believe him? Okay, he said. But you have to promise you won't tell anyone. Neither Aditya-da, nor Chaitanya, nor Shambhogya bhauju. Do you promise?

That bad?

It's bad.

Right then Aditya walked in. What's so bad?

Nothing, Bhaskar said.

Aditya looked at him suspiciously. Both of you became super quiet when I walked in. Is it about me?

Maybe, Prithvi Raj said.

The appointment with PM Papa was set for two days later, in the afternoon at the Humble Abode. Someone at the Humble Abode confirmed that the guests would be seated on the lawn.

—

At Beggar Street, Professor Shrestha asked Bhaskar to wait while she went into Kranti's room. Reaching into the closet, she pulled out a box. It was Dada's box, which Kranti had secretly taken for herself, as though her mother didn't have any right to it. Professor Shrestha had been unaware of its existence until Kranti had married and gone to the Asylum. One afternoon she'd been looking for something else in Kranti's room when she'd stumbled upon the box. Briefly she'd fingered her husband's items, momentarily holding the yellowed watch in her hand. She remembered buying it for him in Hong Kong's Stanley Market. But the gun really captured her attention. She vaguely remembered Dada boasting about buying it in an alley in Old Dilli. She hadn't even realized that he'd kept it all these years.

She gave the gun to Bhaskar.

He held the gun. Ruger, it said on the brown grip. Ruger, Bhaskar read. Just saying the name made it come alive. It had a short barrel, and Bhaskar recalled the Ancient Kalo Bandook with its long snout that PM Papa had brandished. This Ruger, a short gun with a bullet for a short man, thought Bhaskar. He aimed it toward the window. He wondered what Kranti would think of him now.

Where are you going to put it? Professor Shrestha asked.

He inserted the gun into the sock of his right foot. It pressed a bit but didn't feel uncomfortable.

What if there's a metal detector at the main gate?

There isn't. I've heard enough about it at the Asylum. There's one at the front door to the house, but it's confirmed that we'll have tea on the lawn.

What if he suggests you all go inside the house?

His wife doesn't like outsiders in her house. She's a strict Brahmin, worried about being polluted by lower castes.

But you're a Brahmin, too.

I've married a Newar.

Ah. The Hippo's wife is a nutty fruit, I see.

She's now a big fan of Swami Go!swami. Wants to return to the feudal days of caste purity.

Sometimes it's a total mystery to me—how we came to be under the thumb of such idiots.

Soon no more.

What if they frisk you at the front gate?

They won't. I'm a Ghimirey, remember? Even if they do, I'll take the risk.

Professor Shrestha gazed at him with near tears in her eyes. They embraced. They could have been lovers. Had Kranti walked in at that moment she would have thought that something untoward was going on between her husband and her mother. But no, this was merely an embrace of two kindred souls who knew that they didn't have many days together.

I'll pick up the gun right before I go to the Humble Abode, Bhaskar said. I don't want to take this to the Asylum, just in case someone discovers it there.

He handed the Ruger back to Professor Shrestha, who returned to the closet and put it back in the box, just in case Kranti came by in the next day or so and searched the box. Unlikely, thought Professor Shrestha, but they couldn't risk Kranti rummaging through the box and finding the gun missing.

Professor Shrestha suggested she make tea for Bhaskar today. Together they went to the kitchen where she put the water to boil. She was watching him closely. There's something else that you need to know, she said. I don't want you to get upset, especially not now when you're getting ready for this important task. But you need to know.

She told him.

Bhaskar took a deep breath. His face became transformed. That's hard to believe.

You don't think it's possible?

It's totally possible. It just hadn't occurred to me. But it makes perfect sense.

My God, he said, bowing his head. Why? Why?

She put a hand on his shoulder. Maybe I shouldn't have told you this now, Professor Shrestha said, on the eve of this mission.

He raised his head and looked at her. No, you should have told me. No one should be in the dark, ever. Our mission is even more important now.

—

Bhaskar debated with himself whether he ought to confront Aditya-da about what Professor Shrestha had said. What would it accomplish? Nothing, he knew. Aditya-da would either deny it, or perhaps even more to his character, admit it and challenge his brother that there was nothing he could do.

Bhaskar took a circuitous route to the Asylum, playing in his head what he was going to say to his brother. An enormous despondency settled on his head, like a mammoth elephant. This must be the kind of depression that Kranti feels all the time, he thought. Poor Kranti. What had he brought her into? What kind of world was this? He should have never agreed to marry her—that way she wouldn't have been cursed with the fate of association with the Ghimirey family at all. The shame that Bhaskar felt, deep in his bones, about Raddi Tokari was so debilitating that he wondered if he'd simply collapse on the pavement. He'd always thought of himself as a strong person, someone who'd not be deterred by setbacks, major or minor. But now?

At the Brave Hospital, he stood to observe the giant statue of the Hippo. The unveiling of the statue had happened earlier that morning, witnessed by a large crowd—strips of giant green cloths covering the statue had been removed with the help of tall cranes with multiple arms. Gifts from President Corn Hair, the cranes had arrived directly from a factory in Amrika. The "anointing" of the statue, as Motherland TV was calling it, was supposed to happen the next day amidst a religious ceremony.

Bhaskar observed the monstrosity in front of him. The Hippo's face was so high up that you couldn't even see it properly. Families from all over Darkmotherland had come to see the statue. Many of them were staying over for the anointing. Tomorrow it was going to get crazy in this whole area. As Bhaskar watched the statue, he felt its massive presence crowding his consciousness. He imagined the Hippo to have a churlish smile up in the sky. With this giant statue, he had declared his complete control over Darkmotherland. The Hippo had hammered a final nail in the coffin of democracy. He had effectively made himself into a deity. Even the gods of Darkmotherland, who had dwelled among its inhabitants since the ancient times, didn't have a statue as big as this one. Yes, there were large statues of the Awakened One scattered throughout the Valley, often on hilltop monasteries, but they were no bigger than the size of a big bus. Until now, the largest statue in Darkmotherland was of the Pothead God, in his lungi and holding a trident in his right arm, standing on a hill in the eastern outskirts of the Valley, but PM Papa's statue was four times bigger.

Watching the statue, Bhaskar became paralyzed. He tried to move his arms and legs, but found that he couldn't. He tried to move his head, to ask for help, for himself, for Darkmotherland, but he couldn't. I'm done for, he thought.

Then someone bumped into him, cursing him for blocking the way, and he was jolted into movement. He hurriedly left the area and jogged toward the Asylum. He needed to finish the mission quickly. If he didn't do it soon, no telling what was going to happen. As he ran home, he considered whether it was even necessary that he confront Aditya-da about Raddi Tokari. What would be the point? That might prove to be a distraction. Focus, focus on the mission.

But once he saw his brother's face at home, that sneering, mocking face, Bhaskar lost it. Aditya-da was in the living room, watching the large TV, where Hom Bokaw was blathering on about the giant statue, praising its size ("thize doth mather"), saying how the statue would give a further boost to an already thriving tourism in Dark-motherland. "Bettha than Thweejerland," Hom Bokaw said.

"Brilliant, this man is," Aditya said when he saw his brother enter. He jabbed his finger at the TV. "You underestimate him at your own peril."

Bhaskar went to his brother, slowly.

"Look," Aditya said, pointing at the split screen images of the largest statues in the world. Hom Bokaw was showing them to emphasize how they all paled in comparison. "PM Papa is putting Darkmotherland on the map," Aditya said.

When Bhaskar reached him, Aditya said, "Boss move, that's what it is. Total dominance. He's going to crush you Lefties like insects, brother. You better surrender. Now."

Bhaskar grabbed Aditya by the collar and pushed him toward the far corner of the room. "What have you done?" he whisper-snarled. "What have you done?"

They stumbled over a chair, a coffee table, Aditya trying to regain his footing while saying, "What the hell! What's wrong with you?" as Bhaskar gritted his teeth in anger. They both ended up in the far end of the living room, shielded by a wall so that anyone entering the living room would see them only if they peeked around the corner. But no one had come to check out what the noise was about—where was everybody?

If Aditya thought that his younger brother was horsing around, like they used to do in their childhood, he was disabused of this notion when Bhaskar, his mouth close to his brother's, asked, "What's happening at Raddi Tokari? Manchhe marira chha tya?"

Aditya tried to get his brother off of him but couldn't—Bhaskar was always bigger and stronger—so he ended up spitting in Bhaskar's face. But Bhaskar seemed to have become inured to such physical insults, for he ignored the spit sliding down his cheek and said, "Tell me, what really happening at Raddi Tokari? How long? Does Sir know?"

Aditya finally managed to push Bhaskar off of him and whispered back angrily, "Sir? You're asking about Sir? Of course he knows." The two brothers were now sitting on the carpet, underneath a painting of snow-capped peaks with a mountain goat in the foreground, the coffee table askew, the chair toppled next to them. "Sir just pretends he doesn't know, to keep his hands clean. I do all the dirty work for the family." Aditya smiled at his brother. "But I'm proud that I am able to do this for my country, bujhis?" The two brothers were sitting right next to each other, their knees touching. Aditya punched the air in front of his brother's face, as though about to hit him. "Pure Darkmotherland!" he whispered. "Pure Darkmotherland! Do you understand, my handsome Leftie brother? I'm not ashamed of it."

It was surprising that in that household, normally teeming with the Ghimireys and the nokerchakers, no one had come to the living room and peeked around the wall to catch the two brothers, disheveled, angrily whispering to each other. It was as though fate had decided to leave the two brothers to hash it out, like in a climactic moment in a drama.

"You have to face the consequences," Bhaskar said. "You *have to.*" He broke down, cried. "Aditya-da, Aditya-da, why did you do such a thing? Why did you need to go this far when you—we—have everything?"

Seeing his brother so despondent, so desperate, watching him cry—Bhaskar hadn't cried since his childhood days—stirred an emotion in Aditya, for he embraced his brother. "It's okay, bhai, it's okay. You're looking at this the wrong way. All you need to do is adjust your thinking a bit. Also, I urge you to consider the long-term implications of what's going on. Yes, in the short term it does look like something horrible is happening, but is it? When you're purifying an organism, don't you have to get rid of the negativities first? The impurities? That's all PM Papa is doing. He's turning Darkmotherland pure." Aditya lifted Bhaskar's hand and covered it with his palm to make it a fist, then gave it a slight jerk. "Pure Darkmotherland! Say it, brother. Once you say it, all becomes clear and you'll feel good."

Bhaskar told Aditya-da that a reckoning of sorts would be coming to him because "the Hippo is going to be no more." He realized, even as he said it, that he probably shouldn't have said it (he sounded so ominously prophetic). Aditya immediately started grilling him about what precisely he meant by it. Was PM Papa's life in danger? Is that what he meant?

This time it was Aditya who grabbed him by the collar and said, "What are you plotting? What is going on, Bhaskar? Are you planning on doing something to—? If something happens to PM Papa—" The brothers had glared at each other, like the staring contest they used to get into when they were kids, to see who would blink first.

Aditya let go of Bhaskar's collar and pushed him away. "But what am I worried about? PM Papa will crush you like an insect, like this." Aditya rubbed his thumb and forefinger and thrust it in front of Bhaskar's face. "And you know what? I wouldn't care if you got caught and they chopped your head off at Palace High, like they did to those buddies of yours, the Gang of Four. I'll come to watch it with my bag of popcorn, like this." Aditya popped a handful of imaginary popcorn into his mouth and vigorously chewed, as though he were masticating Bhaskar's bones.

Bhaskar, still panting from the brawl, said, "I don't recognize you anymore, Aditya-da. We'll see who crushes whom, but one thing is for sure. You will not escape this. I am going to tell everyone what's happened at Raddi Tokari. Do you not think that media around the world would be interested in publishing this? This level of horror? The *New York Times* would be interested in it. And they will listen to me—you know why? Because I am a Ghimirey."

"Try it," Aditya said, sneering. "Go public and it'll be me who'll crush you like an insect."

Bhaskar stood and straightened his clothes. "I'm beyond caring what happens to me, Aditya-da."

"Then you should care what happens to your new bride upstairs." Aditya jabbed his finger at the ceiling.

Bhaskar raised his eyebrows.

"Have you discussed your plots about PM Papa with her?" Aditya asked. "And if you're not around, do you think she'll survive in this household without you?"

"Don't count on me being gone so soon," Bhaskar had said and left the room.

All night Bhaskar was engulfed in a shroud of shame, replaying his argument with his brother in his mind. He wondered if it had been wise to suggest to Aditya-da that PM Papa wasn't going to be around anymore. Would Aditya-da say something to Sir, who would then suspect that Bhaskar had nefarious intentions about wanting to visit PM Papa? Or would Aditya-da think that Bhaskar was merely bluffing?

When he'd come upstairs, Kranti asked him whether he had been talking with Aditya-da downstairs earlier. Bhaskar said, "No, why?" She said that she thought she heard voices downstairs, an argument maybe, even a scuffle. Furniture scraping. She'd even gone down to check and had stood at the bottom of the staircase to see if there was anyone in the living room. But it was empty.

At some point in the night Bhaskar woke up feeling guilty about the way he'd physically attacked his older brother. Maybe he shouldn't have confronted him like that, maybe he should have been more composed. Then Bhaskar realized the absurdity of it. His brother was complicit in the horrors that were taking place at Raddi Tokari, and here it was Bhaskar who was feeling guilty.

By early morning, he decided that nothing mattered except that the Hippo be exterminated. Just as light hit the sky, he dressed quietly in the graying dark. He needed to get out of the house before there was another confrontation with Aditya-da.

Kranti asked him, sleepily, where he was going, and he responded that he'd be right back. At the door, he thought of something, then came to her and kissed her on the forehead and said, "Don't worry about anything, okay? If anyone tells you anything, don't mind it."

She opened her eyes fully and clasped his hand. "Who? Tell me what?"

"Nothing," he said, "just saying. Things are getting crazy everywhere."

"What crazy?" She sat up now, wide awake, alarmed. "Bhaskar, what are you talking about?"

He leaned over and kissed her, first on the cheek, then on the lips. Then he was gone.

—

That morning the Ministry of Education sent directives to schools to cancel classes so that students could attend the anointing of PM Papa's giant statue. The directives, in a typical Darkmotherlandite fashion, arrived only that morning, when most schools had already started their classes. Many schools hastily shut down and instructed their students to go to the Open Stage. Some schools even recalled their buses to the premises to transport the students. But Streetwise was a poor school, with no buses, and students had already arrived and were in the classroom.

Bhaskar had already started his first period, so he decided that he was just going to ignore the directive and continue teaching. His mind was still reeling from the revelation about Raddi Tokari, from his physical tussle with Aditya-da, and the meeting that was scheduled for later this evening with PM Papa in the Humble Abode. After he finished teaching, he was going to go to Beggar Street, pick up the Ruger, then head on back to the Asylum, where his father would be waiting for him.

Bhaskar wrote four math problems on the blackboard for the students to solve. When he finished writing the fourth problem, he turned to the students to instruct them about the principles they were to apply. That's when the men appeared at the door. There were four of them, wielding khukuris and machetes. They wore the yellow bandanas of Papa's Patriots.

～

The news reached her swiftly, almost eagerly. Kranti likened it to how the news of Dada's death had arrived, through a disembodied voice via a phone call from Hotel Thunderbolt & Diamond. Come quickly, that voice years ago had said, there has been an accident. Now, it was not a stranger but Kabiraj, and the wording had been different. "Something terrible has happened, Kranti," Kabiraj said.

She was in Bauko Bank when he'd called. The entire office had been watching the anointing of the giant statue of PM Papa in Open Stage, on Motherland TV. A smiling PM Papa was cutting the ribbon. Then his short figure, in daura suruwal, made his way toward the front of the statue. Rozy was walking beside him, also in daura suruwal, hair hiding underneath the dhakatopi. They were followed by several members of his cabinet, including Dharma Adhikari. Everyone was sporting a big smile. Had all of Papa's cabinet members become shorter, in order not to upstage PM Papa in the height department? Bhaskar had shown her magazine photos of government officials in Saddam Hussein's regime sporting identical moustaches to look like him. She had joked that Saddam Hussein could easily send the wrong minister to the gallows thinking he was someone else. Then, there were the men in the North Korean dictator's regime: all donned the same bland safari suit, the men fattish and roundish with severe faces. If the dictator laughed, they all laughed. If the dictator scowled, they all scowled.

On Motherland TV, General Tso was marching alongside PM Papa toward the massive left foot of the statue. With his stern face, he looked North Koreanish, thought Kranti. A handful of generals marched behind him, followed by a bunch of swamis. This had become his regular entourage during his public appearances: Rozy by his side, wearing a daura suruwal and a dhakatopi on his head hiding his long hair, flanked by his bodyguards, his cabinet members in daura suruwal, a handful of generals under General Tso's command, and finally, about half of dozen swamis led by Swami Go!swami.

PM Papa approached his statue, then, incredibly, touched his left foot, i.e. the statue's foot—given the statue's size, he could only touch a portion of the toe. He brought his hand to his forehead in a gesture of deference, as one would do to a deity or a respected elder. It was as if the statue of PM Papa in front of him—towering over him like the Giant Beanstalk loomed over Jack in that Angrezi fairytale, the top so high that it disappeared into the sky—was not him but a deity indeed, a figure demanding the utmost reverence. If PM Papa's entourage was perplexed by his action, they didn't show it. They all followed suit by going to the statue, looking up at its disappearing head high, high above them, then reached out with their right arm to touch the toe, which was the size of a small room. Then they touched their forehead with that hand, as though saying, "I only deserve to be the dust of your feet."

Everyone paid their respects except Rozy, who swerved to the side as he approached the statue, and planted himself in a corner. General Tso stood at ramrod attention to the side, as though he couldn't touch the statue's foot because he had to stand guard to ensure that everyone else behaved.

"That is so good," one of Kranti's colleagues in Bauko Bank said, her eyes glued to the TV.

"Aren't we lucky to have PM Papa as our leader?" another colleague said.

"It's a matter of great pride for Darkmotherland to have the largest statue in the world in our great nation," the manager said.

Right then Kranti's mobile, which she had in her hand, buzzed. Kabiraj. She never received calls from him at work; at most they exchanged texts, which Kranti deleted immediately after she read them. As she was debating whether to answer it, she got distracted by the "oohs" and "aahs" and gasps of delight in the office. On Motherland TV, small planes were flying around the statue's head. One of them was filming something strange: the statue's head was rotating, slowly. The plane painstakingly made a ninety-degree turn, then flew until the face was behind it, facing toward the Parade Ground, while its torso still faced the Diamond Park. It was disorienting to look at the statue with its head twisted backwards, even on a TV screen.

The statue's eyes seemed to be alive, as though it had rotated to that impossible angle to observe the Bhureys, and their antics on the Parade Ground.

"PM Papa can see everything!" Kranti's manager exclaimed.

Kranti's mobile buzzed again.

Her supervisor generally disapproved of her employees talking on their personal mobiles at work, but right now everyone was entranced with PM Papa's rotating head, so she stepped into the hallway and answered.

Kabiraj told her something really bad had happened. "Bhaskar," he said.

"What? What happened?" she said. She was next to a window that overlooked a busy street, where a julus, men clad in daura suruwal and women wearing gunyu cholo, were headed to the Open Stage as they chanted, "Pure Darkmotherland!" and "Long Live PM Papa!"

"You better come here quick," Kabiraj said.

"Is it gas? Is it gas?" Kranti asked. She saw herself getting into a taxi and hurtling toward Thunderbolt & Diamond. Why was Bhaskar at Thunderbolt & Diamond? Had he gone to see Dada?

"Kranti," Kabiraj said, "it's not gas. How can I say it?"

"Say it, dallu!" Kranti yelled into the phone. "Say it!"

"Bhaskar is dead."

PART II

PART 4

WIDOW

26.

On her way to meet Kabiraj in Laj Mahal, Kranti came upon a street theater at the edge of the Bhurey Paradise. Darkmotherlandites were still enacting their traumas, nearly a year and a half after the Big Two. Small, impromptu roadside melodramas. Nautanki. Victims of the monster earthquake fainting and screaming, howling and hollering. Women beating their chests, crying "Yo ma! Yo ma!" Young children mimicking being trapped in a giant rubble, that was formed by a bunch of laughing teenage boys who were trying their best to suffocate the little ones inside their huddle. Finally, someone from the audience cried out, "Hey, hey! Stop it! You're going to kill those little naniharu."

On the makeshift stage, the actors sang:

Crash. Boom.
La, la, la, la, la!
OMG, OMG
Bhaga, Bhaga!
Bhuichalo, Bhuichalo!
Ammai! Mariyoni!

A gaunt-looking man wearing a medieval bard's hat, with a long feather flowing out the back, cleared his throat and approached the mic:

The floor jerking like a sieve.
The neighbor's house bowing down.
Trees dancing, swaying, shuddering.
The earth cracks, it swallows.

The audience booed him for taking himself and his poetry so seriously, then, as if in counterpoint to his solemnity, people erupted into revelry, with dancing and gyrating, accompanied by madals, cymbals, and horns:

The Big One, yeah
The Big Two, yeah
The Big One in nineteen thirty-four
That's it, we thought, we won't get no more.
Then the Big Two
The Mother of All Quakes
Crap in our kattoos, it made us too.
Here a goo, there a goo.
Everywhere a goo, goo.

When the nautankis had started soon after the Big Two, there were some worries initially about whether the Rajjya would put a stop to them, simply because they could. But the Rajjya appeared to approve of them. "Cafartic," Hom Bokaw said on Motherland TV as the performances were shown on screen. "Goof for fealing."

Crash. Boom.
La, la, la, la, la!
OMG
Bhaga, Bhaga!
Bhuichalo, Bhuichalo!
Ammai! Mariyoni!
Ah! Ah!
Ah!

Before Bhaskar died, when it had become clear to Kranti that she was beginning to lose him to the Sangharsh, and when her affair with Kabiraj overwhelmed her with guilt, she often woke up to her own soft moans, "Ah! Ah!" as though she had just achieved orgasm.

Some days, when Kranti walked the streets, her thoughts whirled and churned along with the dust that still swirled in the streets. She experienced brief blackouts, and found herself in the middle of the street somewhere, talking to herself, not knowing where she was or whether she was still living in Beggar Street with her mother. She was confused about whether Dada was still alive or whether she was returning to Bhaskar's arms at the end of the day. She could sense the stares and laughter of those nearby, and she would come out of this black hole briefly, hoping that no one who knew the Ghimireys had spotted her in this condition.

She considered returning to Beggar Street. Looking around the Asylum, she thought, there's nothing for me here. Yet she stayed on. She felt nothing for anyone in the house, even Muwa, who was the kindest to her. Then she felt sorry for them, for they too had lost in Bhaskar a son, a brother, a brother-in-law, an uncle. When Kranti considered returning to Beggar Street, she experienced an even greater dread. Filled with memories of Bhaskar, she couldn't return to that life again, amidst the Beggars, thinking that they had a hand in his death.

It would have been logical to restart the Paagalium. She'd stopped taking it for Bhaskar's sake, to try to become normal for him. But he was gone now. Even though she hated the side effects—the tremor in her fingers, the feeling of numbness, the constantly dry throat, the upset stomach—the drug calmed her and made the voices recede. Poe appeared less frequently. She knew it was a mistake to stay off the medicine. When her episodes came, they usually came swiftly. Let them come, she thought. I'll put on a spectacular show for the Ghimireys.

The Ghimireys, for their part, hated her leaving the house. The widow of such an esteemed household walking the streets like a common woman? She could hear them think: we knew she was not one of us. But, they seemed to recognize that in her grief she was unreachable, and they didn't say much.

One time, when she returned to the Asylum after a few hours of haphazard meandering, Aditya eyed her and said, "Don't you get tired, pounding the streets for hours like a common woman?" He hadn't tried to hide his disdain for her, and the suggestiveness of the "common woman" wasn't lost on her, even in her spaced-out mental state.

They had all been sitting in the living room, as though anticipating her arrival, and she thought maybe Shambhogya would take offense at her husband's insult. But no one said anything, so Kranti said, in a deadpan voice, "Oh, have you all been waiting for me? How considerate!" Then she went up to her room.

Bhaskar's body had been brought to the Lord of the Animals ghat completely wrapped in white. The cloth hadn't been lifted from his face, as was customary, because he'd been so badly mangled. She'd wondered if her in-laws were hoping she'd immolate herself in Bhaskar's funeral pyre. Fat chance, she'd thought, the daughter of Madam Mao throwing herself in the fire consuming her husband (this momentary solidarity with her mother hadn't escaped her). Instead, she'd actually cremated him, going against the wishes of the Ghimireys, for a woman wasn't supposed to light the funeral pyre of a man, even a widow mourning her husband.

She had seen Kabiraj at the ghat. Their eyes had met, and that was all.

After the cremation, Kranti had considered leaving the Asylum. But for where? Certainly not Beggar Street, and not with Kabiraj, not yet. Perhaps among the refugees in a corner in Bhurey Paradise at night, sleeping among the dogs and their fleas. There, she would have no responsibility. She could beg for food, for a few coins to be thrown her way. She could wear rags and heckle passersby. She could call them names. Oye fatso! Oye toothless hag! Oye slut! Oye retard! Oye sisterfucker. If Kabiraj passed her way, what would she say? Oye pudgy! Oye dallu! Oye romantic king of poets!

There were days when she was sure that the Ghimireys were plotting something. What exactly, she couldn't be sure. One time, she came out of her room and saw them in the atrium below, huddled next to the statue of Darkmother. She couldn't hear what they were saying, but they were whispering furiously. She continued to watch them, a faint smile on her face, as though saying, what mischief are you all up to. Eventually they looked up and saw her, then they all disbanded. Another time, she thought she heard some noise outside her door. She tiptoed to it and jerked it open. Thulo Maya and Shyam Bahadur were standing there smiling. She was sure they had their ears to her door, listening. To what? Her mumbles about Bhaskar and yellow bandanas? "Congratulations!" she said to Thulo Maya and Shyam Bahadur. "You deserve medals for being superspies."

She was reminded of the days after Dada died, when there'd been voices, whispers, sudden silences after she entered a room—the living room in Beggar Street, in a friend's house, the tea shop at college. Kranti wondered if she had now entered the same darkness that had engulfed her after Dada died. But when Dada died, she was young, and more vulnerable, more naive, than now. Fighting her mother all these years had hardened her.

Kabiraj was napping in Laj Mahal when she rang the bell, opened the flap, and entered. He rubbed his eyes and sat up. "I have missed you," he said.

"No tutoring today?" she asked.

"Later in the evening," he said.

She sat down next to him. She could tell that he wanted to touch her, but he was hesitant. She was in her white widow-dhoti, which, she noted ruefully, was not what she'd been wearing the last time she was here.

"We have to be careful," he said. "Now it's even more dangerous for us to be here together, now that you're a widow."

She was sitting on her haunches, her chin resting on her arms that were crossed at her knees. "I don't care what happens to me anymore," she said. She badly wanted to lean against him, close her eyes, let him soothe her, but it felt wrong to touch him, right now, so soon after Bhaskar's funeral.

"It's hard to believe he's gone," he said. "Human life. So easy to extinguish."

That sounded commonplace. Human life, so easy to extinguish—hardly poetic. And to think that Kabiraj's name meant the king of poets.

He was watching her and she knew that she would soon seek his arms. She had missed him, this pudgy, ugly-looking man with his large, bulging eyes.

"The big man himself is coming to the Asylum," she informed him.

"The big man?"

"The big kahuna. The bossy boss. The whip cracker. The Lord of Us All."

Kabiraj stared at her. "Sachchi?"

"Why would I kid, kiddo?"

"PM Papa?"

"The one and only. But he's come to the Asylum before, remember? For my wedding to Bhaskar. And he'd come to the cremation ghat."

"And you went to visit him in the Lion Palace and nearly got mauled by the Hanu Mans."

"Oh, yes," Kranti said. "My god, that already seems like so long ago. It feels like another era." Well, it was a different world now. One in which Bhaskar no longer existed.

"What is the purpose of the dictator saheb's visit now?"

"To console us all. To console me, I guess."

"Are you going to ask him?"

"Ask him what?"

"Whether?"

"Whether?"

"Whether he?"

"Whether he?"

"Whether he had a hand in it?"

She slapped his arm. "Stop dillydallying, dallu! Come right out and say it."

Kabiraj smiled and nursed the spot where he'd been slapped. In a little while she was going to blow gentle breaths on that arm, then kiss it, then kiss other parts of Kabiraj's portly body. In the immediate aftermath of Bhaskar's murder, she had not thought of Kabiraj as her lover. She had thought of him as tyo moro Kabiraj, that bastard Kabiraj, as though it was his fault that Bhaskar had suddenly been wrenched away from her, as though by calling her about what had happened, he had summoned Bhaskar's murder.

In those initial moments she blamed everyone. Kabiraj, the Ghimireys, PM Papa, the Fundys, the Bhureys, Darkmotherlandites, the khateykids, even the stupid school with its stupid name—Streetwise School—where Bhaskar had been hacked to death. She blamed Motherland TV, Motherland Radio, the dark swirling clouds that seemed ever-present in the skies above the Valley, the dust, the half-collapsed buildings on their way toward full collapse, inch by inch, even now, more than a year after the Big Two.

Now, she found herself becoming slightly aroused and she chastised herself: widow, behave! That led to a soft chuckle, prompting Kabiraj to chuckle. "Are you going to ask PM Papa if he had a hand in what happened to Bhaskar?" Kabiraj finally said.

Even Kabiraj was hesitant to say "Bhaskar's murder," just like everyone else. In the Asylum it was always "the Streetwise incident," or simply "Streetwise." It was okay to say, "Bhaskar's death," giving the impression that Bhaskar had died of natural causes, perhaps a heart attack, a brain aneurysm, a medication overdose, or even a car accident. All of these would be palatable deaths, unfortunate, sad, and tragic, but palatable.

The Ghimireys were not foolish enough to deny the facty-fact of the event. They simply wanted to separate the murder from the death because, in their thinking, the murder defiled their idea of what was an acceptable method of death for a member of the Ghimirey family.

Kranti had learned only later that Bhaskar and Prithvi Raj had an appointment with PM Papa at the Humble Abode the day he was killed. She had wondered why he was going there, but in her grief she hadn't asked why. Whatever it was, she didn't want to know; perhaps he was going to confront PM Papa over the Palace High Beheadings. She wouldn't put it past Bhaskar to have a confrontation with

Darkmotherland's most powerful man in his own residence. Maybe that's why PM Papa had him killed—if indeed he was behind it.

At the Lord of the Animals ghat, Kranti had watched Bhaskar's body burn next to the polluted river. Across the bridge, khairey tourists took pictures with their cameras. She had thought then that it didn't matter who was behind Streetwise. What really mattered was who groomed Bhaskar so that he would then be ripe to be killed. Who filled his head with ideas about injustices in Darkmotherland? Who taught him that dying for the Sangharsh was the only thing that had meaning in PM Papa's regime? That person was her mother, who had also been responsible for leading Dada to suicide. Professor Shrestha had passed on her rage to Bhaskar, told him it was okay to die for the Sangharsh, and Bhaskar, not to be outdone in the specialty of buffoonery, had gone and died on Kranti.

After Bhaskar was cremated, Kranti didn't leave her room for two whole days. The members of this esteemed household into which she had married knocked on her door. She wouldn't open the door to their knocks. They couldn't open it from outside because she'd locked herself in. You shouldn't be alone like this, they said through the closed door. The nokerchakers also came and spoke to her with their hajurs, khaisyos, and garisyos. But she wouldn't bother responding to them either because they were nokerchakers after all. Take away their pay and they would not care whether she lived or died. Harkey especially was extra solicitous. He had that look in his eyes. A strange look. At times it was compassion, other times pity; and sometimes, she couldn't tell what it was. "I think in his previous life Harkey worked for the mafia," Bhaskar had said after they were married and Kranti was introduced to all the nokerchakers. "If you watch *The Godfather* closely, you'll see Harkey in the background, his eyes impassive, ready to do Marlon Brando's bidding." Bhaskar took Kranti's hand, and, bowing his head slightly, said, "Be my friend?" He took her hand and said, "Godfather?" And he kissed it. Then he slobbered all over her hand and up her arm. She slapped him fondly on the cheek.

When Muwa knocked on her door, Kranti considered getting up, but in the end, she didn't open the door even for her mother-in-law.

She knew that she was not the only one suffering. Muwa too was devastated. Bhaskar was my favorite son, she often announced in front of her family—in front of Aditya and Chaitanya, in front of Shambhogya and Priyanka, in front of Prithvi Raj, in front of the nokerchakers.

"He was my favorite son," Prithvi Raj Ghimirey had also said to Kranti when they were downstairs alone in the large living room the day after the cremation. She'd just awoken on the couch from a beautiful nap in which she and Bhaskar were running through a field filled with bright yellow flowers.

"Yes, Sir," she said.

Prithvi Raj sat beside her on the sofa and said, "You know, Kranti, of my three sons Bhaskar held a special place in my heart."

Bhaskar had told her that from their adolescent years his brothers had hungered to be part of the empire their father had built. In their teens, with suits and briefcases, Aditya and Chaitanya had accompanied their father into Ghimirey & Sons' various offices and factories. They observed and copied his business conversations and mannerisms, watching him and how he made decisions. Deals, contracts, bottom lines, bids, negotiations—phrases common in the Ghimirey household—ran through their heads even when they slept. They pondered commissions and profit margins, brand recognition, assets, and cash flow. And, over the years, they had taken what their father had given them and had expanded it. They continued the expansion despite the Big Two, and now, Kranti saw, despite Bhaskar's death. The business can't stop: this sentiment had been expressed by Aditya and Shambhogya, Chaitanya and Priyanka.

Bhaskar had not really been the old man's favorite, Kranti knew, yet his death had broken something in him; something had become unhinged. Kranti pictured a small screw inside his brain that held everything together—she recalled school lessons on the hypothalamus, cerebellum, and medulla, and her favorite, the oblongata—slowly becoming looser by the day. Dimag ko hawa phuskyo, she whispered. And of course, the air had gone out of her mind a long, long time ago.

———

In the hours after Bhaskar's death, everyone thought: PM Papa. After all, the men were wearing the yellow bandanas of Papa's Patriots. There had been instances in the past of Papa's Patriots appearing, suddenly, at a person's doorstep, or in a shop, or a park. Then, either a beating, a push into an idling van, or a slashing of the throat took place.

The Ghimireys, too, had entertained doubts, Kranti was sure.

Kranti heard the silent rebuttals inside her in-laws' heads as Bhaskar's corpse was transported to the Lord of the Animals ghat:

Why would he?

He's a friend of the family.

But what about the fact that they were Papa's Patriots?

They were Lefty instigators. PM Papa loved Bhaskar.

Of course he loved Bhaskar. He came to Bhaskar's wedding, didn't he?

He loved Bhaskar even though Bhaskar was always, always so much against PM Papa. Against him from day one. A Papee.

Papee or not, PM Papa would never harm a Ghimirey.

Unthinkable. They want us to think it was PM Papa.

And PM Papa phoned immediately after it happened, hadn't he? Came to the funeral, didn't he? Filled with sorrow for what had happened, even though Bhaskar was a Papee?

PM Papa had come to the cremation at the Lord of the Animals ghat, his rotund figure, clad in daura suruwal, flanked by bodyguards. He looked at Kranti, gave her an understanding look, and briefly, maddeningly, she'd felt grateful, even in her numbness. He had acknowledged that he had known her, that he had given a stamp of approval to her after she and Bhaskar had visited him in the Lion Palace.

If he was surprised that Kranti was at her husband's funeral, he didn't appear to disapprove. The Ghimireys had at first frowned at Kranti's wish to cremate Bhaskar, as the Fundys often raised a stink about women going to the cremation area, but in the end they had relented. The Fundys didn't prevent Kranti from going to the cremation ghat simply because she was a Ghimirey. However, Swami Go!swami was reportedly not happy.

At the cremation ghat, PM Papa had stood next to Kranti, who was already in her widow-white dhoti. Motherland TV didn't broadcast that image, for it didn't want to anger the Fundys, who'd be loath to see PM Papa next to a widow where the widow wasn't supposed to be. But the image of him with Prithvi Raj Ghimirey was broadcast throughout Darkmotherland, with the caption, "PM Papa grieves with Ghimirey & Sons." Most likely, it had also helped tame speculations that PM Papa might be behind Bhaskar's death.

PM Papa's visit to the ghat had helped dilute the Ghimirey's suspicion about him. "He cares," Aditya said later.

"Of course, he cares," Prithvi Raj said.

"He's always cared," Priyanka said.

"What was he whispering to you at the ghat, Sir?" Chaitanya asked.

In the footage on Motherland TV, PM Papa's mouth had been close to Prithvi Raj's, in a near-kissing gesture, as Prithvi Raj stood in his dhoti, his man-boobs on display, in front of Bhaskar's pyre that was yet to be lit.

"He said to me . . ." Prithvi Raj choked. "He said, 'We will avenge your son's death, I promise.'"

"He's as devastated by this as we are," Aditya said.

"And all these people saying that he had a hand in what happened to Bhaskar," Priyanka said, shaking her head.

"PM Papa is our ally," Aditya said, his voice emotional. "He'd never harm the Ghimirey family, no matter who or what Bhaskar was involved with."

"It's someone else," Shambhogya had said.

Soon enough, it was being said in the state media that it was actually the Son of Yeti who was behind Bhaskar's death.

Why?

Why not? What better way to create confusion? Turn the Ghimireys against PM Papa.

Why not? He wants to show that he can kill someone important
with impunity.

One afternoon PM Papa had called during the mourning period,
when relatives, friends, and associates visited the Asylum to offer
their condolences. The Ghimireys were all in the living room, talking
quietly with about a dozen visitors, including a couple of prominent
businessmen. Kranti was sitting on a sofa beside Prithvi Raj when
his mobile buzzed. It was PM Papa, who asked to be on the speaker-
phone so Kranti could also hear. Prithvi Raj thanked PM Papa and
told him that Bhaskar was a good boy. "He always thought well of
you," Prithvi Raj said, a blatant lie. He praised PM Papa for his support, a message that was intended not only for PM Papa but also
for the visitors. In that instant, Kranti could sense their awe of the
Ghimirey family grow. It was known that PM Papa and Prithvi Raj
were long-time friends, but to witness an actual phone conversation,
in real time? PM Papa's voice was audible, booming in the room, the
same voice that gave fiery speeches on Motherland TV. Kranti, PM
Papa said, I too am suffering your loss, my heart is also heavy with
Bhaskar's absence today.

His voice had choked on the phone, and there were murmurs
in the room. The great PM Papa showing such emotion. He truly
loved the Ghimireys. Everyone's eyes welled up. Such a good man,
such a caring man. At that moment, Kranti too had believed that
PM Papa had cared for Bhaskar—even though Bhaskar had been
against him. Then, later that night she'd thought of the Palace High
Beheadings, and about the time PM Papa had cheered as Bangara Singh had brained Sweej Cheej with his gada. Kranti hadn't

been able to reconcile these two thoughts and had simply stopped thinking about them.

If there had been oblique suggestions prior to the phone call that PM Papa had somehow been involved in Bhaskar's murder, fingers now increasingly pointed toward the Son of Yeti. Aditya thought that a personal visit to the Asylum by PM Papa would put all the ugly speculations about PM Papa to rest once and for all. Initially, Prithvi Raj was doubtful. Wasn't his appearance at the cremation and the subsequent phone call enough? But Aditya had insisted that they try to get him to come, that news reports about the big man's personal visit to the Asylum would be good for Ghimirey & Sons. Besides, it'd be an honorable way to remember Bhaskar, Aditya had added.

—

"Do the Ghimireys know you're here?" Kabiraj asked after their love-making. Both were under the bedsheet, totally naked, his flaccid penis against her belly. His hairy body felt good against her. Caressing his chubby face felt good. God, it felt good to have sex after such a long time. How long had it been? Weeks probably. She couldn't even tell if the last time was with Bhaskar or Kabiraj. Before he died, Bhaskar was spending so much time with the Beggars that he was hardly around.

She and Kabiraj hadn't talked much about what he'd seen at Streetwise. She'd understood that he'd arrived at Bhaskar's classroom only after the men had left. If Kabiraj had wanted to give her the details of the scene at the murder—how Bhaskar's body lay, how the children were screaming—he'd been dissuaded by the look on Kranti's face: she didn't want to know.

She pressed her chest against Kabiraj and said, "Of course, they don't, dallu. They think I'm at my mother's place, in Beggar Street. The Ghimireys will go into a major tizzy if they find out about you and me."

Kabiraj leaned back and looked at her. "Are you sure they don't know already?"

"I would have sensed it if they knew."

But Kranti had a feeling that the time was coming when the Ghimireys would find out. Until now, until Bhaskar's death, they had no reason to suspect her of infidelity. It would not have occurred to their elitist minds that Kranti would actually take on a lover, a nobody poet who lived in a tent in Bhurey Paradise.

"Have you gone to visit her, your mother?" Kabiraj asked.

She shook her head.

"You should," the pudgy poet said. "She's probably grieving as badly as you."

Murti had called Kranti on her mobile soon after the funeral. Kranti, still in a daze, had picked up her phone, not paying attention that the number wasn't familiar. Murti told her that Professor Shrestha wasn't taking Bhaskar's death well. She was even refusing the company of the Beggars. How they must have felt, the Beggars, to be shunned by their goddess. But Murti, who had been with Professor Shrestha the longest, had kept a vigil at Beggar Street, day and night, cooking food for her Madam, trying to coax her to eat, even as her Madam asked her to go away, to leave her alone. Murti told Kranti this, then said, "You must come, Kranti nani." That's when Kranti had hung up.

In the days that followed, her mobile had rung incessantly. The same number. That Murti was a persistent bitch. Murti called on the landline, asking for her. Kranti had told the nokerchakers to say that she was not at home.

Shambhogya had asked Kranti why she wasn't taking the call from Beggar Street. Kranti replied, "My mother has nothing to offer me."

Shambhogya had said, not unkindly, "But she's your mother. I'm sure that she feels for you." Unsaid was this, "Even though she despises us."

Muwa, on one of those rare moments when she'd emerged from God's Room, had said, her own eyes drowning in heartbreak, "You shouldn't act like this with your own mother. I'm sure that all she wants to do is to console you, and perhaps be consoled herself."

First, my husband gets murdered, Kranti mused to herself, and now here I am, a freshly widowed buhari of one of the most prominent houses in this Valley of the Gods, sleeping with a common poet in an even more common tent in a refugee camp smack in the middle of the city. A tent the poet himself, in a moment of poetic genius, had named The Palace of Shame. The Ghimireys, if they ever got a whiff of what she was up to, could come down here any moment, even though they would be loath to set foot in Bhurey Paradise. On second thought, the Ghimireys would probably not come themselves to get her. The Ghimireys would send someone, one or more of the nokerchakers, maybe Harkey, who seemed to be at Aditya's beck and call, willing to do anything for him, perhaps even kill a freshly widowed buhari.

She and Kabiraj could also be discovered by the Fundys, which might not be any better than being discovered by the Ghimireys. They could barge in at any moment, as they often did in Bhurey Paradise. It was usually four or five of them, almost always men, for women in such aggressive roles didn't fit their ideals of the women as the ever-feminine, chaste maternal figures. There were reports now, however, that some women Fundys, increasingly unhappy with the rampant moral decay of Darkmotherland, had formed their own separate group, Yoginis, and were going around harassing women they thought were licentious or uncouth. The rationale was that women telling other women to be more chaste would have more impact than men telling women to be more chaste. And of course, there were jokes about Fundys and Yoginis copulating in the woods of the Lord of the Animals temple.

"Have the Fundys been around lately?" Kranti asked Kabiraj, later, as she put on her dhoti.

"Yes," Kabiraj said, tightening the belt of his trousers. "They have PM Papa's blessings. Who's to stop them?"

"Your advanced warning system doesn't work?"

"Sometimes they're too quick for us."

When the Fundys barged into the tents and houses in Bhurey Paradise they did so with a lot of noise and whoops and hollers. "*Eh! Heh! Geh! Peh! Meh!*" That's what it sounded like, although they were really chanting some Sanskrit verse to juice themselves up. They also flailed their arms and made guttural, animalistic noises. Kabiraj had once said they resembled some type of monkey, some orange breed.

"What was that animal you called the Fundys?" she asked him now.

"Orangutans," Kabiraj said. "With their orange robes."

"Orangutans," she said, bursting into laughter. It was not that funny, but he'd said it so quietly and in such a neutral voice, it was hard not to laugh. And she laughed a lot with Kabiraj.

"Like this?" she said, flailing her arms and legs about and starting with "*Eh! Heh! Geh! Peh! Meh!*" and moving on to "*Ka, ka, koo, koo.*" Kabiraj, now sitting, watched her softly, adoringly, a foam of spittle on his lips.

"Kok koo?" She stopped flailing and stood on her right leg, arms stretched in front and above, left leg raised high, bent at the knee.

"Papakoo ka, koo kwat?" Kabiraj asked softly.

"Krouking kiker kikken krakken."

"Kwat?"

"Krouching tiger hidden kragen," she said. "Kwatch."

Then she started doing slow martial arts moves. Her moves from the karate classes she had taken during her teen years came back to her. What had she earned? A brown belt, green belt, burgundy belt, whatever, she didn't remember. She had stopped going after Dada's death. "Watch what I do to the Fundys," she said. She was in her widow's white dhoti. It was ridiculous. Where in the world would you find a white-dhotied widow enacting kung fu moves on imaginary Fundys? Exactly here, in the sunlit tent named Laj Mahal belonging to a shy, pot-bellied king of romantic and soul-searching verse.

"Aiiieeeee!" she screamed, delivering some well executed kicks and punches to the imaginary Fundys, who emitted many "ouch!"

and "aiya!" and "mercy!" which Kabiraj dutifully vocalized. The bludgeoning of the Fundys continued. Kranti flew through the air, landing deadly kicks. One flying drop kick snapped a Fundy's head so hard that it spun on its axis once, twice, then a third time, finally coming to rest with the neck twisted at 180 degrees so the face looked behind him rather than to the front. Like PM Papa's giant statue! Kabiraj drummed his belly and laughed. The Fundy tried desperately to realign his neck with his hands.

Kranti lunged at the Fundys, as though attacking them, and, as they cowered at the edge of the tent, she conducted a swift sleight of hand and—fhut! fhut! fhut!—their dhotis were on the floor, revealing their saffron undies. Saffron undies? Who wore saffron undies? The Fundys, who else? "Fundys in undies!" Kranti vocalized, pointing at their crotches. One of the Fundys, it turned out, was wearing an undie-in-name-only, a thin strip of loincloth that didn't even bother hiding his package. He had nuts as big as bowling balls, with his micropenis ensconced somewhere deep within.

"Mother, please forgive us!" the Fundys supplicated and begged.

"Don't call me mother, motherfucker," Kranti said, then performed the mother of all roundhouse kicks, jettisoning the Fundys right out of the tent's door. She then climbed up and down the inside of the tent's walls, as Kabiraj watched in awe. After perching upside down on the tent's ceiling like a bat, she flew in circles inside Laj Mahal, poking Kabiraj in the belly, in the chest, and on the arm every time she went past him. Finally, she landed on the bed, closed her eyes, and drifted off into a dreamy sleep.

27.

Something was afoot.

Shambhogya and Priyanka were up to something. They had a furtiveness about them. First, Shambhogya came to ask if Kranti had a chinha.

"I don't think I do," Kranti said. "My mother never believed in such things."

Shambhogya had come into Kranti's room. Both were seated on her bed.

"Could you check?" Shambhogya said.

"Why do you need to see my astrological chart?"

"Sir was requesting it."

"For what purpose?"

"Jyotish Jeevan is back in town after his trip to Amrika. We're all having our charts read."

Kranti wasn't sure she was expected to know that name. "Jyotish Jeevan?"

"He's our family astrologer. Very accurate."

"I wonder if my chart shows my widowhood."

"Shhhh," Shambhogya said and put her finger on Kranti's lips. "It's inauspicious to talk like that."

Superstitious much? But aloud she said to Shambhogya, "Maybe I'm the one who's inauspicious? My father died, and now Bhaskar is also gone. Maybe I'm not right for this family."

Shambhogya faked outrage. "If I hear you say that one more time I'm going to be very upset with you. You belong here. That's why Bhaskar babu brought you here. You're here for a purpose. This is a great family. Would you rather be in any other family in Darkmotherland? I am like your sister, Kranti. Priyanka is like your sister. We'll take care of you."

Before she left the room, Shambhogya reminded Kranti to ask Professor Shrestha for the chinha. "It'll make Sir happy." She paused at the door. "He is very fond of you, you know. He loved Bhaskar so much."

The next day Priyanka came to her room to inquire if she'd gotten the chart from her mother.

Kranti became annoyed. "What is with this chart business?" she said. "It's as if everything hinges on my chart."

"It's not me who's asking," Priyanka said sullenly. "Jyotish Jeevan is coming tomorrow."

"Are you having your chart read too, Priyanka?"

"Of course," Priyanka said. "Jyotish Jeevan is the best in Darkmotherland. He's the one who predicted, years ago, that the king would be kicked out of the palace."

"But he couldn't predict the Big Two?" Kranti asked.

"The Big Two was something else," Priyanka said. "You know what I think, Kranti-di? I think the Big Two was a gift from God. There! I've said it. I know it sounds awful when you hear it like that, but I increasingly think that it's true."

"It's a cruel God, then, isn't it?"

"God is never cruel," Priyanka said. "And you shouldn't talk like that about our Gods. Maybe the Christian God is cruel, what with their hellstone and brimfire."

"Hellfire and brimstone."

"Whatever," Priyanka said. A curious mix this one is, thought Kranti: utterly, stupendously religious on the one hand, and like a teenager on the other.

"The Big Two was necessary," Priyanka said. "Divine intervention. To make us come to our senses. To stop us from sliding into the Age of Darkness." If this wasn't a direct quote from Swami Go!swami, the leader of the Fundys, then it was uttered by a Rajjya official expounding the virtues of Darkmotherland's ancient culture.

"You believe all of that?" Kranti asked.

"Why wouldn't I?" Priyanka said, almost defiantly. "I bet you conveniently forgot the precipice on which our beautiful country was tottering. The riots, the looting, the burning. The ethnic cleansing.

And now look at what our PM Papa has done. He has restored sanity. Now our country is united, once again."

Precipice. Tottering. Restoring sanity. United, once again. These were all PM Papa's words. Kranti herself had been sucked into these words at one point because she thought that PM Papa would protect Bhaskar. But even the big kahuna couldn't prevent Bhaskar from dying. Or the big kahuna himself had a hand in it.

But Priyanka was so young, younger than her actual years, one could almost forgive her for her naivety. And now, as she watched her younger sister-in-law, for a foolish moment, Kranti thought that Priyanka could be the sister that she never had. "What do you want to know about yourself, Priyanka?"

"You know what it is, Kranti-di. You're acting as though you don't know."

Kranti looked at her in confusion, then she understood. Of course. She didn't say anything further.

"I know you don't believe it, Kranti-di, but Jyotish Jeevan can work miracles."

The only way an astrologer can give you a baby, thought Kranti, is by sleeping with you.

Priyanka provided examples of childless women who had conceived by performing pujas, wearing rings with stones of tourmaline and azurite, and chanting siddhi mantras 100,000 times. She reminded Kranti that PM Papa also regularly consulted Swami Go!swami.

Kranti waited for Rozy in a rooftop restaurant in the Queen's Pond area. Rozy had finally called, offered condolences, then said that he wanted to see her.

The restaurant claimed on its signboard the doubtful honor of being "the tallest joint in Queen's Pond that the Big Two couldn't fell." Across the street was the Palace High School, where the beheadings had taken place. She felt a throbbing in her temples just thinking about it—the Charlie Chaplin jallad with his giant khukuri, the blindfolded members of the Gang of Four. That incident had changed Bhaskar, turned him into a different person. But perhaps he had never changed; she'd just deluded herself about who he was. Maybe he was already doomed—and she was doomed along with him—when, two years ago, she fell in love with him after he showed up in Beggar Street with his beautiful face.

Kranti shifted her eyes away from Palace High and observed the masses below: hawkers selling oil from rhino testicles, beggars, hypochondriacs, wrestlers, cyclists, barren women looking for lovers, old perverts eyeing schoolgirls, roadside clowns, soft-bellied rickshaw pullers, etc. The rainy season had bypassed Darkmotherland, and everyone had been praying for the rains so the dust would abate. The sun was out, and its rays felt good on her face, but there was still a bit of a chill in the air. If she looked beyond the Queen's Pond and the Diamond Park, she could see PM Papa's giant statue. Even from the distance, which was about a kilometer away, it was as though he was looking straight at her, grilling her with his eyes, as though daring her to accuse him of Bhaskar's death.

She looked away from his statue toward the north, where the mountains loomed right over the Valley. The Big Two had jolted the snowcapped peaks, pushing them closer to the Valley. "Oye ma!" people had shouted, the day after the Big Two, at the sight of the white mountains that seemed propped up in their own backyards. "Is that the Elephant God Mountain? But it used to be so far away!" And there were others, these giant creatures, at six thousand meters or higher, now all huddled close. Even Mt. Forehead in the Sky, the tallest summit in the world, could be glimpsed from rooftops in the Valley. It was odd to see the mountains crowding the Valley's skies to the north, as though they had hopped all the way from near the Chiniya border and were now squished together so they could keep an eye on the Valley residents. It was also odd that the mountains hadn't brought their cold. In fact, the Valley was as hot and sweltering as it was before. The Fundys tied the new proximity of the mountains to their theory that the Big Two was the result of gods outraged at the moral decay of the country: these mountain gods too were fuming.

Kranti was observing these summits, wondering if they were indeed angry, when Rozy appeared at the top of the staircase. He was wearing tight jeans and a pink shirt, half unbuttoned, showing his dark, smooth chest. On his head was a Make Darkmotherland Great Again cap, and his eyes were hidden behind sunglasses. This was his disguise.

After giving Kranti a hug, he sat down next to her, pulling his chair close to her. He held her hand. "I was devastated when I heard the news," he said. "But I also saw it coming."

Kranti asked him what he meant.

The waiter came and the two ordered smoothies, and resumed talking only after the waiter left.

"He's been on a mission of retribution."

"PM Papa?"

Both spoke in whispers.

"Who else?" Rozy said, smiling wanly. "Who else do I have?"

"I don't know what to believe."

"Just think, Kranti," Rozy said. "Who else would benefit from Bhaskar's death?"

"I don't know. What benefit is it to PM Papa?"

"Your mother."

Kranti shook her head in frustration.

"It's a signal to your mother that he can take her out anytime he wants."

The waiter came with their smoothies. He put the glass down in front of Rozy with a slam, as though he wasn't pleased about serving the likes of him.

"Did you see that?" Rozy said, pointing to the waiter.

Kranti nodded. "I'm going to call him back," she said, but Rozy signaled to let it be.

"Then why wouldn't he take out my mother directly?" Kranti asked. "Why Bhaskar?"

Rozy shrugged. "Maybe he thinks this indirect way is better? He wants to send a message that he won't tolerate any dissent." Rozy leaned back on his chair. "I have no doubt that it's him."

Kranti wasn't totally convinced, but she accepted what Rozy was saying at the moment. After all, Rozy knew PM Papa better than anyone else. More than anything, Kranti was surprised at her own reaction to Rozy's certainty: she didn't feel much. She didn't feel angry, not even upset. All she could think was: if it is PM Papa, it's not surprising. She still blamed her mother.

As if in response to her thoughts, her mobile rang. It was Murti. Kranti rolled her eyes.

"Who is it?" Rozy asked.

Kranti told him about Murti, how she'd been calling since Bhaskar's death.

Rozy squeezed her hand. "You should go see your mother."

Kranti shook her head. "I can't. I simply can't."

"She's your mother, Kranti."

"A fine mother she's been. She's also at fault. She's squarely at the center of this."

Rozy's hand moved to her shoulder, massaging it. "She's not going to be around much longer, then you'll miss her."

Kranti quickly looked at him, and Rozy said, "No, no, I don't mean that I know if he's already put a hit out on her, I just mean in general." Then Rozy seemed to rethink what he'd said. "But, you should be prepared. She might just be his next target. I don't know what he's thinking every moment, who he talks to, what he plans and executes."

A sharp wind of fear passed through Kranti's body. Throughout her life, in moments of anger and frustration, she'd wished death upon her mother, but what would she do if her mother really died?

Her phone rang again, and this time Kranti answered. Murti complained bitterly that she'd been calling for days. She'd even called Bauko Bank and was told that Kranti was still on leave.

"I'm here now," Kranti said. "What do you want?"

"Madam has holed herself up in her room, she hardly speaks to anyone."

"How's that my problem?" But Kranti knew that in a few minutes she'd reconcile herself to the fact that it would indeed end up being her problem. She fought a surge of anger. *Bhaskar was my husband, and even in my grief I can't mourn him in peace.*

Rozy squeezed her hand, as though to say, don't say such things. He couldn't fully hear what Murti was saying, but he'd guessed.

"Kranti nani," Murti said. "Please don't say that. I've never seen her like this. She's also, you know, drinking more than usual."

"All right, all right," Kranti said. "Now be quiet. I'll be there." She disconnected.

"It'll be good for you to go," Rozy said, standing. He snapped his finger at the waiter, who was huddled near the entrance with a couple of other waitstaff, giggling. The waiter brought the check on a tray, which also had some fennel seeds to chew on, and sulkily placed it on their table. Rozy put a thousand rupee note on the tray and dismissed him with a small wave of his fingers. The waiter returned to his coworkers to continue sulking. Rozy and Kranti overheard something about having to serve homos.

"Learn some customer service," Kranti said to the waiter as she and Rozy exited the rooftop.

Down the stairs, Kranti said to Rozy, "I'm glad you came to see me. But tell me"—she lowered her voice—"why are you doing this? Aren't you afraid for yourself?"

"Something is happening, Kranti," Rozy said, stopping at the floor below, next to a window. "Something is happening to me. I am trying very hard not to be afraid." Rozy said that PM Papa had said that he was going to consult doctors abroad, in secrecy, about how Rozy could have his baby. "There's also a woman he knows, called Awnty, that he's contacted." When Kranti asked what this Awnty could do, Rozy shrugged. "He's been pushing it, pushing it. He's not going to stop until he impregnates me." He pointed to the giant statue of PM Papa in the distance, visible through the window. "Look at how ugly that is," he said.

Professor Shrestha wasn't on her usual green sofa in the living room. Murti was cooking in the kitchen when she arrived. She stopped, wiped her hands on her dhoti and gave Kranti a hug. Kranti reluctantly patted her back. "Finally, you're here," Murti whispered. In a low voice, she offered sympathies, told Kranti how her "world came crashing down" when she heard the news about Bhaskar. He was loved by us all, Murti said.

Kranti knocked on her mother's door. At first Professor Shrestha didn't open it, even after knowing it was Kranti. Was she conveying that her own grief was greater than her daughter's? When Professor Shrestha finally opened the door, Kranti saw that her eyes were bloodshot and the room smelled of alcohol.

Professor Shrestha waved her in and sat on the bed. "I've been remembering your Dada a lot lately," she said. "We should have never stopped doing his annual rites. I've wondered if he's happy up there."

"Dada had learned to make himself happy despite his circumstances." And it was not me who stopped with the annual rites, she thought.

Professor Shrestha patted her bed. "Come, sit."

Kranti sat down on the edge, at some distance.

"I also keep thinking how much your Dada would have liked Bhaskar."

Kranti had also thought the same thing, had even conjured imaginary conversations between Bhaskar and Dada, with Dada's jokes sending Bhaskar into uproarious glee. "Annual rites are a hoax anyway," Kranti said.

"Hoax? How are they a hoax?"

"You think that's what makes our ancestors happy? A ball of rice offered to them once a year?"

Professor Shrestha laughed. "True, but we can't abandon our customs."

"You're just feeling guilty about Bhaskar," Kranti couldn't help saying.

Professor Shrestha looked at her. She was about to say something, then rethought, finally saying, "Do you really think I have something to feel guilty about? After I've lost two of my favorite people? First Prakash and now Bhaskar. Poor Prakash, he was thinking about me, and my silly book *Cry the Cursed Country*, around the time he disappeared."

Kranti shook her head, deciding to drop this line of conversation. "Eating well, I see." She pointed to the small bottle of Scotch on her mother's bedside table.

Professor Shrestha nodded absent-mindedly. "It gives me strength," she said. "So, what are they saying at the Asylum? How are the Ghimireys doing?"

"How do you think they are doing?" Kranti asked.

"I hope they believe now the extent to which the Hippo will go."

"They don't believe PM Papa did it."

"They don't?" Professor Shrestha asked. "What stronger message can he send to his enemies? Kill the son of a prominent family, a son who was against him."

There were many things Kranti wanted to say to her mother, but words seemed futile now.

For a while, the two listened to Murti talking to herself in the kitchen as she cooked.

"The Ghimireys think it's the Son of Yeti," Kranti said.

"Of course they do. That's what they're saying on Motherland TV, that all clues point to Son of Yeti. What a crock."

"It's not totally implausible."

"Just think. If the Son of Yeti wants to kill anyone, wouldn't he go for his sworn enemy, that Hippo? Haven't you heard that the enemy of my enemy is my friend?" Professor Shrestha held her head in her hands. "The Hippo has the power to make you believe that your parents are your enemies, and turn them in."

Kranti nearly laughed at that one. She had, in fact, throughout her teenage years and even later, when Bhaskar became more and more enthralled with her mother, fantasized about turning her in to the authorities. Even now, she thought what it would be like to tell PM Papa that Madam Mao needed to be jailed for what had happened to Bhaskar. She pictured herself announcing it during his upcoming visit to the Asylum, watching the horror, and perhaps delight, on the faces of the Ghimireys. But her mother was right. The Rajjya's power can make you believe what it wants you to believe. Among the Ghimireys, suspicions regarding Bhaskar's death had quickly and easily shifted from PM Papa to the Son of Yeti. Kranti couldn't help recalling, again, how even in the Asylum, in the immediate shock after Bhaskar's murder, they had been surrounded by an unarticulated undercurrent that PM Papa might have had a hand in it. Kranti, who was near-delirious, had seen that thought flash on the faces of everyone. But the unarticulated suspicion was there only for the initial few hours and was soon replaced by growing doubts, then, finally, exoneration for PM Papa.

"I wouldn't be surprised if the Ghimireys themselves have a hand in this," Professor Shrestha said.

"Have you lost your mind?" Kranti said.

She watched her mother's face—maybe a screw had indeed become loose inside her.

"Why would that be so outlandish? He was the black sheep of the family. He was getting in the way. Here's another theory: the Ghimireys and the Hippo are in this together, to get rid of their biggest obstacle."

She didn't speak for a while, as though she was too sad to speak. Kranti should have left then but she didn't; she stayed, stewing over the insane pronouncements of her mother.

Professor Shrestha initially didn't want to eat dinner, but Murti coaxed her, and also managed to persuade Kranti to stay for dinner. It was beginning to get dark, and Kranti usually entered the gates of the Asylum before sunset.

They ate at the small dining table next to the kitchen, where Kranti had spent most of her childhood and young adult life eating and doing homework as Dada adoringly gazed at her. Murti had cooked dal-bhat with kauli and saag and mula ko achar. Despite her resentment against Murti, Kranti had to admit the food was delicious. However, Professor Shrestha hardly touched her plate. She wanted another drink, and Murti was about to give it to her when Kranti said, "The one evening I'm here, and you want to spend it in a stupor."

"It's no stupor," Professor Shrestha said, but she signaled no to Murti.

To make small talk, Kranti asked whether the Beggars visited.

"What Beggars?" Professor Shrestha said. "First Prakash, now Bhaskar. The Beggars are finished."

Murti said that Vikram and Chanchal did come by every now and then. "But they're also aware that Madam is grieving, so I've told them to call before they come."

After dinner, as Murti was washing the dishes, Kranti asked whether Professor Shrestha had Kranti's chinha.

"Your chinha? Now why would I have it?"

"Well, most normal families have chinhas, you know. I'm not asking about a six-legged monkey."

Professor Shrestha sighed. "Who has time for such superstition? Besides, what do they need the chinha for? Are they planning on getting you remarried?"

"Why can't you answer a simple question with a yes or a no?"

"But I told you. Why would I have it? If you're just going to come here and get annoyed with me, why come?"

"So, I shouldn't have come?"

Professor Shrestha threw up her hands in the air. "Is that what I said?"

After some silence, Kranti said, "Apparently there's a famous, family astrologer who's coming to the Asylum. Jyotish Jeevan."

"Oh, yes," Professor Shrestha said. "He's an old con. Used to be the royal astrologer when we were under the regime of the royals."

"They say he's been on an astrology tour in Amrika, and has now returned to Darkmotherland."

"I remember him from a couple of talk programs on TV. He is of the belief that women should be submissive. Agyakari—that's what he says is the proper role of women. He'll do well in this age of the Fundys. He'll probably look at your chart and say that you're now the property of Ghimirey & Sons and ought to be auctioned at the market."

I'm no one's property, Kranti thought. Not even yours. But then she felt foolish. She was arguing with her mother as though she were still a teenager. "They seem to believe he makes accurate predictions."

"Of course they do. He probably butters them up, tells them what they want to hear. And he has the ancient scriptures to back them up, now revived and amplified under the Hippo."

Her mother had a point. Since the Palace High Beheadings, the Fundys had become bolder, more strident, as seen in their increased appearances on Motherland TV. They were becoming louder and more aggressive about how the sacred texts were the only true guides to living a harmonious life, bound by traditions and rituals. The man should be the figurehead of the family. The woman should submit to her man. The woman should be chaste. Intercaste marriages pollute our religious heritage. Homosexuality is an abomination, a disease; Swami Go!swami had even begun talking about a conversion therapy that was a mixture of hatha yoga postures, daily meditation, and ingesting rare herbal mixtures.

During the monarchy years, Professor Shrestha had said on live television that religion was a curse on Darkmotherland, an utterance for which, after much hue and cry from religious corners, she had been briefly imprisoned. Dada was still alive then, and he had taken Kranti to visit Professor Shrestha in Monkeygod Gate jail. In her cell Professor Shrestha was surrounded by her minions, likeminded atheists and communists. Even in the crowded cell, someone had procured a chair for Professor Shrestha, and there she sat, legs pulled up and crossed in the lotus position, with the others in a semi-circle on the dusty floor, just like at Beggar Street.

28.

When Professor Shrestha was sixteen, she had joined the Sang-harsh against the autocrats. Then, once they were toppled, and the monarchs came into power, she joined the resistance against the monarchs. When the Shades-Wearing King banned all political groups, sketches of Professor Shrestha's face, along with others from the resistance movement, appeared all over Darkmotherland. She lived in the jungle for a couple of months. Legends about her grew.

She had a pet tiger to whom she whispered about the upcoming revolution, some said.

Others countered: she wasn't talking about the country's revolution, stupid. She was talking about her daughter Kranti, revolution.

But she wasn't pregnant then.

How do you know? How do you know she wasn't?

She hadn't yet met her husband, Chef-ji.

Where is it written that she could get pregnant by only one man?

The timelines don't match. She gave birth to her daughter much later, after she came aboveground and met the chef, with whom she fell in love. If she was pregnant in the jungle, the gestation period would have to have been years, which is physically impossible.

Gestation-festation. She knew she was going to birth a daughter. She told the tiger, a real devotee.

They say he growled at others, but purred when she stroked him.

I'm sure she stroked many other things, made them purr. Wasn't she the only woman among men?

Yes, and she continued to be the only one when she was sang-harshing against the monarchs.

Sangharshing? Is that even a word?

Sangharsh turned into an active verb.

That's when the Beggars formed. She was never satisfied.

Even after the last king was booted out, she wouldn't give up, that one.

She didn't think much of the Maoists either.

No, she didn't. She was highly critical of their tactics when they began the Civil War. She thought their corruption would surface once they grabbed power. She didn't trust them: she was her own person. But you know she once had an affair with a Maoist leader, don't you?

What? That's impossible. She hated the Maoists.

That was later, after the Maoists started slaughtering people like goats. This affair was before the Civil War.

With whom? The Fierce One?

No.

Mr. Cloud?

Guess again.

Get out of here!

Yup.

The PhD Wallah? The Killer with a Brain?

You got it.

But he was already married. To that awful woman with that hideous smile.

Maybe that's why he had an affair with Madam Mao. She had a more Colgate smile.

I'll be damned!

A little-known fact, eh? In any case, she continued with her Beggars. She went on to get her PhD, became a professor, wrote scholarly articles, but in her heart of hearts she's always been a fighter.

Her husband's suicide crushed her, didn't it?

She's a tough one, that Madam Mao. She keeps going, like that Energizer bunny.

⁓

"Wait," Kranti said to Professor Shrestha in the living room, as Murti was washing dishes in the kitchen. "I seem to recall seeing something like my chinha in this house."

Professor Shrestha shook her head dismissively. "There is nothing."

But the memory persisted for Kranti: Dada showing her a parchment of rice paper with diagrams, and his voice, "Your Saturn is in the third house, which means that you have Raja Yoga. Very lucky. And you're going to be a strong woman." Why did she have that image? Dada wasn't an astrologer.

Kranti stood.

"Leaving already?" Professor Shrestha asked.

"No, I'm going to my room for a while."

She went to her room—former room, she reminded herself—and shut the door. Dust had collected on the desk, the windowsills. On the pillow was a poetry book by Khalil Gibran that that she and Bhaskar used to read together, out loud, sometimes to drown out the voices of the Beggars from the living room. Its edges were curled now from lack of use. A couple of cockroaches scurried across the floor. Her mother obviously hadn't done much cleaning since Kranti married and moved to the Asylum. But what did it matter? This was no longer her home. Still, she opened the window to air out the room's musty, suffocating smell.

In the closet she found the box in the far, dark corner, hidden behind old shoes and badminton racquets that hadn't been used since Dada's death. It was under an ironing board behind her clothes. She pulled it out, this box in which Dada kept his things, a box whose existence Professor Shrestha wasn't aware of, even now, because Kranti had kept it hidden from her when Dada's things were disposed of after the funeral. The Grateful Dead jacket was there, inside a plastic bag. She took it out and pressed it against her nose, as though expecting to smell Dada. But he'd died before getting a chance to wear it. She recalled the ruckus with the monkeys at the Lord of the Animals ghat when she'd gone there to burn it. She put the jacket back in the plastic bag.

In the box were his diary with songs and jokes, some old books, a pen he liked, and a watch that Professor Shrestha had bought for him in Hong Kong, now with the glass yellowed. And the gun which he'd purchased in a back alley of Old Dilli when he was younger. It was a small gun, one that fit into his palm when he held it, and on the handle was written RUGER. "I don't know why I bought it, Kranti," Dada had said. "Can you see me shooting a gun, ever?" Kranti had shaken her head and smiled, and Dada had said, "That was even before I met your mother." Perhaps you had a feeling that you'd need to shoot your own wife one day, Kranti had cruelly thought then. And after Dada died, she wondered why he hadn't simply used the gun on himself. Why use gas, at work, to do the job? She'd concluded that because he was such a gentle soul, he didn't want Kranti to discover him dead at home, his brains splattered against the wall.

She took the gun and briefly held it in her hand, then put it back.

Tucked inside one of Dada's books was a sheet of rice paper containing her chart, with symbols for the sun, the moon, Jupiter, and the other planets drawn inside rectangles and triangles. Yes, right, this can foretell my future, she thought. She located Saturn. "How lucky my Saturn is, Dada," she whispered, "to lose first my father and then my husband. Maha lucky. Super lucky."

On the way back from Beggar Street, Kranti found that a portion of the street was blocked off to clear traffic for the passage of a minister. That old Darkmotherlandite government practice, one that existed even before PM Papa, of making life difficult for the public to appease a VIP, was still intact. She was forced to take a circuitous route home, which forced her into Diamond Park. The area had become even more crammed and compact lately, with more people squeezed into the same small space. And still the Bhureys kept arriving every day. The Big Two had caused more damage up in the mountains than what had been reported. A year and a half after the Big Two, Motherland TV and Motherland Radio were still cagey with their answers. One day they said that the situation was improving, that such-and-such road leading to the mountains was beginning to open. A few days later, the situation was improving, but "it takes time." Then, again, "Reconstruction of such-and-such road that snakes its way into the mountains is finally underway. Better Than Sweejerland!" But didn't that road open a few weeks ago, someone asked timidly? Doubts were raised, then quickly dismissed. They must have heard it wrong. Or that the situation changed quickly in the mountains, what with its landslides and the pouring rain and whatnot. "Our Loyal Army has dealt a significant blow to the Yetifolk up in the mountains," Motherland TV would announce. "The Yetifolk are retreating." Then a few weeks later, "The Son of Yeti has occupied a mountain pass close to the Valley. PM Papa, Darkmotherland's fiercest protector, has ordered two Loyal Army battalions to the area to regain control of the mountain pass. Stay tuned."

Today as Kranti navigated her way through Diamond Park, a boy in a hoodie handed her a piece of paper, with the Kaneykhusi logo. A rag, really, that resembled the mimeographed sheets of yonder years, the kind that used to be hawked in the Stone Fish Market when the monarchs reigned supreme. Since Papakoo, a handful of underground newspapers had started, but they couldn't survive PM Papa's regime; some were violently shut down, and some closed after the editors were imprisoned or disappeared. A number of these rags originated in the Bhurey Paradise. One of them, Kranti remembered, was particularly successful, boasting a readership of thousands, and even contained ads for "secret, sensuous massage" and "erection pills." The rag was particularly vicious in its attack of PM Papa. And soon enough, its editor died of purported food poisoning in his tent. His wife, who helped publish the rag, was imprisoned on charges of her husband's murder. Since then, the underground rags had disappeared ("they are now truly buried underground," someone said), with only an occasional pamphlet appearing here and there, encouraging a revolution. Rise up for a kranti! they declared. And Kranti thought: Well, here I am, you morons, rise and kneel.

The Kaneykhusi rag read:

Our country is in trouble.
We're helpless turkeys going gobble, gobble, gobble.
All courtesy of one rascal, a real *mapa*
He should be first hung, then tried, our very own—
PM Papa!

Kranti crumpled up the paper and threw it away.

A little later she passed by Mofo Momos. Kranti walked quickly before Na-Ryan could spot her. He'd want to offer his condolences over Bhaskar, and Kranti simply wasn't in the mood.

She did, however, stop by Tato Chiso to order a cappuccino. She distractedly picked up a *Motherland Daily* that was lying on the table. The headline read: "Mr. Handsome Now Not So Handsome." She didn't pay attention to the words because she was still thinking about her conversation with her mother regarding who might be behind Bhaskar's murder. Briefly, Kranti wondered if that was indeed something that she ought to be doing—going about trying to figure out who was behind it all. Then again, what would be the point? What was the bloody point when it was not going to bring him back?

Then her eyes fell on the first few words of the article in front of her. "Bhaskar Ghimirey, the middle son of industrialist Prithvi Raj Ghimirey." As soon as she recognized what the article was about, she flipped to the next page. Too late. On the next page was a picture: swollen cheeks, blue eyes, closed shut. A deep gash on the jaw. It wasn't Bhaskar, yet it was. A large black dot on the lower lip, which after two seconds she realized was a big fly. A shit fly, with a metallic blue-green body, the type that made its home in outhouses. Beneath the photo it said: "Wanted: The Son of Yeti for Bhaskar Ghimirey's Death."

She stumbled out of Tato Chiso, nearly falling down the stairs. The sun outside was strong. She ought to head to the Asylum; they'd be expecting her, the widowed buhari. Yet, she couldn't go home.

Instead, she meandered through the Tourist District for some time, a hot vomit-like breath rising from her throat.

Right outside the Asylum, just as she was about to enter its gate, a khateykid stopped her. "Auntie," he said, and she recognized the voice but failed to recognize the face, partly because her mind was still reeling from what she'd seen in the *Motherland Daily*. Then it dawned on her who he was.

"Do you know who killed Bhaskar Uncle?" The look on the boy's face was fierce.

"How are you, Subhash? Where have you been?"

"I know who killed him," Subash said.

"Who, babu?"

"That man is inside this house," he said, pointing toward the Asylum. "Your house. How can you be so stupid and not know?"

He glared at her. That boy, he has suffered much, Bhaskar used to say. You can see it in his eyes, Bhaskar had said. Kranti looked into his eyes now, but they were so intense, so filled with something that she couldn't hold his gaze for long. "Where is your little sister?"

"Are you listening to me?" Subhash said. "Bhaskar uncle's killer is in there."

This boy too, just like her mother. "I heard you, babu. Where is your sister?

He pointed vaguely behind him. "She's around. Why did your man kill Bhaskar Uncle?" He pointed to the house again.

"My man?" she said. "Who are you talking about?"

"I'm going to get revenge," he said. "I'm going to cut the throat of all these machikneys."

"Not so loud, babu!"

He leaned forward and said, with gritted teeth, "I'm going to kill that bastard."

She grabbed his arm, quickly looked around, and said, "Shhh! Please, don't say that!"

"I saw it myself," Subhash said loudly. "It was that man in your house."

"What are you saying, Subhash?" Kranti asked. "How do you know all of this?"

"I saw it, and Darkmother came to me and said so herself. In my dreams."

Kranti sighed.

"You don't believe me? You don't believe me?" His voice had gotten louder. "Maybe you are also a part of his gang." He shouted. "You all should be shot."

People turned their heads. Across the street in a corner a couple of Loyal Army Dais were standing, smoking, and chatting. "You all should be hung," Subhash continued shouting.

Afraid that the Loyal Army Dais would hear him, she nearly put her palm over his mouth, but suddenly he was crying. She embraced him, pulling him close to her so that if he shouted again his voice would be muffled. After he calmed down, she took out a thousand rupee note and gave it to him. He refused to take it, saying he wasn't asking her for money.

"For your sister," she said.

With tears streaming down his face, he walked away.

—

A week later, Kranti watched PM Papa talk in the living room of the Asylum. He was standing next to the bar, which was on a slightly raised area, so it looked like he was giving a speech from a small stage. Now he was raising a finger up in the air, and Kranti's eyes flitted to the large painting of the Founding Father on the opposite wall. There he was, the great man himself from the 1700s, his right hand raised with the index finger up: we are one race, only four castes and thirty-six different colors, a veritable garden, let everyone be awakened. Those words from two and a half centuries ago had been drilled into the brain of every Darkmotherlandite schoolchild. And now

PM Papa, who faced the painting across the room, was mirroring that iconic gesture in front of his rapt audience in the Asylum, his hosts with their whiskeys and cocktails and bites of chicken chili and shrimp pierced with toothpicks.

The Hippo. Yes, he did look like a hippo, with a wide jaw and small ears. Clad in his daura-suruwal (what else?), he looked downright ridiculous with that topi desperately trying to cover his large head. His belly bulged from his midsection. After Bhaskar and Kranti had visited him in the Lion Palace, Bhaskar had joked that he had been tempted to rub his hand on PM Papa's belly, tickle him, and make him laugh. PM Papa's legs were short, and so when he walked, he seemed to waddle. Even his fingers, Kranti saw again, as she had when she first met him in person at the Lion Palace, were so thick and short that they looked like meatballs. He had a ruddy face, with near-glowing cheeks, and smallish eyes. He appeared to be smiling when he was not.

A small crew of Motherland TV was there, with their camera and lights. An officious-looking man, presumably the director of the crew, was running around, sweat on his forehead, instructing his people to set up the camera correctly, to position the light at just the right angle. He almost looked panicky, as though if he missed a small detail, he would face a firing squad the next day. Hom Bokaw was standing in a corner, stroking his white goatee, talking with Priyanka. A handful of liveried waitstaff, hired specially for the occasion, were walking around with plates of hors d'oeuvres. The nokerchakers were coming in and going out of the room on the smallest pretext, trying to catch a glimpse of PM Papa. They were scolded in whispers by Shambhogya.

On the big TV screen against the wall, Motherland TV was on mute, with Hom Bokaw hosting a program on PM Papa, who was giving speeches, cutting ribbons, stroking the cheeks of the poor and homeless, riding the helicopter to observe an earthquake-ravaged area, touching the feet of his giant self-statue, and on and on.

Tomorrow this visit to the Asylum would be on the news, in a repeated loop, with images of PM Papa looking like the Founding Father. Not everything PM Papa said would be shown to the public, of course, but the moments when he identified the Son of Yeti as Bhaskar's killer would be emphasized.

PM Papa's bodyguards were also there; among them his chief bodyguard, the legendary Laxman. He had saved PM Papa from an attempted assassination during the Papa Don't Preach rally. Laxman had been shown on Motherland TV receiving a special award for his valor, so it was easy to recognize him among the bodyguards in the Asylum tonight: a good-looking muscular man, big square chin, with eyes that constantly roamed the room.

The one person missing was Rozy. After Kranti had learned of PM Papa's visit, she had texted Rozy, saying she'd forgotten to ask him at the rooftop restaurant, but was he coming to the Asylum? Rozy responded that he wouldn't be. When Kranti asked him why, Rozy texted back: "Sorry."

With the Motherland TV camera on him, PM Papa spoke of the threat of the Son of Yeti, who wanted to unleash an avalanche of terror across Darkmotherland. The Yetifolk had captured many of the villages in the mountains, so that even those who didn't want to leave their homes after the Big Two were forced to do so, deluging the Valley with refugees. PM Papa now had definite intelligence confirming that the Yetifolk were behind the Streetwise incident. "The men who attacked our dear Bhaskar were plants," PM Papa said. "They are called plants in Angrezi." He paused. "Not plants like our flower-pot plants but like double agents. They were planted by the Son of Yeti."

"PM Papa, why is the Son of Yeti after us?" It was Shambhogya who spoke, soft and earnest once the media and others left, and it was just the Ghimirey family with him and the bodyguards.

That the first person to query PM Papa was not Prithvi Raj or Aditya but a buhari of the family wasn't lost on the others. And that it was an intelligent question was also obvious, and in hindsight who else but Shambhogya would ask it—so gently and persuasively without any hint of skepticism?

PM Papa nodded, his rotund head bobbing up and down. "Because he knows how close the ties are between me and this family. A strike at the Ghimireys will also wound me. Which it has."

Prithvi Raj was holding back tears. Aditya had his head down. Chaitanya looked shifty, as though he was battling some inner thoughts that ran contrary to what was being said in the room.

"And the Son of Yeti will pay for it," PM Papa said, now sitting on the sofa that was specially reserved for him. "Trust me."

"Why did he choose Bhaskar babu, PM Papa?" Shambhogya asked, her voice hoarse as if she were about to cry. "Why not target one of us?"

Priyanka, seemingly encouraged by PM Papa's approval of Shambhogya's line of query, added, "Or one of our factories? Or our main office? Or even the Asylum itself?"

The Ghimirey women were taking over this political panel.

"Because," PM Papa said, "it's simple. Bhaskar was, how shall I say, an easy target." Kranti had a feeling that PM Papa had caught himself from saying, "Bhaskar was, how shall I say, a fool."

"My son was not naïve," Muwa said abruptly.

Everyone looked at her, aghast that she had spoken. Muwa, who was sitting next to Kranti, had wanted to go to God's Room soon after greeting PM Papa, but Kranti had held her back, saying she could use the company.

"Muwa," Shambhogya said, "no one's saying that. PM Papa isn't saying that."

"She's been hit really hard," Prithvi Raj said in an apologetic tone to Papa in a low voice, as though Muwa wasn't in the room. "Bhaskar was her favorite son."

Kranti glanced at Aditya and Chaitanya, but they didn't show any reaction to what their father said.

PM Papa nodded, clearly not liking that he'd been contradicted, but demonstrating an understanding that Muwa was speaking as a grieving mother. "We have to face hard truths in life," he said, looking at Muwa. "Bhaskar was an easy target."

"True, Papa, true," Prithvi Raj whispered, nodding.

"What we need to remember," PM Papa continued, "is that the Son of Yeti won't be satisfied with just taking out Bhaskar." He paused again. His lips were thick, Kranti noted. How come she was noticing all the faults with his body now, whereas she'd missed them during the Lion Palace visit?

"He'll come after all of us," PM Papa said. "He'll come after you."

Anxiety rippled through the room.

PM Papa said that Son of Yeti wanted to redistribute Darkmotherland's wealth, a change that some prominent people in the country would be happy about. He meant Professor Shrestha, of course. One of Son of Yeti's prime targets would be Ghimirey & Sons and the Asylum. "In fact, he might know right now that I am here," PM Papa said. When Chaitanya said that Motherland TV says that the Loyal Army is winning the battle against Yetifolk, PM Papa said that of course the Loyal Army is winning, and that it was important to convey that to Darkmotherlandites. "We're winning, yes, but there's no doubt that the Son of Yeti is a formidable enemy. He's recruiting more and more young people every day. Recruiting and radicalizing." He said it again, "Radicalize. The Son of Yeti is radicalizing disenchanted Darkmotherlandites to become Yetifolk."

"Our Bhaskar was also radicalized," Aditya said. He glanced at Kranti. "And we all know who radicalized him."

PM Papa held up his palm. "The Son of Yeti wants to destroy Darkmotherland."

"Bhaskar never believed in the Son of Yeti," Muwa said.

Kranti was, despite herself, glad that Muwa was speaking. It was as though she had decided to channel her son into this room.

"Bhaskar also believed in a lot of nonsense, Muwa," Aditya said. Then he looked at Kranti, pointedly, laying the blame directly on her, on her mother.

PM Papa said to Muwa, "You see, the Son of Yeti is very crafty. He has elevated himself to be a mythical creature." He spoke to Muwa as though he were addressing a child. "He is a master at fooling gullible people."

Muwa didn't meet PM Papa's gaze, but Kranti heard her mutter under her breath, "My son wasn't gullible." Kranti was sure that PM Papa, sitting in the opposite sofa, didn't hear her, but her heart beat rapidly, fearing that PM Papa would deem Muwa was a Papee.

She whispered to Muwa, "Why don't you go to God's Room?" Muwa whispered back, asking Kranti whether that would be okay, and Kranti nodded. The others were watching them, Shambhogya giving them both a stern look.

Muwa stood and slowly but quietly left the room, without even looking at PM Papa.

After she left, there was some silence, then Prithvi Raj said, "Please forgive her, Papa. For the last few years she's become . . . different. Bhaskar's death has sent her over the edge."

PM Papa grunted, then he said, "She doesn't know who she's dealing with." He meant the Son of Yeti, of course, but there was an undertone that suggested that the "who" could be him. He waved his hand to indicate the Asylum. "The Son of Yeti will take everything you have."

There were noises of dismay and disconcertion. PM Papa said they needed tighter security around the Ghimirey & Sons business. And also outside the Asylum. Cheech and Chong and Harkey were not enough; PM Papa was going to ask General Tso to assign a company of Loyal Army battalion for the Ghimireys. Kranti thought of Bhaskar, who, had he been in the room, would have voiced his opposition. He'd been angered by the militarization of Darkmotherland since Papakoo. We're in a junta regime, he'd frequently said.

"And one more thing," PM Papa said, raising his index finger. "I will need the full support of Ghimirey & Sons in what I do."

"You have our support, Papa," Priyanka said. "You have our full support."

There was a chorus of agreements.

"And." PM Papa paused. "You will need to trust me. PM Papa

values loyalty. He will never harm his friends." He looked pointedly at everyone. "Our enemies would want to divide us, sow seeds of distrust. But remember: Bhaskar's death has been like a death of one of my own sons."

"We are so grateful, Papa," said the Ghimireys.

"The Son of Yeti must be defeated, Papa," Aditya said, somewhat loudly. "He must be crushed, like an insect." He rubbed his thumb and forefinger together, just like he had with Bhaskar. His voice was slightly shaking. "We should not be afraid to ask for help from other countries, especially Amrika."

"We will crush him," PM Papa said. He fisted his palm, as though crushing the Son of Yeti there. "We will not allow our enemies to destroy our country." He lowered his voice. "Let me also let you in on something. This news hasn't gotten out yet, as I don't want my enemies to get ideas. But I'm soon embarking on a couple of foreign trips. First, to a Khadi country, where I'll be making some more fabulous deals, especially for our migrant brothers and sisters."

At this, the Ghimireys let out noises of approval and said, "You're already doing so much for our migrant brethren."

PM Papa raised his stubby finger in the air. "Then, more important, I'll be going to Amrika to visit President Corn Hair in a couple of months—I have already received a personal invitation. I will be asking him to give Darkmotherland the largest foreign aid, including military, in the history of our country, and, given the high regard in which President Corn Hair holds me, I expect we will be successful. This will be a major boon to Darkmotherland, and I expect all of us—all of us here as well—to reap its benefits."

"That's amazing news!" Aditya shouted, and he appeared so excited that Shambhogya pinched him on the arm asking him to control himself. But Aditya ignored Shambhogya's pinch and shouted again, "That will do wonders for everyone. You are an amazing leader of this country, PM Papa."

PM Papa smiled and raised his hand, palms toward his face, in the gesture of adab arz, accepting this accolade. The Ghimireys had never seen PM Papa do the adab arz before, and they all laughed joyously and clapped. Watching them, Kranti thought it was hard to believe that a son of this family had not only died, but had been murdered just a few weeks ago.

⁓

She wasn't meant to hear it. It was late afternoon, her usual nap time, so they most likely thought that she was upstairs in her room. But, assaulted by images of Bhaskar's bloated face, she hadn't been able to fall asleep, and had wandered around the house. She'd leaned on the balcony for a while, watching the atrium below. It was a lush green, and the fountain's sound was soothing. Then she'd made her way down the spiral staircase. When she reached the bottom, she heard voices in the living room. She stopped, and the conversation came to her in waves, like she was in a fitful dream filled with disembodied voices.

They were talking about her, that much she could gather, especially since she heard her name mentioned. Suddenly she noticed that she could see them in the mirror at the other end of the living room. Shambhogya sat on the sofa, where PM Papa had sat not too long ago, and Prithvi Raj was seated on the floor in front of her, her knees touching his back. This hierarchical faux pas confused Kranti, then she realized that Shambhogya was massaging Prithvi Raj's head. Priyanka sat next to Shambhogya, helping pour oil from a small bottle into Shambhogya's hands when she signaled. Kranti could only see Priyanka's arm as she extended it to pour the oil.

"We should have talked about this earlier," Prithvi Raj said.

Why the massage wasn't being done upstairs in one of the rooms, Kranti didn't know. It could be that Shambhogya had to chase him, like a mother would a child, in order to coax him to have his head massaged, finally cornering him in the living room. There were days when the patriarch, instead of beginning to heal, appeared to worsen:

he walked about the house in unwashed vests and pants, hair rising in tufts from his scalp, circles under his eyes.

But he sat at her feet now, like a docile child, letting his head loll to the movement of her fingers on his scalp. The two shared a special bond, this much had become clear to Kranti by now, a bond that Prithvi Raj didn't even share with his wife, who had become even more distant from him. Now Muwa spent most of her waking hours in God's Room. Prithvi Raj drifted in and out of his tormented world, sometimes appearing utterly defeated by Bhaskar's death, other times back to his wheeling and dealing self, scion of Ghimirey & Sons.

"We should have consulted Jyotish Jeevan before they got married, but he forbade me," Shambhogya said, repeatedly thumping his head with the fleshy part of her clasped hands. "Now, it's too late."

"Bhaskar dai never believed in such things." It was Priyanka; she had to be part of this conversation, as always. Or was it collusion? But why was Kranti thinking this way? Wasn't it normal for them to talk about her? Yes, it was, but she somehow sensed that this time it was different.

"Could it be that her chart is incorrect?" Prithvi Raj asked.

"She said she remembered her father had shown it to her, and now she found it in a box with her father's other knickknacks."

The massage was now finished. Shambhogya wiped her hands on a towel. Priyanka handed her a comb, and Shambhogya began to comb Prithvi Raj's hair, treating each strand with care.

"I didn't tell you this, but one day in private I too had raised the question with Bhaskar of matching his chart with Kranti's," Prithvi Raj said. "But he told me that despite amassing so much wealth, I was still mired in the old ways of thinking. He told me that there's basically no difference between a so-called leading industrialist, such as myself, and a poor uneducated villager who believes that his stomach flu is caused not by bad water but by an evil spirit that'll be appeased by slaughtering a chicken." Prithvi Raj laughed. "He actually used that word: so-called. A so-called industrialist. All of this meant nothing to him." Prithvi Raj gestured vaguely in the air, indicating the Asylum. They liked to do that, the Ghimireys, point to their palatial mansion as a confirmation of their status and what they'd accomplished.

"There's a huge difference between you and an illiterate hillbilly," Shambhogya said.

"You have built an empire," Priyanka said. "You supply Western toilets to the country. A hillbilly doesn't know how to sit on a commode."

What are they babbling on about? Kranti thought.

"It's a cruel joke," Shambhogya said, working on perfecting the parting on Prithvi Raj's hair. "The very person who didn't believe in astrology ended up marrying a manglik, and look what happened to him."

Manglik. Kranti still didn't fully know its meaning, but it was the way Shambhogya said it, slowly and with dread, that made Kranti wonder if Shambhogya knew she was nearby listening. Or, even if Shambhogya didn't know Kranti was around the corner on the stairs, she knew the word would somehow reach her, upstairs in her room. Or, that even if Kranti wasn't in the house, it would reach her in her mother's house. Or as she walked the Valley streets.

"I still don't know whether I believe in it," Prithvi Raj said.

"I've also had doubts," Shambhogya said. The massage and combing was now complete, and she helped Prithvi Raj from the floor and sat him on the sofa. She sat where he'd been sitting, on the floor, facing him, like a dutiful daughter.

"What's there to doubt?" Priyanka said. "Did I tell you about my cousin who married a manglik?"

"Yes, you did, one too many times," Shambhogya said. "Kranti is not only manglik, Sir, she's what they call a double manglik."

"It's confirmed?" Priyanka said. "Jyotish Jeevan verified this?"

"Unfortunately, yes."

"I told you! I told you so!" Priyanka nearly shouted. "I suspected she was a manglik."

"Yes, you should have been an astrologer yourself," Shambhogya said.

"I wish Bhaskar had thought more about what he was doing," Prithvi Raj said. Suddenly sobs erupted. The old man was crying. "My poor Bhaskar." Sounds were made by the two daughters-in-law—consoling, placating, commiserating, lamenting.

They discussed what Jyotish Jeevan had said, that a manglik wouldn't be satisfied by devouring only her husband. She'd want more. And a double manglik would be violently insatiable. Kranti imagined herself feasting on Bhaskar's body: he was stretched out on a table before her, his stomach cut open to reveal his innards, and she was chewing on his intestines and gizzards, smacking her lips, saying he wasn't enough. Priyanka said that a double manglik would first take her husband and then the entire family. Prithvi Raj was incredulous. If Jyotish Jeevan was such a good royal astrologer, how come he couldn't predict the royal massacre, when the crown prince gunned down most of his family, and hastened the eventual destruction of the monarchy? They have turned into royal ghosts, Prithvi Raj said, lamenting, and probably thinking of his own relationship with the last king, whose large photo adorned the wall of the Asylum.

Kranti briefly remembered visiting the Durbar years ago, when, after the Droopy-Mouthed King had gotten booted out, his furniture and chandeliers were on full display for the public. The visitors to the museum, as it had become, complained that what they saw—the small rooms, the drab furnishings—didn't measure up to how they'd imagined the inside of the palace to look like when the king still ruled. "I've stayed in better hotel rooms in Bangkok," Kranti had heard a businessman say out loud. Some visitors asked for their money back because the show was so disappointing.

"Some royal astrologer," Prithvi Raj added.

"Can an astrologer prevent what's written in your charts?" Priyanka said.

"Didn't you yourself say that your village astrologer foretold your success in the Valley?" Shambhogya said.

"Yes, he did," Prithvi Raj said. "But now look at the state I'm in."

"But what happened to Bhaskar babu was what was in his karma,"

Shambhogya said. "He brought it upon himself. Through her." She meant Kranti.

This was the moment Kranti should have stepped in, coughed, commented on the weather. But she didn't, she continued listening. They talked about what the astrologer recommended but switched to whispering so she couldn't fully catch what was being said.

"But how is that possible?" Prithvi Raj wailed after a minute, and was shushed by his daughters-in-law. "But that's impossible!" the old man said. "I can't do this to Bhaskar."

Then, only snatches and snippets:

"Ludicrous." Prithvi Raj.

"Only solution." Priyanka.

"I will go mad." Prithvi Raj.

"He's good." Shambhogya.

"Agree." Priyanka.

Another silence, then Prithvi Raj: "I don't know what to think anymore. I can't think anymore."

29.

Rozy didn't want to accompany PM Papa to the Khadi country. He genuinely feared being alone with him in a strange location, but PM Papa insisted. "It's so hot there," Rozy complained, "and you know that I can't even think properly when the temperature gets that high." The last bit was true—Rozy sweated a lot and felt dizzy in high temperatures.

"But maiya," PM Papa said, "they have air-conditioning everywhere, even on the airport tarmac. You'll see." He looked at him with his beady eyes. "Please." PM Papa didn't say "please" to anyone. For a moment, Rozy enjoyed the realization that he had that level of power over the most powerful man in Darkmotherland. But he knew that he needed to play the game a little bit more, so he kept saying PM Papa didn't need him.

"Why don't you take Bill Tamang with you?" Rozy said.

Chief Secretary Bill Tamang, a devout Baptist who was active in several Christian organizations and charities, had been with PM Papa from his early days. Soon after PM Papa had gained power, there had been criticism of the selection of Bill Tamang as the Chief Secretary. "A Christian, a traitor to his religion," the Fundys had said, but as PM Papa consolidated his power, those voices had withered away.

PM Papa asked Rozy whether he was serious. How could Rozy think that he would enjoy Bill Tamang's company as much as he would Rozy's? "Besides," PM Papa said, "it'll be our first foreign country visit together. I want to bring you out. What do they say? Out of the closet?" PM Papa laughed.

Rozy said no.

PM Papa's face changed. He looked angry, as though he was about to say, "How dare you say no to me?" Then, he seemed to rethink his response, didn't utter a word, and walked into his cabinet meeting.

In the evening PM Papa came to visit Rozy in his flat. His face was grim. Laxman had driven him. PM Papa wore dark glasses, with a cowboy hat pulled low over his forehead, tight jeans (in which his package bulged), and a T-shirt and jacket, very unlike the daura-suruwal-wearing PM Papa he was in his public appearances, and on Motherland TV.

This was actually his third visit to Rozy's flat. Rozy had discouraged him from coming, told him that it was too dangerous for him to come like this, after hours. There was always a risk that someone would try to assassinate him. There were people, Rozy had advised PM Papa, even within his inner circle, who were waiting for the right moment to dislodge him from his position of power, whether by a koo or by assassination. The two previous times he'd come in the evening after dark, and left quickly, usually not staying for more than an hour or so.

"You could have called for me," Rozy said this time, after ushering him in and offering him a glass of brandy.

"I don't like you saying no to me," PM Papa said.

"But Papa, I told you about the heat. It's like forty or forty-five degrees there. I can barely survive in thirty degrees centigrade."

"You grew up in the Town of Lakes, the hotbed of humidity," PM Papa said.

Rozy said nothing, merely put on an I'm-so-fond-of-you face and gazed tenderly at PM Papa. A thought crossed Rozy's mind: it would be so easy for Rozy, with Laxman as a lookout in the car downstairs, to do something to the big man upstairs in his flat and escape. After all, his back door opened to a narrow alley that would tunnel him to the next neighborhood.

"I've noticed you're saying no to me more and more," PM Papa said. "I don't like it."

Rozy, who'd gone into the kitchen, returned with a bowl of spicy peanuts, which he put in front of PM Papa and said, "And why do you dismiss what I want? My desires?"

PM Papa pulled Rozy into his lap, said, "Why don't you understand that you are my partner? That I'm doing this all for you?"

Rozy laughed and struggled to get away from him. "For me? For real? None of this is for you?"

But PM Papa held on to him tight and rubbed his chin against Rozy's cheeks, saying, "How does this feel, huh? Does this feel good?" Then he picked up Rozy, placed him on the floor, and climbed on top of him. He was hard, and he rubbed his crotch against Rozy. "We're going to fuck like this, in the Khadi country." Despite himself, Rozy was getting hard himself, but he managed to tickle PM Papa and finally push him away. Both were laughing.

"Come on, maiya," PM Papa said. "I so badly want you to come with me."

For the next fifteen minutes, he pleaded and cajoled, and finally, Rozy acquiesced, but not before extracting a promise from PM Papa that they would not sleep in the same room. "It won't look good," Rozy said. PM Papa wasn't happy about it, but Rozy put his foot down, saying that was the one condition.

After he left, Rozy dwelled on the fact that PM Papa was taking greater risks with him, as if he was getting ready to declare something to the world. These days he often called Rozy into the Gufa in the afternoon and latched the door from the inside without any care that Bill Tamang was watching.

Perhaps PM Papa had come to believe the image that he'd created for himself in Darkmotherland, that no one could touch him, that he could do whatever he wanted.

Rozy had never flown on an airplane before. This was PM Papa's private plane, of course, one he'd purchased on discount from Germnee soon after he came to power. Rozy hadn't told PM Papa that he'd never flown before, and he tried not to appear awed by the sound of the revving engine, the leather couches inside, the flight attendants who brought them hot towels to wipe their faces soon after they were seated, the champagne in slim glasses and small bites of potatoes filled with caviar. PM Papa kept looking at his face to gauge how impressed he was, but Rozy kept a neutral face, and only once smiled at PM Papa before closing his eyes as the plane took off.

Throughout the flight, which lasted for about five hours, PM Papa was on the phone, with the embassy officials in the Khadi country, and with his cabinet members back home. He was terrified of being kooed while he was out of the country. He gave orders to tighten the security around the Lion Palace, in the Humble Abode. He put General Tso in charge of everything—the general was, in effect, his security blanket. "I don't like to leave Darkmotherland," he'd confessed a couple of times to Rozy. One time he churlishly hugged the Darkmotherlandite national flag, with its distinct shape of two triangles on top of each other, as though embracing the flag was the ultimate test of one's patriotism. One time in the Gufa, PM Papa, stroking Rozy's cheek, had said, "I have to be very alert, you understand? You and General Tso are the only people I trust. And maybe Bill Tamang."

The heat in the Khadi country was worse than what Rozy had imagined. Yes, the airport tarmac was air-conditioned as they were escorted on a red carpet to the VIP area in the terminal. "It's dry heat," PM Papa whispered to him, but Rozy was sweating inside his shirt, his armpits already showing two broad patches. "It's embarrassing," he whispered back to PM Papa.

From then on, it was one miserable event after another. Rozy hated standing next to PM Papa, with eyes of the Khadi men, and some women, clad in the thobes and their abhayas boring down on him. They were curious about who this feminine-looking person next to PM Papa was, Rozy was sure, and even after Rozy was identified as PM Papa's valet, it was clear that they weren't totally satisfied. Often Rozy was left to the side, perspiring and uncomfortable, as PM Papa talked with the various VIPs and was asked to cut ribbons or accept flowers from Khadi children. Rozy had to sit through long meetings, often bored by the conversation.

But this was an important trip for PM Papa, one that was crucial to filling his coffers. He had been vigorously courting oil-rich nations of the Arab world, citing the contribution of migrant workers from Darkmotherland who toiled under the brutal sun of these countries as construction workers, gardeners, cooks, and drivers. He'd become a master fundraiser. The kings and princes of these Khadi countries liked the tough love that this hippo of a man, in his funny dress, had demonstrated during Darkmotherland's moment of crisis. They saw a little bit of themselves in him—his disdain for unchecked freedom, his clamping down on dissent, his ability to keep the religious right happy (something they themselves often struggled with in their own countries). PM Papa's vigorous lobbying on his country's behalf had worked. The Khadi countries had doubled and tripled their aid to Darkmotherland since PM Papa took over. Only a small portion of which went toward reconstruction and resettlement. A large part was used by PM Papa to solidify and expand the circle of his loyalists.

Toward the end of that first day, in a meeting with the Khadi country's Tourism Minister, PM Papa once again stressed the importance of tourism for Darkmotherland. "We hope you'll continue to publicize Darkmotherland as a premier tourist destination," PM Papa said. He spoke decent Angrezi, better than most previous heads of state of Darkmotherland. The prime minister he'd kooed against spoke such atrocious Angrezi that people used to complain that they were mortified when he gave speeches in international meetings. PM Papa received compliments on his Angrezi, as he did now from the Tourism Minister, himself a graduate of Oxford. They discussed a robust Visit Darkmotherland program that would be implemented in the Khadi country. PM Papa signaled to Rozy, who produced a folder that was filled with materials on Hotel Himalayan Happiness belonging to Ghimirey & Sons. "This hotel will be a special hotel for our Khadi guests," PM Papa said.

PM Papa held a meeting with a contingent of the migrant workers, who chanted "Pure Darkmotherland!" when he emphasized how he was working hard to ensure that their working and living conditions in the Khadi country were vastly improved. Rozy wasn't sure whether they completely believed PM Papa, but their faces made it obvious that they wanted to believe. Some of them stared at Rozy, trying to figure out how he fit into the picture.

Later, at the world-famous mall with its gleaming surfaces and its bou-tique shops, PM Papa walked into an electronics store and bought the latest Samsung mobile phone for Rozy. "For emergency pur-poses," PM Papa had said, handing the phone over to Rozy with his cucumber hand. His words were meant for Bill Tamang, who had accompanied them to the store. But in the SUV as they headed back toward the palace guest house, PM Papa had put his hand on top of Rozy's and whispered, "You understand why I gave you that Samsung, don't you?" Laxman was riding in the front with the driver from the Ministry of Culture, and a thick glass separated the front from the back. The windows of the SUV were tinted so the passengers in the other cars, including the Minister of Culture, couldn't see what was happening inside. That this Khadi country had strict laws against sodomy, punishable by death, had most likely crossed Laxman's mind, as it certainly had Rozy's. Although, would they have enforced their laws against a foreign prime minister, even if he was the prime minister of a small, poor, third-world country that he'd managed after a horrific earthquake?

"This is perfect for our sweet talk," PM Papa had said. He leaned over and licked Rozy's earlobe, making him wince. But Rozy flashed a smile and stroked PM Papa's round cheeks. Laxman, had he glanced at the rearview mirror, would have seen it.

The day had been long, and Rozy was tired. The Khadi city's heat was maddeningly intense, even though most of their time was spent in air-conditioned cars, malls, and buildings. PM Papa took Rozy's hand and put it on his crotch, where he was hardening. "I will call you at night in Darkmotherland on this mobile," he said, "when I'm pining for you." He spoke close to Rozy's ear. "And I'll ache for you every night." He was getting excited by his own words, just like he did when he gave speeches or interviews. Sometimes Rozy thought that PM Papa believed in what he said only after he finished saying it. He had no true convictions, except things that benefitted him, but once the words left his mouth, he became per-suaded of their truism.

"I can taste you in my mouth," PM Papa had said as he nibbled Rozy's earlobes in the SUV, in Khadi country.

"There are people."

"I don't care."

"They'll talk."

"Let them blabber."

"They are cruel here to people like me." He wanted to say "us," but he also knew that in many Khadi countries, men who didn't think of themselves as gay sometimes used more submissive men, even prepubescent boys, for sexual pleasure.

"I don't care."

"The media will catch it."

"Let them."

If Rozy had let him, PM Papa might have sucked him off right there, in the back seat of the SUV. But Rozy pushed him away.

Rozy wondered if PM Papa's boldness came from being away from Darkmotherland. Was he planning something?

Rozy found out later that night. They had been put up in the royal penthouse suite in the world-famous Caliphate Hotel, which jutted out into the ocean, and boasted a spire-shaped top that pierced the sky.

Rozy had his own small room to the side, but once everyone was asleep, his door creaked open. PM Papa's short figure was in the doorway, and even in the darkness Rozy could tell that he was grinning. "You can't come here," Rozy whispered fiercely, but PM Papa quickly closed the door and slipped into Rozy's bed. He nuzzled Rozy, who was genuinely afraid that the door would burst open and the Khadi Poolis Uncles would barge in. Or perhaps the mutawa. "What are you doing?" Rozy asked again. PM Papa was hard, he could tell, and it looked like he'd been hard for a while.

Rozy turned on the bedside lamp and attempted to sit up, but PM Papa reached over quickly and turned it off. "Please, maiya," he said into his ear. "I've been wanting this for a long time."

"It's too dangerous."

"No one will know, I swear, we'll do it quietly." He already had his pajamas down to his knees, and now he was attempting to pull Rozy's shorts down. Rozy resisted, saying it was not a proper place, that they could do it once they were back in the Gufa. Normally, when Rozy resisted this strongly, PM Papa would relent, sometimes petulantly, sometimes with a laugh. Tonight, however, he was pleading, pleading, saying that he had fantasized so long about "loving Rozy" in a foreign land. That was true. PM Papa had talked in the past about what it would be like to fuck Rozy in an exotic location. Then Rozy had thought: In a zoo? A cable car? Where?

Tonight, PM Papa wouldn't take no for an answer, and after a while, Rozy didn't have any strength to fight him. PM Papa was having a tough time getting Rozy's shorts down, so Rozy said, "Wait, wait," and he did it himself. PM Papa was hard—very hard. And it seemed bigger than normal. Had he taken something? Perhaps Viagra? Did Viagra make you bigger than your normal size? Rozy didn't know. "It might hurt a bit tonight, okay?" PM Papa whispered into his ear as he thrust himself into Rozy. Before Rozy could ask why, whether PM Papa had taken a pill to enlarge himself, PM Papa was in. Immediately, Rozy experienced a piercing pain, as though PM Papa had stuck in a needle. He cried out, then felt PM Papa's hand over his mouth. "Shhh!"

The pain subsided, but something was wrong. Rozy felt something glide and slide inside his anus. It was as though instead of PM Papa's cock, a snake had slithered in there and was on a probing mission. "What is that?" Rozy said. "Why does it feel so different?"

PM Papa grunted, and he kept thrusting. But it was inaccurate to call it a thrust because PM Papa's cock wasn't thick enough or hard enough to thrust. It had become more like a rope, like a drain snake—Rozy had seen a plumber in the Lion Palace wiggle it into a hallway toilet to unclog it. PM Papa's cock was now frantically reaching deeper and deeper into Rozy, as though it were on a strict schedule. PM Papa was groaning and snorting, not sounds of pleasure but of strain. Rozy himself wasn't feeling any pleasure—normally, his pleasure during sexual activity with PM Papa was minimal, but today there was nothing, except a feeling of discomfort that increased by the minute at having PM Papa's organ probe his insides. It almost felt like a medical procedure. Then, suddenly, the organ—or the organ's head—seemed to have reached a place that it liked, a place that was so deep inside Rozy's body that even Rozy didn't know that it existed, did a kind of a mad jiggling, discharged, then squirmed its way out.

It was over. PM quickly pulled up his pajamas, planted a kiss on Rozy's cheek, said what sounded like, "Mission accomplished," and left the room.

What was that? Rozy thought. Wham-bam-thank-you-ma'am?

It was so unlike PM Papa, who liked to cuddle after their love-making, even if all Rozy wanted to do was get into the shower, quickly.

Rozy didn't sleep well that night, even in that luxury room with a window that overlooked the well-lit promenade by the ocean where people were strolling until late. The feeling of discomfort in his anus remained, but it was not even the anus—it was somewhere deeper than that. It was as though PM Papa's ejaculation, instead of disappearing into wherever ejaculations disappeared after sex, had found a cave inside Rozy where it was now securely nestled, waiting.

—

As days passed, words and phrases from that moment in the living room—manglik, curse, solution—appeared in her dreams, but there were no perceptible changes in the way Shambhogya and Priyanka behaved toward her; they were solicitous, accommodating, appearing concerned about how Kranti was dealing with Bhaskar's death.

Except for Muwa, who was increasingly aloof, mired in her grief. After PM Papa's speech in their house, Muwa had begun to isolate herself even more in God's Room. She was, Kranti suspected, even more convinced now that PM Papa had a hand in her son's murders. She couldn't understand why the Ghimireys refused to see it and continued to kowtow to the man. She also had even less tolerance for

Priyanka and Shambhogya these days, it seemed. Was Kranti projecting too much of her own perceptions onto her mother-in-law? But there was no doubt that Muwa's face would become strained when Shambhogya entered the room.

Not too long after the wedding, Kranti had casually said to Muwa, who used to visit her in her room, "Sometimes I feel like this household will collapse without Shambhogya didi." In those early days, Kranti had been awed by Shambhogya, her poise, her skills in household management. Her stunning beauty.

"Yes," was what Muwa said. "Shambhogya does everything around here."

There was a penetrating silence.

"I remember when we first went to see Shambhogya," Muwa said. "Me and Aditya and your father-in-law. She was beautiful then."

"She's beautiful now, Muwa."

"Yes, she still is. Hasn't aged a bit. But if you'd seen her that day, you'd have known what I was talking about. She's the one, I'd thought then. She'd been so shy, blushing, barely meeting our gazes. But now, is there a shy bone in her body?"

"What about me?" Kranti asked. "What did you think of me? I know we didn't even have a proper viewing. But when you first heard about me and Bhaskar, what did you think?"

"You?" Muwa reached across and stroked Kranti's face. "Do you really want to know?"

Kranti nodded.

"I worried that you might be a smarty-pants."

Kranti laughed. Smart was the last characterization she would have had for herself.

"I worried you might thumb your nose down at us all."

"But I didn't even act snooty! Why did you think that?"

"Since your mother was a professor, known for her intelligence, I thought you might find us unschooled. I've always regretted not completing my education. Once I married your father-in-law and came to the Valley, all I did was breed children and provide support for this business. Back in the village I had harbored dreams about becoming a daktar. I had seen how hard it was for people in our village to get a daktar to look at them; people had to walk a whole day to a health post in another village where a daktar came once a week. Only the rich could hire porters to carry the sick on their backs. I thought I'd become a daktar and return to my village to serve my people. But once I got married and came to the Valley, I knew there was simply no way I could find the time and the stamina to spend years studying medicine. Besides, I hadn't told my husband about my aspiration. How could I? We hardly talked."

Kranti had heard Muwa's story. Muwa had confided in her about her confusion and bewilderment when she first came to the Valley with Prithvi Raj. Her marriage to Prithvi Raj, the landlord's son, had happened quickly, and the next thing she knew, she was on the bus on a long journey to the Valley.

Now, after Bhaskar's death, often Muwa went into God's Room early in the morning and didn't emerge until after dark. "Has Muwa eaten?" Shambhogya asked the nokerchakers. When they said no, she took a plate to God's Room and knocked. Only after some persistent knocks did Muwa respond. In an irritated voice she asked whoever it was—and she knew who it was—to leave the food outside, that she'd eat it later.

Kranti watched the interaction from the window in her room, which overlooked the lawn, marveling at Shambhogya's continued dedication to Muwa. When the door to God's Room finally opened, it would be dusk, and the food was usually untouched. Yet Muwa's face was serene under the lawn lamp. She had, Kranti thought, gone to another world and returned. It was another type of madness. On occasion Prithvi Raj went to knock on the door to God's Room. While Shambhogya's knocks were gentle and cajoling, Prithvi Raj's were loud and petulant. When he knocked Muwa opened the door quickly. The two spoke in muted tones, and it appeared that Prithvi Raj was the slighted one and Muwa was attempting to mollify him. Once or twice Muwa accompanied Prithvi Raj back into the house. She would then eat with him, which seemed to pacify him.

One afternoon when there was no one on the lawn, Kranti, feeling like a voyeur, had sneaked down to God's Room. What did she want to discover about these people, now that Bhaskar was dead? God's Room had a side window. She stood on her toes, but at first, she couldn't see anything because it was slightly smoky inside from the burning of incense. Gradually her eyes adjusted, and she saw the shape of her mother-in-law, seated in front of the Elephant God's statue. Muwa's eyes were closed, as though in deep contemplation. There appeared to be moisture on her cheeks, but Kranti couldn't be sure because of the smoke. Kranti felt a tingle on the back of her neck. When she glanced toward the house, up in Shambhogya's window, she saw a figure withdrawing.

Muwa came out of her hiding, not too long after what Kranti secretly heard in the living room, and provided Kranti with some additional information. Kranti had just come back from Bauko Bank—she'd returned to work because she was worried that otherwise she would just mope around the Asylum—and had just changed into her stay-at-home dhoti when Muwa knocked and came in. Muwa told her that the three must have thought that Muwa was upstairs in her room, taking a nap because that's what she'd told Prithvi Raj she was going to do. But she'd felt too hot in her room, and had retreated to her cave. "In God's Room I was lying on the floor, cooled down but still restless, when I heard voices. You know where they were talking?"

Kranti shook her head.

"Behind God's Room, where the bushes are. So that you, Kranti, wouldn't hear them from your window." Muwa continued, "I heard whispers, and I thought I was dreaming. His voice—I thought I had entered into the early days of our marriage. And in my dream the voice was sweet, and filled with kindness, which it never had been in real life."

"So, what were they talking about, Muwa?" Kranti asked, impatient now.

Muwa told her. A man was coming to the Asylum.

30.

Highway traffic had become more regular in Darkmotherland, but taking the bus to the Town of Lakes was still risky. Since the Big Two, there had been numerous landslides and cracks on the highway, and every few weeks or so a bus hurtled into a ravine or a riverbed, killing most of its passengers. PM Papa would probably have arranged for a car, had Rozy requested it, and indeed he would be surprised, and probably offended, when he discovered that Rozy didn't. But Rozy didn't want to be beholden to PM Papa for this. This was his own thing, his own journey. He didn't want to arrive at his birthplace in PM Papa's car. He didn't want to visit his parents as someone else's concubine, even if that someone else was the most powerful man in all of Darkmotherland. He also didn't want to hire a taxi. He needed to return as he had come, on a bus.

All morning PM Papa had been calling on the new Samsung phone, and Rozy had been ignoring his calls.

Wearing his Make Darkmotherland Great Again cap, Rozy boarded the morning bus at the New Buspark. He didn't know what he'd find in the Town of Lakes, returning after half a decade.

He knew that the lakeside area, a hub for tourists, had been devastated by the Big Two. Half of the restaurants and shops had slid into the lake. But PM Papa had put a lot of money and energy into reviving the lakeside. PM Papa had visited the Town of Lakes a few times, cutting the ribbons for a new resort, taking foreign donors around to show the Big Two's damage so they'd fund the town's renovation. He'd wanted Rozy to accompany him on these trips, but Rozy had always declined, unsure of what he was going to find in his hometown. "Why don't you want to go?" PM Papa had asked, caressing Rozy's cheeks in the Gufa. "What is it you are afraid of?"

Rozy had said, "I don't want to revisit painful memories from that place again." PM Papa had asked what those painful memories were. Was there anyone in the Town of Lakes that had done Rozy wrong?

Just for a brief moment Rozy had thought about mentioning Bir. Then he thought he could tell PM Papa that his parents had done him wrong. Would PM Papa punish Rozy's parents, like he punished his political enemies? Rozy felt ashamed.

On the bus, Rozy squirmed in his seat. Something was off down there. The feeling of uneasiness in Rozy's rectum had remained even after they'd returned to Darkmotherland from the Khadi. "Last night—that was weird," he'd whispered to PM Papa on the airplane on the flight home, but PM Papa had merely smiled and looked out of the window at the roiling clouds in the sky. "Your thing was so . . . slippery," Rozy had muttered. PM Papa hadn't heard, or had pretended not to hear. "What did you mean by mission accomplished?" Rozy had whispered to PM Papa again a bit later in the flight. PM Papa shrugged and whispered back, "You know what I mean—I told you what I wanted to do on a foreign soil. And what a beautiful place to do it, in the royal penthouse suite of the famous Caliphate Hotel, overlooking the ocean."

Rozy's mobile continued to ring, now at infrequent intervals, as the bus wound its way down the first mountain pass out of the Valley. The woman seated next to him asked him why he wasn't picking up his phone. "Don't feel like talking," he said. She asked then why didn't he switch it off, so he switched it off.

The woman gave him slices from the orange she'd just peeled. She had a shawl on even though it was warm. She had on a tika, and there was sindur on her forehead, so he knew she was married. The woman was going to the Town of Lakes to meet her aunt, then the two would head on a pilgrimage to the Lord of Liberation Temple up in the mountains.

"It's good that the Big Two didn't damage the Lord of Liberation Temple," Rozy said as way of conversation. "Maybe it being so high up saved it. Twelve thousand feet or something, isn't it?"

"Praise be God," the woman said. "It's God himself who has protected that temple."

"You think so?"

"You don't think so?"

"Well, why would God protect one temple but destroy others?"

"These are special places," the woman said. "God also protected the Lord of the Animals Temple in the Valley, didn't he?"

At that moment he should have simply said, "God works in mysterious ways," and that would have been sufficient because it'd have accommodated both his confusion and God's awesome powers.

But he ended up saying, "What can I say? Sometimes it's hard to believe God exists."

"You're speaking like an atheist," the woman said. "Don't speak like an atheist."

Her tone was curt, and he felt like she needed to be answered. "Well, my logic makes sense, though, doesn't it? Sometimes don't we rationalize things to fit our beliefs? If God existed, would the Big Two have happened to us?"

"The Big Two happened precisely because God was angry at Darkmotherland's sins."

"Sins like what?"

"Like Christianity. Like homosexuality. Like intercaste marriage. Like eating beef. Like young girls walking around like sluts."

Her loud voice was beginning to attract some attention. A few youths seated in the front looked back. Yellow bandanas. An old man seated immediately in front of Rozy turned his head and said, "Not believing in God is itself a sin. Who made you if not God?"

Rozy should have stopped talking, or simply moved on to another seat to diffuse the tension; there were a couple of empty ones in the back. But he couldn't stop himself from saying, "These Fundys have brainwashed you." It was getting warm inside the bus, so he took off his cap and shook his hair loose, which soon turned out to be a mistake.

A man across the aisle said, "It's not only the Fundys. PM Papa says the same thing."

"Are you saying PM Papa is lying?" the woman asked Rozy.

Two Papa's Patriots ambled over to the back to listen to the argument.

"Okay, okay," Rozy said to the woman. "You win."

"He looks like a homo," a Papa's Patriot said.

"Face like a girl, look at that beauty-queen hair."

"He was hiding his hair underneath that cap," the man in front of Rozy said.

"Is that rouge on his gala?" a Papa's Patriot said, pinching Rozy's cheek. "He has to be a homo."

Rozy looked down, didn't meet anyone's eyes. He could call PM Papa right now and ask for his help. But it'd be too late for him to send some Loyal Army Dais, stop the bus, get Rozy out to safety.

"Hey everyone, we have a homo in our midst."

There were two or three tourists on the bus, and they were observing the crowd bewilderingly, with somewhat frightened expressions.

"We need to beat the shit out of this unnatural being," a Papa's Patriot said.

"Cut his hair and cut his nose as well. Let that be a lesson to all the homos out there."

There were shouts of yeses and kill him from the other passengers.

The bus driver stopped the bus and asked what the ruckus was about.

"Homo here," someone said, "and an atheist."

"PM Papa jindabad!"

Soon, the bus was saturated with cries of PM Papa jindabad. The Papa's Patriots grabbed Rozy by the neck and hauled him out of the bus. "PM Papa jindabad!" The tourists had caught on to what was going on, and one of them tried to come to Rozy's rescue but she was pushed away and someone said, "Go back to your country, you filthy khairey Christians!" Outside, Rozy was slapped a couple of times, then someone threw his bag at him. They all got back in the bus and it dashed away.

Rozy stood by the side of the road, feeling battered. The mobile rang again. He thought about picking it up, telling PM Papa what had happened, asking that he send Loyal Army Dais to stop that bus, haul everyone out by their necks, except the tourists, and thrash them within inches of their lives. Rozy had memorized the bus's license plate: Ba 26 Cha, 6985, and below it, in Angrezi, God Say Drive Slow. PM Papa would send the Loyal Army Dais. There might be a question about the Loyal Army Dais beating Papa's Patriots, but PM Papa never had to explain things, and the Loyal Army Dais never had to justify any actions they took under PM Papa's direction.

But this was Rozy's journey, and calling PM Papa would mean falling back into the old way of doing things. But the old way was about to give way to the new way, so he couldn't allow himself to become trapped in the old way again. Yes, the new way was coming, and what happened to him right now was also necessary, a required step. He might even have foreseen it, like a psychic with visionary powers. Years ago, when he left the Town of Lakes to go to the Valley, the bus had broken down not too far from here, thereby launching him on his concubine journey. Now, on his return to the Town of Lakes, he'd been harassed and ejected from the bus. There was a symmetry here that pointed to the things to come.

He brushed himself off and stood, then hitched his thumb out for a ride.

In the rearview mirror of the car that gave him a ride, Rozy checked his face for bruises: he had none. Without any hesitation, he applied a thin layer of lip gloss and some rouge, then combed his hair. His cap had been lost when he'd been thrown out of the bus. It no longer mattered.

The driver was a young man, an IT professional, who didn't seem fazed by Rozy's appearance, and the two chatted amiably until they reached the Town of Lakes.

No one from his neighborhood recognized Rozy when he stepped out of the car, but he hadn't expected them to. Before the car entered the Town of the Lakes, however, he had wiped off the rouge with some water at the side of the road and put his hair in a ponytail.

Several of the houses around him had been destroyed by the Big Two, but his ancestral home was intact. The ground floor of it was occupied, as before, by a metal shop that sold pots and pans and vases and vessels made out of tin, brass, and iron. An old man with a severely bent back was puttering around inside. Baje. His back had been relatively straight when Rozy had left the Town of the Lakes.

Rozy's heart beat wildly, and the earlier composure he'd felt disappeared. Why was he here, Rozy asked himself, if he was so afraid? But he knew he had to go through with this.

"Baje, do you recognize me?" he said loudly from the doorway.

Baje turned, squinted at him.

"I am Rozan."

"Who is Rozan?"

Rozy pointed up to indicate he lived on the second floor.

"These days I don't see well," Baje said. "Have you come to buy something?"

Rozy signaled no, then asked whether anyone was upstairs, but the old man had lost interest in him.

The staircase to the second floor was in a corner of the shop, and Rozy made his way there. "Anyone home?" he asked at the bottom. No one answered, but there were footsteps above. He climbed and reached near the top and was about to call out again when his mother appeared at the landing. Her face was wrinkled now, and she too appeared to be stooping, although not as much as Baje.

"Who is there?"

"Rozan. Your son." He waited, hoping for a small cry of delight, or just recognition.

"Rozan?" she said. She peered down the staircase, steadying herself by grasping the railing with her right hand, and he saw how wrinkled her hands had become. After a brief silence she said, "Why have you come after so many years?" He thought he heard her sigh, then mumble something.

Rozy wondered if he should turn back.

"For how long have you come?" his mother asked. She didn't seem pleased, nor displeased. He couldn't even tell if she was surprised. It was as though he'd returned home after a few hours.

"I came to pay respect to the mother and father who gave me birth," he said. "I am going away, forever."

"Come inside. Your father is here."

He took off his shoes at the door and followed her in. His father was sitting on the bed. His cheeks were now shrunken, caved in, and he gave Rozy a vacant look.

"It's Rozan," his mother said loudly. "He's come for a visit. After so many years. We thought you'd died."

"Ra—Ra—" His father had trouble speaking, that much was clear. Did his father remember how cruelly he used to beat Rozy?

Rozy kneeled on the floor next to the bed and took his father's hand in his. "Father, it's me, Rozan."

"Rozan," his father whispered. Then he said something Rozy didn't catch.

"Your father's health is not so good," his mother said. "His mind is also not right. This happened right after the Big Two. He doesn't remember people. It's like the earthquake rattled things inside his head. Now every time there's a noise, he gets frightened." She addressed him loudly again, "Rozan has come, your son."

Rozy's father pulled his hand away and looked in the other direction, toward the window.

"What work do you do in the Valley?" His mother sat next to him.

"A have a job with the Rajjya."

"That's good, that's good," she said. "I hear you have done well for yourself there. That's what people are saying. That you work in the Lion's Palace."

"How do you manage the household, Mother?" he asked. "Where does the money come from?"

His mother talked of their financial troubles, the cost of medicine for Rozy's father. Rozy's previous room was now occupied by a tenant. A real slob, his mother whispered. But they needed the money.

"What about Reshami?" he asked. "Has my sister visited?"

"You didn't hear?"

Rozy shook his head.

"She has been widowed. Her husband died in the Big Two."

Rozy lowered his head. Should he have known? But how would he have?

"Now she has her own struggles. She does call every now and then, unlike you." His mother had raised her index finger toward him, and he now saw that it was shaking. In fact, a slight tremor seemed to be passing through her body, like a remnant from the Big Two.

He looked toward his old room. He wanted to go into it, see what it looked like now, touch things, see if his mom had kept a family photo, of him and his parents at the Wish-Fulfilling Goddess's Temple, that he hung above his bed. There were no photos of him in the main room where they were sitting. There was a large, close-up one of Reshami's face, smiling; it must have been taken before her husband died.

Rozy took out his wallet and extracted a few thousand rupees.

His mother pushed his hand away with her shaking hand. "You keep your money to yourself," his mother said. "I don't need it."

"Take it. Take it, please." He found himself choking.

She stood. "Here, let me make some tea, then you can be on your way. You must have friends to visit here. Isn't that so, Rozan?"

———

He found a hotel in the Founding Father chowk. He ate some chicken chow mein by himself in the hotel's restaurant. He thought about his friend Sangeeta who had sheltered him after the Bir incident. She must have finished her medical degree a long time ago, must have become a daktar. He contemplated trying to locate her, to see if she was still in town, then abandoned the idea, unsure he was up to answering her questions.

After he finished eating, he wandered around the town a bit, recognizing some of the places from his childhood, marveling at other places that had become unrecognizable because the neighborhoods had become so crowded—so many buildings, so many people. He drifted toward the lakeside, went to the spot near the big peepul tree where you could rent boats for excursions on the lake. Bir used to say that in the future he was going to own a house on the side of the hill overlooking the lake, with the glorious white mountains to the north. He used to say that he fantasized about going on a boat with Rozy around the lake, gasping at the mountains and singing romantic songs.

Bir. Rozy felt the knot in his chest again, and he gently rubbed it, trying to loosen it. Yes, he needed to do something about Bir. He needed to take care of Bir. The time was coming. Rozy's relationship with PM Papa had reached its peak. He could feel this transition coming, this shifting into another mind, as if he were going to become an entirely different type of being. He had sensed this in him a long time ago, perhaps even during the time when Bir was raping him, perhaps even when he entered the Valley and sold his body to that businessman. There was a shift occurring inside of him, a metamorphosis. During those times, and even now, the pain made it impossible to see this accumulation of power, but it was there.

He stayed up most of the night, staring at the ceiling in the dark, going over and over in his mind why his mother hadn't taken money from him. He also replayed his father's withdrawal of his hand once he realized who was holding it. By dawn Rozy's heart had hardened even more toward his parents. The person he'd been with them in the past, that Rozan, was also now impossibly distant.

In the morning he took the first bus back to the Valley.

INTERLOPERS

31.

He was a thin, dark man with a bird-like nose. He reeked of cigarettes, even from a distance. He was sitting in the living room with Shambhogya and Priyanka, playing with the ashtray on the side table, shaking it, caressing it, running his index finger in circles on its smooth surface.

Prithvi Raj wasn't there; was he hiding? The young servant Mokshya had come to fetch Kranti, and as soon as Mokshya said, "Shambhogya didi is calling you to the living room," Kranti understood what it was about. For some reason, she didn't feel anxious about meeting this man. If there was any anxiety, it had been numbed over by another feeling—as though she could do anything, go anywhere, defy anything.

She went down to the living room, without bothering to brush her hair, still in her widow-white dhoti.

"Come, Kranti," Shambhogya said, patting the space next to her on the sofa.

The thin man was sitting by himself, and Priyanka sat across from Shambhogya. He stood and did a somber namaste. He looked nervous, his eyes wary—he knew what this meeting was about. Judging from his clothes, he didn't appear sophisticated, or perhaps even well off. What had he been offered in return? A nice bank balance? Or perhaps a stake in Ghimirey & Sons?

"My cousin Umesh dai," Shambhogya introduced him as Kranti sat next to her. "We are distant cousins, but he's more like a brother. We grew up as childhood companions."

Kranti tried to imagine elegant and pretty Shambhogya and this man as childhood playmates, but she couldn't. "You've never talked about him before," she told Shambhogya.

"Perhaps the occasion didn't arise," Priyanka said.

"Umesh dai is the nicest man I know," Shambhogya said. "He would give anything to those he loves."

The man appeared shy. "Shambhogya surely knows how to flatter."
Priyanka laughed, a bit too full-throated.

"You didn't comb your hair today?" Shambhogya whispered to Kranti.

"Feeling lazy," Kranti said in a normal voice, not bothering to whisper back.

Shambhogya looked pointedly at Priyanka, as though saying, See, what did I tell you?

When the three daughters-in-law were together, Shambhogya and Priyanka seemed to be carrying on a private conversation through their eyes, excluding Kranti. I can't penetrate their bond, Kranti told herself. She pitied these two women, knowing their closeness was unhealthy, or even illusionary. One was a passive-aggressive controller and the other was a whispering conniver. The two were made for each other; it was a symbiotic relationship. Kranti could picture the two in their old age, toothless and balding, sitting in rocking chairs on the balcony, whispering, plotting, and scheming, yet also disliking each other.

Shambhogya patted Kranti's cheek and said, "And we are more like sisters than sisters-in-law, aren't we, Kranti?"

"Of course. Sisters."

Priyanka excused herself to get some tea. Soon, Shambhogya would also find an excuse to join Priyanka, leaving the two mangliks by themselves. They could have at least tried to find her a good-looking manglik, Kranti thought sardonically, although no one would say that Kabiraj, the man of her own choice, was good-looking. She noticed now a dark spot the size of a large coin, a skin disfigurement, on this man's right cheek. He kept fiddling with his shirt pocket: he was itching to extract a cigarette from the pack of Surya that was visible through the fabric.

"Why is Priyanka taking so long?" Shambhogya said. She told Kranti to converse with Umesh and left the room.

He met her eyes and quickly looked away. His eyes seemed to suggest that he didn't think he was worthy of her, but that he was desperate. Or was she being too harsh, too judgmental too soon?

"So, what do you do, dai?"

He fidgeted. "You don't have to call me dai. Just call me Umesh. I work at a manpower agency, sending people to work abroad."

"Ah," she said. "Bad condition for our brothers and sisters in those Khadi countries. What's the rate of death now? One a day?"

"Media exaggerations," Umesh said. "Fake news."

"So what's true news? They're doing well in these Khadi countries? No abuses? Everything hunky-dory?"

"The media exaggerates," he said. "PM Papa just visited a Khadi country. You know him—he's going to make everything great again." He was about to speak again, but then he simply picked up the empty ashtray and rolled it on his fingers.

Afraid that he was going to drop the ashtray and break it, she nearly snatched it away from him, then thought: An ashtray breaking in the Asylum is like a drop of rain in a vast ocean—it'd barely make a clink. Dada would have appreciated that analogy. It would have tickled Kabiraj's poetic imagination. "Who else is in your family?" she asked him abruptly, as though he was a candidate being interviewed for a job.

"My parents. They are getting old, though, with many ailments. After my wife and children died." He didn't continue.

A short silence ensued. She asked gently, "The Big Two?"

"Bus accident during the Big Two." His fingers clawed out his cigarette pack. She waved him her permission. His hands were shaking as he lit a cigarette. "My wife had gone to her mother's house in the hills for her father's annual rites, and took our two children with her. The bus . . ." He made a motion with his hand that she took to mean a plunge, perhaps down a ridge or into a river.

"How old were the children?"

"Seven and nine."

The smoke curled up toward his face. His entire body seemed to be quivering with nervous energy. The children hadn't wanted to go, he said. They had complained that their grandmother's village was boring. "I persuaded them, even bribed them, promising them gifts upon their return."

She imagined the kids' faces as the bus hurtled down the ridge, then their heads smashed to pulp.

"The children died instantly. Their mother was taken to the hospital, but for days I didn't know which hospital, and by the time I reached her, she was gone." He took long drags of his smoke.

Kranti wondered when Shambhogya and Priyanka would return.

"I was acquainted with Bhasker babu," he said.

"How so?"

"I'd come here for Shambhogya's wedding. Couldn't make it to your wedding, though."

"I see."

"A fine man."

"Just a moment, okay? I'll be right back." She stood and strode toward the staircase, bumping into Shambhogya at the bottom.

"Where are you going?" Shambhogya said. "Leaving the guest by himself?"

"He's your guest."

"Don't be rude, Kranti," Shambhogya whispered urgently. She gave a quick smile in the direction of the guest, who'd already lit another cigarette. "Priyanka is bringing tea. Just five more minutes, okay?"

"I have things to do."

When Shambhogya didn't move, Kranti pushed past her and went up to her room.

Umesh dai, thin, nervous, chain smoker, the man they had chosen for her, became a regular at the Asylum. Smoke Chimney dai was her name for him. He had, it appeared, also been okayed by Prithvi Raj. One evening after work, Kranti happened to glance out of her window, and there was the fellow they'd chosen for her, a cigarette smoldering between his fingers, talking with the old man on the lawn one story below, near God's Room, as the sun was on its way to set above the roofs of the houses toward the west. For some reason Prithvi Raj was bare-chested and wearing a dhoti, resembling a Brahmin priest about to embark upon an important ritual—such as getting his wid-owed daughter-in-law married, thought Kranti. Both the men were quite animated. Kranti had never seen Smoke Chimney dai so lively before. In her presence he was shy, with a pall of sadness that had, presumably, to do with his grief over his family. But now here he was, smoke twirling in the air as he waved his arms about to make a point. They were not arguing; they were in agreement. Smoke Chimney dai also appeared to slightly grin, an expression she'd never seen on him before. They were conducting a rapid back and forth conversation, completing each other's sentences, nodding ho ho, saying thik thik and bhannai pardaina, no need to say it! A verbal dance that showed no signs of stopping, until Smoke Chimney dai happened to look up at her window with a startled movement, like a small animal suddenly aware of a predator. He stopped talking and turned somber. Noting this change, Prithvi Raj also glanced up. He appeared puzzled, as though at her own window was the last place he expected Kranti to be. "Were we talking too loud? Did we disturb you?" he called to her.

She shook her head.

"Why don't you come down? I need to speak to you about something."

When she got there, Prithvi Raj Ghimirey had left; it was just Smoke Chimney dai. He asked how she was. This was not the same person she'd observed from the window moments ago; there was something made-up about him, how polite he was, how sad.

She was irritated at the ploy to get her alone with Smoke Chimney dai. "Are you Sir's spokesman now?" she asked.

He appeared confused.

"Any messages?" she asked. "Did Sir ask you to convey any messages?"

He finally seemed to grasp what she was referring to, and he sputtered, said something about Prithvi Raj being pulled away by an important phone call.

"Up and down the stairs for me," she said, pointing toward the Asylum. "It's good exercise, hoina?"

He stared at her for a moment, then abruptly threw down his butt and crushed it—on Shambhogya's well-manicured lawn.

She sensed eyes—Shambhogya's, Priyanka's—watching her and Smoke Chimney dai. She scanned the big house, but they weren't there. Her gaze stopped at her bedroom window, noting the after-glow of her own figure from moments ago: there she was, Kranti, the heroine of this saga, watching herself down below with her future husband. Future husband? Had she already accepted this fate?

"Enjoy your smoke," she told Umesh dai as he lit another cigarette, and she headed toward God's Room, which was merely a few feet away.

She knocked, then looked back. Umesh dai was gazing at her, dumbfoundedly, and seemed to be caught off guard that she turned to look back. In his nervousness, he threw the freshly lit cigarette in his hand and crushed it. Another one bites the dust, thought Kranti—one of Dada's songs.

Muwa didn't respond. Kranti knocked again—still no response. Hesitantly, she pushed the door with her fingers. It creaked open, so she entered. Muwa's back was turned to her. She was in the lotus position, meditating.

"What do you want?" Muwa asked without turning around to see who it was.

"It's me, Muwa."

"I know it's you. What do you want?"

"I can wait until after you're finished."

"Too late now, isn't it? I'm already disturbed. Might as well say what you need to."

"They're not going to give up, Muwa."

Muwa finally turned to look at her, almost angry. A vertical stress-line was visible on her forehead. "Why does that surprise you? What were you thinking?"

"I wasn't thinking anything." Kranti felt a lump rise to her throat.

Muwa's eyes softened. "That's what I was trying to tell you. These people are relentless. It's best if you leave this godforsaken place. Go to Beggar Street. Stay there until that awful man stops coming here."

"If I go, I won't come back."

"And if you stay here, they won't leave you alone."

"What can they do to me, Muwa? What can they possibly do to me?"

"Do you want to marry Smoke Chimney?" Muwa asked.

Kranti was pleased that Muwa had arrived at the nickname independently of Kranti. It proved to Kranti that she and her mother-in-law were on the same wavelength. But, this thought was also prominent: To what avail? Muwa was the most helpless of them all in the Asylum, including the nokerchakers.

"No, I don't, but can they force me? Really, they think they can force me? I'd like to see them try."

Muwa didn't speak for a moment, then she said, "You are as crazy as the rest of them. Now I can officially declare everyone in this house crazy. Including me, and I was a lost cause that day I married your father-in-law and came to this godforsaken place." She dismissed Kranti with a wave of her hand and returned to her meditation.

—

Rozy appeared in the Lion Palace after visiting the Town of Lakes, clad in jeans and a leather jacket over a tight black T-shirt, his hair no longer hidden underneath a cap. He was confronted by Bill Tamang, right at the door of the Victorian room, before he could even get to his desk outside the Gufa. "Where did you go?" he asked Rozy in an angry whisper. Some of the other Lion Palace staff—the press secretary, the house manager—were also in the room, watching. Rozy replied that he had not been feeling well. And, because he hadn't been feeling well, he'd stayed with a friend who could take care of him. Then, that friend had taken extremely ill and he'd had to stay to take care of his friend. He gently pushed past Bill Tamang and went to his desk as Jungey, from the painting, looked on sternly.

Bill Tamang seemed slightly offended by Rozy's audacity, then followed him. "Go inside," he said, indicating PM Papa's office. "Why aren't you in your daura-suruwal today? And your hair just loose like that?"

Rozy shuffled some papers on his desk and said, "In a moment." As PM Papa's valet, he had a desk of his own, right outside PM Papa's door, though really there was no reason for him to have a desk—he didn't have to deal with any paperwork. He had a phone on his desk that never rang because most of his communication was with PM Papa and with Bill Tamang, on the mobile phone. Besides, he spent his time inside the Gufa, with PM Papa.

"You are in for some real trouble," Bill Tamang whispered. "Absent for days without notification, and coming back like this. PM Papa has been worried sick. He thought that you'd been abducted by an enemy. We nearly sent the Loyal Army Dais to look for you. In fact, I was preparing to send your photo to the Poolis Uncles." He pulled out a sheet of paper from his pocket and showed Rozy a xeroxed photo of him, where he was wearing a cap, looking large-eyed at the camera, downturned lips revealing his sadness.

Rozy sat at his desk. The others were watching him, waiting for him to knock on PM Papa's door, make deferential noises, and be let in. But Rozy continued working. After about half an hour, PM Papa's door opened. "Rozy," he said.

"Yes, Papa?"

"Can you come inside?"

"Yes, Papa."

Rozy went in. As soon as the door was closed—a huge, heavy door of soundproof mahogany—PM Papa clasped Rozy close to his body and kissed him deep and hard. PM Papa's grip was the strongest that Rozy had felt, as though his hands were iron claws. Rozy struggled. PM Papa didn't release him. He ground his lips against Rozy's—big jaws crushing Rozy's chin—as though getting his fill for all the days missed.

Finally, Rozy pushed him away. "So rough you are," he said.

"Who do you think you are?" PM Papa said, pointing his finger close to Rozy's nose. His voice was a croak. "Even President Corn Hair wants my friendship. Rozy, who do you think you are?"

Rozy's eyes fell upon the cricket bat standing in the corner. After Rakshya Garam's death, it had fallen upon Rozy to get the bat cleaned. He had given it to the Lion Palace custodian, an old woman who'd served several past prime ministers, and she'd looked at the blood-spattered bat quizzically but hadn't said anything. The bat had been returned in Rozy's absence, but he could see that it still had a faint blush of red on its surface.

PM Papa noticed Rozy's gaze on the bat, and Rozy, impulsively, said, "Go ahead, do it. Go ahead and smash my head to bits. I know that's what you want to do."

"Is that what you think?" PM Papa said, raging and complaining at the same time. "Is that what you think?" He strode to his desk and picked up a bouquet of roses—Rozy hadn't noticed the flowers before. "See?" he said, shaking the bouquet. A couple of petals flew off, one brushing against Rozy's cheek before falling to the floor.

Rozy slowly bent down and picked up the petal, turned it this way and that in his fingers. "What's the use?" he finally said.

PM Papa's anger vanished. "Please, maiya, don't do this to me."

"I'm not doing anything," Rozy said. "Why do you always accuse me of things I haven't done?" He threw the petal toward PM Papa, but the petal fell to the floor before it could reach the man.

This time it was PM Papa who picked up the petal and brought it to Rozy. "I'm not accusing you, truly."

Rozy looked at him steadily, then said, "Let's get away from here."

"Where?" PM Papa's face lit up. "Amrika? Let's go to Amrika."

"Right, keep joking."

PM Papa clasped Rozy's hand in his and said, "No, seriously, where do you want to go?"

"Let's get out of the Lion Palace, and I'll tell you outside."

In the Hummer, PM Papa said, "I don't understand. You have everything. I've given you everything."

The backseat of the Hummer was spacious, and Rozy always felt small while seated in it. Right now, however, PM Papa was squeezed against him, as though he were afraid Rozy would open the door and jump out. A sliding glass divider separated them from Laxman and the driver.

Rozy refused to look at his face.

"Is there anything lacking?" PM Papa caressed Rozy's cheek with his thumb. "What's lacking? You know all you have to do is tell me."

Rozy said nothing.

"You know I'm PM Papa, right?" PM Papa said, his voice a bit harder than before. "You know I can do anything, right?"

"You can't do everything," Rozy said flatly. His heart was pounding.

PM Papa grabbed his arm roughly. "What did you say? What did you say?"

Before his Town of Lakes trip, Rozy had grown his fingernails and painted them purple. He looked at them now. It felt symbolic, somehow; he thought of purple clouds forecasting a massive storm. "You won't be able to do what I ask you."

"Try me," PM Papa said, his voice a mixture of rage and bitterness, and, Rozy was glad to note, fear. "Did someone do something to you? Tell me, and I'll kill that person."

Rozy pressed the window button, and a rush of warm air—and the sound of pedestrians talking and cars honking—filled the Hummer. Laxman looked back with alarm, signaled with his hand for Rozy to close the window. Rozy pretended not to have seen him. Laxman spoke through the intercom, and Rozy threw up his hands in the air, but then obliged.

"Rozy," PM Papa said.

"Take me to your residence."

PM Papa stared at Rozy, then, with some relief, laughed, then clasped his hand, said not to joke.

"I am serious," Rozy said. "Take me to the Humble Abode."

PM Papa stopped grinning. "Why are you teasing me?"

"I've become very serious these days, Papa," Rozy said. "And I'm saying, let's go to the Humble Abode, you and me."

PM Papa looked down at his lap.

"Yes, I believe you—you can do anything," Rozy said. He pushed the button that operated the intercom. "Laxman dai, tell the driver to stop the car," Rozy said. "I need to get out."

The driver, without taking his eyes off the road, asked, "Stop, Papa?"

"No, drive to the Humble Abode," PM Papa said.

Since PM Papa had ordered special shock absorbers from Amrika, his Hummer slid smoothly through the pot-holed, earthquake-cracked streets of the Valley. There was a period of silence as they went past the Durbar.

Rozy watched the Durbar, its orange-yellow façade, a picture popping into his head. A white horse snorting. Smell of goat meat rising up in the air.

"Is that what this is about?" PM Papa said, his voice cracking. "You want me to take you to my home? Then I'll take you to my home. I'll have you sit in my living room. I'll even have Shrimati Papa serve you snacks. If this is what you really want."

Rozy continued looking outside the window.

PM Papa held Rozy's hand. "I want you to go to Amrika with me."

Rozy didn't say anything, didn't turn his face toward PM Papa. The thought of going to Amrika was enticing. When he was younger, and in the immediate aftermath of the Bir episode, he had fantasized about escaping to Amrika, where he'd heard LGBTQ people could live openly and love openly, hold jobs and even run for elected positions. But that thought had been quickly quashed, and now, the LGBTQ people in Amrika, too, had lost many of their rights under President Corn Hair, hadn't they? There was no question of going anywhere: his destiny was in Darkmotherland.

They pulled up to the Humble Abode, a large Chiniya-brick house, two-storied, with a pagoda roof and a chaitya on top. At least a dozen national double-triangled flags were fluttering on the roof. Humble Abode boasted a superbly manicured lawn, like the types found in foreign nations. Dozens of men with machine guns roamed the compound and stood on top of roofs and walls. As the Hummer stopped at the front of the residence, several nokerchakers, bent at their waists in submission, came to receive them. A large Alsatian dog came running to Rozy, sniffing his crotch. PM Papa scolded him, then petted him fondly, saying his name was Kukkur.

Shrimati Papa came to the porch, looking worried. "Everything all right? You didn't call to say you'd be home early." She was an average looking woman, about six inches taller than Papa and not as round. She came from a prosperous family and had married PM Papa when he won his first local election. Her eyes fell on Rozy, and instantly Shrimati Papa recognized him as a rival. He was dark but pretty, with a young, lithesome body, with long, curving eyelashes. Was that a hint of kohl around his eyes? And the long purple fingernails. His lustrous black hair touched his shoulders. He was also wearing a tight-fitting leather jacket that an associate had delivered to her husband some weeks ago, Shrimati Papa now remembered, so the jacket had been gifted to this thing by her husband. He resembled, Shrimati Papa thought, a young, beautiful model in a men's fashion magazine. Her husband had brought a sauta home.

"There's some urgent work we need to do at home," PM Papa told his wife. "So, we'll be in the office." He was referring to the small room that he called his home office, where he rarely spent any time because he was often in the Lion Palace, where he was more in control and could monitor the comings and goings of his cabinet members. And obviously, the Lion Palace was a better place for spending time with Rozy.

Rozy didn't bother to look at Shrimati Papa, who, he knew, was aware of his position in the Lion Palace as her husband's valet. Previously, Rozy had greeted her on those occasions when she accompanied her husband for state functions. But all those times he'd been dressed in daura suruwal, and his hair was hidden under a dhakatopi. She had never returned Rozy's greetings, nor smiled. She was not the type to return greetings of those beneath her. Besides, Rozy knew she suspected that he was more than an attendant to her husband. Rozy knew how conservative Shrimati Papa was, and he wondered what mental images ran through her mind when she imagined what her husband did with his male lovers.

Shrimati Papa watched her husband take the young homo, who finally gave her a sideways glance with his pretty eyes, to his home office, where the two were holed up for nearly an hour. Sounds of arguments, then fervent whispers, then, to Shrimati Papa's horror, what sounded like kisses and moans coming from the homo's throat. Laxman and the other bodyguards were outside, by the front door to the house, so they couldn't have heard. The old cook who was standing with Shrimati Papa outside the office door closed her ears with her bony fingers, chanted a prayer, and walked away. A couple of other nokerchakers standing nearby avoided Shrimati Papa's eyes. She could have sunk to the floor. What was her husband doing? So brazen. So blatant. What did he think would be the outcome of it?

She went to her room and lay down.

One moment she was the queen of the castle, and the next moment she was the cuckqueen. Discarded for the sake of this—this *thing*. Shrimati Papa felt humiliation burn through her like a hot liquid. She imagined the entire Darkmotherland laughing at her, she, a Brahmin girl from an upright family. She had sacrificed so much for PM Papa, turned a blind eye to his sexual appetites because she felt that he was, really, going to purify Darkmotherland.

But this? Who *was* this Rozy? Was it a man or a woman? Was it a hijra? Shrimati Papa had seen an occasional hijra in the Valley, and there'd been the encounter with her husband on a pilgrimage trip to Bharat, one of the only times the two had traveled together when he was the Home Minister. Along with them were about three aides who had been making and handling the travel arrangements, and a Brahmin cook because Shrimati Papa wouldn't eat food cooked or touched by outsiders. The entourage had been accosted outside a temple gate on a drizzling afternoon. Clapping their hands and singing, a dozen or so hijras had surrounded PM Papa and Shrimati Papa. When the aides attempted to push them away, they had been attacked with a fury that had shocked everyone. The hijras had grabbed and squeezed their crotches, hit them with their open palms, and even struck them with the umbrellas they had in their hands. "We'll chop off your dicks and feed them to the dogs," the hijras had screamed.

PM Papa stood in the doorway to her room, his stout body barely fitting in the doorway. "We have to fix up my office," he said, "so that Rozy can sleep there."

"I never thought you'd humiliate me in my house like this." Shrimati Papa was lying down on her bed, facing the wall, and she said this without facing him.

PM Papa chose to ignore her. "Make sure that the office gets swept up and there's clean bedding."

"You can do it yourself," Shrimati Papa mumbled.

"What? Can you speak louder?"

"I said if it's that important to you, do it yourself."

"Well, I've told you what needs to be done."

Shrimati Papa rolled over so that she finally faced him. "I never said a word, all these years. At least have the decency not to bring such filth into my home."

PM Papa approached the bed. "Don't talk like that about Rozy."

She sat up, quickly, as though his approach meant he'd realized how he'd wronged her. "I'm your wife!"

PM Papa sat next to her on the bed. "What has that got to do with anything?"

She scooted away from him a bit, even though his body hadn't been touching her. "What has that got to—! Dear God, how can you even say that?"

"You have everything you need."

"No!" Shrimati Papa said, stomping her feet on the floor. "This is not acceptable! What are Darkmotherlandites going to say? Have you thought about that?"

PM Papa placed his hand lightly on Shrimati Papa's knee. "You know we—you and I—wouldn't be here if I paid attention to what people said."

"They will rise up against you. Darkmotherlandites will not let this stand. Wait until General Tso finds out. And Swami Go!swami."

"They've probably known by now, maybe even before you."

Shrimati Papa was so aghast by this last bit that she let herself drop back on the bed, mildly bumping her head against the wall in the process, which elicited a torrent of "aiya!" and "maryo ni!," exaggerating the physical pain, as though PM Papa had somehow made it happen, perhaps even pushed her without touching her.

That evening Shrimati Papa was privy to ferocious lovemaking noises coming from the home office. Entreaties to Rozy and giggles and laughter. Sounds of shuffling, creaking, grunting noises like those made by animals. Soft murmurs. Then, after a few moments of silence, Rozy's voice in the kitchen—Shrimati Papa's kitchen—loudly demanding a cup of lemon tea. She buried her face in the pillow, but there was no respite because the old cook came to her, complaining.

"Today complete darkness has entered this home," the old cook said, standing at the door, not entering, as though now even Shrimati Papa's bedroom, one that she shared with PM Papa, was contaminated. "Such a big man, what is he doing? This is a grave sin. God, why didn't you kill me before you made me witness this?"

"Shut up, old woman!" Shrimati Papa said. "Otherwise, I'll send you to rot in jail."

"So, you're okay with it?"

"Okay with what? Nothing is wrong, and if I hear you say anything more about this, you will be the sorriest hag in Darkmotherland."

32.

Her face shrouded by the white dhoti, Kranti crossed Bhurey Paradise. The pimps and touts knew better than to harass a white-clad widow. They were all afraid of the curse it might bring. Sure, it would be nice to tell her how suckable her mango-ripe breasts were, but try it and you might wake up the next morning with half your face rotted off.

Punishments for sins, big or small, had been frequent and severe since the Big Two.

Rajnikant Aryal had failed to offer a goat sacrifice to the Wish-Fulfilling Goddess, even after the cable car that transported devotees to her mountaintop abode had been repaired. Punishment: his sister-in-law absconded with all the money he'd earned from years of road construction work in the scorching heat of the Khadi country desert.

Kaushik Basnet refused to shave his head after his father passed away. Within days he was overwhelmed by a whooping cough and began to hack up tiny pieces of his lungs. Now he was on his deathbed and the lung tissue he brought up into his mouth was mixed with strips of heart muscle.

Sulabh Pradhan pronounced that the Afro-haired Godman was a fraud and a trickster, that his ability to pluck watches and jewelry from thin air was mere sleight of hand, that the holy ash that supposedly flowed from his photos and statues were fake news. This is what happened to Sulabh: he became incapable of ingesting real food and the only thing he could swallow—the only thing that kept him from starving to death—was holy ash.

The Big Two had convinced Darkmotherlandites that unless they intensified their prayers and supplications and devotions, they were doomed. And then, of course, there was talk of the Big Three, which was coming soon unless people shed their ungodly ways. The Big Three would be nothing like the other two. It would be so calamitous that there'd be no survivors. Astrologers, witches, astrophysicists, and geologists appeared in the media proclaiming that the Big Three would decimate humanity as we know it. A 9.7 on the Richter scale, likely higher. Larger than the Good Friday 9.2 earthquake in Alaska that had rattled the entirety of the Prince William Sound. More devastating than the 9.5 Great Chilean earthquake that created a tsunami that traveled all the way to the shores of Hilo, Hawaii. "You want to build earthquake-resistant houses? Good luck! The Big Three will blow any house to smithereens."

He was chatting with a man near his tent and didn't see her coming. The two were deep in conversation, it seemed, perhaps even mildly arguing. Just for fun, Kranti stood a few feet away, waiting to see if he'd see her, and what his reaction would be. Kabiraj tended to lose awareness of his surroundings when he was engrossed with something—reading, composing a poem in his mind, contemplating a philosophical riddle. She had teased him about it. Pinching his nose, she'd said, "My woo woo dallu!"

"We should change the venue," the man was insisting to Kabiraj, who was saying that it wasn't possible at this last minute, that the invitations had gone out, that guests had been invited from all over Darkmotherland, that hotel rooms had been booked. The man said something that sounded like Poolis Uncles, but Kranti couldn't be sure. Then, the man noticed her and elbowed Kabiraj, who said, "What?" The man elbowed him again, and only then did Kabiraj see Kranti. He told the man they'd have to carry on the conversation later. The man protested a bit but Kabiraj brushed him aside and came toward Kranti. The man walked away, grumbling.

As they entered Laj Mahal, Kabiraj pushed aside the anchal covering her face and kissed her. He was becoming a better kisser: he took longer, and didn't slobber all over her lips.

After they sat down and he set some tea to boil, Kranti asked Kabiraj who the man was.

Kabiraj shrugged. "No one important."

"What meeting was he talking about?"

"Nothing," Kabiraj said. "He's a bit cuckoo." He whistled and pointed to his head to indicate cuckooness.

"I thought he mentioned Poolis Uncles. You're not involved in anything, are you?"

"No, no," Kabiraj said.

She watched his face for a while. He appeared flustered, and she had half a mind to pursue this, but just the thought that Kabiraj might be involved in something covert made her so anxious that it crowded out all her other thoughts. It was best if she didn't even consider the possibility. She also knew that he was not Bhaskar, and she hoped he would not hide anything major from her. They were together now. She had become his, fully, after Bhaskar's death. That was an odd way to think, that he now fully possessed her, this pudgy, pot-bellied poet. I belong to nobody, she said to him in her mind. Nobody, you hear? Not you. Not the Ghimireys, who were now trying to marry her off to Smoke Chimney dai. Not even Bhaskar, although she would have cut some slack for him. She would let Bhaskar possess her if he returned from the dead.

They drank their tea, chatting. Her eyes fell upon his pile of dirty clothes in the corner of the tent.

"Why haven't you washed your clothes?" she asked him. "That pile—it's bigger than when I was here last."

"It's not like we have a private tank deliver water to us in Bhurey Paradise, like in the Asylum," Kabiraj said, smiling. "Most of the taps are dry, and the two that spew out muddy water have lines stretching outside of Bhurey Paradise."

An idea came to Kranti. She debated it internally, but only for a few seconds, then made a decision. What did she have to lose?

They made love. He had turned into such a good lover in recent days. She was proud of him, and she thought it funny that she was proud of him as though she'd trained him. She knew why she was proud of him: he never indicated that he thought he possessed her, although in his shy way he showed a lot of passion while making love to her.

Today, he let her take the lead, as though he were a virgin starting all over again. As she climbed on top of him, as she often did, he smiled and closed his eyes, his lips moist from their kiss. When he closed his eyes it was as though he was a new bride who wanted the lights turned off before she could allow herself the pleasures of the flesh. Spittle flew out of his mouth as he climaxed, which she found strangely adorable.

Afterward, as she dozed, he stroked her forehead, and she knew he was watching her, maybe composing a poem in his mind about her, how beautiful she was, how she compared to the full moon, or the sunlight dappling on the blue surface of the lake, or the heady bliss of a delicious wine.

Abruptly, she opened her eyes and said, "Boo!" He was startled. He turned red, then looked away quickly, embarrassed. Again, she closed her eyes and she knew he was observing her, and she quickly opened them and said, "Goo!" And he covered his face with his palms, then split his fingers so he could look at her through one eye. "Peekaboo!" she said.

Children we are, really, she thought, and she knew that she had been this happy only during her own childhood when she and Dada used to play peekaboo.

Later, she and Kabiraj ate hot samosas from a gaudily decorated cart nearby that was popular with everyone. Many middle-class folks sneaking into Bhurey Paradise to eat them stood up next to the cart, clicking and popping their tongues over the hot chutney. It was not only because the samosas were delicious, which they were, but also because they were some of the cheapest samosas around, given the high cost of everything since the Big Two.

Back in Laj Mahal, Kranti stuffed Kabiraj's clothes in a bag and said, "No reason for you to wait in line now at the Bhurey Paradise tap for hours just to wash your clothes." Kabiraj insisted that she not do it, but she didn't listen.

As soon as Kranti entered the gate of the Asylum in the evening, she saw Shambhogya on her balcony. Shambhogya quickly retreated.

Who else was watching Kranti return? She scanned the house. Did she also spot Prithvi Raj back away from his window? She wasn't sure. Cheech or Chong—when would she able to tell them apart?—was reaching out to take the sack of laundry from her hands, but she told him she'd take it inside herself. She asked him the whereabouts of Muwa. "Where do you think?" Cheech or Chong said. "In God's Room, as usual."

Shambhogya was waiting for Kranti in the living room, her arms crossed. She sported a tight smile. "So where have you been all evening? We were worried when you didn't come home from work." She noticed the sack. "What did you bring?"

"These are clothes."

"That's not a shopping bag."

"Dirty clothes."

"Whose? Did you go to your mother's house?"

"No."

"Whose then?"

Kranti brushed past her and climbed the stairs.

Shambhogya followed. "Whose clothes, Kranti?" When Kranti didn't answer, Shambhogya said, "Umesh dai was here. He was waiting for you all afternoon. He said you two had planned on going out."

Kranti had forgotten that she had told Smoke Chimney dai, teasingly, that they could stroll together in the Tourist District in the evening after she got off work. The Ghimireys would disapprove of them going into the Tourist District, but maybe because they wanted this liaison to succeed so badly, they wouldn't mind this transgression. Smoke Chimney dai had appeared insanely excited at the thought: his fingers had shaken as he'd dragged on his cigarette. The two had been in the living room. She'd asked if she could take a drag from his cigarette. He'd appeared astounded, and said that the Ghimireys would not approve, but she promised it would be their secret, then she took a drag and coughed, which made both of them giggle like children.

"Didn't have time, okay, Shambhogya didi? I was with a friend."

"Oh," Shambhogya said. "So, does the laundry also belong to your friend?"

Kranti didn't bother to answer her.

At the top of the stairs, it was Priyanka who waited anxiously. "Kranti didi, Umesh dai was waiting."

"Heard it already."

They watched her as she went to her room. She felt their eyes on her back. No sooner had she changed into a home-dhoti than Mokshya came to tell her that the others were waiting for her at the dining room table. "I've already eaten," Kranti told her. When Mokshya asked her if food should be brought up for her, she said no. Kranti glanced at the clock. Seven thirty, which was when the family ate, excepting Muwa, who rarely joined them these days. Once or twice Kranti would catch Muwa eating a banana, slowly, while leaning against a balustrade or the door to God's Room. Or she'd eat the skin of an orange, not the orange itself. Prithvi Raj emerged for meals or not depending upon whether he was of sound mind that evening. Shambhogya and Priyanka tried hard to get their father-in-law to join them, thinking the conversation would prevent his mind from wandering. Often they succeeded in getting him to come down for dinner. Lunch in the Asylum was more erratic, with people eating at different times. Aditya and Chaitanya usually ate lunch in the Headquarters; sometimes they came home and quickly left for work again. These days, after the manglik talk and the foisting of Umesh upon her, Kranti too ate mostly by herself in her room. Any semblance of closeness she'd felt with Shambhogya had already disappeared.

The laundry room was next to the kitchen. It was a large room with two taps where the nokerchakers washed the household clothes, with hang lines stretched across for the rainy day. The taps were hooked to a large tank, in service since the Big Two. A water truck pulled into the Asylum's driveway every few days, and thick hoses delivered water, at the insane price of 50,000 rupees for 5,000 liters, to the tank in the laundry room. One of the younger nokerchakers, usually Mokshya, was assigned the laundry duties, but today, after changing into her home-dhoti, Kranti took Kabiraj's dirty clothes to the laundry room herself.

No sooner had she entered it when Mokshya came running in. "Kranti didi, what are you doing? All you had to do was call me. I'd have picked these up from your room."

"I'm going to wash them myself," she said, then took out Kabiraj's dirty clothes and put them on in a pile.

Mokshya splayed her palms. "But why, hajur? What are we here for? I was hired just for this purpose. To wash."

When Kranti turned on the tap to fill the bucket, Mokshya crouched in front of the laundry pile.

"Don't touch anything," Kranti said. She hadn't washed any clothes, not even her own, since she came to the Asylum.

"Whose clothes are these, hajur?" Mokshya lifted a half-soggy pair of pants with her fingers, then dropped them as if she'd contracted a disease. "They're very dirty, and they're a man's." Then, with a sly smile, "Not Umesh dai's?"

Kranti turned off the tap and carried the bucket to the clothes. "You must have other things to do. Now leave me in peace to wash these."

The report that Kranti was washing clothes in the laundry room—none of the daughters-in-law had ever washed clothes; larger loads were picked up every few days by an outside dhobi, who returned them washed, starched, and ironed—must have reached the others. Soon Shambhogya was at the door. "Kranti, what are you doing? Is this really necessary? We're paying these nokerchakers for a reason. You will spoil them, as if they aren't spoiled already."

Kranti's back was to the door, and she didn't bother to turn and look. She continued to rub the collar of a shirt to get the grime out.

"Whose clothes are these?"

Kranti didn't answer.

"Whose, Kranti?"

"You know very well whose they are."

"Okay, let's say I do," Shambhogya said in a patient voice. "But why are you washing them? Since when did we become a laundry shop for the Bhurey Paradise?"

Kranti scrunched Kabiraj's shirt into a ball in her palms and softly battered it against the floor. She had always washed her own clothes in Beggar Street—Professor Shrestha's emphasis on Mahatma-inspired self-sufficiency and all—so now the motion came to her easily.

"Kranti, am I just an idiot standing here blabbering?"

"Then don't blabber," Kranti muttered.

She wasn't sure whether her muttering reached Shambhogya's ears, but Shambhogya's breathing could be heard across the laundry room. "Well, you seem to know what you're doing," Shambhogya said, "so what right do I have to say anything? I am simply here as your shuvachintak, wishing nothing but good for you." She paused. "Umesh dai was very disappointed at missing you, so I've invited him for lunch tomorrow. Tomorrow is Saturday so you won't have to go to work. Please don't disappear like you always do. It'll be embarrassing for me, for this family, if you're not here."

"Tomorrow, I have something else."

"Please, Kranti."

She didn't know why she wasn't repulsed washing Kabiraj's dirty underwear with its yellow patch at the crotch. The only underwear she'd washed had been Dada's when she was a teenager.

"Kranti?"

A thought came to her. "I'll be here."

No sooner had Shambhogya left when Priyanka peeked in. "Aren't you going to eat, Kranti didi?" she asked in a concerned voice.

"I'm not hungry."

"You shouldn't go to sleep on an empty stomach."

"I ate in Bhurey Paradise."

The nokerchakers were pacing outside the laundry room. Prithvi Raj also stopped by. Kranti didn't see him, of course, because she was facing the tap, but she felt his presence, his bulk blocking the light at the door. Even Muwa appeared. "Lots of hullabaloo in this house today, Kranti," she said, and Kranti turned her body to face her. Muwa must have been disturbed in God's Room, for she looked tired, almost ready to fall asleep. "I'm assuming you are the cause of it?"

"I know nothing, Muwa."

Muwa looked at the bucket, the clothes. One pair of underwear, a shirt, and a vest were already on the clothesline. "At least someone is doing some real work around here," Muwa said, and, as she moved on, "Looks like you've kicked up a hornet's nest."

After she hung Kabiraj's clothes on the clothesline, Kranti returned to her room. The exertion had made her hungry, she realized, so she ate a packet of bhujiya she and Bhaskar had picked up in the Tourist District black market after the Big Two. It was at least a year old. When she opened it and started munching, she found it to still be surprisingly piquant, so she chewed and masticated and swallowed with gusto.

33.

Every day Shrimati Papa tried to push Rozy out of her house—"my house!" she said to those around her in disbelief—and every day she didn't succeed. Rozy was a feature in the Humble Abode now, and his power grew. He brazenly, at least as Shrimati Papa saw it, went to the kitchen and ordered the nokerchakers around. "Didn't you put some lemon in?" he'd ask, scrunching his nose, when a nokerchaker brought him black tea, which he pretended to exasperatedly wait for in the kitchen doorway. "You folks certainly haven't been trained well, have you?" he commented as he tasted boiled green tomato achar. "What is this?" he asked as he scooped the achar with his index finger from the bowl that a nokerchaker had presented to him. "Smell this," he said, taking his finger close to the nokerchaker's nose. "Does it smell like tomato achar or someone's diarrhea? Is this how your high lordess there"—he jerked his chin toward Shrimati Papa's bedroom—"teaches you how to make poleko achar? Let me tell you. In my birthplace of Town of Lakes, even the starving street mutt would refuse to lap up poor quality achar like this." Rozy said this loudly, to ensure that it reached Shrimati Papa's ears.

Rozy sunbathed on the roof. He went up late in the morning, stripped down to his underwear, spread a blanket, and lay down. The underwear was not a white kattu underwear but a tight jockey type that clung tightly to the hips and emphasized his bulge. It was bright orange in color, and its glare made the security dais with their machine guns patrolling the roof cover their eyes. Shrimati Papa called her husband in the Lion Palace, hysterical. PM Papa assured her that nothing untoward was happening. Rozy was merely sunbathing—what was the problem?

Shrimati Papa stormed up to the roof but stopped in her tracks at the top of the staircase. One of the nokerchakers, a young girl of nineteen whose name was Nakkali because she had coquettish manners and showed a fondness for facial makeup, was massaging Rozy's back with coconut oil. Shrimati Papa recognized the bottle because it was a special coconut oil from Hawaii that the Amrikan ambassador had gifted her during her last visit when the Grass Knoll Gal had blown herself up.

Nakkali was so focused on the massage, rubbing the fragrant oil on Rozy's smooth, gleaming skin with the utmost devotion, that she didn't even notice Shrimati Papa at the doorway only a few yards away. When she did, a look of fear passed over her face, but only momentarily before she returned her attention to Rozy's back, turning her body slightly away from her employer. Shrimati Papa restrained herself from storming to the girl and dragging her away by her hair. She looked at the security men with their machine guns, as they were pretending that what was happening a few feet away from them wasn't actually happening. Instead, they continued scanning the surroundings for danger—and Shrimati Papa decided to retreat back down the stairs. At the bottom of the stairs, the cook was standing, tears streaming down her face, as though PM Papa was *her* husband who'd brought home a sauta.

That evening when PM Papa came home from the Lion Palace (Rozy hadn't gone because he'd taken an indefinite leave of absence as a valet), Shrimati Papa confronted her husband at the door. "Do you know what people are saying? Do you know how you've tarnished our name forever?"

PM looked past her at the nokerchakers, who were lurking about, and asked them where Rozy was. The nokerchakers pointed to his home office, now Rozy's room. Pushing aside his wife, PM Papa strode to Rozy's room and knocked. Rozy asked lazily who it was. "It's me, Papa," PM Papa said.

"Oui, entre," Rozy said imperiously.

PM Papa opened the door, halfway, and asked, "How was your day?"

Rozy was wrapped in the blanket on the bed. He replied that he roasted himself sunbathing on the roof. "Wanna see?" he asked with a mischievous smile. Without waiting for PM Papa's response,

Rozy flashed him by lifting the blanket. He was hard; his member was ramrod straight. And he was roasted—his dark skin was even darker. More exotic, thought PM Papa. But the hard penis, which was lighter in color because the jockey underwear protected it from the sun, looked like a beautiful white flower standing proud in rich, dark muddy earth.

PM Papa was impressed by his own poetic analogy. He pressed his hand to his lips to say, "Oh, my!" then he mouthed "later" and, with a smile and a wink, shut the door.

Shrimati Papa was in the hallway, her arms crossed. "Well?"

"Well, what?" PM Papa went to his room and sat on his bed.

She followed him and stood next to him. "I got a call from my sister. It's all over Darkmotherland."

He signaled to a nokerchaker standing outside the door, who rushed in and knelt in front of his master, untied his shoes and took them off. He gently massaged his feet. "Should I bring some warm saltwater, hajur?" he asked.

PM Papa ruffled the hair of the nokerchaker, a middle-aged man who'd been with him since his Home Ministry days. "Ramparsad," PM Papa said. "You might be only one in this house who understands what my needs are. Here I am, working hard for Darkmotherland on my feet all day, and what do I get when I get home? Only nagging." He made nagging sounds, "Ngang, ngang, ngang."

Ramparsad called out to another nokerchaker to bring PM Papa some warm water with salt. "Don't make it too hot, hai?" Ramparsad cautioned. He pulled off PM Papa's socks, sniffed them to ascertain their smelliness, then tossed them to the side. Then he sat with his legs crossed on the floor and began to softly knead, rub, and squeeze PM Papa's feet.

Shrimati Papa decided that she was going to say her piece, even with the nokerchakers present. They knew what was going on anyway—they'd all heard the sickening noises that came from the home office yesterday. "My sister couldn't stop crying," Shrimati Papa told her husband. "She said that she's never been as embarrassed in her life. To have to hear these filthy rumors. She said until today she was so proud to tell everyone that she was the sister-in-law of the beloved PM Papa of Darkmotherland, but what is she going to tell people now? People are already stopping her on the street to ask her whether PM Papa had brought a concubine home to the sacred temple of the Humble Abode."

Another nokerchaker brought a tub of warm salted water and set it on the floor. Ramparsad gently guided PM Papa's feet into the water, asking him repeatedly whether the water's temperature was just right. PM Papa groaned and nodded. It felt good to be pampered by Ramparsad, especially when Shrimati Papa's cantankerous voice wasn't letting up. By bringing Rozy to the Humble Abode, he had gone beyond a line that thus far had remained sacrosanct even in his own mind. But Rozy's absence the previous week had triggered something primal in him, clarified things in his mind. Then there was *that*—the seed of which should begin to bear fruit in due time. PM Papa couldn't bring himself to articulate, in his own mind, what *that* was, lest his internal vocalization somehow jinx it.

"Are you even listening to what I'm saying?" Shrimati Papa asked.

PM Papa gritted his teeth, lifted his index finger and said, "One more word about this, and no one will be a worse person in the entirety of Darkmotherland than me."

Shrimati Papa believed him, so she abruptly turned around and left the room. She went to a small room in the corner of the living room where she normally quarantined herself during her menstrual periods so as not to contaminate the rest of the house. She slammed the door shut and sat on the cot, arms around her knees, rocking back and forth to calm herself.

That night Rozy let PM Papa suck him off—"the fairest cock in Darkmotherland," PM Papa crooned as he dove in—but Rozy didn't let him penetrate him, despite repeated pleadings. "Why? Why?" PM Papa asked, and Rozy said, "Not today, maybe some other day." PM Papa watched him briefly, then didn't push further.

Later, they lay in bed together, PM Papa's hand lying fondly over Rozy's spent cock, his other hand holding an unlit cigar that he'd wanted to light after sex but Rozy asked him not to, saying the strong smell would bother him. "So, how is the First Lady doing?" Rozy asked.

"The First Lady will be fine," PM Papa said, waving the unlit cigar about. "She'll just have to adjust."

"Be Best?"

"Right now she's Be Worst." He ran his index finger over Rozy's face, tracing an imaginary line of beauty he saw in it. Rozy of course wanted to slap his hand away but didn't—everything that was happening was moving toward a larger purpose.

"So, when are you going to get rid of her?"

PM Papa stopped tracing Rozy's face and raised his eyebrows. "O-ho, tigress! A bit hasty, aren't we?"

"Well, I'm not leaving this house."

PM Papa snorted nervously.

"You can give my flat to Laxman, or whoever."

"Maiya."

Although PM Papa had stopped tracing his finger on Rozy's face, his palm still cupped Rozy's chin. Rozy swatted his hand away and said, "You are such a bullshit artist." PM Papa placed his hand on Rozy's arm, but Rozy slapped that away too. "Your words don't mean anything."

"Tell that to Darkmotherland," PM Papa said. He sat up a bit and, leaning back on the wall, clasped his hands behind his head. He had such short and stumpy hands it was a miracle that he could make them meet behind his head.

"Well, I'm not leaving. You might as well name this Rozy's Abode now."

"Arre wah!" PM Papa said, smiling at the ceiling. "I like that." He unclasped his hands and made a marquee in the air in front of him, the cigar still clasped between his fingers. "Rozy's Abode. Fabulous. I'm going to have Laxman make a new plaque for the front gate tomorrow."

"Really?" Rozy said, turning to face him and running his purple fingernails over PM Papa's chest hair, making him moan in pleasure. "You are such a doll."

Just hearing the word "doll" from Rozy's mouth seemed to drive PM Papa crazy. He grabbed Rozy's hand and pulled it down toward his crotch. He was already hard.

"My, my," Rozy said, stroking it. "Hello, Little Papa. Or should I say Little Peepee?"

"I want so bad to put it inside you, maiya."

"Will you really mount a plaque with my name at the front gate?"

PM Papa's cock was stubby and thick, just like him. Rozy had given him blowjobs before, reluctantly, gagging as he did so, but lately he'd managed to avoid putting him in his mouth.

"Yes, maiya," PM Papa said, whimpering in pleasure.

Rozy stroked him faster, rubbing his fingers up and down the shaft, almost like he was providing the Hippo with feathery tickles. "Will you kick Be Best out of the house?"

"Yes, yes, maiya." PM Papa's eyes were closed in rapture, and he was as hard as Rozy had ever seen him. Rozy stopped stroking him and clasped his member with his hand, squeezing it with strength. "When?"

"Soon, soon. I promise. Please don't stop."

Rozy continued, moving his hand rapidly, up and down, giving PM Papa a robust handjob until PM Papa, disgustingly, and a bit prematurely, came in his hand. Instead of looking for a hankie or a towel to wipe his hand, Rozy took it to PM Papa's face—his eyes were closed in post-discharge bliss—and said, "Here, this is for you."

PM Papa popped open his eyes. "What? No!"

Rozy placed his semen-slathered hand next to PM Papa's nose and said, "Smell it."

"Smell my own? What the—?" But he did take a small sniff.

"It's not that bad, is it?"

PM Papa sniffed again, then shuddered like he'd taken a whiff of an extra-strong yet tantalizing alcoholic drink.

Rozy lowered his palm to PM Papa's lips and placed it there. Now the semen was touching PM Papa's lips. "Smell it again," Rozy said. "It'll smell different now."

PM Papa inhaled. It wasn't clear from his expression whether he thought it smelled different, but the expression in his eyes softened as though he'd just smelled a baby.

"Now taste it," Rozy said.

"What? No way!" PM Papa shook his head vigorously.

"You won't regret it, I promise."

PM Papa looked beseechingly at Rozy, as though asking him not to make him go through with it. Rozy nodded in encouragement. Tentatively, PM Papa stuck out his tongue, but stopped before it touched his semen.

"C'mon, babua," Rozy said. "Just a small lick. It's not going to bite."

PM Papa did lick it this time. Well, it was hardly a lick: the tip of his tongue barely brushed against the semen before he hastily retracted it. The tongue disappeared inside his mouth for a couple of seconds before it reemerged. This time it was a bit bolder—the tip touched a spot here, a spot there, then retreated again into the mouth. One couldn't be entirely sure what the tongue was doing inside the mouth with its two or three dabs of semen. It appeared to be swirling them around, as one would do to wine during a wine tasting. It emerged shortly, now more eager, more like a gleeful dog who's been offered a heap of rice pudding. Now the tongue started to lick Rozy's hand with abandon—dipping, sliding, gliding, slithering, bouncing, slurping. Every few seconds it retreated into the mouth but only to jump right back out, as though it were afraid that its pudding would be declined if it was late. The tongue skidded across Rozy's palm, then attacked the crevices, leaving no nook and cranny untouched. It slid down under the palm and slobbered on the glaciers of slow-moving semen. Soon there was not a spot of Rozy's hand that had not been licked. Still, the tongue kept going as though sucking up the moisture that had seeped into the skin. Finally, the tongue did a large sweep of the palm, then, satisfied that it was totally dry, retreated into the mouth, giving out an audible sigh.

A bronze plaque stating Rozy's Abode, golden letters in a rich chocolate-brown background, arrived the very next evening, but instead of mounting it at the front gate, PM Papa ordered it to be nailed to the door of his home office, now Rozy's room. "Chicken," Rozy said, then spread his arms out and fluttered them while clucking. But he did so in a laughing way. The nokerchakers were hovering nearby. Shrimati Papa was in her Menstruation Room. She had emerged from the room a couple of times today, but had quickly retreated each time after seeing Rozy lording over the house—ordering the nokerchakers to make him smoothies or lemonade or tea. He walked down the hallways in his half-open bathrobe and lounged in the living room, which directly faced the Menstruation Room.

Laxman nailed the Rozy's Abode plaque on Rozy's door and stepped back. "Nice, huh?" PM Papa said to Rozy, who scrunched his nose.

"Not the location we agreed upon," Rozy said, "but it is passable. For now. I give it a C." PM Papa turned to the nokerchakers and asked their opinions of the plaque. They murmured their approvals while glancing toward the Menstruation Room, where, it turned out, Shrimati Papa was observing them through a partially open door.

"Can you come here?" PM Papa called out to his wife, "and see how this looks," as though asking his wife whether a new photo he'd nailed on the wall was aligned properly.

Shrimati Papa retreated, shutting the door quietly behind her. Since Rozy's arrival, the only nokerchaker who had access to her, whom she allowed in the Menstruation Room, was the cook. Often there was a lot of wailing that wafted out of the Menstruation Room. Mostly it was Shrimati Papa who was doing the wailing. Sometimes though it was the old cook who was wailing. Sometimes it was the both of them. Sometimes it was hard to tell.

That night after dinner, Rozy insisted on sleeping with PM Papa in his bedroom. PM Papa was uncertain, as though debating whether they ought to cross that line.

"What difference does it make?" Rozy said. "She's holed up in the Menstruation Room anyway."

"But we just had that plaque made for you for your room," PM Papa said. They were discussing this outside his bedroom, with the nokerchakers nearby waiting to see if they needed anything. "Don't you want to enjoy your new plaque?"

"I'll just enjoy looking at the plaque," Rozy said and entered PM Papa's bedroom. "I don't need to be on the other side of the plaque to enjoy it." He ordered Nakkali to go next door into Rozy's Abode and retrieve his clothes and toothbrush. Then Rozy opened the closet in PM Papa's bedroom and took out all of Shrimati Papa's clothes—mostly petticoats, dhotis and saris, and shoes (there were only a few pairs—she was no Imelda Marcos) and threw them on the floor, instructing Nakkali to pick them up and deliver them to the Menstruation Room.

—

Nakkali had a vast network of friends and relatives who provided her with information about the talk on the street. Rumors were already circulating, Nakkali said as she massaged Rozy's legs on the roof, that PM Papa had brought home a concubine.

Well, they're not too far off the mark, Rozy thought.

"They're saying that the concubine is a thirdgender."

"Do tell more."

"No one is talking openly about it, but there's a lot of whispering," Nakkali said. "Some of my friends think it's fake news spread by the enemy who wants to bring PM Papa down."

"The Son of Yeti maybe?" Rozy asked.

Nakkali was vigorously massaging Rozy's calves. The security dais were throwing lecherous glances in their direction.

"The Son of Yeti maybe," Nakkali said. "Maybe someone in Papa's cabinet."

"Who in Papa's cabinet?"

Nakkali didn't speak for a while, then she said, "I'll get into trouble, hajur. If I say the wrong thing, then I might be visited by the Charlie Chaplin jallad."

"Your thoughts are safe with me," Rozy said. "A bit more to the left. Yes, do you feel the knot there?"

Nakkali, for the ultra-feminine girl that she was, had good, strong hands. "Do you trust General Tso?" she whispered, her mouth close to Rozy's ears so that the security dais wouldn't hear.

This girl has balls, Rozy thought. She's a good one to keep by my side. "Do we have a reason not to trust General Tso?" Rozy whispered back.

"Well, he's so . . . orthodox," Nakkali said. "He might not like the idea of PM Papa bringing home a concubine, and especially not a thirdgender concubine." Nakkali must have realized that she crossed a line with that utterance, for her face suddenly turned pale. She was silent, then fervently apologetic, saying she didn't know what she was saying, that she was just parroting what she'd heard from others. She hoped that Rozy would forgive her and not report her to PM Papa. She renewed the strength of her hands on Rozy's legs, mauling his thighs like it was her way of showing repentance.

⁓

Instead of dying down, as some rumors did, this one gained momentum. People began whispering about it in more public spaces—in tea shops and bus stops, always careful, always checking, always unsure that the person they were talking to might turn out to be a Papa's Patriot, or a Fundy in disguise.

There was confusion. PM Papa? Really?

There was disgust. "But it's immoral," people said. "It's unnatural."

"It's ungodly," someone said.

People began to speak out.

Something crazy was happening. No one was getting arrested for saying these things.

Then something even stranger happened. The concubine began to be mentioned in the media. A teasing reference in a newspaper, a brief allusion on the TV, first on the private media, then even on Motherland TV and Motherland Radio.

It was as though the media had received permission to broadcast, even rejoice, in this news. One woman appeared on private TV to claim that she was the much-talked-about concubine.

"This lady here, Miss—what did you say your name was?" the TV host asked the woman. She was wearing a bright salwar kameez, and her wrists were sparkling with gold jewelry. She had a mannish face, on which she had lathered ample makeup. Her breasts were also ample.

"Miss Rukshana Rauniar."

"Where did you meet PM Papa?"

"At a function."

"Could you elaborate?"

"At a function!" Rukshana said in exasperation. "PM Papa attends many functions, I attend many functions. We met in one of those. I don't remember which one."

"Do you remember what happened at this function?"

"I was always a big fan of PM Papa. So, I was thrilled to see him at this function. I had heard that someone was coming, but I thought it would be just another politician. But then it was PM Papa, getting out of his limousine. My heart went *dhuk-dhuk-dhuk*, like this." The woman took the host's hand and put it on her chest.

The host smiled embarrassedly into the camera and pulled his hand away. "Do you always get this excited when you see men?"

"Not every man, you idiot. Only someone like PM Papa, a powerful man who knows what he's doing, who has come to the rescue of the country."

The host coughed. "Rescue the country?"

"Do you doubt it?"

"No, no, I don't doubt it."

"For a moment there, I thought you did."

TV viewers across the nation held their breath. Not long after the Big Two a talk show host had been arrested live on television. This was before the media had fully come to grasp their situation. The host had been interviewing Dharma Adhikari, and had asked if a proposed Judicial Selection Act, which would rehaul the judiciary and allow the Rajjya to hire and fire judges at will, wouldn't propel the country toward an autocratic rule. Dharma Adhikari had stiffened, then made a signal to someone at the entrance to the studio. Two Poolis Uncles appeared behind the host, put him in handcuffs, and hauled him off. Dharma Adhikari turned to the camera and said, "PM Papa is very serious about anti-nationalist elements in the media. For too long we've allowed these people to strike at our moral fibers."

Months later, when he left the Monkeygod Gate Jail, the host was unrecognizable, with red splotches on his face, dilated pupils, and chin trembling behind a dirty beard. He would only say, "I was fine. The jailers were kind." For a while he had waited tables at a hole-in-the-wall restaurant, and people weren't sure what had happened to him after that.

Remembering that host, Darkmotherlandites turned up their volumes and shushed their children, waiting to see if this host too would be dragged off in chains.

But the host, perhaps suddenly recalling the other host, began to cough, as though he was sick and therefore whatever he said could be misinterpreted. "Forgive me," he said, as he viciously hacked into his hand. "This cold has been brutal."

"Sounds like you're dying, my dear," Rukshna said, smirking.

The host thumped his chest a couple of times, took a deep breath, and said "forgive me" a few more times. He turned to the camera and said, "Of course he rescued the country." He then turned to Rukshana as though it were she who had doubted that PM Papa had rescued the country. "Who says he didn't rescue the country? Only Treasonists say that." Then the host slowly pivoted to pleading, yet articulate praise of PM Papa about how he saved Darkmotherland from economic and political collapse after the Big Two. The host admitted that every night he thanked God for raising this good son of Darkmotherland.

He slowly stood, as though preparing to exit the studio. Instead, he stood in front of Rukshana and sang the national anthem.

> *More beloved than*
> *Our heart*
> *Our one and only*
> *Venerable PM Papa*
> *His contribution to our nation*
> *As vast as the ocean*
> *As tall as the mountain*
> *This is the country*
> *That makes our chest swell in pride*
> *It's swell*
> *He's swell*
> *Hail, hail, hail*
> *Hey, hey, hey*
> *It's a beautiful day.*

⁓

No matter where she was in the Humble Abode, Rozy made it a point to call out Nakkali's name in a loud, annoyingly nasal, deliberately saccharine voice, "Nakkaleee!" so that everyone would hear, especially Shrimati Papa in the Menstruation Room.

"Nakkaleee! Could you bring me a comb, my dear."

"Nakkaleee! Are you going to make some khasiko masu today? You know how much PM Papa loves your mutton."

"Nakkaleee! Where did you disappear to?"

"Nakkaleee! I am craving sandheko bhogatey. Can you ask the security dai to bring a ripe pomelo from the garden?"

"Nakkaleee! Can you quickly wash my undies please? I only brought a couple from my flat."

And Nakkali would come bounding out from wherever she was, ready to serve. She had abandoned all of her duties toward the house and Shrimati Papa to exclusively attend to Rozy's needs. She had, Rozy thought, quickly figured out on which side her pauroti was buttered.

One morning, seeing that Shrimati Papa's door was slightly ajar, which meant that she was probably behind it, watching the activities in the living room, Rozy sang to Nakkali, who was folding his freshly laundered clothes on the floor. It was a popular old song, the lyrics speaking about someone named Nakkali who had caused a lot of heartbreak for her suitors, including the singer, because she eloped with a flashy dude name Jhilke. Nakkali couldn't help laughing, in embarrassment and in delight. Shrimati Papa didn't approve of singing, unless it was a hymn, let alone a song this vulgar.

Once, sometimes twice a day, Shrimati Papa would open the door of the Menstruation Room—"she's menstruating all the time now," Rozy had commented to Nakkali. Shrimati Papa screamed at the top of her voice, shaking the foundations of the Humble Abode, her screams reaching up to the security dais on the roof.

"This is Big Five level earthquake scream," Rozy commented. "She has skipped Big Three and Big Four."

Shrimati Papa screeched about how she wasn't going to take it anymore. The abomination that had invaded her house didn't know what was in store for it, Shrimati Papa declared. She squawked that Armageddon had arrived at the Humble Abode. She yelled that she was going to unleash her people on the abomination in her dwelling, and everyone else who had wronged her. Shrimati Papa performed her rage-shouting only when Rozy was in his room, meaning Shrimati Papa's bedroom, or when he was sunbathing on the roof. She started and finished her screams within a few seconds and quickly retreated back into the Menstruation Room, slamming the door and latching it from the inside.

"It's hard for her," Nakkali said, while on the roof slathering oil on Rozy's back. "She's so used to being the mistress of her domain."

"Well, *I'm* the mistress of her domain now," Rozy said.

"She's so orthodox—do you know the story of the Gurung driver?"

Rozy had heard snippets of that story in the Lion Palace from the lower-level staff, but the details had been vague. Something about PM Papa's previous driver, something about water, untouchability. Something about an accident in a Khadi country? "I'm sure you're going to tell me, Nakkali."

A few months ago, Nakkali said, one of PM Papa's drivers, a man clearly from a lower caste, stocky and flat-faced with high cheekbones, had entered the kitchen and helped himself to some water from a jug. Shrimati Papa had come upon him as he was drinking, his head titled back, the water going down his throat, his lips carefully not touching the jug's rim.

"Launani, ke gareko yesto!" Shrimati Papa had wailed. "You can't just come straight into my kitchen like this." The driver choked and sputtered. "Out! Out!" Shrimati Papa commanded. She moved toward him as though to push him, then stopped because she didn't want to contaminate herself by touching a bhotey. "If you wanted water," she fumed at him, "you could have asked the cook, who would have placed a jug on the back porch." The old cook was a Brahmin of the purest order, Nakkali informed Rozy, and Shrimati Papa had brought her from her hometown to the Valley because she didn't allow non-Brahmins in her kitchen.

The bewildered and still coughing driver retreated to the driveway, where he was further chewed out by the irate cook, who was worried that she'd be blamed for not guarding the kitchen. This was the day of an auspicious puja Shrimati Papa was conducting at the temple of the Tiger-Riding Goddess, and for which she had already bathed. When PM Papa arrived home in the evening he'd gotten an earful, and the driver was assigned to a minister's office the very next day.

After the Gurung driver drank her water, Shrimati Papa had the entire house mopped with cow dung, then summoned her priest for an impromptu cleansing. Still, she hadn't been satisfied. A week later, her mother had died in the village. Although the dead woman had been surrounded by relatives on her deathbed, for some unfathomable reason, at the precise second she stopped breathing, no one had been in the room to give her water. Shrimati Papa became inconsolable with grief. That bhotey stole my mother's water on her deathbed— this thought hounded her. She told her husband that the driver had cursed her family, that he must be punished. After days of nagging, PM Papa relented and ordered the minister to let go of the driver, who then went to a Khadi country to work construction and died in a freak accident his very first day. The water truck he was driving crushed him under its wheels when, without pulling the parking brakes, he stepped out for a moment to talk to someone. It was reported that the truck, bizarrely, had swerved toward him, as though consciously targeting him. Shrimati Papa had been hugely satisfied to learn about the manner of the driver's death; the water truck was especially symbolic. "The Tiger-Riding Goddess has punished him for what he did to my mother," she said to the nokerchakers at the Humble Abode.

"Wow, just wow," Rozy said at the conclusion of Nakkali's story. "Instead of the convoluted scheme, the Tiger-Riding Goddess could have simply sicced her tiger on the poor driver. Easier and simpler, and the tiger would have gotten a delicious meal."

⁓

At the Lion Palace, General Tso came into PM Papa's office. He pointed at the TV in the corner, where the Rukshana Rauniar interview was being rebroadcast. "This could be a problem," General Tso said.

PM Papa was looking out of the window, his hands behind his back. He was checking out the scores of security people with their machine guns manning across the lawns of the Lion Palace. "Do you think our security is tight enough?"

"We also have plainclothesmen scattered all over the Lion Palace," General Tso said.

"Hmm," PM Papa said. "We don't want to see a repeat of what happened during Papa Don't Preach."

Amidst the chaos of that rally, a member of the Gang of Four had managed to infiltrate the corridors of the Lion Palace and was on the way to the Gufa, where PM Papa had been monitoring the activities outside. His double, a small-time performer who had acted in a few comedies, was giving a speech by the gate of the Lion Palace. But Laxman, who had been with PM Papa, had the sixth sense to check the corridor. He saw the Gang of Four member prowling the hallway. Gun in hand, Laxman stealthily moved toward the Gang of Four member, who didn't see him. Just as Laxman was about to shoot, the Gang of Four member saw him and fired. The bullet grazed Laxman on the thigh, but despite being hit, Laxman had lunged at the Gang of Four member and, wincing in pain, overpowered him. The Rajjya had given Laxman a medal of honor.

"Had it not been for Laxman, I'd have been killed that day," PM Papa said. Lest General Tso think of that as a criticism of him, he added, "Just saying. I'm sure everything is under control now."

"Everything is under control," General Tso said. "This, however …" Once again, he pointed to Rukshana Rauniar talking about functions.

PM Papa walked a few steps toward the TV, watching the host backtrack from his seemingly questioning whether PM Papa rescued the country. "Who's that fool?" he asked General Tso.

"Shall we bring him in, hajur?"

The host was now standing and singing the national anthem.

PM Papa laughed and pointed at the TV. "That's fun."

"We can also shut down the station. Teach them a lesson."

"No. Let them be. We can use that clip of him singing the national anthem." He watched as the host concluded his singing with "It's a beautiful day." Smiling, PM Papa shook his head at the TV. "That's not bad. From now on, have him end his program by standing and singing the national anthem."

"Every day?"

"Every day."

General Tso seemed to crack a smile, but it was hard to tell with him. "What about this Rukshana Rauniar?"

"We'll tell Prapu Ganda to use her more," PM Papa said, now sitting down on a chair and gesturing to General Tso to also take a seat. "Arrange to have her appear on more TV stations, give more interviews to newspapers and magazines. She's our official concubine."

The two men talked some more. General Tso was deferential, but always a bit distant, as he was with everyone. At times PM Papa felt that of all his men, he understood General Tso the least. The man showed very little emotion, but he was tough as nails. And he was on PM Papa's side.

PM Papa said that he wanted even tighter security all around when he went to Amrika in a few weeks. He asked General Tso whether they should shut down the Lion Palace altogether, just so that anyone planning mischief wouldn't be able to access it. PM Papa said "mischief" but General Tso knew what he was talking about. PM Papa was terrified of being kooed while he was away. General Tso told him that shutting down the Lion Palace wasn't a good idea. It might actually motivate the kooers to koo even more strongly. "A shut down Lion Palace would feel like an empty Lion Palace that was ready to be occupied," General Tso said.

PM Papa drummed his fingers on the table. "Well, even if we keep the Lion Palace open, people will know that I'm in Amrika. Wouldn't that give them ideas?"

"Can't you make this a secret trip?"

"No, no, no!" PM Papa said, agitated. He stood and walked around the room. General Tso's head swiveled to follow him. "This is an extremely important visit. It must be heavily publicized. It should be done with great fanfare. Darkmotherlandites must know that I am going to Amrika. Not only that, but I'm going at the personal invitation of President Corn Hair." PM Papa stopped at the other side of the table and said, "Do you even realize how big this is?"

"It's big," General Tso said, nodding. "It's very big."

This was the second time General Tso had remarked that making it a secret trip would greatly reduce the chances of a koo. Why was General Tso bringing it up again? If there was anyone in Darkmotherland who could easily koo him, it was General Tso. Just for two seconds, PM Papa became intensely suspicious of General Tso, then the suspicion evaporated. General Tso was immensely loyal—PM Papa would harbor doubts about him at his own peril. He also couldn't afford to make General Tso angry by expressing doubts about his loyalty. If General Tso turned against him, PM Papa's hold on his power would be in grave peril.

"Do you know why it also can't be a secret?" PM Papa asked General Tso, who shook his head. "Amrikan TV will show me shaking hands with President Corn Hair in the Oval Office. They will show me addressing the Amrikan Congress. They will show me visiting the Arlington Cemetery, the Vietnam Memorial."

"That's true."

"Darkmotherlandites should see me in Amrika, and watch me being treated with respect by President Corn Hair and his cabinet members. Imagine, the most powerful man in the world treating the prime minister of Darkmotherland as if he were his equal. This has the potential to make Darkmotherland a major player in international geopolitics. No, no, no. This can't remain a secret."

"Then we'll use a double," General Tso said.

"What?"

"We'll use a double in the Lion Palace while you're in Amrika."

"But—you mean—use a double even as I'm being shown shaking hands in Amrika?" PM Papa had paused in his pacing and was looking directly at General Tso.

"Yes."

"But how? I mean, I can't be in two places at the same time?"

"Why not?" General Tso said. "Where is PM Papa? He's in Amrika. Where is PM Papa? He's in the Lion Palace, protecting Darkmotherland and leading it to peace and prosperity."

The replacement valet for Rozy while he was on leave, a young man of similar age, appeared at the doorway and asked if they needed anything. PM Papa dismissively waved him away. Nothing compared to Rozy.

PM Papa moved closer to General Tso, who was still seated, upright and immovable, in his position at the table. "But won't my enemies know it's my double?"

"They won't be sure. They might suspect it to be true, but it could also be true that you shaking hands in Amrika had already happened, that you were already back in the Lion Palace."

PM Papa nodded thoughtfully.

"Or," General Tso said, "they won't be sure that it's your double who's in Amrika and you are still here, in Darkmotherland."

PM Papa went to the window and checked the roofs above his office. He could spot the snipers there. He thought he saw a sniper pointing his rifle straight at him and quickly moved away from the window. General Tso saw his sudden movement and said, "What's the matter?"

"Nothing," PM Papa said.

"They're all my men, you know. They're fiercely loyal. They will die for me. Mountain people."

PM Papa sat down again next to General Tso. "It's brilliant, your idea of using a double. I should promote you."

"I'm the highest ranking general in Darkmotherland."

"We can promote you to Supreme Commander General Tso."

Even then, General Tso didn't smile.

"So what about this babe, this Rukshana Rauniar?" Rozy asked PM Papa in bed that evening after the lights were turned off.

"What about her?"

"Are you going to do anything about her?"

"Are you jealous, maiya?"

The house was quiet. All the nokerchakers had gone to bed. Occasionally they could hear murmurs of the security dais outside. Once in a while a soft moan was heard from the Menstruation Room.

"I don't think she gets a wink of sleep in there, our First Lady," Rozy said.

"She's always been a sound sleeper. A snorer she is, big time snorer. Like this." PM Papa closed his eyes, wagged his head, and snored loudly, rattling his breath so that it seemed like something was stuck in his nostrils.

Rozy slapped his arm and said, "You snore too. You sound like this." Rozy brayed like a donkey.

PM Papa grabbed him tight in his arms and mock-threatened him. "Do that again and I'll have your head cut off."

Later, just as they were drifting off to sleep, Rozy asked him, "Are you going to have Rukshana Rauniar arrested?"

"We will let her continue, at least for a while."

PM Papa was confident that his sexual preference, once it became fully public, would be manageable. But it had to be leaked into the public slowly so that it would be imprinted upon their minds as their new reality, and they would accept his homosexuality, like obedient children. PM Papa was above the law. PM Papa was a supernatural leader. PM Papa was chosen by Darkmother herself.

PM Papa also needed an heir. This was also important for Darkmotherland. His people needed to see that there was someone ready to carry on his legacy. This would give him more legitimacy.

PM Papa, who was spooning Rozy, tentatively placed his palm on Rozy's stomach. He softly, oh so very softly caressed it, as though already sensing a baby in there.

⁓

Another day when Shrimati Papa was caterwauling her lungs to high heaven, Rozy said to Nakkali, "Be Best needs to have her head smashed in." Nakkali was in the bedroom, mending a tear in Rozy's jeans. An idea came to Rozy. He called PM Papa, who was in a cabinet meeting but promptly answered the call. In the background Rozy recognized a couple of voices—General Tso and Dharma Adhikari. Rozy told him what he wanted. PM Papa listened. The background voices went silent—they must have realized that they couldn't talk while PM Papa was on the phone. "Do you want it today, maiya?" PM Papa said.

Rozy said he'd be grateful if PM Papa would oblige. "Just send an aide over with it."

PM Papa paused, then said, loudly laughing, meaning for the room to hear, "Your wish is Papa's command."

After the conversation ended, Rozy wondered what the cabinet members were thinking. They knew that maiya was Rozy, they knew the concubine PM Papa took to the Humble Abode was none other than his valet. By not hiding who his lover was, had PM Papa signaled that he was ready to come out?

In an hour, an aide brought the cricket bat that had dispatched Defense Minister Rakshya Garam to heaven. The pink blush was still on the bat's surface. When Nakkali saw the bat, her hand went up to her mouth. "Is that—?" she asked.

"Indeed it is," Rozy said, waving the bat around like a nanchaku. Not too long ago, he'd soiled himself at the violence this bat had unleashed, but now it was almost as though he'd seen a new potential with it. Well, that was a different Rozy. This Rozy had moved into a different dimension. There was no turning back. "How do you know about this bat?" Rozy asked. "The rest of the country thinks that Rakshya Garam simply disappeared, like so many other people."

"PM Papa told us about it," Nakkali said. "He came home and he boasted about it. He meant it as a warning for us, told us there was no room for disloyalty in this house." Then Nakkali, probably thinking about her utterance regarding General Tso, launched into a fervent appeal to Rozy about her impeccable credentials in the loyalty department. "I am willing to die for PM Papa," Nakkali said. "And now for you, too, of course."

Sure you are, thought Rozy.

Rozy walked about the Humble Abode in his half-open bathrobe, orange jockey underwear showing, the cricket bat on his shoulder, like an infantryman carrying a rifle. He sometimes twirled it and jabbed it like a sword at an imaginary enemy. Other times he used it like a cricket bat, swinging it close to the ground to hit the imaginary ball. At one point, he even stood in front of the Menstruation Room, holding the bat in both hands in front of him, his body still, as though waiting for Shrimati Papa to come out. There was absolute silence on the other side of the door. "Not even the squeak of a mouse," Rozy whispered. The nokerchakers watched the hallway, the doorway, every which way. A couple of security dais also came down from the roof to watch what was going to unfold.

Rozy swung the bat to and fro in front of him, making a swoosh-swoosh sound.

Still nothing from the Menstruation Room.

If there had been a window in the Menstruation Room, one could have been certain that Shrimati Papa had already escaped, but the Menstruation Room was created to further punish the menstruatee, so it had no windows. Rozy yodeled, but still no response. "She's playing dead," Rozy announced. "Or she might actually be menstruating." Then he did an about turn and said, "Cricket, anyone?"

All the nokerchakers, except the old hag cook, scrambled to look for a ball (the cricket bat had arrived without an accompanying ball). They found an old tennis ball, its skin frayed, in a corner of the lawn, probably belonging to Kukkur. Soon a small cricket ground was created in the living room in front of the Menstruation Room. Nakkali had suggested that they play on the lawn but Rozy said no. One of the security dais found three sticks in the garden that served as wickets. He made them stand upright by sandwiching them between thick grammar and religious texts—and the game was on!

Rozy was the star cricketer, of course, hitting ball after ball and

bowling away the opposition by striking the wickets. Even a couple
of the security dais had descended from the roof to watch, or perhaps
even try their hand at batting. There was a lot of whooping and hollering. Even the old hag was seen to clap and shout with her toothless
mouth.

It was upon this scene that PM Papa arrived one evening. "Children at play," he said fondly, not even seeming to mind that the
security dais were playing (they quickly abandoned their play and
went upstairs when they saw him). "Go ahead," PM Papa said, sitting
in a nearby chair. "Don't let me ruin your fun and frolic."

Rozy batted and sent the ball "flying" against the wickets. The ball
actually traveled only a few feet until it trundled to the ground. But,
all the spectators exclaimed "it's flying" and "it's soaring in the air."
There were resounding claps everywhere.

"Rozy the cricketeer, everybody," Nakkali said, gesturing grandly
toward Rozy, who took a couple of deep bows as a ballet dancer would
at the end of her performance. He sashayed toward PM Papa, who
stood from his chair and embraced him, then kissed him on the lips,
in front of everyone, a deep long kiss that, given how silent everyone
was, surely must have been heard even in the Menstruation Room.

Rukshana Rauniar became a popular media concubine. It was said
that even the Fundys secretly enjoyed watching her on TV.

Unable to contend with the sauta that her husband had brought,
Shrimati Papa made the decision to leave for her maiti and take the
old cook with her. As Rozy sat in the living room drinking a smoothie
that the cook had made (the old cook had softened considerably
toward Rozy, even though in the presence of Shrimati Papa she put
her finger in her ear and said, "Hare Bhagwan!" every time Rozy was
mentioned), Shrimati Papa told her husband that she wasn't going to
come back to him, which they both knew was a lie even as she uttered

it. PM Papa consoled Shrimati Papa. He even hugged her with his fat arms and said that perhaps going to her mother's house would "cool her mind," make her see the situation in a "more positive light." She had always known what he was like, he reminded her, and so she shouldn't "take it personally" that matters had evolved this way.

She looked at him in utter dismay. But he told her that what was happening was important for the country, for Darkmotherland. "Realize that you're going through this challenge for Darkmotherland. This is what makes me happy. This is important to me. And you are serving the nation by making me happy, aren't you? It is important that I am able to serve our beloved country of ours with a happy and focused mind, wouldn't you agree?" And of course, how could Shrimati Papa disagree with this argument? Hadn't she thought similar thoughts before, when she'd first discovered where his appetites lay? That she was going to tolerate what he did for the sake of this country that she loved so much? And now, although he had done something unspeakable by bringing this abomination home, she had to force herself to think along the lines that it was for the sake of the country. Briefly, just briefly, Shrimati Papa even had patriotic feelings surge through her body: my country, right or wrong. Then she thought of Rozy slurping on that smoothie in her living room—her living room!—and bile rose to her throat. She thought of the way PM Papa had kissed that abomination, on the lips, fully, as though he was slurping a smoothie himself.

"Perhaps what you say is true," she told her husband. "But it's also true that right now I can't stand to breathe the same air as that thing, and I need to go. I'm not coming back to you, as long as that thing is in my house."

"Sure, sure," PM Papa said, patting her on the cheek. "Just call me if you need anything. Always at your service."

After Shrimati Papa left for her maiti, the Humble Abode became a bit charmless for Rozy. PM Papa had the Rozy's Abode plaque removed from the door of his home office and hung at the main gate.

"Now people will know," Rozy said.

Common citizens couldn't come to within half a kilometer of the Humble Abode, but word would surely get around that the Humble Abode had turned into Rozy's Abode. Darkmotherlandites sometimes knew things without even experiencing them in reality.

"For now, Rukshana will keep them occupied," PM Papa said.

By the second day of Shrimati Papa's departure, Rozy was already bored and insisted on returning to the Lion Palace to work. PM Papa was disappointed. Rozy's stay at the Humble Abode, especially with Shrimati Papa gone, had given him a taste for what was possible in the future, at the palace that was being built in the City of Glory.

34.

On Saturday, Kranti was in the kitchen by eight-thirty in the morning. The nokerchakers watched her. Apart from Shambhogya, who supervised all the cooking in the Asylum, and Priyanka, who sometimes acted as her apprentice, or supervised in her absence, the other two women—Kranti and Muwa—didn't spend time in the kitchen. Kranti hadn't stepped foot inside the kitchen since Bhaskar's death, and Muwa no longer even bothered to pretend that she was interested in household matters.

Today Kranti had abandoned her widow garb of white and was now wearing a regular dhoti, slightly orangish in color, as though she were a yogini. The nokerchakers could barely contain themselves.

"Is it a special occasion today?" one of the nokerchakers asked, and Kranti responded that guests were coming.

With the nokerchakers helping her, Kranti began to cook. A strange, afflictive energy had overtaken her body. Wonderful music was playing somewhere above her, directing her movements. The nokerchakers were astounded, harried and excited, even giggly, at the maelstrom in the orange getup that had hit the kitchen this early. Kranti was humming. There had been a period, not too long after she met Bhaskar, when she'd decided she needed to be a better cook, better than she was when she was a teenager, especially if she was going to marry into the Ghimirey family. She had regretted that she hadn't learned more from Dada, the only one who really cooked at Beggar Street. A couple of times when young Kranti had shown some interest in cooking, Professor Shrestha, who abhorred all symbols of women's domesticity, had said, "I hope becoming a chef is not your career ambition." When she and Bhaskar started talking about the possibility of a life together, it occurred to Kranti that she'd want to be able to cook her Bhaskar sumptuous meals, not the jumble she occasionally made when she was younger. The more time she'd spent with him, the more she'd found herself harboring fantasies of domesticity, and she began cooking again with interest. Professor Shrestha, and Bhaskar, if he was visiting, had made fun of her. "I like cooking," she said as way of response, but they teased her, saying that she wanted to be "housewifey."

In the two years Bhaskar and she were together before their wedding, she'd spent enough time in the Beggar Street kitchen that she had become a passable cook. In the Asylum, the kitchen was an efficient and well-run enterprise under Shambhogya, with the nokerchakers slightly breathless—tense, thought Kranti—yet productive—washing, dicing, scrubbing, peeling. Very little extraneous conversation happened. Even after the dishes were cooked, there was hardly any relaxation. Shambhogya went around tasting each item laid out on the table. When Shambhogya paused, pondering the taste of a dish, the nokerchakers held their breath. If she wasn't satisfied, they had to dump the food in the garbage and start over. They all wanted to please her, and they were happy when she praised their cooking, their faces breaking out in relief and laughter.

Kranti, on the other hand, was more of a spectacle herself, she realized. Within half an hour of her beginning to cook, the kitchen was a mess, with vegetable peelings scattered all over the floor, puddles of gravy on the stove and counter, and broths bubbling over pots. The nokerchakers were snickering and giggling, making jokes about Kranti's sudden interest and energy in the kitchen. Tasks were accomplished without much seriousness. At one point, Kranti even waved her ladle in the air like an orchestra conductor, splattering gravy onto the nokerchakers, and sending them fleeing in mirthful alarm.

"What's going on here?" It was Shambhogya at the door. Her voice was soft. The nokerchakers sobered up and avoided her eyes. Thulo Maya frantically tidied up the floor. Shambhogya's eyes took in everything, including the fact that Kranti wasn't wearing white.

"I'm cooking for today's lunch," Kranti said.

"Why is it necessary?" Shambhogya said. "We have all these nokerchakers, drawing fat paychecks, precisely to cook and clean."

Kranti said she felt like cooking. "Do you want to come in and check?"

"The kitchen is a mess." Shambhogya paused. "All this for Umesh dai?"

Kranti flashed her a grin.

Shambhogya observed her. "And why aren't you wearing white?" she finally asked in a whisper.

"I will no longer wear white," Kranti said, also in a whisper.

"Oh?"

"Don't you think it's time? I mean, Bhaskar is gone. I'm sure he wouldn't want to see me remain a widow."

Shambhogya watched her, as though trying to discern if Kranti was pulling her leg. Then, it appeared that she was willing to give Kranti the benefit of doubt, and slowly a hint of a smile materialized on her face. "Hmm, I wonder where the energy is coming from. It's a nice change. Umesh dai will be pleased."

"I hope he likes my cooking."

"Let me help you."

"No, Shambhogya-di. I want to do this all by myself. It'll be my pleasure."

"It's already ten o'clock. Will you be done by noon?"

"Everything will be ready, and I'll have the kitchen spic-and-span."

"I'll make sure Sir and Muwa also eat lunch with us today. They'd want to eat food cooked by you—you've deprived them of this pleasure thus far."

Around noon all the food was carried downstairs to the dining room. Smoke Chimney dai had already arrived and was chatting with Prithvi Raj in the adjacent living room. Both men stopped their conversation to observe Kranti. Prithvi Raj's face was filled with wonder. His cheeks puffed up, and although he had combed his hair, a couple of strands stood up. He must have been thinking that she had finally come around to the idea of marrying Smoke Chimney dai.

Kranti relished the thought that all she had to do was say "No" and the Ghimirey family would fall apart. What did they, Shambhogya and Prithvi Raj, imagine would happen if they didn't neutralize her manglik curse? That their corporate empire would go bankrupt? But the Ghimirey & Sons momentum hadn't stopped since Bhaskar's death. They were expanding, the revenue had increased, and even more factories were planned. Aditya never failed to mention that the waste management facility, Raddi Tokari, was doing extremely well. And Hotel Himalayan Happiness was booming. How could their empire be ruined by what was written in one woman's charts? But they believed it. They believed that something ominous in her chart had led to their son's murder, and worse things would happen if a cure wasn't found. Smoke Chimney dai was that cure.

As the nokerchakers carried the dishes into the dining room, Kranti approached and greeted Smoke Chimney dai and Prithvi Raj, just like Shambhogya would. With smooth, confident, perfect composure, she became even more aware of the power she wielded. Muwa was waiting in the dining room for Kranti's special meal, but her mind was elsewhere. She had only come because Shambhogya had dragged her from God's Room. Perhaps Shambhogya saw this as a pivotal moment? She could be gearing up to make an announcement about Kranti and Smoke Chimney dai, a formal announcement.

There were Prithvi Raj and Smoke Chimney dai, expectantly waiting. Shambhogya watched her from a corner, slightly suspicious, yet also proud, as if she'd groomed Kranti for this moment. Priyanka supervised the nokerchakers in the dining room—this dish here, spoon and fork this way—but with the understanding that she was merely second in command to Kranti. All of these people were under Kranti's control now.

"Shall we commence?" Shambhogya said. Now she was eyeing Kranti with a degree of suspicion, for she obviously noted how Kranti kept glancing out the window toward the front gate. It was fifteen minutes past noon already, and Kabiraj wasn't here. Kranti was checking to see if Cheech and Chong were giving Kabiraj a hard time. The twin guards always kept an eye out for the riffraff that lingered on the pavements outside, especially the glue-sniffing khateykids.

Kranti heard voices from the main gate and stood up to check. Kabiraj had indeed arrived, and, as she expected, Cheech and Chong were engaged in an argument with him.

"Who is it?" Prithvi Raj asked.

"Just a friend I invited for lunch," Kranti said over her shoulder as she went toward the gate. She asked Cheech and Chong to let Kabiraj in.

Cheech and Chong did, reluctantly. Kabiraj slipped in, looking befuddled. He was in his slippers, and although he'd shaved, there were small strands of hair above his lips that he'd missed. His shirt was crumpled, and too tight at his bulging belly so his white vest was showing. God, she thought, mentally rolling her eyes. But she was also experiencing some glee.

Shambhogya had come to the front door, and was watching the entrance of this stranger as he followed Kranti up the driveway.

"Why so late, dallu?" Kranti scolded him, with an extra drip of affection, as she took him past Shambhogya.

"I wasn't sure I would be able to make it," Kabiraj said, whispering. "I was questioned by the Loyal Army Dais a block away."

With Shambhogya following, Kranti took him to the dining room, where the others waited to see who her guest was. They'd heard the voice, they knew it was a man, and silence had come over the dining room, even among the nokerchakers, as Kranti and Kabiraj approached. Kabiraj apparently hadn't expected to see so many people (But why? Kranti thought—he knew the Ghimirey family was large), for Kranti could feel the nervousness in his body as she stood next to him with her body nearly touching his. Kabiraj did a quick, uneasy round of namastes, even greeting the nokerchakers deferentially because he was unable to distinguish who was important and who was not. The nokerchakers at the Asylum were always nicely dressed anyway. Then his eyes returned to Prithvi Raj, who he recognized through newspaper photos or newsreels on TV. But Prithvi Raj could barely decipher why this scraggly-looking man was in his house, why he was Kranti's guest. Shambhogya had caught up to them and was leaning against the doorway, arms crossed at her chest.

"This is Kabiraj," Kranti said, "Bhaskar's friend. Now mine."

The tension in the room was palpable. Aditya turned his face away. Chaitanya seemed to snigger. There were some imperceptible nods, some turning away of heads. Kranti introduced everyone, including Smoke Chimney dai, whom she called a family friend. Clearly out of his element here, Kabiraj did a second round of namastes, his palms close to his face, his head bowed as though he were paying obeisance to a phalanx of fearsome deities.

It was an awkward lunch. Kranti was overtalkative (she wondered if a panic attack was coming—she was perspiring and could feel damp-ness under her armpits—but she doubted it, for it was as though suddenly her mind had become stronger than before), Shambhogya was glaring, Priyanka looked like someone had stolen a big secret from her, and Prithvi Raj appeared shell-shocked. Smoke Chimney dai had a deep crease in his forehead, as if he were inching his way toward a painful realization. Kabiraj ate slowly, his gaze fixed on the food, aware of all the eyes on him. Muwa also focused on her food, not caring what was happening around her. She ate quietly, with no indication that the food tasted of anything. One time she did ask Kabiraj, "Where did you meet my son?" But his answer didn't seem to interest her.

Kabiraj mumbled things that no one heard. Kranti spoke for him, with uncharacteristic energy. She told everyone at the table about the work Kabiraj and Bhaskar did at Streetwise.

Kabiraj kept his head lowered.

"Oh, I see," Shambhogya said. "Sounds like you're on a rescue mission."

Kranti laughed as one does at a witty remark.

Prithvi Raj asked Kabiraj a few perfunctory questions. The meal ended. Everyone looked at Kabiraj, expecting him to leave so that Smoke Chimney dai, who hadn't uttered a word and whose face indicated his great pain, would be united with Kranti. Kabiraj rinsed his mouth at the sink, gargling a bit too loud for the Ghimireys, and wiped his hands and lips with a towel Mokshya provided. With her nose slightly scrunched, Kranti said, "Come, I'll give you a tour of the Asylum."

"Umesh dai has been waiting," Priyanka said, but her voice was so soft that Kranti felt confident in pretending she didn't hear.

Throughout the time she took Kabiraj around the Asylum, she could feel the eyes of the entire household on her. Shambhogya and Priyanka peeking out from Shambhogya's room, and Prithvi Raj in one of the corridors, observing with his windblown look. Smoke Chimney dai was next to him, smoking (Shambhogya, who hated cigarette smoke, allowed him to smoke inside the Asylum—that's how badly she wanted this union to work), trying very hard to pretend that nothing was wrong. Muwa had retreated to God's Room, but the nokerchakers, senior and junior alike, were also alert as they attended to their chores. Kabiraj kept glancing back to see who was watching. At one point, Kranti reprimanded him for his distractedness, loudly addressing him as "dallu," as though she were his garlfren or wife. Then she took him into her room and shut the door.

Holding hands, they lay in her bed. Her stomach was warm, her heartbeat accelerating.

"How am I going to walk out of here?" Kabiraj said. "They are going to skin me alive."

She stroked his back with her palm. "You're not walking out of here anytime soon." She slid her hand inside his vest so she could feel the bare skin on his pudgy tummy. He stiffened. "When the time comes," she said, "I'll walk you out of here. Don't worry."

"I should probably go now."

"You mean you don't care for the Asylum?"

"My God, it's big, innit? It's much bigger than I imagined it would be."

"You'd have known had you attended my wedding."

"I just couldn't, you know that. I'm not comfortable in this type of opulence."

"Well, now you're here, I won't let you go home too soon," she said.

His body had relaxed slightly, but she could tell he was still nervous. He was trembling a bit.

"Look at me," she said, and when he didn't, she said, "I'm not going to eat you."

"I'm just so nervous," he said. "I shouldn't have come."

"No, you should have. Bhaskar would have wanted you to."

Kabiraj looked around as if looking for Bhaskar. "Do you think he's watching us?"

"Of course he is," Kranti said. Lately she'd been troubled by dreams in which Bhaskar appeared to her and asked her who did it to him. When she asked him what he meant, he asked her who killed him. When she said that she didn't know who, he asked her why she wasn't curious. What has gotten into you, Kranti? he asked. Don't you want to know who snuffed out this young life, this life with so much promise? And in the dream, he began to sniff and say, Look, I'm sniffing because I was snuffed out.

"He was a good guy, just born in the wrong house."

She leaned over and placed her chin on his chest. Kabiraj closed his eyes; his trembling hadn't stopped. Her eyes fell upon the bulge in his crotch. If I touch him down there, she thought, he will ejaculate. She moved her chin farther up his chest so that her lips were next to his. His eyes closed; he was breathing heavily. She could hear a muted gurgling sound inside his chest. Dallu is continuing his gargle from earlier, she thought. Her breasts pushed against his ribs. "Doesn't it feel good to do this here, in these hallowed halls?" she whispered. She couldn't help but place her hand on his erection, over his pants. She didn't do anything, simply let her palm rest on his penis, feeling it rise. Then, instantly, he went limp, and his wetness seeped through the cloth onto her palm.

He stayed for a whole hour. She didn't try to revive him. They kissed, and even then his eyes were closed. He said, "This is bad. In the Asylum. On Bhaskar's bed." She shushed him. The whole world was listening outside. There was some rustling outside her door, probably a nokerchaker spying on Shambhogya's behalf. Kranti sucked on Kabiraj's lips.

Shambhogya came into Kranti's room the next afternoon and leaned against the wall. The strain on her face was palpable. "You shouldn't have done that. That was deceitful."

Kranti was propped up on the bed, flipping through a magazine. Well, I'm a manglik, she thought.

"You brought him into your room."

"He's a friend," she said in a deadpan voice. "He was Bhaskar's friend too."

"Yes, we all know what's going on."

"What do you think is going on? Tell me. I want to hear it from your mouth." This was the first time she had spoken to Shambhogya in this manner. It was clear that things were about to take a turn.

"He's your friend from Bhurey Paradise, isn't he? Well, congratulations." Shambhogya said from the edge of Kranti's bed. "All this time I was thinking that you were cooking for Umesh dai because you were finally starting to like him."

Kranti put the magazine down. "I don't dislike Smoke Ch . . . er . . . Umesh dai." It was a partially true statement. She understood Smoke Chimney dai's loneliness, but there was also greed in him, about her, about the Ghimirey wealth. How much of the family coffers had he been promised?

Shambhogya said in a soft voice that was meant to convey patience and reconciliation but was accusatory, "Even if you invited your poet friend for lunch, you shouldn't have brought him into your room."

"Am I not allowed to have friends?"

Shambhogya placed a hand on Kranti's knee and spoke as one might to a troubled teenager, "No one is saying you're not allowed to have friends. We Ghimireys are actually quite forward in our thinking. I know that's not what you believe."

Right, Kranti thought. You are all a progressive bunch.

"But a widow spending time with a male friend? Come on, Kranti!"

"His name is Kabiraj."

"But he's a Bhurey, isn't he? I'm not trying to be a bad person here, but can't you agree with me that once you become a part of this family then you have an obligation to protect the name and prestige of the Ghimireys?"

What was she like, Shambhogya, when she was younger? Did she dream of marrying into a prestigious family? What was she like with her friends? Was she as officious and controlling as she was now? It was hard for Kranti to imagine otherwise. When she imagined a teenage Shambhogya, she pictured the present Shambhogya, with her perfect makeup and skin and flawless enunciation. Did she listen to forbidden music when she was young? Did she sleep in until noon? Did she throw unnecessary tantrums? Did she scatter her clothes all over her room? As she observed her sister-in-law, Kranti realized that she knew very little about Shambhogya's past. She had gathered, mostly through Priyanka, that Shambhogya's mother had been a critical, overbearing woman, and that Shambhogya now had a younger sister with whom she had a cordial yet cool relationship. She had attended an elite boarding school where she had excelled in everything—academics as well as field hockey and volleyball, but had married soon after she began college, then dropped out.

"Did you ever have a boyfren, when you were younger?" Kranti asked her. It was too bold. Former boyfrens were never topics of conversation among the buharis in the Asylum.

Shambhogya appeared startled, then laughed. "What kind of question is that?"

"It's a perfectly normal question. Did you have a boyfren, in school or in college?"

Shambhogya looked at the door. "No."

"No?"

She turned toward Kranti, and her face was crimson. "No."

Kranti had never seen Shambhogya blush before. "You're lying."

"I was never interested in men that way."

Shambhogya denied, and Kranti persisted, tenaciously, almost cruelly, not knowing why the answer had become so important to her, until, surprisingly, Shambhogya relented and said yes, there had been someone at college. "But it was nothing," she said. "I hardly think about him anymore."

"What was his name?"

"Ajay."

"What was he like?"

For a few moments, it looked as if Shambhogya couldn't speak. "He was nice," she finally said.

"How long were you two together?"

Had Shambhogya's eyes turned moist? "We were only together for a year."

"A year? A year? That's a long time, Shambhogya-di. So, he was your beau."

Shambhogya shushed him. "Please, don't speak so loudly. That was such a long time ago. Let it go, Kranti."

"I want you to tell me. I want to hear."

And, gradually, hesitantly, Shambhogya told her about Ajay. He was a quiet boy—"he was beautiful"—but one day her mother got wind of her romance with a Lama boy. "You're going to break up with him," her mother said. "If you don't break up, I'll break it off for you." Shambhogya wept, for she had foolishly woven dreams about herself and Ajay. After her mother's ultimatum, she contemplated running away with Ajay. But in the end, she wiped her tears and met Ajay in a restaurant and ended the relationship. In all the time she'd known him, he'd never been angry. In fact, he was so shy and such an introvert that her friends had expressed surprise that a young woman with her beauty and charm had fallen for him. But Shambhogya liked how gentle he was, how he acquiesced to her wishes, how happy she felt when they strolled the streets of the Valley together. They often preferred hidden alleys to avoid running into people they knew.

In the restaurant, with tears streaming down his face, he called her a coward. She walked out, unable to deal with it all. During the next few days, Ajay walked by her house a few times, and although she saw him, she didn't go out to meet him. He wrote her letters, he called her, but she didn't respond. When her mother informed her that she was finalizing her marriage with the eldest son of Ghimirey & Sons, she paused only for a second before she gave her consent.

The news of Ajay's death came to her a couple of weeks after she got engaged. His body was discovered one morning in the cold courtyard of the Sky Goddess Temple. People spoke of a heart attack. His family rushed him to the ghat to be cremated. The Sky Goddess Temple was Ajay's favorite. He'd taken Shambhogya there. "Isn't the goddess's statue resplendent?" he'd said. Shambhogya had barely been able to see inside the dark room where the shrine was kept, but she had caught the image of a statue of the goddess in a flying pose, her right leg bent behind her, her left leg pulled up to her breasts. Ajay had told her that he always found peace when he climbed the steps up to the temple and lingered in the small courtyard.

HOWL

35.

Soon after returning from their stay at the Humble Abode, PM Papa suggested that he promote Rozy to the role of an Advisor. Rozy laughed, hiding his face with his palms, and PM Papa loved him all the more for it. He loved the small gestures Rozy made—the way laughter broke out of his sad face; the way he scrunched his nose and small, lovely wrinkles appeared on the bridge of it when he disapproved of something; the way his paujebs thrummed on his ankles when he walked the corridors of the Lion Palace, as he went in and out of the Gufa, and now the InnerGufa, the room behind the Gufa that PM Papa had finally constructed.

Wearing the paujebs at work was PM Papa's idea, although it was Rozy who had purchased them. He'd gone to the inner lanes of the Lord of Heavens chowk and bought a pair of paujebs. Intricate in design, with tiny, tiny silver bells hanging from them, the paujebs were quite a pleasure to look at when he wore them around his ankles at the shop. But he hadn't worn them at work, and one day PM Papa found him admiring them in the InnerGufa. "They're beautiful," PM Papa said, snuggling up to him. "Why don't you wear them?"

"I'll wear them at the Humble Abode."

"You mean Rozy's Abode?"

"Yes, my abode," Rozy said.

"Will you reside in your abode? Forever?" PM Papa asked, nuzzling his nose into Rozy's neck.

"I'm only biding my time," Rozy said.

PM Papa closed his eyes, overwhelmed by the image of Rozy walking around Rozy's Abode with the paujebs. "I also want you to wear them here."

"Here? In the InnerGufa?" The InnerGufa had padded walls, and a fortified door. PM Papa also made it soundproof. It had a large queen-size bed with thick mattresses, decorated like it was a bed for newlyweds, with lots of reds and pinks, and a headboard that had a heart carved in it. The ceiling was filled with mirrors.

"Yes, in the InnerGufa."

"Sure." Rozy pulled his ankles up closer to fasten the paujebs.

"Also out there, in the Gufa."

"It'll make too much noise," Rozy said. "Too distracting." Rozy shook his legs a bit, which made the bells jingle.

"Pleasant. Exciting."

"What'll the others say?"

PM Papa, whose face was now buried in Rozy's stomach, said, "I'll shoot them with my Ancient Kalo Bandook."

Rozy smiled. He wouldn't put it past PM Papa to point his gun at a staff member who criticized Rozy. "Bill Tamang isn't going to be happy."

"Fuck Bill Tamang."

"I don't want to fuck Bill Tamang."

"If he lays a hand on you, I will—"

"What will you do, Papa? What'll you do if Bill Tamang makes a pass at me?"

"Let him try."

"What if?"

"I'll shoot him."

"Ancient Kalo Bandook?"

"What else?"

"He won't lay a hand on me. He's a family man."

"He won't because he knows the consequences."

"You have all of them trembling with fear."

"They respect me. So, does that mean you will wear the paujebs for me now?"

"Yes."

"Wear them in the InnerGufa. Wear them in the Gufa."

"Yes."

"Wear them in the Lion Palace. Wear them under the beautiful chalice."

"I wouldn't dare."

"Wear them all over the city. Make your ankles sexy and pretty."

"Ugh."

"Wear them while you're awake. Wear them while you sleep. No one in Darkmotherland will utter a peep."

"How long are you going to keep up with the rhymes?"

"Wear them fully clothed, wear them naked. Wear them when you're with me in bed."

"Will you stop?"

"Wear them when we're in Amrika, wear them with a nice tika."

"One more rhyme, and I'm leaving."

The word "leaving" triggered something in PM Papa, and his breathing became still against Rozy's belly. "Don't say that. You can never say that."

"Then stop with your silly rhymes."

"I'll stop, but don't say that," PM Papa said. "Not after what I've done for you."

Rozy realized that PM Papa was serious. "Okay, I won't say it again. But you should know, I'm not going with you to Amrika." They had a brief argument, with PM Papa expressing deep disappointment about Rozy's decision. He kept asking why, and Rozy kept saying that he had no interest in Amrika, and couldn't envision spending hours inside an airplane. Rozy said that trip to the Khadi had turned him off against all plane rides. "Just let me be. Why don't you take that wife of yours? I'm sure she'd love to go. She is, after all, a big fan of President Corn Hair's wife, that model-turned-first-lady."

When Rozy started openly dressing more like a woman in the Lion Palace, eyebrows were raised, then quickly lowered. At first Rozy wore dark-colored skirts with a boy's shirt on top. Then the dark-colored skirts gradually became more colorful, rainbow-colored, like those worn by the foreign hippie girls. No one said anything. There were stares but people were quiet. Rozy didn't come in wearing women's clothes; he brought a bag with him, disappeared into the InnerGufa and emerged as a woman. The shirt was replaced by a blouse. The men's shoes gave way to high heels. She also put on makeup. Her red lips became redder, thicker. A phuli appeared on her nose. Earrings were added.

There was grumbling, but who was going to say anything out loud? Rozy now also attended cabinet meetings, her paujebs going *chum-chum-chum*, serving PM Papa, bringing him tea (with honey; he wouldn't drink it without honey), fetching documents from the Gufa, retrieving Papa's reading glasses. She stood behind PM Papa's chair, her face gorgeous and impassive, or gorgeously impassive, or impassively gorgeous. Once in a while PM Papa reached behind and patted her hand and eyebrows were raised and quickly lowered. No one wanted to take the risk of saying anything. Everyone in the Lion Palace wanted to please PM Papa. All day long there were whispers and chatter about whether something met PM Papa's approval, whether PM Papa had sanctioned something. If PM Papa wasn't aware of something people thought he ought to be aware of, people—his staff, cabinet secretaries, even ministers—fought with one another like children to be the first to notify him.

PM Papa was pleased when the staff trampled over one another to serve him. A big smile spread across his face when they surrounded him and vied for his attention. He soaked in their adulation, complimenting them back. "You have such good judgment," he said to one staff member, pinching her cheek. Or, "If you always rely upon the sweetness of your words, you'll go far," he'd say to another. And, "I don't know where you get these smarts—they must be a blessing from Darkmother."

As Rozy's transformation into a woman became complete, Swami Go!swami said to General Tso, "The Devouts are talking." He'd come to visit General Tso at the Army Headquarters. It was a sunny day. The two men sat in the general's office, near the window.

Outside, a group of Loyal Army Dais were marching, shouting intermittently.

"Hmm," General Tso said.

"It is not good."

"Hmm?" He was smoking a cheroot, and the smoke drifted toward Swami Go!swami's face.

"I mean, given the Religious Righteous mission."

"All is well. All is well."

But Swami Go!Swami wasn't satisfied. What all is well? he thought to himself. Thus far, the Fundys had feigned not to notice PM Papa's abnormal appetites, but thus far it had also remained hidden. Therefore, they had been able to convince themselves that it would do no one any good to point out that the prime minister himself engaged in behavior that the Fundys considered an abomination, animalistic, and anti-God. Swami Go!swami regularly preached hellfire about homosexuality. He knew of PM Papa's history, and he considered PM Papa ungodly. There were days Swami Go!swami couldn't wrap his head around the fact that the current leader of the country, under whose protection the Fundys had so powerfully risen, was himself gay. It gave him a headache when he thought too much about it, and he had to stand upside down on his head for hours in sirsasana to get rid of it.

He knew the Devouts were bothered by it too, especially after they returned a few weeks ago from a meeting with PM Papa at the Lion Palace. Once back at Kailashram, they had complained to Swami Go!swami without naming the nature of their complaint. The Fundys had known immediately that Rozy was a chakka (and this was before the hippie frock, the excessive rouge, before the paujebs, before Rukshana Rauniar). He had long, manicured fingernails, he wore a shirt that unbuttoned at the chest, showed his smooth chicken-like breasts. His pants were tight, accentuating his buttocks, which swayed suggestively as he walked. And the lips, they were so red and succulent, as though dripping with blood. But also womanly. And it was clear that the eyebrows were plucked, and there was a faint trace of kohl around the eyes. And the hair, although under a dhakatopi, they suspected that it was long, perhaps wrapped in a bun.

"But, General sahib, it might not be that, as you say, all is well," Swami Go!swami said to General Tso. He waved his hand in front of his face to drive away the smoke.

Outside, a lieutenant was disciplining a soldier by slapping him. General Tso mentally nodded in approval. Rozy had been on his mind lately, for a different reason, of course. He turned to Swami Go!swami. "Well."

"It's an abomination," Swami Go!swami mumbled.

"Hmm."

Until recently, General Tso often sought spiritual advice from Swami Go!swami, even though overall he was a bit leery of the Fundys. He hated how they frothed at the mouth, even as he believed in their overall goals, especially their zeal to drive out the Christians and put other minority religions in their places. But, General Tso hailed from the villages in the eastern hills. They were populated by ethnic minorities, and many of them, especially those who had not been lured into Christianity, practiced more tribal religions, or a mishmash of tribal religions and shamanism. General Tso did think that those were inferior practices, but they also had roots in Dark-motherland's ancient heritage. Those people were also simple hillbilly folks, naive but kind. General Tso wanted to leave them alone, but the Fundys were ramping up their efforts to abolish even the shamanistic and tribal practices.

But this is what bothered General Tso the most: the Fundys were rabid casteists, including Swami Go!swami. The top leaders of the Religious Righteous all belonged to the priestly caste, thus everyone was inferior to them—they fervently believed this. One of their complaints about the previous regimes had been the rise of the lower castes, including the untouchables. The Fundys hated that the lower castes and the untouchables had been emboldened to use the village wells, thereby polluting the water for everyone else. When the Fundys talked of the other castes, especially the menials and the laborers, they did it with barely disguised disdain. Because General Tso came from an ethnic minority, he was also considered a lower caste. General Tso sensed it when he was with the Fundys, and it infuriated him. Who did they think they were? But they were also godly people, and he liked listening to them talk about the divine, which they often did:

"Once, when the Pothead God was chased by a demon, the Preserver God transformed into a ravishing lass and distracted the demon."

"When the God of Virtue realized that the Ten-Headed Demon King had kidnapped his wife, he unleashed an army of monkeys upon the demon's kingdom."

"When the Lord of Creation talks about . . ."

General Tso loved to listen to the sound of the hymns. He loved religious ceremonies. He often hosted elaborate purification rituals and fire ceremonies, sometimes conducted by Swami Go!swami himself. Some of these were shown on Motherland TV. Just a couple of weeks ago, General Tso had hosted a monster yagya at the Monkeygod Gate Square amidst the rubble of the monuments that the Big Two had leveled. Celebrities had attended. PM Papa himself even made a guest appearance. He accepted tika from Swami Go!swami. Flanked by General Tso, who was beaming because he absolutely loved these yagyas, PM Papa had given a short speech. The chanting of the hymns had gone on until late in the night. Candles had been lit. It seemed that the gods and goddesses in heaven were smiling upon Darkmotherlandites, courtesy of General Tso.

But among all the gods and goddesses of Darkmotherland, it was Darkmother that General Tso was most devoted to. "As long as I get to cuddle in Darkmother's lap, I wouldn't want anything else in life," he often said. Swami Go!swami responded with a story about Darkmother that General Tso relished, even though he'd heard it many times before. Various gods were having problems slaying the demon Seed of Blood, whose blood, when it fell on the ground, gave birth to duplicates. The frustrated gods ended up appealing to

Darkmother, who materialized, angry, with a skull-garland around her neck, and destroyed Seed of Blood and his duplicates. General Tso loved Goddess Darkmother's visage: the super-dark skin, the bulging, wrathful eyes, and the blood-like tongue hanging from her mouth. Even the Pothead God, the mightiest of all gods, was powerless and was depicted as squashed beneath her feet. General Tso frequently invoked Darkmother in his working hours. "Hail to Darkmother!" he shouted in the corridors of the Army Head-quarters. He sang Darkmother bhajans to himself while seated behind his office desk. He hummed them in meetings, with his eyes closed.

General Tso had never married. He'd devoted his life to the mili-tary; the impulse and the opportunity to marry never came. While he admired beautiful women, he didn't have strong romantic or sexual urges. His parents had died a long time ago, and he'd stopped talking to his brother and sister and their families once they converted to Christianity. He had very few relatives, so there was no one to nag him about his unmarried status, which by now he'd come to consider a blessing. His bachelorhood felt preordained, and lately he'd been convinced that he was meant to devote his life to Darkmother. She often appeared in his dreams in her wrathful form. The day after the yagya at the Monkeygod Gate Square, she appeared to him as a young lass, a young fair lass with red lips. How did General Tso know that she was Darkmother, even though she was more olive-complexioned than dark in the dream? Because she told him, and she also told him that he should be prepared for changes.

General Tso thought of all these things as he watched this reli-gious man in front of him, complaining about Rozy.

"I'm just wondering, that's all," Swami Go!swami said. "How far will this go before there is a public outcry?"

"The public is in our hands," General Tso said, waving his cheroot around, throwing some more smoke toward Swami Go!swami. "The public won't cry if you don't let them."

"Of course, that's what I wish too." Swami Go!Swami stood and went to the window, as though to look more closely at the marching of the soldiers. He was actually feeling asphyxiated by the smoke.

"It's our job to make sure that the public isn't burdened with such stuff. They should only worry about food, shelter, and education."

Swami Go!swami turned around and held General Tso's eyes. "If it explodes, I won't be able to contain it."

"It's not enough to say that," General Tso said. "It's your job. One could even say it was your sacred duty to contain it." There was impatience in his voice.

Swami Go!swami observed General Tso. Something about his tone. It was more commanding than usual, similar to when the general addressed his men. Sometimes when the general spoke to his men, it was as if they were nothing. As small as ants. Or bugs that deserved to be squelched under his feet. He cursed them, saying "lando chus," which, when Swami Go!swami had first heard it, had greatly disturbed his equanimity. "Suck my dick!" Who says that? General Tso often addressed his men as "randi ka chora." Calling people "sons of whores" is an abomination, Swami Go!Swami thought, but decided against saying it to the general. General Tso had so far been nothing but polite to him. He spoke to Swami Go!swami in a soft voice, loved listening to the stories of gods and goddesses, and instructed his men to cater to the holy man's needs.

This tone, however, was different.

"It might get out of hand no matter how hard I try," Swami Go!swami said.

"Then try harder," General Tso said, not as sharply, but the tone was unmistakable.

"Not everything is under my control."

General Tso sat down in this chair and looked across his massive desk, which held nothing but a pen holder and a stack of blank sheets of paper neatly arranged in one corner. General Tso never wrote anything on the blank paper. He also never read anything, apart from his prayer book, which he carried in his front pocket next to all of his medals, the pages with Goddess Darkmother hymns bookmarked for easy opening.

"It should be," General Tso said. He was in an uncompromising mood today, and he knew this could signal a shift in his relationship with the holy man.

The dream last night had been very vivid. Darkmother had appeared to him, in the form of Rozy in her psychedelic skirt, her paujebs, and her lustrous hair. But she was holding a trident and had her tongue out and was standing on a very handsome Pothead God. Is that really you, Darkmother? General Tso had asked in his dream. The trident flew, in slow motion, from her hand toward General Tso. The trident sailed majestically through the air and pierced General Tso's chest. There was a soft, gradual explosion in his body. A white light blossomed into thousands of multicolored lights, which then blossomed into a rainbow of colors of such beauty that General Tso didn't even know they existed—colors that carried with them the sweet taste of honey, of kheer, and childhood laughter. A vista opened up inside him, inside his mind actually. But now his body was one giant mind, a vista that contained the most pleasing things of this world—gorgeous deer strolling through a dense jungle; smiling virgin girls holding fragrant flowers waiting to greet him; kind scholars teaching kindly the secret wisdoms of a kinder world; brilliant gems with curative powers; the moon's silvery glow like a palliative for the ages; beautiful grandmothers from across cultures offering milk and jilebis; leafy leaves from trees providing a breeze that cured incurable diseases.

The blissfulness of this vista lasted a few seconds but also appeared to last an eternity. General Tso thought it would go on forever, that it was the real thing, that he had reached immortality, when pffft!—he woke up. Darkmother stared at him from the poster tacked above the bed on the opposite wall. It was positioned there so he'd see her first thing in the morning and last thing at night, before he shut his eyes.

"Rozy cannot be touched," General Tso said to Swami Go!swami. "She can't be touched in any way—physically or mentally."

Swami Go!swami gave him a befuddled look. "Why?"

General Tso banged the table with his fist, and the sheets of blank paper hurry-scurried down to the floor. "Because I say so." He wasn't going to explain to this Fundy about the vision that Darkmother had given him. General Tso was inundated with negativity toward Swami Go!swami. He'd been annoyed with Swami Go!swami before, but this time it was overpowering. He liked the feeling—there was something to it, and he suspected that Darkmother had a hand in it.

"Talk to your people," General Tso said. He snuffed out his cheroot in the ashtray, signaling an end to the conversation. "Tell them that anyone found saying anything negative about Rozy will be subjected to twenty lashes."

"Lashes? But that thing—"

"Don't call Rozy a thing."

"People ought to be able to speak out about abominations."

"Listen, Go!swami," General Tso said slowly. The holy man couldn't help notice the missing honorific. "Trust me on this."

～

Shambhogya's revelation about Ajay didn't bring her and Kranti any closer. Shambhogya distanced herself even more. A couple of times she was downright angry with Kranti over trivial matters, as if she thought Kranti had coerced the confession about Ajay out of her. It is the likes of you who makes things difficult for no reason—this is what her body language conveyed to Kranti, who in turn became dismissive of Shambhogya.

"You can't carry on with that poet man like this," Shambhogya told Kranti one day. "What has gotten into your head? You are a Ghimirey buhari."

They were speaking on the staircase. Her face pinched in disapproval, Shambhogya had appeared at the top of the staircase just as Kranti was getting ready to leave for the Bhurey Paradise.

"Shambhogya," she said, dropping the didi, pausing to let the lack of respect sink in. "I will meet whomever I want." She no longer experienced anxiety about such confrontations with the Ghimireys, but such a sense of normalcy could also be a delusion, she knew—her mind could turn against her at any moment.

Shambhogya didn't seem to care that she didn't receive the "didi" from Kranti. "I know what you do with him, that so-called poet."

So-called? Kranti thought. Hmm. Shambhogya the expert on poetry. But again, she might be. This woman was multitalented. In fact, Kranti seemed to recall vaguely hearing that Shambhogya had won a couple of poetry contests in the Valley before she married the Ghimireys. A poetess shut down, Kranti thought. Her own voice silenced, now she was ranting against the king of poets.

Kranti crossed the living room and opened the main door of the Asylum, Shambhogya following her. "Sir doesn't understand why you're doing this," she said. "No one does, not even Muwa."

Shambhogya was lying about Muwa. Barricaded in God's Room, Muwa couldn't have cared what Kranti was doing. Kranti was happy for her: What better way to deal with the pain of the death of your son than to turn your mind inward? But it also seemed pathological to shun the world completely, like Muwa was doing. If I reach her state of mind, Kranti thought, I'd know that I need professional help. But Kranti was far from withdrawing. There was an energy that was pushing her outward, an energy that was audacious, with a tinge of anger, unlike anything she'd experienced thus far in life. She was coming out, and she was coming out of the mental fog in which she'd been living.

"Kranti?" Shambhogya was asking.

"I'm going out to meet my poet lover," Kranti said and asked Cheech and Chong to open the gate for her.

That evening when she returned to the Asylum, it was Prithvi Raj, not Shambhogya, who waited for her. He was standing at the door when she entered, smiling at her gratefully, just happy to see her. He asked her how her day had been, then asked that she join him in the corner of the living room.

His strategy was gentle, fatherly. He empathized with her, he said. She was a young woman, with emotional and other needs. He understood why she was with Kabiraj (he didn't say "so-called-poet" or appear to be condescending in any way). He understood the connection, given that Kabiraj was Bhaskar's friend. He understood her "urge," he said. Fate had dealt Kranti a terrible blow, and who could blame her for seeking out companionship among those of her own age, perhaps even younger, someone who was Bhaskar's friend, to keep alive his memory?

He was the most lucid she'd seen him in weeks. Perhaps ever. His hair was neatly combed. He wasn't slurring his words, and the speech didn't appear rehearsed. He'd gone through some effort to compose himself, perhaps arrange himself internally, before he approached her. "It's been so long since we've talked," he said, as they sat in the living room, the voices of the nokerchakers in the kitchen occasionally reaching them. This was the old Prithvi Raj, the charming Prithvi Raj, who made deals worth millions of rupees with this smooth talk and his smiles and nods. Had Shambhogya revived him?

"But we're also thinking long-term, not just the present," he continued. "You are this family's future, Kranti. How much of a future do you see in this Kabiraj? I'm in no position to tell you because you're an intelligent, educated woman—more educated and smarter than I am— and you can make wise decisions about this. You know, I've never said this before, and I haven't told this to anyone in this family because it's not something to be told. But Bhaskar always held a special place in my heart." Prithvi Raj paused. "More special than Aditya or Chaitanya."

He held up his hand, as though warding off Kranti's protestations, although she wasn't going to protest because she'd heard this several times before and it was meaningless to her. "I know, I know," he said. "It's not a thing to announce. And I'm not even saying that I didn't love all three of my sons equally. But Bhaskar, he tugged at my heart, Muwa's heart, a bit more than our other two sons."

Prithvi Raj looked at the floor, fingertips of his two hands touching, seeming to contemplate his sadness, his wife's sadness, before he spoke again. "Bhaskar was always different, as if he should have been born in another family. Even when he was a child. He used to give his toys away to classmates who didn't come from well-to-do families. He never asked for pocket money, like his brothers did. And when we gave him money, he took his friends out for treats rather than spending it on himself. I used to wonder: Where did this little guy come from? Later, when he decided not to follow in the family business, I felt betrayed. I resented him, and—why should I lie to you—that resentment stayed with me until the Streetwise incident. I had been forced to reconcile myself to the fact that my middle son was going to do what he wanted to do, that it was his destiny to chart his own path. And in the midst of my resentment, something made me admire him more than I did my other two sons."

Prithvi Raj paused, wrung his hands, then continued. "Umesh is a good man," he said. "He understands the trauma that this family has gone through. He understands it because he's also a survivor. He's a mature man who, given the opportunity, would bring us some healing, bring you some healing. And we need more children in this house."

Prithvi Raj stood. "I feel like I've talked for too long. More than is good for a man my age, in my condition. You are an intelligent, wise woman, the wisest of all of my buharis, and I'm not saying this lightly. The choice that you make now will be the most important one you'll make for your life. For this family."

He bid her good night and went upstairs.

What a shitshow, Kranti thought.

36.

Something changed between the two men that day, all because of a dream. Swami Go!swami didn't know about the dream, of course, and he wondered why General Tso had changed. Stress, he thought. Dealing with PM Papa's unpredictable ways. Commanding an entire army, especially after Papakoo, which was a Godsend koo, Swami Go!swami thought, chuckling to himself as he exited the Army Headquarters. Hey Bhagwan, your magic is awesome, he said, holding his palms up to the heavens. God exhaled the catastrophe that was the Big Two just so that PM Papa would rise from its ashes. One moment the earth shook as if the planet were about to burst and shatter into a million pieces, and the next moment there was PM Papa and General Tso in power, assuring everyone they were in good hands. And now Swami Go!swami had a shiny black Cadillac with a chauffeur. The nameplate on the Cadillac said, "Go!swami!"

Swami Go!swami moved toward his Cadillac, paid for through Rajjya coffers. The driver, with dark glasses and suited in black, opened the door for him and saluted smartly. Swami Go!swami grunted and slid into the limo, letting out a long sigh as though he'd returned from saving the world. The chauffeur smart-saluted him as though he were a military man. Swami Go!swami liked it. He couldn't believe his own luck, his rapid rise. Before the Big Two, although he was a well-known figure in the Valley, he only had the name, not the money. He used to ride around on a scooty; his primary mode of income was the astrological consultations he did in his small flat in Thirty-Two Butterflies Street, and the pujas he performed for the big shots. And now, his religious show, endorsed by PM Papa, dominated the airwaves, and from his large compound ub Kailashram on Thirty-Two Butterflies Street he ran his Go!swami operations: the TV program, a large pharmacy, and an army of scholarly priests who fanned out to perform pujas and enforce religiosity. There was so much work to do, thought Swami Go!swami, so much of Darkmotherland had

rotted before the Big Two. People had lost their morality. Godless-
ness everywhere. Foreign and untouchable religions. Women acting
like sluts. Perverse sexual desires. With PM Papa, things had been
moving in the right direction.

And now Rozy. Even if Swami Go!swami was willing to forgive PM Papa for having a relationship with a homosexual, it was
quite another matter to forgive him for having a relationship with a
homosexual who was turning into a hijra, and flaunting that transformation. Yet now he was being told by General Tso that no one could
criticize that abominable creature. How was Swami Go!swami going
to handle this, placating the Devouts?

That afternoon Swami Go!swami spoke to the Devouts at the
Religious Righteous weekly gathering in Kailashram's spacious, well-
kept back lawn. Kailashram had a pagoda that had been built after
the earthquake, a structure copied from the great temples of Bharat.
Temple bells rang from somewhere within Kailashram, and saffron-
clad Devouts flocked to the backyard, where a giant, hokey statue of
the Pothead God, made from a cheap plastic-type material, stood tall.
It was the height of a small building, palm raised in blessing, the fearsome serpent curled around its neck, its tongue out, slithering.

Swami Go!swami, after clearing his throat, told the Devouts that
they were forbidden from expressing complaints about Rozy. There
were grumblings.

"We have to think strategically," he told the Devouts.

"It's an abomination!" someone shouted.

"Who was that?" Swami Go!swami said. "Who dares to shout like
that at me?"

Heads turned toward the source of the noise. Fingers were pointed.
"Whoever speaks this disrespectfully to your leader, you need to come
forward," Swami Go!swami said.

The bulky figure of Swami Rudraksha stood, looking around
him proudly. Swami Rudraksha was a troublemaker, an upstart who
always looked at Swami Go!swami as though he couldn't grasp why
he was in such a powerful position in the Religious Righteous. Swami

Rudraksha had been a wrestler in his early years, making his competitors eat the dust in the scorching south. His transformation into a
sadhu had come about because of a broken heart, they said.

"Please come forward," Swami Go!swami said. "Here."

Swami Rudraksha sauntered up to the front, his chest puffed up,
looked around lazy-eyed. His friends among the Devouts sniggered.
Swami Go!swami was surrounded by a few of his own assistants,
sadhus with their own administrative ambitions within Kailashram.
They glared at Swami Rudraksha, even though in private they too
had expressed their concern about Rozy to Swami Go!swami.

Swami Rudraksha came and stood before Swami Go!swami, as
though he was preparing to bump chests.

"You need to offer an apology for what you yelled," Swami
Go!swami said.

"Why should I apologize?"

"You yelled out something after I specifically said it was no longer
allowed."

"No longer allowed? Says who? It's an abomination, and I called
it that."

There were voices in support of his defense, and other voices calling
for respect for Swami Go!swami.

"Besides, who are you to tell us?" Swami Rudraksha said. "Are you
a sell-out?"

"Grab him," Swami Go!swami calmly ordered his assistants, who
looked at him in puzzlement. "Arre, grab him, I said!" he thundered.

The assistants scrambled to get hold of Swami Rudraksha, who
was a handful because of his size. Swami Rudraksha fought gallantly
with his grabbers, throwing off a couple of them with his mighty
arms. But a few more Devouts from the audience had joined to
subdue him, so eventually he was conquered. Three Devouts sat on
him as he breathed heavily.

"Bring the whip!" Swami Go!swami ordered. He could feel perspi-
ration on his forehead, and he hoped it didn't show. He'd encouraged
violence before but only toward the godless or foreign religions and the

untouchable castes. But a lesson needed to be taught here. The Religious Righteous needed PM Papa, and PM Papa needed them. If Swami Go!swami was understanding it correctly, PM Papa, through General Tso, was asking that this one concession, Rozy, be made for him.

A whip, said to be passed down from the Pothead God himself, was stored in a chest behind his statue, and there was a tussle among the Devouts to grab the sacred whip, then to get it to Swami Go!swami. Whip in hand, Swami Go!swami commanded that Swami Rudraksha be made to stand. Much of the earlier swagger had left Swami Rudraksha, who almost looked half-drunk as he staggered to an upright position. His right eye was slightly swollen. Perhaps an elbow jabbed into it during the jostle. Swami Rudraksha swayed as though he was a participant in a bar brawl. "God is watching your every move," he said with cracked lips.

Swami Go!swami couldn't help laughing, and when he laughed the assistant sadhus laughed, and when they laughed many of the Devouts in the audience laughed. Soon there was a ho-ho-ho-ha-ha-ha rippling through Kailashram.

Swami Go!swami raised his arms in the air and looked toward the heavens. "God is watching my every move. Hey God, your miracles are awesome!"

"God is watching!" the Devouts sang. "God is watching."

Swami Go!swami raised the whip in the air and flogged Swami Rudraksha. Again. And again. And again. Twelve lashes. "For first offense," he said. He liked the authority in his voice. Take it, bitches. With this action, he had now fulfilled General Tso's instructions and also subdued Swami Rudraksha, who, he knew, was not going to cause him any more trouble.

Increasingly, the Laj Mahal was beginning to feel like Kranti's real home, more than the Asylum, more than Beggar Street. She loved the sounds that surrounded her, as she did this evening—vendors calling, shrieks of children, guitar chords with music that Dada used to listen to, soft murmurs of housewives standing just outside the tent sharing stories of hardships. In the Asylum, it was mostly silence, with everyone cooped up in their rooms and emerging only for their meals, and the voices of the nokerchakers, working, only served to magnify that dwelling's great divide.

"This is a mad country," Kabiraj said quietly, out of nowhere, as they lay in bed. His finger was on his chin, and he was looking at the tent's ceiling.

"Is that a line from a new poem?" Kranti asked. Then she remembered the man from the other day with whom Kabiraj had been discussing things he hadn't wanted to tell her. "You're not plotting anything, are you?" Kranti asked. "If you are, I won't stand for it."

He looked at her as though she was out of her mind.

Just then, his mobile rang. It was an old flip-open type with buttons so tiny that he punched the numbers with his spikey index fingernail that he'd grown especially for this purpose.

"Why don't you upgrade your phone?" Kranti asked, as she'd asked before.

"How can I," he said, as he noted the number of the caller, "think about upgrading when Darkmotherland is continuously downgraded?"

"Are you going to answer?" Kranti asked, elbowing him.

He looked at her, then at the phone, and finally he pressed the green button.

For the next few minutes he conducted a small-voiced conversation, often just saying hmm, ahh, ho-ho, or "just as I was saying," or "inshallah."

"What? Are you a Muslim now?" Kranti asked after he finished his conversation.

"What?"

"You just said inshallah. Did you convert? You know the punishment for conversion into other religions, right? They passed it only a few weeks ago."

"Yes, I'm aware. Imprisonment only if you convert to Islam or

Christianity. But if you convert or reconvert to our religion, the Rajjya gives you twenty-five thousand rupees."

"Who are these people you're talking to?"

"Friends."

"Why do you need to talk to your friends constantly while I'm here?" She said this with only a mild accusation, although she felt a tinge of jealousy that his mind was elsewhere while she was there. Was this getting to be a repeat of Bhaskar?

"It's not like that," he said defensively. "Okay, here, I'll turn off the phone."

And he did.

Outside, the guitar girl was softly crooning a song about how it would be a mistake to fall in love with a traveler, for one day the traveler would have to depart for another destination.

Two days later, four Fundys came barging into Laj Mahal. Kabiraj and Kranti were under the blanket. The lookout who was stationed near Kabiraj's tent, one of the several young boys and girls stationed throughout Bhurey Paradise to alert their brethren to the arrival of Fundys and Papa's Patriots, must have been dozing. For here they were, the Fundys, with a Yogini amidst them. And she did look like an emanation of a goddess: darkish, oily skin, with a fierce forehead and penetrating eyes. Kranti's first thought was: I'm done. She imagined her identity being revealed, and the next day the news that a Ghimirey daughter-in-law, a widow, was caught fornicating with a Bhurey, being splashed all over the media.

"Eh! Ah! Ooh! Hah!" the Fundys shouted.

On the mattress, Kabiraj was on top of Kranti, who quickly turned her face away from the Fundys so that she was staring at a beetle bug resting near the tent's edge.

"What's going on?" the Yogini said.

"In broad daylight?" Fundy One said.

"Licentious!" Fundy Two said.

"We are a couple," Kabiraj said. He was still on top of her, naked under the sheet. She too was in her petticoat and blouse. She could feel his beard and mustache against her lips, and it was ticklish. She was afraid she was going to sneeze, or worse, giggle.

The Yogini's tone softened. "Couldn't you wait until darkness to fornicate, bhai?" she asked Kabiraj.

"When darkness falls," Kabiraj said, "all the couples in the nearby tents fornicate, Ma, and there is simply too much noise for us to concentrate." Kranti could feel Kabiraj's voice in her bones: boom, boobooboo-boom, boom, boom.

"New bride?" the Yogini asked.

"Brand new, Ma," Kabiraj said. "We are attempting to procreate. Do you have a baby, Ma?"

The Yogini blushed. "How could I? I'm a nun. But I've always wanted a baby."

"Ma!" Fundy Three finally spoke. "That's inappropriate."

"I know," the Yogini said. "You don't have to mansplain it to me."

"Mansplain?" Fundy Three sounded confused.

Fundysplain, thought Kranti.

"Remember"—the Yogini wagged a finger at Fundy Three—"I have been a Devout a lot longer than you have." The Yogini barked at Kabiraj. "Do you know Villyam?"

"Villyam?"

"Yes, the Christian. Villyam. Do you know where he is?"

"William," Kranti whispered, squirming under Kabiraj.

Kabiraj shook his head. Kranti was tickled by his beard. Now she was beginning to feel suffocated by the pressure of Kabiraj's roly-poly body on top of her, and also, frankly, bored with all the conversation.

"Why are you hiding your bride from us?" the Yogini asked.

Kranti stopped breathing.

"She's shy," Kabiraj said.

The Yogini smiled. "Shy with us? Why would she need to be shy with us? We are Devouts, we protect our women from licentiousness, impurity, rape, and debauchery."

"Well, unless you dress provocatively," Fundy One said.

"Or walk late at night by yourself," Fundy Two said.

"Or have boyfrens, especially of a different caste," Fundy Three said.

"Or have liaisons with men you're not married to," Fundy One said.

"Then we won't hesitate to violate you," Fundy Two said.

"And we mean, really violate you," Fundy Three said.

"But we are here to find this Christian Villyam and interrogate him," Yogini said.

Kabiraj feigned anger. "I'm sure Swami Go!swami would love to hear how his people are harassing God-fearing fornicating couples. Are the Devouts in the business of bullying pious folks?"

"Pious? I don't see posters or statues of any gods and goddesses here," Fundy Three said.

Now all of their eyes roamed the tent.

"That is odd," the Yogini said. She asked Kabiraj, "Why is that, bhai? You invoke our gods and goddesses, but you have none in your tent. Huh? You do have a poster of MLK-ji. Why is that?"

"And whose photo is this of this funny-looking man in thick glasses and an enormous beard?"

"He's a famous poet from Amrika."

"If he's so famous, how come we've never seen him before?" Fundy Three asked.

"Do you even read Angrezi poetry?" Kabiraj asked disdainfully.

Fundy Three appeared indignant. "I don't read anything in that cow-eating language." Then he challenged Kabiraj, "Do you read any Sanskrit? I do."

"Is that even a woman underneath you, bhai?" the Yogini asked. "He says it's a woman, but that could be a man." She instructed the Fundys, "Lift him up. Let's have a look-see."

"If it's a man, I'll chop both their schlongs off," Fundy One said as he moved forward.

"I'm a woman," Kranti said in a muffled voice because her face was squished by Kabiraj's beard. "All woman here." She shook her right arm in the air, jangling her bangles, which she'd started wearing again after discarding her white dhoti. "Born and raised a woman."

"She's a woman all right," the Yogini said.

Just then another Fundy barged into the tent and said excitedly, "Villyam has been spotted near Hotel Kyalifornya."

"Let's go get that cow-eating villain," the Yogini said.

"Not villain—Villyam," Kabiraj said.

Kranti poked him.

Fundy Three met Kabiraj's eyes and, in a voice deep and echoing, said, "We'll be back."

The Fundys' threatening, "We'll be back," kept ringing in her ears, but despite the fear of their returning to Laj Mahal, Kranti experienced happiness when she was with Kabiraj in the tent—happiness after a long time, she realized, happiness like in the initial days of meeting Bhaskar, before he slipped away from her into her mother's influence. When she was in the Laj Mahal, there were afternoons when the Asylum felt like a distant reality, even though it was only a few kilometers away. She wished she could stay with Kabiraj forever. She'd help him cook in his small brisket stove outside his tent, then they'd eat dal-bhat together, perhaps even feed rice to each other, like newlyweds.

She didn't know why she didn't sleep in Laj Mahal, experience Bhurey Paradise under the stars along with the common folk. These days, just the thought of returning to the Asylum in the evening made her groan inside. But she also wanted to test the Ghimireys, to see how far they'd go—that's what Bhaskar would have done—and so each evening she returned before darkness fell, like a dutiful daughter-in-law. Moving from Bhurey Paradise into the more well-to-do neighborhoods was like, she thought, moving from a rat-infested war-torn third-world country into the comfort and luxury of a rich Western nation. She walked quickly toward home, her head covered with her dhoti, like a maid from the Bhurey Paradise who worked in one of the big houses. Loyal Army Dais with guns patrolled the wealthier neighborhoods to ensure that Bhureys didn't infiltrate. A sizable population of Bhureys worked for the richer Valley residents, and they had their own identity cards. But Kranti's identity card didn't identify her as a Bhurey, and sometimes she received puzzled looks from the Loyal Army Dais, who gave her a dismissive nod as they let her pass and go toward the Asylum. After PM Papa's visit a few weeks ago, there was a strong presence of Loyal Army Dais outside of the Asylum.

When she stopped by to see Professor Shrestha after work, which she now occasionally did, she saw that Chanchal and Vikram had returned, and joined Murti as they sat on the floor while Professor Shrestha sat on her green sofa, nursing a drink. It reminded Kranti of the time soon after Dada died, when the frequency and intensity of these gatherings had dwindled. It was the same now, weeks after the Streetwise School incident. These folks were depressed, her mother was depressed, but were they also scheming something? Were their strained faces indications of more trouble down the line?

One day, when she reached Beggar Street and was about to knock, she heard angry voices inside.

"I feel like my soul has been crushed." It was Vikram.

"I can't take it anymore!" Chanchal's voice.

"Something needs to happen, Madam," Murti said. "Something needs to give."

They quieted when Kranti knocked. Then Vikram opened the door for her.

"Come, Kranti, sit," Professor Shrestha said, but Kranti didn't sit. She stood for a while, asked how things were, then left. She no longer had the patience for it. She only wanted the sunshine and the brightness and earthy smell of Kabiraj's tent.

When she entered the Asylum, she went straight to her room.

One afternoon when she reached Laj Mahal, she found it empty. Things inside were strewn about, the posters of Martin Luther King

Jr.-ji and the famous bearded Amrikan poet were ripped and lying on the floor.

A thin, middle-aged man who peeked into the tent informed her that Papa's Patriots came and took him away. She recognized the man as Kabiraj's neighbor, Genius. A Genius-in-Name-Only, Kabiraj had said about him.

"Not Fundys?" Kranti asked Genius.

"No," Genius said. "It probably has something to do with the *Howl* group that he runs."

"*Howl?*"

"Aye saw the besta minds afa my gene-rey-shon dees-troyed bye myada-ness," Genius recited. It took a moment for Kranti to realize that the words were in the man's constipated Angrezi. The lines sounded familiar, and Mrs. Joshi's voice from her Angrezi class came to her, but vaguely enough that she couldn't place them. Genius's eyes were closed now, as though he was in a trance. He turned up his palm in the manner of an Urdu poet and continued, "Estar-ving hees-tayreecal naykayd," when Kranti cut him off with, "Enough!"

She then asked, "What is *Howl?*"

"It's a famous poem by a famous Amrikan homo." He continued reciting, "De-ragging them-shelves thuru the neegro estereets."

Kranti punched him hard on the shoulder.

"*Howl!*" Genius cried, nursing his shoulder. "What did you do that for?"

Kranti grilled him: What was the group? What were they plotting?

Genius said that it was only a poetry club and they were plotting nothing. He was still holding his shoulder and emitting small cries. He said that the Rajjya arrested them because it had gays, Christians, Muslims, and Sufis—also one Rasta.

"Were they reciting anti-Religious Right poetry?" She quickly peeked outside to see that no one was listening.

"No!" Genius said. "Their poetry isn't anti-anything. It's pro-my religion and pro-your religion and pro-my sexuality and pro-your sexuality, but it is not anti-anything. *Howl!*"

"Were these anti-Rajjya poems?"

"They weren't anti-Rajjya poems. They were merely expressions of their individuality—their spiritual aspirations, their sexual desires. The Christians wrote poems about their Lord, daily bread, forgiving sins, yada, yada. One wrote a haiku that goes like this:

"Christ my Savior
Like a Ray of Light—
Splash!"

"That doesn't make any sense," Kranti said. She was mildly familiar with Christian tenets, as her high school was run by Jesuit nuns. She knew about confession, the wine as Jesus's blood, the Lord's prayer, etc.

"It's not supposed to make sense," Genius said, grinning despite the pain. "But it does, you see."

Oh, here we go again, Kranti thought.

"The splash, although alluding to the famous Basho poem about the old pond and the frog, is really about that dunking thingy that the Christians do, in the water."

"Baptism?"

"Yes, yes," Genius said excitedly. "And because conversions happen suddenly—one moment you are singing bhajans about the Dimple-Cheeked Flute-Playing Blue God with 1600 Garlfrens and the next your bhajans are about how the Lord is a Good Shepherd roaming in the white-peaked mountains, that he can also grant salvation, go to him now!"

"Splash!" Kranti said.

"The Muslims too yearn to be with their Allah. They keep saying, One and only, one and only, one and only, one and only—"

"Okay, okay, I get it! Don't the Muslims and Hindus fight during these poetry readings? Don't the Hindus chant, 'One and many! One and multi-headed and thousand-armed'?"

Genius shook his head, as though puzzled by Kranti's lack of understanding of true spirituality, and her lack of faith in the group, *Howl*. "They all get along. These are just individual expressions. Nothing more, nothing less."

And dangerous to the Rajjya, Kranti wanted to say.

She wondered in the days to come if she'd encounter Kabiraj's dead body, lying in a gutter. Could Kabiraj have simply disappeared, never to be found? But surely, the punishment for reciting a few poems couldn't be disappearance or death? But much literary activity had already died down in Darkmotherland. What had emerged was a group of nationalist poets, known as the Bards, who constantly sang the praise of PM Papa and the country, and wrote poems mocking the Son of Yeti and other anti-patriotic elements. They ruled the Rajjya Academy, and appeared frequently on Motherland TV and Radio, reciting, chanting, and singing their patriotic poems. The Rajjya had already bestowed prestigious literary awards on these poets who had written rousing poems to the glory of PM Papa's reign. PM Papa himself had penned a patriotic poem that, in song form, was played ad nauseam on the Motherland Radio, and sometimes also on Motherland TV, with PM Papa himself reciting his poem. He's dressed in national garb, standing among the trees, his face partially hidden by the leaves, in his garden in the Humble Abode. It sounded awfully similar to a poem by the Shades-Wearing King that talked about how he wanted his beloved country to live on even if he himself died. PM Papa's poem deviated only slightly: "let my country live on" was changed to "let my nation's heart beat on."

The Bards praised PM Papa's song so much that people preferred listening to the song more than the Bards' eulogy, even though they were tired of the song too. Of course, in shops and restaurants and other public spaces when PM Papa's song was played (there was even a rap version), people nodded their heads in approval and sang with their eyes closed. There were spontaneous outbursts of the song by Darkmotherlandites, in vegetable markets, in the mall, occasionally even inside a cinema hall, and everyone would stop whatever they were doing—the hagglers in the vegetable market would stop haggling as they held the vegetables in their hands—and either listen appreciatively or sing along.

PM Papa's song had completely soaked into Darkmotherlandites' imagination. There had been cases of people losing their minds over "Even When I Die." One time a housewife, while washing clothes in her front yard, began whacking the ground with her husband's wet jeans and yelling: "Even-whack-when-whack-I-whack-die-whack-let-my-whack-nation's-whack-heart-whack-beat-on." Neighbors ran to her, trying to quiet her, but she refused to let go of her wet clothes. She warded off her neighbors by swinging them in the air, shouting, "Even when I die, let my laundry dry." Within minutes, and out of nowhere, Papa's Patriots appeared and took her away. Her husband had to argue a case of patriotic insanity to bring her home.

The Rajjya academy conferred prestigious awards to patriotic writers, often selected from among themselves, and rescinded awards given to writers in the past. They took away the nation's premier literary award that had been given to the editor of a leading daily whose novel chronicled a love story during the Maoist Civil War between an artist and an Amrika-returned Darkmotherlandite. Years ago, when the book had been lauded, some people complained that it had received the award only because the author was handsome and had young women swooning over him. Now in its statement of revocation, the Rajjya Academy wrote that the novel had manipulated the growing fondness for coffee culture in the country by injecting the word "café" in the title—just so that impressionable youths who hung out in cafés drinking Frappuccinos, cappuccinos, and lattes would be inclined to read it. The novel was deemed unpatriotic for its unashamed valorization of individual creativity at the expense of national unity, and for its semi-sympathetic portrayal of the Communist movement that led to the Maoist Civil War.

"What is with these Western-influenced novelists?" the Rajjya Academy statement asked. "They can't pen one word without praying to the idol of individuality, and denigrating our culture and religion. What about that other author, our so-called compatriot who is now a professor in Amrika? Didn't he write books solely designed to bewitch the godless foreigners and arresting God in the ancient city and about orphans belonging to the Awakened One? His characters regularly commit adultery and incest, perhaps even bestiality." All of the professor's books had been banned in Darkmotherland soon after the Bards took over the Rajjya Academy. One afternoon there was a book burning ceremony in front of the Home of the Bell. Copies of the professor's books, especially the one that depicted, in graphic terms, the illicit relationship between a domineering woman and her stepson, were thrown into the fire, for all to see on Motherland TV. "The perverted professor thinks so lowly of our women's attractiveness that he couldn't even make the stepmother beautiful so that the stepson's desire for her, however depraved, could be palatable," declared the Bards as they ripped off pages from these books and hurled them into the fire. One Bard tore off a page from a book, used it to catch a flame from the bonfire, then lit his cigarette as the fire burned away the words on the page.

37.

It was dusk by the time Kranti left Genius, who was now mewling softly as he nursed his shoulder. They should have called it *Mewl* and not *Howl*, thought Kranti.

As she walked between the tents of Bhurey Paradise, the sounds of the evening—babies crying, stoves being fired up for dinner, children shouting as they played on narrow strips of land, old men smoking and debating—drifted to the background and she felt slightly sick at what might have happened to Kabiraj. People could rot in jail for weeks or months for small crimes, unknown crimes, or false accusations. Kranti guessed that Kabiraj has been taken to a jail (many more jails had sprouted across the Valley now—old Rajjya buildings, defunct factories and schools converted into prisons), where he would be beaten senseless, then, she hoped, let go. If Kabiraj, too, vanished from her life, what would she do?

She first went to the Monkeygod Gate Jail, where her mother had been imprisoned and questioned by General Tso after the failure of Papa Don't Preach, and where Kranti had also visited her during her teenage years. The Poolis Uncles guarding the entrance laughed at her when she said that she was looking for a friend. Kranti surreptitiously handed the guards some money as a bribe, which they accepted, then one of them went inside to check. He returned within a few seconds and told her that no one named Kabiraj was inside. When she questioned whether he looked carefully, the Poolis Uncles became enraged and asked her, "Are you accusing us of something? We'll throw you in there too. Now scram!"

As she left, the Poolis Uncles shouted after her, "Vamoose!"

"Skedaddle!"

"Woman begone!"

When she was at a safe distance, Kranti turned around and gave them the middle finger. "Suck on this!" She then quickly bolted into an alley near the Pot Smoking God temple.

She checked two more jails, bribed more guards—well, why not? She was a Ghimirey buhari, after all, with cash at her disposal—but Kabiraj wasn't in any of them. She was getting tired, and weepy. She walked aimlessly through the Valley, not knowing where to go, what to do, peeking fruitlessly into alleys, looking for Kabiraj in local bhattis (he was not even a drinker!). She thought: not again, I can't lose another person I love. Love? She wasn't sure she loved Kabiraj. She loved Bhaskar, with all the bones in her body. But Kabiraj? She was fond of him, felt comfortable with him, could see herself spending her life with him in Laj Mahal.

She also couldn't stand the thought of him suffering under the Rajjya brutality. In many ways Kabiraj was a more sensitive and delicate soul than Bhaskar, and he wouldn't survive any form of hardship or torture, despite living in Bhurey Paradise. She wondered if he had been hauled off to the labor camps that were rumored to have sprouted across the Valley. The Rajjya was on a mission, it was said, to arrest people on the slightest of pretexts so it could populate these labor camps. "Excess prisoners" or "surplus prisoners" were being shuttled off in big trucks lavishly decorated with tassels and flags and signs on the back that said, DARKMOTHER'S BLESSINGS, or TRUST IN GOD, or YOU THE EVIL EYED ONE: MAY YOUR FACE BE BLACKENED. A forced labor camp was called a GULA, a riff on its Russian namesake, but flavored for the local tongue: a GULA was where you were made to burst your gula, your balls.

As if in confirmation of these rumors, in Diamond Park, Kranti saw hobos pushed into a truck with a sign on its back bumper that said, NO GARLFREN, NO TENSION. Some people stopped to watch, but most moved on, afraid that they could also randomly be shoved into the trucks and end up in a GULA. "Yes, yes, plenty of food where we're taking you," the Loyal Army Dais said to the hobos as they were pushed into the truck, which, Kranti noticed, also contained other hobos or destitute men and women.

An onlooker approached the Loyal Army Dais. The crowd held its breath. Who was this fool?

"Excuse me, Sir," the man, who must have been around fifty, said. "Where are you taking these hobos?"

"Where else? Hobo Heaven."

"Where is that?"

"Do you want to find out?" the Loyal Army Dai said. "I have room."

"No, no," the man said. "Just curious."

"Are you sure?" the Loyal Army Dai said. "In Hobo Heaven we have delicious food: goat meat, zucchini curry, thick black dal. We have mariachi music and belly dancing. Not only zucchini but jacuzzies. Beds with Tempur-Pedic mattresses. Massage parlors with imported Thai masseuses who specialize in happy endings."

The middle-aged man smiled shyly and raised his fist in the air. "PM Papa jindabad!"

"PM Papa jindabad!" the hobos inside the truck echoed, before a plastic curtain fell on them and the truck roared away.

A woman in the crowd said that the khateykids were next. "That's what I've heard," the woman said.

"Good riddance," a tall man said. "These khateykids are total pests. Put them to work. Get some use out of them. It'll make them healthy. Lean, mean working machines."

The next morning, she awoke to a commotion at the gate of the Asylum. From the window she saw that Cheech and Chong were yelling at someone who, it seemed, was attempting to get in. "Motherfucking khateykid!" the guards said, pointing their rifles. The target of their wrath was not entirely visible, but Kranti managed to catch a glimpse.

"Hey, hey!" she yelled from the window at them. "Stop!"

Upon hearing her voice, Subhash's figure peeked in further to look at her and shouted, "Didi!"

Cheech or Chong swung the end of his rifle at him and thwacked the boy on the side of the face, sending him reeling outside of Kranti's vision. "Don't hit him!" Kranti shouted, then saw that Harkey had also emerged from the Servants Villa and was looking toward the gate. She hurried out of her door and down the corridor.

Shambhogya peeked from her room and asked what happened. Without responding, Kranti raced down the stairs and reached the gate. She nearly punched Cheech or Chong, the guard who was in front of her. "What did you do to that boy?"

"He was a khateykid trying to get in," Cheech or Chong protested.

"He was looking for me!"

"How would I know that? He kept uttering nonsense that Bhaskar babu's killer was inside."

Kranti went to the street. A small figure was running away in the distance, toward the Tourist District. She shouted Subhash's name but he was too far away to hear her, and even if he heard her, he didn't seem inclined to stop.

Harkey approached. He asked what was going on. When Cheech or Chong told him what the khateykids had said, Harkey said, "If that khateykid appears again, bring him to me. I will set him straight."

Kranti cautioned Harkey not to harm any child. "That khateykid was Bhaskar's favorite, you know."

Harkey stared at her.

Kranti retreated into the house.

Shambhogya was waiting for her inside. "Have some control over yourself. So early in the morning, and you're acting like the sky is about to come crashing down. What will people say?"

Upstairs, Kranti played and replayed in her mind the image of Cheech or Chong smacking Subhash with his rifle butt. What was wrong with these people? Why be cruel when you didn't need to?

Did Subhash really know something? The boy was probably so troubled by Bhaskar's death that he was hallucinating, which was not an abnormal state for him. She felt a close affinity with the boy. Hadn't Bhaskar said that a woman who cared for him had been murdered? Subhash was most likely conflating the two incidents.

But Subhash remained in the back of her mind, and at one point she remembered that Subhash was at Streetwise that day. Bhaskar had been trying to get Subhash to come to classes at Streetwise, and finally, a few days before Bhaskar was killed, Subhash had come. He's a bright boy, Kranti remembered Bhaskar saying happily. So, Subhash must have witnessed what happened at Streetwise, must have seen the faces of the killers. But surely the killers were outsiders, whether they were PM Papa's men, or the Yetifolk or whoever? Why did the boy point to the Asylum? A great cloud of anxiety and apprehension swept over Kranti. She felt her stomach tighten, and a tic-tic-tic started in her mind. She needed to find Subhash.

—

Rozy walked down the hallways in her hippie frock, the paujebs going *chum-chum-chum*. Now she attended all of PM Papa's meetings and sat at the table with him. PM Papa had even begun soliciting her opinions about various matters regarding the Rajjya: replacement of bureaucrats who were not demonstrating ardent, groveling loyalty; injecting an even more patriotic, Rajjya-friendly curriculum in schools; initiating a strong public relations message about how PM Papa was emerging as a leader in the international community.

Questions were asked of Rozy in a half-amused, half-proud way, as though Rozy were a child who had been allowed to claim a position that was not hugely important but one that would make her feel important. "Well, let us ask our Rozy here," PM Papa would say.

Papa's cabinet would look at Rozy with blank faces. A couple of the ministers gave tiny, embarrassed smiles. "Rozy's mind is sharp,"

PM Papa said, pointing at his own head with his index finger, as though he were also calling her crazy. Papa's cabinet, mostly men, nodded.

"You're embarrassing me, Papa," Rozy said, coyly at first. "What do I know about these things?"

"Don't underestimate yourself," PM Papa said. "Recognize the greatness in yourself."

"Yes, yes, recognize the greatness in yourself," the cabinet members said, nodding, a look of discovery on their faces, as if they were wondering why they hadn't thought of such a life-altering maxim before.

"You know everything. You only need to realize that you know it," PM Papa said to Rozy.

There were murmurs of appreciation and tsks of admiration.

"Okay, then," Rozy said. "This is what I think." And she would give her thoughts on what was asked of her. Yes, the manager of National Food Corporation had to be demoted, or even fired. No, a drastic change in school curricula would lead to confusion; maybe implement some of the changes gradually. She was careful in enunciating her thoughts, making sure that her opinions were balanced, that they sounded girly yet intelligent. She made sure that her tone conveyed that her thoughts and beliefs on matters of the state were influenced by her great mentor PM Papa, who looked on proudly. And of course, the cabinet members, wanting to please PM Papa, exclaimed that Rozy's views were extraordinarily astute.

"A born politician," Shiksya Pradan said.

One day, in enthusiastic praise, Artha Shashtri, who'd known PM Papa nearly as long as General Tso, said, "She could easily take over your job, Papa."

There was stunned silence. Artha Shashtri's face became drained of blood. Everyone became ramrod still, waiting for PM Papa's reaction. He turned toward Rozy, who was standing behind him, and said, "Now, isn't that something? Rozy the Prime Minister. I like the sound of that."

There was a huge sigh of relief across the table. "PM Rozy," Prapu

Ganda said softly. He still remembered how close the cricket bat had whished near his head before landing on Rakshya Garam.

"Rozy the Riveter," Minister of Industry Udhyog Bikas said. "We can do it!"

"You were excellent today," PM Papa said to Rozy in the InnerGufa as they both lay on the bed.

"I've learned from the master, haven't I?" Rozy ran an index finger down PM Papa's short nose.

PM Papa pushed his nose gently against Rozy's stomach, feeling a movement there. "Oh, Rozy, Rozy, we're going to have a grand future together."

"All men say that at first, then they get tired."

PM Papa rested his head on Rozy's exposed belly, his right ear listening for something. "If I were getting tired of you, I wouldn't have taken you to the Humble Abode."

"Rozy's Abode."

PM Papa raised his index finger in the air. "I stand corrected. Rozy's Abode. See! I even made Shrimati Papa realize how much you mean to me."

"Be Best, Papa, Be Best." Rozy stroked PM Papa's chin, scratching it a bit. "Is that enough?"

"Be Best is not enough?"

"It's one thing to boss your family around, but what about here?" Rozy waved her index finger in the air indicating the Lion Palace. "What am I here?"

PM Papa raised his head from Rozy's lap to look at Rozy. "I'm even allowing you to opine on Rajjya matters, in front of my cabinet ministers. That's not enough?" He sighed and lay his head down again.

Rozy stroked his balding head, brushing away tufts of hair with her finger. She blew onto his forehead as though soothing away his worries. She didn't speak for a while, then said, "I doubt this is something you're capable of doing, Papa, and I'm not saying this because

I doubt your abilities. You are a powerful man"—yet she was talking to him as though he were a baby—"I've seen your capabilities. What you did to Rakshya Garam, for example." She sighed and stopped stroking his head with her fingers. "But I don't think you have the guts to go beyond." She made her voice turn slightly cold.

PM Papa shifted his position and grabbed Rozy's arm, his fingers digging into her flesh. It hurt, but right now it felt important that Rozy not show her pain.

"Rozy, Rozy," PM Papa said, his voice slightly hoarse, "you under-estimate me. I'm ready to raze Darkmotherland to the ground for you." He moved down the bed to Rozy's feet and commenced sucking her toes, one by one. "Mmm," he said.

"It tickles," Rozy said, laughing, and turning serious again. PM Papa licked the sole of her foot, which made Rozy scream and pull up her leg. PM Papa slid up and, resting his chin on Rozy's shoulder, reached with a hand and put it on Rozy's crotch. "Hmm, looks like Rozy junior needs some attention. Why don't I take care of that? Then you can tell me what's on your mind."

Rozy shoved PM Papa's hand away. "Not in the mood," she said.

PM Papa became silent, then he said, "Rozy, why do you want to torture me like this? You know I'd do anything for you."

Rozy turned her face away.

"Please, Rozy."

Rozy turned her face toward him. Her kohl-rimmed eyes became smaller. "Then make me the Deputy Prime Minister."

PM Papa withdrew his head, then cocked it. "Joking, hoina?"

"Didn't I say that you won't take me seriously?"

"But I offered to make you a Senior Advisor, which I thought would make you happy."

"Pfft! Senior Advisor!"

"You don't think that's a good position?"

Rozy stood from the couch and walked to the chair near the door, where she sat. She crossed her legs and looked at PM Papa a few feet away. "Anyone can be a Senior Advisor. That idiot Bipin is your

Senior Advisor. When was the last time he made a sensible com-ment? And what about Vivekshya? Half the time she garbles her words as if she's drunk. Who knows what she's saying? These Senior Advisors are a dime a dozen. They never offer you good advice—why even call them advisors? Why not call them Senior Lackeys?" Rozy was experiencing some cognitive dissonance. I ought to be careful of what I say to this man, she thought, but then she appeared to have transcended her fear. The naming of Rozy's Abode and the pushing out of Shrimati Papa had elevated her to a different space altogether. This was not the time to be afraid. "None of those lackeys give you good advice," Rozy continued. "Either they're stupid or they want you to make mistakes."

"Why would they want me to make mistakes?" A note of suspicion had entered PM Papa's voice.

"Why not?" said Rozy, who was a Darkmotherlandite after all.

PM Papa swung down from the bed and came to her, knelt in front of her on the floor. It was as though he was now enjoying him-self in this submissive role. "Do you love me?"

She stroked PM Papa's cheek with her long, lacquered fingers. His palms were resting on Rozy's knees. He was waiting for Rozy's signal to go ahead with the fellatio. "You know the answer to that."

"No, no," PM Papa said. "I need to hear it from your sweet lips."

Rozy slightly tapped his cheek. "Oh, come on, I am devoted to you."

"But do you love me?" PM Papa asked, his face showing some anxiety. He looked like a puppy, eager for some reassuring words.

"Of course, I love you, Papa," Rozy said, her eyes closed, her fingers caressing PM Papa's manboobs beneath the daura he was wearing (and boy, did he have manboobs).

"Oh Rozy, oh Rozy," PM Papa said, pressing his face into Rozy's stomach. He was mumbling about moving to the Palace of Glory, starting a family. His face moved down, but Rozy put her other palm over her crotch, like a chastity belt, and said, "Deputy Prime Minister?"

PM Papa pushed his head into Rozy's crotch again, trying to nuzzle his way past the palm. "Of course, whatever you say."

Rozy grabbed hold of PM Papa's hair and pulled his head up. "I'm serious," Rozy said.

"Oh, you've become a tough one, my maiya. There's nothing I'd love more, but pray tell, how will I justify it to the cabinet? How will I justify it to the Darkmotherlandites?"

"Like you have been justifying everything else. You know the cabinet will approve anything you say."

"What about the public?"

"Ah, the public," Rozy said, smiling. "Darkmotherlandites adore you, Papa. You know they do."

"They do, don't they?" PM Papa said, smiling.

Rozy continued her grip on his hair, and PM Papa continued to tilt his head up to look at Rozy. He was enjoying being dominated by her.

"And some of your own people don't like that the public adores you." Rozy let go of his head.

"That's why I passed the Treasonist Act. No Treasonist left unpunished."

Always admiring his own words. "Yes," Rozy said grimly. "But does the Treasonist Act catch everyone? Does it make sure that your eyes and ears are everywhere?"

"Are you hearing something I haven't heard? What aren't you telling me?"

Rozy closed her eyes, as though what she was about to say was difficult for her. Then she said it. The other day when she was passing through the hallway, she heard whispers coming from one of the rooms, but then when she tried to open the door, it was locked from the inside. The whispering stopped, and there were shushing sounds. Rozy quickly fetched the master key from the Gufa and opened the door, but by that time there was no one there.

Rozy could see that PM Papa wasn't totally convinced that the whispering meant much. But the seed had been planted. Now it just needed more watering. For the next couple of hours, Rozy kept the pressure on, returning to the topic, over and over again. She told PM

Papa that she was certain something was brewing. When PM Papa asked who, she was circumspect, saying that since she didn't have any evidence, she didn't want to malign anyone.

PM Papa was insistent. Rozy must tell him whom she suspected.

"But what reward will I get for telling? Nothing. You don't trust me."

PM Papa mulled that over for a moment. "You don't think the Gufa staff are plotting something, do you?" He took hold of Rozy's right foot and started massaging it.

Rozy withdrew her leg and said, "You should ask Bill Tamang."

PM Papa turned his head to observe her quizzically. "Bill Tamang? He knows something?"

Rozy inspected her fingernails.

Then it dawned on PM Papa. "Oh? You're not suggesting Bill Tamang is somehow involved?"

"I don't know," Rozy said in exasperation. "Why do you keep hounding me about things I'm unsure of?"

"Narisauna!" PM Papa said. "You suspect Bill Tamang's involvement?"

"I don't trust him."

"But he's been with me longer than you have."

Rozy threw her hand up in the air, as though to ask why she was even bothering with this conversation.

"Was Bill Tamang one of the whisperers?"

"Ask him," Rozy said. "Just ask him what he's up to."

PM Papa looked perplexed.

"And you're going to Amrika next month," Rozy said. "Wouldn't it be a good time for your enemies to stage something?" Rozy leaned so that her mouth was close to his right ear. "A koo maybe? Koo-koo?"

38.

The first place she went to look for Subhash was in the Tourist District, since that's where he'd run off to. She searched for him for a while, hoping she wouldn't run into any of the nokerchakers from the Asylum, who sometimes came here. Or run into Professor Shrestha herself, although her mother rarely left Beggar Street now. She saw some khateykids by a corner as they chatted in rudimentary Angrezi with tourists, and asked them if they knew Subhash and Rani. One mentioned the Old Buspark next to the Parade Ground. Subhash used to hang out there in a hotel before he came to the Tourist District—maybe he returned to that area again. "It's a funny looking hotel," the khateykid told her, but only after she gave him a few rupees. "All tilted, about to topple over." The khateykid added, "Like that Tower of Peeesa, ke, understand?" Kranti vaguely recalled Bhaskar also mentioning something about this hotel—was it Hotel Kyalifornya?

It was dark by the time Kranti took a taxi to the Old Buspark, and it didn't take her long to find Hotel Kyalifornya. The sign outside declared: "Check out—anytime. Leave—never." She walked into the lobby, which had a few rundown chairs and a counter behind which a young man stood. He sang, welcoming her to Hotel Kyalifornya.

Kranti remembered Dada singing this song in front of the bathroom mirror. She stood still, closing her eyes briefly, savoring the moment. A ticking had already started in her brain. The world was turning a bit brighter, and there was a jerkiness to things, as though the landscape was shifting slightly, every second, so she had to be on alert. She sensed she was about to have an episode. Bring it on, fucker, she said, to her mind, to the episode.

She asked the singing receptionist to give her a room.

He took her to the second floor and opened the door for her. "Did you just arrive in the Valley?" he asked.

"Yes."

"From where?"

Why does he want to know, mmm? She thought. She took a moment to say, "From the southeast."

"Oh, really," the man said, smiling. He introduced himself as Prashant. "I'm also a southeasterner. Whereabouts in the southeast?"

"I've lived in a lot of places."

Prashant assured her that he knew many places, and she kept nodding. He looked her up and down and said, "You look like you're from a good family. You could have found other hotels nearby. You might hear some noises here, at night. If you feel scared, come down to the lobby. I will be there all night."

She watched his face to see if he was proposing something, but he had a fresh, innocent look, hard to find in the Valley anymore.

Once she shut the door of her room, she questioned what she was doing. She realized that she was trembling slightly. She'd come here thinking that she'd look for Subhash, and here she was checked into a hotel in a part of town she barely knew, this part near the Old Buspark with bhalus and halwais and shady characters, where drugs changed hands and people got knifed in narrow alleys. But it was important that she locate Subhash, grill him about why he thought the killer was inside the Asylum.

She called the Asylum house phone from her mobile. She could have called Shambhogya's mobile—that would have been the proper thing to do, but she didn't want to have to explain anything to her sister-in-law. It was Mokshya who picked up the phone, and the lie came easily to Kranti: Professor Shrestha was quite ill and Kranti was going to stay at Beggar Street for a day or two to nurse her mother until she got better. "But Kranti hajur," Mokshya said. "Have you cleared this with Shambhogya-di?" Kranti said that she didn't need to clear anything with Shambhogya and that if Mokshya was so keen on "clearing things," she should clear them herself with Shambhogya-di.

Kranti hung up and went to the window. Out there was the Old Buspark, from where buses departed and arrived from across the country, now of course only to those places that were still reachable and those that the Yetifolk hadn't captured, at least according to the official media. She had never been outside the Valley, and she wondered what it would be like to board one of those buses and disappear.

She pulled up a chair by the window and sat there for about half an hour, watching the activities at the Old Buspark, wondering how many enemies she had out there, waiting for her to make a mistake. The night buses, it seemed, were about to take off, so engines were revving and vendors were roaming around with baskets of cucumbers, bhujiyas, chips, biscuits, and cold drinks. The eateries surrounding the bus stop were brightly lit and alive with customers. Here I am, she thought, in this smelly, dark room, and there is so much brightness outside.

When she began to hear moaning and thumping coming from next door, she felt the need to escape. She locked her room and went downstairs. Prashant asked her where she was going. She told him she needed to eat, and as she spoke, she realized that indeed she hadn't eaten since the morning, when she left the Asylum.

As she stepped out of the front door—Prashant was telling her about the good places to eat and cautioning her not to stay out too late, not venture into dark alleys—it became clear to her that her search for Subhash had to be carried out with utmost secrecy. There were people out there, forces that would want to cause her harm, perhaps even get rid of her.

Thoughts came in rapid succession, each thought substantiating what had gone before, amplifying it, aggravating it, but always pointing to its truth: perhaps the forces that would try to get rid of her for seeking Subhash were the same forces that had gotten rid of Bhaskar. She felt a flutter of wings near her right ear, and she quickly swatted it away. Poe would be a major pain right now—and if he showed up, she'd wring his neck. She stood still, waiting for him to manifest, but he didn't, so it looked like her swatting worked.

A man passed by her, looking at her as he entered Hotel Kyalifornya. She heard him say something to Prashant. Kranti couldn't catch what was said—a bus blasted its horn right as the man began speaking—but it was quite possible that people might already have been alerted to her presence. It would be best if she found a quiet, shadowy corner to eat, then quickly returned to her room to bolt the door. Yet the Old Buspark was bright, she could tell as she neared it, with glaring lights in shops shining on their gaudy wares. Hunger was cramping her stomach now, but she needed to be careful about where she ate. Men with dark intentions were surely lurking about, ready to haul her away. It occurred to her then that quiet, shadowy corners were not the best places for her, as the darkness would embolden these men to assault her.

She was now in the bustle of the Old Buspark. She had to remain watchful. Watch, fool! What she needed was a disguise to blend in with the crowd. Well, she already was wearing her stay-at-home dhoti, and with the bag strapped to her shoulder she looked like someone born to breathe the toxic fumes of the Old Buspark. But her face, her face! That was the main culprit. Flyers and posters with her photos could have already been distributed by Bhaskar's killer, who could have figured out that she was on a mission to learn his identity. The man who'd walked into Hotel Kyalifornya as she came out must have shown Prashant her photo. Kranti had to find a way to camou-flage her face. But how? Was she going to don a false mustache? The thought of herself with a mustache! But this is no laughing matter, Kranti, get a grip on yourself.

She scanned the width of the bus stop. She wondered if there was a chance, even a remote chance that Kabiraj was somewhere in the vicinity. She knew that he had a lot of friends—could it be that he needed a break from Laj Mahal and had come here? Perhaps he was sleeping in one of the buses around her? Oh, Kabiraj, you stupid dallu, where are you? I could use your help in searching for Subhash.

In the far diagonal corner was what looked like a clothing shop. She lowered her head and pretended as if she were searching for something on the ground and quickly walked toward it. The Old Buspark had many potholes, made worse by the Big Two and now filled with the previous night's rain. Her sandals got splattered with mud. On a rack outside the clothing store were sunglasses, and she chose an extra dark pair and paid for them. She put them on and the world became muted. Even the sounds around her became hushed, as though they were happening in the next neighborhood and not right here. Her eyes fell on some limp-looking caps and hats hanging from another rack. "How much are these?" she asked.

"These are men's hats," the shopkeeper said with an apologetic smile.

"How do you know that I'm not buying this for my husband?" Kranti asked the shopkeeper. "Or my brother?" Her voice became strident.

"I only pointed out that they're meant for men."

"Judgmental, aren't we?" She was loud now, and nearby shoppers were looking in her direction. She immediately realized the foolishness of her behavior. "I'll take this," she said, and put a pathetic-looking, wilting, mud-colored hat on her head.

She was aware that some people were watching her, trying to figure out who she was, why she was acting odd, but with her new hat and dark glasses, she felt more secure as she slowly roamed the Old Buspark. Every so often she slowly turned back to look, casually, as if she were merely enjoying the scenery, to check if anyone was following her.

She found an eatery where the fragrant smell of mutton and rice was wafting. A few benches had been placed outside the restaurant, next to a couple of buses that seemed to have finished their journeying for the day. Some people were sitting on the benches and eating their dinner, using their hands to scoop large portions of dal-bhat into their mouths. Others were eating biryani.

"Thali ko kati ho?" she asked in a soft voice. She'd learned her lesson from the hat shop.

The shopkeeper, who had a Muslim beard and cap, cupped his hand over his ear. "Can you speak a bit louder?"

The people eating dal-bhat on the benches glanced at Kranti. She went closer to the restaurateur and whispered, "How much for the thali?"

"Two thousand rupees," the shopkeeper said.

It was stunning how expensive everything was, even so long after the Big Two. But she had the money. Furthermore, this was still cheaper than what a slice of chocolate cake would be at Tato Chiso.

The restaurateur didn't take long in bringing her food, and she fell upon it with gusto. The mutton was stunningly delicious, and as she chomped on the food, she let out a big "ummmmm."

There was a family on the next bench: a father and mother and their little girl aged about seven or eight. The mother smiled at Kranti and said, "That tasty, is it, bahini?"

Kranti smiled back and nodded, then became cautious. She chewed slowly now, her face turned away from the family but still she was watching them from the corner of her eyes. The little girl came toward her and shyly observed her. Kranti pretended that the girl was not there and continued eating. But the girl stepped nearer, her eyes affixed on Kranti, swaying to some internal music. Little girl, go away! Kranti reprimanded her silently, but of course the little girl was obstinate like little girls always are. She appeared to be looking for Kranti's acknowledgement of her pathetic little existence, her *raison d'etre*, and there was simply no way Kranti was going to give it to her. I know how to play this game, little girl. I've been a little girl before. Then she thought: you better be careful. This girl might not be a little girl at all. She could be something else. She could be a decoy. Yes, a decoy! Kranti looked around again, to see if there was anyone, perhaps even the killer, studying her from a distance, ready to move in once the little girl finished her decoying.

"Sita!" the girl's mother called. "Come here, let the lady eat in peace." To Kranti, the girl's mother said, "Sorry about her. She likes people."

Kranti gave her an imperceptible nod.

"You eat with your dark glasses on?"

"Why? Is that a problem?"

The husband interjected. "There might be a problem with her eyes. You're no better than your daughter, being a nosy parker about strangers."

"I was just trying to be friendly."

The little girl mumbled something. She was still swaying to her internal music.

"What?" Kranti asked. "What are you babbling about?"

"I also want a hat."

"I'm not giving you my hat!" Kranti wasn't liking one bit how she had been drawn into a conversation with these country bumpkins. Yet this was the first time she'd felt a sense of kinship since her arrival in this area. Seated on this bench, on her last morsel of dal-bhat, the Asylum and Professor Shrestha seemed so far away. Don't think about them. If you don't think about them, they won't be real for you anymore. Just remember your mission: to find Subhash, to learn what he knows.

She wondered if this country bumpkin family would know about Subhash. The mother had a kind, puffy face, the father looked like a worrywart, the little girl a bit odd but happy.

But were they just waiting for her to utter the name Subhash and then suddenly a dozen men would appear from the shadows?

She had to take the risk. "Do you know one boy?" she asked the family. She delivered the question in a deadpan voice, as though she were addressing no one in particular.

"What does the boy look like?" the father asked.

"He's a khateykid, a classic case of the village boy forced to become the city son."

"I've seen several khateykids around the Old Buspark," the mother said.

"Have you been here for long then?" Kranti asked.

The woman seemed to warm up even more by Kranti's question. "We came here about a month ago," she said. "We are Bhureys. Our village was destroyed by the earthquake, more than half of its population gone. Now the Yetifolk have taken over, so we escaped."

"Oh, so you are one of those who's had Bhureyness thrust upon you," she said. She wondered if Kabiraj would have agreed with this assessment. There was an ache for Kabiraj in her, for his thick lips that were often dotted with spittle.

"What is that, nani?" the woman asked.

"Sexpear, sexpear," she said, then, not wishing to be misunderstood, she said, "No, no, not sex, not sex, I wouldn't utter such a thing in front of your little girl."

The woman exchanged a glance with her husband.

"So, your PM Papa has done nothing for you, eh?" Kranti said, feeling like she was channeling Bhaskar.

The father shushed her, then in a flat, loud voice he said, "Without PM Papa the entire Darkmotherland would have been under the Son of Yeti's control."

"Here in the Valley, we've been looking for work," the mother said. "But there is absolutely no work anywhere, only suffering." Then, realizing that her statement could be construed wrongly, she said, "But it's okay. Darkmotherland is in good hands."

"You expect to find work in the Old Buspark?" Kranti said.

"No, no," the mother said. "We've lived all over the Valley. Now we're thinking about returning to the village."

"What about the Yetifolk?"

The woman whispered, "We hear the Yetifolk don't harm those who pledge allegiance to them."

"Mother!" the father chastised her, then in a loud voice he said, "PM Papa jindabad!"

A chorus of voices around them chanted, automatically, "PM Papa jindabad!"

Kranti wondered if this family had been sent by the killer to spy on her. I understand your types well, she said mentally to the couple. You come here with your sob stories. Hard life in the village. Sob. No food to eat. Sob. Loan sharks after us. Sob. Yetifolk. Sob. You start crowding out everyone in the Valley and you lose your village innocence and you become scheming and greedy and manipulative like the Valleywallahs. You become spies and backstabbers. Then you build a five-story house and buy cars and you lie to everyone. You say that no, you are originally from the Valley itself, born and raised here, you say. You hide your village as if it were a shameful fact of your life.

I know your types like I know the back of my hand. So don't you try to fool me.

"But we're still afraid of the Yetifolk, so we are still here," the mother said, "wondering if there might be an opportunity that'll still open up. My husband is willing to work even though he's lost weight and has been suffering with back problems for many years now. The journey from our village nearly killed him. He was a respected schoolmaster in the village. Ali Miya here has given me a temporary job of cooking and washing dishes in exchange for meals for my family, but this is only temporary."

"Did you cook this mutton?" Kranti asked.

"Yes, I did."

"You are an excellent cook."

The father said, "She's always been very good."

"My Dada was an excellent cook," Kranti said. "He cooked mutton just like you, with plenty of garlic."

"Is he no longer? Is he in heaven?"

"He's in heaven, yes."

"May God bless his soul."

"Talk about God all you want," Kranti said, "just don't turn into a Fundy." She should watch her mouth; this family could be big Fundy supporters, and she'd be in a whole lot of trouble.

"We are just simple common folk," the mother said. "We believe in live and let live."

"Live and let die," Kranti said.

"What?"

"It's a song from my teenage years," Kranti said. The words came to her, and she sang it softly, as though she were channeling Dada.

Singing that bit, even though it was so nihilistic, made her feel good because it reminded her of Dada.

"Hoina," the father said. "My Angrezi isn't that great, but are you saying you should let others die?"

"It's talking about how the world is," Kranti said. "And it's taking a jab at your God."

"So you are not a Bhurey?" the woman asked. "You look like an educated woman, from a good family."

What was with the people of this country, Kranti thought, with their constant talk of good families? Yes, I come from a good family, she wanted to say, but my life turned bad. I even married a great family, a fabulous family, a supercalifragilisticexpialidocious family, and here I am, talking with Bhureys, looking for a khateykid.

Kranti finished eating, gave a loud burp—she was turning into a rube—and paid Ali Miya. The little girl was once again eyeing her, so she said, "What? You want some money?" She knelt in front of the girl. "Enough with this shyness," she said. "You need to speak up if you want something. Girls have to work twice as hard. I'm sorry, but that's the way the world is."

"She's always been shy," the father said.

"Stop saying that," Kranti said. "You've made her this way, don't you see? Don't force your daughter into a preordained fate. She's shy, she has to be a revolutionary—poppycock! She has to be nothing she doesn't want to be." To the girl she said, "What do you want? Speak up. Speak up!"

"I want ice cream."

"Then ice cream you shall have."

Kranti took the girl's hand and marched her to the next stall, where she got her an ice cream bar. Later, as they watched the girl slurp on the ice cream, clouds began to rumble up above. Kranti asked them where they slept at night. The mother pointed to the small area under the restaurant's awning. What if, Kranti thought, someone comes and violates the mother? Or even the little girl? She made a decision and told the family that they were going to come with her that night to sleep in Hotel Kyalifornya. The parents protested, but Kranti wouldn't take no for an answer, saying that she didn't want the girl to catch cold in the rain.

After some protestations, the mother and the father finally agreed, although before they agreed, they whispered to each other, and Kranti thought she heard the father say, "Somewhat of a cuckoo bird," but she couldn't tell whether that was a voice inside of her instead or the husband's.

"Don't tell Ali Miya that you're going with me," Kranti told the mother in a low voice. "Just tell him that you've found a place to crash for the night, that you'll return tomorrow morning to cook and do the dishes."

The mother told Ali Miya, who eyed Kranti, then he begrudgingly let them go.

Kranti and the family started making their way across the station. Now Kranti was filled with a mission. But she still had to be careful. The crowd in the Old Buspark had lessened, partly because it was late and partly due to the threat of rain, but there were still people milling about. Bus drivers were relaxing inside their buses, or were perched on their roofs drinking liquor, making catcalls at women who came into view. If the Fundys walked by, the drivers hid their bottles and whistled innocently into the night.

"Ah, I'd love to scale the peaks of your titties," they catcalled to a teenage girl passing by.

When they saw Kranti and the family, there were a few appreciative whistles.

"Who is this old-time beauty?" they said. "And why is she hiding her face in that hideous hat?" One driver nimbly jumped off the roof and came close to them. He was a scrawny fellow, with a gaunt face and bulging eyes. Like a bad guy in a film, he took a swaying swig of his rum before he spoke to Kranti, "You look like you've just arrived from a movie set. Why don't you take off your glasses and your hat? So we can behold your fetching face and dream of you tonight?"

"With our hands on our crotches?" said one of his buddies from the roof.

"Now, look, brothers," the father said.

Another bus driver jumped off the roof and came toward them. "What seems to be the problem, old father?"

"We don't want any trouble."

The second bus driver stood very close to the father, who became quiet.

"Goondagirdi?" Kranti said.

"We're not hooligans," the driver said. "We're ashiks, lovers."

Kranti kicked him in the shin. The driver buckled and fell to the ground. Two more drivers jumped from the roof. Kranti took a karate stance: legs spread apart, arms in front of her in a defensive posture. An animalistic fierceness had come into her; along with it a sharp-ened sense of smell. She sniffed the air.

"Jackie Chan, here I come," a bus driver said and strode toward her.

Kranti did some very rapid movements with her hands, her throat producing blood-curdling sounds; the driver received a blow to his shoulder and a slap to the chin.

"Arre!" another driver said. "She's a madwoman."

Kranti's heart was pounding. She was less afraid of these men than the fact that the commotion had attracted a crowd, which meant that someone—the killer?—could recognize her. She scanned the faces to see if there was anyone whispering into a phone or perhaps even a walkie-talkie, identifying her, calling for backup. The bus drivers converged upon her and she was thrown to the ground, but by then a couple of Fundys had come between the goons and her. "Arre, what is this? Beating up on a woman?" the Fundys shouted, and other men in the area also began to circle the goons, crying about a woman being molested in broad daylight, even though it was night. The bus drivers made a hasty retreat, disappearing into the shadows of Diamond Park and the Parade Ground. The Fundys, two men with dark beards and shawls with mantras printed like flies on them, looked triumphant. Kranti picked herself up off the ground. Her clothes were muddy. Her left cheek felt swollen—had she been slapped? She found her hat, dusted it, and put it back on, afraid that any moment someone would come to her and say, "You're Kranti, aren't you? The Ghimirey buhari?"

The Fundys began to scold Kranti, asking her whether she was a

Christian, given her ridiculous hat. "And what are you doing fighting men at night?" they queried. "You are not a honey, are you?" They raised their eyebrows.

"Fuck off," she told them. "So what if I am? Why don't you go home and call your own mothers and sisters honeys."

"Arre, she has a mouth on her!" one Fundy said and raised his hand as though to strike her.

The crowd protested.

"Go ahead," Kranti said, curling her upper lip. "Make my day."

The Fundy took a step back, visibly shocked. "Here we are, we saved you, and you're quoting Clint Eastwood-ji? Ingrate!"

"No one asked for your help, Mr. Holier Than Thou," Kranti said. "I'd have handled those drivers on my own. And I'll handle you Fundys on my own."

The crowd was stunned into silence. They'd never heard anyone speak to Fundys like this. Then there were some guffaws and chortles. Finally, someone had the courage to shout, "Leave her alone. She's gone through enough already."

The Fundys turned sharply toward that voice. But they sensed a slightly tense mood in the faces that surrounded them, and they muttered to themselves.

She grabbed the little girl's hand, said, "Come!" to her parents, and led them toward Hotel Kyalifornya.

The little girl's family knew that Kranti wasn't from the southeast, as she'd claimed; that she was from somewhere in the Valley, that she was in hiding. They had even guessed that she was from a well-to-do family, that she was an unhappy woman who had taken refuge in this shady part of town.

That night she mumbled in her sleep and they listened to her, hoping to find clues about who she was, what she was. But her mumblings were illogical, incoherent, like a child's ramblings:

"The sunlight is like butter."

"A mother's love is a love greater than love for a nation."

"Schoolchildren in uniform—a delight to see."

"One thousand and one nokerchakers."

She thrashed in her sleep, cried out what sounded like "Dada" and "Bhaskar" and "Kabiraj," and, most frequently, "Subhash."

A NEW BODY

39.

So the seed was planted. PM Papa became more guarded around Bill Tamang. He observed Bill Tamang closely, and a couple of times when PM Papa's eyes met those of Rozy's while in Bill Tamang's presence, Rozy looked away, in an I-told-you-so manner, even though what Bill Tamang might have been saying or doing was quite innocuous. PM Papa began snapping at Bill Tamang for no apparent reason. With PM Papa, Rozy was at times emotionally aloof, at other times affectionate. She knew it drove him crazy, this not knowing what state of mind he'd find her in. Thus, he was left in a constant state of cajoling and wheedling, wanting to please Rozy.

Rozy was discovering her own power, and it was greater than what she had anticipated it to be, but it was coming to her in slow increments, almost painfully slow, she thought, as though she was growing into a new body, inch by inch.

One morning Rozy announced to the staff that PM Papa wanted an emergency staff meeting that afternoon. Bill Tamang wasn't in the Lion Palace; he had gone with Prapu Ganda to visit some ministries to inspect the installation of new statues of PM Papa on their premises.

Rozy made the announcement in the main office outside the Gufa. The staff sat around a large table; Rozy sat at its head. The staff—there were about fifteen or so—were terrified. Jungey's painting on the wall looked at them ferociously, as if telling them that they ought to be terrified. They all knew that at this point in Darkmotherland, Rozy had more access to PM Papa's mind than anyone else, even Shrimati Papa, who was still hiding with her maiti.

"PM Papa is not happy," Rozy told the Gufa staff upon their constant pestering.

"What happened? Did we do something wrong?" Color drained from their faces. A couple of them looked like they were ready to cry. Visions of being fired passed through their minds—the shame, the embarrassment. Their jobs were a source of enormous prestige for them among their friends and relatives; after all, how many people could say they worked for PM Papa in the Lion Palace? But it could be more than merely being fired. Their properties could be confiscated; they could be transferred to remote districts, or even sent to the GULA.

"All that whispering and fush-phush, tiptoeing and shushing, and eye-signaling," Rozy said. "PM Papa is fed up with it."

At once there was intense pleading and whining and blame-deflecting, which in other circumstances would have left Rozy in stitches. This time she managed to maintain a grim face and ordered, "Be quiet!"

There was pin-drop silence, then some shuffling of feet and guilty, imploring looks. Rozy observed them one by one. "Things have to change in the Gufa." She stood, and suddenly they noticed that in her hand was PM Papa's cricket bat. Rozy inspected the cricket bat, as though inspecting whether it was up to whatever task it was meant to do. Although they hadn't actually witnessed what had happened during the Rakshya Garam cricket bat incident, the staff had heard the sounds—the thwack, thwack of the bat hitting the minister's head—from the next room, and later had to help with the cleaning.

With the bat propped on her right shoulder, Rozy walked around the table, slowly, pausing near each staff member. "For too long you have acted like whispering, conniving children, and you have sat around and dawdled and loitered and shilly-shallied. All of that is going to change now."

There was no question among PM Papa's staff that they had committed a grave error. But they were too afraid to ask for clarification, afraid that if they asked what their crime was, it would end up amplifying the nature of that crime, and the cricket bat would come descending down on their heads. That they had erred in a major way was a foregone conclusion now. The question was: What would the punishment be? Whisperers and connivers, Rozy had called them. Did that mean that they could now be labeled as Treasonists? Or had they already been labeled? One of them had already peed in his pants, a trickle, enough that it didn't show but left a dampness on the insides of his thighs.

"I don't know what punishment PM Papa has in mind for you," Rozy said, "but it can't be good." She swung the bat in the air lightly, making a whoosh-whoosh sound.

"Rozy Miss, we love and adore PM Papa," they said, "and we want to serve him until our dying days."

"Not only us," one staff member added. "Our children and our grandchildren pledge to serve PM Papa, and his children and grandchildren, until they die."

"So, you all are loyal to PM Papa?" Rozy asked.

"Yes, yes," the staff cried in unison, seeing a ray of sunshine inside their anxiety-numbed minds. "PM Papa jindabad!" they chanted and continued chanting until Rozy mock-slashed her throat, which brought the chants to an abrupt stop.

"Are all of you going to stop your whispering and conniving?"

"Yes! Yes! Yes!"

"From now on you report directly to me."

"To you?" they asked. "And Bill Tamang Sir?"

"To me," Rozy said. She observed them again, as though she doubted they could follow this simple instruction.

"Is Bill Tamang Sir being transferred?" one of them meekly asked.

Without answering, Rozy sashayed back to into the InnerGufa.

"Fire Bill Tamang," Rozy said to PM Papa in the InnerGufa.

"Fire him? Did you discover something?" PM Papa eyed the cricket bat Rozy had just put on the coffee table in front of the couch. He had formally gifted the bat to Rozy at the Humble Abode after the game the other day, declaring her as Rozy the Cricketeer. Had she been playing in the hallways of the Lion Palace?

"I just talked to the staff. There's something going on," Rozy said, coming to sit on his lap.

"What, maiya?"

"Do you really want to know?" Rozy asked, blowing softly into his face, as though she were soothing away his worries, which he loved. "Bill Tamang has forbidden the staff to say PM Papa jindabad in his presence." It sounded trivial when she said this, but she knew that saying something too big might lead to complete dismissal by PM Papa.

PM Papa stared at her. "He did? Bill Tamang?"

"Yes, your favorite Bill Tamang, the one you've known longer than you've known me."

PM Papa stroked Rozy's arm. "Do you want me to fire him? But if I do, how will I find a replacement quickly?"

"Sagar," Rozy said.

"Sagar?"

"Sagar Rajbhandari."

"That Sagar? Are you sure he's qualified for this position?"

"You think Bill Tamang is qualified? The man knows nothing." Rozy pretended to wriggle out of his lap, but PM Papa held on tightly.

"Bill Tamang has been with me for a long time. He's led a hard life."

Rozy stroked PM Papa's cheek. "Bichara! My PM Papa is getting all teary-eyed now?"

"Hard to believe Bill Tamang would do this," PM Papa said, shaking his head. "What is wrong with these people? When they have it so good?"

"He's jealous of me."

PM Papa leaned his head back. "Really?"

"He's never liked that you're spending so much time with me. He's hated me from the start."

"Then he must go," PM Papa said.

Rozy paused. "You want me to do it? Fire him?"

PM Papa nodded. "I can't bring myself to look at his face anymore. If I see him, I will become angrier." He paused, as though he was rethinking his decision. "No, actually, confiscate his home. We need to send a message."

"Doesn't he have a wife and kids?" Rozy said, suddenly unsure about this course of action. "Oh, and a mother who's going senile."

"I know," PM Papa said. "But a betrayal is a betrayal. He can't occupy that position anymore, and he needs to be punished."

"He'll want to see you, Papa," Rozy said. "He'll want to plead and whine with you."

"Call Papa's Patriots. Let them do this work for us. It'll be easier."

—

When Bill Tamang returned from a meeting at the ministries, five Papa's Patriots were waiting for him. It only took him a few seconds to realize what was happening. He looked at Rozy, half beseechingly, but he didn't plead or whine. The rest of PM Papa's staff was solemnly watching. None of them pitied him. The fact that he was being hauled away meant that they were safe, at least for the moment.

Papa's Patriots escorted him to his house and told him that he had a few minutes to gather his valuables. His demented mother thought that the boys were her sons and asked if they had eaten their morning rice.

"No, mother, we haven't," they said. "But we will as soon as this task is over."

The old lady asked where they were taking her son and the family.

"To paradise," Papa's Patriots said.

The old lady clapped her hands and gave them a toothless grin. She even attempted to hug them. Bill Tamang, who was putting some clothes in a bag, said, "Don't you all have mothers?" His wife and two children were crying, saying they didn't want to go to paradise. The old lady asked through whose grace were they going to paradise? When Papa's Patriots said PM Papa, the old lady became overwhelmed with emotion and genuflected and beseeched the heavens with her arms. "God bless PM Papa," she said, wiping her tears.

Papa's Patriots dumped Bill Tamang and his family in Bhurey Paradise.

A chair was placed for Rozy next to PM Papa during cabinet meetings. She sported a grimmer face now. Gone were her coquettish manners from earlier, those facades of Oh-I-don't-know-if-I'm-qualified-to-speak-about-this. Now when she spoke, she spoke sternly, as though she were tired of the incompetence and tomfoolery in the Rajjya administration. PM Papa was part bemused, part worried by her. He squelched any misgivings he had about the authority with which she was conducting herself in these meetings. And it was clear that the others—the ministers, the secretaries—were developing a new deference for her. They snuck glances toward her frequently, even when she wasn't speaking, as if to gauge her thoughts. They all knew what had happened with Bill Tamang. They knew Rozy was behind it, but they had also been fed the information that Bill Tamang had turned against PM Papa. They'd been told that he might even have been scheming a plot to oust PM Papa.

During a cabinet meeting, after PM Papa had left early to spend time with Rozy, Minister of Agriculture Kisan Karmi said, "Bill Tamang is lucky he wasn't declared a Treasonist. I think PM Papa spared him only because he's worked for PM Papa for so long. At least he still has his family. And let's be honest. Bhurey Paradise isn't a bad place to live." The members of Papa's cabinet believed in what they said about Bhurey Paradise, and they cited evidence to back up their claim. The Rajjya had recently distributed tarpaulins to put over the tent tops in anticipation of a freezing winter. New pumping dharas had been installed at strategic spots in the Parade Ground and in Diamond Park for easy access to water, and the old taps that sputtered out muddy water had been repaired. A tented medical dispensary had also opened up in the middle of the Parade Ground, with a Red Cross flag proudly flying in the air, even though the dispensary was sparsely stocked, and most of the medicine they carried had long expired.

"Why are they carrying expired medicine?" some Darkmother-landites asked.

"Why not?" others answered. "Let's not discriminate against expired medicine. We are a third-world country, where expired medicine gets a new life."

So, PM Papa's cabinet concluded, Bill Tamang wasn't in a bad place, as far as bad places went. Yes, his life would be harder now, what with those children and a demented mother, but he should have been careful about going against PM Papa.

The Gufa staff knew now, beyond any doubt, that to curry favor with PM Papa, they had to first please Rozy, who could then put in a word for them with PM Papa in the InnerGufa. Often Rozy made unilateral decisions about the staff, and a couple of weeks after Bill Tamang's firing it was obvious that Rozy had assumed the position of Chief Secretary. Or at minimum, Acting Chief Secretary.

"If Bill Tamang can do this job, any donkey can do this job," Rozy told PM Papa in the InnerGufa. PM Papa had just sucked her off, and Rozy had helped him unload with a handjob. Both were lying on the bed, watching their mirror-selves on the ceiling. "But I am capable of even more than this. I need to be more, Papa."

PM Papa became somber. "What you are asking from me will piss off a lot of people."

"Since when did you become afraid of pissing off people?"

"I'm not afraid," PM Papa said indignantly.

"You're afraid," she said, talking to the PM Papa on the ceiling, not the one next to her. "There's no other reason for it."

"If I were afraid, would I be in the Lion Palace right now?" PM Papa too was now talking to the Rozy on the ceiling.

"Make me the Deputy PM. It'll be good for you. I'll be good for you, for us. It'll be good for Darkmotherland." Talking to the PM Papa on the ceiling felt like a performance, as though she were on stage.

PM Papa became silent. Then he said. "All right, but it won't be easy. I'm taking a considerable risk here."

"What risk?" Rozy said. "You are PM Papa. Look what you've been able to achieve. Look at what you've gotten away with."

"You are so much meaner than before, maiya."

And you've become weaker, thought Rozy. She looked away from the ceiling toward him, then sidled up to him and rubbed her body against his. "Once you make me the Deputy Prime Minister," Rozy said, "it will be amazing, won't it? They will call us Paprozy. The Paprozy Administration."

"Paprozy," PM Papa whispered, liking how it sounded. "Paprozy," he said, then said it again, as he nibbled on Rozy's ear.

⁓

The next morning, Kranti looked for Subhash in the Old Buspark area. She quietly asked around, sometimes barely mumbling his name. But she had only his first name to go by, no last name, no pedigree. She knew he was from the western hills, somewhere near where the Founding Father first launched his mission to unify Darkmotherland. "A boy named Subhash from the western hills?" people said. "You need to give us more." When they asked for more, she became suspicious of them.

Late in the morning a boy in his teens—or perhaps more a young man, as he had an adult face—came to her as she was strolling the Old Buspark, arms crossed at her chest, incognito in her sunglasses, and her Indiana Jones hat pulled down over her forehead. Indiana Jones's garlfren, some shopkeepers were already calling her.

"Are you looking for a boy named Subhash?" the boy-man asked.

She stopped, standing still, like children do when they play statue. "Who wants to know?" she asked, her mouth barely moving.

"No one," he said, trying hard to hide his smirk, thinking: this one is like a cartoon character. "I heard that you were looking for a boy named Subhash, and I was wondering if it was someone I knew. I used to know a Subhash here."

"Who sent you?"

"Mukeshbro."

Why did that name sound familiar? "Mukesh what?" she asked.

"Bro. It means brother in Angrezi."

The puny fucker was teaching her Angrezi! It was only a few seconds before she had a vision of a coat of some sort, garishly colored, odd speech, jerky movements. Then it came to her: the pimp from Bhurey Paradise. Kraymah, he called himself, after a TV show.

"Mukeshbro is a big man in town," the boy-man said. "A very good friend of IGP Chhetri. Soon you'll be hearing even more about Mukeshbro."

Why was it that in Darkmotherland every Tom, Dick, and Mukeshbro was a big man, or was on this way to becoming a big man, or was already a big man on his way to becoming an even bigger man? Why not more Dada, Bhaskar, or Kabiraj, small men with aspirations of becoming even smaller, humbler men?

The boy-man asked her what her name was, and unwilling to give him her own name, she said, "Shambhogya." He clapped, and said he'd never heard such a fancy name before. He introduced himself as Riteshbro. She asked him where Subhash was, but cautioned him that others couldn't know that she was looking for him. Riteshbro thought for a moment and said that Mukeshbro would surely know where Subhash was. Would she be willing to follow Riteshbro to him?

The flat was a three-storied building at the edge of the neighborhood where Hotel Kyalifornya was, near Tiger Market. Riteshbro had brought her here through a maze of alleys that had confused her. "Where are we?" she kept asking him, and he kept saying, "We're nearly there, we're nearly there." After a while she didn't know where east was, where west was, which direction Hotel Kyalifornya was, which direction the Asylum was. The alleys seemed to get narrower and narrower, more zigzaggy and meandering. But even in these narrow lanes there were Bhureys, tented by the side of the house. People hurried past her, as though they were trying to get somewhere fast. The houses around her seemed to get taller, blocking the sunlight. In the windows above, heads and arms poked out, murmuring about her and pointing at her.

At one point, she realized that they'd passed an area they'd already passed before: she recognized a woman she'd glimpsed through a doorway, cooking in her firewood kitchen. "We're moving around in circles," she told Riteshbro angrily.

"That's a different woman, different kitchen." He said, "Lot of people get confused here, but you don't step into the same river twice."

Finally, standing before a three-storied building, he said, "We're here." A drain ran alongside the house, throwing a stink into the air. People who squeezed past them covered their noses with their hankies.

"This doesn't feel right," she said. She took off her hat because her forehead was damp with sweat and removed her dark glasses so she could see better.

"You look beautiful without your hat and glasses," Riteshbro said.

"If this is a trap," she said, "I'm going to cut your tongue off." From her bag she took out a small Sweej Army knife she'd bought at the Old Buspark. Now she wished that she had a bigger knife in her hand. This knife would barely cut this boy's nails. Was he even a boy? He acted like a man and spoke like one, with a deep, gravelly voice.

Upstairs, in a small room, Mukeshbro was sitting on the bed with a skinny khaireyni. They were smoking ganja. "And who is this beauty?" Mukeshbro asked. Riteshbro said that her name was Shambhogya, the one to be enjoyed or used.

"Giddyup!" Mukeshbro said, grinning. "Then we shall both enjoy her and use her, as her name implies."

The khaireyni laughed, as though she understood, but it became clear to Kranti shortly that the woman only spoke a smattering of Darkmotherlandese.

"Why do you look familiar?" Mukeshbro asked, hand on chin. "Were you one of my honeys?" He laughed. "Of course, if you were a honey of mine, I'd have remembered. I never forget my honeys."

"Honey," the khaireyni said to Mukeshbro, "pass me the light. My doobie is snuffed out."

Mukeshbro passed her the light, then patted the mattress next to him, but of course Kranti didn't go. "Oh, come on, dearie," Mukeshbro said. "I ain't bitin'."

What was with these idiots and their dearie business? First Poe, now this pimpy joe.

Mukeshbro asked Riteshbro whether he'd gone to IGP Chhetri to deliver a document. Riteshbro said he had. Mukeshbro asked him whether IGP Chhetri said anything in return. Riteshbro responded that IGP Chhetri said he expected the special Khadi clients to arrive next month at the hotel, and that they wouldn't stay long and "the special items" needed to be ready. "Everything will be super ready," Mukeshbro said. "I've got everything under control." Mukeshbro and Riteshbro were talking partly in codes, and Kranti got impatient.

"Your man-boy," Kranti said, pointing at Riteshbro, "said you know where Subhash is."

"Why are you looking for Subhash?" Mukeshbro asked.

"He's my . . . He's a . . ." Kranti didn't know what to say. She somehow felt that to say anything more to this dirty man would sully any relationship she had with Subhash. She knew this pimp was not a good man.

"Hold on," Mukesh said, peering at her face. "You're—aren't you the Poet King's garlfren? The widow? The horny widow?"

"Call me what you like," Kranti said. "Just tell me where Subhash is. And if you can't, I'll go on my merry way."

The khaireyni snickered. "The merry widow."

"Oh, that Subhash," Mukeshbro said. "Is he still pining after that Jharana?"

Another name that sounded familiar. Jharana. Tato Chiso.

Waterfall. Mocha Java. Bhaskar's voice saying that Jharana was the name of the honey who'd loved Subhash and had been murdered. By a pimp.

"Oh, so you're that nasty halwai," Kranti said.

Mukesh stared at her, "What, my pretty? Oh, I see. Is that puny fucker still going around blaming me for what happened to that bitch?"

"Do you know where he is? If not, I'm leaving."

"What's the hurry?" the khaireyni said. She'd been smoking non-stop since Kranti's arrival, and her head now seemed to dissolve and lose focus in the smoke swirling around her.

"Fucking assholes," Kranti said. "Wasting my time." She turned and pushed the door to leave, but it didn't budge. It was locked from the outside. Then she noticed that Riteshbro wasn't in the room. He must have left and locked it from the outside. She kicked the door; it didn't budge, but she did feel the sharp pain of a stubbed toe.

Mukeshbro stood from his bed, but the way he was tottering, he was smoked out of his mind—it just wasn't as obvious when he was sitting.

"Chill, my pretty," he said to Kranti. "Smoke some cannabis." He came toward her, swaying, and lurched and grabbed at her. There was a scuffle.

She felt a sting on the face—the pimp had slapped her. Kranti kicked him in the groin. Mukeshbro grabbed his crotch and kneeled, his mouth open in a silent *wow, wow.*

"Randi!" the khaireyni said in Darkmotherlandese, leaping from the bed, with surprising agility for a shit-stoned woman. But Kranti pushed her and she fell back on the bed and instantly began bawling.

The door opened an inch. Riteshbro. He was probably checking to see if it was Kranti who was bawling. Kranti pushed at the door, hard, with both her palms, until it swung outward, slamming Riteshbro's face.

"Fucking halwai's sidekick!" Kranti shouted and made her escape.

When she returned to Hotel Kyalifornya around midday, feeling depleted and bruised, she went directly to the reception desk and paid Prashant a week's stay in advance. When Prashant said that she didn't need to, she insisted. Then, she left the hotel.

Her inability to find Subhash had further confirmed her feeling that he knew something, a dark truth that she needed to uncover. She didn't want to think too hard about what that truth might be because it made her anxious to even consider the possibilities. She wished Kabiraj was with her so she could tell him everything, and enlist his help in finding Subhash. That damn Kabiraj! How long might he be jailed for his stupid *Howl?* She hoped that the Rajjya didn't think Kabiraj's crime was big enough to warrant a long imprisonment. She also hoped that he wasn't taken to a labor camp, like those beggars she'd seen the other day near Diamond Park. Kranti's idea of labor camps came from the Soviet-era camps in Siberia, with men in crumpled jackets digging in the freezing cold. Or people working for excruciatingly long hours in a grim factory. Or in Nazi camps where Jews in striped shirts dug trenches for their own graves. What kind of a labor camp were they running here in Darkmotherland? What were they making? Perhaps these beggars and prisoners were forced to repair roads in the mountains damaged by the Big Two? Kranti imagined men and women hammering away at pebbles and stones by the side of the road. And now khateykids were being used for the same?

Subhash! Could it be that the reason she couldn't find Subhash was because he had been taken to a GULA?

40.

When General Tso ran into Rozy at the Lion Palace, he began to bow to her slightly, just a small tilt of his head so that no one other than Rozy would notice. General Tso had asked Darkmother, in his dream, how he should acknowledge her when she appeared to him in the mortal form of Rozy.

"Mortal?" Darkmother laughed and repeated, "Mortal? I am never mortal, even when I appear to you humans in your pathetic forms." Then Darkmother's tone turned affectionate. "Chora Dinesh," she said, and General Tso was thrown back to his childhood, when that term of endearment was often used by his mother and grandmother back in the village. In Darkmother's affectionate "Chora Dinesh" he heard the loving voices of the kind women who had been such a strong presence in his life, a presence no woman had been able to fulfill for him until now. That love was real, and this love from Darkmother was very real. General Tso, with tears flowing down his cheeks, understood that it was not only Darkmother who was speaking to him but also his mother and his grandmother.

"Dinesh babu," Darkmother said. "Just acknowledge me. Don't let the others see you."

And that's what General Tso did.

Until now, General Tso had remained neutral when it came to Rozy, as though he didn't have any opinions about his boss's lover, even though he thought, like many, that homosexuality was an abomination. Once Rozy started transitioning, General Tso was puzzled, but had still convinced himself that it was none of his business who Rozy was, or what Rozy was becoming, as long as PM Papa trusted her. General Tso believed that PM Papa was the right man at the right time for Darkmotherland. General Tso believed in order, and PM Papa had restored order in a very dark time in the country. General Tso was devoted to PM Papa, but he was more devoted to Darkmother. He would do anything for Darkmother.

At first Rozy didn't understand General Tso's deference, then she realized that something had shifted inside him, and it had to do with her. It was positive, this something. She didn't know exactly what it was, but the quality of the energy between the two of them had changed. Before, it was dumb, uninterested, neutral, and now it was infused with warmth, unspoken affinity, and reverence. The realization of the last quality made Rozy thoughtful. Even with PM Papa in the room, as the two men conferred, or when PM Papa addressed General Tso, or when General Tso spoke to PM Papa, Rozy sensed that General Tso's attention was on her—an upward gaze, a tilt of the head, a super-attentive posture, a newly awed discovery, as though the General were looking for guidance. If Rozy moved a few feet away, General Tso's awareness followed her, not with his eyes, which remained focused on PM Papa or whomever he was talking to, but with an inner eye that was longing and devotional.

Does he want to fuck me? She dismissed this thought instantly. It was not a sexual gaze. General Tso was not a sexual creature—that had been clear right from the start. He was a strange, asexual man, a bachelor for life, from what she'd heard. A man of steel. A warrior with a purpose. His single-minded devotion to the army had made him rapidly rise through the ranks. And it was during those years when PM Papa was making incursions into the political world and General Tso was turning into an admired military leader that they had come together. Without General Tso's help, PM Papa wouldn't have been able to grab and maintain power. The Loyal Army Dais were loyal to PM Papa because they were loyal to General Tso, who in turn was loyal to PM Papa.

Kranti hadn't meant to go there, but that afternoon as she searched for Subhash, hoping that the folks at the Asylum hadn't called Beggar

Street and discovered that she'd never been there, she ended up out-side the Supreme Adalat. A large crowd had already gathered in the compound of the highest court in the land, with people spilling over to the street. The Loyal Army Dais were there, but they weren't doing anything to control the crowd. The Rajjya had realized that during such events, the more the crowd was unmanaged, the more the general populace became afraid. An unmanaged crowd gave the appearance of street justice, as if the public itself had come to the conclusion that the accused was guilty of treason. An unmanaged crowd provided moral indignation, thereby granting a conclusive stamp to the guilt of the accused pronounced by the judges inside. Wig-wearing judges. Yes, the kind worn by the judges in England.

Why wig-wearing?

Why not wig-wearing? A judge wearing a traditional Darkmother-landite topi looked a lot less authoritative than a judge wearing an Angrezi wig.

What was Dharma Adhikari's crime? Treason. What did he do? No one knew.

The arrest of one of PM Papa's most trusted sycophants had taken Darkmotherland by surprise. Immediately after Papakoo, PM Papa had brought him into his cabinet, appointing him the Home Min-ister. The two were frequently seen together at functions, ceremonies, and around the table in important meetings, with Dharma Adhikari often seated right next to PM Papa. Dharma Adhikari had been at the forefront of crushing the Gang of Four, and had personally super-vised the Palace High Beheadings. People remembered watching live videos of him knocking on the doors of the enemies of PM Papa and hauling them away to jail. Now he was being arrested as a Treasonist.

The footage of his arrest was shown on the six A.M. newscast on Motherland TV, narrated by Hom Bokaw with his slurred speech. There was Dharma Adhikari, being led away by the Loyal Army Dais from his quarters at four A.M. Watching him, Kranti remembered that day in the Lion Palace when she and Bhaskar had gone to see PM Papa. Dharma Adhikari had briefly come into the Gufa for a signature. PM Papa had said that his loyalty was like that of a dog's. What had happened?

The entire Valley was abuzz with the news. At eight A.M. it was announced that Dharma Adhikari was to stand trial that afternoon in the Supreme Adalat. It had become the norm, this quick justice. Arrest in the morning, trial in the afternoon, which invariably led to the verdict of guilty, then imprisonment by the evening. Many political prisoners were said to be incarcerated in Khor, the massive jail beneath the Durbar thought to have been built during the Shades-Wearing King's reign. He was the one with autocratic tendencies, and the Durbar had been constructed during his time. But it was also equally possible that Khor was built during the time of the subsequent Benign King. People said that the Benign King's benign appearance was only that, an appearance, and that he too had decimated his political enemies who had perished in Khor.

Under PM Papa, it was rumored that Khor was already crammed with prisoners. Some were kept there for a few days after the trial, then taken out and executed with much fanfare in public, which seemed to thirst more and more for the beheadings or hangings.

Kranti was going to shove her way past the crowd that had spilled outside the Supreme Adalat gate when she was pushed inside the gate by those around her badly wanting to get inside. Trapped in a swirl of bodies, she found herself moving closer and closer to the big carved doors of the court. "No, no, I don't want to go in," she shouted, thinking of Subhash, but the people around her were laughing and swirling as though they were performing some type of a whirling dervish. Up the steps she was pushed, until she was inside the courtroom. It happened quickly: one moment she was outside on the street, and the next she was inside, looking at the three judges on their benches, wearing massive wigs. The wigs were so big that they resembled snowy animals perched on top of these brown-skinned men. Their mean eyes, pursed lips, and the limbs and tails of the wig-animals hung down to the floor. "Hoarder! Hoarder!" all three men said at once, banging their gavels in what sounded like vaguely Angrezi accents to Kranti.

"Hoarder! Hoarder!" she mimicked to herself, trying to figure out their accents. Those people around her shushed her. "Pfft!" she said back to them. "I don't even want to be here."

But before she could elaborate, shouts of "Treasonist! Traitor! Gaddhar!" were heard, and Dharma Adhikari, the now ex-Home Minister with a giraffe-like neck, was brought into the courtroom through a side door. He was in handcuffs, and judging from his dancing walk (Kranti couldn't see below his knees), in feet cuffs. He was taken to the dock, his head hanging low.

"Proceed, wakilji," the chief judge in the middle said to a lawyer in a shabby black gown and a wig that was obviously bought third-hand. The government-appointed lawyer for the accused made some ineffectual noises, which sounded like whining, coughing, pleading, gargling, and whimpering. In between came words that sounded like, "poor sod," "doing his best," "not the brightest," "family to feed," "Lawd have mercy"—words that were even more shabbily dressed than the lawyer.

"Lock him up too," someone in the audience shouted, "that dashing wakil!" Laughter and shouts followed, then a chant, "Lock him up! Lock him up!"

The courtroom was so crowded that Kranti could only see Dharma Adhikari and his barrister by standing on her tiptoes. A chubby man in a checkered shirt in front of her, his backside damp from sweat, kept blocking her view. Then, as the chants of "lock him up" died down, the chubby man farted, a thin but elongated squeal that was meant for the nostrils of whoever was right behind him. The fart landed directly in Kranti's face, where it detonated in such a large explosion that Kranti thought she had been bombed. The smell of the fart was out of this world—rotten eggs, dead cat, acrid vomit, and cheap perfume. She shoved the chubby man, saying, "Donkey, what did you eat today?"

The chubby man turned. "What is your problem, woman?" he

said. He grabbed Kranti and pulled her toward him. By this time, the chubby man's fart had spread to the surrounding area and there was a mad scramble to get away from it. As a result, Kranti was pushed even more to the front, putting her within a few feet of Dharma Adhikari. Now she had an unobstructed view of the judges, the accused, and the Loyal Army Dais with their big machine guns strapped across their shoulders, their forefingers ready on the triggers. Dharma Adhikari looked up briefly at her; did he remember her from that day?

"Before we pass the verdict under the Treasonist Act," the chief judge said, "what do you have to say for yourself, Dharma Adhikari?"

After a delay, as if he were carefully weighing his words, Dharma Adhikari said, "I have given my life to the service of Darkmotherland, and this is the reward I get." His chin was trembling. "The accusations hurled against me aren't true." The courtroom had become silent. "I have been a faithful servant to PM Papa, who is the greatest leader this country has ever seen. I consider it a privilege to have had the chance to learn at his feet. In fact, I don't even consider myself worthy to have been the dust at his feet, so why would I betray him? I am a patriot, not a Treasonist."

To this there was a chorus of response, "Treasonist! Treasonist!"

"But what have I done?" Dharma Adhikari asked the court. "How have I treasoned against Darkmotherland? Against PM Papa?"

For a brief moment, there was silence. Then the thunderous response of "Treasonist" resumed.

The prosecuting lawyer for the Rajjya, whose robe was sleek and shiny as though designed by Versace, had a ruddy face that was gleaming and smiling. He hadn't had to utter a single word to enumerate the crime of the accused. He was sprawled out in his chair, chewing paan, hands behind his head, watching the proceeding as though it were a wrestling match on TV. The shabbily dressed defense lawyer, however, was muttering into his hands.

"And now the Rajjya has confiscated my property and my land," Dharma Adhikari said. "My wife and children have been thrown out of their home. How are they going to feed themselves? How are my children going to survive?" He covered his face with his palms and wept. "PM Papa! PM Papa!" he wailed. "Please save me." The very act that he'd advocated and helped pass was now being used against him. The very man who was sending him to the gallows was now being invoked. Then Dharma Adhikari stopped crying and looked around the room, his shoulders shuddering in anticipation of what was going to happen to him. His eyes came to rest on Kranti's. Everyone in the courtroom followed his gaze, and they too landed on Kranti.

I need to get out, I need to get out, a part of Kranti's mind screamed. She saw herself turning and pushing past the crowd to exit through the gate, then out, and away, out of the Valley, Darkmotherland, Asia, the Earth, the galaxy, the universe. But no, she was still rooted to the spot, looking up at Dharma Adhikari.

"She knows all about me," Dharma Adhikari said. He lifted his arm and pointed at her. "She knows how loyal I am to PM Papa."

No, no, no, thought Kranti.

"Who is she?" the chief judge asked, looking suspiciously at Kranti.

"She's the buhari of Ghimirey & Sons," Dharma Adhikari said.

At the mention of Ghimirey & Sons, a hushed awe came over the spectators.

"And how would she be able to vouch for your loyalty?"

In the courtroom were whispers about "Ghimirey buhari" and "widow." Then, "Streetwise incident." Soon, someone would remember that the widow was the daughter of Madam Mao. And in a courtroom filled with nationalists and Papafans and the Fundys, who knew what they could do to her?"

"Because she has seen my devotion to PM Papa, so she knows I couldn't be a Treasonist."

Okay, Kranti thought. I know that the man is in dire straits, but what in the world is he talking about? She'd seen him on Motherland TV, and then that one time in person in the Lion Palace. What would she know about his devotion to PM Papa? She didn't even know about his devotion to his wife. He was hoping that Kranti would step up to save him, but no one except PM Papa could save this man at this juncture. He was, for all practical purposes, already dead. She felt like shouting: dead man walking!

She was afraid that Poe would flutter by her shoulder any moment now, and she would feel his claws clamp her flesh, but he was nowhere.

"Please, Krantiji, tell them how loyal I am to PM Papa."

It was as if the man had known her for years, as though he expected her to respond, "Why, certainly, Dharma Adhikariji, you and I go a long way back. I will do everything in my power." Idiot! Kranti couldn't believe that she was having such thoughts about a man about to die, but he had put her in a tight spot. Then it occurred to her that he hadn't singled her out because she was a Ghimirey buhari but because she was her mother's daughter: he assumed that Kranti would have Professor Shrestha's savior complex. It irked her that Dharma Adhikari thought she was like her mother, that he so readily had identified her as a Ghimirey buhari, in public, in front of this potentially hostile crowd, when in truth she hadn't even come into the courtroom out of her own volition. Why couldn't he leave her alone? Why must she be dragged into everyone's affairs?

"Well, Ghimirey buhariji," the chief judge asked. "What can you say about this that will tell us that this man deserves mercy?" The way the judge's cheek jowls were moving, it could have been that he was trying not to burst into laughter.

The courtroom crowd watched her in anticipation, as if indeed she had the power to change this man's destiny, whereas everyone knew that even if Kranti cut off her arm to prove the accused's innocence, Dharma Adhikari would still be executed. Not only that, but most likely Kranti herself would face charges for aiding and abetting a Treasonist. But Dharma Adhikari certainly seemed to think Kranti had some power, because he broke into fervent blabber, "Please, please, Krantiji, may all of your descendants be blessed with uncountable good fortunes. I have been a slave to PM Papa, don't you know, the greatest man on earth, nay the galaxy, nay the universe, an incarnation of the Pothead God himself, this gorgeous country, land of beautiful flora and fauna and all that. My son is just six years old, my wife is fair-skinned and beautiful and shouldn't be a widow, I studied in the best school in the country, scored the highest marks in physics, I just bought my son a toy the other day, jayanti mangakalai bhadrakali kapalini."

"I don't know this here man," Kranti said.

The courtroom crowd went wild with shouts and whoops of "Treasonist!" A teenager fisted the air in front of him repeatedly and said, "Yes, yes, yes!" Some shuffled toward the prisoner as though they were waiting for the go-ahead to attack a sumptuous wedding buffet.

"Hoarder, hoarder," the chief judge said, banging his gavel.

Dharma Adhikari looked at her as though he couldn't believe what she'd said. And she couldn't believe it herself, when she could have said a number of things:

"Why, your honor, I know Dharma Adhikari very well, and he wouldn't even dream of being disloyal to PM Papa."

"Your honor, as a Ghimirey buhari, as a daughter-in-law of the eminent house, I can unequivocally declare, with no shred of doubt, that this man here, the accused, doesn't have an unpatriotic bone in his body."

"No, your honor and the esteemed audience in the courtroom, I don't believe this man to be capable of backstabbing PM Papa."

Or even, "Your honor and my fellow Darkmotherlandites, although I don't know the accused very well, I did glimpse him once, when I and my now-dead husband (who might, just might have been killed by PM Papa, if you would allow me to add), visited the Lion Palace. Although I saw him only for a few seconds when he came in to get PM Papa's signature, just when PM Papa was showing us his black gun, I could tell, through my great instinctual powers, that he was someone who was utterly, magnificently, unequivocally devoted to our beloved prime minister."

But she didn't say any of this, and now the judge said, "Why, Ghimirey buhariji, I am utterly grateful for your kind words. And your sense of civic duty. You have now proven beyond any doubt that the accused is guilty of every crime that he has been charged with. And for that he shall face the appropriate punishment."

What? All she said was that she didn't know him, and now she was responsible for sealing his fate? But the judge had already signaled the Loyal Army Dais to take Dharma Adhikari away. When they grabbed him, he slumped into their arms.

———

Kranti was so exhausted from the whole thing, first the skirmish with Mukeshbro and his garlfren in that apartment, then the farting man and Dharma Adhikari in the Supreme Adalat, that she went to Laj Mahal to take a nap. She could have gone to Beggar Street but the thought of seeing her mother seated on the green couch surrounded by her pathetic Beggars depressed her. Besides, Kranti was still resentful that Professor Shrestha rarely took the initiative to inquire after her. It was always Kranti who was texting her, calling her. Had Dada been alive, he would have called Kranti every day. He would have called even when Kranti didn't want to talk.

At Laj Mahal, she felt some comfort in knowing that she was still inhabiting Kabiraj's space, wherever he might be. In her exhaustion, she was beginning to fear that he was dead. She tried not to think about it. Her heart had already hardened after Bhaskar's death, and she wasn't going to allow herself to be sucked into that pit again. Another one bites the dust, she thought about Kabiraj. But she had to maintain her sanity. Ha! Ha! That was a hoot: maintain your insanity, you mean, she told herself.

Late that afternoon in Laj Mahal she was aware that she was incoherently muttering herself to sleep:

"My bonnie lies over the ocean."

"Herda ramro macchha, puchchre mari, ramro macha."

"The Ghimireys, my matapita, my sarbesarba, my everything."

She felt breathing on her face and opened her eyes and there was Kabiraj's large, puffy face staring at her.

"Oh, good, now also in my daydreams, dallu," she said.

Kabiraj sighed and slumped his shoulders. "I know, I know, you probably thought I had died."

Kranti touched his face, stroked his beard. "Oh, my God," she said, "you're really here." Then she slapped him. Not very hard but enough to generate a *thwack*! He nursed his cheek. "Do you realize how I ransacked this town to look for you?"

"I was afraid you'd be very worried," he said. "I even tried to see if I could send you a message, to let you know I was fine."

"Were you?" She realized that she should have asked this question first.

He nodded. "I wasn't treated too badly. We were expecting a lot worse."

"We who? Your Meowl group."

"*Howl*," he corrected her. Then he said, "So, you found out, huh?"

"You thought I wouldn't? Especially after you disappeared on me like that? Why didn't you tell me about this *Howl* business?"

He hung his head, then he said, "But you're always making fun of my poetry, of me as a poet. I thought if you heard a name like *Howl*, you would tease me until the day I died."

He told her the *Howl* members were taken and locked up in a warehouse. But it turned out that the Poolis Uncle in charge of their captivity was a closet poet himself, and after a couple of days of beatings and starvation, asked them to recite their poetry, as if it were a joke meant to poke fun at their love for their art. But soon it became obvious that the Poolis Uncle, who said he went by Udaas, a nom de plume frequently adopted by poets to connote the weltschmerz state of their artistic existence, derived much pleasure out of these recitations. One day Udaas himself recited poetry he had written. Despite the sadness inherent in the Poolis Uncle's work, he was happy because it was all in his service to Darkmotherland and PM Papa. All in all, Kabiraj and the Howlers had been treated better than they expected during their confinement. Udaas had even provided them with milky tea and some fritters during one of these recitations. But before he let them go, he turned tough. He hit them with his batons and said that they were using their art to express and promote anti-nationalist elements. Why didn't they also compose poems to describe the splendor of Darkmotherland? To praise PM Papa and his glorious reign?

Kranti told Kabiraj about her search for Subhash, what he might know about Bhaskar's killer. Kabiraj said that he'd help her look for Subhash, asked her whether she'd heard about khateykids being taken to labor camps, and she said that she had.

They watched the dust motes float by the evening sun. They both lay on the floor, cheek against cheek. He hadn't shaved for a few days now and his bristles were rough against her skin. She fell asleep for twenty minutes, then woke up embarrassedly to find herself drooling against his neck. He was reciting something inside his head—poetry?—and his eyes would brighten every now and then. She rubbed her palm against his cheek and asked him what he was thinking.

He said that he wanted to bring Subhash and Rani to live in Laj Mahal, in honor of Bhaskar. She said that she'd help him take care of them, that she'd come to the Laj Mahal early in the morning before work, and also in the evening after the bank closed.

"We need to find them, Kabiraj," Kranti said. "We need to make sure that they are okay, and I need to know what Subhash knows."

That evening as Kranti left Laj Mahal to go to the Asylum, Dharma Adhikari's body was hanging from a tree next to the Temple of the Civil Goddess, a placard saying "Treasonist" tied to his chest.

—

At the Asylum, Shambhogya came into her room, without knocking— Kranti had forgotten to lock it—and, leaning against the door, asked her what sickness was Professor Shrestha suffering from that required Kranti to stay over at Beggar Street. Kranti told her that her mother was old, and her ailments were numerous. She was scrolling through her phone, where the news of Dharma Adhikari's death was prominent. He had been on a mission to sabotage PM Papa for a long time, it was reported.

"You know it's not done, your staying away like this," Shambhogya said.

"It's not done," Kranti mimicked Shambhogya, without wanting to.

Shambhogya stomped her feet, made it as though she was about to leave in a huff, but she stayed. "Next time, please let me know in advance."

Even as Shambhogya was plying her with questions, Kranti found herself wondering if Shambhogya was somehow behind what had happened to Bhaskar. It was awful, this line of thinking, this notion that the Ghimireys would even take out one of their own. But, and she thought of this with a shudder, Bhaskar himself wouldn't rule out his family from being behind such a heinous act.

"When you stay away like that, it's hard for us to think something bad hasn't happened."

Kranti taunted her—would Shambhogya care to elaborate on how her imagination had run wild with what might have happened to Kranti? Maybe Shambhogya had a repressed desire to have those things happen to herself?

"What? You think I too would want to spend time in Bhurey Paradise with your filthy poet?"

"Wouldn't you, Shambhogya? I bet that's precisely what you'd love to do. Rub your face against the filthy beard of my dallu."

She was about to say more, but then, in a huff, Shambhogya left the room.

Shambhogya was probably thinking that if Kranti wasn't brought in line soon, her behavior would get out of hand. Well, what would the Ghimireys do to her if she indeed spun out of control and openly associated with Kabiraj? Would they kill her? Perhaps her death wouldn't be as gruesome as her husband's?

Maybe just some rat poison in my food, eh, Shambhogya?

Kabiraj and Kranti hunted for Subhash and Rani all over the Valley. Whenever they saw a group of khateykids, they stopped to inquire about them. Most of the khateykids that hung about the Tourist District were new, so they didn't know who Subhash and Rani were. One khateykid opined that Tarjan might know where Subhash was. But where could they find Tarjan? He was a khateykid who had turned into a smalltime pimp in the Diamond Park, the other khateykids said. Kranti told Kabiraj that Tarjan's name didn't sound familiar; he was not among the khateykids Bhaskar had befriended.

Kranti and Kabiraj discovered that many of the khateykids were in hiding, or they'd already been taken to GULAs in the outskirts of the Valley. There were reports now that some khateykids were being sold as sex slaves in auctions held at night under candlelight. Once they were sold, they were known as khateybabes. The underground rag *Kaneykhusi* had even published a photograph of a nighttime auction taking place in an alley in the City of Devotees. It showed a man's hand on a girl, no more than eleven or twelve, and a man's back, the purported buyer of the khateybabe. Young prepubescent girls were in high demand, according to *Kaneykhusi*, so slave traders now kidnapped young khateykid girls and sold them in these auctions for lakhs of rupees. Kranti shuddered at the thought of Rani bought by a grown man.

It took Kranti and Kabiraj another day to get hold of Tarjan, who said that Subhash and his little sister used to hang out with him in the Tourist District, but one day disappeared. Only after receiving some money from Kranti did Tarjan reveal that he'd seen Subhash in the Self-Arisen Chaitya area a few days ago. "He didn't look right up here," Tarjan tapped his head with his finger.

They found Subhash on the back hill of Self-Arisen Chaitya the next day. He appeared to be foraging in a small bushy area. He was carrying a rice sack, but judging from how loosely it hung over his shoulder there was nothing in it. At the sound of his name, he appeared startled, ready to bolt, but he stayed still and with wary eyes, watched them approach. Close up, Kranti could tell that he'd lost weight, and his eyes and face had a yellowish hue.

After much prodding, Subhash remembered Kranti as Bhaskar uncle's wife. Subhash touched the side of his head, and Kranti saw the bruise from the Asylum guard's rifle butt.

At first Subhash said that his sister Rani was dead, but he refused to provide specifics. Then, abruptly, he asked them to follow him. He took them to an indentation, like a small cave, next to the wooded area. The girl was there, sleeping next to a dog, who lifted his head as they approached and wagged his tail. The dog's ribs showed through its skin. When they called her name, Rani opened her eyes, only partly. She appeared to be drugged. Kranti lifted Rani and carried her down the hill, with Kabiraj and Subhash following. Subhash was speaking to himself, muttering. Kranti thought he said something about a waterfall, and also thought he mentioned Mukeshbro.

They took Rani to a clinic near the Self-Arisen Chaitya, where the daktar said that the girl had pneumonia. They asked him to check Subhash, who was found to be in the early stages of jaundice.

41.

Something was happening between Rozy and General Tso that neither could properly identify. Yet it was there, a magnetic pull, a coming together, a fusion. When General Tso ran into Rozy in the hallway, his face became transformed, his expressions docile. His body softened, and he stopped and bowed. He didn't do so when others were present, but every time they were alone, perhaps in the Gufa, he bowed. He did this with an expectant facial expression, as though he were anticipating Rozy to bless him. Or acknowledge him. Or something.

Three days before his departure for Amrika, in a last-ditch effort PM Papa tried to persuade Rozy to go with him, but Rozy was adamant about not going this time, she said.

"What's the point of me going with you?" Rozy said. "Things are never going to change. These people will always see me as your valet." They were in the Gufa. For a couple of days, Rozy had come up with excuses not to go into the InnerGufa with him.

Now PM Papa watched her in dismay. "You're already acting like the Chief Secretary. Everyone thinks you're Bill Tamang's replacement."

Rozy stared at him, as though she couldn't believe the nonsense that came out of his mouth. "A donkey," Rozy said. "A donkey can replace Bill Tamang."

"But you're so much better than a donkey, my maiya," PM Papa adopted a cajoling tone.

"I'm not going."

"So, it's come to this now?" PM Papa said. "You're openly disobeying me?" His tone had turned menacing, but Rozy wasn't moved. She knew that unless she crossed a big line—she didn't know what that was—she didn't have to worry. She didn't bother to answer him and went to the window to look at the pigeons cooing on the roof.

"Maiya, look at me. You don't believe I'm trying?" He came toward her and clasped her arm. Was there a flash of anger in those tightening jaws?

But Rozy couldn't give in, not now. "I believe you, but I also see that nothing has happened."

"Rozy, how can you say that? I even got rid of Dharma Adhikari at your behest."

"At my behest!" Rozy said. She kept shelled peanuts in a bowl by the window. She threw a handful of them at the pigeons, who rose in a great flurry of wings to snatch the treats. "Dharma Adhikari was bad news. He treated me as though I was nothing, and he had bad intentions about you, I could tell."

PM Papa ground his teeth imperceptibly. "I believe you, I believe you. But we've discussed this before. I need time."

"Okay. Time."

"Rozy."

Rozy didn't turn to face him.

"Okay, we'll do something when I return," Papa said.

Rozy threw some peanuts into her mouth. "Don't count on me being here when you return."

The morning Papa flew to Amrika, Rozy went into the Gufa, sat in PM Papa's chair, and put her feet up on the desk. She picked up one of PM Papa's Cuban cigars. It was so fat it looked like a giant's thumb. PM Papa claimed he'd been given a box of these by none other than El Comandante himself when PM Papa had visited Cuba. "Dese are da best Cuban shigars in Cuba," PM Papa had even feigned what was supposedly El Comandante's accent. But if PM Papa had visited Cuba when he was a minister, what was the likelihood that Castro had not only hosted a small-time minister from a small-time country but also personally gifted him a box of cigars? If it was after he became PM Papa, when did he sneak off to Cuba without Rozy's, or anyone else's, knowledge?

Rozy smelled the cigar, ran it under her nose, then pretended to drag on it and blow the smoke out, just like she'd seen PM Papa do. Papa was not a smoker, but every now and then he lit a cigar.

On the wall behind the chair was a photo of PM Papa that a Rajjya photographer had recently taken. It showed him seated in his chair, a fat cigar clamped between his lips with its smoke twirling in the air. PM Papa "enjoying a cigar," the caption read. The photo with the caption had become unexpectedly popular, and Rozy had seen the photo everywhere—in shops, in homes, alongside the WANTED poster of the Son of Yeti—after Prapu Ganda had made it available to the media and the public. There was even a movie out, the hero chomping on a thick cigar, a sidekick asking whether he was "enjoying" it. Cigar sales had increased nationwide.

Yes, I am enjoying my cigar, Rozy thought as she swiveled in the chair and blew imaginary smoke out at PM Papa's photo on the wall. The smoke hit him in his face, attacked his nose, and spattered across his cheeks.

Rozy clicked the remote to turn on the TV on the wall. PM Papa was giving a speech today at the newly opened Pure Darkmotherland Economic Forum, which was created with the sole purpose of always singing praises of the unbounded economic prosperity that PM Papa had ushered in. PM Papa's double could have fooled Rozy herself— that's how uncannily he resembled the real man.

A knock on the door. "Enter," Rozy said, waving her cigar imperiously in the air.

The door opened and it was General Tso. In her mind, Rozy saw herself scrambling to her feet, cigar back in the box, profusely mumbling apologies. In her mind she also saw General Tso barking at her, "What the hell is going on? Who do you think you are, you little pervert?" But, Rozy, incredibly, remained in her position, feet up on the desk, cigar casually between her fingers, her heart hammering in her chest. And General Tso, instead of barking at her, said softly, "I'm sorry, Rozy Miss, but I wasn't aware you were here."

"Didn't the staff tell you?"

"No one was outside the door. Maybe the typist went to the bathroom."

"If you ask me, she goes to the bathroom one too many times."

"I came to see if the file on Dharma Adhikari was in the drawer."

Rozy waved him in, said, "You're welcome to look in his desk."

But General Tso didn't move, apparently not comfortable approaching.

"Awful," Rozy said, "how Dharma Adhikari turned out to be a Treasonist."

"We can take no one for granted," General Tso said.

Rozy sighed.

"Are you unhappy, Rozy Miss?"

Rozy observed General Tso as he stood by the door. She waved for him to come closer. General Tso took a few steps and stood in front of the desk, his hand clasped in front of him as a sign of deference.

"How are things at home?" Rozy asked.

"They are fine, Rozy Miss. Thank you for your concern."

"Do you feel lonely, General Tso?"

General Tso hesitated.

"You know you can be open with me."

General Tso didn't speak. Some type of emotion made General Tso's shoulders shake slightly. Something stuck in his throat.

Rozy pulled deeply on her cigar and blew out the imaginary smoke. General Tso's eyes followed the smoke up to the ceiling.

"I know what you're going through," Rozy said. The words were coming to her from somewhere. She didn't know what she was going to say next, yet there was a rehearsed quality to what was emerging from her. This was all planned out beforehand—this thought flew to her, flapped its wings, and flew away. She was aware of the dangers of what she was saying, and doing—feet up on the desk, cigar in her mouth. This strange, yet familiar conversation with General Tso, the commander in chief of the entire army, the man without whose help PM Papa wouldn't have been able to koo in Darkmotherland—he had now become so overwhelmed with something that he was mildly shaking. What was it? Rozy didn't know, but she was beginning to feel it, too, in her supremely confident posture, in the daring words she was breathing out, in the quivering figure of General Tso, who was now in tears.

"You know that things need to change around here, don't you, Dinesh babu?" The name had simply popped into her head. Or had she heard it on one of Motherland TV's broadcasts?

General Tso nodded.

"The people are suffering, Darkmotherland is suffering."

General Tso made a gurgling sound.

"Don't you agree, Dinesh babu?"

"I do, Rozy Miss. I do, Mata."

It didn't feel odd to hear General Tso call her a Mata. Yes, I am a Mata, thought Rozy. I am everyone's Mata, and even if I'm not, I'll be everyone's Mata soon.

"The Big Two has brought a lot of pain into people's lives. And their lot hasn't improved."

General Tso tilted his head.

"Rich insanely richer, poor pathetically poorer. The Son of Yeti still out there plotting an attack. What happened? Where are all the promises? Kya hua tera bada?"

General Tso shook his head sadly. "Yo kasam, woh irada."

"Exactly, promises made but not kept. Is this the fate Darkmotherland deserves?"

"It certainly isn't, Mata."

"Then what are we going to do about it?"

"We need to do something, Mata. But I don't know what to do." It was almost as though he had regained his speech; the words were spilling out of him now. He was opening up to her, as Mata had predicted. "I don't know what to do and I need your guidance."

"You are a good boy, you always have been." A memory came to her, suddenly, of when Dinesh babu was a kid. He had gone to spend his holidays with his grandmother, who lived by herself on the other side of the mountain. That rainy season, while Dinesh babu was visiting, his grandmother had been very sick. The local jhankri had been called, but the remedy he had prescribed—drinking goat milk with a holy rudraksha dipped into it, sacrificing a yellow-footed green pigeon by the river while making sure that none of its feathers floated away—had done no good. The neighbors had given up on his grandmother and had exhorted Dinesh babu to give up as well. In fact, the neighbors were already preparing a stretcher and purifying the ground floor. Because of mudslides, Dinesh babu's family hadn't been able to come over from across the mountain. Dinesh babu, his eyes filled with tears, had shouted at his neighbors, telling them his grandmother wasn't dead yet and that he'd be damned if he was giving them permission to kill her before her time. He'd kicked them all out, and devoted the next seventy-two hours to her, neglecting to eat, sleep, or even visit the bathroom, caring only for his grandmother. Throughout this time, he'd prayed to the poster of Darkmother that hung on her kitchen wall. On the fourth day his grandmother had opened her eyes and said, "How long was I out?" The neighbors said it was a miracle; the shaman said the boy had healing powers.

All of this floated in front of Rozy like a clip from a movie. She then recounted it blow-by-blow to General Tso, who at the end of the story, fell to the floor and prostrated. "Jai Mata! O Goddess Darkmother!"

"Good boy, General Tso."

"Anything, Mata. Anything you say. This humble nokerchaker is at your service. I have been waiting for this day forever. Today I am the happiest I've ever been. If Mata wishes, I will cut my head off right now and present it to you."

"No need for melodrama. I'm not into human sacrifices."

"Whatever you wish, Darkmother."

Rozy stood from her chair and came out from behind her desk. General Tso was still prostrated, his lips close to the floor, mumbling, reciting prayers from his Goddess Darkmother hymn book. Rozy observed him, then put her right foot on top of General Tso's head and spread her arms up in the air, emulating the iconic Darkmother pose. Then she said, "Okay, get up, my child." But General Tso kept blubbering and mumbling. Rozy reached down and encouraged him to stand. He did, slowly, his body in the throes of some divine influence, tears streaming down his cheeks, his eyes closed because he was unable to meet Rozy's. "It's okay," she said. "You can let it all out now. You don't need to hide anything from me."

General Tso vigorously nodded his head.

"From now on I will take care of you."

General Tso cried.

"And you will protect me."

General Tso opened his eyes. "Of course, Mata. Anyone who tries to harm you will have his throat slit open."

Rozy recognized that from now on, blood and slit throats were things she'd have to get used to. "Let's make some changes," Rozy said. She no longer needed PM Papa to make her Deputy PM upon his return from Amrika. She needed to move faster. "Where are the most beautiful horses owned by the Loyal Army? Take me to them."

⁓

On Motherland TV, Darkmotherlandites saw this:

PM Papa walking on Manhattan's Fifth Avenue. Shrimati Papa by his side, looking happy and content. The couple is accompanied by aides carrying bulging bags from Macy's and Saks Fifth Avenue. After it became clear that Rozy wasn't going to accompany him to Amrika, PM Papa had, as a peace offering, asked Shrimati Papa whether she wanted to go with him. Thrilled, Shrimati Papa had said yes, although initially she made it seem as though she was going only because he was pressuring her.

PM Papa and Shrimati Papa are cruising on a private boat, courtesy of the Mayor of New York, the Statue of Liberty looming in the background. Shrimati Papa is pointing to the statue, as though Lady Liberty was her lost auntie.

PM Papa and Shrimati Papa are eating in a restaurant that serves spicy Darkmotherlandite food. Darkmotherlandites living in the New

York area are seated at other tables. There are protesters outside, and Hom Bokaw on Motherland TV tells viewers that these protesting expats are enemies of Darkmotherland, and, once they are identified, their families back in Darkmotherland will be taken in for questioning. There are cries of alarm from the street, and the Motherland TV cameraman filming inside the restaurant goes out, where Amrikan Poolis Uncles in riot gear, accompanied by tanks, have arrived. Under President Corn Hair, Poolis Uncles in riot gear, escorted by army tanks, are often used to squash public displeasure at his administration. There are fewer and fewer protests in Amrika now. People have simply exhausted themselves protesting. President Corn Hair only seems to be getting stronger. Now he's hinting at cancelling the next election to make up for the lost time of his presidency due to the "witchhunts"—various probes and the impeachment efforts by the opposition party. Outside the Darkmotherlandite restaurant, the militarized police are face to face with the protestors, many of whom have already left, because they don't want to be identified by either the Rajjya or the Amrikan law enforcement. The few remaining brave ones are shouting, holding signs that say "PM Papa Murdabad." The militarized Poolis Uncles are holding a megaphone into which they yell that if the protestors don't disperse immediately, more drastic steps will be taken. When the handful of protestors show defiance, the Pools Uncles move in and start beating them with electric-shock batons. Sounds of pain and alarm fill the air.

The camera returns inside, where the participants are enjoying their meals; some are even eating the dal-bhat with their hands in a nostalgic nod to how things are done back in Darkmotherland. PM Papa speaks. He thanks his supporters in the diaspora. A poet gets up and sings a fawning poem, written in perfect meter. PM Papa speaks again, this time raising his index finger in the gesture of the Founding Father. He talks about the "leaps and strides" Darkmotherland is making in every aspect under his leadership. The economy is booming, he says. "Boom!" he adds loudly for effect.

"The Son of Yeti," one of the patrons says out loud, not as a challenge but just as an observation.

PM Papa pauses and looks at the man. "The Son of Yeti is on his way to extinction," he says, "except he doesn't know it." This draws great applause and laughter. PM Papa holds up his hand. "We finally have law and order in Darkmotherland," he says. Then he urges the diasporic Darkmotherlandites to come and invest in their ancestral homeland. One restaurant patron, a rich multimillionaire Darkmotherlandite who owns a large number of gas stations in New Jersey, is so moved by PM Papa's words that he stands up and pledges a ten million dollar investment in his homeland's cyber sector. A couple of other pledges of monetary investments follow.

PM Papa and Shrimati Papa get a tour of the Mall in Washington, DC. They are filmed fingering the names etched on the Vietnam Veterans Memorial, gazing up at the Washington Monument, and admiring the Hubble Telescope in the National Air and Space Museum.

But Darkmotherlandites are most riveted by PM Papa's meeting with President Corn Hair that's shown on Motherland TV. The two leaders are shaking hands in front of reporters in the Rose Garden. President Corn Hair is screaming at the press. "Chopper talk" for years during the impeachment process, when he brayed at the press with the deafening sound of a running helicopter in the background, has turned him into a permanent screamer, with his tongue inside his mouth sliding in and out visibly. President Corn Hair calls the press the enemy of the people. He no longer needs to do so because the Amrikan press has lost its teeth and has been cowed and tamed. They now ask only the most benign questions, or questions that are worded in favor of the president, such as, "Given the enormous, historically unprecedented success of your economy, do you see any reason why you should hold elections? Why would Amrikans want an alternative when what's happening under your presidency is the best deal they've ever received in the history of this nation?"

In between the questions and answers, President Corn Hair, who is wearing a red Make Amrika Great Again cap, takes it off and, accepting a Sharpie pen from an aide, signs it, then reaches over and lifts up PM Papa's native topi and places the MAGA cap in its stead.

The entire room bursts into a thunderous applause. Camera flashes go off for what seems like an eternity. PM Papa flashes a wide smile at everyone. Shrimati Papa, who is seated next to him, says, "Suits you so well. Make Amrika Great Again, hoina?"

"Ladies and gentlemen," President Corn Hair says. "I present to you a great friend of Amrika, PM Papa. This man, a strong man." He points to his temple. "A smart man. The smartest one gets to the top." He punches his fist the air in front of him and says, "Pure Darkmotherland!" He turns to PM Papa. "Isn't that how you say it?"

PM Papa says, "Yes, exactly." And he too punches the air in front of him and says, "Pure Darkmotherland!"

Then, everyone in the Rose Garden—President Corn Hair's cabinet, PM Papa's entourage, even some reporters—are shouting "Pure Darkmotherland!" as they pump their fists. Amrikan TV programs show how people in Darkmotherland are reacting to their beloved PM Papa's meeting with President Corn Hair in Amrika. Cameras show a huge swarm of Darkmotherlandites in the Monkeygod Gate Square watching the Rose Garden meeting on a giant screen, and as the Rose Garden crowd shouts, "Pure Darkmotherland!" so do the Darkmotherlandites in the square back in Darkmotherland. Since there are big TV screens scattered throughout the Rose Garden, the Rose Garden crowd sees Darkmotherlandites in Darkmotherland shouting "Pure Darkmotherland!" in the square, and they respond with a new wave of "Pure Darkmotherland." Thus, for a while, there are boisterous "Pure Darkmotherland!" shouts across the two countries.

Shrimati Papa gets to spend time with the First Lady.

"I haf alvais vanted to wisit Darkmoderlant," the First Lady says.

"Then come, na!" Shrimati Papa says. "Darkmotherland very, very beautiful. Unique, ke, unique. Most beautiful. High mountains very close, ke. Darkmotherland food also very, very good. Dal-bhat. You know dal-bhat? I cook for you, I very good cook."

PM Papa is shown wearing the Make Amrika Great Again cap as he enters the plane to depart for Darkmotherland.

DARKMOTHER IN DARKMOTHERLAND

42.

There had been no warning of her appearance. No radio or television announcement, no posters on walls. Despite the proximity of the mountains, the day had been hot, and the Valley residents had welcomed the evening breeze, even though it was still filled with dust and masks were unavoidable.

She appeared in the heart of the Tourist District, in the vibrant main chowk. Amidst the tourists and hawkers, there appeared a big white horse. Riding the horse was a woman in a psychedelic hippie frock, so bright that it appeared to glow in the dusk. She was surrounded by men in black suits and dark shades, who eyed people and murmured into their walkie-talkies, just like in the movies. They had machine guns and glistening swords strapped to their bodies. Behind the men a couple of black limos were gliding past. No one knew where the horse with the woman, the men in black, and the black limos came from; no one saw them approach from any of the four directions that fanned out from the chowk. They were just there—a gigantic horse with a radiant, dark woman on top, and black-suited men followed by black cars. A miraculous appearance, it was later said. The horse was whinnying, raising its front legs, but the woman in the hippie frock was born to ride the beast. With her fierce, kohl-rimmed eyes, she was surveying the crowd that had gathered around her, guiding her horse to face all four directions so everyone could see her clearly. Her security personnel were keeping the crowd at bay, pushing people back gently if they came too close. Also with her were some Loyal Army Dais, with their big machine guns. General Tso was there as well, casting about stern looks.

Both the tourists and Darkmotherlandites were taking photos with their cameras and mobile phones. "No flash," a black-suited man commanded. They adjusted their gadgets so that the flashing stopped. Local residents appeared at their doorways and windows. Merchants stopped attending to their customers, but it hardly mattered because the customers were also distracted. It was the tourists who first identified her as Darkmother (later some of the locals expressed embarrassment at the fact that it was the khaireys who were more keyed into this glorious moment, even though it was the locals who had waited for this prophecy to materialize since time immemorial). "Darkmother? Is that her?" the tourists whispered to one another.

Still not believing that the prophecy had come true, the locals tried to correct the foolish tourists. "No Darkmother, no Darkmother," they said. But the refrain of Darkmother, even as a negation, rippled through the crowd. What started out as a correction turned into its opposite. Whispers of *Darkmother, Darkmother* buzzed among the multitude. Even those who were initially skeptical became quickly persuaded that this was indeed Darkmother. She was dark, she had long black hair. On her forehead she wore what looked like a headband, but could have been a tiara or a crown. The white horse added to the effect. Heavily decked in ornaments, the horse seemed to have dropped from the heavens. People even wondered if it had wings, perhaps wings that the naked eye couldn't see.

The first one to prostrate was Na-Ryan of Mofo Momos. "The moment I've been waiting for," he shouted and promptly fell on the ground, his arms stretched out, palms pressed together.

His action had a contagious effect, and soon everyone was prostrating, even those in doorways and windows. A waiter who'd been serving beer in a nearby rooftop restaurant stopped serving and lay down on the floor, his palms raised in supplication. A farmer carrying radishes, potatoes, and kauli set down his baskets and kneeled. Someone shouted, "All hail Darkmother!" and the crowd shouted, "All hail Darkmother!"

⁓

The procession wound its way through the alleys and the lanes. There was a somber tone to it, a hushed quality, as if the participants, who had already begun to see themselves as Bhaktas, were afraid that too much noise would get on the nerves of Darkmother, who was leading their way. No one was going to argue that she was indeed Darkmother. The dark, radiant beauty, the solemn eyes, the snow-white horse, and the whispers of "Darkmother, Darkmother" that filled the air as more people joined the procession. People streamed from houses, shops, restaurants and bars. They walked with their eyes lowered, as though they were afraid to look at the brilliance riding the giant horse. Many were softly chanting mantras, or syllables that spontaneously arose in their minds. Some listened closely, heads bowed to their neighbors, followed along, mangling some words, getting others right. No one chanted loudly. A low hum rose from the Bhaktas that echoed against the sky, where even the birds seemed to sway.

At a snail's pace the procession moved. There was all the time in the world. Darkmother had appeared out of her free will, on a gorgeous steed, as described in the ancient scripture. She was here for a purpose. She was here to shine light on the Age of Darkness. For now, what was important was that they followed her. There was no doubt that they were being blessed, perhaps multiple times for being in the right place at the right time. It was important that they stay by her. She was going to work miracles.

General Tso walked alongside the white horse, his hand occasionally patting its rump. They were flanked and followed by smooth-skinned men in black suits, their eyes alert, roving. The crowd tailed behind, heads bowed, chanting, keeling, murmuring. Housewives threw flowers from windows. The entourage inched forward so slowly that at times it hardly seemed to be moving. But there was indeed movement—the houses and shops were imperceptibly sliding back.

With this snail-like pace, amassing more and more Bhaktas, Darkmother moved away from the Tourist District toward the Durbar. When she stopped in front of the Durbar gates, people remembered another ancient prophecy. Didn't the sacred texts also mention a divine being coming down to occupy the Durbar after its original inhabitants, i.e. the royals, were destroyed?

With Darkmother on her white steed facing the Durbar, the other two roads that merged also quickly became filled with people. Durbar Marg, the long avenue that faced the Durbar and was filled with fancy shops and flanked by posh hotels, was already teeming with Bhaktas.

The palace, built during the time of the Shade-Wearing King, was a series of buildings that appeared to be haphazardly stacked on top of one another, a looming pagoda building in the front. Next to the pagoda was a structure that resembled a smaller version of the Empire State Building. Fronting the palace was a large lawn, about three or four soccer fields in length, and enclosed by a big gate with sentries.

The sentries, now faced with cries of "Open the gates!" from the thousands who had gathered outside, quickly did so. Darkmother moved into the Durbar grounds.

———

The mass swarmed into the Durbar compound. Darkmother was allowed space to lead her horse. She approached the front façade of the Durbar calmly. A hum rose from the crowd. Helicopters appeared in the sky—extra security for Darkmother. One of the helicopters belonged to Motherland TV. To the pilots of the helicopters in the sky, the Bhaktas clogging the three streets leading to the Durbar looked like crawling maggots.

A handful of people emerged from inside the Durbar, carrying a palanquin. They lowered it to the ground in front of the horse, which stretched its neck to sniff it and discharge a derisive snort. Darkmother patted the horse and dismounted. She turned around to face her followers, then slipped into the palanquin, like a queen ready to be ushered into her palace. Just then, struggling against the surge of the masses, a young girl appeared in front of Darkmother, even as the men in black tried to block her way. Nakkali. She was beaming, glowing, from head to toe, as though she too had plopped down from the heavens above. Nakkali curtseyed to Darkmother, who snapped her fingers at her, acknowledging her presence and allowing her to stay by her side.

Men lifted the palanquin and carried Darkmother inside. Nakkali, her hand on the window of the palanquin, didn't leave Darkmother's side. The palanquin bearers took her to the second floor, into the former monarch's bedroom, which had large glass windows overlooking the boulevard and stretching all the way toward the Home of the Bell seen in the distance, and beyond, to the Diamond Park and the Parade Ground. Workers dismantled and hauled away all signs and symbols that suggested the Durbar had been a museum. No turning back now—Darkmother was the occupier of the Durbar. This was relayed to the helicopters above, and announced on Motherland TV and other private media. Scholars and pundits appeared on television and radio, expounding on the deep connection between the royal lineage and the Darkmother lineage. It was only natural that they merged. "No better moment for this to happen than during these degenerate times." The phrase "degenerate times" echoed across all the media channels.

With a flick of her fingers, Darkmother ordered food be prepared for her Bhaktas. "All of them, hajur?" the attendants asked. Darkmother nodded. Panic ensued. There were not enough cooks to prepare meals for the thronging masses. Nakkali, the bright girl that she was, came up with a solution—why not enlist from the Bhaktas themselves? A loudspeaker was used to announce the call for good cooks and chefs. A near-riot ensued, with people climbing on top of one another to volunteer. The helicopters swooped down, like giant birds, to maintain order. They flew close to the people, blasting them with the fierce winds from their propellers.

Finally, about fifteen men and women were chosen. Giant cauldrons were brought in from outside, along with vegetables and live goats. Where did all this food come from in a country that had been suffering from food shortage since the Big Two? This bounty, too, was attributed to Darkmother's miraculous powers: she had literally made the food materialize.

In no time dozens and dozens of cauldrons and vats simmered with freshly cut meat and chopped vegetables. Among the chosen chefs was Ali Miya, who began cooking aromatic biryani, filled with cardamom, cloves, and saffron. People swooned to an internal music only they could hear. Na-Ryan, wearing his lungi and juice-soaked vest, prepared momos in steamers the size of small cars. He grinned widely and regaled the others with stories of Darkmother. People sang paeans to their beloved goddess. Moved by the songs, folks danced, and semi-circles formed to allow space for these hundreds of revelers. The singing and clapping intensified, creating a ripple of singing and clapping in all directions.

By now all three streets were jammed with people. More Dark-motherlandites were leaving their homes and their workplaces to join the excitement. People congregated even outside the high northern walls of the Durbar, a useless act because they couldn't see anything. But they could hear the chants and the songs from the other side of the wall. The helicopter pilots reported that the singing below was making their helicopters vibrate with amplified bass. Dozens of goats had been butchered on the front lawn, creating a red damp patch on the grass the size of a badminton court. Once slaughtered, these goats were skinned with boiling water, and turmeric was applied to them before they were chopped into pieces for cooking. The heads were cooked separately, so the beheaded goats sported silly, teeth-baring grins. The goats' ears, tongues, and testicles were roasted on open fires, the pungent smell of burnt meat filling the air. "I can smell the goat meat all the way up here," one pilot happily reported over the radio.

When the food was ready, there were cries for Darkmother to bless it. Darkmother stepped onto the balcony next to her bedroom and surveyed her domain. The Bhaktas lowered their heads and joined their palms together in supplication. Darkmother raised her hand in blessing. Silence descended upon the crowd. After Darkmother stepped back into her room, the crowd erupted into a loud cheer and the festivities began.

Goat gravy, rice, and vegetable curry were doled out in plates made of leaves, sown together by grandma and auntie types, as the food was being cooked. Large canisters were loaded onto the trucks and taken to the masses gathered on the streets. Those who were lucky enough to be at the front of the Durbar were already pitching their tents there, as though they no longer cared for their own houses and simply wanted to be closer to Darkmother. Some had also spread out their blankets and sleeping bags and were determined to spend the night there. Evening was approaching. A haze had drifted into the air, not unlike the dust bowls that roamed the city after the Big Two. But this time the people were gratified and satiated, especially after eating the blessed goat meat and Mofo momos. They talked about how Darkmother was going to bring even more happiness—and more biryani and momos—to this country that had suffered so much.

Darkmother conveyed her wishes mostly through the movements of her eyes and hands, like a Kathak dancer. Often, she didn't even have to say anything; her attendants intuited what was asked. Nakkali, of course, acted like her main nokerchaker—fetching things for her, passing messages—and referring to herself as her valet. But Darkmother's chief attendant was an officious-looking man who was the caretaker of the Durbar. He had been a royal priest, Rajguru, during the monarchial rule. His father, grandfather, and great-grandfather had also served as royal priests to the kings. The disintegration of the monarchy more than a decade ago had been a major blow to Rajguru. Before the monarchy collapsed, he had been grooming his son to carry on his legacy, teaching him important rituals and mantras. His son, who had wanted to be a musician but had reconciled himself to the path of priesthood out of family allegiance and greed (the priests received substantial perks—property, jewelry—from the king), had left his family and gone to pursue a musical career in Bharat. After the Durbar turned into a museum, Rajguru, through the grace of PM Papa, had been allowed to stay as a caretaker. All day long he had walked about the museum, dusting the old paintings, vases, and chandeliers. Darkmother's grand entry into the Durbar was a god-send, or rather, a goddess-send, to him. Without missing a beat, he fell into the role of priest-attendant. He recited mantras in Dark-mother's presence with a great deal of self-importance. He ordered the ex-king's throne, which had been on display on the first floor, be brought up to the room next to Darkmother's bedroom. The room then served as the audience room, where visitors could come and get a darshan of Darkmother. Because he knew mantras, the other people surrounding Darkmother gave him room, even though he was fussy and overly protective of her. Darkmother's security personnel initially regarded him with suspicion, but they soon saw that he was merely a sycophant, and the only one who knew the mantras, so they let him do what he needed to do.

All day people flocked to receive blessings from Darkmother. She sat majestically on the throne, sometimes raising her palm to bless the believers, other times not bothering, maintaining a stoic face. They came with gifts and flowers and fruits, which she signaled be distributed among the poor. The festivities on the palace lawn con-tinued. The streets surrounding the palace were still clogged, and when Darkmother looked out and saw her subjects, ideas began to cohere in her mind.

~

It hadn't been easy to persuade Subhash and Rani to come live in Laj Mahal. Subhash had been paranoid, agitated. He resisted going with Kabiraj and Kranti, and for a short while there was a scene on the street outside the clinic near the Self-Arisen Chaitya, with Sub-hash insisting that they were Mukeshbro's agents, here to sell Rani into prostitution at a slave auction. A group of spectators gathered, making Kranti nervous. But the onlookers were overwhelmingly in support of Kranti and Kabiraj, with some not even knowing what the fracas was all about. This was common in Darkmotherland—the public sided with one party or another armed with little or, often, no information. One woman offered caution: "Watch out for these khateykids. They'll knife you in the back when you're not looking."

Right after that woman spoke, Kranti saw in the distance that a group of Loyal Army Dais, smoking and chatting casually, were approaching. She grabbed Rani from Subhash, who'd been holding her, and briskly walked away. The crowd dispersed, and Kabiraj followed, with Subhash a few steps behind him, carrying on his paranoid ranting, now more muted, like an old man talking to himself. They couldn't find a taxi, so Kabiraj took Rani from Kranti and carried her in his arms, her head lolling over his shoulder. As they neared Bhurey Paradise, Subhash became more fearful, looking all around him, as though he might run into Mukeshbro or Riteshbro. Kranti had to coax and counsel him before he agreed to enter Laj Mahal.

Inside, Kabiraj began to give her panipatti while Kranti fed Subhash some sorry-looking samosas she'd purchased on the way. She watched him while he ate. He appeared to be a different boy from what she remembered. Worse. Much worse. He reminded her of herself a few weeks back, when she had that psychotic episode at Hotel Kyalifornya. There had been a wounded look to him when she and Bhaskar had first met him, but now he looked unmoored. Of course, the skin turned yellow by jaundice made him look even more sickly. "He's a sad sack," Bhaskar used to say about him. "His mother's neglect, his stepfather's abuse, then, once he came to the Valley and learned to love Jharana, her disappearance." Kranti had sensed even then that Subhash spent too much time inside his own head. She wanted to ask him why he'd pointed at the Asylum and said that Bhaskar's killer had been inside. Who was he pointing to? But she was unsure that she ought to ask him right now; it could aggravate him further, perhaps fuel his paranoia even more. But now her own paranoia had also been ignited, and she had begun to look at the Ghimireys with eyes of suspicion. She had begun to see cover-ups and evasions in their mannerisms and their conversations. She recalled stories of fratricide, filicide, and parricide from Darkmotherland's deep historical past, when the oligarchs ruled the country and killed their own blood for power. Why would it be a surprise?

The suspicion and hostility at the Asylum these days was mutual. The Ghimireys barely spoke to her anymore. The nokerchakers, too, became quiet in her presence. When she asked them to do something, they pretended they didn't hear. Prithvi Raj had begun to look at her forlornly, as though she were a daughter of his who had become totally estranged over the years. Shambhogya glared at her every time she passed by. Priyanka avoided her eyes, telling her silently that she couldn't bring herself to look at someone who had caused so much hurt in this good family. Dinner times were awkward. The rest of the family talked amongst themselves, and communication with Kranti was kept to a minimum.

But Kranti was determined not to leave the Asylum, at least not yet. Let's see how far they'll take this, she said to herself as she continued to endure their shunning. At the dining room table, it was often as if she were in solitary communion with her food. But she didn't care. She wasn't going to bow down to these people, or let them throw her out. That they weren't going to do—she was certain of this. They were too afraid of what she would do once she was completely out of their control. They still harbored hope that she'd eventually agree that Smoke Chimney dai was the best thing that could happen to her, given her circumstances. She was perfectly willing to let them have that hope for now.

In Laj Mahal, as Subhash ate, Kranti casually asked him, as though she were merely making conversation, "Do you remember how Bhaskar Uncle used to take you and the other khateykids to Tato Chiso?"

Subhash, chewing on his samosa—he was masticating slowly, as if it hurt to move his jaws—nodded.

"Mocha Java was your favorite, I remember." Kranti stroked his arm, which had darkened because of the dirt caked on it. The boy needed a bath, for sure.

"Mock-a-java," Subhash said.

"Yes, maybe one of these days we can all go to Tato Chiso for some drinks."

"But Bhaskar Uncle won't be there."

"True," she said. "Babu, the other day you said that the person who killed Bhaskar was someone from my house, remember? Can you tell me who it is?"

"He didn't do it alone," Subhash said.

"Who didn't do it alone, babu?"

"The man at your house."

"But which man? Until you tell me which man, how can I understand?"

"You will never understand it," Subhash said. "All of these people are very powerful. And let me tell you something else. It will blow your brains away."

"Tell me please."

"Mukeshbro is also involved."

Kranti sighed. There it was, Mukeshbro again. "No, babu, you were talking about someone else. I know Mukeshbro is a bad man. He did something bad to you, didn't he?"

Subhash raised his eyebrows at her. "How do you know what bad thing Mukeshbro did to me? Who told you?"

"Bhaskar told me, babu." She didn't want to freak him out by saying she'd gone to Mukeshbro's flat, foolhardily, thinking she could find him and Rani. The tussle with Mukeshbro and his khairey garlfren in the flat came to her, in fragments. She didn't want to think about it.

Subhash studied her with mild contempt. "You know nothing then. Mukeshbro is the one who killed Jharana."

"I believe you, I believe you," Kranti said. "But you're thinking about Bhaskar, hoina? Mukeshbro doesn't have anything to do with Bhaskar, does he?"

Subhash leaned closer, looked suspiciously at Kabiraj, who was napping next to Rani, and whispered, "Because I saw the man."

"The man? Mukeshbro?"

Subhash nodded, then shook his head, then nodded again, this time more slowly. "He's Mukeshbro's man."

"Riteshbro?"

Subhash shook his head and snorted. "Riteshbro couldn't kill a fly if he wanted to. Riteshbro is a moron."

"Who then?"

"The man at your house."

"Who?"

"Mukeshbro's man."

"At my house? The big house? The Asylum?"

"Mukeshbro has people everywhere. I'm telling you, he's a big shot. If he finds out I've been talking to you—" He sliced his throat with his hand.

"Don't do that," she said, reaching out to stroke his cheek, but he pushed her hand away.

After that, Subhash wouldn't say anything more. He kept glancing toward the tent's door, and whenever he heard voices outside, he startled, as though he thought someone was coming for him. Kranti didn't want to aggravate his paranoia further, so she reluctantly stopped talking to him about Bhaskar.

—

When Kranti came to Laj Mahal the next day after work, Kabiraj was performing in front of Subhash and Rani, who were seated on the bed, sharing a bag of popcorn. Kranti stood by the door and watched.

"I was walking in the Tourist District, you know, minding my own business." He made an exaggerated sauntering movement, swinging his arms, whistling casually. Rani giggled. "I had gone to Tirthayatri Book House, you know, the one that burned down and was resurrected, and was returning with some books on the Beatnik poets when . . ." He stopped, arms and legs frozen in shock, mouth agape, as he looked at Kranti, as though she were Darkmother. "There she was on a big white horse."

"How big?" Subhash said. He sounded like an adult, like a teacher quizzing a cheating student.

"Very big," Kabiraj said, stretching his arms wide. "As big as an elephant."

"Elephant," Rani said, clapping. It was one of the few utterances she'd made since coming to Laj Mahal.

"But bigger than a regular elephant, like an Afrikan elephant, huge."

"White?" Subhash asked. "Milky white?"

"Not just any milk, pure-cow-mother-pure-grass-fed-churning-milk-white."

"Neighing?" Kranti asked from the doorway.

"Neighing like it was the sound of the universe opening. Like the sound of OM itself."

"OM!" Rani shouted.

Oh, the girl is capable of shouting too, Kranti thought.

"Front legs raised," Kabiraj said, lifting his arms in front of him. "Then rearing and neighing." Kabiraj neighed, "Neeeeiiigh! Neee-iiigh!" He looked bona fide ugly, with his upper lip raised, his facial hair lifting up as his neighing echoed inside Laj Mahal.

"But it was more beautiful—"

Kranti shushed him. "Listen!"

They heard sounds outside. Neighing. People in the surrounding tents were also neighing, as though agreeing with Kabiraj's neighing.

"Neeeeiiigh! Neeeiiigh!" Kabiraj neighed again.

He was responded to with a chorus. Rani also neighed. Then she stood and hopped around in circles in the tent, neighing, or just saying, "Nay, nay," which passed for neighing.

"What good neeeiiighbors," Kabiraj said, wiping the spittle from his lips, then joining Rani, his hand on her shoulders from behind as the two pretended to gallop like a horse.

"You're backing the right horse, for sure," Kranti said, pointing at Rani.

Rani was giggling and neighing, even as she coughed occasionally.

A smile had even appeared on Subhash's face as he watched how happy his sister was.

"Won't you be a good neeeiiighbor and join us?" Kabiraj asked Kranti. Rani didn't look like she was going to stop. Kranti hesitated, then she joined them, placing her hand on Kabiraj's shoulders from behind. "Come on, babu!" Kranti exhorted Subhash, who hemmed and hawed, then reluctantly joined them, saying, "I can never say neeeiiigh to you."

The chorus of neeeiiighs outside hadn't stopped, and, after a couple of rounds inside the tent, Kabiraj shouted that they should go out, which they did.

All across Bhurey Paradise, Bhureys were out galloping and neighing, either in small groups or individually, in the small pathways in between tents. It was as though thousands of horses had broken loose from a stable run by a cruel farmer and were celebrating their freedom.

43.

Kranti told Kabiraj that the Ghimirey household had been in a bit of a panic since the rumors about Matakoo began. It was a name that was on everyone's lips in describing this phenomenon of Dark-mother's divine appearance. Prithvi Raj had been calling the Lion Palace to talk to Papa but thus far he'd been stalled: PM Papa is in a meeting, he's on an inspection trip of new highways in the far west, he just flew to Bharat to finalize a bipartisan agreement, and once, he's flown to the mountains in a helicopter to search for the Son of Yeti. Aditya even went to the Humble Abode, but they wouldn't let him in, even after he told them who he was. Aditya returned home fuming. How dare they! They hadn't let him past the main gate, as if he were a commoner, a peasant or a day laborer. "Do you know who I am?" he shouted at the Loyal Army Dais, who told him that if he made more noises, they'd be forced to apprehend him.

"The old days are over," the Loyal Army Dais told him.

What days were these two-penny sipahis referring to? Aditya asked his family. The days of civility and people in their proper places? "I am the eldest son from Ghimirey & Sons," Aditya told the Loyal Army Dais. "Go inside and tell PM Papa that. Tell one of his assistants. Tell that faggot, Rozy. He knows who I am."

But in the end the Loyal Army Dais said, "Move on, Sir, before we take a drastic step against you."

"Against me? Against me?" Aditya was furious even in the retelling of the story. "Drastic step against me for doing what? For wanting to visit an old family friend, the man who'd come to our house for parties, who previously had met us in his pajamas, without appointments?" Aditya paused. "There was an old man in rags at the gate, a bhikhari type who'd come to bring a petition to PM Papa. You know, one of those entitled ones who think they are owed things without having to work at all. When I had reached the Humble Abode's gate and got out of the car the bhikhari bowed down to me as if I were PM

Papa himself. But once the ingrate saw that the Loyal Army Dais weren't showing me respect, his expression changed and he asked me questions as one might ask a fellow bhikhari on the street. What my name was, where my house was, who was in my family. He looked me up and down as if I didn't deserve the nice tie and the Armani suit I was wearing, like I was some kind of an upstart. You know what the bhikhari did next? As I was getting into my car, he waved his finger in front of my nose and said, 'As of now, there's no difference between the likes of you and me, so no need to be a big showoff with your fancy car and the shiny cream on your face. Just be warned: one day you'll lose all of it and I'll be the one driving this car.' And he slammed his hand on the hood of my car! What is it with these people? One moment they're ready to lick the dust off your shoes, and the next moment, they catch you in a vulnerable moment and they'll stomp on you. That's why I say: never trust the nokerchaker class. They plot to stab you when your back is turned."

Aditya continued, "On my way back I happened to notice that they're constructing all these flats near Ring Road. Have you noticed them? Ten or twelve large concrete buildings, ugly-looking but capable of holding many flats. They weren't there even a week ago. I asked the driver to stop, as I'd not been aware of this development. I mean, we're in the construction business. We're aware of the new bids, tenders, and contracts. So, where did this come from overnight? There was a man in a hard hat instructing some workers, so I approached him and asked, 'Bhai, who is behind this big construction project? Who is the builder?' You know what this guy, this mamuli worker did? He spit the pan he was chewing right next to my shoes and said, 'Rajjya.'

"'The Rajjya is building this? What is it, like a dormitory or something?'

"'Does it look like a dormitory to you?' he asked, his lips snarling in contempt.

"What is it with these people, I wondered. Where were they getting the nerve to behave like this?

"'No,' I said. 'They appear to be flats, but there was no announcement of this, no public bidding.'

"Now it was this construction worker's turn to look me up and down, as though I didn't deserve the suit I was wearing, as if given the chance he'd rip my suit off my body and force me to wear garb made up of the empty cement sacks lying around his feet. He said, 'Everything doesn't have to be done through a public bid so that the likes of you can immediately sink your teeth into it. This is a Rajjya project.'

"'But for whom? Who is going to stay in these apartments?'

"'The Rajjya is working on a resettlement plan. All the poor people without proper homes will be migrated to these apartments.'

"I cried out in disbelief. 'How come this was not announced in the media? And where is the money for all of this coming from?'

"The construction worker looked at me like I was some crazy fool.

"'It's going to come from me, of course,' I said. "From my taxes."

"And you know what this guy, this piddly-assed nobody, said? He said, 'Finally the sun is shining on your bald head.' Bald head! I'm not even bald!"

While Aditya was telling his story about the guards and the construction worker, the Ghimirey family, including Kranti, were in the living room. Everyone was drinking, except Kranti. Harkey was serving drinks and snacks. When Aditya finished his story with that warning about nokerchakers, everyone's eyes fell on Harkey. But he continued to serve with the same deference as before, as though he didn't have the mental capacity to know what his employers were talking about. Aditya continued saying what an ungrateful bunch the nokerchaker class was, how businesses like Ghimirey & Sons were providing so many lower-class people with a living so that they could feed their families and send their children to school. Kranti's eyes kept drifting toward Harkey's face, to see if it would register an ounce of anger, shame, discouragement—to show that he was human. But there was nothing. In fact, he took the whiskey bottle next to Aditya and said, "Shall I pour more, hajur?"

Chaitanya said that he too had been hearing that things were about to get topsy-turvy in Darkmotherland. "Where are these speculations coming from?" he asked. "Is there any truth to them?"

"What are you hearing?" Shambhogya asked.

"Chaitanya has not been able to sleep at night," Priyanka said. She was sitting next to her husband. She tousled his hair. She wouldn't have done this if Muwa had been present, but Muwa was in God's Room. Prithvi Raj was drinking whiskey. He appeared shell-shocked. The smooth-talking man who'd counseled Kranti some days ago had disappeared.

"There are rumors of an uprising," Chaitanya said.

"This has always been a country of rumors and hearsay," Prithvi Raj said. "I wouldn't put much stock in it. There have always been whispers about revolts, koos, and collapse."

"But what about those apartment buildings?" Aditya asked. "Something is afoot. We have to be careful."

"Yes, something is definitely up," Chaitanya said. "Where is PM Papa? He's disappeared completely. All we hear about now is Darkmother this, Darkmother that. I think the rumors are true: there has been a Matakoo."

Right then Harkey came with a fresh bowl of roasted peanuts. Everyone turned silent. He replenished the drinks, and as he was leaving, Aditya said that they wouldn't be needing anything for a while. Aditya shut the sliding door behind Harkey, fastened the latch and leaned against the door, facing the others. "I think we have to be careful about what's happening in the Asylum," he said softly.

"What do you mean?" It was Shambhogya.

Aditya jerked his head toward the door.

"What, dai?" Chaitanya asked.

"Is it just me, then?" Aditya said.

"What are you talking about?" It was Prithvi Raj. His face was swollen, as if he'd been stung by a bee.

"I think I know what Aditya dai is referring to," Priyanka said. "I also sensed it the other day. But I thought maybe it was just me, imagining things. But now you've confirmed it, Aditya-da."

"What on earth are you going on about?" Prithvi Raj said.

"Something is going on with the nokerchakers," Aditya said. "They're behaving strangely."

"How?" Shambhogya asked, clearly offended that she, the grand master of the nokerchaker domain, had been left out of the loop, and by none other than her husband.

Aditya observed everyone gravely. "I think they are plotting against us."

"Plotting?" Shambhogya said. "Plotting what?"

"I don't know what," Aditya said. "If I knew, I'd tell you. But there's something going on."

"If you don't know what they're plotting, how do you know they're plotting?" Shambhogya said.

"They're plotting something," Priyanka said, smugly, looking sideways at Shambhogya. "I'm also certain of it. This morning, I woke up around four-thirty, very thirsty, and noticed that I'd forgotten to put a water jug by my side before I went to sleep last night. So, I went to the kitchen. As I approached, I heard some whispers. I thought maybe they were robbers. But how? They couldn't have gotten past Cheech and Chong. Then one of them said, 'Shhh! Someone's here,' and the whispers stopped. I was terrified and wondered if I should scream, when suddenly, two figures bolted from the kitchen. One of them was that young Mokshya, I swear. I couldn't see who the other one was, but the figure didn't look familiar. I went into the kitchen, and Harkey was there, lighting the stove. 'What are you doing here so early?' I asked. Harkey rarely starts that early, and why wasn't he making tea in the kitchen in the Servants Villa? I asked him who was in the kitchen with him just then and he said no one. When I pressed him, he said in an irritated voice that the darkness must have confused me. But I knew I was not confused. I had distinctly seen shadows fly out of that kitchen this morning."

"They could just have been gossiping," Shambhogya said. "You know these nokerchaker types—they live more on gossip than they live on food."

"At four-thirty in the morning?" Priyanka said.

"Have you noticed the way they've begun to look at us?" Aditya said.

"I find it hard to believe," Prithvi Raj said. "Thulo Maya has been with us for decades now. She came with us from the village, before all of you were born."

"What difference does that make, Sir?" Aditya said. "These nokerchaker types will switch loyalty at the drop of a hat."

Priyanka said, "There was the recent case of the maid who worked in several houses and was acting as reconnaissance for some robbers. When the owners were out, the robbers came and emptied the house."

"Forget thievery," Aditya said, raising his index finger for emphasis. "What about that case last year when the old nokerchaker murdered both his master and mistress, after working for them for thirty years? There's your example of long service, Sir."

"Are you saying," Shambhogya asked, "that our nokerchakers are getting ready to murder us?"

"I don't know what they're getting ready for," Aditya said. "Whatever it is, it's not good. It's all brought about by this Matakoo, or whatever."

Chaitanya said, in one long whine, "I've also been hearing things. You know Hriday, son of the Baba Company? He was saying that the laborers and menial workers at his Hotel Laligurans have staged a near-revolt, so don't be surprised if it happens soon at our own Hotel Himalayan Happiness. Hriday happened to walk into the bathroom of the hotel lobby and saw water on the floor everywhere. When he located the head custodian in the garden, smoking a cigarette, the man was uncharacteristically lackadaisical about the whole thing. He walked toward the bathroom slowly, as if he were being pressed into a task that was not in his job description. When Hriday

asked what would the khairey guests think when they saw the state
of the bathroom in one of the most luxurious hotels in the Valley, the
custodian said something to the effect that Hriday shouldn't make
it his life's mission to always worry about what his white masters
from foreign countries think. That's the kind of attitude, the head
custodian said, that keeps us brown folks in servitude. The custodian
pinched his own arm when he said 'us brown folks,' emphasizing
the color of his skin. So, this two-penny custodian was lecturing the
son of the Hotel Laligurans owners on how to run his hotel. We
are not anyone's nokerchaker, the head custodian said. Those days are
over. The head custodian's 'we,' Hriday deduced, meant all of the
workers at the hotel."

Chaitanya continued, "But that was not the end of it. The next
morning Hriday found most of his kitchen staff enjoying the break-
fast buffet in the restaurant. The remainder of the kitchen staff,
three or four of them, were waiting on them, acting exaggeratedly deferential and asking them, in Angrezi, whether they wanted
Thai coffee or chamomile tea, or whether their pleasure would be
butter or marmalade for their bread. The kitchen staff who were
waited on were trying hard to suppress their laughter. The foreign
guests, who were obviously being neglected, were watching with
partly bewildered, partly amused, and partly annoyed expressions.
The kitchen staff didn't stop their nonsense even after they spotted
Hriday at the restaurant's entrance. The restaurant manager ambled
over, perspiring, and explained to Hriday that he tried to dissuade
the kitchen staff from this activity, but they accused him of being
a toady. Hriday asked him to get the custodial staff to serve the
foreign guests. Meanwhile, he went to talk to his kitchen staff, who
were stuffing strawberry pancakes and croissants into their mouths.

"'Are they tasty?' he asked them.

"'They're yummy,' they said. 'After all, we made them.'

"'Okay, people,' Hriday said. 'I'm glad to see you're enjoying your
own food. But there's a time and a place for everything.'

"Hriday was being very polite, but he could feel a clicking in his head—he was literally ticking, like a bomb, about to blow up. 'Can somebody explain the meaning of this?' he asked.

"'Why?' the senior chef said. 'Do you think we don't deserve to eat the food we cook with our own hands?'

"'That's not it,' Hriday said. 'But this is a restaurant for hotel guests.'

"'It's our restaurant too. Does it also not have our sweat and blood?'

"'Of course it does. But you could have received approval before-hand.'

"'Do we need permission from you to exercise our rights?'

"'I'm just saying that all you needed to do was come to me and I'd have organized a grand buffet for all the hotel workers.'

"'Oh, so you're going to feed us a buffet now, is that it? You're going to throw some food at us—is that what you think, Mr. Hriday Kumar, big-shot son of Baba Company?'

"A couple of the kitchen staff had aggressively gotten into Hri-day's face. Until a few days ago, all these people were saying, 'Yes, sir?' and 'Right away, hajur,' and now they were like snarling animals. The situation was brought under control only by allowing them break-fast time for forty-five minutes before the restaurant opened in the morning. Whoever had heard of such a thing?

"Hriday tells me," Chaitanya said, "that his kitchen staff are still not satisfied, and they and the other lower-level staff continue to break the rules and be rude to their superiors."

The room was quiet for a few minutes after Chaitanya stopped talking. Then Shambhogya said, "Well, what do you think it means? Why are the nokerchakers acting this way?"

After a pause, Chaitanya spoke as if it pained him to utter these words, "Hriday has heard that the Durbar is behind it."

There was a pin-drop silence in the room. From the street, the windy conversation between two riders on a motorcycle could be heard.

"Why would the Durbar be behind it?" Shambhogya finally said. Her body was still, but her eyes were attentive.

Prithvi Raj was shaking his head, like a man who's finally had confirmation that he is to be taken to the gallows. "That's impossible," he mumbled. "All of this is nonsense. Hogwash." His voice continued to rise. "All of you"—he pointed his finger, waving it at them—"have lost your mind." His finger came to a stop at Kranti. "You, what do you have to say about all of this?"

Kranti waved her hand dismissively, indicating she had nothing to say. What she really did want to ask them was: did one of you have a hand in what happened to my husband?

"What?" Prithvi Raj said, his finger still on her. "You have nothing to say?"

She should have stood and left the room then, but something kept her there. Perhaps she was worried about coming off as rude. Funny. Here was her father-in-law pointing his finger at her, and she was the one worried that she was appearing rude. She was the one who had remained quiet throughout the evening.

"Yes, Kranti." It was Aditya now. "Why are you depriving us of your words of wisdom?"

"I guess she doesn't consider herself a part of our family anymore," Priyanka said.

Kranti still couldn't speak. Talk about being tongue-tied. She could feel herself sinking into the couch, like prey folding into itself at the approach of a predator.

"Perhaps her mind is elsewhere," Priyanka said.

"Where?" Aditya said. "Where is her mind?"

"Perhaps Kranti didi's mind is with her wannabe poet," Priyanka said.

"Ah, Kranti's friend," Aditya said, leaning back against the couch and fixing his eyes on her. "The poet-king, the chronicler of the ills of our times. Tell me, Kranti, what do you two talk about? Do you talk about how much you miss Bhaskar?" He laughed. "What a riot. Bhaskar's friend, now your good friend." He said "good friend" in air quotes.

"I never thought I'd live to see such a day," Prithvi Raj said.

"What day, Sir?" Priyanka said. She knew already where he was headed; she was merely goading him.

"A day when my own daughter-in-law would go against my wishes." He was wiping his eyes—was he crying?

"You've broken Sir's heart," Shambhogya said to Kranti.

A weight was preventing Kranti from speaking—a strong pressure on her chest.

"Kranti didi no longer has any shame," Priyanka said. Something had been released inside her. It seemed she was inching toward a leadership position, or at least she was already on an equal footing with Shambhogya. If Kranti were Priyanka's mother, she'd have been proud of her daughter right now—this absurd thought went through Kranti's head. But she couldn't articulate any of it, not even a whimper to express her distress at being the brunt of their attacks. She had really withdrawn into herself, crouched in a near-fetal position, her face blank. She appeared to have floated up to watch herself. There she was, sunk into the couch, contracting into herself as if she were about to be eaten alive.

"What, Kranti, you have nothing to say now?"

"She's a manglik, after all," Priyanka muttered. It was a mutter, but loud enough for everyone to hear.

"It's not enough that she's a manglik," Chaitanya said. "She's a double manglik."

There it was, out in the open now. No holds barred. No whispers and innuendos.

"It's like this curse is upon us," Shambhogya said. "First Bhaskar's death, now this scheming and plotting by nokerchakers."

Had Muwa been there, Muwa would have risen up to defend her. Then again, she wasn't sure. Muwa could have remained quiet, too weak to fight.

"I don't know about this manglik-fanglik business," Aditya said. "But I don't want to see her male friends in this house. And I don't want to hear from anyone about how a Ghimirey buhari is hanging around with a lafanga who recites poetry for a living."

"Why, your highness," Chaitanya said, "you don't like poetry?"

"Poetry makes me snooze."

"Me—it makes me run for booze," Chaitanya said. He took a sip of his whiskey.

Aditya stood and gestured at Kranti:

"Hark, the beautiful maiden,
asleep over yonder.
Take a good look,
isn't she a wonder?
She's our dead brother's keeper,
but the poet king—
He's conned her."

"Poor Umesh," Prithvi Raj said. "We gave him so much hope."

"Forget Umesh dai now, Papa," Aditya said. "My main concern is that our family reputation is being sullied. Even if she doesn't agree to marry Umesh dai, she shouldn't be hanging around with these Bhurey chow mein–types."

"Kranti, you cannot see that Kabiraj anymore," Shambhogya said firmly, sternly.

"Is she really sleeping while we're talking to her?" Priyanka cried.

At some point Kranti must have closed her eyes, but even with them closed she could see them clearly, as though she were observing them in her mind's eye. I'll see them even when I'm dead and have turned into a corpse, she thought. Even as I'm cremated at the Lord of the Animals ghat.

"She's pretending to sleep," Aditya said. "Let her. She's got the message about the two-penny verse guy." He raised both his arms in the air. "Enough of her! I don't want to waste my time on such selfish women."

"Selfish!" Priyanka said.

Kranti was half-dead, or deeply sleeping, or something like that. She was aware of her body on the sofa. The air around her was hot from all the heated words that were flung about.

"We need to focus on the more pressing situation here," Aditya said. "What are we going to do about the nokerchakers?"

"Even more pressing, dai," Chaitanya said, "is this Durbar thing. If the Durbar is indeed inciting this discontent, the next stop will be our factories."

"Nothing will happen to our factories," Aditya said, grimly.

"Well, I'm hearing grumblings," Chaitanya said.

"Who is grumbling?"

"I don't know, but I am hearing from our factory supervisor, Pratyoush, that the workers have expressed their dissatisfaction."

"About what?"

"About everything and nothing."

"Ingrates!" Aditya said.

"Reprobates," Priyanka hissed.

"We need to do something," Chaitanya said. "We need to take care of it before it gets out of control like it did at Hotel Laligurans."

"In my time," Prithvi Raj said, "factory workers used to come touch our feet. They were grateful that we provided jobs for them so they could feed their families. To them we were like gods."

—

The nokerchakers everywhere were getting bolder, ruder, and more demanding. They organized protest marches, and were often flanked by Poolis Uncle cars (sometimes even the Loyal Army Dais) acting as security for them. Bums and khateykids banged pots and pans and blew on conches. Hijras, honeys, homeys, and frens took to the streets, singing and clapping. Their faces were lathered with makeup and they made kissy lips at the television cameras and threw colorful powders into the air like they were celebrating the holi festival. The streets were blocked or barricaded for hours, causing even snarlier traffic jams in a Valley already known for its snarly traffic jams. Khateykids danced on the tops of cars, imitating the latest Bollywood moves.

Motherland TV and Motherland Radio now openly talked about equality, particularly class equality. They advocated, softly at first, becoming increasingly louder, with compassion and justice for those on the margins, especially those belonging to the thirdgender. In public buses, the radios blasted out songs about revolution. They praised the janjatis and others who had been historically oppressed. A gay singer who had been banned under PM Papa was heard again, with a song about rising up. But the Rajjya also never directly mentioned Matakoo, nor did it mention PM Papa. It was as if it still wanted to impart the impression that nothing had changed in the power structure, that the gays and the minorities had always enjoyed full rights in Darkmotherland. However, it was hard not to notice that the billboards with PM Papa's face were slowly disappearing from the Valley. Those that were still left standing appeared faded and colorless, as though they were ancient, remnants from the country's antiquated past.

Kranti defied the Ghimirey injunction against seeing Kabiraj. She left the house early in the morning and spent the day at Laj Mahal with Subhash and Rani. She rarely ate with the Ghimireys. The last few days, Professor Shrestha had been trying to communicate with her through SMS messages, which Kranti didn't respond to. What is happening, chhori? Where are you? Everything going well? When her texts weren't answered, Professor Shrestha called, but Kranti didn't pick up the phone. Let her stew, she thought. Kranti had been through so much—the entire Old Buspark episode, the disappearance and reappearance of Kabiraj, her own private ordeal at the Dharma Adhikari trial, her lingering suspicion, despite her doubts about Subhash, that the Ghimireys might have had something to do with Bhaskar's death. It looks like I can survive fine without my father, Kranti thought.

At the Asylum, tension was also brewing between the masters and the nokerchakers. The nokerchakers were becoming more visible, louder, their laughter ringing through the corridors more often. They continued to cook, clean, and do the laundry, but now everything was done half-assed. The meals were burnt, or watery, sometimes tasting faintly of petrol. The kitchen floor was often sticky, with food crumbs everywhere. Cockroaches had moved in. One morning when Kranti went to the kitchen to make tea for herself—the nokerchakers had begun taking their time waking up in the morning—she heard a rustle at her feet. She looked down and saw what appeared to be a rat. But it couldn't have been a rat with a head that looked like that of a small kitten's. It screeched before it scampered off, its tail swishing. She went to the Servants Villa to tell Harkey about the monkey-rat, and he sleepily replied, "Well, we are out of meat today, anyway. I'll catch it and cook it for lunch. Should I fry it or should I grill it?" Shyam Bahadur, sleeping on the next bed, laughed as he turned over.

All over the Valley there was bewilderment over what was happening. Men dragged on their cigarettes in tea shops and said philosophically, "The nokerchaker has become the master."

One man told the story of how he was beaten by up his young male nokerchaker.

Women shopping for vegetables complained, "Now I have to serve bread and tea to my kanchi, instead of the other way around."

There were tales of nokerchakers who were already making major decisions in the households, such as kitchen renovations and children's schools, even signing property documents and carving their names into the plaques at the front gates.

It was like a koo by the nokerchakers, they said. Or Nakoo. It was hardly a koo, merely a revolt that was showing reasonable signs of success, but Nakoo had a nice *up-yours* ring to it, as the word referred to the male genitalia in the language of the Valley's original inhabitants.

~

In Laj Mahal, although she still coughed, Rani was gradually getting better. But Kranti worried about Subhash. While he had fully recovered from jaundice, he smiled more often, and even participated in the conversations, he still exhibited signs of paranoia. He startled every time the cowbell rang at the door, and at night Kranti had to hold him in her arms because of his nightmares. He had a running narrative about the pimp Mukeshbro.

Another mattress had been added to the existing one to create sleeping space for the two kids. Subhash and Rani slept together, with Kabiraj next to them. During the day, the bedding was folded and put away in the corner so that there was more room when Kranti came after work. At times, it seemed like even with four people, Laj Mahal was crowded. Yet that didn't prevent Kabiraj and Kranti from bringing more kids into the tent's cramped space.

Mamata, a blind girl Rani's age, was abandoned by her alcoholic parents. Nilesh was a talkative eight-year-old who sang Bollywood tunes with gusto; he was short and round, with a pockmarked face, but he was filled with a lot of firepower. Sunaina was close to Subhash's age, the smarty-pants of the group. She could read quickly, recite useless trivia, and tell half-funny jokes. Kranti called her Professor Sunaina. In the village, her mother had been accused of witchcraft and was murdered. Zero was the nickname for Jogendra, a sweet kid but always a bit slow at understanding things. The other kids said that he was that way because he'd been squashed under a tree in his village during the Big Two. But no one knew where his village was, or who his parents might have been. "His history is zero," Professor Sunaina opined.

Bimala was an indigenous girl who had been sold by her parents to a husband-and-wife daktar team in the capital. She wanted to attend school, but the daktars made her work nonstop in the house from four A.M. to ten P.M., so she had run away. She didn't want to return to her impoverished village because it didn't have electricity or television. Pepsi was a six-year-old boy Kranti and Kabiraj had found cuddled between stray dogs near the Holy River. Hira, age unknown, was so quiet that at times they forgot he was even around. He and Subhash seemed to have formed a bond, for the two spent time together, often in silence.

Of course, it was no surprise that Laj Mahal proved to be woefully small for all these bodies, as small as they were. Fights frequently broke out over shared space or toys. They'd borrowed beddings from their neighbors in Bhurey Paradise, but one of them turned out to be filled with lice, which meant that everyone in Laj Mahal caught lice, including Kranti. Lice wasn't uncommon in Bhurey Paradise, but this was a full-fledged infestation. She and Kabiraj washed everything— clothes, bedding—and Kranti sneaked a vacuum cleaner from the Asylum and vacuumed the tent thoroughly. While Laj Mahal was being cleaned, Kabiraj struck a deal with the neighbor next door to buy the man's tent. The neighbor had made a decent amount of money with a food cart and was moving out of Bhurey Paradise into an apartment. Kabiraj had apparently helped him a number of times in the past, so he agreed to sell his tent to Kabiraj at a discount. Once the neighbor vacated his tent, some of the khateykids moved into the other tent, which helped with the spacing issue.

Kranti continued to dwell on who might have killed Bhaskar. She had nightmares about it. Blurry figures coming toward her and Bhaskar as they sat next to a pond feeding the ducks. The blurry figures stabbed Bhaskar in the back. Giant birds with big talons swooped down on Bhaskar, who looked a lot like Subhash, and carried him away, eating him on a mountain top. Even now, she wanted desperately to believe that it was PM Papa who had orchestrated Bhaskar's death. But, more and more, that theory rang false. Why would PM Papa have the son of Ghimirey & Sons killed, even if that son turned out to be a Treasonist? If PM Papa wanted anyone killed, it would have been Professor Shrestha, wouldn't it? Cut off the head of the hydra, or whatever that expression was. Then there was Subhash, convinced that someone from inside the Asylum was behind it. Kranti increasingly realized that she too had come to believe it. But who? All of them? They'd planned it together? Even Shambhogya? Whatever one could say about Shambhogya, she was no killer.

How Kranti wished Subhash would say who he'd seen. But since that day when he'd talked about the Asylum, he had clamped up, and no longer spoke of Bhaskar Uncle's killer. Kranti had even thought about taking him aside and sternly wagging a finger in his face, so he'd cough up the identity of who he thought was behind it. But she was never the stern type. Besides, it could backfire: he might never speak to her again, or worse, he might run away.

She told herself not to care, that it wasn't necessary for her to know whether the Asylum had a hand in her Bhaskar's death. What mattered now—she told herself over and over, sometimes successfully, sometimes futilely—was that there were these khateykids, and too many of them roaming the streets. Every time she saw one of them, she saw Bhaskar. And no, it wasn't merely a metaphorical expression. She actually believed that Bhaskar, or at least his spirit, had descended from somewhere—heaven? up above? the clouds?—and entered the bodies of these khateykids. And every time her eyes fell upon one of them, she saw a part of Bhaskar in them. Perhaps the eyes, or the tilt of the head, or the way they spoke— a phrasing or an intonation. If a khateykid happened to stare back at her, it was Bhaskar staring back at her, as though mocking her. Once, in an alley near the Tourist District, she chanced upon a young boy, about eleven or twelve years old, who was sitting against the wall, his head down, sleeping, or just depressed. Something about the cut of the boy's hair reminded her of Bhaskar. The cut of the boy's hair! She couldn't believe how desperate she'd become.

"Bhaskar!" she'd cried.

The boy had uncomprehendingly looked up at her. His eyes were cloudy, distant. Drugged. She knelt in front of him. "Bhaskar, is that you?"

"Who are you?" the boy asked in a slurred voice.

"It's me, Kranti. Don't you recognize me?"

"Are you my garlfren?"

"Yes! Yes!" She laughed. Of course it wasn't Bhaskar, but it was okay to pretend, to believe that Bhaskar had returned to her in these various forms.

"Ah, you are a crazy woman, I see," the boy said. "Get out of here! I don't have time for such nonsense!"

On some days her longing for Bhaskar, and to know who had killed him, was so acute that she couldn't focus on anything else. She descended into a funk where her body ached, and her soul only cried out for Bhaskar. Kabiraj sensed this, and often left her by herself to deal with it. He realized that she was exorcising her own guilt, and Kranti was grateful that he understood and left her alone. On other occasions he held her closely and said, "It's okay, it's okay. Everything will be fine."

She would rock in his arms, like a child seeking solace.

"You know that he is gone but that he'll always be with you," Kabiraj said softly.

"I need to know what happened to him," she said. "Who do you think killed him?"

"Providence," Kabiraj said. "Sometimes shit happens."

She pushed him away from her. "Shit happens? Shit happens? That's your hifalutin poetry?"

Professor Shrestha's calls kept coming and Kranti didn't pick them up. One day they simply stopped. Then there was a flurry of calls from Murti, and Kranti didn't pick up those calls either. Then they also abruptly stopped. Good riddance, Kranti thought. I don't need those people anymore. I have my own family here in this Palace of Shame.

44.

It was utter foolishness, but Chaitanya barred Kranti's way at the front door of the Asylum as she was on her way out. "What are you doing?" she asked.

"You can't leave today, bhauju," he said. He gave her a pleading look.

"And you're going to stop me?"

He didn't answer. She felt a presence behind her and looked back. Priyanka.

"You heard him," Priyanka said. "We forbid you to leave this house today."

"Forbid?"

"Yes, forbid. You are a Ghimirey buhari and it's time you behaved like one."

It was not just Kranti's imagination. A hardened look had come over Priyanka's face in the past few weeks, a tightening of the jaw, a more upright posture, an edge to her utterances. Some type of inner fury was clawing its way out, making her resemble Shambhogya more and more. Good for Priyanka, thought Kranti. But bad for her that she couldn't arrive at this point on her own without mimicking her oldest sister-in-law.

Kranti tried to push past Chaitanya, saying, "I have to go to Bauko Bank," but he wouldn't budge. "Bhauju, please don't." His face was flushed. Kranti felt Priyanka's hands grab her wrists and twist them behind her. There was a flash of silver. Priyanka tightened her grip on Kranti's hands, and metal was clamped around her wrists. Handcuffs.

They led her up the stairs in handcuffs, one on each side, clasping her arm. Where did you get the handcuffs? she wanted to ask Priyanka. She wondered if Chaitanya and Priyanka were into kinky stuff in the bedroom.

For some reason, the house was empty. Shambhogya and Prithvi Raj didn't appear. Kranti suspected they were lurking behind pillars and walls. Had Shambhogya handed this task to her assistant Priyanka, or had Priyanka taken charge on her own? Was this a major breakthrough for Priyanka in unshackling herself from Shambhogya's tight grip?

Kranti allowed herself to be propelled forward, like she was being taken to the gallows. But no, at her door, they un-handcuffed her and gently shoved her into her room. Priyanka said, "From now on there is no need for you to walk the streets, shaming our family." She paused. "If you feel hungry, you can just knock on the door and either Shambhogya or I will bring you food."

Shambhogya! Not Shambhogya-di! This was indeed progress.

"Don't even try anything funny, Kranti," Priyanka said. Kranti! Not Krant-di! Wah! Wah!

"What funny thing could I try?"

Priyanka merely looked at her, then she shut the door and Kranti heard her bolt it from the outside.

Stunned, and yet also paradoxically calm, Kranti contemplated her situation. It was as though ever since she got to know Bhaskar and prepared to be his life partner, she was getting ready for such a moment. But she had to admit that she hadn't anticipated being *handcuffed*. It was a sign that things were reaching a climax. She wondered what Bhaskar would have thought of his wife behind bars like this. Bars? There were no bars, and the window was wide open. If she wanted to, she could try jumping to the lawn below and make her escape. Could she bribe Cheech and Chong to allow her to flee? A few thousand rupees might suffice. Cheech and Chong, like the other nokerchakers, were also moving toward rebellion. They were balking at the day-and-night vigilance they had to maintain. They too had managed to finagle a hundred percent increase in their wages, yet were still derelict in their duties. A few days ago Kranti had come home early in the evening to find the gate unmanned, with a few shady types lingering outside on the pavement. One lafanga was about to enter the gate when he saw Kranti and stopped. He leered at her, barely moving so that her body was forced to graze against his as she went past him. Inside, she shouted the guards' names, but no one came. The men outside had entered the gate and were studying the house.

Right then Harkey strode out from the garage and asked in a commanding voice what was happening. When Kranti asked him where Cheech and Chong were, he made a small, dismissive gesture with his hand, which she took to mean that she should mind her own business and go inside. As she left, she heard whispers behind her.

"Idiots!"

"But Harkey dai—"

"I warned you."

"But the gate was open."

". . . not ready yet . . ."

The next morning when she left to go to Bhurey Paradise, Cheech and Chong were back at their station. As she walked past them, their eyes followed her.

She had been drugged—she realized this only in the afternoon when she tried to wake up from what she thought was a nap. Priyanka had come into her room late that morning with a plate of dal-bhat and a tall glass of lemonade. "You need to eat," she said, as she sat on the bed and pushed the tray toward her. It was still a command, but some of the earlier anger appeared to have melted away.

"What do you think you're doing, Priyanka?" Kranti asked. The whole thing was ridiculous. Here she was, imprisoned in her room, with this formerly mousy woman acting as her jail warden, when there were khateykids in Laj Mahal needing her.

Priyanka reached out and stroked her cheek. "Nothing bad is going to happen, dear. I think you know exactly what you are up against."

"And what is that?" She wanted to add, "You mousy little piece of shit," but restrained herself.

"You need to be taught a lesson."

"A lesson? What kind of lesson?"

"You need to be disciplined."

"How? Who will discipline me? What am I, a child?"

"You're certainly acting like one. Here, you want me to drink your lemonade? Here." Priyanka took a sip.

Thirsty, Kranti drank the lemonade, knowing that something wasn't right, but a pleasant numbness had come over her body. The lemonade tasted delicious, minty. When she'd drunk halfway, Priyanka said, "Okay, now you eat some food." She set the glass down, picked up the plate and began feeding Kranti.

"I'm not a baby," Kranti said with a giggle. The room seemed to have become more fluid. Everything felt nice.

Priyanka's voice was filled with honey as she rapidly fed Kranti, as efficiently as if she were born feeding children. She made a small scoop, with her fingers—combining rice, dal, kauli, and chicken—placing it in Kranti's open mouth. There was hardly any time to breathe between one swallow and the next. "More?" asked Priyanka and Kranti lazily shook her head. "Then finish the lemonade," Priyanka said.

"I need to sleep," Kranti said. Her body was heavy—what was in that food? Maybe she shouldn't have eaten it.

"The lemonade will make you feel better." She scooted close to Kranti, placed her palm on Kranti's spine to prevent her from toppling back, and placed the glass to her lips so she would be forced to drink.

"Mmm, mmm," Kranti said, attempting to shake her head. But, in the end, it was just easier to drink.

"Yes, Kranti, that's the way," Priyanka whispered. Ah, now she's sweetly calling me Kranti—this thought, like a lazy balloon, drifted through the vast expanse of her mind. She finished the drink. Priyanka eased her back on the bed. "You've left us no choice," Priyanka said.

～

When Kranti awoke, her body was sluggish. Her mind felt heavy and she drifted back to sleep again.

She was decked out and bejeweled in a red sari. She was dreaming, except that it was not a dream. Before she could take stock of the situation, Priyanka and Shambhogya barged into the room and said that everyone was waiting for her downstairs.

"What's happening downstairs?" she asked, but her tongue was so thick that it seemed she was pushing a giant marble around the inside of her mouth. She swallowed—her throat hurt—and she asked again.

"We have something in store for you," Priyanka said.

"I don't want to go down," she said, sounding like a petulant child.

"Come, Kranti," Shambhogya said. "Otherwise, it'll be too late."

"Late for what?" She had been propped up on her feet now by Priyanka. Kranti could barely keep her eyes open, yet she knew she must—the khateykids! Nilesh, Zero, Bimala, all the rest. They must be wondering where she was. But what time was it? She tried to loosen herself from Priyanka's clasp so she could consult her watch, but then she wasn't even sure whether she was wearing a watch—her wrists were jangling with gold bangles—or whether this was even the same day. She searched for her mobile, but it wasn't on her person, nor nearby. She might have slept for a couple of days, there was no way to tell. "I need to go," she said, trying to wrench herself away. But she could barely stand, so there was no question of escaping the claws of these women. "My khateykids," she said.

"They'll be fine," Shambhogya said. "They have your so-called dallu to look after them, don't they?"

"They'll be worried."

"We'll send someone to check on them." Of course, they wouldn't, Kranti knew. They hated everything about those khateykids.

They were now outside her room, walking down the hallway. Across the open space above the courtyard, on the other side of the house, she could see blurred images—nokerchakers, they were watching.

Chaitanya had come to fetch them. "What's the delay?" he asked in an irritated voice. "The lagan is about to expire. We can't let that auspicious moment pass us by."

"She drank too much," Shambhogya threw an accusatory glance at Priyanka. "She's too sleepy," she explained to Chaitanya, who asked them to hurry.

"Priyanka," Shambhogya said. "Could you fetch a towel? I want to wipe her face."

In the living room a wedding pyre—a large bronze bowl with a fire—was burning. All the windows had been opened to enable an easy passageway for the smoke, but the room was still smoky. A pundit was intoning mantras. Prithvi Raj was seated next to the pundit and was wearing a dhoti so that his ample chest hair, whitened around the nipples, was there for everyone to see. Even in her grogginess, Kranti remembered the time she'd seen him like this with Smoke Chimney dai on the lawn. Smoke Chimney dai. Smoke from the wedding pyre. What the hell!

Prithvi Raj Ghimirey waved them over. Aditya was standing by the window, looking out, and he turned upon their arrival with a bemused expression.

"No, no," Kranti said, but her own words sounded feeble and inconsequential. Besides, the smoke was stinging her eyes so badly she could hardly make sense of her own thoughts.

"We need a fan in here," Prithvi Raj said.

Priyanka brought a wet towel and forcefully wiped Kranti's face. Kranti cried out in pain when the rough towel passed over her lips.

"I still don't understand why this is being held in our living room," Aditya said, "when we have a perfectly good lawn."

"And announce to the whole world what's going on?" Shambhogya said.

"Who can see, huh? Who can see?" Aditya pointed outside, to the high compound walls that blocked visibility from the street.

"All the panhandlers and the hangers-on outside the gate will know something is up," Priyanka said. "Besides, Muwa shouldn't get a whiff."

"With all this smoke, a whiff is exactly what she'll get," Aditya said.

"Bring a fan, I said," Prithvi Raj commanded.

"Tell Harkey to bring a fan," Chaitanya said.

"As if he will," Priyanka said. "He'll tell me to get it myself."

"Shh!" Shambhogya said. "He might hear."

"Given how arrogant they've become," Aditya said, "I won't be surprised if they try and charge in here and create a ruckus."

Priyanka and Shambhogya exchanged glances. "That's taken care of," Priyanka said.

"How?" Aditya asked.

"How, he asks," Shambhogya said. "How do you think?"

Understanding seemed to dawn upon Aditya. "Sweetener? How much?"

"You'll probably faint when you hear."

"This is turning out to be an expensive affair, isn't it?" Aditya angrily said. "And all for what? So that this donkey's so-called curse is lifted."

"Aditya, you fool," Prithvi Raj said calmly. "Once we get this accomplished today, then the black cloud that's hanging above us will be lifted."

"Maybe," Aditya said. "But will it change what's happening outside?" He told them that the Loyal Army Dais had come and shut down Raddi Tokari. General Tso's orders, Aditya was told. And Himalayan Happiness was now effectively under seige by its staff. "What about Matakoo, then?" Aditya asked his father. "Is your ceremony going to change the fact that PM Papa is effectively gone now?"

"Are you sure that's what has happened?" Prithvi Raj asked. "PM Papa knows all kinds of tricks. Remember he plays five-dimensional chess while his enemies play checkers. This could be a giant hoax he's playing on the country."

For a moment, all of them pondered whether PM Papa was behind Matakoo. Maybe he had something grand planned that was going to have the country in shock, and likely in stitches, once it was revealed.

"For now," Prithvi Raj said, "I'm going to take care of this first."

"And you're going to do that by forcing this brainless woman?" Aditya said.

"At least I'm doing something," Prithvi Raj said, the veins on his neck bulging. "I have to protect this." He pointed to the house. "I have to protect us."

"It's not auspicious to get into arguments now," the priest cautioned.

"Aditya, it's past the time for debates," Shambhogya said. She turned to Priyanka. "Go fetch Umesh dai."

Shambhogya steered Kranti to sit in front of the fire, opposite Prithvi Raj, who looked away. Kranti realized that she hadn't eaten anything; a sudden pang of hunger struck her, and she whispered, "Food." Shambhogya whispered back that food would come later, that she could eat only after the ceremony.

Smoke Chimney dai entered in a groom's suit, a pagadi adorning his head. Pagadi! What did he think this was, a Bollywood movie? He was smiling, and didn't look like his nervous self. As soon as he sat next to Kranti, the priest increased both the volume and speed of his chants. Ihemabindra samnuda chakrawakeba dampati, prajayaurau swastako biswamayurbashanutam.

The room filled with smoke and the priest's incantation. A shadow lurked outside the windows on the lawn. Muwa! She had indeed caught a whiff. Shambhogya dispatched Aditya, who quickly left to distract his mother. A brief argument was heard outside, Muwa's querulous voice drifting in through the windows. It was not clear whether she knew the exact nature of what was happening inside, but it was obvious that Muwa suspected Kranti was involved. "Muwa!" Kranti shouted, but it only came out as a whisper, barely audible even to herself.

That night in bed, she was still groggy, but gradually, hour by hour, her mind appeared to be moving toward clarity. Still, sometimes she mistook the body next to her as Bhaskar's, and at other times she thought it was Kabiraj, who had somehow managed to sneak past Cheech and Chong and make his way to her room. Kabiraj was spending the night with her in the Asylum—what a message that would send to the Ghimireys! But no, it was not Kabiraj but Smoke Chimney dai, wearing his pajamas, his eyes on her, a cigarette smoldering between his fingers. By now she had begun to hate how he reeked of cigarettes: his clothes, his body, his breath. Wait, what was he doing here, in her room? The events of the morning and the afternoon began to cohere in her head: the handcuffs, the lemonade, the smoke-filled living room, Muwa's figure outside the window, Prithvi Raj's fatty cheeks, the priest joining her hand with Smoke Chimney dai's.

He was watching her, smoke spiraling out of his nostrils. She laughed in disbelief. He took it as a sign of her happiness.

"This is the best day of my life," he said.

"Even better than when you first married your wife?" she couldn't help asking.

"She was somewhat of a dunce. A good woman, but no education, so a bit dim that way. And certainly not as beautiful as you."

"She gave you your children."

"That's all past now," he said. "Today is a new beginning." His cigarette burned down to the butt. He stretched and smiled.

Her mind was a lot clearer now but her body still felt sluggish and sore. Umesh leaned over with his smoke-breath and said, "Kranti, you are so beautiful. You can't imagine how long I've waited for this day."

"I'm having my period."

"What?"

"I'm menstruating. Nachhune bhaeko chu ke!"

He expressed disappointment. "So we can't do it? Even a little?"

"You'll just have to wait." And she turned over and closed her eyes.

She could feel the disappointment in his heavy breath as he turned off the light and slipped next to her. He put his hand on her arm, and she tolerated it.

She tried to imagine what Bhaskar would have thought of her situation now. She was in bed with this chimney of a man, smoke-breathing down her neck. She held her breath; Smoke Chimney dai didn't move. He was snoring. The best day of his life had tired him out.

She too closed her eyes, and Bhaskar appeared before her. "You can't say I didn't warn you about my family," he said, grinning.

"Yes, you warned me, then you abandoned me."

"You have Kabiraj now."

"It's not the same." Yes, it was not the same, but it was still nice. She was deeply appreciative of the calmness she felt when she was with Kabiraj, with the khateykids, how she felt everything was all right with the world.

The khateykids! Her heart thudded, and her mind snapped to a startling clarity. She slid herself out of Smoke Chimney dai's grasp and quietly stood by the side of the bed. She had people who were waiting for her, who needed her.

Kranti took out a dhoti from the cupboard. The full moon's large silver disc was shining right outside the window; she could even see the rabbit ears on the moon's surface. She loved watching it when she was a child. She unfurled the dhoti, then wrung it so that it turned into a thick rope. She continued to keep an eye on Smoke Chimney dai as she did this, but he didn't even stir. She tied one end of the dhoti-rope to the windowsill, flung the rest down the side of the house, climbed up on the window and, grabbing the dhoti with her hand, descended. Halfway through, the dhoti began to slide down—the knot must have started to loosen—and before she knew it, she was on the ground with a thump, the dhoti cascading after her. Fortunately, it wasn't a long fall, and apart from a rattling of her stomach, she didn't experience any hurt. The lawn was wet, and since she didn't have her shoes on, her feet were damp. She stood still, listening to the sounds around her. To her right was a movement, and a shadowy figure abruptly appeared.

"Kranti?" It was Muwa.

"Shhh."

"What is going on?"

Kranti clasped her mother-in-law's arm and took her to the nearby bushes. The lights were on in the guards' cubicle by the gate and she could see that Cheech was awake. Or was it Chong? He seemed to be scrolling through his phone.

"I can't stay in this house any longer," she whispered to Muwa.

"What happened?" Then Muwa didn't seem to need any more explanations. "Doesn't matter. Wait here for now. When I give you the signal, run through the gate."

Before Kranti could ask what she meant, Muwa went toward the gate and asked Cheech (or Chong?) to come out. Cheech (or Chong) asked her why and she said she needed to show him something. "Go away!" Cheech (or Chong) said. "I don't have time for such nonsense."

"Please."

"Crazy old woman. Go back to God's Room!"

Muwa disappeared into the shadows near the garage, which was at the end of the driveway. Soon, a wailing sound, like the cry of a disturbed cat, could be heard.

"Motherfucking hag!" Cheech (or Chong) cursed and left his post and went toward the garage. His brother Chong (or Cheech) seemed to have woken up inside the cubicle and said, "Who? What?"

Then both the twins rushed toward the garage to silence Muwa.

Muwa had created Kranti's moment of escape. Kranti headed toward the gate, cringing at the possibility that Cheech (or Chong) might hit Muwa to bring her in line.

"Help! Help!" Muwa cried.

"Shut up!" both Cheech and Chong shouted.

Kranti slipped out of the gate into the night.

⌣

The Loyal Army Dais went to the Town of Lakes in the middle of the night and hurled Bir out of bed, while his wife and two children watched in befuddlement. A helicopter hovered above. The army captain who headed the mission was the best of the lot, someone decorated in multiple skirmishes and peace-keeping missions in Aafrika and the Khadi countries. He quickly put a hood over Bir's head and shoved him into the waiting jeep. Bir had realized his dream as he was growing up: he lived on the side of the hill next to the magnificent lake. He had done well for himself. He was a major contractor in town; he'd married a former Miss Mountain winner; and he had two adorable children. He amassed more and more money every day. The house where he had been apprehended was built just a few months before. It was a large bungalow, with a wide circular balcony that overlooked the expansive lake below and the stunning Fishtail Mountain to the north. On a clear sunshiny day with no wind, you could see the mountains reflected on the lake's pristine surface, just like in the postcards.

"What did I do wrong? What did I do wrong?" he asked the Loyal Army Dais as the truck barreled down the hill. He wondered if this arrest had to do with his bribing an official for a construction deal, but that type of bribery was commonplace. This felt like something else. A distant memory came to him: he and Rozan locked in an embrace. Rozan? But how? Why was he thinking of Rozan now?

By the time the army plane lifted up from the runway, he had already vomited twice in the paper bag that the Loyal Army Dais had provided for him.

It was dawn when the plane landed in the Valley, and he was driven to the Durbar, still in handcuffs, but without a hood. In one of the inner rooms the priest-attendant was chanting a morning hymn dedicated to the Pothead God. Bir worried about his wife and children. He was a good father, a good husband. He had worked hard to construct new buildings in the Town of Lakes, especially after the Big Two, and had earned a name for himself. This was a mistake, and soon he'd be exonerated.

He was thrown into Darkmother's room, handcuffs intact.

Darkmother was sitting on her bed, wearing her psychedelic hippie frock, her face heavily made up to accentuate her rosy lips, the brightness and roundness of her eyes. "Chinyau malai, Bir?"

Bir recognized her immediately, the heavily caked face or not.

He'd thought about her for years, even though there was no question in his mind that he loved his wife and children. Even in the midst of loving his family, he'd thought that if that gorgeous creature from his past were to materialize, his desire would be reignited. And now this. Bir relaxed. "What a pleasant surprise."

Intuiting that he was about to utter her name, Darkmother raised her finger to silence him. "Don't utter that name, don't make that mistake."

After Darkmother's ascension to power, the Town of Lakes too, had rallied, with people singing her praises. Bhaktas had flocked to the Boar Goddess temple on the tiny island in the middle of the lake. From his balcony, Bir had watched as hundreds of boats, red, blue, and yellow, had converged on the water, ferrying Bhaktas who had gone to the temple with offerings.

Observing Darkmother, Bir thought it funny that they had had a relationship at one point. And now, another opportunity had opened up for him, for further success. "I'm beginning to understand." Bir smiled. "All these years. I didn't know."

"All these crazy ideas swirling in my head," Darkmother said.

"You've done well for yourself."

"So have you, from what I hear. A wife, two cute kids, a house overlooking the lake and a clear view of Fishtail Mountain." Darkmother left her bed and sat with him on the floor. He thrust his handcuffs toward her.

Darkmother untied a knot in her frock and pulled out a key. She opened the handcuffs and let them slide to the floor. Bir massaged his wrists to get the blood flowing again, and moved his arms about. "For you, I'd have come willingly," he said. "There was no need for this."

Darkmother ran a finger across Bir's lips. "I didn't want to take any chances."

Bir grabbed Darkmother, pulled her toward him and kissed her hard on the lips. It was a long, rough kiss, the kind he used to give her when they were younger. He was gentler with his wife, for she would have otherwise thought he was a low-class junglee. When he finally let Darkmother go, she was breathing hard. "I see," she said, "that you haven't forgotten your old ways."

Bir moved closer and nibbled at Darkmother's ear. "And I haven't forgotten you." He lowered his voice to a whisper, even though there was no one else in the room. "Every time I make love to my wife, I think of you. It gives me a terrific hard-on. Like this one." He took her hand and placed it on his crotch. "Feel it?"

Darkmother nodded. "A raging bull you are." She massaged his cock. "I don't know how much of this, how much of you, I can take anymore."

Bir knew then that in a couple of days he'd be able to return to his wife and kids. "It was just a big misunderstanding," he'd say to his wife. "They thought I was someone else. But no worries, it's all clarified now. They're very apologetic." He wouldn't need to give his wife all the details, but he would tell her, "And guess what? Now I have connections in the Durbar, so we can expand our business to the Valley." His wife, in her wide-eyed eagerness for more money, for more fame, more prestige—I've married someone exactly like me except prettier, Bir often joked with his business associates—would be delighted at this turn of events. Then Bir would come to the Valley every few weeks, a guest of the Durbar, to spend time in Darkmother's bedroom.

All of this unfolded before his mind as he allowed himself to be massaged by Darkmother. Then she stood and moved to the bed, where she lay down and buried her face in the pillow.

He followed her and stroked the back of her head. "What's the matter?" All these years when he'd been building his own life and enjoying it with his wife and kids, this woman—yes, he'd begun to think of her as a woman now—had been pining for him. Look at her now, overwhelmed by this reunion. I should have loved her more before, he thought kindly. I should have been gentler. Then, mirthfully: I would have, had I known she'd end up wielding this much power.

"I'm sorry," Bir whispered. He had to make amends. "I was mean to you." He added, "But I never stopped thinking about you all these years." It was partly true: she hadn't been on his mind *all* the time. But he'd thought about her often enough that at this point he could persuade himself into believing that she'd been on his mind day and night.

Darkmother turned to him, tears making black rivulets on her heavily made-up face, and said, "And I am sorry that I have to do this to you. But I must."

45.

Nothing had changed in Hotel Kyalifornya. The same worn-out lobby, the same building with peeling paint and moss around the windows. The noises from the Old Buspark still infiltrated the hotel. Prashant was asleep at the front desk, his head resting on the counter. "Welcome to the Hotel Kyalifornya," Subhash whisper-sang from a distance, then sneaked past him and went to what used to be Jharana's room. The door was shut. He gently knocked, not sure who'd open it. It was Gunekeshari, an old honey, still in her nighttime maxi, a toothbrush in her mouth, her hair uncombed. Gunekeshari had hated Jharana, considered her a rival who was undeservedly favored by Mukeshbro. Gunekeshari stared at him for a moment, then a grin spread across her face. She pulled out the toothbrush and said through a foamy mouth, "Arre! Stinkface. What brings you here so early this morning? And what happened to you? Why do you look so pale?"

"Just passing through," Subhash said. He didn't tell her that he'd roamed the Valley all morning, his mind a jumble of images from his days with Jharana and what he'd seen at the Streetwise School that day when Bhaskar Uncle was killed.

Gunekeshari signaled to him to come in, then coughed into the sink that was in the corner. She rinsed loudly, making *pichik-pichik* sounds as she forcefully spat out the remaining paste from her mouth. Then she held her nose between her thumb and forefinger and jettisoned a menacing-looking mucus from her nostrils. "Ahh!" she proclaimed in satisfaction, wiped her hands on her maxi, then turned to Subhash and asked him whether he wanted fried eggs, his favorite.

Subhash nodded.

Gunekeshari fried an egg for him while he chewed on a piece of bread. She asked him where he'd been all this time and what he'd been doing. Then she gave him a glass of hot milk, for which he was grateful. Jharana also used to insist that he drank hot milk every day, as milk was crucial for growing bones. As he sipped the hot milk, he realized how hungry and thirsty he was. He'd sneaked out of Laj Mahal after a night of fitful sleep, his mind wracked by images of Streetwise and Jharana. Kranti Aunty had stirred a bit as he'd opened the tent door, but she'd merely turned to the other side and gone back to sleep. Subhash knew she too hadn't slept well because he'd observed her peeking out of the flap at odd hours during the night.

"Where is Mukeshbro?" he asked Gunekeshari.

"Why?" Her eyes narrowed. "So you can go to him with your crazy talk blaming him for what happened? Telling the world that he killed your Jharana? Listen, Subhash, that whore ran away because she was an ungrateful, unscrupulous bitch. She didn't care a whit about anyone, including you. The sooner you realize it, the better it'll be."

Subhash gave an imperceptible nod.

"You still pining after her, Stinkface, after all this time?"

Close to two years, Subhash thought, but it felt like yesterday that Jharana had found him stumbling through the streets, delirious, and taken him under her wing in Hotel Kyalifornya.

"No longer pining," he said to Gunekeshari. "Outta sight, outta mind." He'd heard that expression used by a khairey in the Tourist District, and although it had taken him a moment to understand what it meant—the words contorted by the khairey's accent, sounding at first like attaside attamine—once he understood, he'd loved how pithy it was. "That's the past."

She stared at him, then smiled. "Now light is finally shining on your thick skull. You're even using Angrezi on your Aunt Guneke-shari now. Go see Mukeshbro, apologize to him. He'd be happy to see you."

"Where is he?"

She handed him the egg and he began eating. "He has a garlfren now."

"Garlfren?" Subhash plunged his spoon into the egg—Guneke-shari somehow knew that he liked his eggs with runny yolk.

"A young khaireyni, with hair as yellow as that egg yolk you're eating, and skin as pale as an albino's. I don't know what he sees in her—she has no meat on her bones, no boobs, she's as thin as bamboo, and there's always a god-awful smell about her. I think they call that smell sugandhara but to me she stinks as though she's just wrestled with a hog."

"The khaireys call it patchouli," Subhash said, shoveling the last bit of egg into his mouth. That was another term he'd heard in the Tourist District.

"Patchouli-fatchouli whatever, don't lord your Angrezi over me. Mukeshbro is besotted with her. He's even named her Goriramri. Yes, gori she is, given the fact that she's a fair-skinned khaireyni. But ramri? I'm no longer in my prime age, and no one in my life called me pretty, but my God, even I'm easier on the eyes than that skank."

"Is he going to kill her too?" Subhash couldn't help saying.

Gunekeshari stared at him, then snatched the plate away from the table, as though taking the egg away from him, even though he'd already licked the plate clean. "Keep thinking that, keep saying that, it's your own mind that you torture." Subhash didn't respond, so Gunekeshari sat next to him on her bed and put her arm around him, her breasts pressing against his shoulder. "Listen, Stinkface, I know that Jharana and Mukeshbro fought. Often they fought over you. He thought that you distracted her from her pilgrims. And he was right, hoina? She doted on you, to the detriment of her pilgrims."

"Mukeshbro always told her that he was going to kill her."

Gunekeshari slapped him on the head. "That's how men talk, you idiot! That's how Mukeshbro talked. But he loved her, don't you see? He wouldn't do anything to harm her. All would have been forgotten had you not gone to the Poolis Uncles to lodge your complaint."

"The Poolis Uncles are all Mukeshbro's friends," Subhash said dryly.

"Were. That's also in the past now, so it makes sense that you also let bygones be bygones."

"What happened to Mukeshbro's Poolis Uncle friends?" Subhash asked.

Gunekeshari explained that after Matakoo, the Poolis Uncle chief, IGP Chhetri, was quickly replaced by another top-dog Poolis Uncle, and everything fell apart. No luxury hotel, no Khadi clientele. Mukeshbro never recovered from the blow. He'd turned into a fulltime pothead loser. Now, more and more often, Riteshbro was handling his business, trying to get back all the honeys who now had gone to work for Badal, Mukeshbro's old rival. Most of the time Mukeshbro hung out in his flat, stoned out of his mind. "But he'd appreciate an apology from you, Stinkface, and he'd be happy to see you. Maybe your stinky face is precisely the kind of thing that'll lift up his spirits. He's mentioned you a few times."

Maybe because he wants to kill me? Subhash thought.

"Talk to Riteshbro too. I'm sure he'll be able to use you some way, just so you can earn a few rupees and not starve. Riteshbro says that he always liked you, thought of you as a younger brother, until you went totally berserk. Is it true that you physically attacked Mukeshbro in Diamond Park? That's why you were forced to escape to the Tourist District?"

Subhash nodded. He'd received a sound thrashing then. His jaw had felt twisted and his teeth had ached for weeks.

"What were you thinking? You could have ended up dead in a gutter. I couldn't believe it when I heard it. My dear Subhash going for the bossman himself."

"Kraymah!" Subhash said, imitating Mukeshbro. He stood and jerked his body, as though he'd been electrocuted, drawing laughter from Gunekeshari.

"I love it when the joker comes out in you," Gunekeshari said. "I heard you were living in the Tourist District for a while. Are you now in Bhurey Paradise?"

"I've been here and there," Subhash said, unwilling to disclose his whereabouts to Gunekeshari in case she'd tell Mukeshbro.

"And I hear you have a sister now, some little tramp you found in the garbage dump. Where is she?"

"She ran away a while ago," Subhash said.

"Too bad. I was going to say that I could teach her some tricks of the trade. You know, they like them younger and younger these days." Gunekeshari fingered his shirt, then ran her hand over his chest a bit longer than he liked. "The clothes you're wearing are nice. Where did you get them?"

"I worked as a nokerchaker for a woman," Subhash lied, "but then she kicked me out."

"And you didn't cut her throat, like all nokerchakers are doing to their mistresses now? But of course, you wouldn't do something like that." She caressed his chin. "So gentle, my Subhash, such a sad story, to have been betrayed once by your mother in your village and the second time by that harlot Jharana."

"Do you think this Nakoo will go anywhere?"

"Who knows? Anything can happen in Darkmotherland. I sympathize with these rebelling morons, though. Nothing as bad as working as a nokerchaker for someone, understand? Even working for the richest person in the world. You lose your freedom, your dignity. When I hear about all my fellow sisters being tortured and raped in those Khadi countries, my heart weeps. Here, even though I'm in this crummy hotel with a singing receptionist whose song I've never understood, I'm in control of my life. I can slice off a man's cock if he starts acting funny."

"I think I'll go now."

She tousled his head. "After you see Mukeshbro and Riteshbro, come and tell me what they say, okay? If I'm free this afternoon, we can go to the movies together." She gave him directions to Mukeshbro's flat, which she said he'd bought recently. All courtesy of Riteshbro's hard work.

The flat was not too far away—in the next neighborhood, in fact, on the top floor of a tall, thin building. Clutching his bag, Subhash climbed the stairs. The neighborhood around him was already awake and active. He had to move quickly.

~

Just as light broke in the sky, Harkey appeared at Laj Mahal accompanied by Shyam Bahadur, Cheech and Chong, and a few other shady types that Kranti had seen lurking around the Asylum the other day.

Kranti had barely slept a wink all night. She had laid her bedding on the floor near Laj Mahal's door, frequently lifting the flap at the bottom to look out. She had dozed a few times but had been startled awake by the slightest noise: a child's cough, voices and groans from the other tents. Seconds before Harkey and his men arrived at Laj Mahal, she had been seized with a premonition and parted the tent flap to look. There he was, Harkey, in the distance of the dawning light—she could tell it was him by his stocky figure—at the front of a group of men striding toward Laj Mahal on the pathway between the other tents. "Kabiraj!" she shouted, and Kabiraj, who was at the other end of the tent, awoke and punched a number on his mobile.

As the men dashed toward the tent, Kranti regretted putting Kabiraj and the khateykids in harm's way like this. She ought to have taken them elsewhere as soon as she got here last night. Or, she shouldn't have left the Asylum. She ought to have stayed with Smoke Chimney dai for longer until she figured a way out of her situation.

The men came wielding sticks, and—Kranti saw with horror—khukuris. They were holding the khukuris above their heads, as though ready to use them at a moment's notice, or strike at any Bhurey that dared to get in their way.

The khateykids were stirring awake, and she fervently prayed that these invaders, these marauders, wouldn't go to the next tent, Laj Mahal II, as the khateykids had come to call it, where four of the older khateykids were sleeping. Kabiraj should have slept in Laj Mahal II, so that there was at least one adult in each tent. What a mistake they'd made!

Again, she peeked out through the tent flap: the men were only a few feet away now. And no one had come to their rescue—Kabiraj's phone call had not worked.

Through the flap she saw that Harkey and his men were right outside the tent.

"Open up!" Harkey shouted.

"The rope!" Kranti whispered to Kabiraj, who was attempting to simultaneously console and shush the khateykids. The khateykids had sensed that something bad was about to happen and were looking bewildered and whimpering. Kabiraj leapt to the door and criss-crossed a rope, fastening it to small hooks protruding from the edge of the flap. They had practiced fastening the rope last night to secure the flap, knowing full well that it was only a very short-term solution. How hard would it be to slash open a tent?

Apparently, Harkey had the same thought, for now he was yelling, "If you don't let us in, we'll rip open this tent."

The men struck at the tent with their palms and their fists, and Kranti saw the imprints of their hands on the fabric. The men's foot-steps sounded all around them, even on the opposite side of the tent, toward Laj Mahal II. A part of Laj Mahal seemed to cave in—one of the men had hurled himself at it—and they saw the body on the fabric before it bounced back out. "*Mierda!*" she heard someone curse, and she was sure it was either Cheech or Chong.

The khateykids huddled together in the corner opposite the door. but it seemed that some of the men outside had figured out where they were because Kranti saw their shadows in that corner outside. "Didn't you call?" she shouted at Kabiraj. "Where are they?"

"No response!" Kabiraj yelled back.

The khateykids were wailing now. The always silent Hira was so afraid that he was standing in the corner of the tent, covering his face, weeping. Kranti shouted at Subhash to console Hira; it was then she noticed that Subhash wasn't there. "Where's Subhash?" she said. "Did he go out?"

"I hope he's not outside, or in the toilet. Those men—"

"Whore!" Harkey's voice boomed outside. "Open up now."

"Kabiraj, maybe I should go out, go with Harkey to the Asylum. Otherwise, who knows what they'll do."

"No, wait. Let me try something." Kabiraj cupped his palms next to his mouth and let out an ear-splitting yodel. His previous yodels had sounded like yodels, but this one sounded like a cry of distress, like dozens of goats crying out during the Ten-Day Festival the moment before they were slaughtered.

Right then, the men outside sliced the door open with their khukuris, and stumbled in, falling on the ground. Cheech and Chong shouted *"Aye, caramba!"* simultaneously, lost their balance, and became entangled with each other as they fell upon the khateykids in the corner.

—

Subhash stood observing the two figures sprawled on the bed. The window was open, ushering in a cool breeze. He could see a room in the adjacent building, where a portly man was looking into the mirror and slowly dressing.

The knife, which was about six inches long, was in Subhash's hand. He had picked it up from Laj Mahal and stuffed it in his school bag on the way out.

He was grunting in the outhouse, swatting at horseflies, when he heard his classmates screaming from the main building at Streetwise. Initially he thought that Bhaskar Uncle had made a raucous joke, but the screaming continued, and he stood and lifted the jute curtain that covered the small window in the outhouse that provided a view of the school's yellow building.

The khaireyni's face had scars and pimples. Goriramri—that's the name Mukeshbro had given her. Fair beauty. Her arms, from what Subhash could see, were mutilated with needle marks. He'd seen similar marks on several honeys and homeys in the Diamond Park.

A group of men emerged from Streetwise. A couple of them held weapons in their hands. He could see that one was a machete and another was a

khukuri. Subhash thought he saw some red—blood?—on the glinting sur-
face of the machete. Then he noticed the Jeep slowly emerge from next to
the tree to his right, and stop on the lawn. The men casually got into the
Jeep. When the Jeep turned around to leave, Subhash saw the driver, the
man with the high cheekbones he had seen at the Asylum, a man he knew
worked for the Ghimireys.

Mukeshbro had lost weight—his cheeks were hollow and his arms
thinner than how Subhash remembered them.

Subhash had seen the man with the high cheekbones—what was his
name? Hari? Harsha? Harka?—talking with Mukeshbro outside the
gates of the Asylum. He'd also seen him enter and exit the Asylum a couple
of times before that, and also briefly during Bhaskar Uncle's wedding,
when he was instructing the serving staff who were walking around with
small appetizers.

—

There were five of them—Harkey, Cheech and Chong (who was
guarding the Asylum then?), and two other lafanga-types she'd
seen hanging outside the mansion's gate. They immediately attacked
Kranti and Kabiraj. While they didn't use the khukuri, they beat
them with the sticks they had, repeatedly striking them on their
heads, backs, and arms. The khateykids wailed, probably thinking
that the same fate awaited them. Cheech and Chong trapped Kabiraj in a corner of the tent and hit him repeatedly with their sticks
as he tried to shield his head with his arms. One of the khateykids,
Nilesh, leapt upon the back of a man, who then swung his body
wildly to try to dislodge him.

Harkey grabbed Kranti by her hair and attempted to drag her
out of the tent as she kicked and screamed. Another group of bodies
then charged into the tent. Thirdgenders, more than a dozen of
them, burst into an already overcrowded and chaotic Laj Mahal.
They made a lot of whooping and hollering sounds. They even yelled
"Eh! Heh! Geh! Peh! Meh!" like the Fundys did when they raided

the tents in Bhurey Paradise—the thirdgenders knew the power of those words firsthand!

"What the hell?" Harkey shouted in confusion, wildly swinging his khukuri at the thirdgenders. But he had barely landed a couple of swings when he was overpowered by them. Harkey and his men were quickly pushed against the corners of the tent, which had become so crowded now that it was impossible to stand upright without stumbling over the next person. The thirdgenders weren't armed, but there were twice as many of them than Harkey and his gang—and more had gathered outside the tent, calling to thrash the invaders and to slice off their cocks. Harkey and his men knew that it would have been foolish to fight the thirdgenders. If you struck one down, it was likely that more would instantly rise in their place, like how in one ancient battle depicted in the scriptures, the Ten-Headed Demon King sprouted a new head every time he was decapitated.

Laj Mahal was filled with fluttering saris and dupattas and loud voices, and arms waving and gesticulating, as though the Ten-Headed Demon King was right there with his multitude of limbs. Harkey and his men were paralyzed in their corner. The leader of the thirdgenders, Pyari, asked Harkey what his intentions were. Harkey said he was merely following orders.

"How much money were you paid?" Pyari asked. She had picked up a stick that had fallen on the floor during the melee and was tapping it against her palm, like a Poolis Uncle in a B-grade movie. Many of the thirdgenders had tucked their dhoti-ends into their waist for the fight. So had Pyari. Two big patches of sweat were spreading in her armpits.

At first Harkey denied that they were paid any money. "We are nokerchakers," he said, appearing contrite. "We have to do what our masters tell us. We didn't want to come here to get Kranti bhauju forcefully, but we had no choice. They'd have fired us if we hadn't."

The other men, including Cheech and Chong, solemnly nodded (Cheech and Chong were muttering "*Perdoname, perdoname*"), but it was clear that even Harkey was having trouble keeping a straight face as he talked about being a nokerchaker at the Asylum.

Pyari banged the lathi on the tent wall next to Harkey's head, making him flinch. "Shut up!" she said. "If you don't tell me how much you were paid, I'll strike each of you like this." She whacked the knees of the lafanga next to Harkey, and the man screamed, doubling up in pain. "Are you going to tell me or not?" Pyari asked Harkey.

"Two lakh rupees."

"Only?" It was Nilesh, who was apparently energized by the conversation.

"Three lakh rupees."

"Only?" Now it was all the khateykids who were enjoying being the victors.

"I swear. I swear." Harkey was perspiring because Pyari had raised the stick again. "They were going to pay only two lakh, but I raised it to three."

"Ah, the perks of Nakoo," Pyari said.

Pyari signaled to her colleagues, who leaped upon Harkey and his men as if they were attacking them, whereas they were really searching their pockets. Harkey had a lot more money than the others. Pyari held Harkey's one lakh in her hands and said, "What is this?"

"Where did you get that money?" Shyam Bahadur asked his uncle.

"Ah, betraying your own men, eh? There are consequences to betrayal." She handed the money to her colleague who shoved it into her blouse. Harkey argued that the thirdgenders had no right to take all the money, but he became quiet after Pyari struck him twice on the legs, making him scream in pain.

"How many of us here?" Pyari asked Harkey.

"Many." The area outside the tent had crowded even more, and now there were perhaps thirty to forty people, not only thirdgenders but honeys, homeys, and Bhureys, itching to get inside to lay their hands on the goons.

"And how many of you?"

"Five."

"Are you going to return here again?"

"No."

"What will happen if you return?"

No answer.

"Okay, let them go now," Pyari said.

Harkey and his men left. Once they were out on the street, they hurled threats at the entire Bhurey Paradise before sprinting out of the Parade Ground toward the Diamond Park.

—

All Subhash had to do was plunge the knife, perhaps a few times, into the chest of this scoundrel, who looked so drugged out that he most likely wouldn't even open his eyes.

"Look away, I'm hideous!" Subhash whispered, hiding his face with his right arm. It was a line that Mukeshbro often used in his performance as Kraymah. Subhash didn't understand the reference, but the words had always seemed to fit Mukeshbro ("He is hideous, isn't he, Subhash?" Jharana used to say), and it seemed to apply even more now as he slept with his garlfren.

Subhash sat at the edge of the bed, which lurched a bit under his weight, but neither Mukeshbro nor the khaireyni fluttered their eyes. So, it wasn't Mukeshbro who was coming after Kranti Aunty—Subhash had misunderstood the conversation between her and Kabiraj Uncle last night. This fool sleeping in front of him with the filthy khaireyni could not swat a fly if he wanted to. How long, he wondered, before Riteshbro took complete control over the pimping business and pushed Mukeshbro out of the way?

Subhash couldn't let himself be weakened by Mukeshbro's pathetic state. He couldn't let himself be swayed. This was the man who had taken away sweet Jharana. At her memory, tears welled up in his eyes. And he couldn't forget that he was also involved in Bhaskar Uncle's death. "Motherfucker," he whispered. "Your sins are howling from the mountain." It was an expression he'd heard his mother say—paap dhuribata karaunchha—and it seemed appropriate for the situation. He lifted the knife in the air.

46.

Since the morning there had been rumors that another big earthquake was coming. Tremors had been felt throughout the day, signs of the Big Three, people said, even though in the past the tremors had remained tremors and no monster earthquake had followed. Still, these rumors had a force of their own, and once a rumor started, it gained momentum by the hour. What would be merely a suggestion in the morning about the possibility of a giant shaker, often triggered in the media by a Fundy guru, a celebrity, a politician, or an astrologer, would turn into a sure-shot possibility by mid-morning. By early afternoon the entire city would be in a type of mania, with the residents of old, teetering houses fleeing their homes for open spaces and sometimes, inexplicably, for crowded markets. With Darkmother in power, the frequency of these rumors had diminished. The Durbar had announced that Darkmother was using her spiritual powers to hold the Big Three at bay. Darkmother Slays the Big Three, it was said on Motherland TV. The slogan had become popular, but for a citizenry traumatized by hundreds and hundreds of tremors, even Darkmother's promise didn't allay all fears. So, every few days there was a scare. Some lasted a few hours, and others much longer, until the entire city was in a frenzy.

At Laj Mahal, Kranti and Kabiraj were arranging the bedding for the khateykids before turning in for the night.

"Aren't you worried about your mother?" Kabiraj asked. "It's been weeks now, Kranti, since you've checked in with her."

The rumors about the Big Three had been particularly vicious that day, and even as the city prepared to sleep, a buzz circled over it like electricity. Many people who'd escaped their houses in fear that they'd collapse were congregated at the Bhurey Paradise. The khateykids, too, had been hyper all day, and it had been a challenge putting them to sleep. Along with the rumors of another big one had been a rumor that Darkmother was ready to squelch those who were rising up against her. The Beggars had been mentioned in this regard.

"What am I expected to do?" Kranti said. "It's not like she cares, anyway."

"Aren't you at least curious how she's doing?"

"Not particularly," Kranti said.

She had to admit, her mother had been in the back of her mind, like an annoying mosquito that's hovering and buzzing behind your ear. Yesterday evening at the Lord of the Heavens chowk an old friend of Professor Shrestha spotted Kranti buying vegetables and came rushing over. "Is it true? Is it true?" she whispered. "Have they taken her?"

"What? Who?" Kranti pretended she didn't know what Mrs. Misra was talking about.

"Your mother? She's disappeared?" Mrs. Misra looked about quickly.

"Who told you that?"

"Have you looked for her?"

Kranti inspected the radish in her hand more closely for blemishes.

"Aren't you worried for her?"

Kranti asked the vendor why the radish looked so jaundiced.

"A strange daughter you are," Mrs. Misra said. "Strange woman."

Kranti acknowledged now, but only to herself, that she had been worried about her mother. However, when the worry had surfaced, she'd quickly squelched it. Now that Kabiraj mentioned it, she felt another stab of anxiety about her mother. Kranti had heard it in a tea shop in Bhurey Paradise that Darkmother had already dispatched her people to go around the Valley apprehending those critical of her koo.

The next morning, after a restless night of sleep (every hour or so someone from another tent shouted, "It's coming! It's coming!" and someone nearby would ask them to shut up), Kranti went to Beggar

Street. The Big Three had turned out to be a bust. Everyone credited Darkmother. It was said that another big one was already rumbling underneath Darkmotherland, but Darkmother would gather her magic and slay it.

The front door was padlocked. Mr. Sapkota was on his roof, watching. Kranti didn't want to engage with him, but he shouted, "Kranti! O Kranti!"

Kranti looked up sharply.

"Where are you these days?"

"Here and there."

"I hear you've gone to live in Bhurey Paradise. True?"

"True."

"You left the Ghimireys? La hera! A buhari of such an esteemed household, now living among the rats. What has the world come to?"

An answer surged up inside her, but she squelched it. "How long has my mother been gone?"

"Three weeks to this day," Mr. Sapkota said, chuckling. "The Loyal Army Dais came. Your mother, you know, I thought after Bhaskar's death, she'd give up, but she's proved to be incorrigible. Your Dada, on the other hand, was such a fine man. Your mother crushed his spirit. God bless his soul."

"Did they say where they were taking her?"

"You think the Loyal Army Dais gives out such information? I've heard they're even stricter now, with Darkmother at the helm. Jai Matadi!"

"So, it was the Loyal Army Dais?"

"Yes," Sapkota said, grinning. "Did you notice that now they have Darkmother patches on their arms? Jai Matadi!"

Kranti hadn't seen the Loyal Army Dais close enough to notice. "They took only her?"

"No, they also took that butterfly guy, what's his name, the flitty one."

"Chanchal?"

"Yes, and that buff-boy Vikram."

When Kranti gave the padlock a tug, Mr. Sapkota said, "Come to think of it, that poseur Murti wasn't here."

"That's odd. She's always here."

"A poseur, isn't she? I heard that she was visiting a sick relative, thus not in attendance at your mother's subversive activity that day." Mr. Sapkota smiled. "Pity. That Murti was the one I disliked the most among the Beggars."

Kranti made a move to go, and Mr. Sapkota said, "The one I liked the most was your husband. Bhaskar." Mr. Sapkota crouched down and asked Kranti to come closer. Reluctantly, she went to the wall next to the roof. "So, who do you think offed Bhaskar, huh?"

Kranti shrugged.

"Now there are rumors that it might be the Ghimireys." He was watching her face closely. "Any truth to it?"

"Sapkota Uncle, aren't you ashamed? This early in the morning, you are spouting such gibberish?"

Kranti walked away.

"I blame your mother," Mr. Sapkota said loudly after her. "Madam Mao. I blame her entirely for what happened to him. If she hadn't sucked him into her subversive activities, he'd still be here. Handsome Bhaskar."

As Kranti moved toward the Tourist District, where shops were just beginning to open, she wondered if her mother was dead, just as she'd wondered whether Kabiraj was dead a couple of months ago. Things change, yet they remain the same, she supposed. If her mother wasn't dead, then she was rotting in a prison somewhere, perhaps in that giant Khor underneath the Durbar. If she was dead, she was dead—Kranti could do nothing about it.

At the crossroads in the Tourist District, she saw some Fundys arguing with a group of young men with long hair. Briefly, she stood to watch. The Fundys had apparently made some comments about the long hair and the tattoos on the youths, who had, instead of walking away quietly this time, decided to fight back. They had now surrounded the Fundys, and although both groups were equal in number, the Fundys were already beginning to sound conciliatory. Kranti couldn't help but think that once people smelled weakness in others, as these young men did, they were instinctually aggressive. In this case, the aggression was even more pronounced because the Fundys had been the aggressors for so long. Kabiraj had told her that just the other day he'd seen a boyfren-garlfren team slap a couple of Fundys around because the Fundys had said something about how they were "too amorous" on the street. Or, it was possible that the Fundys might not have said anything at all, and that the couple had attacked them because, well, now they could.

On the way to see Murti, she caught a glimpse of General Tso on TV inside a shop. General Tso was talking animatedly about Dark-mother's divine appearance. There was no trace of his tough military demeanor.

Murti's house was not too far away, stacked tightly with other houses, in an alley at the bottom of the hill near the New Market. Her door was padlocked. Of course, if the Beggars who'd been arrested had been tortured by the Loyal Army Dais, then they would have squealed on the whereabouts of Murti, who was probably also already apprehended by now. As Kranti stood at the door wondering what to do next, she heard someone urgently whisper her name from around the corner of the alley, two houses down. She turned toward the voice, but she couldn't see the person's face, only a beckoning hand and another whisper. Kranti moved closer.

Murti was a ghost of what she had been; her eyes were now sunken deep into their sockets and her hair was matted. She was wearing a crumpled up dhoti, looking as though she'd slept in it for days. Murti appeared relieved to see her. "They've taken everyone away, Kranti nani."

"How long have you been in hiding?"

A couple of people walked by them, and Murti covered her head with the dhoti and turned toward the wall. "Too dangerous here," she whispered. "Come." She grabbed Kranti's hand and pulled her deeper into the alley.

"Where are we going?" Kranti asked. It occurred to Kranti that being seen with Murti could also get her into trouble. With all the khateykids to take care of, Kranti couldn't take that risk right now, but it was too late. They were speeding through the alleys. Even though she'd disliked Murti all her life, she now felt sorry for her and trailed alongside her. Murti dragged her through one alley after another, this way and that. After some time, Kranti couldn't tell which was north or south, east or west. It seemed that they went deeper and deeper into the bowels of the Valley, places that Kranti didn't even know existed. Finally, they reached a crumbling, dilapidated house that was probably already in bad shape before the Big Two, but now was worse. The front of the house tilted forward at a severe angle, the tiles of the roof ready to come showering down on the pedestrians, electric wires on nearby poles crazily crisscrossing close to its windows.

"Here?" Kranti asked.

"Yes, it's fine. Besides, I don't have a choice." She led Kranti into a room that had a sukul on the floor. A rat stood up on its haunches in the corner, looking at them expectantly as one might look at the arrival of generous aunts. "I don't sleep here every night," Murti said, "just in case Mata's Matriots end up coming."

Ah yes, overnight Papa's Patriots had become Mata's Matriots, who wore black because Darkmother's color was black. Mata's Matriots did not harass people like Papa's Patriots used to. They walked around in groups with stern gazes, shouting "Jai Matadi!" Overnight "Jai Matadi!" had replaced "Pure Darkmotherland!"

"Where has she been taken?" Kranti asked.

Dust rose from the sukul when the two sat down on it. Kranti also smelled garbage—there must be a dump nearby, she thought.

"I don't know," Murti said. "I hope nothing has happened to her." Murti's face became distorted, and Kranti thought that she was going to start ranting about the injustice of it all, but, surprisingly, she wept, silently at first, then with small heaves. "It's been hard, really, really hard," she finally said. "I've always thought of myself as a strong woman, but I really miss Madam. I feel unmoored. I had taken for granted my reliance on her for everything, how close she is to my own soul." She took a deep breath. "But this time she has vanished. With Matakoo, we thought things would be better, but some things never change."

"Were you planning something?"

Murti didn't answer.

"Were the Beggars plotting something, Murti?"

"We had been talking."

"What?"

"We had been saying that nothing had changed."

"But there was Matakoo. Isn't that change?"

"Yes, but we wanted our rights back," Murti said.

"But Matakoo has just happened! You don't know what Dark-mother is going to do. You don't know whether she's going to turn out like PM Papa."

"You are so naïve, Kranti nani. Madam has been arrested and we don't know where she is and what's going to happen to her. What more evidence do you need?"

Murti had a point, and for a moment Kranti wondered if history was repeating itself. Actually, since Matakoo more people had enlisted in the Loyal Army, thus the army's presence had multiplied in the Valley. The age for joining the Loyal Army had been reduced from eighteen to fifteen, so now suddenly youths, the Loyal Nanis, many of whom looked like they should still be playing Seven Stones in their neighborhoods, marched the Valley streets. Military junta. That's what Bhaskar would have said had he been alive to see these new near-children recruits marching down the streets with their rifles and their khukuris.

"So what was the plot?"

"We were going to storm the Durbar."

Kranti couldn't speak for a moment. "You were going to do what? How?"

"There was talk that we might be able to turn the guards at the Durbar's northern gates. One of the guards was Vikram's cousin, and he was going to convince the others."

"But how?"

"Money."

"How much?"

Murti was hesitant.

"How much, Murti?"

"Ten crore rupees."

Kranti sucked in her breath.

"It's a lot of money, I know, but there were five guards to be paid."

"Where did the money come from?"

Again, Murti was reluctant to say more.

"Murti, who financed this?"

"Madam arranged it."

"From where? The sky?"

"She depleted her savings, sold all of her jewelry."

Kranti laughed in disbelief. "And how was she going to live the rest of her life? Was she going to eat her freedom for her daily meal?"

"We were all desperate."

"But you all didn't use *your* money. It was my mother's money you used."

"We don't have any money."

"How convenient," Kranti said, suddenly so angered that she couldn't stay seated on the sukul. She got up to pace the room, but the room was so compact, with old boxes and piles of clothes taking up much of the floor, that she could barely move, so she abruptly sat down again. "Come to think of it, that was my money. I would have inherited it once your Madam passed away." She didn't like the way it sounded when she said it, and she hadn't really thought about inheriting her mother's property or wealth until now. What was there, anyway? Throughout her life, Professor Shrestha had reached into the family savings to fund the Beggars. Now, with this act her mother had given away something without a thought to what she might have passed on to her daughter. For the millionth time, resentment toward her mother flared up inside of Kranti. Then she thought: What if she's already dead? What would all of this matter then? "Do you think they've already executed her?" she asked Murti.

"I don't know, I don't know. Who can rely on rumors? Poor Madam. If she's alive, she must be greatly suffering."

For a moment both of them were lost in the possibility of Professor Shrestha being tortured. It was General Tso who had jailed Professor Shrestha a few months ago. She thought of the clip she'd seen of him earlier in the shop. He had looked like a child excited at having seen the most awesome of kites in the sky during the long season of the Ten-Day Festival and the Festival of Lights.

"So, what was the plot you all had devised?" Kranti asked Murti.

"The guards were going to let us in, and we were going to storm the Durbar."

"With what? Your bare hands?"

"No, we bought guns."

There had been a dozen or so firearms of various shapes and sizes spread out on the Beggar Street living room floor that afternoon. All from the black market—three rifles, several revolvers that seemed to have been excavated from an armory during the time of the eighteenth century Angrezi colonials, and even a pair of muskets, along with a little pile of swords and khukuris.

With the weaponry thus assembled, the Beggars' operation was feasible. They called it Operation Cry Motherland, after Professor Shrestha's seminal *Cry the Cursed Country*.

Chanchal argued that their weaponry, if and when they managed to get inside the Durbar compound, was not adequate. The Durbar had to be teeming with the Loyal Army Dais. How were they going to get past all of them? And even if they did, where would they find Darkmother? And wouldn't she be surrounded by her own bodyguards? It was clear that Chanchal had become squeamish, despite his original enthusiasm for Operation Cry Motherland. "Aren't we inviting divine wrath upon ourselves for going after Darkmother?" he asked the others.

"You don't really believe in that nonsense that she's a goddess, do you?" Professor Shrestha asked.

Chanchal hemmed and hawed. No, he didn't believe it a hundred percent. A live goddess wouldn't appear on the street like that. And what was the symbolism of the white horse? It seemed to be the stuff of movies. Or perhaps the goddess atop a white horse was made to resemble Jhansi ki Rani, a woman warrior goddess type, you know. No, he didn't really believe that she was a goddess. But what if she was? What if there was a chance that she was indeed the real Darkmother? Wouldn't the Beggars then be fighting a divine being? Besides, how would you explain the reverence that people had for her?

Murti pointed out that a large part of the population had the same reverence for the Hippo, and where was he now?

They discussed what might have happened to the Hippo. Vikram said that his cousin, the guard, had told him that the Hippo was already dead, that he was killed during Matakoo and buried in a cemetery underneath Khor.

"There's a cemetery underneath the Durbar? I thought there was a prison, Khor."

"The cemetery is underneath Khor."

"And what's under the cemetery?"

"The purgatory!"

"Ha! Ha!"

The Beggars even discussed the possibility, which had been floated around the Valley, that PM Papa was behind all of it: Matakoo, the rumors of his death, everything. He was the mastermind.

"The Hippo might be playing three-dimensional chess," Murti said. "There's a long-term strategy to this."

"For what purpose?" Professor Shrestha said. "What does he gain by fabricating a koo against himself?"

"So he can come back and gain even more power. He'd have conquered even Darkmother, which could elevate him in the public eye, perhaps even give him a divine status."

Professor Shrestha put a stop to these endless speculations. "Whether it was a real koo or a fake koo, we are left with an authoritarian power, again. We are going to act, and we are going to act now. If you're not with Operation Cry Motherland, you need to leave now."

Instead of leaving, they wrapped the weapons in a blanket and put them in a closet next to Kranti's room, after which they began to discuss whether they should make spicy muri, which was Chanchal's specialty, or go down the street to fetch samosas.

To minimize the presence of the Loyal Army Dais inside the compound, the attack would take place at night during a shift change. The bribed guards would let them in, and the Beggars, led by Vikram, would stick to the inside walls as they made their way toward the front door of the Durbar. Vikram's cousin had given them a map of the Durbar interior.

"And what were you going to do once you entered the Durbar premises, if you weren't mowed down by then?" Kranti asked Murti after she finished talking.

"Our mission was to assassinate Darkmother," Murti said. Avoiding Kranti's eyes, she stood and went to the window, where she fingered the paper-thin curtain, twisting it in her hand, as though she realized the folly of their thinking, the sin they were plotting.

But Kranti wasn't concerned about the sinful aspect of Operation Cry Motherland. She realized now that she had never believed, for a second, that Darkmother was a divine being of any sort, endowed with supernatural powers that a common person needed to be afraid of. Kranti was merely stunned by how harebrained they'd been in devising their scheme.

"I can't believe the stupidity of your operation," Kranti said to Murti. "This kind of stupidity, only God can hand down—just to demonstrate the level of stupidity humans are capable of. Just the name Operation Cry Motherland sounds like a failure, just like your Mothercry Press was a failure. And what's with this mothercry, mothercry business anyway? Why not motherlaugh for a change?"

"We were caught in a fever," Murti said. "Madam was in a kind of fever. Her eyes were on fire when we discussed storming the Durbar."

"She was going to go in herself? With her cane?"

Murti nodded. "Yes, we tried to dissuade her from going, saying she would slow everyone down, but she wouldn't listen. I need to go, she kept saying, I must go, I must lead the way. We said that she didn't need to go in the actual mission, that her blessing was enough. But she said that she couldn't just send us into such a risky venture and sit back in Beggar Street twiddling her thumbs. Her heart wouldn't allow it, she said. She was in a do-or-die kind of mood. We all were. We even evoked your name to prevent her from going."

Kranti rolled her eyes.

"We said what would Kranti do if something were to happen to you? And you know what she said?"

"Pray tell."

"She said, Kranti is fine without me. She's an independent woman who has created her own world. She won't miss me."

Kranti felt something, a shard, a pinch.

Murti continued that the evening before the operation, the Loyal Army Dais came and arrested Madam, Vikram, and Chanchal. One of the guards wimped out and snitched, Murti was certain. Murti escaped the arrest because she was visiting an ailing relative at that time.

Both of them sat in silence for a few moments. Then Kranti noticed an assortment of objects on a small mat in a corner—a small skull, like that of an animal, perhaps a monkey or a raccoon; two or three long, slim bones; one bowl with some powdered stuff inside; and some feathers. "What's that?" she asked, pointing.

"Nothing," Murti said quickly. "Just some stuff."

The objects, obviously for a ritual, were right below a poster of Goddess Darkmother tacked on the wall next to it.

"Your witchcraft stuff?"

Murti hung her head in shame.

"You still practicing?"

"I tried to find out Madam's whereabouts."

"And?"

"I got fuzzy answers."

"Why not simply use your witchcraft to get her out, have her materialize before us, right here?"

"You're making fun of me." Murti looked like she was about to cry. "I was good at this work, and now my powers are weak."

"Maybe she has something to do with your diluted powers," Kranti said, pointing at Goddess Darkmother's poster. It was the fiercest image of Goddess Darkmother Kranti had seen. She was seated in a crouching position, possessing deep blue skin, face distorted in rage, an overly long tongue hanging out and down to her naked breasts, her multitude of arms holding skull, rope, trident, and a chopped-off head. "She doesn't like you no more, Murti."

"But she's supposed to help. Goddess Darkmother is the benefactress of all the witches."

Kranti had no time or inclination to get into an elongated conversation with Murti about the finer points of witchcraft. She gave Murti some money, asked her to take care of herself, then left her and headed toward the Durbar. On the way, she had the option of avoiding the Asylum but she deliberately took the alley that brought her next to its side walls. The high walls of the Asylum made it impossible to see the first floor, but she could see the window of Aditya's and Shambhogya's room on the second floor. As she watched, she saw two blurred shadows behind the curtain. From the shapes she could figure out that they were Shambhogya and Aditya. Then it unfolded like a theater scene, or perhaps a dramatic moment in a puppet show:

The couple is talking, then their talk intensifies. Sharp words are exchanged, but for a viewer at some distance the words are dully muted, as if they were coming from behind a heavy oak door. The shadow figures tremble, then the man abruptly raises his hand, as though to strike the woman. The woman, instead of recoiling, as most would expect, stops trembling and stretches to become taller as if she's going to meet the man's hand. Strike me, she appears to be saying. It's clear from the tone and texture of the shadowy figures that the argument started a long time ago, perhaps even before it was an argument, and it is coming to a head now, a climax when everything that has been built up breaks.

Faced with the defiance of the female figure, the male figure stops, his hand dropping. More words are exchanged. Now they seem to be softer words, aimed at compromise and reconciliation. Then the couple embraces, awkwardly. It is not an embrace of love, only temporary truce.

A BLESSING AND
A SHEHEADING

47.

Bhaktas packed the streets surrounding the Durbar. Some of them were sprawled on the pavements, just happy to be in the proximity of Darkmother. There was also a long line of petitioners and appealers at the Durbar gate, stretching all the way down the wide boulevard to the Home of the Bell. The line didn't seem to discriminate according to class. Businessmen in suits and ties were standing next to day laborers with their headstraps, and alongside housewives holding babies. Kranti faced angry glares as she pushed her way to the front of the crowd. Once she reached the front, she attempted to talk to the Loyal Army Dais, who shouted at her to get back in line. Kranti didn't dare say that she was looking for her mother who was imprisoned inside the Durbar; the crowd could easily turn on her. "I have an urgent appeal! I have an urgent appeal!" she repeated to the Loyal Army Dais. But they simply shooed her away, saying no appeal was considered more urgent than anyone else's in Darkmother's reign. Those already standing in line, squished and sweaty, growled at her, and threatened to "cut her to pieces and feed her to the vultures." This forced Kranti to go to the back of the line. As she listened to the clang of the Home of the Bell, tears threatened to spill from her eyes. She watched the students stream out of the Tri-Moon College. What were they studying? What did students study these days? Earthquake relief? Motherland TV was already showing images of books that adulated PM Papa being burned to ashes in empty oil drums in neighborhoods across the Valley. Had new college books already been printed to show PM Papa as a ruthless and corrupt leader?

Kranti saw her younger self, a young Kranti, and Bhaskar walk out of the Tri-Moon College, gazing into each other's eyes. She saw them as they were before the Big Two, except the backdrop was the present moment, with the chaos of the Bhaktas waiting for a darshan of Darkmother. The two young lovers were highlighted, with a transparent glow to them as they exited the college in front of Kranti.

"But the tea is much better there, Bhaskar," Kranti was saying, pointing toward the Tiger Market.

Bhaskar leaned against her. "Then we'll go to the Tiger Market. After tea, what then?"

The two young lovers didn't look at the older Kranti standing fretfully in line. They didn't know of her existence in the future, this Kranti with the khateykids and her mother imprisoned by Dark-mother. Hell, they didn't know of Darkmother. Or they didn't want to know. Or they didn't care, about this future, about this Kranti. It upset her. Then she imagined them talking about her, behind her back, as they strolled toward the Tiger Market: Did you see her? What a sorry figure. Who would have thought!

She argued with Bhaskar and Kranti from the past: I am not pathetic. I am not the shiny, neon-lit tight jeans-wearing versions that you two are. You two are what you are because you two are still trapped in the time before the Big Two, before PM Papa, before you were sucked into the Asylum and spit out.

The line wasn't moving, and she had been stuck in the same spot underneath the Home of the Bell for an hour now. It was all a sham. Darkmother had no intention of meeting the Bhaktas. Or per-haps Darkmother did, just not today. Around her she heard people talk about those who'd already been granted an audience with Dark-mother, how they'd described the experience as beyond imaginable:

"My uncle said it was as if he'd reached the heavens."

"A tremendous calm came over her—that's what my sister reported."

"Yes, he cried, my old professor did. And he said he'd never cried in his life, not even as a baby."

"My best friend said that she was blinded by the glow around Darkmother's body!"

Some had swooned in Darkmother's presence; others had fainted, the Bhaktas said.

After about an hour of being crushed in the jam-packed line, Kranti asked a Loyal Army Dai who strolled by with his rifle, "Loyal Army Dai, I don't think this line is moving, is it?"

"It's moving," the Loyal Army Dai replied without paying her much attention.

"But Dai, I've been in the same spot for the past hour."

"No, you haven't!" Bhaktas near her corrected her. "The line is moving, we're making progress."

Kranti tried to explain: an hour ago she and the people near her were next to the gate of the Home of the Bell, and now they were in the same spot. But she was thunderously drowned out by the Bhaktas. Not true, not true! The line has been moving steadily. But that was not even the point, they said: the queue is the destination. How dare she complain when she was fortunate enough to be in the queue to see Darkmother. Had she no shame? Even if the line was moving backward, she should feel only gratitude at the possibility of paying homage to Darkmother.

Then Kranti made the mistake of saying that she was not in line to pay homage but to find out if someone she knew was imprisoned inside. She realized her mistake as soon as she said it, for the crowd turned aggressive. "You're not even a Bhakta and you're complaining about the line?"

"Besides, have you considered that you're taking up someone's space?"

Then, suspicions about the person imprisoned inside. A Treasonist, obviously. Otherwise, why would Darkmother imprison this person? What is your relation to the Treasonist? Are you also a Treasonist? Or an aspiring Treasonist?

People were in her face. Men rubbed their crotches against her, women called her a cunt. An ancient-looking man, drooling, swayed in front of her, glassy-eyed, raising his cane as though she was an incarnation of the devil herself. She had no choice but to leave.

In Bhurey Paradise, a nautanki was being staged in a clearing next to the communal tap. Kranti watched a large man in a Darkmother mask glower and glare at the onlookers as he waved his arms and pranced around. He appeared to be flailing and flapping. A man with blue paint on his face and a heap of fake matted hair on his head was mumbling to himself—which could have been a song praising Darkmother. A man in a gray animalistic mask—boar? rodent?—was writhing on the ground.

O Darkmother, a man stepped forward to sing. It was the same thin man in a medieval bard's hat that had a long feather sticking out from it, the one who had been booed by audiences all over the Valley.

O Darkmother, he said solemnly. You are the most glorious.

The crowd booed the feather-capped man yet again, and the writhing man leapt to his feet and pushed him back into the crowd. Then, above gyrating hips and flailing arms, beady-eyed masks howled and boomed forth with an ecstatic song of praise to Darkmother.

By the next morning, tea shops, banks, disco bars, and colleges were all buzzing. The speculation also rippled through Bhurey Paradise. Kabiraj didn't say anything to her. He couldn't meet her eyes, as though he were afraid of what she might say to him, or what he might say to her. She had told him about her unsuccessful attempts to get into the Durbar, and he'd said perhaps there was another way. However, the conversation had fizzled out because there really was no other way. And now, this rumor. When she reached Laj Mahal, it was already circulating in the Valley.

"Who is Madam Mao?" Rani asked. She must have heard the name when she was playing near Laj Mahal.

Kabiraj told her that Madam Mao was a political figure.

"I want to go see her," Rani said.

Kabiraj shushed her.

When she stepped out of Laj Mahal that afternoon, she felt the glances of the people in Bhurey Paradise. They knew who she was. She felt the speculations that trailed her as she went to buy vegetables and stopped to collect some money she'd loaned a neighbor. She felt them growing in force, until a heavy protective armor descended upon her, and she returned to the tent clad in iron.

In the evening, Motherland TV announced that there was going to be a public execution of a big-catch Treasonist. "Fe fi fo fum," Hom Bokaw said. "We don't know who that person is going to be, but we are being told"—he cupped his ear as though receiving instructions from high above—"that it is going to be a major public figure, an old hand."

Kranti wondered if folks in the Asylum were ecstatic over what was going to happen to Professor Shrestha. Serves her right, they must be saying. Serves her bitchy daughter right, especially given how she brought us dishonor by shacking up with a deadbeat poet in Bhurey Paradise. Or were the Ghimireys too worried about their own problems, and about how Matakoo and Nakoo had changed their own standing now in Darkmotherland?

Whether it was going to be a firing squad, a hanging, or a beheading, Kranti didn't know. The Palace High Beheadings had proved the crowd's bloodthirst for public executions. There had been a couple of public beheadings after Palace High, but they weren't as high profile, and they didn't involve the Charlie Chaplin jallad. Initially, Madam Mao's impending execution was called The Palace High Beheadings II, but someone suggested The Palace High She-heading, and the name stuck.

Kabiraj confronted her in Laj Mahal. "You can't avoid this."

She turned away from him, but he shifted positions so he was facing her again. She shuffled away from him to a corner of the tent, but he followed and hovered over her. Finally, she turned to him, eyes filled with tears and said, "What can I do? What should I do? I don't know what to do."

Kabiraj held her, consoled her.

Motherland TV announced that the public execution was to be held at the same spot where the Palace High Beheadings had been held—in

the compound of the Palace High School. "Thymbolic," Hom Bokaw
said. Treasonists during the previous autocratic regime were executed
here, so the major Treasonist of Darkmother's benevolent reign is
going to be executed here. How fitting!

New spiritual gurus cropped up in the media and they talked
about how this execution brought everything back to a circle. The
Treasonist who had run amok during the previous autocratic regime
would now be executed by Darkmother. In fact, Darkmother doesn't
even need to execute anyone, whether it was Madam Mao or a goat
named Rao. She can slay enemies by digging into their necks with
her awesome fangs. So, understand that she is doing this for the benefit of us mortals. In her divine existence she has already slayed all of
her enemies. Just like the Awakened One, who was already enlight-
ened, but wanted to guide us on the path. He chose to be born as a
royal prince, leave his wife and child to meditate under a tree, and
suffer hardships, just to show us how liberation was achieved. So, this
execution was an act of blessing from Darkmother.

And celebration there was, for three full days before the execution. Colorful balloons floated into the air. Small bands of people
came out in the streets, boogieing and playing loud music—cymbals, saxophones, guitars, sitars, harmoniums, ukuleles. Professional
dancers entertained the viewers with ballet, samba, salsa, kabuki,
Bharatnatyam, tango, and the waltz. There were parades with giant
floats of Darkmother and other gods and goddesses—the Elephant
God, the Pothead God, the Goddess Playing the Beena. Actors and
actresses made special appearances and took pictures with adoring
fans. Children showed off lewd, hip-thrusting moves they learned
from videos and films. The festive atmosphere reminded people of
past years during the coronation ceremonies of the monarchs. But
Darkmotherland had moved far from those days of the monarchy,
and now, amidst these celebrations, even the Big Two seemed far
away. And of course, the autocratic regime of PM Papa had vanished so quickly. Oh, he was a real character, that PM Papa. How
did we even allow such a nincompoop to rule us? People partook in

reflections and analysis, self-evaluations and conjectures, rationalizations and mea culpas. In the end, the overwhelming consensus was that this excessively roly-poly man had nearly taken the country to ruin, had it not been for the divine appearance of Darkmother.

The Hippo. Wasn't that his nickname among those, obviously patriots, who opposed him? What an apt name! We should have been calling him the Hippo right from the start. The Hippo, they chanted. The Hippo!

The name stuck. And after a while it became bad form to call PM Papa anything other than the Hippo. He was no longer PM and he was no longer anyone's Papa, so why should he be afforded the dignity of that name? If someone mistakenly called him by the former name, that person was immediately corrected. Within days the new name was picked up by the media. Even Motherland TV and Motherland Radio referred to him as the Hippo.

There was a new call to root out those who had been ardent supporters of the Hippo's regime. But whenever a finger was pointed, the ones who were pointed at vigorously shook their heads and denied any and all involvement. "I knew he was bad news right from the start," they said. "And I tried to warn people. But did anyone listen? No! Instead, I had to be careful about who I talked to."

More fingers were pointed, and more people denied complicity. They either completely denied any involvement with the previous regime, or they simply pointed their fingers at others, who then had to shake their heads and point their fingers elsewhere.

It wasn't too long before a narrative emerged that a majority of the country had been opposed to the previous regime while the Hippo was in power.

Yet another narrative emerged: Darkmother's divine appearance was a result of months and months of subterranean planning and scheming by patriots like General Tso, who, when he realized what a monster the Hippo was, worked to undermine the Hippo from within and to pave the way for Darkmother.

Then, another narrative sprouted, and unsurprisingly, gained credibility: the Hippo and Madam Mao were in cahoots. She was, in reality, the Hippo's accomplice, not his enemy. She was acting as his bogeyman but in truth they were partners. The two snakes had pretended sworn enmity so that the public would be distracted and the Hippo would consolidate his power. Darkmotherlandites had been hoodwinked. What a schemer and conniver the Hippo was. And that Madam Mao. No wonder Darkmother had imprisoned her. It seemed appropriate then, that Madam Mao would be the first one on the chopping block.

> Madam Mao
> This is her death song—gao! gao!
> To Darkmother she must bow.
> We'll crush all Treasonists, this is our vow.
> We will execute her—how?
> Chop off her head—now!
> Or bullet chalau,
> And her head will explode. Wow!

Kranti became sickened as the celebrations continued. Kabiraj tried to pull a few strings to see if he could get Kranti inside the Durbar, but it was like a sad joke. No one was going to listen to a small-timey poet living in Bhurey Paradise. Kabiraj said that it had been easier to see the Hippo in the Lion Palace.

A day before the Palace High Sheheading, without telling Kabiraj or any of the khateykids, Kranti made her way to the Asylum. She hadn't slept all night, hounded by images of her mother's death. Once, in the middle of the night, she had stepped out of Laj Mahal to retch. But nothing had come out. When she returned to bed, Kabiraj reached out and stroked her back. "Try to get some sleep," he said.

On the way to the Asylum, she passed by the Durbar. The line that she had stood in had barely moved. The same Bhaktas who had shouted at her the other day had moved only a couple of feet from the Home of the Bell. But the Bhaktas were still patient, laughing and joking and anticipating their darshan with Darkmother. As she moved toward the Asylum, she glanced nervously around—now that her mother was in custody, wouldn't the Poolis Uncles also come after her?

At the Asylum, Cheech and Chong wouldn't even let her in, and they refused to go inside to call anyone. She begged and pleaded with them, and finally Harkey came outside. With gritted teeth he said, "You have the nerve to return here after what you and your thirdgenders did to me?"

"Please, I need to see someone. Shambhogya didi or Aditya dai."

Harkey imitated her. "Please, Shambhogya didi or Aditya dai. Who do you think we are? Your nokerchakers?" And he laughed, joined by Cheech and Chong. He leaned forward as if he was going to kiss her lips. "But haven't you heard, you little bird? It's not like before."

"Is Muwa in? Can I talk to her at least?"

The three of them laughed for a long time, as though they'd been waiting for this moment since the last century. It was a laugh of deep satisfaction, of victory, a laugh of I-told-you-so, of triumph, a laugh that told Kranti that all the rich types who'd treated those below them with contempt were now themselves going to face contempt and ridicule. "Where have you been, dearie?" Harkey asked. "Oh, yes, with that filthy beer-bellied poet of yours. I guess you haven't heard? Your Muwa left the Asylum a couple of days ago."

"Where did she go?"

"Who knows? She told no one. Left in the middle of the night. When this lazy duo was sleeping."

Cheech and Chong cursed him with a flurry of *putas* and *pendejos*.

"Didn't anyone go look for her?" Kranti asked.

"Who is going to go? I don't think it's even registering with the old man that his wife has flown the coop. And the sons. They are so shocked about everything."

Kranti spotted the shadowy figures of Aditya and Shambhogya at their window. "Shambhogya didi! Please!" she shouted at them.

The shadows at the window disappeared. Harkey was observing

her. "See? This is about your mother, isn't it? Did it ever occur to you that she, the invincible Madam Mao, deserves what is coming to her? What has she done all her life except bother other people, become a pain in the butt for everyone?"

"She fought for people like you, you imbecile!" Kranti said.

"Did she?" Harkey said. "I think she fought only for herself, and for people like her. Only after Matakoo have we found our voices."

She walked away. No one here was going to do anything for her.

On the way back, Kranti feared that the Loyal Army Dais that guarded the Durbar would recognize her as Madam Mao's daughter. She avoided that route altogether and took to small alleys that led to the Queen's Pond area. At the Palace High School, the stage for the next day's execution was being assembled on its front lawn. It was bigger than the stage that had been set up for the beheadings of the Gang of Four. This stage had two platforms, and amplifiers and sound boxes set up on the first platform. There was going to be a concert on the first platform, to be followed by the execution on the second. Traffic was already being blocked from accessing the roads adjacent to the Queen's Pond, and vendors with their carts had begun to sell fritters, momos, eggs, goat testicles, Darjeeling noodles, and ducks' entrails. One vendor was selling 4D sunglasses for viewing the beheading from the street. He claimed that the beheading would make blood splatter on your face. A small group of men and women were engaged in yogic contortions; they believed that the energy surrounding the execution would propel them onto a higher spiritual plane. Young hippies, who seemed to have broken open a time barrier and emerged straight from the seventies, were banging madals and playing flutes, the smell of patchouli and ganja wafting around them.

From across the street Kranti watched the workers on the Palace High lawn hammering away at the poles, roofing the stage with canvas, and adjusting the beams. Her eyes roamed all over the stage, then right behind it, where the Big Two-ravaged building of the Palace High School was located. Its long arches spoke proudly of a bygone era's musty knowledge. The building itself was thin and rectangular, with corridors running along its length. On the narrow, pathetic lawn in the front, students gathered in groups during breaks, their shouts and play-noises vying with the honks and hoots of the traffic only a few feet away.

Classes were being held in this school, despite the damage to its structure by the earthquake. In fact, a number of students had suffered grave injuries not too long ago because the windows had simply given way and collapsed, hurtling them to the lawn below. Even now, blue-uniformed kids were crammed near those same weak windows, chattering excitedly and pointing down at the workers setting up the stage. At one window, a kid raised an imaginary khukuri and sliced the head off of another kid, who pretended to writhe and flail now that he was headless.

But tomorrow the kids wouldn't have classes. The day of the execution had been declared a national holiday, and the Palace High School would be empty. The window where the kids were enacting the beheading was directly above the second level of the stage. One could easily jump down a few feet onto the stage from the window. But would the Loyal Army Dais be stationed at the school's windows tomorrow? If Darkmother was going to attend the execution (there was talk that she would) then this entire place would be swarming with Loyal Army Dais, Poolis Uncles, and Mata's Matriots. Why would Darkmother attend the execution? Why had this become so personal for her? What had Professor Shrestha done to her to face this type of punishment? Had Darkmother thought about what Kranti might be going through? Or had Darkmother changed into a completely different being, one who had thrown away all of her compassion? And to think, ironically, Darkmother was supposed to be the embodiment of compassion.

Kranti nearly cried out Darkmother's previous name, but she couldn't bring herself to say it. It was as though the name had been blotted out from her mind, even though she could visually see it. Oh, Darkmother, didn't you think of me?

Kranti went to a shop on the next street and bought a six-pack of

Coca Cola, smarting at the four thousand rupees that she had to pay for them. She carried them in a plastic bag. When she tried to enter the premise of the Palace High School, the couple of Poolis Uncles stationed at the gate said, "Hey, hey, where do you think you're going?"

"Just going inside."

"What for?

"I want to give our hardworking construction bhais, working on that stage, some Coca Cola."

"What for?"

"Don't you see how hard they are working? Sweating and cursing?"

"Are you a Coca Cola model or something?" the second Poolis Uncle asked Kranti.

The first Poolis Uncle made a coquettish face, batted his eyelids, and said in a falsetto voice, "Namaste, look at me, I am a Coca Cola model."

"You Poolis Uncles are such jokers," Kranti said and slapped them lightly with her palm.

"Ai hai!" the first Poolis Uncle said. "Ees kudiya ney mera dil nu chori kita hai."

"He thinks he's the actor Dharmendra," the second Poolis Uncle explained to Kranti. "What about Coca Cola for us? We are thirsty too, sis. And with our salaries, we can't even afford an effervescent bottle of piss, let alone Coca Cola."

Kranti took out one bottle and gave it to them. "You can share, my dear Poolis Uncles."

"Of course, it's a day of sharing, isn't it?"

The first Poolis Uncle popped open the bottle and glug-glugged the drink down his throat. With the afternoon heat and the stunningly blue sky and small puffy clouds behind him, he looked like he was filming a Coca Cola commercial. Kranti even thought that she saw the frizzy dark drink sexily slide down his gullet.

They let her through.

The construction bhais inside were grateful for the drinks that Kranti had brought them. They seemed to be on the verge of complaining about their harsh working conditions—toiling in that incredible heat with little protection from the sun, the pittance that were their wages—but they quickly shut up. Kranti chatted with them, extracting useful information, as they took a break and drank the Coca Cola. Yes, they were sure Darkmother would attend—this was her idea. Kranti asked, injecting her voice with awe, even happiness, whether there'd be Loyal Army Dais with snipers on the roofs. One construction worker pointed across the street to the north and said that the snipers would sit on the rooftops of surrounding restaurants. Palace High School, after the workers finished this evening, would be shut down and locked for the night and be guarded by Loyal Army Dais.

Kranti had to move fast. She bade the construction bhais goodbye and went to Beggar Street, hoping that the Loyal Army Dais wouldn't be there, waiting for her. It still surprised her that as Professor Shrestha's daughter, she'd yet to be arrested. The front door was still padlocked. After quickly ascertaining that Sapkota from next door wasn't watching from his roof or his window, Kranti made her way through the side of the house to the lawn behind Beggar Street. Although the back door was secured from inside with a latch at the bottom of the door, she knew a trick. She lay on the ground, on her side, and inserted her fingers between the bottom sill and the threshold. The opening was wide enough that she could squeeze in her entire palm. Once she had a firm grasp of the bottom of the door, she shook it with vigor, making a rattling sound, and gradually, after about a minute or so, the latch jiggled open.

She went inside the house to the closet, found Dada's box, opened it, and took out the gun. The Grateful Dead jacket was still in the plastic bag, and a wave of melancholy wafted over Kranti. She nearly reached in to take out the jacket—no, she couldn't let herself soften right now.

She stood, and, holding the Ruger in her hand, wondered if she could shoot her mother before the jallad got a chance to execute her. A daughter killing her own mother to spare her the trauma of an execution. Briefly this possibility seized her. A mercy killing would be a fitting end for Madam Mao. Laid to rest by none other than her daughter in an act of kindness. Professor Shrestha would rather die at the hands of her daughter than at the hands of the Rajjya—Kranti was certain of this. Then she was thrown in doubt again. Her mother might actually want the Rajjya to execute her—it would be a perfect final symbol of her lifelong fight against injustice and oppression.

The afternoon was beginning to slip away, but Kranti sat there immobile, in Beggar Street, holding the gun. Things could go wrong at every step. She was going against the big state apparatus, and the monster was simply too big and overpowering. She felt small, and for the first time she had an idea of how her mother might have felt all of her life fighting the powers. Kranti now understood that her entire life Professor Shrestha had fought against feeling small at the hands of the Rajjya. The only problem was that in the course of that fight she'd ended up making the loved ones in her life also feel small and powerless.

But that was in the past. What was happening now was wrong—her mother didn't deserve to be executed. She deserved to know that someone still cared about her.

Kranti held the gun in her hands and lifted it up, as though it were a spiritual offering. "This is for you, Dada," she whispered. "This is for you, Bhaskar." She touched the grip of the gun to her forehead. She knew what she was going to do.

48.

In Laj Mahal, Kabiraj was waiting. The khateykids surrounded her, and she gave them the chocolate bars she'd purchased in the Lord of the Heavens chowk. Eating their chocolate bars, they went to the "park" close to Laj Mahal, a small clearing that had been created in the Bhurey Paradise after much hue and cry about a lack of play areas for children.

Kabiraj watched her carefully. "Any news?" he asked.

"Nope," she said. The gun was bulging out a bit from her waist, so she had her hands casually clasped together in front her. But Kranti had never been a hand-clasping type, and Kabiraj seemed to notice that something was off in her posture.

"What's going on inside your head, Kranti?" he asked.

It was late afternoon, and the sunlight filtered through the tented roof of Laj Mahal. For a brief moment, Kranti was transported back to her childhood, when a shard of sunlight came in through her window in late afternoon as Dada hummed and cooked snacks for her in the kitchen next door. Before he became a rock music fan, Dada was into Bharati music. He especially loved the "I am turning alcoholic" or the "this alcohol is my only salvation" lyrics popularized in songs and ghazals. "This red drink, when is it going to leave me alone?" Dada wailed as he fried some pakoras. "Please, world, don't think of me as an alcoholic!" he cried as he ground some cardamom to sprinkle in the tea for Kranti.

Kabiraj saw the resolve in her eyes, and he knew that it would be futile to argue with her. "Whatever you are planning, you can't do it alone. Let me help you." He argued with her, but she wouldn't budge. And eventually she told him what she was planning.

When she finished, Kabiraj stared at her. "A suicide mission," he said finally. "You'll be like one of those whatchamacallit pilots."

"Kamikaze. There's no alternative," Kranti said.

They went back and forth, softly, and in the end Kabiraj gave up.

Tears had come to his eyes. "I know I won't see you anymore," he said. He cried.

She also wanted to cry but she felt numb, and her eyes were dry. She hugged Kabiraj.

"I can feel it," he said.

"Feel what?"

"Your gun."

She laughed, thinking that she ought to be crying. "Wanna check out my gun?" She seductively thrust her hips at him.

"May I stroke your gun, hajur?" He put his hand on the gun and caressed it over her dhoti, then he pulled it out. It didn't look threatening in Kabiraj's hand at all. It looked more like a toy, designed to pump out colorful ribbons if the trigger was pulled. A gun in the hands of a poet transforms it, she supposed.

"Does this thing even work?" Kabiraj asked.

"It works," Kranti said, and took it away from him, not totally sure that it did. "If I'm going to get into Palace High, I better be going, before they barricade it for the night."

Kranti and Kabiraj went out to look for the other khateykids. Kranti hugged and kissed them, then searched for Subhash, who was off by himself. He seemed more subdued than usual; he let Kranti hug him, but he didn't hug her back. "Babu, are you feeling all right?"

Subhash nodded.

Tousling his hair, Kranti left him.

As he watched Kranti leave Bhurey Paradise, Subhash sensed that she was also on a mission of resolution, like he had been that day when he'd gone looking for Mukeshbro and had held his knife above him, certain that he was ready to plunge it into the halwai's neck. But his mission hadn't concluded with the outcome Subhash had so badly wanted. His hand shook, and he couldn't bring himself to strike Mukeshbro with it. He had remained like that for a couple of minutes, thinking all he needed was one small push of encouragement, and this man, who'd taken Jharana away from him, would be no more. But no matter how much he willed himself to thrust the knife into Mukeshbro, he couldn't do it. His mother's phrase about sins, screaming from the mountain, kept ringing in his ears. But this time, it seemed that the sins being referred to were not only Mukeshbro's sins, of which there were plenty, but also his stepfather Puru's sins, for forcing Subhash to leave home, and his mother's, for not loving him enough to protect him from a man like Puru, and not wanting her own son around. But the paap could also be referred to as what Subhash was about to do, the sin that would follow him for the rest of his life, if he were to take this bastard's life right now.

Subhash had then left Mukeshbro's room, the knife clasped in his hand all the way to Laj Mahal, drawing stares from others on the street.

—

Kranti made her way to Palace High. It was already quarter past four. She hoped that the gates hadn't been closed already. There had been heavy talk that the Charlie Chaplin jallad was going to perform tomorrow. The entire Valley had been in a kind of delirious glee about it. "He's awesome!" people had gushed.

Hom Bokaw had said on Motherland TV, "Fee fi fo fum. The Charlie Chaplin jallad or shomeone else? Shtay fumed." But the way Hom Bokaw had smiled, his lip-ends curving, revealed that he had inside knowledge that the public wouldn't be disappointed.

The execution was going to be broadcast live on Motherland TV hosted by Hom Bokaw. Giant screens had been set up across the city— in shopping malls, palace squares, restaurants—like a city hosting the World Cup. In small parks and chowks, neighborhood associations were going to throw parties with chicken and goat barbecue and free milk. And in some cases, even free cans of Carlsberg beer. The Fundys had also come out from the shadows and were claiming that the execution would be a major victory against atheism and Western influence, for Professor Shrestha was an ardent atheist who valorized the decadent ways of the West. The Fundys had planned on burning copies of *Cry the Cursed Country*, but Mata's Matriots put a stop to it, saying that under Darkmother's rule, no book would ever be burned, not even pornography.

As Kranti approached the area she saw that the two-platformed stage was nearly complete; the construction bhais were putting on the finishing touches. Once again, she went and bought some Coca Cola, then approached the Poolis Uncles at the gate. They looked at her in surprise. "Again?" they said. "You have nothing better to do?"

"My heart goes out to those construction bhais slogging in this heat. They deserve better, don't you think?"

"They're working for Darkmother," one Poolis Uncle said. "Are you suggesting there's something better than this?"

"Jai Matadi!" Kranti declared.

"Jai Matadi!" the Poolis Uncles shouted.

"Jai Matadi!" the construction bhais sang in unison without pausing their work.

"Jai Matadi!" shouted the vendors on the street.

The Poolis Uncles let her in after pilfering two Coca Cola bottles from her.

Using thick ropes, the construction bhais were securing the poles holding the platforms on the stage. They paused and wiped their faces and necks with their gamchas when they saw her approach.

"You sure you're not looking for more from us?" one construction bhai said when she climbed a small ladder to the stage and handed them the Coca Colas.

"More like what, bro?" another construction bhai said. "Can you be more specific?"

"You know, up in the mountains there are villages where a woman can sleep with up to five men."

"Rubbish!" Kranti said, laughing. "You are all like bhais to me. I was nearby again and saw you all toiling in this incredible heat."

"But we still have energy for the night," a construction bhai said to chortles from the others, "if you'd care to come with us."

"Don't mind him," a construction bhai said. "I think his wife has been neglecting him lately."

"I don't mind," Kranti said. "I'm just so happy you're working so hard for Darkmotherland."

She continued to praise them, and their chests swelled as they drank their Coca Cola. Then they returned to work as they chatted with one another, and she slipped away, mumbling something about needing to pick some flowers growing near the entrance at the other end of the long building (there were no flowers in this dusty, crumbling wasteland of a school).

"We need to hurry before that dickhead supervisor returns," one construction bhai said. They all picked up their paces.

After climbing down the ladder, Kranti darted toward the southern end of the school. She slipped into the corridor that ran its length, crouched, then scuttled back toward where the stage was. She was now inside the school, hidden by the stone balustrade that ran the corridor's length. Kranti found some stairs, then quietly went up and slipped into a classroom on the first floor. She hid behind the door and watched. The Poolis Uncles at the gate were yawning and smoking cigarettes. Near eye level the construction bhais were hammering some nails into wood. The supervisor came and scolded them for not having finished the job sooner, so the construction bhais moved even faster. In about half an hour they were done, and no one asked where the didi who brought them Coca Cola was—they had all forgotten about her.

Kranti listened to the sounds of footsteps on the stage above her, then saw the construction bhais and the supervisor uncle descend the ladder to the ground. It was when they were exiting from the gate that the Poolis Uncles asked them, "Where is the Coca Cola bahini?"

"Didn't she already leave?"

"No."

The construction bhais looked around the compound. "She must have. She's not here."

"If she left, we'd have seen her," the Poolis Uncles said. "This is the only gate."

"Oh come on," the construction bhais said. "You guys were lazing around all day while we worked. One of you even went to the store to fetch pan parag. She could have easily slipped past you."

"Maybe we should go look inside the school," a Poolis Uncle said worriedly.

"I'm not going back in there again," the supervisor said. He addressed his workers, "And you guys are also finished. This is not our problem, let's go."

The construction bhais and the supervisor left.

Just then a handful of Loyal Army Dais arrived and talked about locking everything up until tomorrow. They asked if anyone was inside. The Poolis Uncles said that there was a woman who'd brought them Coca Cola earlier, but they hadn't seen her leave. The Loyal Army Dais were furious. They admonished the Poolis Uncles, and brushed them aside to go into the building to search.

As she saw the men make their way into the school, Kranti frantically looked for a place to hide inside the classroom, which was dusty and had long, poor-looking desks and benches. In the distance she could hear the footsteps of the Loyal Army Dais climbing up to the open corridor. There was no way she could hide in the classroom. She went to the corridor, where she risked being seen. Right next to the classroom was the girls' bathroom. She slipped inside, just as the Loyal Army Dais turned the corner and marched in her direction.

The stench inside the bathroom had the force of a hurricane, capable of blowing her right out to the corridor at the feet of the Loyal Army Dais. It was as if dozens and dozens of schoolgirls were in the stalls, all crapping simultaneously after eating basketfuls of boiled eggs. Even in the midst of her panic—the footsteps and voices were closer now, just a couple of dozen yards away—she couldn't help but feel angry for such inhumane bathroom conditions for the girls of Palace High. Bile was threatening to rush out of her throat.

She darted into the last stall at the far end of the bathroom. The stench in the stall was so strong that she wanted to run out screaming. She pinched her nose and flattened herself against the wall, behind the door. There was a gap at the bottom of the stall, which meant that her toes could be visible to someone looking from outside, so she curled her toes in.

Now there were voices right outside the bathroom. "I'll check in here," a Loyal Army Dai said, then entered and immediately started cursing. "What the fuck! What bathroom in hell smells like this? Motherfucking suck my dick, and fuck this job!"

Kranti held in her breath and kept still. Swearing and ranting, the Loyal Army Dai kicked open the first stall, then loudly gagged at the godawful smell that assaulted him. In rapid succession he kicked open the other stalls, and Kranti's mind raced to offer explanations to the Loyal Army Dai, once he kicked open her stall, for why she was hiding. Simultaneously, she saw herself taking out the gun from her waist and shooting the man.

The Loyal Army Dai kicked her door, and it violently swung inward, slamming her in the face. The sharp pain in her nose was unbearable, disorienting. The world turned red, as though someone had poured blood over her head. She was about to stagger out of the stall, pleading forgiveness, when she heard footsteps leaving. There was some more cursing by the Loyal Army Dai, now outside the bathroom, about having walked into hell.

Voices sounded outside.

"Checked the bathroom?"

"Yes, I did. But you should check again."

"Why?"

"So that you can also experience purgatory."

"That bad, eh?"

"Why don't you give it a shot?"

"No, thank you very much. What about upstairs?"

"Clear."

"Check under the stairs?"

"Roger."

"Checked the ceilings?"

"Ditto."

The voices moved away, and after a few minutes, only the traffic and voices of pedestrians could be heard from outside.

Kranti stayed in this torture chamber of a bathroom for another fifteen minutes or more, wondering if a Loyal Army Dai had stayed behind to pounce on her as soon as she left. But she couldn't stay in the bathroom much longer than that, unless she wanted to die because of toxic inhalation. She exited the stall, inch by inch—the stall door creaked at the hinges when she pushed on it—then finally the bathroom door. She stood still for a couple of minutes outside the bathroom, crouching, ready to bolt back inside if she heard voices or sensed any movement. The corridor allowed a view of the street and beyond. Directly across from her was the Queen's Pond, and beyond the pond was the Tri-Moon College and the Home of the Bell. She could also see the Loyal Army Dais with their machine guns stationed at either ends of the blocked-off street. The gun at her waist had been poking into her stomach for a while, so she took it out and, still crouching, held it in her hand. Now that dusk was falling and it appeared that the first part of the mission had been successful, the gun felt odd in her hand, as though she were holding an injured bird. She'd most likely be mowed down by a barrage of gunfire even before she leapt from the window to the stage. But whatever might happen, she had to try.

Still crouching, Kranti headed toward the stairs for the second floor. She used the flashlight in her mobile to light her path, holding the phone low to the ground, so the Loyal Army Dais on the street wouldn't see the speck of light slowly moving inside Palace High.

Her palms and knees had suffered some scraping from the crouching and crawling. On the second floor she found the window that overlooked the stage. The good news was she had only a few feet to jump down tomorrow. The bad news was that she had no idea how many Loyal Army Dais would be onstage along with the jallad and her mother. She imagined herself as a woman warrior, like Mulan or Jhansi ki Rani, yelling "yeeeha!" and leaping onto the stage. Silly fantasies! Except for what she'd seen and heard in movies, she didn't even have a conception of what kind of noise a gun made when fired. Did it sound like a firecracker? Or like a balloon popping? She should have tested the gun to see if it worked when Kabiraj had asked her. Or perhaps she could have shot Kabiraj himself when he asked. Bam! She laughed. Why would she shoot her poor dallu? Why was her mind doing a number on her like this? The gun had been sitting in that box for so long that it could easily jam when fired. Images of guns jamming in movies—cartoonish images, with the shooter appearing totally baffled—ran through her mind. Kranti realized that all her knowledge of guns was from movies—cocking the gun, pulling the trigger, the recoil (was the recoil only with rifles but not with hand-guns?), the puncture of a bullet. Then there was the pain of being shot. She should expect to be shot tomorrow, perhaps killed. What was the pain like when the bullet entered your body? Kranti had low toler-ance for physical pain. Even the slightest cut or bruise made her flail and yowl. She remembered breaking her arm in the third grade while doing long jumps on the school playground. The pain had engulfed her so badly that she had writhed on the ground for minutes until a teacher had arrived. Her classmates, instead of helping, had laughed at her.

Activities started at Palace High around dawn. Scores of Loyal Army Dais, who'd arrived to replace the ones who'd stood guard overnight, stationed themselves throughout the length of the street. Vendors and hawkers from the previous days had been shooed off, and a large crowd of onlookers had already gathered at both ends of the street, pushing and shoving as they waited for the barricades to open. Kranti had observed everything from her crouched position on the balcony. But now, with the increased activities outside, she had to be care-ful about not being detected. Thankfully the two-platformed stage, with its canvas and poles, concealed her to a great extent. Her body ached from the hard floor of the classroom where she'd tried to catch snatches of sleep during the night. Squatting behind the balustrade as she massaged her lower back with her knuckles, Kranti could tell that a type of mania had already infiltrated the crowd. Their faces were contorted in anticipation, some of them slobbering and drooling like hungry wolves.

At seven A.M., the barricades were lifted. It was as if the floodgates had been opened. Within minutes the street was jam-packed. Masses of people still thronged at the both ends of the street, howling at the injustice of not being allowed a closer vantage point.

The immediate space in front of the double-platformed stage was reserved for VIP seating and the media. Hom Bokaw was there already, decked in daura suruwal, speaking in front of the camera. He was monologuing, and it appeared to Kranti that he was situating today in Darkmotherland's long history, going back to its mythological times. Although from inside the school, Kranti couldn't make out his exact words, it sounded like he was talking about the time when the bodhisattva Gentle Glory had drained the Valley's water by lacerating the mountain with his wisdom sword. Watching Hom Bokaw's pontificating figure, Kranti recalled a similar sermon from Na-Ryan of Mofo Momos. For a moment, Kranti, disoriented by her lack of adequate sleep, thought that Darkmotherland's immortal television host would soon start juggling momos and plopping them into his mouth after he regaled his viewers with Darkmotherland's magical past.

At eight, the musical performers arrived. The first was a folk-dance troupe. It got the crowd going but the enthusiasm level wasn't all that high. Then a stand-up comedian appeared. He made some really bad jokes that had the crowd in stitches. A rock group singing "Stairway to Heaven" followed, but the music was too loud and discordant and the lyrics incomprehensible, the refrain sounding like *a stale way to heaven*. Finally, there was a rapper in daura suruwal, surprisingly the biggest hit of the morning.

The entire area was swarming with Loyal Army Dais, in shinier uniforms than normal, it seemed. At times they deliberately pointed their guns at the crowd. Why? Why not? Everyone needed a good scare now and then. The crowd giggled when the guns were pointed at them, as though they thought it might actually be *fun* to get shot at this momentous time in Darkmotherland's history, the import of which Hom Bokaw was solemnly reminding his home-viewers a few feet away. At one point, a child of about ten lunged at a Loyal Army Dai, to the alarmed, and a few delighted, cries from those nearby. The child grabbed his rifle and clung to it. The Loyal Army Dai attempted to wrench his weapon away from the rascal but couldn't. He ended up swinging his rifle in the air, with the child cleaving to it. And for a few seconds there was an impromptu show of a child being swung about at the end of a rifle like in an amusement park. The Loyal Army Dai swung his rifle back and forth, as though building momentum, then he rotated on his heels a few times, circularly spinning his rifle in the air, like an Olympic hammer thrower, turning the child into a blur. Once he had enough velocity, the Loyal Army Dai released his rifle into the air—the child with it. The rifle and the child shot into the air above the Palace High School and disappeared into the clear blue sky above.

At ten o'clock a figure in handcuffs, with a sack over its head, was led to the stage by four armed Loyal Army Dais. Kranti held her breath, then began to silently and fervently chant the Monkeygod Forty Verses—*you charged toward the golden sun, even though it was thousands of miles away, thinking it was a sweet fruit*—as the crowd began to shout: "Cut it off! Cut it off! Cut it off!"

49.

Months ago, the video of the Palace High Beheadings with the Gang of Four had been shown on Motherland TV, ad infinitum, accompanied by the soundtrack of Beethoven's Fifth Symphony, a fine video shot in HD that zoomed in at the moment of decapitation, and zoomed out again. This time, the production for the Palace High Sheheading was even bigger. Several Motherland TV cameras, manned by consummate professionals, were stationed right in front of the stage, as though it were a music festival like Woodstock, and Santana was going to make his guitar loudly weep, and Joe Cocker was going to go into conniptions about getting help from his friends. A large yellow crane had been brought in to stand right at the edge of the VIP section. A cameraman precariously dangled from the hook, swaying to and fro, up and down, at times filming a panoramic view of the ecstatic crowd (that already extended all the way to the Bhurey Paradise). At times he swung below for a close-up of the moving lips of Hom Bokaw, who had covered the Ice Age, the three Dinosaur periods, the Bronze Age, the Vedic Period, and was enumerating the glorious 105 years of the Oligarchs and singing praises of its vicious progenitor Jungey. Across the street at the rooftop restaurant that advertised itself as "the tallest joint in Queen's Pond that the Big Two couldn't fell," where Kranti had met Rozy not too long ago, more professional cameras jostled for space with snipers from the Loyal Army Dais.

But the clip that went viral, and that eventually made its way to Motherland TV, was an amateur video taken with a smartphone, an iPhone 5 or even a 4. The phone must have shaken nearly the entire time because the camera kept jerking, and there were background voices—a conversation between the phone owner (male) and a friend (female). After the video became a hit, people identified the spot from where the video was taken. The Home of the Bell. The Loyal Army Dais never let anyone go up the Home of the Bell. How in the hell—or as someone quipped: How in the bell—did they allow entry for this group?

The phone-wielder seems to be a young man or a boy—he has a young person's voice—who apparently has little regard for human life because he keeps saying, "*Khachak!*" mimicking the sound that the giant khukuri would make at the exact moment it sliced off Madam Mao's neck. "I can't wait for the *khachak!*" he says to the young woman (his garlfren?), as the camera irreverently shakes in his hand.

"Alee focusma rakhana!" the girl says complainingly. "You're jerking all over, like a jerk."

The young man laughs.

"They're bringing her now," the girl says.

There is a cacophony of excited voices close to the camera. (About twenty people had squeezed into the Home of the Bell, people guesstimated later).

"Do you see?"

"Blindfolded."

"Where?"

"Right there."

The camera swings crazily to the right, briefly showing crowded rooftops to the north of the Queen's Pond, including the Worldlight Cinema Hall's top, where people are cheering at what's happening onstage. The camera swings back to the stand, then incredibly swings 180 degrees again, this time to settle on the girl's face. Slightly chubby, smiling with shy, yet mischievous eyes. The girl squeals. "Don't focus on me. Focus on that tauko."

"You are prettier than any loose head," the boy says.

A couple of strangers, older men with mustaches, try to get into the camera's view. The girl becomes annoyed. "Don't push, please na, uncles." The men, looking somewhat lecherous, grin at the camera.

The girl pushes the men away, and the young man loudly says, "Not uncles, but grampas, actually."

Suddenly, the girl's eyes widen; she puts her hand over her mouth and lets out a scream. Squeals, howls, and hoots are heard around the camera.

"Charlie Chaplin! Charlie Chaplin."

"Charlieeeeeee!"

The camera swerves wildly, jerking maniacally, capturing the sounds of raucous cheering all around, before it settles, trembling, on the stage, where the dark-skinned Charlie Chaplin jallad, holding the giant khukuri behind his back, is sneaking slowly up to Madam Mao, who is kneeling at the front of the stage, flanked by two Loyal Army Dais. The Charlie Chaplin jallad puts his finger to his lips and tiptoes, oh ever so slowly, toward her. About five feet away from her, he makes a sad face, then lifts his khukuri high up and brings it down, the weapon making a swoosh sound that is heard even across the Queen's Pond in the boy's video. But at the very last minute, the Charlie Chaplin jallad lets the khukuri drop, which makes a loud claaaang as it falls on the stage floor. Then he clutches his neck dramatically, mimes that his head has been severed from his neck and is now beginning to slide away from him in the air, as he runs after it. The crowd becomes frenzied. But the Charlie Chaplin jallad grabs his head, puts it back on his neck, and heaves a giant sigh of relief and again picks up the khukuri.

Madam Mao is still alive.

On the iPhone video: "Kasto hasaunchha hagi, Charlie Chaplin jallad ley?" the girl asks. "I can't stop laughing."

"Stop, Charlie, you're killing me!" her boyfren says.

Right then the Charlie Chaplin jallad stops in his tracks, a surprised look on his face, and slowly turns around and bows. The voices around the cameraman turn into murmurs and whispers.

"Darkmother!"

"Jai Matadi!"

"I am so blessed—to get a darshan of our mother on this glorious day."

There are a few loud cries of Jai Matadi all around, then silence.

⌒

From her vantage point inside the classroom, Kranti hadn't been able to see Darkmother's entry, but the surrounding hush had alerted her. Then she saw the palanquin. Any moment now, she had to be ready to jump. And then what? She didn't know. Shoot the Charlie Chaplin jallad? Shoot the Loyal Army Dais surrounding her mother? Her palm around the gun was so sweaty that it could easily slide out of her hands when she lifted it up. Even if she managed to shoot everyone on stage, including the men in black—Wham! Bam! Thank you Madam Mao!—then what? How was she going to get her mother away from all of this?

———

The out-of-control camera zooms in on Darkmother, who is surrounded by men in black. A giant hush falls over the spectators. The murmurs and whispers around the camera are barely audible.

"Jai Matadi!"

"General Tso is here."

"Stop moving the phone so much!" the girl commands her beau, who then complies and steadies the camera. Darkmother steps out of the palanquin. Her face is somber, her eyes lined with kohl, almost sad. She takes stock of the crowd, then the men in black surround her, protecting her.

———

Watching from the balcony, Kranti was thinking—now! Now! But she was paralyzed. Was her mother drugged? The figure of her mother, kneeling, seemed to be swaying slightly. Perhaps she was trying to see who was behind her.

———

Suddenly, there is a gasp from the spectators inside the Home of the Bell, and the boy says, "I'll be damned," and his garlfren says, "OMG."

This time the boy tries very hard, and the camera remains focused on the stage. The official Motherland TV version captures this more clearly: A few steps behind the now-alighted Darkmother is General Tso, and next to him is a short, fat man in daura suruwal, wearing a red cap instead of a dhakatopi, a figure who is stumbling slightly, as though he is attempting a two-step. This is the first sighting of the Hippo since the koo, and his appearance unleashes a surge of murmurs. Why is he here? Is he drunk? Drugged? A witness to the Sheheading? He is not handcuffed. General Tso is walking close to him, holding his arm as though accompanying an inebriated friend. The camera zooms in on the Hippo: his red cap says Make Amrika Great Again.

There is a purple couch on the stage, where Darkmother sits. She is in her hippie frock, and today, for some reason, she is wearing a tiara. She looks regal, slightly frail, and of course petite as usual. Her skin has acquired an even darker hue than when she first appeared in the Tourist District on her giant white horse. General Tso leads the Hippo to the fold-out seats that have been placed toward the front of the stage. The Charlie Chaplin jallad is standing close to Madam Mao, ready with his giant khukuri. General Tso and the Hippo sit on the fold-out chairs.

Someone near the iPhone cameraman whispers, "Is this Darkmother's gift for him?"

"For whom?"

"The Hippo."

"She's letting him watch the execution of his arch-nemesis."

"Khatra."

"Shhh."

Darkmother raises her hand as a signal. The Charlie Chaplin jallad raises his giant khukuri. The spectators await breathlessly. But the Charlie Chaplin jallad remains frozen, as though he had turned into a statue, the khukuri raised high above Madam Mao's neck.

"*Khachak!*" the boyfren urges in a whisper.

—

Now! Kranti screamed silently at herself. But she still couldn't move. Her heart was beating so fast that it seemed to be from a soundtrack of a Pink Floyd song that Dada used to listen to. She stood, ready to jump.

—

On the iPhone video: Darkmother raises her hand again, and the crowd waits for the Charlie Chaplin jallad to spring into action.

But there is no movement.

"What's happening?" the garlfren asks.

"I don't know."

"What's happening?" more voices ask.

"What's happening?" There's a chorus of whispers.

The iPhone clip doesn't capture this clearly, but the Motherland TV edition does: General Tso turns back to look at Darkmother. Then he gets up and goes to her. He bends his head, listening to Darkmother's instructions. Still, her lips are close to General Tso's ear, and, although his face is as unreadable as always, General Tso is attentive, absorbing her message. He returns to the Hippo and says something to him. The Hippo's face breaks into a smile and he vigorously nods.

General Tso leads the Hippo to the kneeling Madam Mao, who can't see who is behind her. The Hippo says something to her. Charlie Chaplin is right next to the two of them, frozen, the giant khukuri raised in the air. General Tso says something to the Hippo, who nods again and kneels next to Madam Mao. He speaks to her some more, then looks back at General Tso, who, standing behind the two, gestures with his palm for the Hippo to continue, that he is doing well. The Hippo speaks some more. His head is about a foot away from Madam Mao. He is relishing what he is saying; there is a faint smile on his lips.

General Tso takes out a gun from his holster—from her spot, Kranti recognized it: the Ancient Kalo Bandook; she knew who gave it to the general—and fires it in the air. Charlie Chaplin startles and comes alive.

What happened next took only three seconds, but when it was shown on Motherland TV, it was played in slow-motion so that everyone would savor those final moments.

The giant khukuri descends as though from heaven. It glints in the midmorning sunlight. The background voices, because the tape is in slow-motion, are also in slow-motion so they sound like *glib, goo-ga, wham, gham, blu, club, chin vee choo*. It is impossible to tell whether these are sounds of shock, alarm, delight, or disapproval, at least from the slow-motion clip; for all purposes they could be discussing the price of radishes in the Lord of the Heavens chowk one spring morning.

The giant khukuri descends. On the professional Motherland TV version, one can almost see the air molecules parting to make way for the khukuri's passage. Now it is only inches above Madam Mao's head. Then, a slight turn, and along with it a slight turn of his head by the Hippo, whose left eye seems to acknowledge the glint of the descending giant khukuri. The left eye then narrows—what the heck is this thing doing so close to my neck?—and then it widens. The giant khukuri makes contact with the Hippo's neck and in the slow-motion version it slowly cleaves it—first a quarter, then half, then three quarters, then the head reluctantly disengages from the body and rolls away, still wearing the red MAGA cap. Blood sprays from the neck, raining on Madam Mao.

HAPPY ENDING

50.

She had known this day would come. She had not known until she had known. Now, when she looked back, it was clear to her that this had been her destiny right from the start, when she had been a child and played in the dust in the Town of Lakes. Goddess Darkmother had appeared to her then, fangs showing, asking:

> Rozan, Rozan, where have you been?
> You will become me, one fine deen.

Goddess Darkmother had laughed and had bared her white teeth, and Rozan had known then that he ought to have been scared but he wasn't because she was, after all, a kind mother. Kindness oozed out of her pores and eyes. You could say that there was a halo of kindness around her. Everything she touched became a symbol of kindness. The breath she exhaled turned into kindness and soothed those it touched. The words she spoke split into thousands of atoms as soon as they emerged from her throat, and it didn't even matter what she said because at the core of those words was a nucleus of kindness.

———

She had work to do. Darkmotherland had truly been dark for the last two years. She had many problems to solve. Oh, these mortals and their problems. What mess were they capable of getting themselves into, then falling into the same mess again and again, then somehow surviving those messes and plunging right back into them again. Poor sods. And how gullible they were, how vulnerable to suggestions and coercions. How readily they had been duped by the Hippo. How easily cowed. No guts.

But it wasn't guts that had brought Darkmother this far, was it? Look at the price I've had to pay, she said to the mirror as she gazed at herself. Her eyes—the white parts were getting whiter and the pupils were getting darker so that even in the mirror her eyes appeared to be "flashing."

Good, good, she thought to herself as she observed herself.

She wandered around the halls of the Durbar in her hippie frock, her paujebs going *chum-chum-chum*. That was going to be the official sound of Darkmotherland from now on: *chum-chum-chum*. Darkmother had to be careful that all this didn't go to her head. She was not another Hippo. She wasn't going to allow herself to be another Hippo. Remember the kind Goddess Darkmother, she told herself. It cannot be anything but a kind Darkmother, the Darkmother of the prophecy who had come to untie knots, to soothe, to heal, to strengthen the people under her protection.

But there were still vulnerabilities. Moments of weakness. She experienced, for example, instances of rage that left her body shaking. Just yesterday she had gone down to the gardens of the Durbar, the very place where about a decade and half ago, the crown prince had chased and killed his mother and his younger brother, after he shot dead the rest of his family inside, including his father, aunt, and uncle. Darkmother had spent some time in the spot where the argument had started. The one that had sparked the fuse in the crown prince's brain as he'd adorned himself in military gear to butcher his family. She had touched the floor of the party room, now gutted, where the king had supposedly lain in disbelief, all bloody and dying, saying to his son who was clad in army fatigues, "What have you done?"

This was the bloody legacy of the rulers of this country, and now she, Darkmother, was a part of it.

Darkmother hadn't meant to order that execution. But the Hippo deserved it. She wanted him to shit in his pants. What was that ditty about the Big Two?

The Mother of All Quakes
Crap in our kattoos, it made us too.

Darkmother wanted to be the mother of all quakes for the Hippo. She wanted him to feel the fear that Darkmotherlandites had felt during his reign.

Darkmother had been conflicted about having Professor Shrestha arrested. It was not her idea, and in retrospect, she wished that she hadn't okayed it. But General Tso had come to her saying that Madam Mao needed to be taken care of. When Darkmother raised her eyebrows, he told her he'd learned that Madam Mao and her ragtag band of the Beggars were plotting to storm the Durbar, imminently. Darkmother rolled her eyes. "Maybe it'll come to nothing, General Tso," she said. "Maybe it'll fizzle out? Remember how long it took for the Beggars to get that stupid rally off the ground?"

"Possible," General Tso said. "But these are crazy times, Mata. Madam Mao has expressed great frustration over what has happened. She's now given interviews saying that a dictatorship is a dictatorship, and that the only thing we've done is switch genders."

Darkmother felt insulted that Professor Shrestha would compare her to the Hippo. The first thing Darkmother had done after coming to power was open up the press. The media could, once again, say anything they wanted. It was another thing that they chose not to say anything bad about Darkmother. Oh, there was an occasional "what has happened?" or "how did Darkmother gain power?" type of articles, but they were more analytical than critical. The media, too, seemed cognizant of the public sentiment toward Darkmother, the awe and reverence with which she was held. Also, Darkmother's appearance had been so miraculous that even the media, and even atheists and skeptics, were fearful that speaking out directly against Darkmother might mean something bad would rain down upon them. Darkmother herself didn't know what she would have done had there been negative media coverage of her. She might have put her foot down, like the iconic visage of her with her foot on the chest of the Pothead God.

"I think it's better to nip it in the bud," General Tso said.

Darkmother nodded, then said, "But make sure she's not harmed."

General Tso briefly looked at her.

"I know what you're thinking," Darkmother said. "You want to harm her, don't you, Dinesh babu?"

General Tso scratched his head, and eventually nodded.

"Well, those days are gone, do you hear me? Do you understand?"

General Tso bowed. "I will not harm Madam Mao, Darkmother."

Darkmother flicked her fingers in dismissal.

She had thought about Kranti, how worried she must be for Professor Shrestha. Darkmother could see her combing the Valley for her mother. There she was, at the gate of the Monkeygod Gate Jail, pleading with the guards. There she was, showing a photo to a shopkeeper, asking him if he'd seen her mother. As if! Darkmother thought. How would a shopkeeper of all people know where Madam Mao was? Kranti knew damn well her mother was imprisoned. But, she was in denial because she didn't want to think that Darkmother, her friend in her previous incarnation, could have had her mother imprisoned. Kranti hadn't even wanted to admit that her mother was missing for those many days; it was that pudgy poet of hers who had to awaken her to reality. This was also something that Kranti needed to understand: she was inextricably tied to her mother, no matter how much she abhorred it. We cannot escape our pasts, we cannot escape our parents, regardless of how much we wish it otherwise.

It was at this point that Darkmother thought of her own parents, and tears welled up in her eyes. Did they miss her? Okay, if not miss, then did they think about her? Did they remember their teenage son, the one who put on lipstick and preened in front of the mirror? Did they remember the child that they gave birth to, the one they held in their arms and made cooing sounds to? The pain she experienced at the thought of her parents was so sharp, so piercing that even in the divine body of Darkmother, she felt she'd collapse to the floor. But she wouldn't do that; she couldn't do that now. She was Darkmother. She had to be strong for her people. She had toyed with the idea of bringing her parents over to the Durbar from the Town of Lakes, let them see what had become of their child, the power that their progeny wielded now. But she was also afraid that the sight of her parents would weaken her. And they would be befuddled. Or perhaps even uncaring, no matter who she was now. This thought pained her even more, that her parents could reject her, even now, even after she had turned into Darkmother—even when the entire country kissed the ground that she walked on.

Darkmother had not gone to see Professor Shrestha after she was arrested, sensing that the meeting would be difficult. Professor Shrestha, she knew, would not be respectful toward her. She would question Darkmother's legitimacy, and Darkmother didn't know what she would do about it. Could she be sure that there were no authoritarian tendencies inside her that would flare up at a real or perceived insult?

Don't let it get to your head, don't let it get to your head—you're Darkmother.

Professor Shrestha had been kept in a little room in a corner of the Durbar, with a nice bed and nokerchakers who brought her the same meals that Darkmother ate upstairs. The nokerchakers also delivered to Professor Shrestha the newspapers of the day; there was even a small TV in the room.

Looking out of the large windows of Durbar, in the distance Darkmother saw the figure of Kranti, at the end of the long line that had formed outside the palace. She looked desperate, was pleading with the Loyal Army Dais. Darkmother had half a mind to send someone to fetch poor Kranti, allow her to see Professor Shrestha and put some sense into her so that Darkmother would have a ready excuse to have her released. Some sense! Hadn't Kranti been trying to do precisely that—put some sense into Professor Shrestha—all her life? Had Professor Shrestha listened? Had she listened to anybody her whole life? When Darkmother thought about Kranti, details of her life came to her in glimpses, like those from a jerky movie projector, details that Kranti hadn't told her. Darkmother saw the tearful walks to the bus stop between Kranti and her father, the I'm-going-to-die-laughing jokes in the kitchen regarding the Beggars, the screaming matches between Kranti and Professor Shrestha and the subsequent days of silent resentment, the jacket with the skull, the rush to Hotel Thunderbolt & Diamond in a taxi following an urgent phone call, the fight with the monkeys, and on and on.

I understand you perfectly, saathi, Darkmother whispered to Kranti in the solitude of the bedroom.

That's when the idea of using Professor Shrestha as a decoy had come to Darkmother. It was a devious idea, full of cunning, but wasn't the mythological Darkmother a resourceful one, unafraid to use deception in order to make a point? What point would this make? Darkmother didn't know. She was moving forward by intuition, which arose inside her like a powerful flame these days, tearing through the gap between thought and action.

51.

What happened at the Palace High Sheheading was talked about throughout Darkmotherland, in whispers, of course, for no one was sure how and when or even if it should be talked about. Darkmotherlandites still feared that they could say the wrong thing and land in trouble. They could be slapped around by the Loyal Army Dais or by Mata's Matriots, or both. They could be dragged off to jail. They could be flogged in public as a demonstration of what happens to people who are discovered plotting—and whispering could easily be deemed plotting—which could turn into accusations of being a Treasonist. They feared that simple-minded, innocuous whispers about the Sheheading could lead to their own beheading, making them clasp their throats in instinctive gestures of protection. They tried to laugh it off, saying, "What? We're going to be beheaded for talking about the Sheheading? That's absurd. Darkmother isn't like that." But no one could be sure. The Sheheading had effectively managed to silence Darkmotherland. Even the first Palace High Beheadings hadn't inspired this much fear.

Things had changed inside her mother's brain, thought Kranti. Some of her older self was still there—the slightly controlling, critical, scoffing self—but a new, somewhat fearful Professor Shrestha had emerged since the rescue. Kranti always put the word "rescue" in air quotes, and initially Professor Shrestha, too, used air quotes or mockingly exaggerated it, but as time passed, she insisted that no, Kranti had indeed rescued her. "If it weren't for you—" Professor Shrestha said, then made a gesture of her head being sliced off.

"But what happened to you would have happened whether I was there or not." Watching the iPhone clip on Motherland TV later, Kranti had tried to see if the camera, when it jerked around haphazardly, also detected her, Kranti, on the second floor, waiting to jump to rescue her mother (the official cameras had unflinchingly fixated on the stage). She must have been in the direct line of the iPhone, but the camera, even when it moved up, had somehow rendered the Palace High building blurry, although she could even pinpoint the area on the balcony where she hid. At the time that Charlie Chaplin jallad was going through his miming act, she had been wondering, gun in hand, whether she should make her move right then, or wait.

"No, no," Professor Shrestha said emphatically, wagging her index finger. She had shrunk a bit and lost weight since the Palace High Sheheading. The Sheheading had done something to her. She now had the nervous habit of touching her throat, as though she couldn't trust that it was still intact.

Every now and then Professor Shrestha had a deer-in-the-headlights look, her mind frozen in that moment when, blindfolded and handcuffed, she was waiting for the Charlie Chaplin jallad to finish his task. She was reliving that moment, over and over, like a stuck film reel, except her mind had substituted what did happen—her rescue—with what nearly happened, her execution. Professor Shrestha had gotten thinner and straighter, as though she'd been kicked in the back to rectify her spine. Gone was the cane: she no longer needed it. She no longer sat for long stretches on her favorite green couch in Beggar Street. Kranti noted when she visited her mother that she now paced the living room, her body lithe and more agile than before. More nervous. Laughing at odd moments. Sleepless. A bit like Murti, Kranti thought, an older version of Murti, who stayed away from Beggar Street now. Vikram and Chanchal had also been released along with Professor Shrestha. Those two had also been forced to watch the Sheheading that morning at the Palace High, with the clear intention to traumatize them. It worked; they didn't return to Beggar Street either after their release. Murti was still living in that crumpled building, from what Kranti had heard. Still cooking for herself, still living like a true beggar. Still practicing her failed witchcraft? Kranti didn't know. Professor Shrestha hadn't asked why Murti, Vikram, or Chanchal hadn't come to visit. She'd avoided mentioning their names. The fight—the Sangharsh—had gone out of Professor

Shrestha, at least for now. The Sangharsh has been *harsh* on her, Dada, Kranti couldn't help thinking. Every now and then Kranti thought she caught a glimpse of the old Madam Mao, with that fire in her eyes. The blaze was still there, and one day it would emerge, like a slow volcano erupting. Madam Mao, the lifelong fighter, had merely gone dormant for a while.

But for now, Beggar Street was no longer a place for secret meetings and hatching revolutions. Now, on those days when Kranti and Kabiraj visited with the khateykids, it resembled a Dickens novel: khateykids sprawled on the sofa, khateykids hanging by the doorway, khateykids playing hopscotch in the cramped yard in the back, khateykids chasing one another through the kitchen, khateykids hiding under the beds. "They are the Neo Beggars," Kabiraj joked. No, Kranti said, they were not Beggars at all and they weren't going to be groomed as such, Kranti would make sure of it. That's why she was resisting her mother's urgings to move back to Beggar Street. "If I do, I will bring my khateykids with me," Kranti had replied when Professor Shrestha suggested that Kranti move back to Beggar Street.

"That's fine," Professor Shrestha said, to Kranti's surprise. Her mother was willing to be surrounded by all the khateykids if it meant getting Kranti away from Bhurey Paradise.

"And Kabiraj, of course," Kranti said. "Kabiraj is their father. He also comes." Kabiraj, who had come by to pick her up after he finished tutoring some rich kids nearby, was standing by the door.

Kabiraj, with his unkempt beard, his beady eyes, and his pig-snout face, sheepishly smiled. Professor Shrestha didn't have any problems with Kabiraj before, when he had visited Beggar Street when Bhaskar was alive. Now, however, after Bhaskar's death as it became clear that her daughter deeply cared for the poet, she appeared to have grown a dislike for him. She especially couldn't seem to understand why Kranti lived with him in Laj Mahal when she had a perfectly fine home, with her own room, in Beggar Street. "You don't belong in Laj Mahal," Professor Shrestha had murmured to Kranti a few times. Madam Mao, a lifelong fighter for equality and justice, letting it be known that she didn't think Kabiraj was up to the standard of Beggar Street, of Kranti, of being Bhaskar's equal.

"Laj Mahal is more reliable than this house," Kranti told her mother. "Remember how close you were to losing this one in your cockamamie scheme? What was that—Operation Cry Motherland?" Although her mother hadn't sold the house to finance her failed plans to storm the Durbar, Kranti had thought that she would have, if she felt it was necessary. Luckily, the Rajjya had been able to get most of the money back from the bribed Durbar guards—upon the instruction of Darkmother, Kranti learned later—and returned it to Professor Shrestha.

"Why does Kabiraj need to move here?" Professor Shrestha said as though Kabiraj wasn't standing by the door. "Doesn't he have a family of his own?"

"If he had family, he wouldn't be living in Bhurey Paradise, in a tent whose name means the palace of shame."

Scoffing, Professor Shrestha shook her head. Kranti couldn't tell whether she was disgusted at the name Laj Mahal or at the fact that Bhurey Paradise was where Kabiraj and Kranti lived. Kranti had been somewhat annoyed, and disappointed, frankly, that Professor Shrestha had been prejudiced against Kabiraj right from the start. Not up to par, Professor Shrestha was suggesting about Kabiraj. Not good enough for my Kranti. Not like Bhaskar.

Only Kranti knew what Kabiraj brought to the table in order to compensate for Bhaskar's charisma and good looks: her dallu had an earthiness, a man-of-the-soil quality, he didn't want to change the world, only to live happily in the small world around him, and, unlike Bhaskar, he gave his full attention to Kranti. Most important for now: he was extremely good with the khateykids. While Bhaskar had been dynamic with his band of khateykids, like a dashing and brilliant uncle who awed them with his joie de vivre and his generosity, Kabiraj's devotion to them was less showy, more steady. He was ready to do what each khateykid wanted him to do, whenever the khateykid wanted him to do it. He washed their dirty clothes, cooked their meals, took them to the daktar in the Bhurey Paradise health post, gave them baths in the communal tap, oiled, braided, and combed their hair, read them books, took them for soccer practice, stayed by their bedside when they became sick, got them ready for school, packed their lunches. He was born to take care of these kids, be a father to them—he rarely raised his voice at them; never punished them for anything. He was consistent and loving. A stable parent.

"If I come to Beggar Street, then Kabiraj also comes," Kranti made clear to Professor Shrestha on a day when Kabiraj wasn't present.

Although clearly unhappy, Professor Shrestha said, "Okay, we'll talk more." It was obvious, however, that every time Professor Shrestha's eyes fell upon Kabiraj she thought of Bhaskar, and her mind immediately began comparing them and seeing flaws in the oinky-looking man with the unkempt beard and mustache.

—

One afternoon the cowbell rang outside Laj Mahal. It was Shambhogya, though she looked different. Instead of a glittering sari, she wore a simple dhoti. No makeup, so her face looked windblown. She stared at Kranti as though it was Kranti who'd rang the bell outside the Asylum.

"O-ho Shambhogya didi!" Kranti was genuinely happy to see her.

But Shambhogya didn't smile.

"Please come in, didi," Kranti said. "It's been so long." She stopped herself from saying that she'd been thinking about visiting the Asylum. It was true. One time she'd even walked all the way to the Tourist District with that purpose, then changed her mind and returned to Laj Mahal. She had forgiven—or at least tried hard to forgive—the Ghimireys for not raising a finger to help her when she was in a panic about her mother.

Shambhogya lowered her head and slowly entered, as though she were being coerced. Once inside, she cast a disapproving look at the mess: clothes draped over boxes and chairs; chess pieces scattered; books and magazines strewn on the floor; half-eaten food on plastic plates. The khateykids had all been taken to the zoo by Kabiraj, even though the zoo had been in shambles since the Big Two with half the animals dead or injured. Professor Shrestha hadn't needed much encouragement to tag along with Kabiraj and the khateykids. Kranti had stayed behind, saying she'd tidy up the tent, but as soon as the children left, she'd made a cup of tea and relaxed with a book on the green couch that Professor Shrestha had had delivered to Laj Mahal because she no longer used it.

"So, this is what you left the Asylum for?" Shambhogya said. She nodded as her head moved around to scrutinize the room. Her eyes, however, had a dull look, as though their juices had been sapped out of them. She had also lost weight. There had been stories of noker-chakers across the Valley not giving enough food to the masters of their home. Was that what was also happening at the Asylum?

A small shudder appeared to pass through Shambhogya's body every few minutes.

"Didi, please sit down. I'll make some tea."

"No need."

"Please."

"No need."

Still, Kranti scooted to the corner and boiled water for tea. Shambhogya continued standing, arms tightly wrapped around herself, looking at the ceiling, as if there was something there.

"Do you have any idea where Muwa is?" Kranti asked.

"She came back a couple of days ago," Shambhogya said, shaking her head. "Where would she go? I knew it was a sham when she disappeared—it was all a big act to prove she's superior to the rest of us."

"Still," Kranti said. "I'm relieved to hear it. What about Sir? He's fine? Aditya-da? Chaitanya? Priyanka? Are they all fine?" After the Palace High Sheheading, Kranti had stopped wondering whether the Ghimireys had a hand in Bhaskar's death. It seemed highly improbable. Now she had once again begun to think that it had been the Hippo. Still, every now and then she recalled Subhash's conviction that the man who killed Bhaskar was inside the Asylum.

"Fine, fine, fine, they're all fine, why wouldn't they be?"

After tea was ready, Shambhogya still refused to sit, so the two sipped their tea standing, their slurping noises loud as they struggled for things to say. There was more awkward silence after they finished. Kranti then decided to end it. She set her glass down on the floor, took Shambhogya's empty glass and did the same, then took her sister-in-law by the hand and led her to the green couch, where she forced her to sit. Kranti sat on a plastic stool in front of her and continued to hold her hands. She could feel the tremor in Shambhogya's body through her fingers. They both looked at each other. Shambhogya's eyes were dry, defiant.

"Didi."

"The Palace High Sheheading—you must be very glad. You must have been worried."

"I'm glad nothing happened to my mother." Was Shambhogya going to mention how the Asylum had refused to help? Was that a slightly guilty look on her face? Was this visit an atonement of some type? It was hard to tell—all Shambhogya's face displayed was misery and anger.

After a while, Shambhogya looked around and said, "Where are the khateykids? And your—dallu?"

"They've gone to the zoo. How is Shaditya? Is he on vacation from the boarding school?"

Shambhogya didn't answer her about her son. Instead, she asked, "Are you happy here?"

"I am very happy."

"Are you trying to rub it in? Gloat in your happiness? I don't need your pity."

Shambhogya said it so quickly that for a brief moment Kranti didn't understand. Then she did, and she said, "But I don't pity you."

"I know what you are thinking. I know the likes of you. You think you are above us now, don't you, Kranti? You think you are better than me. I have felt this from you since the first day you entered the Asylum." Her lips were quivering. She was wheezing out her words, but she didn't pull her hands away from Kranti. "Well, I came here to tell you that you are not above me. You don't know how much I've suffered to make sure that no harm befalls the Ghimirey family, to make sure that things are taken care of. You think it's easy for me? You think it's easy to live with someone like Aditya, who doesn't think of anyone but himself? Do you know that he has a mistress? And Muwa, she didn't like me from the start—I could tell from her eyes. No matter how hard I tried, no matter how much I took care of this cursed family, her dislike never diminished. After you came, she disliked me even more. Have you ever considered what that must have felt like for me? And the big man, Prithvi Raj, the Sir of the family—he totally fell apart about Bhaskar's death. In the end, a weak, weak man, despite all the wealth he has amassed."

What about Priyanka? Kranti wanted to ask.

As if reading her thoughts, Shambhogya said, "You want to know what I feel about Priyanka, don't you? Do you know that I can't stand her? I've never been able to stand her, that conniving mouse. Imagine how hard it has been for me to have Priyanka follow me around. Shambhogya didi this, and Shambhogya didi that. I've wanted to slap her many times, but I've held back. You know why? Because I've thought that if I did, everything would simply fall apart. With each of these people I've felt that if I didn't hold things together, things would collapse. That's why I was furious when you resisted getting married to Umesh dai. I thought: That bitch, who does she think she is? Do I believe in all that manglik business? I don't know, Kranti. At times I've thought it was all hooey. Bull crap, I thought, we make our own destiny. How can the alignment of stars at the time of your birth dictate your marriage? My stars match perfectly with Aditya's. I know this because my parents had consulted both the charts before they married us. Yet he keeps a mistress on the side, and I am sad and alone. Some match! But for the longest time I was seized with the idea that your being a manglik had everything to do with Bhaskar's death and the sorrow that had descended upon this family. I convinced myself that the family disintegration started the day your name was first mentioned in the Asylum. Hell, I even painted a rosy picture of my own marital life, making myself believe that my marriage was fine until you came, that Aditya started keeping his mistress only after you began to see Bhaskar, whereas the truth is that he'd bought that flat for her long before you and Bhaskar met. But I persuaded myself that only after you entered our lives did Aditya start to neglect me.

"When you started resisting Umesh dai, there was a point when I thought it would be nice if you no longer existed. I wondered how that could be turned into reality. I wondered if there was something I could do so you'd no longer be in our lives—my life—anymore. I recalled stories of women who'd consumed rat poison to kill themselves, and I debated whether I should put some rat poison in your food. You'd simply not wake up the next morning. Everyone would think that you committed suicide, quite logical for a recently widowed woman, especially given her husband's gruesome murder. I rummaged in the storage room to see if I could find any rat poison, and when I couldn't, I went to the market—yes, one afternoon I slipped away to the Lord of the Heavens chowk, and bought some. That nosey parker Priyanka saw what I had bought, and she asked me whether I'd seen a rat in the house. I didn't tell her that I thought she was one herself. She was looking at me strangely; she might have thought I was going to consume it myself.

"But every time I thought about grinding it and slipping it into your food, I couldn't bring myself to do it. Because I admired you. I hated you, but I was jealous of you and I admired you. I was jealous of the mother you had, who let you be what you wanted to be. I would have worshipped a mother like that. And I admired you for following the beat of your heart and finding love with Bhaskar. I admired you for not caring a whit about his wealth, for remaining true to yourself even after you came into the house with all the expectations of a Ghimirey household. Can I make a confession to you, Kranti? You won't think I'm a witch after I tell you?"

Kranti shook her head. She glanced at her phone to check the time, hoping that Kabiraj and Professor Shrestha wouldn't return with the khateykids soon to disrupt this narrative.

"But you already think I'm a witch, so what does it matter? Perhaps I am indeed a witch. When I first learned of Bhaskar babu's death, my first thought was: khuchching! Serves her right. Can you believe that? Who else but a witch would think these thoughts? For a few days I carried that thought inside me. A part of me was secretly self-congratulatory at what had happened, even as another part mourned for your loss, for Bhaskar, whom I genuinely liked because he treated me with respect. 'Loosen up, bhauju,' he used to tell me and massage my shoulders. 'You don't have to be the general manager of the world.' After my secret jubilation at Bhaskar babu's death, another thought clutched at me: Why couldn't it have been Aditya who'd been killed? I laughed, then cried. But it seemed logical. I was in an unhappy marriage, and if he died, I could live out the rest of my life as a widow. I would no longer have to be the general manager of the Asylum. I could retreat into a cocoon, as a widow would be expected to do. Or, if I felt like it, over time I could take on a secret lover, perhaps keep a young stud in a flat. When I pondered this further, I thought I was a loser. Even in the area of losing one's husband, you had come out on top."

"I wish you'd come to talk to me," Kranti said, tears welling up in her eyes. "I had no idea you were feeling, thinking these things."

"I didn't want your pity. I don't want your pity." Shambhogya lifted her hand as though to wipe away Kranti's tears but let it drop halfway. "Are you happy here?" she asked.

"I am very happy here."

Shambhogya let out a sigh of exasperation. "Well, I better get going. I have to go home and cook dinner for everyone."

"So it's true that if you want decent food at the Asylum you need to cook it yourself?"

"If you want *any* food, you need to cook it yourself." Shambhogya laughed wryly. "It's amazing how far we've fallen. I don't mind the cooking, but sleeping in such close proximity to the nokerchakers makes me feel dirty all the time. They demanded that we vacate a couple of rooms upstairs because the Servants Villa was too cramped. So now four of them stay up there with us, two in your former room and two in what used to be Muwa's room. She hasn't been using it for months anyway. Not only does Muwa now sleep in God's Room, she barely comes out. And when she does, she paces in that small area behind God's Room so no one can see her."

"Who takes her food?"

"I used to, but we noticed that whenever I took the food to her it remained untouched. So, now Thulo Maya takes it. She tells me that she does so not because she's a nokerchaker, but because of their bond from the village. She's the only one that Muwa talks to anymore. A word or two, that's all Muwa speaks, according to Thulo Maya. 'I think she's losing her speech,' Thulo Maya told me. 'All because of you folks.'

"That's the way the nokerchakers speak to us these days. Blunt. Rude. Well, they're hardly our nokerchakers anymore. Gone are the 'ji,' 'hajur,' or even 'tapai.' The other evening Harkey called me 'timi,' and when I said that he was taking it too far, he became confrontational and ended up labeling me a whore. The nokerchakers called a meeting and we all sat in front of them. I had to offer an apology to Harkey for my disrespect. We were told that they, the nokerchakers, were on equal footing with us now. 'If you cling to the old reality,' they told us, 'you will make yourselves even more miserable.' We can no longer call them nokerchakers, or workers. They are now coworkers. Coworkers, my foot! We do most of the housework now. Priyanka and I cook for the family. If we need help in the kitchen, we have to very politely request them to give us a hand, and that also goes for other chores, like shelling peas or chopping kauli. Once, I asked Mokshya to cut some onions for me. As soon as she started cutting, she began to snivel and weep. I brought her to the Asylum when I got married—she was a starving little girl then. Her mother, who was a cook for my mother, had told me that their family was indebted to me for life, for allowing their girl to work for such a prestigious family. And here she was crying as though I had asked her to clean the septic tank. Harkey came into the kitchen and berated me for making Mokshya cut the onions. 'Don't you see that she's suffering?' he asked. 'Why didn't you give her something lighter to do?" When I tried to explain to him that the other day Mokshya had a similar problem peeling potatoes, he loudly called me names. Aditya came to see what the problem was, but the rest of the nokerchakers also quickly arrived and their voices dominated our meek appeals. Our husbands have been rendered impotent. Cuckolds. That day Harkey made me chop the onions, in front of everybody, including Aditya.

"They no longer wash our clothes, and they don't allow the outside washerwoman to come anymore, so Priyanka and I have to do all the laundry. It's exhausting work. The other morning as I squatted on the floor of the laundry room, soaping, rinsing, and wringing, Harkey came by and dropped a pair of his shorts on the floor. 'Can you get these done immediately and put them out to dry? I need them by this afternoon.' When I looked at him in disbelief, he said, 'Is there a difficulty with what I asked?' I sputtered something about how the clothes wouldn't dry on such a cloudy day, and he said that in that case I should iron his shorts to dry them."

Kranti asked Shambhogya whether she was hungry, whether she could fry her an egg or make her aloo sandeko, which she knew Shambhogya liked.

Shambhogya continued as though Kranti hadn't spoken, "Aditya tells me that every day is a battle now in the Ghimirey & Sons factories. But it's happening in all the big places, Shakya Inc., the MOM Group. Workers are riding roughshod over the management. All the employees at Ghimirey & Sons have received a two hundred percent pay increase. Two hundred percent, can you imagine? We now are paying for all the medical bills of their families. Huge losses, Aditya says. We're going to become bankrupt soon. Then cut down on the expenses, I want to tell him. Get rid of that whore in that expensive flat. But I no longer care. In all likelihood his mistress has also demanded a two hundred percent increase. He could be pondering whether it's wise to keep her, or given how things are crumbling all around us, maybe she is his only solace. He looks depressed all the time, my Aditya. When I observe him, I experience only a hardening in my chest, and I look away."

"And Sir?"

"He's been reduced to a bumbling idiot. The nokerchakers openly mock him. He has lost comprehension of much of what's happening around him. But who's going to take him to a daktar for diagnosis?"

"What about Daktar Pant?"

"He's stopped coming, saying that we haven't paid him for his last visits. But it's a waste of money, paying a daktar who comes, monitors your pulse, then advises you take a sleeping pill or Cetamol."

Kranti thought that it sounded much like how she'd complained to Kabiraj recently about the daktar in Bhurey Paradise who had to be fetched when one of the khateykids got sick. "What are you going to do now, Didi?"

"What can I do? This is my family. This has been my family for years. I think soon we'll lose everything, and we'll be out on the street. No matter what, I'll continue to serve the Ghimireys, do the best I can. I am a good buhari, after all. Aditya is trying hard to see if he can funnel some money to a separate account so that if we lose Ghimirey & Sons and the Asylum we can move elsewhere, perhaps the Town of Lakes, and try to at least have a roof over our heads. But it's really hard now because they're hawkishly watching everything, the noker-chakers and the workers, and demanding rationales and proof. But I don't care. I will deal with whatever fate throws my way."

Shambhogya stood. "You're probably getting bored listening to me talk. You've set up a nice life for yourself." She pointed to the mess around her.

"Didi, please, whenever you feel like talking, please visit me."

"I told you, I don't need your pity." They were at the tent's door now.

"Shambhogya-di, can I ask you something?" Kranti asked, a bit hesitantly.

Shambhogya splayed her palm, as though saying, what are you waiting for?

"Promise you won't get mad?"

"What? Out with it! I have to get back to the Asylum, otherwise the nokerchakers will get mad."

"There's been talk, I'm not saying that there's any truth to it, but still, I thought I'd ask. Some people are saying that perhaps Bhaskar's murder was an inside job. I don't know."

"Inside job?"

"You know," Kranti said. "From inside the Asylum? It's all poppycock talk, I know, but—"

Shambhogya laughed. "Are you asking if Bhaskar babu was killed by one of us, Kranti?"

"I just thought—if you'd heard anything—if you knew anything."

Shambhogya continued to look at her, with such hatred that Kranti thought she was about to be walloped. "How dare you?" Shambhogya said, finally. "How could you even think this?"

Without another word she opened the flap and walked out of Laj Mahal.

52.

Darkmother sat on a duvet in her bedroom in the Durbar. She'd had her bed put right up against the window so she could look out at the boulevard at night when she couldn't sleep, and these nights she didn't sleep well.

Darkmother had imagined, without pleasure, how the Hippo had learned of Matakoo. He had just landed at Tri-Universe International Airport when he saw what was happening on the TV inside the airplane. He had had a restful sleep on the airplane, dreaming of a new alliance with President Corn Hair that would make Darkmotherland truly great, and would allow him to go down in the history books as the most transformative ruler of the country, even more revered than the Founding Father. He would perhaps even be in contention as one of the greatest political leaders in the history of the world, like Churchill or Nehru. He'd dreamed of this on the flight back with his red MAGA hat on, which he'd come to think of as a talisman of good luck. An aide had turned on the TV just as the plane touched down on the tarmac at Tri-Universe International Airport.

Shrimati Papa was sitting next to him, knitting a sweater for him. The trip had put her in good spirits as well, especially after getting to meet the First Lady. So beautiful, so kind. Hadn't she been a naked model for dirty magazines sometime in the past? Shrimati Papa thought that she'd read something to that effect somewhere, but what did it matter now? What clearly mattered was that PM Papa had formed a partnership with the most powerful man in the world. Things could only get better. Shrimati Papa hoped that the euphoria of this trip would also do something to change the relationship between her and her husband, that she'd be able to move back into the Humble Abode and kick that abomination out of her house.

As PM Papa's plane taxied toward the terminal, PM Papa watched with alarm at what was unfolding on Motherland TV.

PM Papa saw the incredible crowd that had gathered outside the Durbar, and the palanquin that had been brought for Darkmother.

Shrimati Papa stopped sewing and stared at the television. "That's General Tso," Shrimati Papa said. "That's—that's—that's—your pashu—"

"Shut up!" PM Papa's jowls were quivering.

It could be nothing. A stunt that he and Rozy could laugh about later. A practical joke that Rozy and General Tso could be playing on PM Papa, on Darkmotherlandites.

The plane reached the terminal.

Shrimati Papa stood from the sofa, her eyes on the TV screen. She began pacing inside the small airplane, saying, "Hai Ram, Hai Ram."

"Sit down," PM Papa said.

"What are you going to do?" Shrimati Papa asked in a quivering voice.

PM Papa dialed General Tso's mobile number. On the TV screen he saw General Tso reach into his pocket, take out the phone, glance at it, then drop it back into his pocket.

"Is Go!swami in on this?" Shrimati Papa asked.

"I don't know."

"Call him!"

PM Papa did.

"Allo?" Swami Go!swami picked it up right away.

"What is going on?"

"Are you back in Darkmotherland?"

"At the airport. Swami Go!swami, what is going on?"

"Yes, I heard, I heard. I saw, I saw."

"Are you a part of this?" PM Papa had to control himself from screaming.

"What? Am I a part of what?"

Through the phone, PM Papa could hear voices in the background at Kailashram. Other Fundys talking as they watched Motherland TV, where Hom Bokaw blathered on about how impressive the crowd was outside the Durbar. Even in his panic, PM Papa couldn't help but think that there seemed to be two Hom Bokaws: one on his Motherland TV channel inside the airplane, and the other, on the TV in Kailashram, streaming through his mobile phone. He shouted into the phone, thinking there was still hope: "Could this be a practical joke?"

"A joke, yes, yes." But there was fear in Swami Go!swami's voice.

"Come to the airport immediately."

"Hahn-ji, hahn-ji."

"And can you assemble an army of the Devouts?"

But Swami Go!swami had already hung up.

"I'm going to have the Devouts go en masse toward the Durbar," PM Papa said to Shrimati Papa, his voice hoarse. He was fully aware that a small army of Devouts would be crushed immediately by the Loyal Army Dais if indeed this was another koo, which it looked like it was. A small, now diminishing part of PM Papa clung on to the hope that it was all one giant ha-ha-hee-hee hoax. Who was the idiot who said that hope springs eternal?

The plane had stopped. When an aide opened the airplane door, there was Laxman, waiting right outside. PM Papa's heart sank. Rozy had asked that he not take Laxman with him to Amrika, that Laxman be left behind to be her bodyguard. There'll be Amrikan Secret Service for you, no, Papa? Rozy had said. And PM Papa, the fool that he was, had listened to her.

"Laxman," PM Papa said. "You see what's happening?"

Laxman nodded. Behind him were four or five Loyal Army Dais holding machine guns.

"I have been instructed, PM Papa," Laxman said, "to take you to the Durbar."

Shrimati Papa began wailing.

Laxman brought PM Papa to the Durbar in Papa's Hummer. It was followed by other cars that were filled with Generals and Colonels of the Loyal Army. Laxman kept a stoic face throughout. It was hard to believe that this same man had been by his side day and night ever since General Tso appointed him as his bodyguard. He had even saved his life during Papa Don't Preach. PM Papa knew that Laxman had a wife and two small children. He liked to watch Amrikan wrestling on TV. And he had a particular weakness for sukuti, PM Papa was well aware of this fact. On two occasions he had ordered Rozy to send big packets of dried deer meat to Laxman's house when Laxman was home sick.

PM Papa thought of saying something to Laxman. Political fortunes change, PM Papa wanted to say, meaning that by the end of this ride PM Papa could be back in power again. Was Laxman sure he wanted to do this? Did Laxman want to be a part of something that, once it turned into its opposite, would lead to his execution?

Once they entered the gates of the Durbar, however, panic gripped a tired and jet-lagged PM Papa. He looked at Laxman and said, "There is still time. I can still forgive you."

Laxman only slightly shook his head.

"Think of your children," PM Papa said. "Think of what'll happen to them."

It didn't even occur to PM Papa to ask where they'd taken Shrimati Papa.

The Loyal Army Dais didn't talk to him as they descended underground. They passed through dimly lit corridors, then went down more staircases. He heard moans. They passed through a corridor with prison-like cages on both sides. He saw them: skeletal figures clutching on to bars, staring at him. Some were so emaciated that they looked like Holocaust victims, and it was hard to tell what their skin color or their ethnicity was. They were mostly men, some women, some whose gender couldn't be distinguished. In the air was a heavy odor of urine and excrement. Inside a cell he saw a man crouching— he was defecating. It became clear then: there were no bathrooms in the cells. In another cell he saw a pile (animal meat?) around which angry flies buzzed; the flies also hovered around the faces that were watching PM Papa from behind bars.

"No dignity, Laxman?" PM Papa said. "Have they ordered you to imprison me here, like these animals?"

Laxman finally said, "This might be temporary, I don't know." Then he looked pointedly into PM Papa's eyes, as if in response to his comments about Laxman's children. "Or it may be permanent."

Rage was building up inside PM Papa. Once he regained power—and he was sure that he would; in days or weeks he would orchestrate something that would turn this around—he was going to punish General Tso. He would personally watch that bhotey be tortured. He would order his men to insert needles into the general's fingertips. He would order his men to burn him with cigarette butts. He would make General Tso hang upside down, then flay the skin off of his face.

Laxman took him into a cell where there was another prisoner, an old man sitting on a bench, his legs crossed. He was so thin that the flesh on his body seemed to have dried up and blackened against his bones. His cheekbones jutted out, and there were hollow caves where his eyes were. There was something vaguely familiar about him.

"Not even a house arrest, Laxman?" PM Papa said. "Okay, I'll remember this."

Laxman and his men left.

PM Papa held the bars with his hands and looked out. He closed his eyes, then opened them, half expecting to find himself back in the Humble Abode, perhaps back with Shrimati Papa knitting a sweater for him. But even in this imagining he found Shrimati Papa highly unappealing. Then, he saw in his mind's eye the prisoner who was sitting right behind him in this cell. And the man's previous face came to him, before Khor had reduced him to this pathetic state.

PM had no choice but to turn. The man appeared to be donning a small smile, but it was hard to tell amidst all that fucked-up skin and the lack of flesh on his face.

"Recognize me now, mahanuvab?" the prisoner asked.

PM Papa said to the previous prime minister, the one against whom he had kooed, "Everything well, Subba-ji?"

For a couple of hours, PM Subba talked to PM Papa as though they were reunited long-lost friends. Then, gradually, PM Subba talked about Papakoo, how unfairly PM Papa had disposed of him, even though PM Subba had done nothing but support PM Papa throughout his political career. PM Subba became even more agitated as he spoke and time went on. When PM Papa lay down to sleep on the bunker (he knew he couldn't sleep, but he had to at least close his eyes), PM Subba continued talking to him, standing by the cell door, pacing the room, looming over his body. "You ruined me," PM Subba wept. "My son committed suicide after I was shoved in this Khor. My wife became paralyzed from shock. You are a monster, you know that?" At one point, PM Papa thought that he should simply wake up and strangle the man, but he was too tired, and he continued to think that once he got out of Khor and regained his power, he'd order his men to take PM Subba out to the yard of this very Durbar and shoot him. The man didn't deserve a voice, if he was going to go on a harangue like this. PM Papa even thought that once he regained power, he would make this Durbar his home, live atop Khor, leave the Humble Abode to his unhappy wife. He imagined the havoc he would cause once he regained power. He would slaughter half of Darkmotherlandites if he had to. He would rule the country with utter ruthlessness. He would never trust anyone again. He would hang General Tso next to the Home of the Bell and not remove his body, even after the flesh fell away and only the carcass remained.

Sometime in the early morning, PM Subba, who had been muttering invectives against him all night, attacked him. PM Papa was in a somnambulant state when he felt the punches. For two seconds he thought he was dreaming, then knew he wasn't and started throwing his arms and legs about. Finally, he managed to kick PM Subba, a solid kick that landed in the former prime minister's groin, forcing him to sit on the floor, clutching his balls. PM Papa fell atop him and had pinned his arm to PM Subba's throat, thinking he might as well kill this man right now, when the prison guards came in and separated them. PM Subba was sniveling and crying as he was led away. PM Papa shook his head and tried to return to sleep but he was wide awake now.

He thought of ways he could regain his power. Darkmother was his last hope. General Tso had corrupted her brain, fed her stuff, perhaps drugged her. PM Papa had to talk to her and turn her against General Tso. This thought comforted PM Papa a bit, and he managed to sleep for a couple of hours.

—

When Darkmother went to see him, PM Papa, unlike the other prisoners, was in old-fashioned Western-style prison garb, the kind with black-and-white stripes. It was someone's idea of a joke, perhaps General Tso's. It was speculated that the uniform was imported from Amrika. The prison cell had two benches nailed against the walls. PM Papa sat on one of them. His skin had turned translucent in the past week. He smiled when he saw Darkmother approach.

"Behold His Sovereign Excellency PM Papa," Darkmother addressed him, genuflecting.

From somewhere there was the tinny sound of a radio—surely not from inside the prison? It must be coming from outside, thought Darkmother. Perhaps the Durbar gardener had a radio playing while he worked, although it was impossible for the sound to have penetrated the Khor's thick walls. It was a folk song, sung by a woman. Darkmother couldn't make out the words because the volume was low, but she recognized the tune. It took her back to her youth, when this song was popular.

PM Papa was wearing the MAGA cap. Why the hell was he wearing the MAGA cap in prison, along with his prison garb?

"Bravo," PM Papa said. "I knew you were smart, but I didn't know you were this smart."

"Not as smart as you," Darkmother said. "You taught me everything. You were my guru."

"The Guru of Love?" PM Papa asked. It seemed like he wanted to reach out and touch Darkmother. But he restrained himself. He had to be careful. More than anything, he had to get her on his side now. She had been brainwashed; he had to get rid of whatever junk General Tso had put inside her brain. That was the only way out of this hellhole. Easy does it.

Darkmother, bright as usual in her hippie frock, sat on the opposite bench and observed PM Papa.

"I thought you and I had something," PM Papa said.

"Did we? Was it a relationship based on love?"

PM Papa's throat tightened. If there was anything in his life he could have claimed to love, apart from power, it was this woman.

"Did you love me, Papa?"

Now Darkmother was standing before him. PM Papa wanted to take her hand.

"I would have done anything to have you by my side," he said. He thought of her taking care of him in his old age, in that mansion, Palace of Glory. He thought he would love to kneel on the dirty cell floor to unhook her hippie skirt and . . . He felt a chill, a wisp of air enveloping him, as though a warning: he couldn't think in those terms anymore.

"You are going to miss me, aren't you?" Darkmother said. She bent her knee, and put her leg up on the bench. The other leg was stretched out so her panties showed. Darkmother knew PM Papa could see the bulge. There was something pleasurable about laying yourself open like this to PM Papa. The man had treated her like a queen, showered her with gifts, even taken her home to shame Shrimati Papa. And look at what he got in return: imprisonment in the dungeon of the very Durbar where he had thrown the former prime minister to rot. And all it took was a big white horse.

"Have you been eating well?" Darkmother asked. "Is there anything you'd like to eat? Khasiko masu khana man chha?"

PM Papa nodded.

Darkmother straightened and snapped her fingers. Out of the shadows, Nakkali appeared.

PM Papa stared at her, then said gently, "Nakkali? How are you doing?"

Nakkali curtseyed him and said, "Couldn't be better, Papa." Then she turned to Darkmother, who told her what she wanted. Nakkali vanished.

PM Papa took Darkmother's hands in his and asked her what had brought this all about. He was about to use her previous name when Darkmother abruptly dropped his hand, stood, and walked out of his cell. Nakkali approached with a tray bearing khasiko masu; its fragrance elicited cries of distress from other prisoners, many of whom were former members of Papa's cabinet.

Nakkali set the tray down on the floor of the cell and said, "Bon appetit."

Only after she left did PM Papa realize that this was his last meal request.

53.

Shambhogya wandered around in the Tourist District. She had slipped out of the Asylum, a break from the laboring in the kitchen she had to do all day. Funny, she thought, that not too long ago the Ghimirey buharis didn't step into the Tourist District because it was a place for low-class people. Now for this Ghimirey buhari it had become a refuge.

She only had about half an hour before someone noticed her absence. Then she'd have to return to the Asylum, cook and feed Aditya, and do some other chores, including laundry. And she might even have to cook for the nokerchakers—one never knew these days. She didn't mind. I don't mind, she said to herself with conviction. I really don't mind it. She tried out various ways of saying it, in different accents and with different intonations, like she and her classmates used to do when they mocked the speech habits and mannerisms of the Sisters and the Mothers at their boarding school.

"Why, I don't mind it at all, Harkey," she said in a British accent. "Have a cup of tea?"

"Eh, why I mind, no?" she said in a Bharati joker accent.

Like an Australian, she said, "Don't mind it, mate."

German: "I zont minz."

She could go on entertaining herself like this forever. Kranti had been the mad one, the one who talked to herself, but here was Shambhogya now, like a commoner, jabbering away to herself in the middle of the Tourist District.

Oh, what did it matter? Who cared? The Ghimirey family was falling apart, and she could no longer hold on to it. It was a relief, actually. She felt it as an opening up in her chest, a release in her body that allowed for an easier flow.

Shambhogya had gone to Kranti to reveal the secret, but even after Kranti asked, she couldn't bring herself to tell her. She had fully intended to confess, but she'd chickened out. Was she going to continue pretending nothing was amiss?

But nothing was amiss, she told herself. She pointed with her hand to indicate the Tourist District, still somewhat ravaged by the Big Two, yet bursting with tourists. The Durbar, a couple of blocks away, was now getting a fresh coat of paint for Darkmother. Its gardens were being revitalized; the boulevard in front of it was also getting a facelift. New boutique shops were opening up, and the pavements were being widened. Further down the road in the Open Stage, the giant statue of PM Papa was demolished and was now replaced by a ginormous Goddess Darkmother statue. It was equally as high as the previous statue—touching the clouds, replete with a garland of skulls, with the Pothead God squished beneath her feet.

She realized that some people stopped to observe her talking and gesticulating to herself. She felt like turning to them and saying, what are you lookin' at? Or shouting, oye fatso! Oye toothless hag! Oye slut! Oye retard! Oye sisterfucker!

But she didn't shout at anyone. She wasn't a screamer. She didn't even scream at Aditya when he told her what he'd done. She merely trembled a bit as she sat on the bed and listened to him.

After Aditya revealed the unspeakable thing he'd done, Shambhogya understood that he had been waiting for days, itching in fact, to tell her. Basically because he wanted to punish her. He knew she wouldn't be able to take it. It'd destroy her. Except he was wrong. She was going to absorb this secret. She was, after all, Shambhogya.

The other day, Aditya returned from Ghimirey & Sons depleted because the workers had barged into his office, demanding more fringe benefits on top of the two hundred percent raise they'd received just a few weeks ago. He had literally been held hostage in the office all day; they hadn't even let him use the bathroom. Belligerent workers shouted at him and slammed their fists on his desk, scattering his documents and contracts around the room. Aditya had appealed to the new IGP who had replaced IGP Chhetri. However, the new IGP had expressed his helplessness, explaining that the Poolis Uncles had been asked not to get involved in "such internal disputes" and to "let them play out." But who was giving such asinine orders? This is a matter of law and order. Darkmotherland is going to devolve into anarchy, Aditya said. After some hesitation, the IGP admitted that the orders were from the very top.

Shambhogya sat on the bed, head down, listening to Aditya rant. The Ghimirey & Sons workers hadn't calmed down until Aditya assured them that their demands would be considered by the executive board of Ghimirey & Sons the very next day. The board consisted of all the male members of the Ghimirey household.

The factory workers laughed. "Consider, eh?" their leader, Pratyoush, the factory supervisor, questioned. Until recently Pratyoush had bowed down and groveled like a sycophantic rodent to the Ghimireys. "Like one would hold up a potato for inspection in the vegetable market, that type of consider?" he asked.

"We need to follow the company policy. As it is, you've already received a gigantic raise."

Pratyoush slapped Aditya.

Stunned, Aditya held his cheek.

"Does this also follow your company policy?" Pratyoush asked.

"You're all fired," Aditya said.

They all laughed, as though it was a joke.

"Try it, boss saheb," Pratyoush said. "We will burn this place down."

"Okay, I won't fire you, but you have to understand. Until yesterday—"

"Forget yesterday," Pratyoush said. "We're in a Brave New World now."

"Ah, Aldous Huxley," a worker, who was casually smoking a cigarette by the window, said. "An important novel, I would say."

They wouldn't leave, or let Aditya leave, until he said that yes, he would agree to their demands and tomorrow's board meeting was only a formality.

"What is happening?" Aditya cried to Shambhogya, raising his hands up in the air. "What the fuck is happening to Darkmotherland?"

He covered his face with his palms for about a minute, then let his hands fall to his side. "We're going to lose everything, Shambhogya." It was as if he'd come to that realization for the first time. "We're going to lose everything that Sir and I built with our blood and sweat."

Of course, you're not going to credit the rest of your family, thought Shambhogya. You're not going to credit us.

"We have to do something!" Aditya cried. "That fool. The Hippo. How could he have not foreseen this? We all thought he was so powerful. Invincible."

The higher you rise, Shambhogya thought, the harder you fall. She was beginning to sound like Kranti.

"Are you listening to me?" Aditya asked. He came close and stood in front of her. "You have nothing to say?"

Shambhogya remained silent, then, simply to prevent him from uttering another word, she said in a low voice, "What is there left to say?"

Aditya's voice acquired an edge. "Not a word of sympathy? Your husband has been going to a war zone every day, coming home bruised and battered, and nothing?" He kneeled in front of her. She kept her head lowered. "All shy now, my pretty?" He reached out and touched her chin, coaxed it up so he could see her face, like a besotted groom would to a shy bride on their wedding night. She closed her eyes, tightly, and clenched her jaw. She was trembling. He stroked her cheek and she leaned back. "Oh, you're going to act like that, eh? Oh, too good, yaar. You too good for me?"

Shambhogya, eyes still closed, felt for his hands and clasped them tightly, lest he use his hands to slap her, punch her, choke her, or poke out her eyes.

"I'm not going to hurt you," Aditya said, "but I'm going tell you a secret."

She stopped trembling. She had been anticipating this moment ever since things started breaking down, since the Matakoo. The day that Darkmother's procession had moved from the Tourist District toward the Durbar, she knew. She had watched the procession from her window as it passed by the Asylum. It was such an unusual sight. This woman—or was it a man dressed as a woman?—on a giant white horse, flanked by FBI-type men in dark suits and darker glasses, leading a throng of people who were caught up in what appeared to be religious fervor. "What is that? A man or a woman?" she'd asked Mokshya, who was dusting in Shambhogya's room right then.

"That's Darkmother."

"Darkmother?"

"Yes, she's made her divine appearance."

Hogwash, thought Shambhogya. Probably one of Swami Go!swami's stunts. But then Darkmother's giant white horse stopped in the middle of the street and she turned her head to look at Shambhogya. Darkmother was looking directly at Shambhogya, not just vaguely in her direction—that's how she had described the sensation to Aditya. "She turned her head to look at me."

Aditya scoffed. "She probably just happened to look this way. It's the Asylum, after all. Even the gods and goddesses know this address."

Darkmother's gaze had been severe. The procession was probably a hundred yards away, but the intensity of Darkmother's focus on Shambhogya had made her shiver. I've done something wrong, she'd thought. That's when she'd known that everything was soon going to fall apart around her, in the weeks and months to come—this house, this family, this business. That was her punishment. She also knew that in the not-so-distant future she was going to hear a god-awful secret. And that it would come from Aditya.

The moment had arrived; Shambhogya was calm. Their hands were clasped. "Before the secret, here's some news: my mistress is coming here to live with me."

That wasn't surprising. She had known this was coming.

"Don't you want to know the reason why?"

What could she say?

"Harkey wants my mistress's condo for himself. Can you believe it? And I can't throw her out in the streets, can I? We have such a big house here." He looked toward the ceiling. "It's quite likely we're going to lose everything. But until then, she needs a place to live." He clasped her hands even more tightly. "It's okay, she can stay in a guest room. I won't make this harder for you than it has to be."

He smiled, but his voice quivered. "Now onto the more important stuff." And he told her.

—

Shambhogya wondered if she could simply disappear, right now, from the middle of the Tourist District chowk. Instead of heading toward the Asylum, she could go in the opposite direction, toward the Self-Arisen Chaitya. She'd heard that a large number of people had settled there, at the base of the hill on top of which was the stupa for the Awakened One. But then, she'd have to live like Kranti did, wouldn't she? The living conditions around the Self-Arisen Chaitya could be worse than at Bhurey Paradise.

Shambhogya knew she couldn't do it. She couldn't live like a Bhurey. Her place was in the Asylum. *I cannot escape my past,* she thought. *I am chained to it, like a dog chained by its owner.*

Aditya had told her Bhaskar had sniffed out how Raddi Tokari was being used to get rid of Papa's enemies and confronted him with it. "My own brother physically tackled me downstairs in the living room," Aditya said. "I proudly told him that I was doing it as a service to Darkmotherland. These Treasonists—that's exactly how they should be dealt with. All those incinerators. Easy burning. Sometimes the garbage compactor was used, and the bodies would literally turn into minced meat. And to top it off, there are woods behind the factory. Many times even General Tso came, in a truck with the Treasonists, and his men took care of these poor slobs in the woods. Or General Tso sent one of his top Colonels. We were notified beforehand when they would arrive. Usually, once a month, I'd clear the factory premises and let all the facility workers go to Himalayan Happiness to enjoy the buffet, indoor swimming pool, and sauna while the Loyal Army Dais did their work at Raddi Tokari.

"One day one of the Beggars, someone named Prakash, was brought to Raddi Tokari. I was about to get into my car, to head out of the facility, when the Loyal Army Dais dragged him past me on their way to the incinerators. His face was bloodied, one of his eyes was totally shut, and at least one of his legs was broken. I asked the Colonel in charge what he had done, and he told me that Prakash was caught gathering evidence of PM Papa's crimes. He called it the Dojjier, or something like that. The Colonel and I had a good laugh about it. Dojjier—what will they think of next?

"Bhaskar threatened to take what he called my 'politicide' to the international media. My own kid brother. The one I used to give piggyback rides to when we were young. The one I protected from bullies at school. But now, with his blackmailing face in front of me, I realized I didn't know the motherfucker. And I didn't care what happened to him. It's really strange, Shambhogya, how alienated I felt from him, how emotionally disengaged. Bhaskar had become the enemy. He was our biggest enemy. So, I told Harkey, 'Take care of him.'

"Harkey stared at me. 'Bhaskar babu?' he asked politely. Unlike now, he spoke softly, like all nokerchakers used to speak then.

"'Yes, take care of him.'

"He looked down at the carpet and contemplated this for a moment. Then he asked, 'You mean?'

"'Do what you need to do.'

"He could have asked me what precisely I meant, but he didn't—perhaps he saw an opportunity here to have something on me he could use later. I also could have clarified what I wanted, but I didn't. All I knew was that I wanted Bhaskar to stop being a bother. I wanted him to be taught a lesson.

"I think a part of me thought that Harkey would have his goons take Bhaskar to a deserted alley to beat the crap out of him. Give him a black eye, shatter his ribs, break an arm or two. But I also knew it wouldn't change Bhaskar's mind about me. He would still spill the beans on Raddi Tokari. So, I thought, let Harkey—I don't know what I thought.

"And now Harkey has something over me. The Russians have a name for it—kompromat, or something like that. I can feel it from Harkey without him having to utter one word. He never told me what exactly transpired that day. He doesn't need to. I can well imagine it. This is his modus operandi: he sits back and lets his goons take care of business. He's usually nearby, in a shop, in a car, watching, making sure nothing goes wrong. So, I'm sure Harkey was watching from somewhere nearby, perhaps peeking from behind a curtain in a tea shop near the Self-Arisen Chaitya, or hiding in his car, when his men went after Bhaskar in his classroom at Streetwise School."

—

Shambhogya tittered as she pivoted toward the Asylum from the Tourist District chowk. You coward, she rebuked herself. You don't have the guts to walk away from all of this. You don't have the guts to tell the world what Aditya did. She wasn't going to utter a word about it. She was going to go home and make preparations for the arrival of her son, who was returning home from his boarding school because they could no longer afford his studies. She also had to make the guest room ready for her husband's mistress, who was moving in tomorrow.

54.

Kranti was beginning to realize that Kabiraj resembled Dada in many ways. The same body shape: small, portly yet agile, the same waddling walk (when Kranti first realized this, she nearly uttered a cry of dismay, then she was amused). The same self-effacing smile even in the face of disapproval or criticism. The same devotion to Kranti. In fact, if Dada were alive, he would be taking care of the khateykids in exactly the same manner as Kabiraj. I've found my father, Kranti said to herself, remembering the days when her school-bus friends teased her as a daddy's girl. This realization bothered her for a day or two, until she realized she had become fond of a man who resembled her father. And her father was the best person she knew, the kindest and the most accommodating. She couldn't help wondering what it said about her mother that even in her old age she looked down on a man who resembled Dada. Despite herself, despite the recent semi-reconciliation and the let's-live-in-peace philosophy she and her mother had adopted, Kranti couldn't help but visit her old resentment. It erupted like a tiny, searing flame she'd thought had been extinguished. Professor Shrestha's attitude toward Kabiraj was further proof that she'd always held Dada in low regard.

Kranti tried hard to extinguish the flame. For the most part she succeeded, and there remained an awkward, but tolerable peace between mother and daughter. This truce had been aided by her mother's acceptance of, and even joy in, the khateykids. Professor Shrestha was the last person that Kranti would have pegged as child-friendly, and yet here she was, reveling in their presence when she visited the Laj Mahal and Laj Mahal II. And there were so many of them now that Kranti herself lost count. She had to use the fingers on both hands to name them: Sanjay, Rani, Bishnu, Sushma, Binita, Mamata, Lisa and her brother Joshua, Zero, Sunaina, Rad (short for Radical, real name unknown), Okie, Bimala, Dokie, Khan, Pepsi, Hira. There were nights that Kranti found herself reciting the names of the khateykids in her sleep, and when she woke up she recited their names, and sometimes in the afternoons too the names spilled from her lips. Sanjay, Rani, Bishnu . . . even when the children were right in front of her eyes. She recited their names silently, sometimes whispering, sometimes out loud, for no reason, and the khateykids would look at her in surprise as though she were addressing them, and they smiled when they realized that she was merely singing their names. When they smiled she also couldn't help but smile widely and they would laugh because it was hard to really smile widely and call out names at the same time without the names coming out all odd, and when they laughed she also laughed and then the names hiccupped into the air and bounded around the walls of the tent.

55.

The boulevard stretched out before Darkmother. It was close to midnight. She knew she wouldn't be able to sleep for at least another two hours, if not more, and even then it would be a few hours of fitful sleep. She'd experience drowsiness in the wee hours of the morning, but not total sleep. There would be no real oblivion for her from now on. Such was the price of leading a nation. There were moments when she wanted to laugh at her own predicament. How did she end up in this situation? She checked her own body to see if she was indeed real. She patted her thighs, pinched her stomach, and moved her hands up to her chest. She was growing breasts. This had started happening not too long after she moved into the Durbar—tiny buds that were growing in millimeters every day, so slightly that no one else would notice.

When she checked herself in the mirror, she found that she was becoming prettier, more feminine. Her face had become fuller, her eyes more doe-like, and her lips plumper. She jutted out her tongue. It reached down to her chin now, and it was blood red, as if she'd just devoured a beast.

She had thought about where all of this was going to go, where she was going to take the country. Right now, there was chaos, what with Nakoo and the confusion surrounding it. But chaos was essential before order could emerge. After all, didn't the scriptures say destruction and creation were two sides of the same coin? And wasn't her counterpart, the Pothead God, the lord of destruction? So, let things destruct, then she would impose order. And it would be a benevolent order. People needed to believe that the world was a coherent place where truth and justice mattered. More than anything, Darkmother wanted to ensure that there was no fear in people's lives—fear of being subjugated, of being oppressed, of being imprisoned, of disappearing. Fear not, she told her Devotees with a gentle gesture of her palm. She was, after all, the goddess of liberation.

But all of what she wanted to do wasn't going to happen overnight. She had to be patient. She had to take her time, so things happened gradually, in increments. First, the Fundys needed to be neutered. She was already in the process of doing it. Swami Go!swami had been to the Durbar twice, requesting to see her, possibly to complain about how the Fundys were slowly losing their power. Both times she had denied his requests for an audience with her. No, she had shaken her head. Her aides had indicated that Swami Go!swami looked like he was in utter disbelief that she would not even see him. She met with many who showed up at her door, especially the poor and the downtrodden, and those still seeking relief from the Big Two. Sometimes she would spend hours with a family, especially if they had traveled a long distance to see her. She always had her door open to the LGBTQ crowd because she knew their stories even before they opened their mouths.

Then there was this "thing." Darkmother's hand moved to her stomach. Recently it had begun to stir. There was no protrusion, yet, but in the coming weeks there would be. People would notice. Nakkali already suspected something, for when she gave Darkmother her daily massage, her fingers spread oil gently and with the utmost care over her belly, as though she were comforting and soothing what was inside.

Darkmother didn't know how it happened, how it was even possible. But she knew when it happened—in that Khadi country, in the Caliphate Hotel. She'd felt it drop then. She suspected it had something to do with Awnty. She also suspected it had something to do with them being in a foreign location. She was curious about it, and had considered interrogating the Hippo, but she didn't want to give him the satisfaction, before his execution, of knowing he'd managed to leave his seed inside her. Couldn't she just get rid of it? Drink something, eat something so that it would simply disappear somewhere inside her body? She might. For now, she was going to let this thing grow. Her Little Hippo.

ACKNOWLEDGMENTS

It takes a village to write a book, and a book of this size wouldn't have been possible without the support and love of many kind-hearted beings. I am greatly indebted to Indiana University, especially my colleagues and students in the English Department and the Creative Writing Program, for embracing and encouraging this immigrant's imaginative endeavors for more than two decades. A fellowship from IU's wonderful College Arts and Humanities Institute afforded me much-needed time to work on this novel. Many thanks to J.T. for providing critical feedback on an early draft. I am deeply grateful to my readers and friends in Nepal, whose interest in my work has sustained me over the years. I am lucky to have Eric Simonoff as my literary agent—this book would not have been published without his abiding belief in my fiction. Mark Doten's brilliant editing lifted this novel to another sphere, and I am grateful to the entire Soho Press team, especially Rachel Kowal, for their care and attention.

Lastly, I want to express my deep gratitude to my family for their rock-solid support for everything I write—even before I write them! Babita, Shay, Ammi, Sangeeta, Mummy: this book is also yours.